# 挑戰 NEW TOEIC
# 新制多益
## 閱讀滿分
### 模擬試題1000題

作者 Choi Young Ken ｜ 譯者 蘇裕承 / 關亭薇

解析版

試題本

# 目錄

# 新制多益介紹

## 新制多益於2018年3月正式實施

### ✔ 改制後如下

| 類別 | Part | 舊制多益 題型 | 題數 | 新制多益 題型 | 題數 | 時間 | 分數 |
|------|------|------|------|------|------|------|------|
| 聽力 | 1 | 照片描述 | 10 | 照片描述 | 6 | 45分鐘 | 495分 |
| | 2 | 應答問題 | 30 | 應答問題 | 25 | | |
| | 3 | 簡短對話 | 30 | 簡短對話 | 39 | | |
| | 4 | 簡短獨白 | 30 | 簡短獨白 | 30 | | |
| 閱讀 | 5 | 句子填空（文法和單字） | 40 | 句子填空（文法和單字） | 30 | 75分鐘 | 495分 |
| | 6 | 段落填空 | 12 | 段落填空 | 16 | | |
| | 7 | 閱讀 單篇閱讀 | 28 | 閱讀 單篇閱讀 | 29 | | |
| | | 雙篇閱讀 | 20 | 多篇閱讀 | 25 | | |
| TOTAL | | 7 Parts | 200題 | 7 Parts | 200題 | 120分鐘 | 990分 |

### ✔ 題型變更重點

#### 聽力測驗

- Part 1, 2 題數減少（**Part 1**：10 題→ 6 題／**Part 2**：30 題→ 25 題）
- Part 3 題數增加（**Part 3**：30 題→ 39 題）
- 部分對話長度減短、對話次數增加
- 部分對話中將出現母音省略（如：going to → gonna）
- 新增三人對話 NEW
- 新增對話、說明加上圖表（表格或曲線圖等）的整合題型 NEW
- 新增詢問說話者意圖的題型 NEW

#### 閱讀測驗

- Part 5 題數減少（**Part 5**：40 題→ 30 題）
- Part 6, 7 題數增加（**Part 6**：12 題→ 16 題／**Part 7**：48 題→ 54 題）
- 文法題比例增加
- 新增判斷上下文意的題型（句子插入題） NEW
  1. 在文章內放入符合上下文意的句子
  2. 將句子放入適當的段落位置
- 新增文字簡訊、線上聊天、通訊軟體多人對話題型 NEW
- 新增整合三篇文章的閱讀題型 NEW
- 新增詢問說話者意圖的題型 NEW

# PART 5–6 高分策略

## PART 5–6 命題趨勢

**01** PART 5 從 101 至 130 題，總題數為 30 題；PART 6 從 131 至 146 題，共有四個題組，每組四題。PART 5 的題目為商業情境或日常生活中經常使用到的短句（由 13–25 個單字組合而成），要求填入適當的單字，或符合文法結構的選項；PART 6 的題目則是在信件、電子郵件、備忘錄、報導等中篇文章中放入四個空格，要求考生根據文法和上下文，選填適當的單字或句子。

**02** PART 6 每個題組都有一題要根據上下文，從四個選項中選填適當的句子插入文章中。
扣除這四題，每次多益測驗的 PART 5 和 PART 6 有 40% 屬於詞彙題；60% 屬於時態和文法題。

**03** **詞性題：**此為兩大題常見的題型，考生要確認句型結構，並選出正確的詞性（名詞、形容詞、動詞、副詞、介系詞、連接詞）填入空格當中。

**04** **詞彙題：**要求考生從數個詞性相同的單字中，根據文意選出正確的答案；此類題型的比例與難度逐漸增加。

## PART 5–6 重點題型

多益測驗中，**PART 5** 和 **PART 6** 的題型有：

❶ 詞性變化　　❷ 動詞相關題型　　❸ 其他文法概念
❹ 詞彙題　　　❺ 句子插入題

**01** **詞性變化**
此題型的數量少則 6 題，多則 9 題，只要確認名詞、形容詞、副詞、介系詞、或連接詞扮演的角色與放置的位置，就能輕鬆解題。最重要的是，此題型為節省時間的好幫手，可以讓你迅速找出答案並進展至下一題，同時增加 PART 7 長篇閱讀的解題時間。

**02** **動詞相關題型**
包含語態（主動／被動）、分詞、不定詞、動名詞和時態等動詞變化的題型，只要將文法概念歸納整理，便能輕鬆解決。

其中主詞與動詞的「**單複數一致**」為 100% 必考題型，主詞人稱的單複數必須與動詞單複數保持一致，也是學習英文句型結構的出發點。多益考題中，為了加深題目難度，常在句子中加入修飾語，使得主詞長度增加，讓主詞和動詞的距離變得遙遠，使考生不易選出正確的動詞。

**03** **其他文法概念**

其他文法概念指的是英文基礎文法概念，除了主詞與動詞單複數一致，還有代名詞的三種格（主格、受格、所有格）、關係代名詞、假設語氣、比較級、倒裝句等。

**04** **詞彙題**

多益測驗中的詞彙題分成四大類：

① collocation（選擇常用的搭配詞）
② nuance（懂得區分同義詞的細微差異）
③ interchangeable words（選擇可互相通用的單字）
④ 掌握文意（根據文意選填適當的單字）

也可以依詞性分成：

①名詞題　②形容詞題　③副詞題　④動詞題　⑤介系詞題

**05** **句子插入題** (NEW)

PART 6 中，考生要根據上下文，從四個選項找出適當的句子插入文章段落。

## PART 5–6 高分Point

### ✔ 徹底熟悉各大題必考的文法概念。

尤其是動詞單複數判斷的題型，當主詞與動詞距離過遠，一時難以選出正確的動詞時，可以**遮住英文句子中的修飾語**，學會找出句子中的主詞和動詞。只要能確認主詞的單複數，就能選出正確的動詞；此題型為 100% 必考的文法題。

### ✔ 不斷學習單字和其相關用法。

包含介系詞和名詞的用法、與動詞的搭配、動詞各類變化、慣用語等題型。此外，考生必須不斷記憶理解新的單字和用法，因為幾乎每次的考題都會出現新的單字。

### ✔ 要練習掌握前後文的脈絡。

針對 PART 6 的新題型「句子插入題」，要學習從前後文找出相關線索，或從後段使用的代名詞、連接詞等，推理出前後文的關係，並將符合文意的句子填入空格中。例如：在前句未知的情況下，若後句以代名詞 It 開頭，即可立刻判斷前句應已提過某事物，故後句再次提及時才會僅以代名詞指稱。

# PART 5-6 高分策略

## PART 5 題型綜覽（句子填空題）

PART 5 的題型要根據句中的文法或是單字，從四個選項中選出一個最適當的答案填入空格中，使其成為完整的句子。新制多益的命題方向不變，但是總題數從 40 題減少為 30 題。

---

# READING TEST

In the Reading test, you will read a variety of texts and answer several different types of reading comprehension questions. The entire Reading test will last 75 minutes. There are three parts, and directions are given for each part. You are encouraged to answer as many questions as possible within your time allowed.

You must mark your answers on the separate answer sheet. Do not write your answers in your test book.

## Part 5

**Directions:** A word or phrase is missing in each of the sentences below. Four answer choices are given below each sentence. Select the best answer to complete the sentence. Then mark the letter (A), (B), (C), or (D) on your answer sheet.

**101.** The fundraising event recorded such high ------- that there will be more than expected proceeds.
   (A) attendant
   (B) attended
   (C) attend
   (D) attendance

**102.** Sky Motors offers a variety of training programs to help enhance ------- in the workplace.
   (A) productivity
   (B) produce
   (C) productive
   (D) productively

**103.** All the employees are asked to report all the expenses incurred ------- business trips.
   (A) during
   (B) so
   (C) meanwhile
   (D) while

# PART 6 題型綜覽（段落填空題）

PART 6 的題型要根據上下文，從四個選項中選出一個最適當的答案填入空格中，使其成為完整的段落。新增加的「句子插入題」也需根據文意，從選項中找出最適當的句子填入空格中。新制多益中本大題新增了 4 題變成 16 題，每篇文章有四個題目，共有四篇文章。

---

## Part 6

**Directions:** Read the texts that follow. A word, phrase, or sentence is missing in parts of each text. Four answer choices for each question are given below the text. Select the best answer to complete the text. Then mark the letter (A), (B), (C), or (D) on your answer sheet.

**Questions 135-138** refer to the following notice.

### Important Notice about Hatter Industries

Please note that the contact information for Hatter Industries changed on March 21. Due to the closure of our Dabbley office and the ----135---- of our operations in Buena, all correspondence concerning our products and services should now be sent to the following address: Hatter Industries, 642 Mandela Lane, Buena, CA. Our employees' e-mail addresses, as well as our website's address, www.hatterindustries.com, remain ----136----.

However, we are still waiting for our new telephone and fax numbers. ----137---- will be updated on our website as soon as the new numbers are assigned as of March 25. ----138----.

135. (A) decision
     (B) relocation
     (C) suspension
     (D) result

136. (A) assigned
     (B) even
     (C) formal
     (D) unchanged

137. (A) Yours
     (B) Another
     (C) These
     (D) Theirs

**句子插入題** NEW

138. (A) We apologize for any inconvenience and thank you for your understanding.
     (B) Refer to the side of the packet for full details of instructions before applying.
     (C) Her office location will also remain the same.
     (D) For more information about the forthcoming event, visit www.lizard.org.br/events.

# PART 7 高分策略

## PART 7 高分Point

**01** **邏輯式速讀 → 找出主題句**

新制多益最明顯的特色就是題數增加、文章篇幅變長，同時新增通訊軟體對話以及多篇閱讀。閱讀的分量遠超過解題的時間，因此務必將文章的閱讀重點擺在找出主題句。要有效率地找出主題句，**邏輯式速讀**是解決之道！無關文章的長度和種類，只要找出將眾多句子濃縮成一句精華的（simplified）**關鍵主題句**，便能在短時間內掌握文意。

**02** **掌握文章脈絡**

為了傳達主題句的理念，眾多句子集合成文章。因此閱讀文章的關鍵並非以句子為單位一句句閱讀，而是要掌握句子之間的走向，也就是「脈絡」。新制多益中新增**判斷說話者意圖**，以及**段落填句**兩題型，更加強調掌握文章脈絡的重要性。因此在閱讀多益文章時，不可使用單句翻譯（translation）的方式，過度執著於單一句子或是單字的意思，而應該要**確認文章脈絡及想要表達的重點理念**。

**03** **迎戰新增的題型**

### 1. 段落填句題

> We are currently looking for an experienced, creative, and dedicated environmental expert to work in our office in Vienna, Austria. —[1]—. With employees from all over the world, the FOE is a linguistically diverse community. —[2]—. Applicants must also possess a degree in environmental science, hydrology, or biology, and have at least three years of international work experience. —[3]—.
>
> Please e-mail your application with a current resume, a letter of recommendation, and a writing sample to Clifford Samuelson by September 30. —[4]—.

**Q.** In which of the positions marked [1], [2], [3] and [4] does the following sentence best belong?

"However, English is the working language of the organization and fluency in written and spoken English is a must."

(A) [1]　　　　**(B) [2]**　　　　(C) [3]　　　　(D) [4]

解說 由「With employees from all over the world, the FOE is a linguistically diverse community.」，可以得知此團體使用多種語言。再看到題目句：「However, English is the working language of the organization」，表示「然而」此團體的共通語言為英語。本句剛好與前述句子的概念相反，因此可以使用 However 連接兩個句子。

另外，題目句後半的 fluency in written and spoken English is a must 表示必要條件（a must）為精通英文，緊接在後方的 Applicants must also possess a degree in environmental science ... 中的 also，可知為補充說明應徵的條件。綜合上述，題目句最適合填入的位置為 [2]，故答案為 (B)。

## 突破解題障礙SOLUTION

● **多次閱讀仍無法選出適當的插入段落**

破解此題型要採用**速讀技巧**（skimming）。請先找出**主題句**，推敲（guessing）文章的主要內容，並快速檢視文章的起承轉合。經由速讀的過程確認文章的架構後，再依照上下文邏輯順序（logical sequence）找出**前後語意轉折、突然轉換主題**或**未完成的段落**，即可在此段落的空格中插入題目句。

**速讀→找出主題句→推敲內容→檢視邏輯→發現轉折、缺漏→填入句子**

● **總是選錯選項**

閱讀文章時，請特別留意句子之間的**轉承語**（discourse marker）。轉承語包含**連接詞、連接副詞、代名詞、指示代名詞**等用語。此類用語在句子間作為連接或轉折的角色，使得文章以主題句為中心，順利延伸出後續的內容。只要學會判讀轉承語，就能輕鬆掌握句子之間的邏輯關係，例如因果關係、補充說明、語意轉折、突然轉換主題或未完成的段落。

## PART 7 高分策略

### 2. 判斷說話者的意圖題

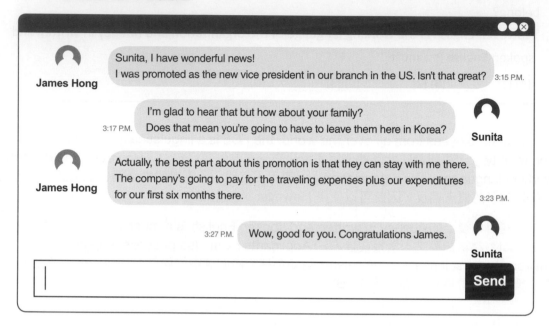

**James Hong:** Sunita, I have wonderful news!
I was promoted as the new vice president in our branch in the US. Isn't that great? 3:15 P.M.

3:17 P.M. **Sunita:** I'm glad to hear that but how about your family?
Does that mean you're going to have to leave them here in Korea?

**James Hong:** Actually, the best part about this promotion is that they can stay with me there.
The company's going to pay for the traveling expenses plus our expenditures
for our first six months there. 3:23 P.M.

3:27 P.M. **Sunita:** Wow, good for you. Congratulations James.

**Send**

**Q.** At 3:27, why did Sunita write, "good for you"?

(A) James can work as a CEO in the US.
**(B) James can bring his family with him abroad.**
(C) The company pays for James' retirement plan.
(D) The company will pay for James' expenses until he retires.

解說 — 前文提到 James 可以帶他的家人一同前往國外工作，公司還會提供最初六個月的補助金，故 Sunita 此時說「good for you」應是在向他祝賀，因此答案為 (B)。

### 突破解題障礙SOLUTION

● **難以找出隱含的意圖**
先刪除出現與該段對話毫無相關用詞的選項，再從剩下的選項中選出最符合前後對話脈絡的內容。

● **難以找出對話主旨**
請注意每段對話開頭的**稱呼語**（I/we/you/here/there），掌握對話者之間的關係。
由對話者的相互關係可以看出對話內容的重點，進而得知對話的主旨。

## 3. 多篇閱讀題

The Nature Tour, in Costa Rica, is ideal for anyone who wants to explore the incomparable beauty of Costa Rica's rain forests.

Tour price includes:
- 1 Night hotel accommodations
- Round-trip in an air-conditioned bus between San José hotel and Nature Lodge
- All meals, entrance fees, and activities listed in the itinerary (except for rafting)

San José hotel stays not included in tour price

| Itinerary | |
|---|---|
| Day 1 | Transfer from San José to the Nature Lodge. Visit a volcano and natural hot spring along the way. |
| Day 2 | Morning rafting on the Corobici River and then head to Playa Coco on the Pacific Coast. |

To Nature Tour:

I saw the ad of your tour service in Costa Rica. I really enjoy rafting so I want to know what I should prepare for this activity in advance. I would like you to call me in person ASAP. I usually work during the daytime. Therefore, is it possible to contact me after 6 PM? I'm looking forward to your response.

Mark Pitt
Supervisor at National Fitness Center

**Q.** Where is Mark most likely preferred to experience?

 (A) Corobici River    (B) Nature Lodge

 (C) Pacific Coast     (D) San José

 本題要綜合第二篇行程表和第三篇文章的內容解題。Mark 在信中寫道：「I really enjoy rafting」，而柯羅比西河（Corobici River）的行程包含泛舟活動，因此答案為 (A)。

## 突破解題障礙SOLUTION

### ● 難以負荷三篇文章的閱讀分量
多篇閱讀的每篇文章都可以**相互連結**，因此可以視為一篇文章分割成三篇短文。練習試題時，請勿忘記這個解題關鍵。先找出第一篇文章的**主題句**，並徹底掌握文章的脈絡，同時確認各篇章之間的關係。

### ● 無法整合分散至三篇文章的資訊
在多篇閱讀題型中，會將首篇文章的部分內容，進行補充說明、或是濃縮成重點精華，也可能將首篇文章中的內容轉換成數字或其他名稱，延伸出圖表、電子郵件、表單等第二、三篇文章。由於三篇文章都在闡述**相同的資訊**，通常會用**換句話說**（paraphrasing）的方式，傳達重複的資訊，所以考生不用緊張，只要找到整合三篇文章的**共同重點**，便能輕鬆找出答案。

# ACTUAL TEST

## 答對題數表

| | |
|---|---|
| PART 5 | |
| PART 6 | |
| PART 7 | |
| 總題數 | |

01

# READING TEST

In the Reading test, you will read a variety of texts and answer several different types of reading comprehension questions. The entire Reading test will last 75 minutes. There are three parts, and directions are given for each part. You are encouraged to answer as many questions as possible within the time allowed.

You must mark your answers on the separate answer sheet. Do not write your answers in your test book.

## PART 5

**Directions:** A word or phrase is missing in each of the sentences below. Four answer choices are given below each sentence. Select the best answer to complete the sentence. Then mark the letter (A), (B), (C), or (D) on your answer sheet.

101. All of the new employees receive training packets that ------ details about their duties.
    (A) contains
    (B) to contain
    (C) contain
    (D) containing

102. ------- just two miles remaining in the race, Ms. Kaufman had a sizable advantage over the next runner.
    (A) With
    (B) Though
    (C) But
    (D) Added

103. Mr. Shaw is not able to participate in the committee convention in Shanghai, so Ms. Jeon will attend in ------ place.
    (A) him
    (B) he
    (C) his
    (D) himself

104. The executive director at All Day Department Store is ------ to any changes to the company logo.
    (A) eager
    (B) interfered
    (C) opposed
    (D) anxious

105. The conference center is on Brooklyn Street, ------ across from the new post office.
    (A) directs
    (B) direct
    (C) direction
    (D) directly

106. ------- the rise in steel prices, FTX Builders will most likely revise the bid for the Golden Bridge construction work.
    (A) Given
    (B) Provided
    (C) Namely
    (D) Regardless

107. The office complex ------ on the outskirts of the pedestrian shopping area.
    (A) will be built
    (B) built
    (C) are building
    (D) builder

108. In the past twenty years, clothing designers have become ------ aware of customer needs and preferences.
    (A) increasing
    (B) increased
    (C) increase
    (D) increasingly

109. ------- the last four months, Miracle Theater attendance has improved significantly.

(A) During
(B) Above
(C) Behind
(D) Into

110. Temporary workers from Adrian Recruitment Inc. have proven to be highly ------ employees.

(A) competent
(B) competence
(C) competency
(D) competently

111. Revenue from sale of outdoor furniture has been ------- higher than expected over the last six months.

(A) optionally
(B) considerably
(C) eagerly
(D) informatively

112. Please complete all items on the checklist ------ submitting your entry for the photography contest.

(A) as for
(B) mainly
(C) before
(D) so that

113. Many ------ farmers sell their produce at Pemberton Green Market.

(A) close
(B) around
(C) local
(D) near

114. Owing to predicted bad weather, tomorrow's outdoor concert has been ------- to next Saturday.

(A) postponed
(B) eliminated
(C) prolonged
(D) implemented

115. In order to ensure a timely response, please include your account number on all -------.

(A) are corresponding
(B) correspondence
(C) corresponds
(D) correspond

116. Lunch will be catered by Welco Café ------ Haqri Grill.

(A) but
(B) nor
(C) and
(D) yet

117. Timothy Darlton is highly qualified for the managerial role, ------ requires extensive experience.

(A) whoever
(B) who
(C) which
(D) whatever

118. We'd really appreciate your ------ in the Nathan Apartment Complex improvement survey.

(A) participant
(B) participation
(C) participate
(D) participated

119. Mr. Lopez will assist with the manuscript, so it is not necessary to do all the revisions by -------.

(A) yours
(B) yourself
(C) you
(D) your

120. Midora Manufacturing reserves the right to delay further deliveries ------ the customer has made all outstanding payments.

(A) until
(B) next
(C) then
(D) later

Go on to the next page

121. Blico Marketing Group ------ provides clients with updated information about its services.

   (A) equally
   (B) perfectly
   (C) substantially
   (D) regularly

122. Nortize Interiors has quickly gained a ------ for excellence among real estate agents in the city.

   (A) pursuit
   (B) reputation
   (C) center
   (D) design

123. The board members of Cistal Inc. ------ to make a hiring decision for the executive officer position by the end of next week.

   (A) indicate
   (B) allow
   (C) assume
   (D) expect

124. Please notify the training session instructor of your anticipated absences ------ different dates can be scheduled.

   (A) ever since
   (B) due to
   (C) in spite of
   (D) so that

125. Mr. Miller ------- that only the loan advisors should take part in the meeting on new trends in lending.

   (A) specify
   (B) to specify
   (C) has specified
   (D) is specified

126. Employees of Leading-Edge Machinery were amazed to receive an ------ bonus in July.

   (A) inexperienced
   (B) indefinite
   (C) equipped
   (D) unexpected

127. Ms. Diana must determine ------ or not to submit the proposal to the North American bureau.

   (A) whether
   (B) neither
   (C) either
   (D) unless

128. Staff members who have not ------ submitted their time sheets must do so by 5:00 P.M. today at the latest.

   (A) only
   (B) earlier
   (C) yet
   (D) rather

129. At last month's company banquet, 11 workers were ------ for having served the company for 25 years.

   (A) recognized
   (B) advocated
   (C) resumed
   (D) administered

130. Because of its ------ to major tourist attractions, Casey Hotel in Singapore is frequently fully booked.

   (A) proximity
   (B) exclusion
   (C) efficiency
   (D) availability

## PART 6

**Directions:** Read the texts that follow. A word, phrase, or sentence is missing in parts of each text. Four answer choices for each question are given below the text. Select the best answer to complete the text. Then mark the letter (A), (B), (C), or (D) on your answer sheet.

**Questions 131-134** refer to the following press release.

Charles Burrow, founder and president of Burrow's, Crosstown's largest clothing retailer,

announced that he ------- $4,000 to the city's new community center. The funds derive from the
      **131.**

sale of tickets to a party held last night at his company's -------. Mr. Burrow will present a check
                                                           **132.**

to the center tomorrow at its opening ceremony.

------- the past thirty years, Mr. Burrow has organized several fundraising events for charitable
**133.**

institutions and community services. ------- .
                                    **134.**

131. (A) will donate
     (B) donated
     (C) might donate
     (D) donating

132. (A) museum
     (B) hotel
     (C) residence
     (D) store

133. (A) Despite
     (B) Over
     (C) Between
     (D) Beneath

134. (A) The opening ceremony will begin at 10:00 A.M.
     (B) The community center offers classes for adults and children.
     (C) Last night's event was the most successful thus far.
     (D) Mr. Burrow plans to open a new location in London next year.

*Go on to the next page*

August 30 — After two years of construction, the largest hotel in Pittsburgh history is almost

ready to open. The Rivertop Hotel, on the banks of the Allegherry River, will have 1,500 rooms

for visitors. -------. The first guests will arrive on September 12 as part of a medical technology
      **135.**

conference. The project is among four downtown area hotels -------. According to Kristofer
                    **136.**

Walsh, president of the Pittsburgh Hotel & Lodging Association, these new developments are

a -------. "We've had a massive influx of visitors over the past few years," said Mr. Walsh. -------,
  **137.**                                                  **138.**

almost all the hotels in the city are completely full. Clearly, additional hotel rooms are needed.

**135.** (A) It is unclear when it will be ready to accept reservations.
(B) Building renovations will begin next month.
(C) It will also have seven meeting rooms for groups of up to 200 people.
(D) There are multiple companies bidding on the project.

**136.** (A) to construct
(B) are constructing
(C) were constructed
(D) being constructed

**137.** (A) necessity
(B) nuisance
(C) risk
(D) bargain

**138.** (A) On the other hand
(B) In other words
(C) In the first place
(D) As a result

**Questions 139-142** refer to the following e-mail.

---

**To:** Seth Ortega <sortega@xeroxmail.net>

**From:** Jake Morris <jmorris@fubmanufacturing.com>

**Date:** May 21

**Subject:** Factory Manager Position

Dear Mr. Ortega,

You are officially invited to a second interview. This time, I will be meeting only with the top

candidates to determine who is most ------- for the manager position. I believe you possess
                                          **139.**

many of the ------- we are looking for.
              **140.**

I trust that you remain interested in this job opportunity. -------, would a 3:00 P.M. appointment
                                                              **141.**

next Tuesday work for you? Please prepare a proposal that explains how you would increase

production at our plant without decreasing quality. -------.
                                                     **142.**

Jake Morris

---

**139.** (A) suiting
(B) suitable
(C) suit
(D) suits

**140.** (A) agreements
(B) performances
(C) qualities
(D) promotions

**141.** (A) Despite that
(B) If so
(C) However
(D) For example

**142.** (A) I would be happy to write a job reference for you.
(B) My assistant will train you in your new duties.
(C) I look forward to hearing your vision for an efficient workplace.
(D) Your new product ideas were especially informative.

*Go on to the next page*

**Questions 143-146** refer to the following article.

August 3

By Chris Garneau

The Noxville Transportation Committee (NTC) will hold a public meeting at City Hall on

Tuesday, August 10, at 6 P.M., to discuss its proposal to extend light rail service to Noxville

Industrial Park.

-------. Residents of the community have complained that the extension will cause too much
**143.**

noise during the rush hours. -------, the NTC has been researching the possibility of installing
**144.**

noise barriers along the tracks. At the meeting, Alex Khan, chief executive officer of Typhoon

Builders, will explain how much noise reduction the NTC can ------- getting with the barriers.
**145.**

A ------- by Mayor Charlie Hoffman will follow.
**146.**

143. (A) The NTC finished the project ahead of
schedule.
(B) The rail line will run through a
residential area.
(C) The committee chairman will run for
mayor election next year.
(D) The NTC has decided to hold monthly
meetings.

144. (A) In addition
(B) In time for
(C) In response
(D) In conclusion

145. (A) remind
(B) accept
(C) persuade
(D) anticipate

146. (A) to present
(B) presenter
(C) presenting
(D) presentation

# PART 7

**Directions:** In this part you will read a selection of texts, such as magazine and newspaper articles, e-mails, and instant messages. Each text or set of texts is followed by several questions. Select the best answer for each question and mark the letter (A), (B), (C), or (D) on your answer sheet.

**Questions 147-148** refer to the following letter.

We are aggressively looking for a receptionist for a local law firm in Crimson Shore. Duties include connecting calls, welcoming clients, answering telephones, handling meeting schedules, and sending out the daily e-mail. The qualified applicant should have an outgoing personality and be proficient in document preparation software. A university degree is required. Pay begins at $100 a week. Send your résumé to <u>danielhickman@fairlaw.com</u>.

**147.** What job is most likely available?

(A) Teller
(B) Lawyer
(C) Supervisor
(D) Assistant

**148.** What type of qualification is NOT included as a requirement for the job?

(A) Accounting
(B) Word processing
(C) Client service
(D) University degree

*Go on to the next page*

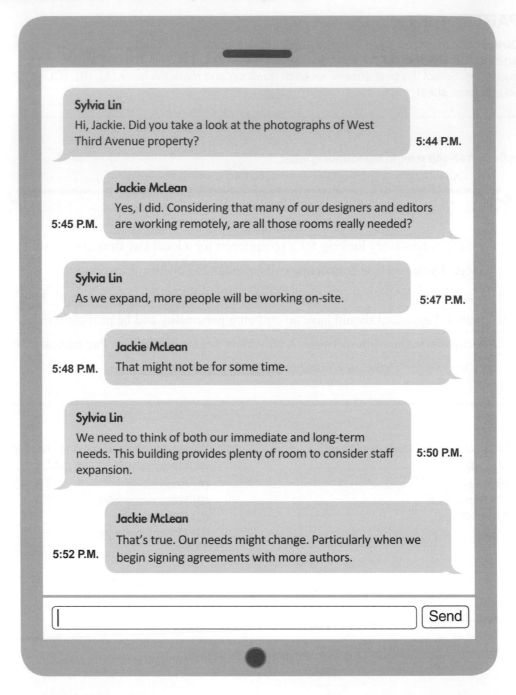

**Sylvia Lin**
Hi, Jackie. Did you take a look at the photographs of West Third Avenue property?
5:44 P.M.

**Jackie McLean**
5:45 P.M.
Yes, I did. Considering that many of our designers and editors are working remotely, are all those rooms really needed?

**Sylvia Lin**
As we expand, more people will be working on-site.
5:47 P.M.

**Jackie McLean**
5:48 P.M.
That might not be for some time.

**Sylvia Lin**
We need to think of both our immediate and long-term needs. This building provides plenty of room to consider staff expansion.
5:50 P.M.

**Jackie McLean**
5:52 P.M.
That's true. Our needs might change. Particularly when we begin signing agreements with more authors.

Send

149. What kind of business do the people probably work for?

(A) A relocation company
(B) A publishing company
(C) A property agency
(D) An exterior design company

150. At 5:52 P.M., what does Ms. McLean most likely mean when she writes, "That's true"?

(A) A different place should be rented.
(B) A new place will be too expensive.
(C) The property may meet the company's needs in the future.
(D) The property needs overall improvements.

**Questions 151-153** refer to the following memo.

**To:** All staff members
**From:** Dwight Howard, Director of Operations
**Date:** June 5
**Subject:** East Wing Closure

This is to inform you that the east wing of the main office building will be temporarily closed at the end of next week. The maintenance staff will be replacing all ceiling lights in the offices and meeting rooms with high-quality fluorescent lights. Safety regulations stipulate that no staff members be allowed in the area while the work is in progress. The work is due to begin Friday, on June 9, and be finished on Saturday, June 10. The affected offices are 200–262. Staff members in these offices should plan to finish assignments at home or, if necessary, use a temporary work area in another section of the building. To reserve a temporary work area, you may contact Administrative Assistant Michael Kane at extension 242. Please note that temporary work areas are limited and requests must be submitted by 5:00 P.M. on June 7 at the latest.

**151.** What does the memo mainly report?

(A) Staff members are being relocated to new offices.
(B) Meeting space is being added.
(C) A safety inspection is being conducted.
(D) Office lighting is being upgraded.

**152.** When will the closure begin?

(A) On June 5
(B) On June 7
(C) On June 9
(D) On June 10

**153.** What are some staff members asked to do?

(A) Call a manager
(B) Work from home
(C) Vacate the offices
(D) Complete work ahead of time

*Go on to the next page*

**Questions 154-155** refer to the following e-mail.

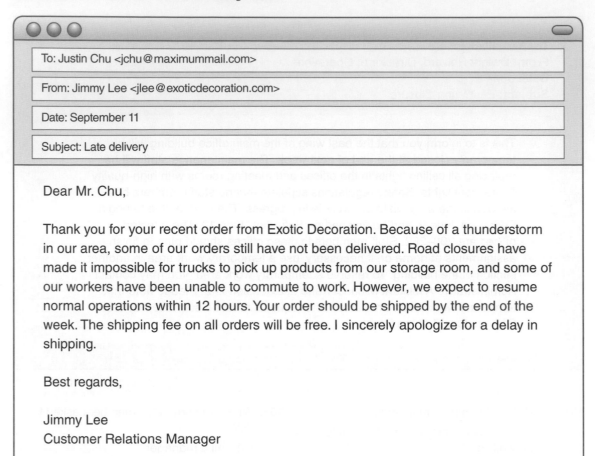

To: Justin Chu <jchu@maximummail.com>

From: Jimmy Lee <jlee@exoticdecoration.com>

Date: September 11

Subject: Late delivery

Dear Mr. Chu,

Thank you for your recent order from Exotic Decoration. Because of a thunderstorm in our area, some of our orders still have not been delivered. Road closures have made it impossible for trucks to pick up products from our storage room, and some of our workers have been unable to commute to work. However, we expect to resume normal operations within 12 hours. Your order should be shipped by the end of the week. The shipping fee on all orders will be free. I sincerely apologize for a delay in shipping.

Best regards,

Jimmy Lee
Customer Relations Manager

**154.** Why was the order late?

(A) Payment has still not been received.
(B) Severe weather affected the delivery schedule.
(C) The product that was ordered is not in stock.
(D) The firm used an inaccurate mailing address.

**155.** What will Mr. Chu receive?

(A) A discount coupon for his next purchase
(B) A cash refund
(C) Complimentary shipping on his order
(D) A replacement part

**Questions 156-158** refer to the following e-mail.

| From: | Tim Daily <tdaily@sunflower.com> |
|---|---|
| To: | Derek Hamilton <lhamilton@goodcaterer.com> |
| Date: | June 12 |
| Subject: | Re: Floral centerpieces |

Dear Mr. Hamilton,

This e-mail serves as confirmation of our telephone conversation this morning about your request for 12 flower arrangements for your company awards ceremony. You had asked that they be comparable to the floral centerpieces that we made for your last event. However, my supplier for the rose of Sharon has notified me that, due to a delay at the greenhouses, they won't be available until the end of this month.

Because you need the flower arrangements finished by June 17, I think it would be best to select an alternative flower. I recommend the hollyhock, which is comparable in appearance. Please let me know if this is acceptable by replying to this e-mail. I will then fax you the finished agreement and pricing list. If you have any other questions, please contact me at 432-234-2345.

Thank you,

Tim Daily
Manager, Sunflower

---

**156.** What is suggested about Mr. Hamilton?

(A) He is a friend of Mr. Daily.
(B) He is preparing a private party at his house.
(C) He has asked for a change to his order.
(D) He has used Sunflower's services previously.

**157.** Why does Mr. Daily recommend replacing the rose of Sharon?

(A) They are out of stock.
(B) They are the wrong size.
(C) They are not cheap.
(D) They are not fresh.

**158.** What does Mr. Daily ask Mr. Hamilton to do?

(A) Sign a contract
(B) Talk at the shop
(C) Respond to an e-mail
(D) Send a partial payment

*Go on to the next page*

# The Museum of Fine Arts

The Museum of Fine Arts will host Ed Harrison on Wednesday, April 5, at 6:00 P.M. Mr. Harrison will talk about his most recent book, *The American Dream's Painting*. Published by Neo Publishing, the volume provides a detailed description of the history of art in North America. The talk is open to the public. No reservation will be taken. Guests must arrive at least half an hour before the start time because seats are limited to 100. For additional information, call 287-333-2422 or go to our website.

**159.** Who is Mr. Harrison?

(A) An author
(B) An artist
(C) A bookstore supervisor
(D) A museum staff member

**160.** How should seats for the event be obtained?

(A) Online
(B) By telephone
(C) By mail
(D) In person

**Question 161-164** refer to the following article.

## Expansion Project Moving Forward in Shanghai

July 5 — Roland Technology finished the first stage of its expansion project two weeks ago. Roland Technology, one of the largest manufacturers of components used in computer monitors and projectors, began construction on its three new factories to be built over the next eight years. —[1]—. The first of the factories to be built, in China's Shanghai, is the company's largest factory and will ultimately produce 60% of the company's production quota every year.

The new plant has brought with it a rise in jobs for local citizens. —[2]—. Over 1,500 construction workers were employed to build the large-scale factory and its surrounding structures. Roland Technology President Takahashi Miyuki said, "This is the largest project for our company. When we began construction, we realized that it was going to need plenty of money, resources, and staff. —[3]—. We employed locals to expand the physical plant as well as adding a number of employees to our full-time payroll. We hope to do the same thing in Japan. We plan to start building in Tokyo soon." The company's main office is now located in Tokyo, Japan.

Extra factories will be constructed in Roland Technology's other locations, including in Thailand and Korea. While the remaining plants will not be as large as the Shanghai factory, they will still need resources and labor. —[4]—.

**161.** What is mentioned about Roland Technology?

(A) It produces monitor elements.
(B) It was recently acquired by its competitor.
(C) It is remodeling its company headquarters.
(D) It sells construction materials.

**162.** What is inferred about the Roland Technology factory in Shanghai?

(A) It was the third new factory which was built last year.
(B) It is the biggest factory the company has.
(C) It manufactures a quarter of the company's output.
(D) It took over six years to construct.

**163.** Where will the next Roland Technology factory be constructed?

(A) In China
(B) In Thailand
(C) In Korea
(D) In Japan

**164.** In which of the positions marked [1], [2], [3] and [4] does the following sentence best belong?

"We were delighted to see the influence the project had on local laborers."

(A) [1]
(B) [2]
(C) [3]
(D) [4]

**Questions 165-167** refer to the following article.

Situated on the corner of First Avenue and East Street, Variety opened a decade ago and rapidly became a popular eatery. As its name suggests, Variety features a large collection of dishes prepared with several international recipes. Variety had been closed for two months while undergoing an improvement in management. It reopened its doors two weeks ago. The new chef, Matt Shelian, has made a remarkable menu with an even wider selection of gourmet soups, salads, and delicious entrées. Some of his specialties include excellent seafood dishes, such as the smoked halibut with mango and the shrimp with chili sauce. Please be sure to try the outstanding dessert—caramel apple pie. With so many delicious items to select, Variety is certain to be a new favorite.

**165.** What is the purpose of the article?

(A) To review a restaurant
(B) To promote a cooking class
(C) To compare two restaurants
(D) To announce a new location

**166.** What is mentioned about Mr. Shelian?

(A) He is proficient in making seafood dishes.
(B) He uses only local produce.
(C) He has refurbished a restaurant.
(D) He started working at Variety six months ago.

**167.** What is suggested about the restaurant?

(A) Its management replaced most of the staff.
(B) It serves an excellent dessert.
(C) Its most popular dish is the halibut.
(D) It has relocated to a new building.

**Questions 168-171** refer to the following e-mail.

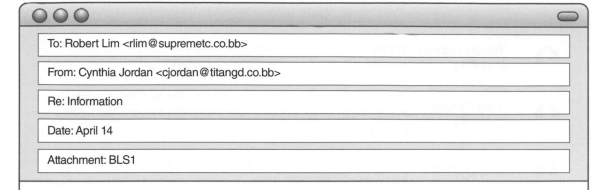

To: Robert Lim <rlim@supremetc.co.bb>

From: Cynthia Jordan <cjordan@titangd.co.bb>

Re: Information

Date: April 14

Attachment: BLS1

Dear Mr. Lim,

I am following up on the Titan Gardening service proposal I sent on 22 March. —[1]—.

We are one of the best in Queensville, and we want to add you to our list of satisfied clients. Our clients include numerous local businesses like hotels, restaurants, and resorts. —[2]—. In the event you overlooked the original proposal, I am attaching it again here.

The proposal is based on the service you asked about, namely the maintenance of the grounds around Supreme Tennis Courts twice a week. —[3]—. If you are interested in more extensive work, such as replacing trees, extra charges would apply.

I'm looking forward to hearing from you. I hope our company will have the chance to be beneficial to you in the future. —[4]—.

Sincerely,

Cynthia Jordan

**168.** Why was the e-mail written?

(A) To schedule a meeting
(B) To explain new prices
(C) To resend a previous estimate
(D) To send in a corrected proposal

**169.** What is suggested in the e-mail?

(A) Mr. Lim is a satisfied customer.
(B) Titan Gardening is a new business.
(C) Ms. Jordan had a meeting with Mr. Lim.
(D) Mr. Lim asked Ms. Jordan for some information.

**170.** What type of business does Mr. Lim probably work for?

(A) A hotel
(B) A tennis facility
(C) A restaurant
(D) A gardening center

**171.** In which of the positions marked [1], [2], [3] and [4] does the following sentence best belong?

"Additionally, we would reevaluate your requirements on an ongoing basis and relay recommendations to you twice a month."

(A) [1]
(B) [2]
(C) [3]
(D) [4]

*Go on to the next page*

**Questions 172-175** refer to the following online chat discussion.

| | | |
|---|---|---|
| 👤 | **Tyrone Gibson**<br>[1:32 P.M.] | Thank you for participating in the virtual sales meeting this morning. Do you have any other questions? |
| 👤 | **Judy Chung**<br>[1:35 P.M.] | George and I are not certain about how the new sales territory maps influence established customers. Will the new territories apply exclusively to new customers? |
| 👤 | **Tyrone Gibson**<br>[1:37 P.M.] | Of course not. The new territories apply to first-time and established customers alike. |
| 👤 | **Judy Chung**<br>[1:38 P.M.] | So, does that mean I will no longer obtain commissions from my French customer, YDV Mechanism? |
| 👤 | **Tyrone Gibson**<br>[1:39 P.M.] | That's right. All established customers in northern France go to George. |
| 👤 | **George Kim**<br>[1:41 P.M.] | But why don't I just allow Judy to keep YDV Mechanism? |
| 👤 | **Tyrone Gibson**<br>[1:42 P.M.] | YDV Mechanism is a big customer. |
| 👤 | **George Kim**<br>[1:44 P.M.] | Yes, but I want to avoid disrupting a productive partnership. Plus, this customer is unimportant to me. |
| 👤 | **Tyrone Gibson**<br>[1:45 P.M.] | I don't see it as disrupting, really. However, if you feel strongly about this, George, I might be able to bend the rules if our president approves of it. |
| 👤 | **Judy Chung**<br>[1:47 P.M.] | Why don't I speak to the customer? |
| 👤 | **Tyrone Gibson**<br>[1:48 P.M.] | I don't think that's suitable. |
| 👤 | **Judy Chung**<br>[1:49 P.M.] | Understood. |
| 👤 | **George Kim**<br>[1:49 P.M.] | All right. We're looking forward to hearing back from you about this matter. |

Send

**172.** Who most likely is Mr. Gibson?

(A) A president
(B) The head of sales
(C) A tour guide
(D) A personnel director

**173.** What is inferred about Ms. Chung?

(A) She has a good rapport with YDV Mechanism.
(B) She is being relocated to an office in France.
(C) She is delighted with the new territory assigned to her.
(D) She did not take part in the sales meeting.

**174.** At 1:48 P.M., what does Mr. Gibson most likely mean when he writes, "I don't think that's suitable"?

(A) He is doubtful that Ms. Chung can meet YDV Mechanism's requirements.
(B) He thinks Ms. Chung has misunderstood.
(C) He would like Ms. Chung to visit France.
(D) He doesn't want Ms. Chung to contact YDV Mechanism regarding this matter.

**175.** What will probably happen next?

(A) Ms. Chung will go over the new map of the sales territory.
(B) Ms. Chung will speak with her customer.
(C) Mr. Gibson will call the company's president.
(D) Mr. Kim will accept a job offer from YDV Mechanism.

*Go on to the next page*

From: Mary Cho <mcho@dtu.com>

To: Peter O'Malley <pomalley@dtu.com>

Date: June 3

Subject: Worldwide Design Conference

Dear Peter,

Thank you for volunteering to fill in for me at the Worldwide Design Conference in Boston on June 10. I need to stay at the San Francisco main office to meet with some visiting French clients. When I was there last year, I found it extremely worthwhile and was able to make some business contacts with prospective designers.

I've already handled your airplane ticket, hotel, and rental car. These have already been paid for by DTU, and you'll receive $50 a day for meals after you return here. If you decide to take some designers out for dinner, please retain receipts for your records and hand them in to the Accounting Department after you come back for reimbursement.

The timeline for the conference is as follows:

|  | 10 A.M. – 12 P.M. Innovative Graphics |
|---|---|
| **Monday** | 12 P.M. – 2 P.M. Web Design World and Luncheon |
|  | 3 P.M. – 5 P.M. Gigantic Logos 4D |
| **Tuesday** | The entire day is scheduled for the design exposition |

Best regards,

Mary

From: Peter O'Malley <pomalley@dtu.com>

To: Mary Cho <mcho@dtu.com>

Date: June 10

Subject: RE: Worldwide Design Conference

Dear Mary,

I came back from the conference earlier this afternoon. The Monday morning presentation was canceled because the speaker's flight had been delayed. However, the other presentations went smoothly. I heard and experienced many things and will finish a report in two weeks. I really appreciate your giving me the opportunity to represent DTU's advertising department at the conference.

Sincerely,

Peter

176. Why did Ms. Cho write an e-mail to
Mr. O'Malley?

(A) To show her gratitude for his
suggestion
(B) To give him some information about a
business meeting
(C) To check his conference reservation
(D) To issue him a refund

177. What does Ms. Cho indicate about the
conference?

(A) It is renowned for presentations by
leading business owners.
(B) It took place in San Francisco last year
for the first time.
(C) It offers opportunities to meet
business acquaintances.
(D) It is the best location to meet French
businessmen.

178. What expenditure will DTU NOT pay for
beforehand?

(A) Food expenses
(B) Hotel charges
(C) Airfare
(D) A car rental charge

179. What presentation was called off at the
conference?

(A) Innovative Graphics
(B) Web Design World
(C) Gigantic Logo 4D
(D) Design Exposition

180. What department does Mr. O'Malley most
likely work for?

(A) Sales
(B) Advertising
(C) Personnel
(D) Accounting

**Questions 181-185** refer to the following e-mails.

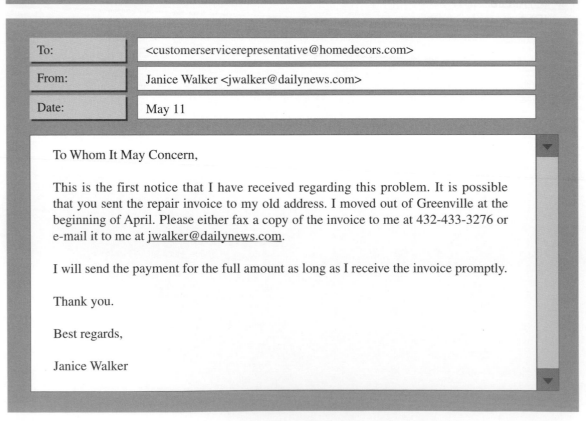

| To: | Janice Walker <jwalker@dailynews.com> |
| From: | Rachel Hunter <rhunter@homedecors.com> |
| Date: | May 10 |

Dear Ms. Walker,

According to our database, your account is overdue at the moment. You have a balance of $735.40 for the work done at your residence. Five workers were at your home to fix the hole in the roof on March 13. An invoice was sent out to you on April 5 and was to be paid by April 23. There is a late fee of $50, but if full payment is made promptly, this late fee will be waived. If you have already submitted payment, contact our main office as soon as possible. Would you please send all correspondence to me because I am monitoring your account?

Thank you.

Sincerely,

Rachel Hunter
Account Manager, Home Decors

| To: | <customerservicerepresentative@homedecors.com> |
| From: | Janice Walker <jwalker@dailynews.com> |
| Date: | May 11 |

To Whom It May Concern,

This is the first notice that I have received regarding this problem. It is possible that you sent the repair invoice to my old address. I moved out of Greenville at the beginning of April. Please either fax a copy of the invoice to me at 432-433-3276 or e-mail it to me at jwalker@dailynews.com.

I will send the payment for the full amount as long as I receive the invoice promptly.

Thank you.

Best regards,

Janice Walker

**181.** Why did Ms. Hunter send an e-mail to Ms. Walker?

(A) To notify her of mistakes in an invoice
(B) To ask for an overdue payment
(C) To apologize for an unsatisfactory job
(D) To charge a late fee

**182.** What does Ms. Hunter ask Ms. Walker to do?

(A) Copy a billing statement
(B) Meet the deadline
(C) Check her account
(D) Pay for the invoice in full

**183.** What does Ms. Walker request that customer service do?

(A) Send a document of her fees by fax
(B) Deposit the payment
(C) Check her current address
(D) Call her right now

**184.** What is inferred about Ms. Walker?

(A) She built a new house.
(B) She recently relocated to a new home.
(C) She lost her billing statement.
(D) She went on a business trip in April.

**185.** What detail did Ms. Walker NOT include in her e-mail?

(A) The former residence
(B) The e-mail address
(C) The name of the account manager
(D) The fax number

*Go on to the next page*

From: <jasonkang@resisdente.com>

To: <bills@planpower.com>

Date: June 17

Subject: Invoice A893-06

To Whom It May Concern,

Hello, I am writing about my electricity bill for May. The amount due was much higher than I have paid in previous months, which is normally $350. I do not plan on missing the deadline for the payment, but I would like to know why the substantial increase in my bill occurred. If the change is incorrect, I would appreciate an adjustment to my account. I know that my meter is nearly obsolete, so I also wonder if it should be replaced with a new one.

If a technician needs to check it, the best time would be before noon on any weekday. I am at home then and would prefer to be present, if possible, while the work is being done.

With my best regards,

Jason Kang

## Service Technician Log Sheet — New Year Residences
*June 30*

| Technician name | Address of service | Start time | Service |
|---|---|---|---|
| Paula Morreja | 2249 Keystone Blvd. | 10:52 A.M. | Meter repaired |
| Gini Padovani | 2809 Redhill Rd. | 12:38 P.M. | Meter replaced |
| Barak Hilton | 76 Ellington Ave. | 1:40 P.M. | Meter replaced |
| Brad Hopkins | 8100 Saint Rd. | 3:52 P.M. | Meter inspected |

| From: | <bills@planpower.com> |
| To: | <jasonkang@resisdente.com> |
| Date: | June 30 |
| Subject: | invoice A893-06 |

Dear Mr. Kang,

Thank you for contacting Plan Power. I am writing to let you know that the sudden increase in your bill was caused by a faulty meter. The technician who visited your Redhill residence found out that the old device had registered your use of electricity incorrectly.

The device has been replaced, and this type of problem should not take place again. The malfunction affects your bill for May only; the total amount of $127.18 will appear on your next bill. Should you have any questions, please feel free to contact us.

Sincerely,

Mark Dillon
Plan Power Customer Support

**186.** Why was the first e-mail sent?

(A) To change a deadline extension
(B) To ask for a receipt
(C) To inquire about the amount
(D) To sign up for online billing

**187.** What is suggested about Mr. Kang?

(A) He correctly identified the problem.
(B) He recently moved to a new place.
(C) He has contacted Mr. Dillon several times.
(D) He plans to close his account with Plan Power.

**188.** Who visited Mr. Kang's house on June 30?

(A) Paula Morreja
(B) Gini Padovani
(C) Barak Hilton
(D) Brad Hopkins

**189.** In the second e-mail, the word "registered" in paragraph 1, line 3, is closest in meaning to

(A) attended
(B) permitted
(C) recorded
(D) allowed

**190.** What does Mr. Dillon indicate in his e-mail?

(A) That the payment is already overdue
(B) That the problem was limited to only one month
(C) That the new service is being provided
(D) That the new meter was ordered

*Go on to the next page*

# Melody Academy of Music
## 32 Saint Street, Seattle, WA 98105
## www.melody-music.ac

Melody Academy of Music is delighted to announce its next season of performances — from classical music to jazz, hip hop, and pop.
Please join us to see all that we have to offer! You can buy all kinds of tickets for the entire season or for an individual performance. Tickets can be purchased at half of the original price for Season Ticket buyers.

　※ The Mozart Group gives an impressive jazz performance. 18 – 22 March
　※ Eugene Ryu performs his award-winning pop songs. One day only — 7 April
　※ The Seattle Ensemble plays classical music. 15 – 22 April
　※ Catherine Winslet sings while accomplished by live guitar. 23 – 27 April

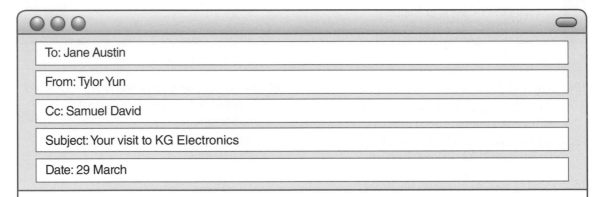

To: Jane Austin

From: Tylor Yun

Cc: Samuel David

Subject: Your visit to KG Electronics

Date: 29 March

Hi Ms. Austin,

On behalf of the personnel department at KG Electronics, I'd like to let you know how happy we are to adopt the personnel management software you will be teaching us about on 21–23 April. As you requested, I reserved the room and necessary devises such as a desktop computer, projector, and microphone. If you need any further assistance with your presentation, do not hesitate to let me know.

As a token of appreciation, Mr. David, our department head, has made special plans to make your visit more memorable. He made a dinner reservation at a very famous Italian restaurant on the first evening of your visit. On the second day of your visit, we will be able to go to see an outstanding performance at the Melody Academy of Music.

Sincerely,

Tylor Yun
KG Electronics

**Tylor Yun's phone**

*From: Samuel David*
*Received: 8:45 A.M.*

Hi, I just got words from Ms. Austin. Her original flight has been delayed. Therefore, her new arrival time has been changed. However, we're going to still be able to hold the meeting today. She requested that the entertainment be moved to tomorrow, so there is no rush now. If I order the tickets myself rather than have you do it, we can receive a considerable discount. Could you postpone the dinner reservation? If that is not possible, please cancel it. I apologize for the inconvenience this may cause.

**191.** What is suggested about Melody Academy of Music?

(A) It has an on-site museum.
(B) It is employing a new conductor.
(C) It offers music lessons to young children.
(D) It offers different styles of music performances.

**192.** How much discount will Season Ticket buyers get?

(A) 20%
(B) 30%
(C) 40%
(D) 50%

**193.** What is Ms. Austin scheduled to do during her visit?

(A) Revise legal documents
(B) Demonstrate how to use some software
(C) Repair presentation equipment
(D) Conduct a survey

**194.** What performance was Ms. Austin originally scheduled to attend?

(A) The Mozart Group
(B) Eugene Ryu
(C) The Seattle Ensemble
(D) Catherine Winslet

**195.** What is Mr Yun asked to do?

(A) Make a flight reservation
(B) Set a meeting time
(C) Train new employees
(D) Call off a meal reservation

*Go on to the next page*

# OHQ Containers
# Mobile Refrigerated Storage Units

OHQ Containers provides refrigerated storage units to restaurants, cafés, grocery stores, and other businesses that are currently looking for cold-storage solutions.

**All the units below include :**
1. Lockable door latches, non-slip flooring, and interior fluorescent light fixtures
2. A 20-metre power cable

**Service for your business :**
Our delivery service is available to any location in Scotland.
All the units are available for short-term, monthly, or annual lease.

**Our storage options are:**

| Unit | Door Type | Length (metres) | Floor Space (square metres) | Internal Capacity (cubic metres) |
|---|---|---|---|---|
| Economy | Single | 3.0m | 7.5m² | 18.75m³ |
| Standard | Double | 6.0m | 15.0m² | 37.5m³ |
| Supreme | Double | 9.0m | 22.5m² | 56.25m³ |
| Supreme Plus | Plus Double | 12.0m | 30.0m² | 75.0m³ |

Should you need any help with making a decision, our outstanding customer service representatives will recommend the ideal storage solution for you. For further information, please visit http://www.OHQ.com.

---

http://www.OHQ.com/inquiry

# OHQ Containers—Customer Inquiry Form

**Name:** Aiden Park
**Business:** Park's café
**E-mail:** <parkscafé@plantomorrow.com>
**Date:** Oct. 14

Hello, I was told about your company from my friend, Bill Folder, who is currently using one of your units for his own business. I am also the owner of a restaurant, and our freezer can no longer accommodate our food storage needs. Thus, we require an OHQ unit that can be placed near the back entrance of the building. We don't need a lot of extra storage space, but we do need a unit with double doors so we can easily load everything in and out. Please tell me which unit you recommend and also the possible date of delivery. Also, I was wondering if your units are equipped with a digital temperature display. We need to be able to closely monitor the temperature at all times.

Thank you.

## Customer Review

I have been using OHQ Containers for about four months now, and I am fully contented with my choice. And I was pleased to have my first month's rental fee waived thanks to OHQ's refer-a-friend programme, which allowed my friend and me to receive a free month's rental each. I started with a smaller 37.5 cubic-metre storage unit, but it became clear this month that I would need something one size bigger to serve the increasing guests. The day after I called OHQ, a company representative delivered a new unit that meets my needs perfectly. I highly recommend OHQ Containers to everyone that is in need of efficient cold storage for their business.

Aiden Park, Owner, Park's Café

**196.** What information about OHQ Containers is NOT given in the advertisement?

(A) The total number of doors
(B) The type of lighting
(C) The range of temperature settings
(D) The size of the interior space

**197.** What is indicated about Mr. Park?

(A) He used to be a coworker of Mr. Folder.
(B) He supports the local community.
(C) He plans to switch to a new delivery company.
(D) He got a discount from OHQ Containers.

**198.** What is suggested about Park's Café?

(A) It features organic produce.
(B) It is located near OHQ Containers.
(C) It plans to extend its business hours.
(D) Its business continues to grow.

**199.** Which unit is Mr. Park currently using?

(A) Economy
(B) Standard
(C) Supreme
(D) Supreme Plus

**200.** In the review, the word "contented" in line 1, is closest in meaning to

(A) pleased
(B) angry
(C) dismayed
(D) astonished

# ACTUAL
# TEST

## 答對題數表

| | |
|---|---|
| **PART 5** | |
| **PART 6** | |
| **PART 7** | |
| 總題數 | |

02

# READING TEST

In the Reading test, you will read a variety of texts and answer several different types of reading comprehension questions. The entire Reading test will last 75 minutes. There are three parts, and directions are given for each part. You are encouraged to answer as many questions as possible within the time allowed.

You must mark your answers on the separate answer sheet. Do not write your answers in your test book.

## PART 5

**Directions:** A word or phrase is missing in each of the sentences below. Four answer choices are given below each sentence. Select the best answer to complete the sentence. Then mark the letter (A), (B), (C), or (D) on your answer sheet.

**101.** Salespeople at Cedarville Grocery Store receive extra pay when ------ work extended hours.

(A) they
(B) their
(C) them
(D) theirs

**102.** Ms. Juntasa has been ------ recommended by her former employers.

(A) high
(B) highly
(C) higher
(D) highest

**103.** The use of high-quality but ------ mechanical components resulted in a decline in costs for Mr. David's factory.

(A) unhappy
(B) incomplete
(C) unaware
(D) inexpensive

**104.** The publishing conference has been rescheduled ------ tomorrow due to the worsening weather conditions.

(A) in
(B) by
(C) for
(D) out

**105.** Alpha Tech's most recent software makes it ------ than ever for publishers to create newspapers.

(A) easy
(B) ease
(C) easily
(D) easier

**106.** A limited ------ of time for questions will be provided subsequent to Mr. Yamaguchi's talk.

(A) amount
(B) number
(C) value
(D) record

**107.** Customers ------ purchase merchandise from Easy-To-Go.com typically receive their orders within three business days.

(A) whomever
(B) whom
(C) whose
(D) who

**108.** The ------ of this training session is to provide business owners with the tools to make informed decisions.

(A) guide
(B) experience
(C) objective
(D) solution

109. Ms. Lee is ------ responsible for supervising quality assurance procedures at the Hawksdale facility.

(A) primarily
(B) nearly
(C) slowly
(D) previously

110. ------- for the Valleywood Photography Contest must be received by May 25.

(A) Being entered
(B) Entries
(C) Enters
(D) Entered

111. Riley Textile Corporation reported a 10 percent rise ------ profits last year.

(A) off
(B) at
(C) in
(D) up

112. Because of the decrease in the cost of materials, the price of Supreme Laboratory's cutting-edge microscope will be lower than -------.

(A) anticipated
(B) organized
(C) experimented
(D) inclined

113. Admission to the Maxwell Botanical Garden will be free every Thursday from 10 A.M. to 2 P.M. ------ the spring.

(A) beneath
(B) throughout
(C) without
(D) down

114. All staff members who ------- drilling equipment must wear safety goggles.

(A) operate
(B) operates
(C) operating
(D) is operated

115. A replacement key for your car may be ordered directly from our dealership, ------ you demonstrate proof of ownership.

(A) as though
(B) provided that
(C) regardless of
(D) instead of

116. We encouraged guests to leave ------- for improving the service at our airline.

(A) suggest
(B) suggested
(C) suggesting
(D) suggestions

117. An uncommonly large number of employees in the Accounting Department retired last year, leaving 13 positions -------.

(A) dedicated
(B) hollow
(C) invalid
(D) vacant

118. Kane's in Denversville is a full-service photography studio ------ in family portraits.

(A) specialist
(B) specially
(C) specialize
(D) specializing

119. Larkhill Health Center is always ------ to consider the certified specialists who are interested in joining our organization.

(A) possible
(B) willing
(C) necessary
(D) useful

120. Government ------ on the import of construction materials were temporarily lifted so as to meet increasing demand.

(A) authorities
(B) treatments
(C) restrictions
(D) supplies

*Go on to the next page*

121. Spring Deli's fruit and vegetable tray is popular now that it is appealing and ------ priced.

(A) afford
(B) afforded
(C) affordable
(D) affordably

122. Mr. Davidson volunteered to help at the reception desk ------ he has not ever worked directly with clients.

(A) even though
(B) or
(C) until
(D) so that

123. Smith's Plumbing has eight company-owned trucks, four of ------ are currently in the auto repair shop.

(A) whose
(B) other
(C) whom
(D) which

124. Hampton Accounting has ------ costs by restricting international travel and encouraging the use of online video conferencing.

(A) reduced
(B) stated
(C) qualified
(D) examined

125. Dawson Corporation announced in a press conference that it is planning to expand ------ Europe.

(A) of
(B) into
(C) around
(D) at

126. As ------ a month has passed since the products were sent, we should ask the delivery company for an update.

(A) nearly
(B) immediately
(C) partially
(D) thoroughly

127. Seeking new sources of revenue, many local orchards ------ catering to tourists in the past five years.

(A) to begin
(B) have begun
(C) will have begun
(D) will begin

128. Meteorologists forecast three ------- days of rain, which should provide a welcome relief from the unseasonable heat.

(A) sensitive
(B) refreshed
(C) consecutive
(D) deliberate

129. Caribbean Bay Hotel's kitchen is open 24 hours a day, making sure that you have the dining service you need ------ you desire it.

(A) wherever
(B) even if
(C) whenever
(D) in order that

130. Jacob Lee told his manager about the complaints from overseas clients, and she promised to ------ the problem.

(A) look into
(B) pick up
(C) show up
(D) turn off

# PART 6

**Directions:** Read the texts that follow. A word, phrase, or sentence is missing in parts of each text. Four answer choices for each question are given below the text. Select the best answer to complete the text. Then mark the letter (A), (B), (C), or (D) on your answer sheet.

**Questions 131-134** refer to the following information.

Hightech staff members who have been working full time for more than two years are ------- **131.** to apply for internal transfers and job advancement opportunities within the firm. -------. Those **132.** interested will be considered together with external -------. Staff members who have essential **133.** qualifications to fill the open positions will be given ------- if outside recruitment isn't considered **134.** to be in the company's best interest.

131. (A) eligible
(B) collaborative
(C) exclusive
(D) prominent

132. (A) Staff members who wish to apply should first meet with their managers.
(B) Actually, all staff members are required to report their work hours daily.
(C) For instance, a competitive benefit package is given to full-time workers.
(D) We are delighted to welcome new staff members to our Hightech team.

133. (A) factors
(B) candidates
(C) occupations
(D) suppliers

134. (A) preferring
(B) preferred
(C) preference
(D) prefer

The Michael Theater will be extending its run of Shining Stars, a play by Justine Kay.

Due to an unexpected rise in ------- for the tickets, the last performance will now occur on
**135.**

March 18. The move comes as something of a surprise, considering the ------- reviews written
**136.**

by critics after the show's opening on February 2. -------. However, the show has abruptly
**137.**

become popular among younger people, most of whom get their news through the Internet.

They are ------- interested in the play's exploration of economic issues and career choices.
**138.**

**135.** (A) demanded
(B) demanding
(C) to demand
(D) demand

**136.** (A) brilliant
(B) deep
(C) harsh
(D) prompt

**137.** (A) Actors from the show are local residents.
(B) The premiere was attended by local business leaders.
(C) The initial box office sales had also been weak.
(D) Moreover, the theater company has been around for several years.

**138.** (A) apparent
(B) more apparent
(C) apparentness
(D) apparently

On April 5, Emerson Radio will celebrate its twenty-fifth anniversary. That's a quarter

of a century of stimulating -------. Over the years, we ------- our listeners breaking news,
                     **139.**                             **140.**

thought-provoking stories, and popular music throughout the world. Now, we encourage

you to celebrate with us during an open house from 7:00 P.M. to 9:00 P.M. on April 5 at our

Charles Avenue studio. Take a tour and see some of the behind-the-scenes magic. Watch a

demonstration of our digital audio equipment. -------. The open house is free, but registration is
                                              **141.**

required. We hope you can join us for this ------- event.
                           **142.**

139. (A) concerts
    (B) development
    (C) programming
    (D) discussions

140. (A) offers
    (B) will offer
    (C) offering
    (D) have offered

141. (A) We hope to merge with another local
        radio station in the coming year.
    (B) You can also meet some of your
        favorite broadcasters.
    (C) This is the second event in our April
        schedule.
    (D) This station continues to be an
        essential part of your neighborhood.

142. (A) special
    (B) specialize
    (C) specially
    (D) specialization

*Go on to the next page*

**To:** David Kim <dkim@eleganthotel.com>

**From:** Albert Lee <alee@eleganthotel.com>

**Date:** 22 June

**Subject:** Good Afternoon

Dear David,

I was recently notified of your upcoming -------. Though the new position as general manager
                                       **143.**

in our New York location formally ------- on 1 August, I wanted to offer my best wishes to you
                                   **144.**

now.

The transition can be -------, so please don't hesitate to contact me if you need any assistance.
                      **145.**

Your performance as assistant general manager at the Elegant Hotel here in Singapore has

been outstanding. -------.
                  **146.**

Congratulations!

Sincerely,

Albert Lee

---

**143.** (A) promotion
(B) award
(C) event
(D) trip

**144.** (A) began
(B) begins
(C) could begin
(D) has begun

**145.** (A) challenging
(B) challenges
(C) challenge
(D) challenged

**146.** (A) The New York hotel is bigger and has additional amenities.
(B) I'm presently interviewing candidates for all the positions.
(C) In the meantime, inquire about staff member discounts at the hotel.
(D) I am confident that you will succeed in your new role.

# PART 7

**Directions:** In this part you will read a selection of texts, such as magazine and newspaper articles, e-mails, and instant messages. Each text or set of texts is followed by several questions. Select the best answer for each question and mark the letter (A), (B), (C), or (D) on your answer sheet.

**Questions 147-148** refer to the following text message.

**From: Montera Hassan**
**To: Grace Kim**

Grace, my smartphone battery is almost dead. I think I left my power cord at the office.
Would you please call my customer and tell him I'll be roughly 20 minutes late?
I'm heading back to the office to get the cord right now.

**147.** Why did Mr. Hassan send a message to Ms. Kim?

(A) To inquire whether she found his power cord
(B) To ask that she contact a customer
(C) To remind her to recharge a battery
(D) To check the location of an accounting division

**148.** What will Mr. Hassan probably do next?

(A) Find his computer
(B) Return to his office
(C) Purchase a power cord
(D) Contact the technical support department

*Go on to the next page*

Dayton Café owner, Brandon Ehret, has signed a lease for a second restaurant at 623 Smithon Avenue.

The building, close to Rolling Concert Hall, previously housed a branch of Carol Financial Group. Mr. Ehret's most recent venture, to be called Tiara Snacks, will begin service on August 1. At first, however, the small restaurant will be open only during the evening hours. The idea is to build a customer base, particularly among concertgoers, prior to adding a lunch service. Mr. Ehret's original restaurant, Dayton Café, is located on First Street, near the Winning Grocery Store bus stop. Executive Chef Jessica Choi will supervise the two locations.

**149.** What is the article about?

(A) The opening of a new restaurant
(B) An outstanding real estate agent
(C) A change in prices
(D) A restaurant's relocation

**150.** What is suggested about Tiara Snacks?

(A) It is situated adjacent to a public transportation route.
(B) It is expected to receive business from concert patrons.
(C) It is supposed to start serving lunch on August 1.
(D) It is Mr. Ehret's third restaurant.

**Questions 151-153** refer to the following memo.

**From:** Alex Baldwin
**To:** Garrison Builders employees
**Date:** 15 June
**Subject:** All-staff meeting

To all of the employees,

Next Monday, 29 June, we will have a guest speaker at our all-staff meeting in room 304. Dee Ihibramvich is a senior architect at the Extraordinary Firm in Bern, where she has worked for the last ten years. She led the design project of Bern's Bundle House as well as the Titan Skyscraper in Rome. These two buildings received international awards for their innovative designs.

Before making a name for herself in Europe, Ms. Ihibramvich spent six years in San Francisco at the Dynamic Architect Organization (DAO). It was at the DAO that I had the opportunity to cooperate with her on many projects. Ms. Ihibramvich will be here in London for two weeks and has consented to deliver a speech at our meeting about many of her internationally admired design projects.

All employees are required to participate.

**151.** Why was the memo written?

(A) To announce a plan to open another satellite branch
(B) To employ a new employee
(C) To suggest a construction project
(D) To introduce an architect's accomplishments

**152.** What does Mr. Baldwin suggest about Ms. Ihibramvich?

(A) She will lead a design project for his company.
(B) She intends to open her own business.
(C) She is a former coworker of his.
(D) She is relocating to a new city.

**153.** Where is Garrison Builders located?

(A) In London
(B) In San Francisco
(C) In Rome
(D) In Bern

*Go on to the next page*

**Questions 154-155** refer to the following text message chain.

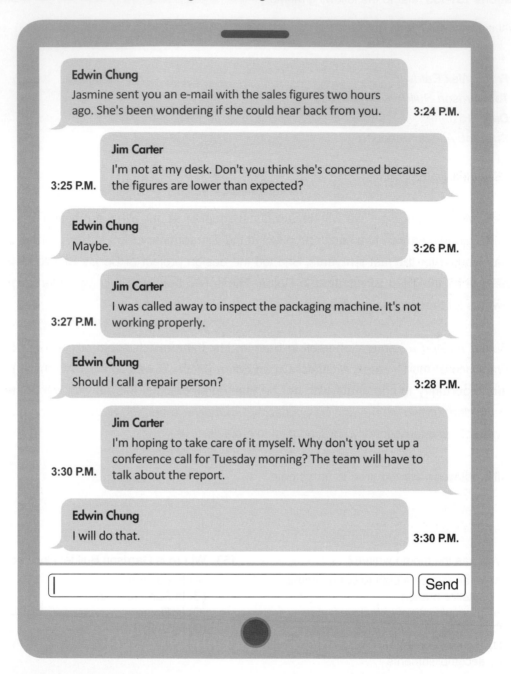

**Edwin Chung**
Jasmine sent you an e-mail with the sales figures two hours ago. She's been wondering if she could hear back from you. **3:24 P.M.**

**Jim Carter**
**3:25 P.M.** I'm not at my desk. Don't you think she's concerned because the figures are lower than expected?

**Edwin Chung**
Maybe. **3:26 P.M.**

**Jim Carter**
**3:27 P.M.** I was called away to inspect the packaging machine. It's not working properly.

**Edwin Chung**
Should I call a repair person? **3:28 P.M.**

**Jim Carter**
**3:30 P.M.** I'm hoping to take care of it myself. Why don't you set up a conference call for Tuesday morning? The team will have to talk about the report.

**Edwin Chung**
I will do that. **3:30 P.M.**

Send

**154.** At 3:25 P.M., what does Mr. Carter probably mean when he writes, "I'm not at my desk"?

(A) He got off work early.
(B) He will miss a deadline.
(C) He is stopping by Mr. Chung's office.
(D) He cannot reply to Jasmine.

**155.** What is Mr. Chung requested to do?

(A) Go over documents
(B) Arrange a meeting
(C) Check travel plans
(D) Fix some devices

**Questions 156-158** refer to the following letter.

# Rachel Artwork Museum

_15 March_

_Ms. Jennifer Baek_

Dear Ms. Baek,

As a Rachel Artwork Museum member, you will shortly be able to make use of our special appreciation deals. —[1]—. From 1 to 28 April, members will receive an additional 30 percent discount on all gift shop products. Members will also be offered a free beverage with their meal in the on-site café. Furthermore, people who become new members no later than 28 April will be offered a 15 percent membership fee discount. —[2]—. So invite your family members, friends, and colleagues to go to our website and register.

—[3]—. The formerly closed fourth-floor galleries, which feature sculptures and paintings by ancient Persian artists, will be open to all visitors until 7:30 P.M. every Tuesday of this month. Images of select artwork from these galleries can be seen on our Web page. —[4]—.

We look forward to seeing you soon.

Sincerely,

Justine Liu
Director of Membership Management

---

**156.** What is mentioned about the Rachel Artwork Museum?

(A) It has a place to eat.
(B) It will be closed down for one month.
(C) It will have photos on exhibit.
(D) It has a workshop for art courses.

**157.** What will be different on Tuesdays?

(A) Admission to the museum will be free.
(B) Extra galleries will be open.
(C) Operating hours at the restaurant will be extended.
(D) People will buy some Persian artwork.

**158.** In which of the positions marked [1], [2], [3], and [4] does the following sentence best belong?

"April is a great time to come by the museum for another reason."

(A) [1]
(B) [2]
(C) [3]
(D) [4]

# Notice

September 8 — An article about the upcoming remodeling projects in the public library network, published in our September 7 edition, incorrectly listed the closure date of the library's Kirkstein and Dodgeville branches as October 15. However, according to the library's spokesperson, only the Kirkstein branch will be closed from October 15 through November 20. The Dodgeville branch will keep operating as normal until the Kirkstein branch reopens on November 21. From that date, the Dodgeville branch will be closed until December 25. Please go to the library's website for further information. We sincerely apologize for any inconvenience our mistake may have caused.

**159.** Where would this notice probably be found?

(A) In a library's yearly report
(B) On a schedule of gatherings
(C) In a remodeling plan
(D) In a local newspaper

**160.** When will the Dodgeville branch close for the renovation project?

(A) On October 15
(B) On November 20
(C) On November 21
(D) On December 25

**Question 161-164** refer to the following article.

# Farther Rider is gone!

By Jamal Lopez

On Tuesday, Typhoon Motors, the producer currently manufacturing Farther Rider motorcycles, announced a delay in the launch of the new Fast DM model. Industry rivals responded in surprise at the news. —(1)—. And Farther Rider motorcycle enthusiasts went to its website to express bewilderment with Typhoon Motors for calling off May's eagerly awaited release.

It appears the determination to equip the Fast DM with a hybrid system, which uses gasoline and electric power alike, is to blame. Typhoon Motors admits that the current prototype was rejected due to its huge dimensions and heavy weight. This design of the power system would have needed a larger motorbike body than planned. They had concerns about the durability of its exterior. —(2)—.

Besides the design difficulties, the Farther Rider plant, having been equipped to manufacture previous models, is not ready for production of the Fast DM hybrid. —(3)—. New machines will need to be purchased, and the assembly line will have to be reconfigured.

Two years ago, Typhoon Motors was widely complimented by motorcycle fans after it intervened to save Farther Rider from going bankrupt. What a difference two years has made? —(4)—.

**161.** What is suggested about Typhoon Motors?

(A) It owns the Farther Rider motorbike brand.
(B) It intends to sell a model at a discounted price.
(C) It is relocating its main office.
(D) It will introduce a new motorbike in May.

**162.** What is NOT mentioned as a difficulty with the power system?

(A) It weighs a lot.
(B) It isn't cheap.
(C) It isn't strong.
(D) It is too big.

**163.** Why will the factory be remodeled?

(A) It does not conform to a new regulation.
(B) It has not been updated in over two decades.
(C) It had been outfitted to produce older models.
(D) It is so small that it cannot produce two models at the same time.

**164.** In which of the positions marked [1], [2], [3], and [4] does the following sentence best belong?

"From now on, they will have to bring back the goodwill of these prospective customers."

(A) [1]
(B) [2]
(C) [3]
(D) [4]

*Go on to the next page*

# Hair Style Salon

9 August — Hair Style Salon had an impressive grand opening earlier last week. Owner and hair stylist Arthur Lee mentioned that the event was well attended, and many appointments in the salon have been reserved during the past week. James Morgan, who came by the salon for the first time yesterday, said that he is not surprised that Hair Style Salon is already popular. "It offers quality cuts," he said, "And it's within walking distance because it's situated on the same street where I and many people in the commercial area work."

In fact, Hair Style Salon is situated on crowded Madison Avenue, down the street from Darlington University. "I selected Madison Avenue as a result of its proximity to the campus, and I want to appeal to university students and faculty members," said Lee at the salon opening.

Another new client mentioned that the rates for the salon's services and hair care items were not that expensive. "I was happy to find a good hair salon that is affordably priced," said Michelle Lin, a satisfied customer. "I will absolutely be returning."

Please don't hesitate to call 031-532-4343 or visit www.hairstylesalon.com for additional information or to set up an appointment.

**165.** What is the purpose of the article?

(A) To inform people of the relocation of a business
(B) To encourage hair stylists to attend an event
(C) To introduce the neighborhood to a new business
(D) To notify students of a special discount

**166.** What is mentioned about Mr. Morgan?

(A) He works on Madison Avenue.
(B) He owns the Hair Style Salon.
(C) He participated in the salon's grand opening.
(D) He made an appointment through the Internet.

**167.** Why did Mr. Lee select a particular site for his business?

(A) There is no competition in the community.
(B) There are many parking garages nearby.
(C) The rent is much lower than other locations.
(D) It is adjacent to a university.

**168.** What is suggested about Hair Style Salon?

(A) It is looking for a new stylist.
(B) It sells hair products at a reasonable price.
(C) It offers a discount to new customers.
(D) It provides complimentary hair care vouchers.

---

## *Company World* Subscribers!

Right now, you can register to receive personalized e-mails every Wednesday morning with the latest in business and financial news. You can get the same exhaustive coverage you expect from *Company World* magazine each month without having to wait for 30 days. Select your favorites from a comprehensive list of topics and receive various fascinating articles on those topics every week. This service is available exclusively to subscribers of *Company World*.

It's simple to get started. Just go to www.companyworld.com. Click Sign Up for Personalized E-mails, provide your e-mail address, and select your preferences for the service, knowing that you can change them whenever necessary. You can also keep having access to subscription information online.

---

**ACTUAL TEST**

**02**

**PART**

**7**

**169.** What is being advertised?

(A) A discussion with a financial specialist
(B) A method of paying bills through the website
(C) A weekly online newsletter
(D) A class in corporate investment

**170.** What is suggested about the service?

(A) It is designed for subscribers of a publication.
(B) It will be available 30 days from now.
(C) It is already popular with business owners.
(D) It is the third in a series of the latest services being offered.

**171.** What are interested people asked to do in order to receive the service?

(A) Send in an application
(B) Register online
(C) Make a call
(D) Mail a request

*Go on to the next page*

**Questions 172-175** refer to the following text message chain.

**Dominic Flores**
Ms. Han, it looks like there will be a storm tomorrow, so the roof work on your hospital's new east wing will need to be postponed.
2:26 P.M.

**Sooji Han**
2:27 P.M.
Does that mean no work all day?

**Dominic Flores**
Absolutely not! My employees can help Tony Lim's workers fix the support beams inside the old building.
2:27 P.M.

**Sooji Han**
2:28 P.M.
How long will it take to fix them?

**Dominic Flores**
Let me find out.
2:28 P.M.

**Dominic Flores**
Tony, how close are you to completing your project?
2:29 P.M.

**Tony Lim**
Everything was fine until this morning, when the structural engineer visited with some updates. We'll be working overtime for the next ten days.
2:31 P.M.

**Dominic Flores**
What do you think about my employees assisting you tomorrow?
2:32 P.M.

**Tony Lim**
That's terrific! Then, we could maybe finish in three days.
2:33 P.M.

**Sooji Han**
2:35 P.M.
So, will your employees require access to the old building?

**Dominic Flores**
For tomorrow, yes. Would it be all right for them to park their vehicles in front of the old building?
2:36 P.M.

**Sooji Han**
2:38 P.M.
Of course. There should be sufficient places near the main entrance. And could you please tell them not to drive their cars on the lawn?

Send

60

172. What does Mr. Flores indicate will disrupt work tomorrow?

(A) A defective machine
(B) Late shipping
(C) Inclement weather conditions
(D) A shortage of employees

173. At 2:31 P.M., what does Mr. Lim most likely mean when he writes, "We'll be working overtime for the next ten days"?

(A) His workers have not been arriving at work on time.
(B) His workers' plan is to get off work early on Thursday.
(C) His workers are needed at two separate work areas.
(D) His workers' construction project was made more challenging.

174. Who most likely is Ms. Han?

(A) A gardening designer
(B) A hospital manager
(C) A transportation supervisor
(D) A construction materials supplier

175. What is one thing Mr. Flores inquires about?

(A) The building entrance for their use
(B) Directions to the newest building
(C) Suggestions for the structure's new wing
(D) Permission to park

**Questions 176-180** refer to the following e-mails.

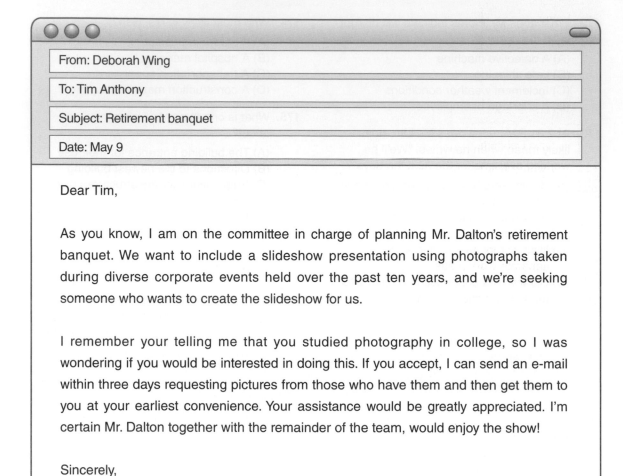

From: Deborah Wing

To: Tim Anthony

Subject: Retirement banquet

Date: May 9

Dear Tim,

As you know, I am on the committee in charge of planning Mr. Dalton's retirement banquet. We want to include a slideshow presentation using photographs taken during diverse corporate events held over the past ten years, and we're seeking someone who wants to create the slideshow for us.

I remember your telling me that you studied photography in college, so I was wondering if you would be interested in doing this. If you accept, I can send an e-mail within three days requesting pictures from those who have them and then get them to you at your earliest convenience. Your assistance would be greatly appreciated. I'm certain Mr. Dalton together with the remainder of the team, would enjoy the show!

Sincerely,

Deborah

| From: | Tim Anthony |
| To: | Deborah Wing |
| Subject: | RE: Retirement banquet |
| Date: | May 10 |

Dear Deborah,

I would like to create the slideshow for Mr. Dalton's retirement banquet. I think we both agree that he's been a great supervisor here. However, I don't think I'm the best person for doing that. I took pictures at one event, but, in fact, I majored in journalism in college. There's a woman whom I want to recommend for creating the slideshow. Her name is Catherine Heinz. I believe she may be interested in doing it. I know she previously created a slideshow for a training session. If Ms. Heinz can't do it for the event, please contact me and I'll recommend another person to you.

Sincerely,

Tim

**176.** How do Ms. Wing and Mr. Anthony most likely know each other?

(A) They work for the same company.
(B) They attended the same university.
(C) They live in the same apartment complex.
(D) They collaborated on a special project.

**177.** What does Ms. Wing offer to do?

(A) Order invitations to a retirement banquet
(B) Make a copy of materials for a training session
(C) Gather pictures from employees
(D) Participate in an upcoming show

**178.** Why does Mr. Anthony say that he studied journalism?

(A) He'd like to relocate to another position.
(B) Ms. Wing needs assistance with an article.
(C) Ms. Wing asked him to confirm his qualifications.
(D) He'd like to correct a misunderstanding.

**179.** What does Mr. Anthony indicate about Ms. Heinz?

(A) She is more experienced with an assignment than he is.
(B) She is more flexible about a schedule than he is.
(C) She will replace Mr. Dalton after he leaves the company.
(D) She has a university degree in journalism.

**180.** Why might Ms. Wing contact Mr. Anthony again?

(A) He sets up Ms. Heinz's schedule.
(B) He can enroll her in training sessions.
(C) He takes photographs at all of the company events.
(D) He can recommend other people to assist her.

*Go on to the next page*

# Innovation Centre

Overlooking the shore, Innovation Centre combines a relaxing resort with the services to fulfill your business needs. In addition to 10 meeting rooms for large conferences, the Opal Room and Sapphire Room provide the perfect solution for small groups of a maximum of 10 people.

Innovation Centre has both a formal dining room and a more comfortable eatery. One-, two-, and three-bedroom suites have high-speed Internet access, fax machines, and coffee makers. Guests can also make use of the indoor and outdoor swimming pools. For more information, contact Randy Frederick at 424-2769 or randyfrederick@innovationcentre.com.

TO: Cameron Gee <camerongee@bronzejournal.com>

FROM: Randy Frederick <randyfrederick@innovationcentre.com>

DATE: March 21

SUBJECT: Reservation

Dear Ms. Gee,

Thank you for your partial deposit of $300.00 for a one-bedroom suite for June 12 and June 13. We have reserved the Opal Room for your event on June 13, but we'll need a total deposit of $500.00 by April 1 to put it on hold for you.

Please let us know what equipment you will need for your presentation so that we can prepare the conference room for you beforehand.

Moreover, to talk about the luncheon for your group, you must contact our catering manager, Lilly Pontiac, at 424-4327, extension 22.

Sincerely,

Randy Frederick
Reservations Manager, Innovation Centre

**181.** Who is the advertisement probably intended for?

(A) Family members
(B) Hotel supervisors
(C) New employees
(D) Business specialists

**182.** What is NOT mentioned as a feature of the Innovation Centre?

(A) A fitness facility
(B) Restaurants
(C) An indoor pool
(D) In-room fax machines

**183.** What is indicated about Ms. Gee?

(A) She is the CEO of a large company.
(B) She has stayed at the Innovation Centre before.
(C) She assumed the responsibility for a presentation.
(D) She received a discounted rate for the conference space.

**184.** What is suggested about Ms. Gee's event?

(A) Full payment for the conference space has been made.
(B) Ten or fewer people will participate.
(C) Attendees will be offered a discount on rooms.
(D) It will be held on April 1.

**185.** What will Ms. Gee ask Ms. Pontiac to do?

(A) Cancel a reservation
(B) Review her presentation
(C) Prepare a food service
(D) Make a payment

*Go on to the next page*

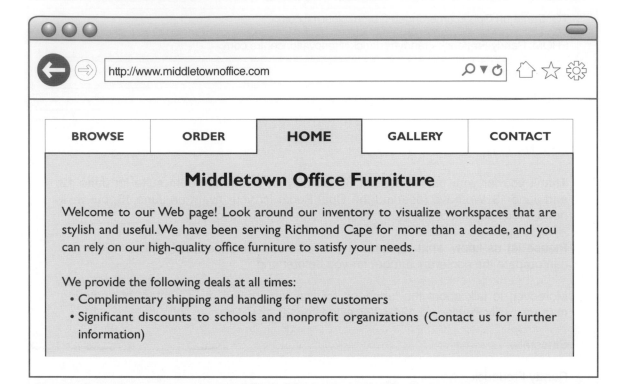

From: James Harley <jharley@standardlawfirm.co>

To: Lemington Chen <lchen@standardlawfirm.co>

Date: 15 April

Subject: Office furniture upgrade

Hello Mr. Chen,

I've completed some research and would like to recommend that we choose Middletown Office Furniture for the desks and other items for our office remodeling. Although we've never bought from them before, they provided references that offered excellent recommendations.

I think we should decide on a larger desk type for our main workspace (15 desks), with corresponding filing cabinets and bookshelves. For the support team and interns who work upstairs, I recommend a simpler desk style.

If you approve of these recommendations, I'd like to place the order as soon as possible so that the products will be shipped while almost all of our employees are away at the meeting in New York.

However, our work areas will seem quite dirty because we will clear out the old furniture and wait for the arrival of the new products.

Please inform me what you think of the plan I have summarized above.

James

**Order Number:** F2465Z
**Contact:** James Harley (067) 523-4352
**Delivery to:** Standard Law Firm, 252 Square Street, San Francisco, CA 94108
**Delivery Date & Time:** 8–9 August, 11:00–18:00

| Quantity | Item Code | Description |
|----------|-----------|-------------|
| 15 | CDF4524 | Dayton Office Desks |
| 15 | FCT1275 | Prime Filing Cabinets, light brown |
| 6 | AA2042 | Crystal Bookshelves, light brown |
| 7 | GE3182 | Versatile Desks |

*Note:* Due to demand, we are out of ITEM AA2042 at our Casey Town store. These products will be shipped to your office directly from our production site, so they will be delivered into San Francisco from Charleston rather than from Casey Town. This might delay the delivery by two or three days. Every effort will be made to have the entire order shipped on the same day.

PART 7

**186.** What is suggested about Middletown Office Furniture?

(A) It offers free interior design services.
(B) It provides special discounts to educational organizations.
(C) It has recently expanded its type of products.
(D) It has just opened a satellite branch.

**187.** What is most likely true about Standard Law Firm's furniture order?

(A) It will be shipped free of charge.
(B) It includes a product which is no longer manufactured.
(C) It was placed too late for shipment in August.
(D) It includes a style selected by the support team.

**188.** Why does Mr. Harley want to schedule a delivery during the particular period?

(A) He will receive an extra discount.
(B) He requires some furniture for an important conference.
(C) He needs additional time to shop for the new furniture.
(D) He would like to alleviate inconvenience for colleagues.

**189.** What product will probably be placed upstairs at Standard Law Firm?

(A) Dayton Office Desks
(B) Prime Filing Cabinets
(C) Crystal Bookshelves
(D) Versatile Desks

**190.** According to the form, where is the furniture made?

(A) San Francisco
(B) Charleston
(C) New York
(D) Casey Town

*Go on to the next page*

67

From: Nathan Jerome <njerome@happydiningarea.com>

To: John McNeil <jmcneil@happydiningarea.com>

Date: Tuesday, July 11

Subject: Menu tasting

Hello Mr. McNeil,

It's hard to believe that Ms. Theresa will be here in only two weeks! Since her review will be published in the local newspaper, why don't we make sure that our selections are reflective of the best of the Happy Dining Area? To get advice on the menu we'll be serving her, I've determined we should host a special menu-tasting event on Thursday of next week.

I have several recommendations for what we can serve at the menu tasting. What about arranging a satisfying fish dish? Maybe our baked sea bream would be a good choice. On the other hand, I insist on providing the new special pizzas we intend to release on our regular menu. Of course, that is assuming construction of the brick oven is finished by that time. Additionally, I think we can serve a minimum of two of our fruit desserts that are popular at all times. However, I have complete confidence in you, as head chef, to finalize the menu choices.

Finally, I want to provide our menu-tasting patrons with an opportunity to visit the kitchen while they are here. Please inform me of what you think about this and how best to prepare for it.

Thank you.

Sincerely,

Nathan

## Happy Dining Area Tasting Menu
### *Thursday, July 20*

*Baked sea bream in garlic sauce*
*Beef steak with cucumber salad*
*Roasted chicken with chili sauce*
*Cheesecake with walnuts*
*All of the steamed shellfish in a broccoli soup*
*Smoked salmon with mashed potato*

# Tasting Feedback Card

Name: Jessie Jackson

Please remark on your tasting experience at the Happy Dining Area.

I was pleased by the gentle sweetness of the cucumber dish; the sauce was a little sour for my taste, though. The sea bream, on the other hand, surpassed all my expectations. The roasted chicken was tender, yet overall it was not tasty. Concerning the dessert, it was very delicious, although a bit dry. I was very impressed by the useful design of your kitchen. I look forward to tasting the new brick-oven pizzas when they're released. I'm disappointed that you couldn't offer them today.

**191.** Why is the menu tasting being conducted?

(A) To prepare for a visit from a restaurant reviewer

(B) To choose dishes to enter in a cooking competition

(C) To assess a chef who is applying for a job

(D) To select dishes to add to the daily menu

**192.** In the e-mail, the word "satisfying" in paragraph 2, line 2, is closest in meaning to

(A) deep

(B) plentiful

(C) gratifying

(D) creative

**193.** What is mentioned about the tasting menu?

(A) It lists dishes that were provided free of charge.

(B) It includes a dish suggested by Mr. Jerome.

(C) It was served to patrons in the eatery's kitchen.

(D) It isn't available every weekday.

**194.** What menu item was probably Ms. Jackson's favorite?

(A) The sea bream

(D) The soup

(C) The cucumber

(D) The chicken

**195.** What is indicated about the brick oven?

(A) It is extremely big for the kitchen.

(B) It has to be fixed.

(C) It didn't pass a safety inspection.

(D) It is still being constructed.

*Go on to the next page*

To: Students

From: Jamal Crawford

Subject: Presenter series

Date: May 5

Dear students,

There's good news! Ms. Ito Hirosa has agreed to attend our Presenter Series this summer. As part of your student internship responsibilities, you will have to prepare her lodging here at the university for August 19–21 and get the relevant document completed and approved so that Ms. Ito can receive her honorarium. Also, please reserve a room for her presentation. I suggest the Dynasty Auditorium because it can accommodate the most people, but any other presentation room in the business building would be fine as well.

Additionally, if Ms. Ito provides her summary, you will have to design a leaflet and post it in the common areas throughout the building. I believe you will be able to assign the job duties among the six of you without any problems.

Thanks!

Dr. Crawford
Professor, Dickson School of Business

## Dickson School of Business

### Presenter Series featuring

Ms. Ito Hirosa
Vice President, Tokyo Investment, Japan

Establishing Different Finance Relationships
August 20, 6:00 P.M.
True-Blue Room

In the past two decades, numerous financial organizations have limited lending to minimize their risk. This policy, however, leads to unfavorable market conditions. How can banks reduce their risk while still offering ideal funding opportunities to business owners? One possible solution that is becoming popular is "Alternative Finance." I will give an abstract of "Alternative Finance," share some persuasive materials gathered by researchers at Tokyo Investment and Dickson School of Business, and talk about how this worldwide banking change can revive our field.

From: Jim Curry

To: Lisa Presley

Received: May 16, 7:00 P.M.

Lisa, I'm in the media room about to print the leaflet you created, and I've noticed a mistake. Ms. Ito's bio was partially omitted from the leaflet! Could you please correct the leaflet promptly and resend it to me? The media room is closing in 20 minutes, and Dr. Crawford emphasized that the leaflets must be posted no later than tonight.

**196.** What is suggested about the True-Blue Room?

(A) It is not situated in the business building.
(B) It is the place for all events in the Presenter Series.
(C) It is smaller than the Dynasty Auditorium.
(D) It is made available on August 21.

**197.** In the e-mail, the word "problems" in paragraph 2, line 3, is closest in meaning to

(A) declarations
(B) inquiries
(C) shipments
(D) conflicts

**198.** What is the topic of Ms. Ito's presentation?

(A) The most recent trend in banking
(B) A job opening in finance
(C) Unique methods of collecting materials
(D) Biographies of experienced business owners

**199.** What difficulty does Mr. Curry mention?

(A) A number has been incorrectly marked.
(D) The leaflet is missing some details.
(C) The leaflet will not be posted online.
(D) The room booked for the presentation is not open.

**200.** Who most likely is Ms. Presley?

(A) A repair person in the media room
(B) A secretary to Ms. Ito
(C) A speaker from the Presenter Series
(D) A student at Dickson School of Business

# ACTUAL
# TEST

## 答對題數表

| | |
|---|---|
| **PART 5** | |
| **PART 6** | |
| **PART 7** | |
| 總題數 | |

**03**

# READING TEST

In the Reading test, you will read a variety of texts and answer several different types of reading comprehension questions. The entire Reading test will last 75 minutes. There are three parts, and directions are given for each part. You are encouraged to answer as many questions as possible within the time allowed.

You must mark your answers on the separate answer sheet. Do not write your answers in your test book.

## PART 5

**Directions:** A word or phrase is missing in each of the sentences below. Four answer choices are given below each sentence. Select the best answer to complete the sentence. Then mark the letter (A), (B), (C), or (D) on your answer sheet.

101. ------- the heavy snow this morning, the company picnic will proceed as planned.

   (A) Due to
   (B) Despite
   (C) Because of
   (D) Regarding

102. The school ------- was an alumnus of the school, so he is very popular with the students.

   (A) principal
   (B) principles
   (C) principals
   (D) principle

103. In his report, Young-Ho pointed ------- several mistakes that had been made by the developers when building the new Civic Center.

   (A) over
   (B) under
   (C) out
   (D) from

104. If Marsha ------- in charge of the project, we probably would have had more success.

   (A) has been
   (B) is
   (C) was not
   (D) had been

105. John was disappointed because, out of all the reports, the director singled out ------- as needing more work.

   (A) he
   (B) his
   (C) him
   (D) himself

106. After the last class, Mr. Morris had each of the students ------- the test from last year before taking the final exam.

   (A) will review
   (B) review
   (C) was reviewed
   (D) to review

107. The team's performance on the assignment was ------- poor, so two of the team members were fired yesterday.

   (A) unaccepted
   (B) unacceptably
   (C) unaccepting
   (D) unacceptable

108. ------- we work all weekend, we will not likely be able to have the presentation slides completed by Monday morning.

   (A) Even so
   (B) Evenly
   (C) Eventually
   (D) Even if

109. The company gala was in full -------, and all of the employees seemed to be having a fantastic time.
   (A) swing
   (B) team
   (C) moon
   (D) party

110. The team leader asked ------- all employees do an exceptional job on the project, as the client is an important one for the company.
   (A) what
   (B) to
   (C) that
   (D) where

111. Five of the new hires, in fact all those hired by the Marketing Department, performed beyond expectations last quarter, but the other three new employees -------.
   (A) did not
   (B) do not
   (C) did
   (D) will not

112. It is ------- for each member of the sales team to expect large bonuses this year because company profits increased so much.
   (A) reasonable
   (B) reasoned
   (C) reasonableness
   (D) reason

113. The passenger was advised to ------- to the check-in counter to have a boarding pass issued.
   (A) returned
   (B) returning
   (C) returns
   (D) return

114. ------- this morning, he would have been able to participate in our strategy meeting.
   (A) Simon did arrive
   (B) Simon will arrive
   (C) Had Simon arrived
   (D) Simon is arriving

115. After a couple of slow years for our company, our sales really ------- last year.
   (A) took off
   (B) fell down
   (C) took on
   (D) outran

116. -------, Nathan submitted the report in time for the meeting, even though he was sick all week.
   (A) Undeniably
   (B) Rarely
   (C) Absolutely
   (D) Surprisingly

117. According to Jason, the projector still has ------- the problems that were mentioned by the mechanic last week.
   (A) both of
   (B) every
   (C) either
   (D) seen

118. The guest speaker ------- next Monday, so please reach out to him this week to confirm his travel schedule.
   (A) has arrived
   (B) arrive
   (C) is arriving
   (D) is arrived

119. The president of the company was excited to have negotiated such a ------- deal, so he let all of the employees go home early yesterday.
   (A) terrify
   (B) terribly
   (C) terrific
   (D) terrified

120. Even though Rachel ------- with the company for very long, she is already thinking of moving on to another job.
   (A) weren't
   (B) hasn't been
   (C) could be
   (D) will be

*Go on to the next page*

121. It was strange that Takashi was late to the meeting because ------- he is extremely punctual.

(A) usually
(B) eventually
(C) more
(D) seldom

122. CraneSteel is committed to ------- the highest levels of customer service and is dedicated to its philosophy of social and environmental responsibility.

(A) providing
(B) provision
(C) provided
(D) provide

123. When Janet announced that she will ------- in May, nobody was surprised, given her age and poor health.

(A) have retired
(B) be retired
(C) retire
(D) retires

124. As ------- earlier, we do not intend to talk about issues that we have already covered in previous meetings.

(A) discuss
(B) discussed
(C) discussing
(D) discussion

125. -------, our weekly staff meetings have been very productive, so let's continue to keep up the good work.

(A) This Wednesday
(B) Always
(C) Of late
(D) Soon

126. ------- of the companies is focusing on teamwork, diversity, and trust in this year's workshop.

(A) Every
(B) Many
(C) Much
(D) Each

127. Interviews ------- all day Thursday in the second-floor conference room.

(A) conduct
(B) have conducted
(C) will be conducted
(D) are conducting

128. Makoto has been with the company more than twice ------- any of the other employees, so she is the best person to answer any questions you may have.

(A) as far as
(B) in comparison to
(C) as long as
(D) relative to

129. It is truly ------- that Pro Consulting was not chosen to undertake the advertising campaign, but Amway Design Co. will do just as good a job.

(A) regrets
(B) regretting
(C) to regret
(D) regrettable

130. Mr. Simpson was a horrible -------, so none of the executives had any intention of hiring him.

(A) interviewer
(B) interviewed
(C) interview
(D) interviewee

# PART 6

**Directions:** Read the texts that follow. A word, phrase, or sentence is missing in parts of each text. Four answer choices for each question are given below the text. Select the best answer to complete the text. Then mark the letter (A), (B), (C), or (D) on your answer sheet.

**Questions 131-134** refer to the following e-mail.

**From:** Gordon Iwatani <gordoniwatani@fastermail.com>
**To:** Recruit Manager <recruit4@mtlanguage.com>
**Date:** April 14
**Subject:** Re: Japanese language teacher

Dear Sir:

I am writing in response to a notice I saw that said your language school is seeking a Japanese

instructor. As ------- be clear from my credentials, which I have attached to this e-mail, I spent
    **131.**

most of the last decade as a Japanese language teacher in China, ------- almost eight years as
                                  **132.**

an instructor at the most prestigious language school in Shanghai.

In addition to my work experience and academic qualifications, I enjoy a number of hobbies,

which you may find interesting. I have spent most of my life playing the violin, and I currently

play in an ------- orchestra. I also have a black belt in judo and enjoy going on long runs and
    **133.**

cycling in my free time. I have a bright personality and adjust well to new environments.

-------. Please let me know if I can provide you with more information.
**134.**

Sincerely yours,

Gordon Iwatani

131. (A) can
(B) would
(C) should
(D) was

132. (A) I spent
(B) having spent
(C) will spend
(D) be spending

133 (A) amateur
(B) ordinary
(C) emerging
(D) odd

134 (A) I appreciate your time in considering my application.
(B) I look forward to meeting you tomorrow.
(C) I graduated from high school in Tokyo.
(D) I very much look forward to meeting my new students tomorrow.

*Go on to the next page*

**Questions 135-138** refer to the following e-mail.

To: slivingston@kmail.net

From: marsvideos@mars.com

Subject: Your order

Dear sir,

We are in receipt of your e-mail regarding the products you purchased from Mars Videos ------- 
**135.**
July. Unfortunately, we have not yet been able to locate the shipment.

Based on our records, you purchased four Blu-ray discs and two DVDs amounting to a total of

$83. Factoring in shipping costs, this amount ------- to a total order of $97. -------.
**136.** **137.**

We would suggest that you do one of the following things. (1) If you hold tight and wait just a

little bit longer, you may receive the products. We have seen instances where bad weather or

other mishaps created delays in shipments. (2) If you would not like to wait, we can cancel the

order now and provide a full -------.
**138.**

Yours sincerely,

Kyle Johnson

Customer Services Manager

135. (A) in
(B) on
(C) when
(D) or

136. (A) increase
(B) increased
(C) will increase
(D) has been increasing

137. (A) You are a valued customer, and we will ship your products today.
(B) Our records show we charged your credit card for this amount on July 17.
(C) Please let us know what you think of this policy.
(D) We will go ahead and charge your credit card for the total amount.

138. (A) refund
(B) shipment
(C) order
(D) apology

**Questions 139-142** refer to the following notice.

Attention employees:

I have received several complaints regarding usage of the employee break room. This notice serves as a reminder of the rules we all must follow.

First, please remember to wash, dry, and put away in its appropriate place any plate, bowl, cup, or utensil that you've used. This should be done immediately after -------.
                                                                                        **139.**

Second, there have been complaints about smoking in the break room. As you all know, we have a strict policy against smoking in the building. If you want to smoke, you ------- to do so in
                                                                                        **140.**
the designated smoking area on the back patio or elsewhere outside the building.

Finally, please do not take food that is not yours. All food kept in the refrigerator should be properly ------- with the owner's name. Take only food that is yours. -------.
               **141.**                                                                 **142.**

Grace Ikawa

Manager

ACTUAL TEST 03

PART 6

139. (A) be used
     (B) using
     (C) use
     (D) to use

140. (A) would request
     (B) requested
     (C) will request
     (D) are requested

141. (A) labeling
     (B) labeled
     (C) label
     (D) to label

142. (A) We will be holding tomorrow's staff meeting in the break room.
     (B) We will be shutting down the break room beginning next week.
     (C) Let us all enjoy the food in the refrigerator together.
     (D) It is important that we keep the break room a pleasant place to use.

**Questions 143-146** refer to the following review.

Maya Gordon's new guide to doing business in the Middle East is an interesting and comprehensive

journey through the Middle Eastern business world.

In this book, readers are provided ------- a unique yet clear understanding of what the business
**143.**

culture is like in several key Middle Eastern countries. Among the many topics covered by Professor

Gordon are essential ones like proper greeting etiquette, proper etiquette during business meals,

the use of business cards, and the intricacies of negotiating with Middle Eastern counterparts.

If you are just getting acquainted with the business scene in the Middle East, this book is

------- reading. No other guide delves into so many critical aspects of Middle Eastern business
**144.**

conduct in such depth and with such detail. -------, Professor Gordon has organized her book by
**145.**

business center (including Dubai, Qatar, and Abu Dhabi), allowing readers to focus on the specific

area they are interested in. -------.
**146.**

Once you have read *Doing Business the Middle Eastern Way*, you will have no trouble conducting

yourself appropriately in the Middle East.

**143.** (A) with
(B) on
(C) in
(D) at

**144.** (A) absolute
(B) ridiculous
(C) compulsory
(D) confident

**145.** (A) By comparison
(B) Unfortunately
(C) Moreover
(D) As a result

**146.** (A) The chapter on Dubai is particularly enjoyable.
(B) Professor Gordon has also written on Asia.
(C) This guide is not as interesting as some of the others on the market.
(D) Book critics have been lukewarm on the book.

# PART 7

**Directions:** In this part you will read a selection of texts, such as magazine and newspaper articles, e-mails, and instant messages. Each text or set of texts is followed by several questions. Select the best answer for each question and mark the letter (A), (B), (C), or (D) on your answer sheet.

**Questions 147-148** refer to the following order form.

## MEGA DEPOT, INC.

Taking care of all of your home and office needs

**Contents:**

# 2 color ink cartridges

# 1 black and white ink cartridge

# 10 packs of letter-size paper (50 sheets each)

# 1 postcard for re-orders

Use the enclosed postcard when re-ordering these products.

If you would like to speak to a customer service representative, call 301-555-1999

Mon.–Fri. 10 A.M. to 6 P.M.

NOT FOR CONSUMPTION

**147.** What most likely is the reason for buying these products?

(A) To print documents
(B) To place an order for supplies
(C) To write letters
(D) To create artwork

**148.** What is true about the order form?

(A) It warns people not to eat the product.
(B) It includes a receipt for the product.
(C) It does not describe the contents of the order.
(D) It provides an address for the store.

*Go on to the next page*

**Questions 149-151** refer to the following text message chain.

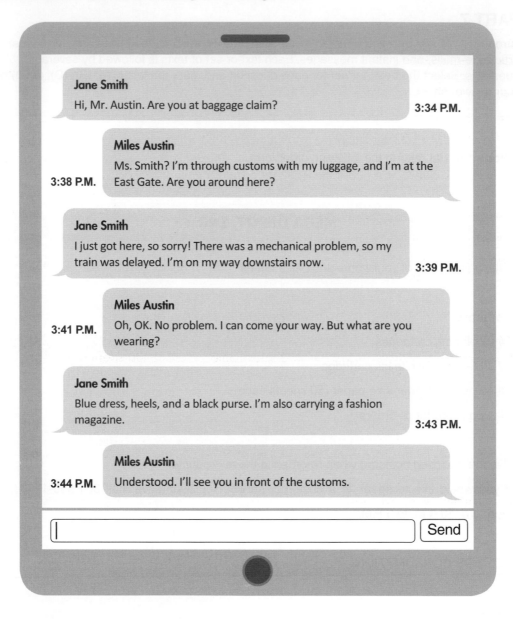

**Jane Smith**
Hi, Mr. Austin. Are you at baggage claim?
3:34 P.M.

**Miles Austin**
3:38 P.M.   Ms. Smith? I'm through customs with my luggage, and I'm at the East Gate. Are you around here?

**Jane Smith**
I just got here, so sorry! There was a mechanical problem, so my train was delayed. I'm on my way downstairs now.
3:39 P.M.

**Miles Austin**
3:41 P.M.   Oh, OK. No problem. I can come your way. But what are you wearing?

**Jane Smith**
Blue dress, heels, and a black purse. I'm also carrying a fashion magazine.
3:43 P.M.

**Miles Austin**
3:44 P.M.   Understood. I'll see you in front of the customs.

Send

---

**149.** What is suggested about Mr. Austin and Ms. Smith?

(A) They have never met before.
(B) They have a meeting tomorrow.
(C) They both took trains.
(D) Jane Smith has just bought a magazine.

**150.** Where is Mr. Austin waiting?

(A) At a magazine stand
(B) At the customs
(C) On a train
(D) Upstairs

**151.** At 3:44 P.M., why does Mr. Austin say, "Understood"?

(A) He just saw Ms. Smith.
(B) He'll be able to recognize Ms. Smith.
(C) He is also chairing the meeting.
(D) He does not want to be late.

Questions 152-154 refer to the following blog.

### February 24

We moved ahead another 25 km on our trek today. My feet are killing me. —[1]—.
I really should not have worn my new boots. My knees are a little sore, too, but all in all
it was a good day. We got off to a bit of a slow start by sleeping in. Keiko was on alarm
duty, so that one is on her! All downhill after that, though. The view was unbelievable.
We took tons of photos. I can't wait to show them to you when we're back. —[2]—. We
even saw a snow leopard! Those are extremely rare and almost impossible to actually
see live. It was hard to see it amidst all the snow—it came into view for about three
seconds. It looked beautiful. Keiko missed it—sweet revenge for failing to wake us up in
time for the sunrise, ha ha! —[3]—.

### February 26

Sorry for not checking in yesterday. It rained all day, and there wasn't much
interesting news to tell you. We found a quaint little café and just spent the entire day
there. The staff was giving us dirty looks, but they never actually asked us to leave.
—[4]—. Well, tomorrow's the last day. I'm really looking forward to seeing all of you the
day after!

**152.** How are the two people most likely
traveling?

(A) On roller skates
(B) By motorcycle
(C) On foot
(D) By plane

**153.** On what date will the blogger return?

(A) March 2
(B) March 1
(C) February 28
(D) February 27

**154.** In which of the positions marked [1], [2],
[3], and [4] does the following phrase
belong?

"We ended up just lounging around all
day, talking, eating, and playing games."

(A) [1]
(B) [2]
(C) [3]
(D) [4]

*Go on to the next page*

# NON-DELIVERY FORM

---

**Date:** 5/16                              **Time:** 11:08 A.M.
**Delivery person:** Sam

**Package number:** 3494-836636-92
**From:** General Office Supplies

**Reason for non-delivery**

**Item too big** ☐                    **Resident not home to sign for delivery** ☑

**Notes:** Item sent by express delivery

**Options:**

(A) Dial 1-800-555-2215 toll free 24 hours a day to reach our automated service.
    You will need to have the package number.

(B) Dial 1-401-555-2216 during office hours (9 A.M.–5:30 P.M., closed on Sundays.)

**_Remember:_** _We will keep the package for only five days from the date of failed_
_delivery, after which it will be returned to the sender._

---

**155.** Who filled out this form?

(A) The sender
(B) An automated service
(C) A courier
(D) The resident

**156.** What will happen after five days?

(A) Sam will come back with the package.
(B) The resident will call the delivery
    company.
(C) The item will be sent back.
(D) The resident will come home.

**Questions 157-158** refer to the following letter.

Zebra Car Rental
1154 West Avenue
San Francisco, CA 85445

Dear customers,

Due to the increasing demands for our cars and vans, Zebra Car Rental is expanding its operations. This will involve a new front yard plus office and warehouse extensions, which will enable us to stock and store more cars and vans.

These changes will take place next month. Especially, we will be closing the warehouse from 8 to 11 of November. However, you can still see a list of our available vehicles for rent online. Please use this website to book a test drive at www.zebracars.com during this period. We hope that you have a good winter and look forward to greeting you at our new facilities in December.

Chris Murphy
General Manager, Zebra Car Rental

157. What is the main purpose of this letter?
   (A) To advise on new prices
   (B) To announce renovations
   (C) To introduce a website
   (D) To offer discounts

158. What is stated about the company?
   (A) It has reduced its stock.
   (B) It sells items from around the world.
   (C) It allows customers to reserve test drives.
   (D) It will be closed throughout the winter.

*Go on to the next page*

| | | |
|---|---|---|
| **Tyler Wood** [5:10 P.M.] | It's incredible! I love the updated graphics. Much better than the last one. | |
| **Sarah Brooks** [5:11 P.M.]: | Are you kidding? For $95, they'd better come up with better quality than that. | |
| **Tyler Wood** [5:11 P.M.] | It is a bit expensive, I know. But I'm sure you were blown away by the soundtrack. | |
| **Gavin Ward** [5:12 P.M.] | Totally! The music was really great. Didn't you think so, Sarah? | |
| **Sarah Brooks** [5:14 P.M.] | Well, I wouldn't say "blown away", but it was alright. The thing I did like was the character voice acting. They really stepped it up on that one. It annoys me when a good story just crumbles under terrible performances. Speaking of which, the story was pretty good, too. | |
| **Gavin Ward** [5:15 P.M.] | Ha ha, I think she might finally be caving, Tyler! | |
| **Tyler Wood** [5:16 P.M.] | About time. Superior graphics, music, and story—with a solid 80 hours of entertainment, including all of the extra missions. What more can you ask for? | |

**Send**

159. What is the conversation most likely about?

(A) A musical
(B) A movie
(C) A video game
(D) A book

160. At 5:14 P.M., what does Sarah Brooks mean when she writes, "They really stepped it up"?

(A) The company did a good job.
(B) The participants walked away.
(C) The users went upstairs.
(D) The performers stopped acting.

**Question 161-163** refer to the following article.

Yesterday, both the governor and the state attorney general joined hands in urging for changes to what they called a "broken" public education system in the state. Governor Wayne Johnson and Attorney General Vicki Perez spoke at length about the issue when it was brought up during a debate on education held at Silver Town City Hall yesterday. It was the first time this state has seen the governor and the state attorney general make such a joint statement.

The problems discussed by Mr. Johnson and Ms. Perez can be easily summarized into three key points, which were:

1. The quality of teachers has deteriorated significantly in public schools across the state. Mr. Johnson and Ms. Perez noted the reason for this being that budget cutbacks had been made, which led to teacher salaries steadily decreasing in recent years.

2. Standardized test scores for students across the state have also been steadily decreasing in recent years. The average scores in the state are now below average when compared to other states across the country.

3. The curriculum for middle and high school students has not changed sufficiently over the past decade to keep up with changes being made in other states. Students who have not been exposed to evolved curriculums have been struggling in college when studying with students from schools in other states. The problem starts early on in each student's education and is a fundamental one, Mr. Johnson and Ms. Perez said.

The State Ministry of Education has yet to issue an official response to the statement made by Mr. Johnson and Ms. Perez.

**161.** What was NOT mentioned about yesterday's statement?

(A) It was about issues with the school system.
(B) Mr. Johnson and Ms. Perez are from different states.
(C) Three key issues were discussed.
(D) The State Ministry of Education did not respond.

**162.** What is one of Mr. Johnson and Ms. Perez's main points?

(A) The state has too many schools.
(B) Students have been doing better in college.
(C) The quality of teachers is lower than it used to be.
(D) The students are unhappy with the new policy.

**163.** According to the two officials, what has caused a change in teacher quality?

(A) Teacher salaries are decreasing.
(B) Many teachers are moving to other states.
(C) The teachers are not happy with the schools.
(D) It is the Ministry of Education's fault.

*Go on to the next page*

Sunny Shiny Daycare Center has been caring for children for more than thirty years. Our reputation continues to grow as the center that provides quality learning and playtime in a warm, friendly, and safe environment for children.

We would like to announce the opening of our newest daycare center next month, right here in Orange County. It is planned to be our largest center yet, able to accommodate up to 50 children. Of course, the newest center will have all of the fun-filled game centers and facilities that parents are used to seeing, including a fortress playground, swimming pool, and state-of-the-art computer corner.

We will be holding an open house from January 27 to 31 next year, and all interested parents are invited to join us for a full tour of our facilities and an open dialogue with our award-winning staff. Please don't hesitate to bring your children with you so that they can truly take a "full" tour by immersing themselves in a number of fun activities that will give them a taste of what life at the center would be like every day.

We hope to see all of you in January. If you would like more information, please call 201-555-8765 or e-mail us at sunnyshiny@mnet.org.

At Sunny Shiny, you are always in good hands.

Lucy Mason
Managing Director
Sunny Shiny Daycare Center

---

**164.** What is NOT a purpose of the notice?

(A) To announce the opening of a new daycare center
(B) To inform parents about an open house
(C) To discuss the history of Sunny Shiny
(D) To provide contact information to parents

**165.** What is a feature of Sunny Shiny Daycare Center?

(A) A tennis court
(B) A swimming pool
(C) A rock-climbing wall
(D) A water slide

**166.** How long will the open house last?

(A) 2 days
(B) 4 days
(C) 5 days
(D) 6 days

**167.** Why might some people call Sunny Shiny?

(A) To talk to their award-winning staff
(B) To buy tickets to the swimming pool
(C) To make a reservation for the open house
(D) To ask for more information

Devastating wildfires spread throughout California today, causing enormous damage to homes and farmland. —[1]—. Reports show that five people were injured, with hundreds more people having to abandon their residences as fires spread as wide as 8 kilometers and slowly moved towards the city of Los Angeles. David Meyer, Chief Firefighter in the suburb of Annandale, said that this year's fires may be the worst he's seen in his long and storied career, but that his team of firefighters is up to the challenge. "Just the sheer speed with which the fire spread was unbelievable," he said. —[2]—. "My guys have really been battling out there, and we still have a ways to go."—[3]—.

It is not clear how these fires got started. It is usually the case, though, that wildfires are the product of human negligence, such as a careless cigarette or unattended campfire, or of natural causes, such as lightning hitting a dry patch of wood or grass.

—[4]—. Last year, parts of Northern California suffered heavy losses following almost two weeks of rampant forest fires, which ultimately caused injury to three people. Two years ago, the same area saw fires injure 40 people.

ACTUAL TEST

03

PART

7

**168.** To whom is Mr. Meyer most likely referring in his comment?

(A) His friends
(B) Other firefighters
(C) His classmates
(D) His sons

**169.** Which cause of wildfires is NOT mentioned in the bulletin?

(A) Failure to extinguish a campfire
(B) Carelessly dropping a cigarette
(C) Lightning striking dry grass
(D) Someone intentionally starting a fire

**170.** According to the bulletin, how many people have been injured in wildfires over the last 3 years?

(A) Forty
(B) Forty-five
(C) Forty-eight
(D) Forty-three

**171.** In which of the positions marked [1], [2], [3] and [4] does the following sentence belong?

"Wildfires have been an annual tradition in California."

(A) [1]
(B) [2]
(C) [3]
(D) [4]

*Go on to the next page*

Please be advised that our annual company workshop will take place this year on Saturday, April 30. I know many of you will be disappointed that we are holding the workshop on a weekend, but we really had no choice this year. You will be happy to know, however, that all employees may choose any day the week after the workshop to leave work at lunchtime, except Thursday.

Each of you will have received a copy of a report this morning. We ask that you read each of the case studies contained in the report carefully prior to the workshop. Also, this year, we are asking each of the supervisors of the five departments to prepare and give a 10-minute presentation. The presentation should cover the strategies discussed during last year's workshop and how they were implemented throughout the past year.

We will be having a special guest join us this year. Joan Mitchell, whom you all know for having just recently won the Businessperson of the Year Award, will be joining us in the morning to talk about marketing tips that have helped her during her career and to lead group bonding sessions. While you enjoy your lunch, I will be presenting on client management, followed by the presentations from each of the department supervisors.

We are planning to have light cocktails and snacks available at the end of the workshop for those of you who do not need to rush home.

Thanks,
Gregory A. Manning
Manager

**172.** What is Mr. Manning's main purpose for writing this message?

(A) To prepare cocktails and snacks for staff
(B) To introduce Joan Mitchell to everyone
(C) To ask supervisors to prepare presentations
(D) To give information about an annual event

**173.** What is NOT true about this year's annual workshop?

(A) It is again scheduled to be held on a Saturday.
(B) There will be refreshments for the employees at the end.
(C) Client management will be discussed at the workshop.
(D) A guest speaker will join in the morning.

**174.** In total, how many minutes will the supervisor presentations take?

(A) 10 minutes
(B) 25 minutes
(C) 30 minutes
(D) 50 minutes

**175.** What is suggested about Joan Mitchell?

(A) She is a department supervisor.
(B) She was at the annual workshop last year.
(C) She will be presenting during lunch.
(D) She has been successful in the industry.

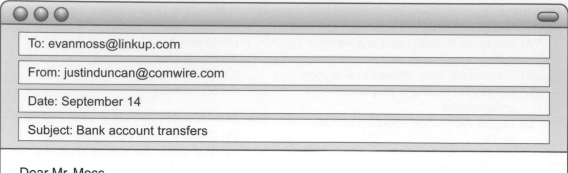

To: evanmoss@linkup.com

From: justinduncan@comwire.com

Date: September 14

Subject: Bank account transfers

Dear Mr. Moss,

Before I temporarily relocated to Hawaii, I asked Linkup Bank to transfer my bank account to the branch here on the island. Although I intended to be here for six months, I have completed my research and will be returning home. Can you now transfer my account back to my initial branch, as from today, September 14? When I return, I would also like to apply for a mortgage. I would appreciate some advice on the most suitable mortgage. I have tried to access the home buying page on your website. However, there is a message that says it is being upgraded at present.

Many thanks for your help.

Yours faithfully,

Justin Duncan

To: justinduncan@comwire.com

From: evanmoss@linkup.com

Date: September 15

Subject: Your e-mail message

Dear Mr. Duncan,

Thank you for your e-mail message yesterday. Please note that your bank account has now been restored to the original branch as you requested. Secondly, we will need to discuss your financial circumstances before we can offer you a mortgage. There are many factors to take into consideration including your income, monthly outgoings and existing loans. May I suggest that you make an appointment to see the mortgage advisor regarding this matter at the Bradford branch when you have a convenient time? Lastly, I must apologize for the error on the website. We are currently upgrading the system and have had to take the page you are seeking off-line until the upgrades have been completed. We hope it will be operational within two days.

Kind regards,

Evan Moss
Customer Service Representative

**176.** What is the purpose of the first e-mail?

(A) To complain about a transaction
(B) To close an account in Bradford
(C) To transfer money to a third branch
(D) To change an arrangement with a bank

**177.** What most likely is true of Mr. Duncan?

(A) His permanent residence is in Bradford.
(B) His transfer to Hawaii was for a year.
(C) He is renting an apartment.
(D) He had previously worked for Linkup.

**178.** What does Mr. Moss suggest that Mr. Duncan should do?

(A) Call the Hawaii branch for advice
(B) Contact the IT department for help
(C) Close his account
(D) Meet with one of the bank's lending officers

**179.** What is NOT mentioned as a factor that Mr. Duncan should consider in deciding on a mortgage?

(A) His monthly expenditure
(B) The amount of his salary
(C) The number of existing loans he may have
(D) The length of time he would need to repay

**180.** In the second e-mail, the word "matter" in line 6, is closest in meaning to

(A) concern
(B) substance
(C) result
(D) oversight

*Go on to the next page*

## Sale of the year! DON'T MISS OUT!

You all know it's sale season, and Brady's Bargain Bin is having the biggest sale of them all! You have to see it to believe it! Here are just a few of our bargain deals:

- 50% off our entire line of TVs, featuring the most popular brands in today's market. We have all kinds, from hand-held portable TVs to mega-screen monsters, all for half off! Whatever kind of TV you are looking for, look no further than Brady's.

- Sampson washer/dryers for only $1000. Sound too good to be true? These popular products usually sell for up to $2500, but we're selling them for less than half that price! We have all of the latest models, and we'll even ship them right to your front door free of charge!

- Top-end cameras and camcorders up to 75% off! That's right—75%! All of our stock of recording devices needs to go, which is music to your ears. What's more—if you buy one of our cameras or camcorders, we'll throw in a black canvas bag you can carry it around in.

So hurry on down to Brady's Bargain Bin. These deals will only last for five more days!

From: hjjang@kmail.net

To: jameskim@vogmail.com

Subject: Bought a camcorder!

Hey James,

I just got back from Brady's Bargain Bin. The crowd was unbelievable. I'm not going to visit there again anytime soon!

The camcorders they had left were definitely not top-end—even mid-range is a stretch. The prices were pretty cheap, though. I ended up buying the Morson camcorder, which they were selling for $150. I know the reviews say the Kell camcorder is of higher quality, but I had one before, and it barely lasted me two years before breaking apart—definitely not worth the price, which is more than double that of the Morson. For the tripod, I bought the one that comes with the Kell instead of the matching of one for the Morson. That one looks much better than the one for the Morson.

Anyway, I look forward to seeing you soon.

Best,

Hyuk-Joon Jang

**181.** Which of the following is true?

(A) The sale will only last for one more week.

(B) Most of the televisions at Brady's are on sale.

(C) The largest discount mentioned in the ad is for cameras.

(D) Products not mentioned in the ad are not for sale.

**182.** Which sale products also come with free shipping?

(A) Televisions

(B) Washers

(C) Camcorders

(D) Roller skates

**183.** How much will the black canvas camera bag cost?

(A) $1,000

(B) 75% off of the normal price

(C) 50% off of the normal price

(D) Nothing

**184.** Why was Brady's Bargain Bin so crowded?

(A) There is a sale at Brady's Bargain Bin.

(B) The store has just recently opened.

(C) People came out to see Mr. Jang.

(D) The store will close soon.

**185.** Which of the following is NOT true?

(A) Mr. Jang has never owned a Kell camcorder.

(B) Camcorders and tripods are sold separately.

(C) Kell camcorders are more expensive than the Morson brand.

(D) Mr. Jang bought the Morson camcorder.

*Go on to the next page*

# Seeking a General Sales Manager

A leading electronics retail chain is looking to hire a bright, diligent, and motivated person to take the position of General Sales Manager, a role that will have the person be in charge of all 22 of our stores throughout Asia. The successful candidate should have a degree from a prominent business school, as well as at least six years of comparable managerial experience, ideally in the electronics retail industry. We primarily sell high-end electronics, so the successful candidate will be someone who is willing and able to grow the market for such products in the Asian region. Candidates must have a valid driver's license and have some experience living in more than one country, as the position will require quite a bit of travel. For anyone interested in the position, please send your résumé (with photograph) and a list of references to mlinton@kmail.com by no later than March 31.

---

**Name:** Daniel Shin
**Date of Birth:** November 5, 1981
**Place of Birth:** Seoul, Korea
**Nationality:** American
**E-mail:** dshin@kmail.com

## Education
| | |
|---|---|
| 1993–1997: | Andover High School |
| 1997–2001: | Harvard University (BA) |
| 2006–2008: | Brussels Business School (MBA) |

## Work Experience
| | |
|---|---|
| 1995–1997: | Andover Deli (Stockroom) |
| 1998–1999: | Sandwich Center (Waiter) |
| 1999–2001: | Pierre Valentine's (Waiter) |
| 2009–2010: | Xenith Electronics (Assistant Manager, Hong Kong) |
| 2010–2012: | Steinway Electronics (Retail Manager, Singapore) |
| 2012–present: | Self-employed |

## Other
I hold a valid driver's license, and I am fluent in Mandarin and Korean.

To: Gregory Smith

From: Matt Linton

Re: General Sales Manager (3 attachments)

Date: March 18

Greg,

Thanks again for the wonderful dinner last night. Please also thank Julie and let her know how much I enjoyed the evening!

Anyway, did you have a chance to look at the latest applications for GSM that I sent you this morning? I've attached them here again in case you haven't had time. We have three new candidates. I know we still have some time, but take a look at this Daniel Shin fellow. He looks like he might be perfect for the job. Yes, he's short of one of the requirements from the ad, but he's got everything else and more, right?

The one thing that concerns me is his most recent experience. Self-employed? That has to mean something else. Let's bring him in for an interview and ask him about it. What do you think?

Best,

Matt

**186.** Which of the following is NOT a requirement for applicants?

(A) A photograph
(B) Relevant work experience
(C) Fluency in Mandarin
(D) A list of references

**187.** Which requirement is NOT met by Mr. Shin?

(A) He has only lived in one country.
(B) He does not have six years' managerial experience.
(C) He does not have a driver's license.
(D) He does not have a business degree.

**188.** What appears to be true about Mr. Linton?

(A) He thinks highly of Daniel Shin.
(B) He has not yet met Julie.
(C) He is Greg's boss.
(D) He is from Korea.

**189.** Why did Mr. Linton attach the applications to his e-mail?

(A) He forgot to send them to Mr. Smith this morning.
(B) He wants Mr. Smith to show them to Julie.
(C) Mr. Shin's résumé does not include a photo.
(D) He thinks Mr. Smith may not have seen them.

**190.** What does GSM most likely stand for?

(A) General Sales Manager
(B) Greg's Sales Memo
(C) Global Sales Mechanism
(D) General Staff Management

*Go on to the next page*

*More Improvement Ahead*

At Wednesday's city council meeting, the Manchester City Council unanimously voted to explore options for more renovations to be conducted on city infrastructure. According to Michael Mann, the City Treasurer, the recent renovation of the Manchester Public Library surprisingly came in significantly below budget. Council members, therefore, decided to put together a short list of other improvement projects that could be completed with the excess funds.

The most well-received suggestions include adding a wheelchair ramp to Manchester Community Center, replacing broken streetlamps in downtown Manchester, and repairing the parking areas in Manchester Park. According to Mr. Mann, the council has decided to open the decision up to public opinion. Those interested in putting forth their ideas may do so at the next council meeting on Wednesday, April 22 at 5 P.M. or can send an e-mail to City Hall by no later than April 29. After April 29, the city planning committee will put before the council a final list for discussion. A final decision is expected shortly thereafter.

From: sshort@hostmail.com

To: citycouncil@manchester.org

Date: April 24

Subject: Improvement projects

Dear City Council Members,

I understand that you are accepting suggestions for improvement projects to city facilities. I had a doctor's appointment, so I was not able to attend the council meeting on Wednesday, but I wanted to express my strong support for replacing broken streetlamps in the downtown area. I work downtown, and when I get off work late, I've noticed that quite a number of streetlamps are in need of replacement. The dark streets are actually a bit frightening. Brightening the streets again should bring more people downtown and reduce crime. This will benefit all of the residents of Manchester. I hope that you will choose this project.

Susan Short

From: mchoi@hostmail.com

To: citycouncil@manchester.org

Date: April 27

Subject: City projects

To Whom It May Concern,

Finally, a renovation project that was actually completed under budget. Although the public library is open to everyone and people of all ages, it tends mostly to be young adults and parents with young children that go to the library. I was hoping we could use the leftover funds on a project that would benefit the senior citizens of Manchester.

The community center is where most older citizens gather, and it is a crime that there are no wheelchair ramps at the entrance to the center. Many of the citizens that frequent the center are in need of wheelchair assistance and have difficulty or need assistance from others just in order to get into the building. Choosing this as the improvement project would really be applauded by people who didn't feel they gained much from the renovation of the library. It is important that the chosen project benefit the entire Manchester community. Thank you for your attention.

Milton Choi

**191.** Why does the city of Manchester have funds available?

(A) The city council raised taxes last year.
(B) It received a generous donation.
(C) It canceled a renovation project.
(D) Its previous project cost less than expected.

**192.** In the article, the phrase "put before" in paragraph 2, line 7, is closest in meaning to

(A) move fast
(B) do first
(C) provide to
(D) place on top

**193.** When did Ms. Short have a doctor's appointment?

(A) April 22
(B) April 24
(C) April 27
(D) April 29

**194.** What does Mr. Choi mention in his e-mail about Manchester Public Library?

(A) It hasn't been renovated for years.
(B) It is used mainly by young citizens.
(C) It has many good programs for senior citizens.
(D) It is in need of further renovations.

**195.** On what point would Mr. Choi and Ms. Short most likely agree?

(A) The chosen project should be beneficial to the entire community.
(B) The city should save the extra funds instead of doing a project.
(C) The city council should push back the deadline for receiving public opinions.
(D) The downtown streetlamps are not really in need of replacement.

*Go on to the next page*

Over the past two days, our two local high schools (Grand Park and Fontana) came together to put on a joint fundraising festival to help raise funds for those affected by the recent devastating earthquake that left more than 30,000 people homeless in Ridgewood.

Never before in our community have the two schools joined together to hold a charity event, and it was a smashing success! The schools were able to raise more than $150,000 to help the disaster victims. Mayor Jeremy Irons graciously accepted the money, thanking each member of the two schools who participated in the event, and he promised that the entire amount would go towards constructing new homes for the victims of the earthquake.

Those who attended the two-day festival will have a few memories they will never forget. Groups of students put on quite a show on the stage at Fontana High School, consisting of unforgettable song and dance performances, comedy skits, and dramatic plays. Each performance was done by a group intentionally composed of students from both schools. This was to symbolize the need for all of us to join together in times of difficulty. There was also a basketball tournament that took place at Grand Park High School on Sunday. Non-student members of our community were also free to take part in the tournament, and everyone said they had a blast.

For the most popular event at the festival, however, the karaoke singing competition on the second day. Contestants were staff and students from each school. One of the students from Fontana High School, Mark Saint, ultimately won the competition, and from the sounds of the cheering, you could tell it wasn't close. When speaking at the closing of the festival on Sunday evening, Mayor Irons emphasized how proud he was of the entire Ridgewood community. This paper would also like to thank everyone involved for providing a ray of hope during what would otherwise be a dark time.

From: Jeremy Irons

To: pjones@fontana.co.edu; mthacher@grandpark.co.edu

Subject: Thank you so much!

Date: Tuesday, October 1

Dear Priscilla and Mary,

I wanted to thank both of you again for your incredible efforts and success this past weekend. You have brought so much joy to our community by collaborating on this amazing event. Please take a moment during your next school day to pass on my appreciation to everyone who took part.

Unfortunately, all-day meetings kept me from joining in the festivities on Saturday, but I was told it was a lot of fun—I heard great things about the display of world foods even though I missed it. That was truly a great idea!

I know Sunday was wonderful because I was there to take it all in. Mary, that Mark is quite a talent. Maybe we will see him on television someday! He could make a good musician, and a proud alumnus of Grand Park High School. Anyway, again, my heart-felt congratulations. On behalf of Ridgewood, I thank both of you.

Jeremy Irons, Mayor

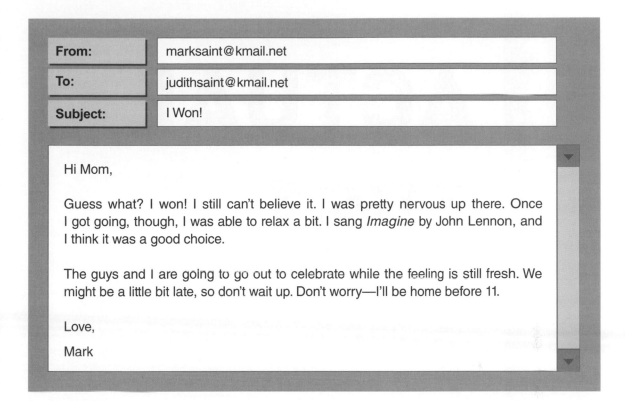

| From: | marksaint@kmail.net |
| To: | judithsaint@kmail.net |
| Subject: | I Won! |

Hi Mom,

Guess what? I won! I still can't believe it. I was pretty nervous up there. Once I got going, though, I was able to relax a bit. I sang *Imagine* by John Lennon, and I think it was a good choice.

The guys and I are going to go out to celebrate while the feeling is still fresh. We might be a little bit late, so don't wait up. Don't worry—I'll be home before 11.

Love,

Mark

**196.** In the first e-mail, the phrase "took part" in paragraph 1, line 3, is closest in meaning to

(A) attended
(B) enjoyed
(C) achieved
(D) completed

**197.** Which of the following happened first?

(A) The mayor, Mr. Irons, attends the fundraiser.
(B) The local residents take part in the basketball tournament.
(C) Mark Saint sings "Imagine" in the singing contest.
(D) A variety of world foods are displayed in the festival.

**198.** On what day did the event begin?

(A) Tuesday
(B) Monday
(C) Sunday
(D) Saturday

**199.** According to the article, what mistake did Mr. Irons make?

(A) He thought they had raised only $100,000.
(B) He wasn't able to attend the event on Saturday.
(C) He thought Mark Saint attended Grand Park High School.
(D) He addressed his e-mail to Judith Saint.

**200.** In the second e-mail, what is implied about Mark?

(A) He is disappointed about not winning the contest.
(B) He was on a TV program.
(C) He has sung "Imagine" before in other contests.
(D) He went out with his friends after the festival.

# ACTUAL TEST

## 答對題數表

| | |
|---|---|
| **PART 5** | |
| **PART 6** | |
| **PART 7** | |
| 總題數 | |

04

# READING TEST

In the Reading test, you will read a variety of texts and answer several different types of reading comprehension questions. The entire Reading test will last 75 minutes. There are three parts, and directions are given for each part. You are encouraged to answer as many questions as possible within the time allowed.

You must mark your answers on the separate answer sheet. Do not write your answers in your test book.

## PART 5
**Directions:** A word or phrase is missing in each of the sentences below. Four answer choices are given below each sentence. Select the best answer to complete the sentence. Then mark the letter (A), (B), (C), or (D) on your answer sheet.

101. Because the regular building inspection will be conducted, please use the side ------ to the main lobby for next week.

(A) entering
(B) entered
(C) entrance
(D) to enter

102. National Council of Teachers and Education states that all in-state instructors are dedicated to ------ their students from in-school violence.

(A) save
(B) saving
(C) saved
(D) safety

103. The marketing department must ------ reliable information to other companies for securing the copyrights they have reserved in their book publishing sector.

(A) influence
(B) provide
(C) register
(D) remain

104. All the employees must follow the current workplace policies ------ otherwise directed from the manager on-site.

(A) below
(B) either
(C) unless
(D) while

105. If you have any problems with the purchased items, please contact the technical support team and tell them the current conditions -------.

(A) most precise
(B) precise
(C) more precise
(D) precisely

106. Applicants who have more than 5 years of experience in marketing will ------ the opportunity to be promoted to a managerial position.

(A) give
(B) be given
(C) be giving
(D) have given

107. A marketing director at Samhwa Electronics carefully reviewed the terms of contracts with the huge ------ company, Whale Co., known as the leading enterprise in Canada.

(A) distribute
(B) is distributed
(C) distribution
(D) distributes

**108.** Ms. Watson submitted two proposals to encourage employees of Allo-Plus Batteries to create a good working environment, but the management declined to accept -------.

(A) fewer
(B) one another
(C) either
(D) much

**109.** Standard Property Realty has benefited financially ------ the well-prepared contract with the worldwide development company.

(A) about
(B) as
(C) from
(D) for

**110.** In order to increase sales figures, employees at Mobby Telecoms ------ to work overtime until they recover the former amounts.

(A) to agree
(B) agreeing
(C) have agreed
(D) agreement

**111.** ------- who purchased the brand-new smartphone T-Star 7 in advance online can receive a refund in full if the model is sold out in the early stage.

(A) They
(B) Them
(C) Which
(D) Those

**112.** Over the past seven years, Xvid Clip Productions ------ the rules about reserving the right to protect its own contents.

(A) set
(B) has set
(C) will be setting
(D) to set

**113.** The total damage caused by inside information leakage is ------ to billions of dollars, which is likely to be a third of annual revenue.

(A) profitable
(B) equivalent
(C) considerate
(D) preventable

**114.** The candidates have stated that they accept their respective ------ for their promotions to Lecovo Technology's overseas branches.

(A) venues
(B) registration
(C) nominations
(D) suspension

**115.** Our county offers you exceptional and fantastic attractions such as Sea Land, Character World, and Fun Driving Park, ------ that you have a memorable vacation.

(A) ensure
(B) ensures
(C) ensuring
(D) ensured

**116.** Employees who have not yet enrolled in the on-the-job training should submit their applications -------.

(A) previously
(B) immediately
(C) closely
(D) roughly

**117.** Economic analysts have devised three ------ approaches to the current problems related to the long-term financial downfall.

(A) difference
(B) differ
(C) different
(D) differently

**118.** In an effort ------ sales of newly released items in an e-commerce market, the company has suggested doing viral marketing by using various SNS channels.

(A) increase
(B) increasing
(C) to increase
(D) increasingly

**119.** Those who get a refund in full should first contact the sales manager ------ they want to receive it by check.

(A) then
(B) if
(C) despite
(D) shortly

*Go on to the next page*

**120.** ------- you find any errors in those articles for the next issue, please report them directly to the chief editor before publishing them.

(A) Had
(B) Should
(C) Were
(D) Have

**121.** We are sorry to inform you that we cannot use the photo that was sent ------ the application in the mail package.

(A) along with
(B) in addition
(C) on account
(D) instead

**122.** Each division and executive at Hans Corporation has a framework document that contains the ------ of responsibilities and accountabilities for each position.

(A) statement
(B) department
(C) increment
(D) enforcement

**123.** Giant Mall has newly developed the rapid order processing system to ------ shipping to customers.

(A) obtain
(B) reduce
(C) expedite
(D) increase

**124.** ------- the firefighters arrive at the scene of the crime, the building will have been totally destroyed by an arsonist.

(A) Because
(B) By the time
(C) In spite of
(D) Furthermore

**125.** His comments on the article that dealt with the environmental issues ------ the need for the conservation of our ecological environment.

(A) acquire
(B) emphasize
(C) customize
(D) sophisticate

**126.** Last year, New York Modern Art Supplies was relocated to Macy Avenue beyond 42th Street ------ its previous store.

(A) on
(B) from
(C) with
(D) about

**127.** Our goal is to attract ------ sensitive customers to the item design when they consider purchasing something.

(A) highly
(B) properly
(C) much
(D) far

**128.** Many salespeople were disappointed because the sales figures were ------ lower than they expected.

(A) significance
(B) significant
(C) significantly
(D) more significant

**129.** Before installing the security program on your computer, please delete the former version of any antivirus software as ------ as possible.

(A) quicken
(B) quick
(C) quickly
(D) quicker

**130.** Giantbook Publishing provided Mr. Dany with a full refund ------ there was a trivial printing error on the cover page.

(A) although
(B) as though
(C) whether
(D) if

# PART 6

**Directions:** Read the texts that follow. A word, phrase, or sentence is missing in parts of each text. Four answer choices for each question are given below the text. Select the best answer to complete the text. Then mark the letter (A), (B), (C), or (D) on your answer sheet.

**Questions 131-134** refer to the following article.

## EGE buys FilaGas

Exron Gulf Energy announced this morning that it had acquired FilaGas in an effort to gain

entry ------- the Permian Basin oil field. EGE spokesperson Jarvis Meeks said they wanted to
     **131.**

take advantage of FilaGas' firm foothold in the recently discovered oil-rich area, given FilaGas

already operates half a dozen drilling concessions in the basin. -------.
                                                       **132.**

Ray Littman, an expert in the energy sector, predicts that the acquisition will make EGE the

leader in oil exploration in the Permian Basin, head and shoulders above its -------. EGE's
                                                    **133.**

early move also saved the oil giant millions of dollars, as the cost of buying land in the area

continues to skyrocket. -------, land prices per acre in the Delaware field rose from $14,516 to
     **134.**

$49,000 in just two years.

131. (A) into
(B) with
(C) for
(D) of

132. (A) FilaGas is still considering the offer.
(B) All six are drilling at full capacity.
(C) EGE will acquire more companies soon.
(D) The purchase cost is higher than EGE expected.

133. (A) buyers
(B) observers
(C) investors
(D) competitors

134. (A) In this instance
(B) After all
(C) Despite this
(D) As a matter of fact

*Go on to the next page*

**Questions 135-138** refer to the following notice.

---

We highly recommend early bookings as flights to the remote Finnish village of Ivalo are very

limited. Thomson Airways offers ------- flights to Ivalo direct from the U.K. The rest of the year,
**135.**

one can take Finnair flights from Helsinki. In case you choose to cancel a flight reservation,

Thomson requires a seven-day notice, while Finnair only asks for three for your ticket ------- in
**136.**

full. Both airlines serve meals and drinks to first-class travelers for the ------- of the flight. -------.
**137.** **138.**

---

**135.** (A) season
(B) seasons
(C) seasoning
(D) seasonal

**136.** (A) are refunding
(B) will be refunded
(C) to be refunded
(D) had been refunding

**137.** (A) length
(B) degree
(C) site
(D) month

**138.** (A) Frequent flyers to Ivalo can fly year-round via Thomson Airways.
(B) This service does not apply to those in the economy class.
(C) Flights to and from Ivalo can be canceled without prior notice.
(D) We recommend morning flights so that they serve meals to all passengers.

---

### Industrial Park Gets Go-ahead

Drastic changes ------- to the residents of Fairbank. On Monday, a real estate developer,
**139.**
Ultima Holdings, announced that its 30-acre Industrial and Technology Park has been given

the go-ahead by the Fairbank Town Council. -------. The park will include the construction of
**140.**
several high-rise office buildings as well as manufacturing and warehouse facilities. ------- of
**141.**
the acreage will also be devoted to recreational purposes, such as a golf course and a driving

range. Most local residents protested during talks on the proposed development, ------- it as a
**142.**
future source of noise, traffic, and pollution.

---

**139.** (A) will have come
(B) came
(C) are coming
(D) comes

**140.** (A) The approval was announced on
Monday, June 2.
(B) The plan will be welcomed by the
town's members.
(C) Residents and developers both await
the council's decision.
(D) Nonetheless, Ultima Holdings
withdrew its plans to develop.

**141.** (A) Some
(B) Many
(C) One
(D) Few

**142.** (A) see
(B) sees
(C) seeing
(D) seen

*Go on to the next page*

Questions 143-146 refer to the following letter.

---

July 12

Ms. Amanda Pickwick

Origami Paper Company

278 East Road

Teaneck, NJ 07666


Thank you for your inquiry about purchasing four bottles of Iron Gall Ink from Collins Supply

Company. We are happy to inform you that we have the ink in stock and can ship it to you if

you fill in the enclosed order form today. -------. As you are a regular customer of more than
                                        **143.**

two years now, we are also pleased to provide you with a 5 percent discount on this and other

------- orders. -------, you can earn store credits with every purchase. When you have -------
**144.**        **145.**                                                              **146.**

store credits, you can use these to purchase other products. This is our way of thanking you for

your continued patronage.

Sincerely,

Dave Earnshaw

Customer Relations Manager

Enclosure: #Order Form.pdf

---

**143.** (A) You may want to choose it from our online catalog of calligraphy inks.
(B) However, we will ask you to return the product in its original package.
(C) You can expect that you can receive your order within 5–7 business days.
(D) Unfortunately, we have no records of any order of Iron Gall Ink.

**144.** (A) upcoming
(B) preceding
(C) preliminary
(D) sequential

**145.** (A) However
(B) In addition
(C) Nonetheless
(D) Of course

**146.** (A) accumulates
(B) accumulating
(C) to accumulate
(D) accumulated

## PART 7

**Directions:** In this part you will read a selection of texts, such as magazine and newspaper articles, e-mails, and instant messages. Each text or set of texts is followed by several questions. Select the best answer for each question and mark the letter (A), (B), (C), or (D) on your answer sheet.

**Questions 147-148** refer to the following notice.

The Oregon Prime Association (OPA) is opening a local chapter in Eugene in October. This organization will be gathered on every Friday at the Culpepper, 305 Washington Drive, at 8:00 P.M. It is open to the public at any time.

If you are interested in this and want to use public transportation, Eugene Red Bus leads to the site, two blocks away, at the corner of James Boulevard and Fleming Avenue. If you plan to drive yourself, the parking lot, Hopkins Park, is free for all citizens after 7 P.M.

We have a lot of topics for next year's events for our community, so we hope you will be about to join our activities together. For more information about topics and presenters, visit our website at www.opaeugene.org.

**147.** Where would the notice more likely be posted?

(A) At a community center
(B) At a parking lot
(C) At a local restaurant
(D) At a residential hotel

**148.** According to the notice, what is available on the online homepage?

(A) Some videos regarding local promotion
(B) Procedures about local parking
(C) Documents for the registration
(D) Some details about the meeting

*Go on to the next page*

Sigma Network Corporation: 2018 Biennial Event!
Thank you for your interest in the COD Network Conference at Sigma Network Corp.
Please complete the request form below.

# 2018 COD Network Conference

## Conference Registration Form

Millennium Hotel St. Louis

October 10–14, 2018

### Name Badge and Mailing Information (use a separate form for each person)

Name _____ (for POD database)

Badge Name _____ (this name will appear on your name badge)

Title _____

Department/Unit _____

Institution/Organization _____

Mailing Address _____

City _____ State/Prov. _____ Postal Code _____

Work
Phone _____ Fax _____ E-mail _____

### Conference Registration

| | Early Bird (postmarked by 9/21) | Regular (postmarked after 9/21) | On-site | Registration Amount Enclosed |
|---|---|---|---|---|
| **Member** (must have paid 2018–2019 dues) | $180 | $220 | $240 | $ _____ |
| **Non-member** (includes 1 year membership) | $255 | $295 | $315 | $ _____ |
| **Student or Retired** | $130 | $160 | $180 | $ _____ |
| **One Day Only** ___Thurs ___ Fri ___ Sat | $130 | $140 | $150 | $ _____ |

** If you need to get a temporary parking permit during the conference, please stop by our reception desk and pick it up from our personnel for the event.

**149.** What is implied about the 2018 COD Conference?

(A) It offers in-advance payers some discounts.

(B) Its members should register for participation online.

(C) It provides the conference with just regular members.

(D) It has been held in St. Louis once a year.

**150.** What will Sigma Network staff do?

(A) E-mail potential clients their conference details

(B) Accept participants' papers for the conference

(C) Deliver short-term parking permits to attendees

(D) Organize and designate the conference rooms

Questions 151-152 refer to the following e-mail.

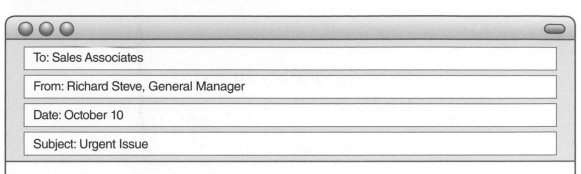

To: Sales Associates

From: Richard Steve, General Manager

Date: October 10

Subject: Urgent Issue

Dear Sales Associates,

Our advertisement in the recent issue of *Cal-State Post* has some errors. It indicates that our date for the half-price sale is November 11 instead of November 1. Although a correction of the error appears in the next month's issue of paper copies, our customers cannot be aware of this error on the Web. Therefore, if they ask whether it is November 1 or November 11 for the sale, first apologize for this inconvenience and then offer them a coupon for 10% off any item they want to buy, at both off-line stores and online ones. If consumers have more questions about it, please direct them to the floor manager. Thank you for your understanding.

Richard Steve,

General Manager, Kingswhite Clothing

151. What is stated about *Cal-State Post*?
(A) It publishes articles and advertisements every week.
(B) It posted an apology for the error of their promotion date.
(C) It attached a discount coupon on the page of Kingswhite's advertisement.
(D) It misprinted the date of Kingswhite Clothing's sale.

152. What does Mr. Steve require the associates to do?
(A) Advise customers to discuss extra issues with a supervisor
(B) Tell customers about problems with an item's malfunction
(C) Explain the reason why they made a mistake
(D) Send the correction of the misprinted date to the magazine

*Go on to the next page*

# ANNUAL SPRING MEETING

**Central Pennsylvania University**          **Mellon Board Room**
**April 13, 2018**                                          **9:00 – 12:00**

**8:30 – 9:00**      Registration & Breakfast
**9:00 – 10:30**    Panel Discussion: *Expanding the Teacher Toolbox*

Peggy Daniel, Director, Intercultural Communication Center, & Rebecca Oreto, Associate Professor, Carnegie University
*Technology in your hands: using creative materials and building academic fluency*

Steve Lin, English Language Program Coordinator, Chatham University
*Highlighting some collaborative group activities in a "Glee" syllabus*

Jane Piadget, ESL Teacher & ELL Coordinator, Franklin Regional School District
*Teacher Technology Tips–Using Puzzlelet.com and Mobile Devices*

Christopher Pierce, Instructor, Pittsburgh City University, English Language Institute
*Using Jigsaw Puzzle to generate and share vocabulary activities*

**10:30 – 11:15**    Interest Groups Gathering Sessions & Networking
**11:15 – 12:00**    General Business Meeting and Elections

**Free to members of Three Rivers TESOL**
**$5.00 for non-members**

Map: http://www.cpu.edu/campusmap/
Directions: http://www.cpu.edu/about/directions.cfm
Parking at the Terrace Parking Lot

Special thanks to Central Pennsylvania University for hosting our 2018 Spring Meeting!

**153.** For whom is the workshop most likely intended?

(A) Human resources experts
(B) Business analysts
(C) Educational graduate students
(D) New employees at local colleges

**154.** Whose topic involves web-based learning?

(A) Ms. Daniel
(B) Mr. Lin
(C) Ms. Piadget
(D) Mr. Pierce

**155.** What is NOT indicated about the workshop?

(A) It is a half-day event.
(B) It includes free lunch.
(C) It introduces new items.
(D) It may require a fee to attend.

**Questions 156-157** refer to the following text message chain.

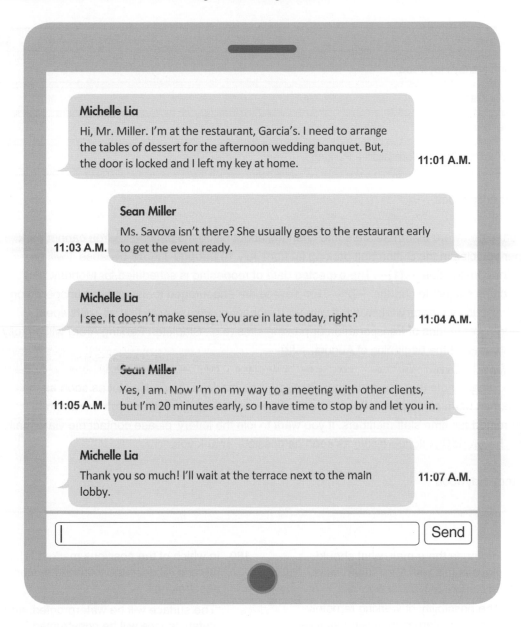

**Michelle Lia**

Hi, Mr. Miller. I'm at the restaurant, Garcia's. I need to arrange the tables of dessert for the afternoon wedding banquet. But, the door is locked and I left my key at home.

11:01 A.M.

**Sean Miller**

11:03 A.M.　Ms. Savova isn't there? She usually goes to the restaurant early to get the event ready.

**Michelle Lia**

I see. It doesn't make sense. You are in late today, right?　11:04 A.M.

**Sean Miller**

11:05 A.M.　Yes, I am. Now I'm on my way to a meeting with other clients, but I'm 20 minutes early, so I have time to stop by and let you in.

**Michelle Lia**

Thank you so much! I'll wait at the terrace next to the main lobby.　11:07 A.M.

Send

**156.** Who most likely is Mr. Miller?

(A) A café waiter
(B) A restaurant manager
(C) A café cashier
(D) A restaurant chef

**157.** At 11:04 A.M., what does Ms. Lia most likely mean when she writes, "It doesn't make sense"?

(A) Her peer doesn't show up in advance.
(B) She does not understand what Mr. Miller said.
(C) The situation is unsuitable for the event.
(D) Event attendees are already there.

*Go on to the next page*

**Questions 158-160** refer to the following e-mail.

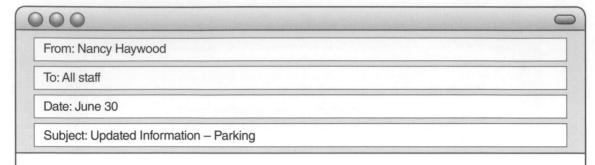

From: Nancy Haywood

To: All staff

Date: June 30

Subject: Updated Information – Parking

Dear colleagues,

Please be aware that there are some changes about using the parking lot. You cannot park your vehicles in the Sutton Hall parking lot from July 10 through July 15 because it will be under construction. —[1]—. The expected date of reopening is scheduled for Monday, July 16, but is subject to change. —[2]—. Employees are encouraged to use public transportation and discuss temporary teleworking with your managers. Please note that all costs spent using other means of transportation or parking sites (e.g., Stapleton Parking Area) will be fully reimbursed at the beginning of August. —[3]—.

Also, please note that two additional spaces will be made in the parking lot as soon as the work has been completed. —[4]—. These places will be designated through a drawing to interested full-time staff members. If you want to join the lottery, please contact me via e-mail at n.haywood@suttoncorp.com as soon as possible. Thank you.

Nancy Haywood

---

**158.** According to the e-mail, what should employees talk with their supervisors about?

(A) The possibility of working remotely
(B) The best alternative parking spaces near the company
(C) How to participate in the parking space lottery
(D) The amount of reimbursed expenses they can get

**159.** What is implied about the Stapleton Parking Area?

(A) It will be closed on Sundays.
(B) It has the latest equipment.
(C) It was recently expanded.
(D) It charges drivers for its use.

**160.** In which of the positions marked [1], [2], [3], and [4] does the following sentence best belong?

"The surface will be waterproofed, and safety fences will be constructed."

(A) [1]
(B) [2]
(C) [3]
(D) [4]

Question 161-164 refer to the following online chat discussion.

| | | |
|---|---|---|
| **Chris Paul**<br>[3:30 P.M.] | | Jim and I are grabbing an early meal after work around 4:00. Anyone want to join us? |
| **Jeremy Lavine**<br>[3:31 P.M.] | | Maybe. I still have something more to do on a report for my boss. Where are you going? |
| **Chris Paul**<br>[3:32 P.M.] | | We're thinking of going to the Mexican bar on Washington Avenue. It's called TACO Ring. |
| **Danny Rivera**<br>[3:33 P.M.] | | Oh, you are unlucky! That place closed last week. |
| **Chris Paul**<br>[3:34 P.M.] | | Really? That's too bad. I heard there are a variety of great things to eat there. |
| **Danny Rivera**<br>[3.35 P.M.] | | How about Romeo Pizzeria near Carnegie Street? They have a lot of delicious dishes and snacks on Tuesdays. |
| **Chris Paul**<br>[3:37 P.M.] | | That sounds great. Does anyone want to go there with us? |
| **Jeremy Lavine**<br>[3:38 P.M.] | | OK. But I won't be able to get there until around five, I guess. |
| **Brad Triana**<br>[3:39 P.M.] | | It will be great for me. Lavine, I just sent you the modified reporting documents. |

**Send**

**161.** What are the chat participants discussing?

(A) The place to go for dinner
(B) The meeting for a weekly sales report
(C) The menu at TACO Ring eatery
(D) The introduction of new members to others

**162.** What information does Mr. Rivera provide about TACO Ring?

(A) The taste of the food is not good.
(B) The menu is very diverse.
(C) The restaurant has gone out of business.
(D) They are gathered there for a meeting.

**163.** At 3:34 P.M., why most likely does Mr. Paul write, "That's too bad"?

(A) He cannot go with his colleagues for dinner.
(B) He wanted to eat at TACO Ring.
(C) He has a lot of things to report to his boss.
(D) He has had a delicious meal at TACO Ring.

**164.** What does Mr. Lavine decide to do?

(A) Join his coworkers for a meal
(B) Request a food delivery
(C) Work overtime on a task
(D) Look for another cafeteria

*Go on to the next page*

# Pennwholeissue Co.
### *We value your opinion!*

The Pennwholeissue Corporation has been conducting open polls of the public about current issues for over two decades. All of our questions are based on phone interviews with adults, who are eighteen years of age or older living in our designated polling areas. To ensure the same opportunity for participation for these adults, potential respondents are chosen by a computer at random.

To find information on what people think about recent world issues, please visit our Latest Poll Issues tab on our website. New polls are created weekly, and all of them are saved and accessible through the Internet. If you want to find polls by subject, use the sorting tools for a specific topic or Subject on the banner on the right. Should you want to copy the tables, graphs, charts, or other graphics made by Pennwholeissue, click the Contact Us banner and request them through our Permission Division. You can easily find the information about an easy-to-use online manual form with specifications about how and where to use them. Usually, we can respond to your request within 24 hours after you submit it.

**165.** What is NOT mentioned about poll participants?

(A) They are interviewed via the phone.
(B) They are randomly selected.
(C) They should be adults.
(D) They should be interviewed in a group.

**166.** What is indicated about Pennwholeissue Co.?

(A) It publishes books about world-historical issues.
(B) It posts new poll results on the Web every week.
(C) It is seeking new employees for Web management.
(D) It has more branches in other locations.

**167.** How can readers be permitted to get graphics?

(A) By submitting a paper form
(B) By calling a Web master
(C) By sending a request letter
(D) By contacting them on the Web site

**168.** The word "current" in paragraph 1, line 2, is closest in meaning to

(A) contemporary
(B) tentative
(C) momentous
(D) appropriate

# Need to take a break?

## Come along on the Rocky Mountains Trip!
## with Bluespruce's Tips for "Best Southwest Vacation!"

### Bluespruce Co. Offers:

The Great Outdoors!

See incredible views of oak groves and valleys along the ranges while you breathe fresh mountain air. Over 20 km of off-road biking and riding a cable car to the mountain top, which is offered for an additional fee, is prepared for you. Travel along this beautiful ridge on your own or with a trained guide. The Extreme Sports Activities program allows you to enjoy a variety of sports such as rock-climbing, white-water rafting, and so on. Indoor Unity Day is also provided by having a barbeque party, Bingo game, and live music performance in our condominium If you want to join us in this group, we offer a special price based on the number of participants in our events. Should you have more questions about our activities and costs, do not hesitate to contact us at 750-8103.

ACTUAL TEST

04

PART

7

**169.** What most likely is Bluespruce?

(A) A travel agency
(B) A national park
(C) A recreational area
(D) A sports complex

**170.** What is indicated about the Rocky Mountains?

(A) They include a variety of waterfalls and lakes.
(B) They are located in the Southwest.
(C) They have a lot of complimentary activities.
(D) They require visitors to get a license for activities.

**171.** What is offered at an extra cost?

(A) A cable car
(B) A Bingo game
(C) Live entertainment
(D) A rock-climbing activity

*Go on to the next page*

# Hopkins Apparel

Weekly Reports about Management Status, April 7–11
Assigned: Jose Mackerry, Project Manager

This week's achievements:

* Talked with five manufacturing companies in Hochimin, Vietnam, with experience of making handbags. —[1]—. Gave them our brand-new bag designs and asked questions about minimum order amount, costs of production, and shipping and processing time. —[2]—.

* According to initial data about contacted manufacturers, Staple Industries is the most suitable for our needs in terms of time and cost. —[3]—. In addition, Jim Bommer, an account manager, called me first. He was very passionate and professional, and gave us immediate answers to all our requests. I strongly believe that Staple Industries could have a good relationship with us in this business.

* The other companies we contacted were unable to accept our schedule or meet our pricing requirements. —[4]—. Therefore, we do not need to consider them.

Plans for the week of April 15–20

================= [an intentionally blank page] =================

**172.** What is suggested about Hopkins Apparel?

(A) It has a branch in Vietnam.
(B) It plans to acquire other companies.
(C) Its project manager will retire soon.
(D) It is planning to introduce some new items.

**173.** According to the report, what did Mr. Mackerry do during the week of April 7?

(A) He chose the best partner possible.
(B) He got a permit to make a product.
(C) He called a shipping company for negotiation.
(D) He held training sessions for new recruits.

**174.** What is mentioned about Mr. Bommer?

(A) He is willing to work with Hopkins Apparel.
(B) He needs more information about new bags.
(C) He has worked as a project manager at Hopkins Apparel.
(D) He wanted to meet Mr. Mackerry for pricing negotiation.

**175.** In which of the positions [1], [2], [3], and [4] does the following sentence best belong?

"The company is too small to produce our request, but it is willing to hire additional employees to carry out the work."

(A) [1]
(B) [2]
(C) [3]
(D) [4]

*Go on to the next page*

**Questions 176-180** refer to the following e-mails.

To: Steve Jack <stevejack@fastmail.com>

From: John Dewy <jdewy@aaco.com>

Dear Mr. Jack,

Your application for the managerial position of the Accounting Department at Arizonas Accounting Co. has been carefully reviewed by our department. This year's application process was highly competitive, and we were able to offer a position to only two of those who applied. Based on their recommendation, I regret to inform you that we cannot act favorably on your application and go with you at this time.

If you wish further information regarding this action, please feel free to contact the recruiting division of the Human Resources Department.

Recruiting Office
Telephone: (480) 965-3344
e-mail: recruit@aaco.com
URL: http://recruit.aaco.com/manger-apply

If you wish to be considered for other positions at Arizonas Accounting Co., more information and Web links are available at http://www.aaco.com/departments.

We thank you for your interest in Arizonas Accounting Co. and wish you success in your future endeavors.

Sincerely,

John Dewy
Arizonas Accounting Co.

To: John Dewy <jdewy@aaco.com>

From: Steve Jack <stevejack@fastmail.com>

Dear, Mr. Dewy,

I am writing this e-mail inquiring about your e-mail. I am sorry to hear that the position I applied for was not given to me, but thank you for informing me so kindly. However, I wonder what other departments are dealing with monetary issues at your company. Because I majored in business at the University of Arizona, I can handle any other matters related to accounts, budgets, and distribution management. Would it be possible for me to apply for these relevant positions in your company during this season? If so, please let me know at your earliest convenience.

By chance, the duties that I currently perform for SYSMATIC Ltd. are exactly the same as the responsibilities mentioned above. So, I would like to know very quickly about other job openings at Arizonas Accounting Co.

I look forward to becoming a valuable member of Arizonas Accounting Co.

Regards,

Steve Jack

---

**176.** For what kind of company does Mr. Dewy most likely work?

(A) A law firm
(B) A financial business
(C) A publishing company
(D) A governmental office

**177.** In the first e-mail, what is the recipient NOT asked to do for more information?

(A) Send an e-mail to the personnel division
(B) Click some links on the Web
(C) Call the company directly
(D) Post questions on the Web

**178.** What is suggested about Arizonas Accounting Co.?

(A) It had a lot of remarkable candidates.
(B) It has entered into a partnership with SYSMATIC.
(C) It has increased its sales figures in distribution.
(D) It employed a lot of new employees for the assembly lines.

**179.** Why was the second e-mail written?

(A) To advertise the applicant's merits to the manager
(B) To negotiate further conditions for the position
(C) To recommend a suitable person for a position
(D) To ask whether other related positions are available

**180.** What most likely is NOT indicated about Mr. Jack?

(A) He has a bachelor's degree.
(B) He studied business law in college.
(C) He can do various monetary tasks.
(D) He wants to transfer to a new company.

*Go on to the next page*

*Issue 100, June*

# Table of Contents

*Monthly Cover: 100th Issue Anniversary*

From: jdoris@royalrecipe.com

To: t-daven@lycoos.com

Date: 20 May

Subject: Contest Winning

Dear Mr. Daven,

I am happy to inform you that your entry of Daven's Sweety & Breeze-to-Make Pudding is the winner of our contest. Your innovative recipe will be published in the June issue of our magazine. However, the title may be shortened by our editors due to limited space in the column of the Winner's Recipes section.

Before we publish your recipe in our magazine, I would like to ask some additional information. In the recipe you submitted, honey could be used instead of sugar as a sweetener. Could you tell me how much honey is used in comparison with using sugar? Is there any other replacement if there is no honey at home? In addition, the recipe shows that the pudding should be frozen in the freezer before eating. What is the minimum amount of time and proper degree for freezing it? Thank you for giving us this information.

It is also usual for us to include a picture of the author when we publish a recipe. Please attach a clear half-length photograph of you in your reply e-mail to this.

Thank you,

Jane Doris

**181.** Why was the e-mail sent to Mr. Daven?

(A) To point out errors in his submission
(B) To encourage him to register for a cooking class
(C) To tell him about the winning process
(D) To discuss the publication of a recipe

**182.** In the e-mail, the word "entry" in paragraph 1, line 1, is closest in meaning to

(A) front of building
(B) new staff member
(C) contest submission
(D) lowest degree

**183.** What does Ms. Dorris NOT ask Mr. Daven to provide?

(A) A modified recipe title
(B) An amount of an ingredient
(C) A length of time for a process
(D) A photograph of himself

**184.** On what page does Mr. Daven's recipe appear?

(A) 16
(B) 20
(C) 36
(D) 38

**185.** What can be inferred about the recipes?

(A) The artichoke is cooked with lamb cutlet.
(B) The Oriental Balsamic Salad has a sweet flavor.
(C) A key to making pudding is the place it is cooked.
(D) All of the recipes are made by head chefs.

*Go on to the next page*

Questions 186-190 refer to the following Web page, list and article.

[http://www.m-survival.it]

**Event Name:** Long-Night-Summer Song Festival
**Location:** Daytona Beach, Florida
**Dates:** 1–14 August
**Contact:** Sabrina Anne: sanne@musicsurvival.com

**About:**

This annual event, in its fifth anniversary, brings in over 100 solo and group contestants from around the southeastern area of the United States of America. In particular, there are a lot of competitive and competent applicants in diverse fields of music. In addition, Music Survival, an organizer of this event, expects that more than 2,000 audience members will be gathered in Daytona Beach, Florida, which is nearly double that of the previous year. This contest has become one of the largest beach events in Florida. Daytona Beach, one of the longest sandy beaches in Florida, is located about one hour from Orlando. During this week, the city of Daytona holds the 40th World Grand Prix Championship, which is internationally recognized in car-racing sports. Visitors can get a chance to attend these fantastic events for free, with just $5 for parking.

## The Winners of the Fifth Annual Long-Night-Summer Song Festival

[Solo Section]

| Placement | Name | State | Title |
|---|---|---|---|
| 1st Prize | Ashton Jane | Alabama | **Cooling Summer Night** |
| 2nd Prize | Justin Moore | Georgia | **The End of the Moon** |
| 3rd Prize | Simon Rick | North Carolina | **Mixed Bowl in the World** |
| 4th Prize | Tyler Smith | Florida | **Catcher in the Lie** |

[Group Section]

| Placement | Group Name | State | Title |
|---|---|---|---|
| 1st Prize | Tina Band | Tennessee | **Don't Bully the Rustic** |
| 2nd Prize | South Life | South Carolina | **Never Stop Exploring** |

# What's New in Northeast Florida?

By Donald Scott

The annual Long-Night-Summer Song Festival took place last week, and it was the perfect way to say farewell to the hot summer season. Because of the beautiful weather, the number of visitors was over double that of the preceding years, even more than the host anticipated.

The contest drew music artists for both the solo and group sections. They introduced themselves to visitors by stimulating their emotions with their great voices. All people on the Daytona Beach fully shared their emotion. I strongly believe that this is the reason why we consider music as one of the composite arts. A feast of songs made the festival more and more exciting and helped everyone to relax.

As a result of this contest, Ashton Jane, with the amusing song, Cooling Summer Night, won the first prize in the solo section, and Tina Band from Tennessee did it in the group section with Don't Bully the Rustic, which deals with anti-social issues. The winning process consisted of both judges and audience members at the rate of fifty-fifty voting.

With the success of this festival, John McKayno, the state governor of Florida, announced that the Department of Culture in Florida will expand the scale of this event all over the country in the near future. By doing so, the state intends to advertise its region to all citizens as one of the most prosperous culture states in the U.S.

**186.** What is indicated about contestants?

(A) They are from a certain group of states.
(B) They are all professional musicians.
(C) They are requested to register early.
(D) They are all in-state residents.

**187.** What is indicated about this year's event?

(A) It is the largest festival ever.
(B) It costs $5 per person to join.
(C) It took place in Daytona Beach for the first time.
(D) It was the last event be held.

**188.** Who is the second prize winner in solo category?

(A) Ashton Jane
(B) Justin Moore
(C) Tyler Smith
(D) South Life

**189.** What does Mr. McKayne intend to do?

(A) He will develop the event into a nationwide event.
(B) He will never accept the following events.
(C) He will run for election to the National Assembly.
(D) He will change the event into a charitable one.

**190.** Which song was performed by an in-state participant?

(A) Cooling Summer Night
(B) Mixed Bowl in the World
(C) Catcher in the Lie
(D) Never Stop Exploring

*Go on to the next page*

# Borough of Ebensburg
### *Continuing Education Classes – June*

Continuing education classes are open to all residents in the Borough of Ebensburg aged 19 and over. Classes are held at Mount Aloysius College unless otherwise notified. For the registration process, please see page 4 of this brochure. There is more detailed information about tuition, fees, and payment options.

| *How to Start Your Own Business* | |
|---|---|
| Mondays, 1 P.M. – 3 P.M. | Sutton Hall, Room 101 |
| Instructor : M. Judies, Co-chair of Indiana Retailer Association | |

| *Taking a Photo — Easy and Fun Photography World!* | |
|---|---|
| Tuesdays, 2 P.M. – 5 P.M. | Stapleton Library, Room 202 |
| Instructor : S. Kenneth, Manager of Narin-Arto Pictures | |

| *Become a Real Estate Agent — Preparation for the License Test* | |
|---|---|
| Wednesdays, 1 P.M. – 4 P.M. | Leonard Hall, Room 305 |
| Instructor : K. Peter, President of Jack's Realty Firm | |

| *To Make Your Car Perfect! — Self-Care Tips* | |
|---|---|
| Thursdays, 3 P.M. – 6 P.M. | Lael Auto Lab, Monroeville Campus |
| Instructor : T. Schenider, Mechanic of Heinz Auto Parts, PA | |

---

TO : Gloria Park (and 12 others)

FROM : Jerry Gebhard <jgebhard@ebensburg.gov>

SUBJECT : [URGENT] Class Canceled

DATE : June 19

To All Class Participants:

Ms. Judies asked me to let every student know the class has been canceled due to an important issue she should attend to, so it will be rescheduled soon. Once we know the date and time, we will inform you of it via e-mail and send a new parking permit too, because your current permit is no longer valid. Sorry for this inconvenience.

Regards,

Jerry Gebhard
Manager, the Department of Local Welfare, Borough of Ebensburg
Telephone: 743-8917

# Mount Aloysius College Facility Division

## TEMPORARY ONE DAY PASS
## FOR TODAY ONLY

**SOUTH BLUE LOT**
**Valid Date:** June 22
**Time Stamp:** 1:30 P.M.

\* *Please display this permit on the front window of your vehicle so it is visible from the outside.*

---

**191.** Who most likely is T. Schenider?

(A) A repairman
(B) A council member
(C) A local business owner
(D) An association chair

**192.** What is NOT indicated about participants in the continuing education classes?

(A) They live in the Borough of Ebensburg.
(B) They paid class tuition and fees.
(C) They should be at least 19 years old.
(D) They graduated from Mt. Aloysius College.

**193.** What is Ms. Park most likely interested in?

(A) Real estate
(B) Owning a business
(C) Photography
(D) Car maintenance

**194.** In the e-mail, the phrase "attend to" in line 2, is closest in meaning to

(A) participate in
(B) take care of
(C) bring up
(D) sing up for

**195.** On what date will the rescheduled class take place?

(A) June 20
(B) June 21
(C) June 22
(D) June 23

## Richmond Daily Post

### In Brief  17 March

As reported earlier this year, Giant Hawk Grocery is going to open its additional distribution center. Completion of construction was delayed for a time because there were some problems with the ground conditions at the site. However, these matters have been completely resolved and the 20,000-square-meter area will be fully operational starting on April 5, when the opening ceremony is held with numerous citizens.

The warehouse has a special section with state-of-the-art equipment to wrap up packages with a vacuum pack system. In addition, other equipment can keep foods frozen or cool by applying quick-cooling technology.

The new distribution center is expected to create more than 200 new jobs, according to Chuck Conrad, General Manager of Operations. Due to the size and scope of the work, a variety of new employees will be needed from loaders and drivers to office clerks.

| TO: | Chuck Conrad <chuck@gianthawk.co.ca> |
|---|---|
| FROM: | Mallory Blaniar <mblaniar@gianthawk.co.ca> |
| SUBJECT: | Notification Company |
| DATE: | 20 April |

Dear Conrad,

Thanks for inviting me to the grand opening at the beginning of this month. It's unbelievable that I have seen such a well-organized event. We should get Mr. Andrew something to show our appreciation for preparing it.

I think that it is time to choose a company that sends automatic notifications to employees' cell phones. This service would enable us to deliver messages to our staff promptly and prevent some mistakes. I have the contact information of a company working with customer service at Sending to You. I guess that this is a good company, but Unitas Notification also looks great, and its monthly fees are lower than the former. Anyway, I attached the information for both companies to help you decide. Please let me know what you think.

Regards,

Mallory Blaniar

# UNITAS NOTIFICATIONS

**2:20 P.M.**

To Giant Hawk Employees,

The frozen-item deliveries expected to arrive on Monday will not arrive until Wednesday. Employees who had volunteered to work overtime on Monday and Tuesday night at the Richmond Distribution Center will not be needed. However, we will need help for the overnight shift on Wednesday night. If you are willing to work additional hours at that time, please contact Sue Trinity in the Personnel Division.

**196.** What is the purpose of the article?

(A) To introduce a start-up venture
(B) To report on a business index
(C) To provide information on a new local issue
(D) To demonstrate the latest equipment

**197.** What is most likely true about the Richmond Distribution Center?

(A) Its opening ceremony was very impressive.
(B) Mr. Conrad will soon be retired from the site.
(C) Ms. Blaniar is one of the volunteer workers.
(D) Some technical issues took place.

**198.** What is the e-mail mainly about?

(A) Celebrating the opening ceremony
(B) Organizing the upcoming event
(C) Helping choose a company
(D) Breaking off a business connection

**199.** What company was selected by Mr. Chuck?

(A) The company that Ms. Blaniar works with
(B) The company that employees want to join
(C) The company that operates an overnight service
(D) The company that is cheaper than another

**200.** What does the message ask the employees wishing to work extra to do?

(A) Contact the human resources department
(B) Work for another distribution center
(C) Go to the warehouse from Tuesday
(D) Reply to the message within a day

# ACTUAL TEST

## 答對題數表

| | |
|---|---|
| **PART 5** | |
| **PART 6** | |
| **PART 7** | |
| 總題數 | |

05

# READING TEST

In the Reading test, you will read a variety of texts and answer several different types of reading comprehension questions. The entire Reading test will last 75 minutes. There are three parts, and directions are given for each part. You are encouraged to answer as many questions as possible within the time allowed.

You must mark your answers on the separate answer sheet. Do not write your answers in your test book.

## PART 5

**Directions:** A word or phrase is missing in each of the sentences below. Four answer choices are given below each sentence. Select the best answer to complete the sentence. Then mark the letter (A), (B), (C), or (D) on your answer sheet.

101. Mr. Robertson was concerned that the suggested hotel was not ------- enough to the airport.
    (A) close
    (B) closer
    (C) closest
    (D) closely

102. The University of Texas at Arlington provides residents ------- various recreational programs.
    (A) for
    (B) at
    (C) with
    (D) as

103. Office supplies should be ------- only for business-related purposes.
    (A) purchase
    (B) purchases
    (C) purchased
    (D) purchasing

104. In order to stick to the ------- of Omega Fashions, buyers ought to present a valid receipt when getting a refund.
    (A) product
    (B) sales
    (C) manual
    (D) policy

105. Anyone attending the mountain climbing activity has to prepare proper -------.
    (A) equip
    (B) equipped
    (C) equipping
    (D) equipment

106. The state-of-the-art program will ------- reduce the amount of time it takes to meet the deadline.
    (A) significantly
    (B) recently
    (C) inappropriately
    (D) approximately

107. Promising candidates should possess a license to operate ------- bulldozers and excavators.
    (A) either
    (B) both
    (C) during
    (D) after

108. We are scheduled to ------- the final results of the survey conducted last week with our customers on our website.
    (A) share
    (B) split
    (C) ask
    (D) improve

**109.** The department of human resources replaced its chairs with ------- ones to decrease noise in the office.

(A) lightly
(B) lighter
(C) lightest
(D) lightness

**110.** The schedule for the conference call has been changed, so those involved will attend on Monday -------.

(A) alike
(B) yet
(C) likewise
(D) instead

**111.** ------- of Mr. Anderson's telephone messages is to be left with his secretary while he has a meeting with his clients.

(A) Everyone
(B) Other
(C) All
(D) Each

**112.** Given the nature of the meeting, formal attire is considered -------.

(A) useful
(B) appropriate
(C) affirmative
(D) indicative

**113.** General Electronics plans to start a new business that ------- its customers to access more information.

(A) enabled
(B) enable
(C) has enabled
(D) will enable

**114.** The managers at Lion Autos award a prize to employees who continuously ------- their expectations.

(A) exceed
(B) command
(C) desire
(D) suggest

**115.** The recently released film by Astro Enterprises has received customer reviews and ratings that are ------- positive.

(A) except
(B) exception
(C) exceptional
(D) exceptionally

**116.** At Berkshire Hardaway, managers of each department are chosen based on their expertise and experience in a ------- area.

(A) granted
(B) provided
(C) particular
(D) substantial

**117.** Valuable, fragile or perishable items would be much more expensive to ship ------- they need greater care.

(A) because
(B) nevertheless
(C) however
(D) even

**118.** McKain and Mae is a full-service law firm that can help clients with a ------- of specialized legal needs.

(A) kind
(B) range
(C) way
(D) direction

**119.** The newest version of our computer program for business expenses, ------- contains various functions, is relatively easy to use.

(A) it
(B) which
(C) whose
(D) those

**120.** ------- you encounter any problems regarding assembly or operation, please call our customer service center.

(A) If
(B) Whether
(C) As
(D) Nor

*Go on to the next page*

121. The following document details the statistics the government will need for its ------- of next year's budget.

(A) analyze
(B) analyzes
(C) to analyze
(D) analysis

122. ------- a lot of people in Salt Lake City showed interest in the lifelong education program, none have yet enrolled.

(A) Even though
(B) As though
(C) However
(D) Likewise

123. Sales in North America are expected ------- most of the company's profits.

(A) generate
(B) generated
(C) to generate
(D) will generate

124. Lawyers process a sizable number of cases at the same time ------- strict time limits.

(A) near
(B) toward
(C) following
(D) within

125. The feasibility for the construction of the new museum is heavily ------- upon the city authorities' ability to pass the budget.

(A) depend
(B) depended
(C) dependable
(D) dependent

126. To prevent dairy and other ------- products from going bad, all trucks for Andy's food delivery service company are refrigerated.

(A) perishable
(B) pervasive
(C) adverse
(D) solid

127. The Ministry of Finance reported that many small and medium-sized businesses are ------- strapped during their first year of business.

(A) finance
(B) financial
(C) financing
(D) financially

128. Mr. Nakamoto recommends that travel expense reports be submitted ------- after employees return from their trip.

(A) measurably
(B) vaguely
(C) uniquely
(D) promptly

129. After careful -------, we decided to move to a larger location to accommodate more tourists.

(A) deliberate
(B) deliberated
(C) deliberately
(D) deliberation

130. With her outstanding performance, Ms. Ashley has already ------- herself from her colleagues.

(A) differentiated
(B) designated
(C) featured
(D) performed

# PART 6

**Directions:** Read the texts that follow. A word, phrase, or sentence is missing in parts of each text. Four answer choices for each question are given below the text. Select the best answer to complete the text. Then mark the letter (A), (B), (C), or (D) on your answer sheet.

**Questions 131-134** refer to the following e-mail.

**To:** Brian Nixon <bnixon@futuresky.co.au>
**From:** Jessica Hepburn <jhepburn@cardinalfargo.org.au>

Dear Mr. Nixon,

We have received your application for a photographer at Cardinal Fargo Studio. The ------- is
**131.**
still available. -------.
**132.**

I was quite ------- with your previous experience of working at other major studios, so you must
**133.**
be accustomed to some of the job duties we require. -------, our main business would be quite
**134.**
different from what you have done before, so you need to spend some time getting to know

about this. I have scheduled a job interview for 15 September at 10:00 A.M. To confirm the

schedule, please call my office at (01) 444-0125. I am looking forward to seeing you soon.

Sincerely,

Jessica Hepburn, Personnel Manager
Cardinal Fargo Studio

---

**131.** (A) document
(B) position
(C) operation
(D) appointment

**132.** (A) Could you give us additional information regarding reimbursement?
(B) To be specific, do you have any experience in designing unique styles?
(C) Directions to the room for the interview can be found on our website.
(D) If you are still interested in this job, an individual interview is the next step.

**133.** (A) impress
(B) impressed
(C) impressive
(D) impression

**134.** (A) However
(B) Therefore
(C) Consequently
(D) Moreover

*Go on to the next page*

April 20

Leonardo Cruise
111342 Main Street
Kroger, CA 91101

Dear Mr. Cruise,

We are delighted to inform you of the fact that Kroger Recycling Program will start in our area

on May 1. Residents who would like ------- in the program will be offered a blue container with
135.

wheels. To ------- a container, please call 800-111-1217.
136.

As scheduled, the program will take place once a week instead of twice a week. -------, this will
137.

reduce greenhouse gas emissions and provide us with a better environment.

If you need further information, such as a list of recyclable materials and maps, visit our

website at www.krogerrecycling.com. -------.
138.

Sincerely,

Dwayne Damon, General Manager
Kroger Recycling Program

135. (A) participate
(B) participated
(C) to participate
(D) participating

136. (A) request
(B) reinvent
(C) review
(D) remove

137. (A) However
(B) Consequently
(C) Meanwhile
(D) On the other hand

138. (A) The program has raised significant funds thanks to generous donors.
(B) We hope that you take part in this important program.
(C) You will get the blue container within 10 days.
(D) Please make sure that you do not put fragile materials in your container.

**Questions 139-142** refer to the following article.

City Mayor Alexandra Smith made the announcement that Robin Williams Tunnel ------- to
                                                                                          **139.**
better accommodate larger trucks. Drivers using the tunnel have increased significantly over

the last few years due to the growth of freight transportations in this area. It is expected to take

approximately ten months to finish this expansion project. -------.
                                                                **140.**

Jacksonville Road, which runs ------- the tunnel, is to be closed and traffic congestion between
                                **141.**
Amitiel and Hennatown will increase during that time. " -------, it is the only possible option we
                                                          **142.**
could have," said mayor Smith.

139. (A) expand
     (B) to expand
     (C) was expanded
     (D) will be expanded

140. (A) Robin Williams Tunnel was completed
         one hundred years ago.
     (B) Those living in Amitiel have
         complained about traffic jams.
     (C) Freight service companies hope to
         recruit graduates from Hennatown
         University.
     (D) The provisional estimate of eighteen
         months has been reduced as a result
         of accurate measurement.

141. (A) along
     (B) next
     (C) while
     (D) over

142. (A) Surprisingly
     (B) Accordingly
     (C) Therefore
     (D) Unfortunately

ACTUAL TEST **05**

PART **6**

*Go on to the next page*

**To:** Sarah O'Connor <sarah_oconnor@pinghwacorp.com>

**From:** Jim Lennon <jim_lennon@ams.com>

**Date:** November 11

**Subject:** AMS

**Attachment:** AMS Brochure

Dear Ms. Sarah O'Connor,

We would like to express our gratitude for your inquiry on AMS. Our most advanced software

program has helped a great number of companies streamline their performance appraisal

process, ------- time and money.
       **143.**

We would recommend that you ------- the attached file. It contains information about five top-
       **144.**

notch companies taking advantage of AMS. As you are aware, the ability to browse through

evaluation sheets based on ratings has been exceptionally helpful to them. -------, they can
       **145.**

easily find all candidates who are eligible for promotion with our software program. In addition,

after the entire digital sorting process is done, there is no paper clutter. -------.
       **146.**

If you have any questions regarding this, please let me know.

Sincerely,

Jim Lennon

AMS Marketing Manager

143. (A) save
    (B) saves
    (C) saved
    (D) saving

144. (A) review
    (B) make
    (C) prepare
    (D) throw

145. (A) As a result
    (B) As long as
    (C) In the meantime
    (D) In keeping with

146. (A) Our software will be updated next week.
    (B) It will be a difficult task for you to sift through qualified candidates for promotion.
    (C) All the sheets are well organized in the computerized database.
    (D) Candidates should have at least 3 years of experience in a related field.

# PART 7

**Directions:** In this part you will read a selection of texts, such as magazine and newspaper articles, e-mails, and instant messages. Each text or set of texts is followed by several questions. Select the best answer for each question and mark the letter (A), (B), (C), or (D) on your answer sheet.

**Questions 147-148** refer to the following text message.

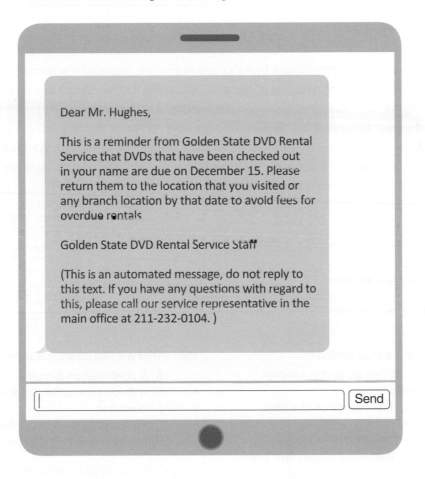

Dear Mr. Hughes,

This is a reminder from Golden State DVD Rental Service that DVDs that have been checked out in your name are due on December 15. Please return them to the location that you visited or any branch location by that date to avoid fees for overdue rentals

Golden State DVD Rental Service Staff

(This is an automated message, do not reply to this text. If you have any questions with regard to this, please call our service representative in the main office at 211-232-0104. )

Send

**147.** Why did Mr. Hughes receive the text message?

(A) Because the items that he borrowed should be turned in soon
(B) Because he should pay late fees by December 15
(C) Because the items he requested are already sold out
(D) Because his membership card is set to expire on December 15

**148.** According to the text message, what could Mr. Hughes do if he has any questions?

(A) Visit the rental service company's website
(B) Speak with a service representative
(C) Send a text message to a service representative
(D) Go to any branch location of the rental service

**Questions 149-150** refer to the following e-mail.

From: Tom Affleck <affleck@valerofurniture.com>

To: Scarlett Lawrence <lawrence@smail.com>

Date: March 11

Subject: Shipping delay

Dear Ms. Lawrence,

Thank you for your recent purchase from Valero Furniture. Some of the items have yet to be shipped owing to the heavy snow in our area. Closures on the roads have also made it harder for items to be delivered from our warehouse. To make matters worse, the snow has caused power failures in our region. We, however, promise that we will get back to normal within 12 hours. Thus, your order will be shipped no later than Wednesday. The shipping fee on all affected orders will be fully refunded. We do apologize for any inconvenience this may cause you.

Sincerely,

Tom Affleck
Customer Service Manager

**149.** Why was the e-mail written?
(A) To give an update on the weather conditions
(B) To inform Ms. Lawrence of a late shipment
(C) To advertise furniture
(D) To report that some roads have been closed

**150.** What will Ms. Lawrence receive?
(A) A confirmation e-mail
(B) A discount voucher for a future purchase
(C) Free shipping on her order
(D) An additional new product

## New Rules for Trash Collection

Krudenwald City will set a limit on the number of trash bins, which starts on April 25. Therefore, residents can now put no more than three trash bins outside for each curbside pickup, even though the monthly fee for trash collection is still unchanged. The sum of all trash bins should not exceed 100 liters in size.

City officials said that encouraging residents to take advantage of the city's free collection and recycling services for metal, plastic, and paper is part of the city's efforts to reduce the cost of trash collection. This will decrease landfill dumping fees as well.

**151.** What is the purpose of the notice?

(A) To provide a new service
(B) To announce a policy change
(C) To complain about recycling fees
(D) To recommend a landfill site

**152.** According to the notice, what can residents use free of charge?

(A) A recycling service
(B) A trash collection service
(C) A trash bin
(D) A landfill site

Go on to the next page

---

## MEMO

**To:** All employees

**From:** Christian Diesel, Director of Operations

**Date:** Thursday, July 28

**Subject:** West Wing Closure

The west wing of the building will be closed in the first week of August. The maintenance department will be in charge of replacing all the chairs and desks with environmentally friendly ones. According to the safety regulations, the site is off-limits to all employees while the maintenance staff is at work. The replacement schedule will start on Tuesday, August 1, and it will be finished on Saturday, August 5.

The affected offices are 1201–1235. Employees involved should work at home or, if necessary, a temporary workspace can be prepared for them in another part of the building. You may call administrative assistant Natalie Johansson at extension 51 to request a temporary workspace. Please note that we have limited temporary workspaces, which will be provided on a first-come, first-served basis. Thank you for your cooperation.

---

**153.** What is the reason for the closure of the west wing?

(A) A regular inspection will be taking place.
(B) The headquarters will be moved to a different location.
(C) Office furniture will be replaced.
(D) Space for meetings will be added.

**154.** Which of the following offices will be temporarily unavailable?

(A) 1200
(B) 1224
(C) 1236
(D) 1240

**155.** What should employees do if they would like to request a temporary workspace?

(A) Contact their supervisor
(B) Write an e-mail to Mr. Diesel
(C) Apply online
(D) Call Ms. Johansson

Questions 156-158 refer to the following e-mail.

From: Angelina Grant <agrant@lowecatering.com>

To: James Hardy <jhardy@uig.com>

Date: June 11

Subject: Catering service

Dear Mr. Hardy,

This e-mail is to confirm your telephone conversation yesterday with respect to your request for a catering service for the annual corporate conference. My understanding is that it should be similar to what you requested for last year's conference. Unfortunately, my food supplier has notified me of the fact that due to a shortage of beef, they are unable to provide it until next week. As you will hold the conference on June 15, I think it would be necessary to choose a different type of meat. I recommend chicken, which could be ready in time. So, if this is acceptable, please let me know by responding directly to this e-mail. Once you agree to the alternative, I will send you the contract and estimate sheet. If you need more information, please call me at 514-212-0114.

Thank you,

Angelina Grant, Manager
Lowe Catering Service

156. What is suggested about Mr. Hardy?
(A) He is Ms. Grant's colleague.
(B) He is planning a dinner party for his friends.
(C) He has requested a service from Lowe Catering Service before.
(D) He has asked for a change to a service.

157. Why does Ms. Grant recommend replacing the food item?
(A) It is out of stock.
(B) It is very expensive.
(C) It lacks freshness.
(D) It doesn't taste good.

158. What does Ms. Grant ask Mr. Hardy to do next?
(A) Send a contract
(B) Call her immediately
(C) Reply to an e-mail
(D) Cancel a meeting

●⊡⊗

| | | |
|---|---|---|
| | **Seneca Co. Agent**<br>[5:15 P.M.] | Hello, this is Seneca Co. Service Center. What's your problem? |
| | **Martin Ford**<br>[5:15 P.M.] | I am having trouble with updating the newest version of software for my desktop. |
| | **Seneca Co. Agent**<br>[5:16 P.M.] | What kind of desktop do you have? |
| | **Martin Ford**<br>[5:17 P.M.] | It's an XPS 8910. In order to download the software, I have to enter the correct serial number, but I can't find it. |
| | **Seneca Co. Agent**<br>[5:18 P.M.] | Here's how to find the serial number on your product. It is printed near the barcode on your product packaging. |
| | **Seneca Co. Agent**<br>[5:18 P.M.] | It could be too small to read, so take a photo of the number with your mobile phone, then zoom in. |
| | **Martin Ford**<br>[5:19 P.M.] | Yes, there is a ten-digit number on it. Is that it? |
| | **Seneca Co. Agent**<br>[5:20 P.M.] | Yes, that's right. Is there anything else that I could do to help you? |
| | **Martin Ford**<br>[5:20 P.M.] | No. Thank you so much. |

**Send**

**159.** What is Mr. Ford trying to do?

(A) Find his password
(B) Create an account
(C) Buy a computer
(D) Download software

**160.** At 5:19 P.M. what does Mr. Ford most likely mean when he writes, "Is that it"?

(A) He wanted to check what he was looking for.
(B) He didn't understand the agent's idea.
(C) He has not used the online service before.
(D) He wanted to end the online chat.

| From: | Bradley Cooper [bcooper@sysco.com] |
|-------|-------------------------------------|
| To: | Robert Gosling [rgosling@sysco.com] |
| Date: | January 4 |
| Subject: | Donation program |

Dear Mr. Gosling,

I have looked into the documents you gave with regard to Sysco's new donation program. —[1]—. At the next department meeting, you should share the information in the documents with our members. —[2]—. Moreover, I will encourage them to check the list of recommended organizations and participate in the program by selecting at least one of these to donate to before the program starts in February. —[3]—.

Please give me a call at your earliest convenience to discuss some issues about the program. —[4]—. Thank you in advance for your cooperation.

Sincerely,

Bradley Cooper
The Department of Human Resources

**161.** What does Mr. Cooper want Mr. Gosling to do?

(A) Discuss details about the program
(B) Make a donation to some organizations
(C) Reschedule a department meeting
(D) Create a donation program

**162.** What is suggested about Sysco's new donation program?

(A) It is scheduled to go into effect in February.
(B) It is limited only to employees.
(C) It is held twice a year.
(D) It allows for employees to choose only one organization.

**163.** In which of the positions marked [1], [2], [3], and [4] does the following sentence best belong?

"This will take several weeks to decide."

(A) [1]
(B) [2]
(C) [3]
(D) [4]

May 1

Ryan Eastwood
Pinewood Apartment #1299
Orange County, California 562

Dear Mr. Eastwood,

Your Pinewood rental apartment is subject to a regular maintenance assessment. We are scheduled to visit on Tuesday, May 15, at 2:00 P.M. What we request is that tenants be present. Please let us know a time that works for you if this time is inconvenient for you. —[1]—.

During the assessment, we check several important items to make sure that they are working properly, which include appliances, the gas line, and plumbing. —[2]—.

According to our check-up lists, the interior of your apartment has not been painted for five years. If you want your house to be repainted, our maintenance staff will handle the task. We will make the utmost effort to finish the work in a timely fashion. —[3]—. We have a range of colors for painting, and you can see them by visiting our website at www.pinewood.com/colorsforpaint. —[4]—. Finally, our records indicate that the furniture in your house was fully replaced last year, so the replacement is not available at this time.

If you have any questions, please call me anytime.

Best Regards,

Chris Hemsworth
Office Manager

164. Why was the letter sent to Mr. Eastwood?

(A) To provide him with information on a rental promotion
(B) To notify him of a late payment
(C) To inform him of upcoming check-ups
(D) To suggest an annual event in an apartment

165. What is Mr. Eastwood asked to do on the afternoon of May 15?

(A) Visit a Website
(B) Choose paint colors
(C) Reply to an e-mail
(D) Stay at home

166. What home improvement work is Mr. Eastwood currently eligible for?

(A) Painting a house
(B) Changing to new appliances
(C) Fixing doors
(D) Replacing furniture

167. In which of the positions marked [1], [2], [3], and [4] does the following sentence best belong?

"If necessary, maintenance work will be performed."

(A) [1]
(B) [2]
(C) [3]
(D) [4]

## Moonlight Questionnaire

Thank you for participating in the preview of the film tentatively named *Moonlight*. As the film is in its final stages, it would be a great help for the final editing if you could give us your opinions about the film. Please take a few minutes to answer to the following questions.

Name: Rachel Jane
Address: 2885 Sanford Avenue Grandville 28912

**What was your impression of this film?**

I loved it! I enjoyed watching the same characters and scenes that I had imagined when reading the original novel a few years ago. It was a perfect adaptation of the novel.

**How about the sound quality? Please elaborate.**

It was very clear. Especially, I loved its soundtrack. In general, there was no part where I could hardly understand the dialogue.

**If there are any parts that seem too long, please elaborate on this.**

It seemed that this film was a bit longer than any other films that I have ever seen. However, all scenes were necessary for its storyline and flowed together smoothly. I would personally recommend not making any cuts.

**Do you have any other comments?**

Emma Aniston and James Niro gave quite excellent performances. I have never paid attention to Jessica Watson before. This time, she was amazing, and I hope she wins an award for this film. Just one thing I would like to mention is that what she wore in the movie didn't seem true to the original. The film is set in the mid-1880s. I think she should have worn something historically accurate.

168. To whom was the questionnaire given?

(A) Professional writers
(B) Acting class members
(C) Directors in the film industry
(D) Audience members at a film screening

169. What is indicated about *Moonlight*?

(A) It has a relatively short running time.
(B) It is based on a book.
(C) It is filmed in a documentary style.
(D) It was completed a few years ago.

170. What can be inferred about Ms. Watson?

(A) She recently starred in several films.
(B) She dropped out of the film.
(C) She was participating in the preview of the film.
(D) She had an impressive performance in the film.

171. What does Ms. Jane recommend?

(A) Enabling the dialogue to be understood more easily
(B) Making clothing more authentic
(C) Including more soundtracks
(D) Shortening the film

**Sandra Lopez**
[9:02 A.M.]

Good morning. The board of directors approved our company's merger at the December meeting. I would like to know what you heard from the managers' meeting at the headquarters.

**Kate Lively**
[9:03 A.M.]

At first, it caused a lot of confusion, but everything is restored to normal now. People seem to know what is going to happen.

**Cameron Winslet**
[9:03 A.M.]

Employees here are convinced that the merger will lead to changes in personnel. Everybody is expressing concerns about any moves in February. That's because it is our busiest time of the year. When are we going to get detailed information on this?

**Cate Adams**
[9:05 A.M.]

I am not in the right position to answer these questions without knowing more information from the head office.

**Sandra Lopez**
[9:07 A.M.]

I'll keep working on this. I will get more information before long. In February when the four of us meet together, I will make a report.

**Cameron Winslet**
[9:08 A.M.]

It seems that some of our employees will move boxes in March.

**Sandra Lopez**
[9:09 A.M.]

It could be possible. The personnel department is still figuring out which offices will receive employees from the other teams.

**Cate Adams**
[9:10 A.M.]

There must be plenty of decisions to be made.

Send

**172.** Why did Ms. Lopez start an online chat with the managers?

(A) To cancel a meeting
(B) To announce an upcoming merger
(C) To gather some opinions
(D) To change the date of the relocation

**173.** At 9:07 A.M., what does Ms. Lopez most likely mean when she writes, "I'll keep working on this"?

(A) She is trying to get an update.
(B) Employees increased substantially last year.
(C) The headquarters will be moved in February.
(D) She is making an effort to get back to normal.

**174.** When will the managers receive the updated information?

(A) In December
(B) In January
(C) In February
(D) In March

**175.** What is the personnel department expected to do?

(A) Reshuffle some employees
(B) Provide employees with office supplies
(C) Introduce new employees
(D) Replace the old personnel system

*Go on to the next page*

Questions 176-180 refer to the following letter and e-mail.

**Statewide Insurance Co.**

848 Main Street, Fresno, CA 93721-2760

April 8
George Hanks
2451 Inyo Street, Fresno, CA 93721

Dear Mr. Hanks,

Thank you for applying for the position of junior associate with Statewide Insurance Co. We regret to inform you that we decided to select another applicant after much consideration. However, we were very impressed by not only what you have done in the past few years, but also the knowledge and expertise you showed when you are interviewed. Therefore, we would like to offer you a vacant position that we believe suits you.

The position that we offer you is a part-time job, unlike the one you applied for. The working hours are from 2 P.M. to 6 P.M. on Tuesday and Thursday, and 3 P.M. to 7 P.M. on Monday, Wednesday, and Friday. Your primary responsibilities will be gathering and analyzing information and data, providing potential clients with tailor-made plans, and planning insurance products.

If you are interested in this position, feel free to call me at 515-217-0121 or email me at markchan@statewideinsurance.com.

From: George Hanks [ghanks@atmail.com]

To: Mark Chan [markchan@statewideinsurance.com]

Date: April 10

Re: Your letter

Dear Mr. Chan,

Thank you for your letter in which you offered me a job. I am very delighted to join Statewide Insurance Co. I am wondering, however, if the company could adjust my business hours.

At the interview session, I mentioned that I have been working as a volunteer with the International Insurance Society (IIS). There could be a scheduling conflict on Monday and Tuesday since I am now working for the organization Monday and Tuesday from 9 A.M. to 3 P.M. So, I would really appreciate it if your company would allow me to work from 4 P.M. to 8 P.M. on Monday and Tuesday.

I am looking forward to hearing from you soon.

Best wishes,

George Hanks

176. For what kind of company does Mr. Chan most likely work?

(A) A law firm
(B) An auto manufacturer
(C) A publisher
(D) An insurance company

177. In the letter, the word "select" in paragraph 1, line 2, is closest in meaning to

(A) go with
(B) receive
(C) depend on
(D) account for

178. What is mentioned about Mr. Chan's company?

(A) It has joined with the International Insurance Society.
(B) It recently signed a great number of clients.
(C) It has never hired full-time employees before.
(D) It offers an insurance planning service.

179. Why was the e-mail written?

(A) To ask for a change of working hours
(B) To make inquiries about benefits for employees
(C) To recommend someone else qualified for the position
(D) To request a pay increase

180. What most likely will NOT be a responsibility Mr. Hanks takes at Mr. Chan's company?

(A) Collecting materials
(B) Counseling customers
(C) Introducing products
(D) Interviewing job applicants

Go on to the next page

## New York Media Corporation
**Research and Development Team**

Annual Performance Appraisal Report
Name: Kim Barrymore
Title: Research Associate

Please write all major events and projects in which you took part this year.

1. Offered four-week course of media law for students at New York University majoring in mass communication (February 2–28)
2. Represented Research and Development Team at the 10th anniversary of News Media Conference, New York City (March 2–3)
3. Acted as a guest speaker, *"Current Status of Internet Media"* at the World Journalism Forum, London, England (May 12–15)
4. Carried out a research project on a new wave of Internet broadcasting (January — November). Study submitted to *Broadcasting Trade Journal*, accepted for publication.
5. Led public tours of new headquarters at New York Media Corporation (December).

## NY Media's Kim Barrymore Receives Award

by David Stewart, JSP Journalist

December 17—Kim Barrymore from New York Media Corp. has been named Journalist of the Year for her research project on a new wave of Internet broadcasting.

Margot Green, editor-in-chief of New York Media Corp., mentioned that it is unusual for the award to be given to a researcher. She went on to say, "It is attributable to Barrymore's hard work and dedication. And we're very delighted to have her on our team."

Ms. Barrymore joined New York Media Corp. 10 years ago after earning a doctorate degree in mass communication from New York University. She received her undergraduate education at Brooklyn Latin School in New York.

The award ceremony will be held on 23 December at the New York Conference Center.

**181.** According to the report, why did Ms. Barrymore go to England?

(A) To report a case
(B) To study mass media
(C) To deliver a speech
(D) To tour a new research facility

**182.** What does the report suggest happened at New York Media Corp. in December?

(A) An international forum was held.
(B) New courses for university students were given.
(C) A new head office was opened.
(D) The cost for public tours decreased.

**183.** Where most likely did Ms. Barrymore's article first appear?

(A) A magazine published by New York University
(B) On the website of New York Media Corporation
(C) In an industry publication
(D) In a scientific journal

**184.** What does Ms. Green imply about the Journalist of the Year award?

(A) It offers both a medal and prize money.
(B) It is presented by New York Media Corp.
(C) It is rarely presented to a researcher.
(D) It is only for New York residents.

**185.** What is mentioned about the News Media Conference?

(A) It is usually organized by the government.
(B) It was not held for the first time this year.
(C) It gives university students complimentary tickets.
(D) It is held every two years.

*Go on to the next page*

## Honeywell International's Offices to Be Relocated

March 1 — Honeywell International is scheduled to move its offices in Sydney, Melbourne, and Brisbane into company-owned properties. The significant increase in rental costs forced the company to make such a decision.

"We came to realize that building our own offices would result in saving money in many ways," said Elizabeth Lohan, Honeywell International's general director. She also mentioned that sharing space with other businesses has caused discomfort and inconvenience when doing businesses. Construction of its headquarters in Sydney, which began two years ago, will finally be finished this month.

Construction of the other branch offices in Melbourne and Brisbane will be finished in one year, and then employees will be moved accordingly.

A representative of the company said that its entire workforce, which totaled approximately 1,000 employees last year, will be relocated to the new buildings no later than July.

## TIAA Relocation Services

We will handle everything for you. TIAA makes your move easier.

A relocation consulting service will be provided free of charge. Our consultant will visit your office or your home to give an estimate for the move. We will send you a written estimate by e-mail within two to three days after the visit.

Whenever you need us during the move, we will always be there for you.
• Do you need help packing? Our team members can help you with anything.
• Do you want to move any classified materials? We will arrange a schedule with your security staff to make sure that confidential files and documents are monitored without interruption.
• Do you need some space to hold your belongings? Our strictly-controlled warehouse is prepared for you.

We will fulfill our tasks. We will do our best to make all items neatly arranged.

# TIAA Relocation Services Estimate Sheet

**Please complete the following request form to schedule a visit for an accurate estimate.**

| | | | |
|---|---|---|---|
| **Company Name :** | Honeywell International | **Name of contact person :** | Elizabeth Lohan |
| **Telephone number :** | 128-01-2821169 | **E-mail :** | el0800@atmail.co.au |
| **Pick-up address :** | 680 George Street, Sydney | **Delivery address:** | 458 Harris Street, Sydney |
| **Pick-up date :** | April 3 | **Delivery date :** | April 3 |

**Preferred date and time for an estimate:** <u>March 3, 10:00 A.M.</u>

---

**186.** In the article, the word "forced" in paragraph 1, line 2, is closest in meaning to

(A) compelled
(B) acted quickly
(C) broke down
(D) made a difference

**187.** What is inferred about Ms. Lohan?

(A) She was promoted to general director this year.
(B) She has worked for Honeywell International for five years.
(C) She will move to the new headquarters in April.
(D) She works in Honeywell International's Brisbane office.

**188.** What kind of service does TIAA offer?

(A) Constructing buildings
(B) Transporting sensitive items
(C) Maintaining computer systems
(D) Strengthening security

**189.** What is implied about the Harris Street location?

(A) It will accommodate nearly 1,000 employees.
(B) It was constructed in approximately two years.
(C) It has recently been remodeled.
(D) It is now rented by other firms.

**190.** What will most likely happen on March 3?

(A) A TIAA employee will visit George Street.
(B) Items will be properly arranged.
(C) Ms. Lohan will check an e-mail to review an estimate.
(D) Classified documents will be moved.

*Go on to the next page*

**Questions 191-195** refer to the following Web page, list, and article.

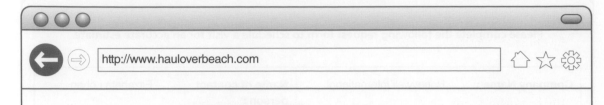

| Home | Events | Location | Contact Us |

**Event Name:** International Sand Sculpture Festival

**Location:** Haulover Beach, Miami

**Date:** 28–29 July

**Contact:** Denzel Freeman: dfreeman@hauloverbeach.com

**About:** The oldest and largest sand sculpture contest in Miami, which brings in over 50 master contestants from all over the world creating sculptures from 10,000 tons of sand. The festival marks the 7th anniversary this year. Last year alone, more than 20,000 visitors went to the Haulover Beach International Sand Sculpture Festival, which has become one of the largest beach events in Miami. In addition to the contest, the two-day festival features live music and sand workshops for children. When darkness falls, the sculptures will appear in a different light. Even though the event is free for all, $5 for parking will be charged.

## Winners of the 7th International Sand Sculpture Festival

| Placement | Name | Title of Piece |
|-----------|------|----------------|
| First Place | Humphrey Washington, England | Dinosaurs |
| Second Place | Jack Nicholson, Canada | Spaceships |
| Third Place | Johnny Spacey, U.S. | Castle |
| Fourth Place | Russel Pitt, Denmark | Pirates and Princesses |
| Fifth Place | Lonardo Travolta, Argentina | Sea Creatures |

## WHAT'S NEW IN MIAMI

By Christian Winslet

(1 August) — The 7th International Sand Sculpture Festival was held last weekend and was the best way to enjoy the summer. Due to the exceptionally fantastic weather, the event attracted more visitors than last year. This year, there was a competition for solo masters. They created eye-catching sand creatures and turned mere sand and water into genuine art. Masters depicted everything from sea creatures to castles and even spaceships in a somewhat exaggerated way.

Humphrey Washington from England beat three-time champion Jack Nicholson from Canada with his "Dinosaur" sculpture, which dazzled the judges with its absolute artistic realism. All the sculptures were attractive, but my personal favorite was "Pirates and Princesses," which vividly expressed comic gestures through the characters' arms and faces.

Children could participate in the sand class led by sand sculpting experts who were not participating in the contest. Live music pleased visitors' ears as well. This must be the perfect way to enjoy the hottest season.

**191.** What is mentioned about the contestants?

(A) They are all amateurs.
(B) They have an acquaintance with Mr. Freeman.
(C) They had to sign up online in advance for the event.
(D) They are from various countries.

**192.** In the article, the word "attracted" in paragraph 1, line 3, is closest in meaning to

(A) moved
(B) drew
(C) won
(D) participated

**193.** What is indicated about this year's event?

(A) It cost 5 dollars to attend.
(B) It had over 20,000 visitors.
(C) It took place at Haulover Beach for the first time.
(D) It had adult-only programs.

**194.** What is indicated about Mr. Nicholson?

(A) He has won the contest before.
(B) He has led a sand class.
(C) He just moved to Canada.
(D) He is a member of a national team.

**195.** Whose sculpture did Ms. Winslet like the most?

(A) Mr. Washington's
(B) Mr. Nicholson's
(C) Mr. Spacey's
(D) Mr. Pitt's

Go on to the next page

# International Financial Investment Forum

Nairobi Conference Center, Kenya
Thursday, November 8

The 1st International Financial Investment Forum in Kenya will be a venue for discussing the current state of financial investment industry. Africa is one of the fastest growing markets in the world. The tourism and building infrastructure have brought a huge influx of money into Africa. World-renowned presenters will bring their expertise, passion, and enthusiasm to their session and share their insights on various issues. To participate in the forum, all involved are required to have their names registered. Anyone who would like to attend, please feel free to visit our website at www.ifif.org and fill in the sign-up form. No participation fee is charged.

Please note that applications for participants will be accepted entirely on a first-come, first-served basis because of the limited number of seats.

| Time | Presenter | Title |
|---|---|---|
| 9:00 A.M. | Keira Jane | Current Status of Africa |
| 10:30 A.M. | Catherine Jones | Economic and Market Outlooks in Africa |
| 12:00 P.M. | Lunch Break | |
| 1:00 P.M. | Clive Gibson | Strategic Investment |
| 2:00 P.M. | George Bloom | Quality Decision-Making Process |
| 3:00 P.M. | Sandra Ryan | Risk Management |

From: Sandra Ryan <sryan@ryaninvestmentgroup.com>

To: Megan Diaz <mdiaz@ifif.org>

Subject: November Forum

Date: September 15

Dear Ms. Diaz,

Thank you for giving me the opportunity to be a part of this meaningful forum. First of all, I have to say that the international forum will have a great impact on the industry in Africa, which needs more investment across the board.

I have received the full schedule of presentations. Unfortunately, I have an important commitment in Kenya after the lunch break, so I have to leave the venue by 11:00 at the latest. The schedule indicated that I am the last presenter. Although I already reported the issue to the organizing committee, I want to get a definite answer. So if it is possible to change my presentation schedule, please send me a revised schedule and distribute it to everyone.

Thank you.

Sincerely,

Sandra Ryan
Ryan Investment Group

**196.** What are participants required to do?

(A) Arrive at the event site 30 minutes early
(B) Register online
(C) Receive name cards
(D) Take a designated seat

**197.** Who will make a speech on economic forecasts?

(A) Keira Jane
(B) Catherine Jones
(C) Clive Gibson
(D) George Bloom

**198.** When will Ms. Ryan probably speak at the forum if it is rescheduled?

(A) 9:00 A.M.
(B) 12:00 A.M.
(C) 2:00 P.M.
(D) 3:00 P.M.

**199.** What is indicated about Ms. Ryan?

(A) She has to go to the airport after her presentation.
(B) She has an appointment during the forum.
(C) She changed her topic before the event.
(D) She is a member of the organizing committee.

**200.** What does Ms. Ryan request that Ms. Diaz do?

(A) Extend the registration date
(B) Get approval from the hotel
(C) Update an event document
(D) Change a location

# ACTUAL TEST

## 答對題數表

| | |
|---|---|
| **PART 5** | |
| **PART 6** | |
| **PART 7** | |
| 總題數 | |

# 06

# READING TEST

In the Reading test, you will read a variety of texts and answer several different types of reading comprehension questions. The entire Reading test will last 75 minutes. There are three parts, and directions are given for each part. You are encouraged to answer as many questions as possible within the time allowed.

You must mark your answers on the separate answer sheet. Do not write your answers in your test book.

## PART 5

**Directions:** A word or phrase is missing in each of the sentences below. Four answer choices are given below each sentence. Select the best answer to complete the sentence. Then mark the letter (A), (B), (C), or (D) on your answer sheet.

---

**101.** As one of the company's events, GLK-Auto provides complimentary auto parts to ------ loyal customers.

(A) they
(B) their
(C) them
(D) theirs

**102.** Taking advantage of Power-Shoulder to ------ goods can prevent people from getting injured on their shoulders.

(A) achieve
(B) cause
(C) lift
(D) culminate

**103.** Some ------ coast communities are totally dependent on the shipping and fishing industry to earn a living.

(A) locate
(B) local
(C) location
(D) locals

**104.** Ruby's Friday restaurant is always ------ to provide exceptional dishes to our customers by hiring professional chefs.

(A) delicious
(B) ready
(C) experienced
(D) complicated

**105.** If you have a problem with the item, please return it to the nearest store ------ seven days of the purchase to get a refund.

(A) until
(B) out of
(C) within
(D) from

**106.** A ------ of products targeted for the winter season has been gradually piled into stockrooms in Portland stores.

(A) series
(B) lack
(C) frequency
(D) length

**107.** According to the monthly financial report, these results of increasing loans on properties accord ------ with predictions in the popular magazine, *Jerry's Economy*.

(A) newly
(B) lately
(C) closely
(D) drastically

**108.** A policy without any discussion among the management should not ------ the decision-making process regarding expanding their branches internationally.

(A) act
(B) remind
(C) influence
(D) confess

109. Premium Ltd. has made an extensive
------ to its assembly line to increase its
productivity, which had caused a lot of
mechanical problems.
(A) modifying
(B) modification
(C) modify
(D) to modify

110. Mr. Terry has sent the loan application
to several banks for securing funds
displayed on the proof of bank statement
------ to purchase a new house in Austin,
Texas.
(A) require
(B) will require
(C) required
(D) requiring

111. Ms. Yoon has started the research project
on second language writers by -------,
but recently asked peers to help with
collecting reliable data.
(A) her
(B) hers
(C) herself
(D) she

112. ------- this year's annual profits are lower
than expected, the management at
Johnny Index Distributions is not willing to
approve employees' annual pay raise.
(A) Owing to
(B) Given that
(C) With regard to
(D) In case of

113. The Maxi Department Store has attracted
a lot of people due to its ------ to many
urban transportation.
(A) arena
(B) field
(C) proximity
(D) width

114. ------- advance ticket sales number more
than three thousand, Penn Entertainment
uses its main auditorium at Kovalchick
Convention Center in Flint City.
(A) Whether
(B) If
(C) That
(D) Despite

115. Candidates are ------ to submit their
portfolios to apply for the position at Alex
Cooper Appliances.
(A) will ask
(B) asks
(C) asking
(D) asked

116. The award committee of Selex Security
Service nominated the top 10 employees
------- are entitled to get the Employee
of the Year Award at its 20th anniversary
banquet.
(A) those
(B) anyone
(C) who
(D) which

117. The newly installed program for the staff
payroll system will be operational ------
on Friday, March 17, unless otherwise
directed by a general manager.
(A) beginning
(B) to begin
(C) will begin
(D) beginner

118. As of next year, UPT Electronics ------ its
branches into other countries, especially
Eastern Asia, for diverse businesses.
(A) have expanded
(B) are expanding
(C) will expand
(D) is expanded

119. You can easily find the Stapleton Library,
which is located slightly ------ the Oak
Grove on the IUP Campus.
(A) over
(B) among
(C) between
(D) past

120. If you purchase the latest items from
Savannah Electronics, please thoroughly
------ the manual that comes with the item.
(A) program
(B) gather
(C) direct
(D) review

*Go on to the next page*

121. Whenever ------ with prospective clients, please keep in mind that you should tell them about approaching special offers such as online discounts.
(A) to speak
(B) speaking
(C) spoke
(D) spoken

122. Recruitment experts will help to distinguish a ------ candidate from other applicants by using tools for assessment of aptitude.
(A) selling
(B) promising
(C) reminding
(D) proposing

123. Montgomery Corp. is ------ to confirm that they achieve a diversity of positive results from distribution, exclusive sales, and service sectors.
(A) pleasure
(B) please
(C) pleasing
(D) pleased

124. Working as a senior manager at Punxtwaney City Museum two years ago, Mr. McNab has ------ been in charge of directing main exhibitions.
(A) since
(B) yet
(C) ever
(D) too

125. Premier Investment Co. was forcibly operating inefficient production lines at a deficit, which might be damaging the company's ------ for maintaining its rank in the financial world.
(A) reputation
(B) negotiation
(C) consideration
(D) rotation

126. After parliament members reach an agreement to the amendments, the new regulations will be fully understandable to ------ concerned about the election.
(A) each other
(B) whatever
(C) anything
(D) everyone

127. ------ all the prerequisite courses have been finished, the graduate students should prepare for their comprehensive written and oral test.
(A) While
(B) So that
(C) As soon as
(D) In that

128. The board of directors has already recognized ------- of the issue when all sales figures started to take a downward curve in the budget report.
(A) specifically
(B) specify
(C) specific
(D) specifics

129. Once you submit the application for the position, you are ------ to hear the interview schedule from the Personnel Division.
(A) limited
(B) sought
(C) bound
(D) covered

130. If the item you purchased had been damaged, you ------ to return it to a nearby store for exchange.
(A) would have been opted
(B) would have opted
(C) has opted
(D) is being opted

# PART 6

**Directions:** Read the texts that follow. A word, phrase, or sentence is missing in parts of each text. Four answer choices for each question are given below the text. Select the best answer to complete the text. Then mark the letter (A), (B), (C), or (D) on your answer sheet.

**Questions 131-134** refer to the following e-mail.

**To:** Brad Triana

**From:** John Fontainne

**Date:** 17 March

**Subject:** A request for advice about theater renovation

Dear Mr. Triana,

We have spent a lot of time dealing with the recommendations you gave at the last meeting.

Above all, we ------- a wide black curtain that blocks the noise from the outside of the stage. For
**131.**
testing its degree of blocking, our worker stood ------- near the stage, and we couldn't hear any
**132.**
sound during pre-practice. We also have plans to comply with your recommendations to expand

the control console, enabling experienced staff to work closely together. -------.
**133.**

We are pleased ------- your useful and informative guidelines and look forward to meeting you
**134.**
next time.

Sincerely,

John Fontainne

131. (A) purchase
(B) purchased
(C) will purchase
(D) are purchasing

132. (A) shortly
(B) hardly
(C) only
(D) rather

133. (A) This can enable us to manage our lighting and sounds more effectively than before.
(B) The prior curtain is too thin to screen noise from the outside.
(C) There is only one improvement we made among your recommendations.
(D) We want to increase the number of ticket sales for the next performance.

134. (A) to
(B) with
(C) for
(D) on

*Go on to the next page*

---

### *Indiana Tribune – Business Briefing*

Clarion (20 October) – Tyler Srinogil has been promoted to the chief editor of the *Indiana Tribune*. The board of directors ------- his promotion on Friday. -------. As of next month, he
                                 **135.**                             **136.**

will supervise the featured columns and inserted images. -------, he will manage the overall
                                                   **137.**

operations for IndianaTribune.com, the company's online website. Tyler Srinogil is an

industrious staff member ------- the improvement of IndianaTribune.com last year.
                              **138.**

---

135. (A) confirmed
    (B) indicated
    (C) provided
    (D) rewarded

136. (A) Tyler Srinogil has served as assistant editor for two years.
    (B) The chief editor position will stay open until filled.
    (C) The *Indiana Tribune* has just leased a new building space downtown.
    (D) The management is offering him a new position as the webmaster.

137. (A) However
    (B) In addition
    (C) Meanwhile
    (D) For instance

138. (A) who contributed to
    (B) that contributes to
    (C) whose contributes to
    (D) contributing

**Questions 139-142** refer to the following information.

Thank you for your order from Elliezon.com. We sincerely hope that you are content with

the quality of our products. If you are not -------, you can return and refund the products with
**139.**

the original receipts and boxes you received within 10 days of the delivery date. In order to

get a refund, you should complete the form in the box and sent it to us with the items. All

merchandise ------- in the original packaging. -------. This is because a credit card cancellation
**140.**                                                        **141.**

takes more time than a cash transaction. We appreciate your business and hope that you will

continue to ------- with us.
**142.**

---

**139.** (A) satisfying
(B) satisfied
(C) satisfy
(D) satisfaction

**140.** (A) will ship
(B) have been shipped
(C) are shipping
(D) should be shipped

**141.** (A) We extend an apology for the inconvenience.
(B) The items you ordered are out of stock.
(C) We have confidence in the quality of all the items.
(D) It takes one or two weeks to process the refund.

**142.** (A) shop
(B) learn
(C) place
(D) compile

Questions 143-146 refer to the following article.

After three years of ------- growth, Korean smartphone retailer SLP is planning to expand its
143.

business into the U.S. and Canada. -------. On November 11, SLP's CEO, Jeremy Kim,
144.

announced that the company intends to open more than 100 branches in North America. -------,
145.

SLP is looking for passionate individuals with an adventurous spirit and dedication to customer

service to become franchise owners. Future ------- are advised to contact Christine Jung at +82-
146.

2-333-8282.

143. (A) appropriate
(B) advisable
(C) steady
(D) beneficent

144. (A) The U.S. needs to attract more
smartphone users for boosting its
domestic economy.
(B) The company has already operated
many stores in Asian areas.
(C) SLP is recognized worldwide in the
smartphone field.
(D) The weather in Korea is similar to
eastern America in many ways.

145. (A) Moreover
(B) Nonetheless
(C) However
(D) Therefore

146. (A) candidates
(B) residents
(C) experts
(D) architects

# PART 7

**Directions:** In this part you will read a selection of texts, such as magazine and newspaper articles, e-mails, and instant messages. Each text or set of texts is followed by several questions. Select the best answer for each question and mark the letter (A), (B), (C), or (D) on your answer sheet.

**Questions 147-148** refer to the following advertisement.

**Posting Item:** XA-360 Deer Power Lawn Mower

**Price:** $700

**Location:** Fairfax, VA

*Item Description:*

Bought at LEX store a year ago. Paid $1000 for it. Had a two-year warranty.
Fuel box is not working and should be replaced by the buyer.

In good condition. (No image available)
The price is fixed. (Not negotiable)

If you have any questions about the item, please feel free to contact me.
(fairJohn@horrisnet.com)

**147.** What is NOT indicated about the lawn mower?

(A) A part should be purchased.
(B) A manual is included.
(C) The price cannot be changed.
(D) It is a pre-owned item.

**148.** What is the seller likely to do?

(A) Respond to an inquiry
(B) Extend the warranty
(C) Attach some pictures via e-mail
(D) Send the item to a buyer directly

Johnstown City has planned to recruit a new financial planner in order to replace Mr. Kevin Davis, who has lately expressed his intent to retire. Mr. Davis will hand over his responsibilities on October 31 after holding the role for fourteen years. —[1]—.

The city finance director reports to the city manager and is in charge of supervising the monetary issues of the city. —[2]—. This position is a complex one, requiring the ability to enhance or put into effect a huge range of policies and steps to support the city's aims and to organize and keep the entire city's financial records.

"The new planner will have a lot of things to do," said city manager Cindy Fetterman. "The prospective staff member must have extensive experience managing the finances of an organization or a company."

According to Ms. Fetterman, the application screening period will begin soon, and interviews for the position begin in early September. —[3]—. The new employee will be confirmed at the end of October. —[4]—.

**149.** What is the information mainly about?

(A) Johnstown City has a plan to rebuild the city hall.
(B) There is a job opening for a city position in finance.
(C) The city's financial issues have not yet been resolved for two consecutive years.
(D) To celebrate Mr. Davis's retirement, city officials organized a banquet.

**150.** According to the information, what is required for the position?

(A) A master's degree in finance
(B) A willingness to work on weekends
(C) A capacity for finance-related issues
(D) Moving to Johnstown City

**151.** In which of the positions marked [1], [2], [3] and [4] does the following sentence best belong?

"Applications received after August 20 cannot be considered."

(A) [1]
(B) [2]
(C) [3]
(D) [4]

**Questions 152-153** refers to the following article.

Bremerton, March 6 — Bremerton has recently invited local property developers to bid for constructing a business complex on a 30,000-square-meter area in the northern area of the town.

The business complex will be built near 81 Penn Highway, on the site that used to be an industrial complex that formerly included Waxon Generator, Bill's Auto Parts, and Ulus Steel Manufacturing. The new buildings will be equipped with the latest energy- and water-saving systems. The town also plans to erect a small residential section near the area within three years.

"We are pleased about this opportunity to bring new business to our town," said Mayor Gilford Hubric. "The business complex will be located in the best area, adjacent to a national main highway and many popular accommodations." He also mentioned that the space will be distributed among occupants based on their needs after the first blueprint is designed.

Most of these activities in Bremerton have been prompted by the recent expansion of the local sports complex in the Millner neighborhood.

**152.** What is suggested about the northern area of Bremerton?

(A) It is close to the sports complex.
(B) A variety of metal products were made there.
(C) It is currently a residential area.
(D) Its population has suddenly increased.

**153.** What characteristic of the business complex is NOT mentioned?

(A) Its location near a major highway
(B) Its proximity to hotels
(C) Its energy-efficient structure
(D) Its country-operated area

**Questions 154-155** refer to the following text message chain.

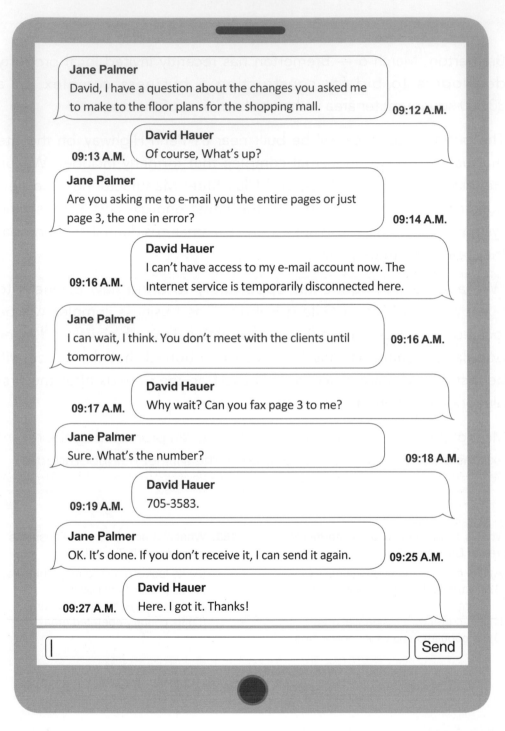

**Jane Palmer**
David, I have a question about the changes you asked me to make to the floor plans for the shopping mall.
09:12 A.M.

**David Hauer**
09:13 A.M.
Of course, What's up?

**Jane Palmer**
Are you asking me to e-mail you the entire pages or just page 3, the one in error?
09:14 A.M.

**David Hauer**
09:16 A.M.
I can't have access to my e-mail account now. The Internet service is temporarily disconnected here.

**Jane Palmer**
I can wait, I think. You don't meet with the clients until tomorrow.
09:16 A.M.

**David Hauer**
09:17 A.M.
Why wait? Can you fax page 3 to me?

**Jane Palmer**
Sure. What's the number?
09:18 A.M.

**David Hauer**
09:19 A.M.
705-3583.

**Jane Palmer**
OK. It's done. If you don't receive it, I can send it again.
09:25 A.M.

**David Hauer**
09:27 A.M.
Here. I got it. Thanks!

Send

**154.** Who most likely is Ms. Palmer?

(A) A computer programmer
(B) An architect
(C) An attorney
(D) An Internet service manager

**155.** At 9:17 A.M., what does Mr. Hauer most likely mean when he writes, "Why wait"?

(A) He wants to get the paper now.
(B) He thinks he had better postpone the meeting.
(C) He asks about the Internet connection.
(D) He needs to download the form.

**Questions 156-157** refer to the following letter.

Shirley Eye Care
#203, 151 Fleming Avenue
Bayside, NY 11361
March 17

Heather Lory
#403 West Gate Apartments
333 Lancaster Boulevard
Bayside, NY 11361

At Shirley Eye Care, it is our priority to continuously provide the best service for you. Starting on August 1, all payments will not be made at the time of service but must be paid within 15 business days. Enclosed you will find the details about the reason why we changed the billing policy.

The new policy enables us to continue to offer the best eye care service to you and your family without any rate increases in the upcoming 2 years. If you have more questions about this payment policy, please call our client account manager, Kevin Loyce, at 715-6534.

Sincerely,

Jane Shirley

Enclosure

**156.** What is the purpose of this letter?

(A) To recruit licensed nurses
(B) To publicize a clinic's service
(C) To inform a customer of a policy change
(D) To make a correction to a billing statement

**157.** What is suggested about Shirley Eye Care?

(A) It makes an effort to keep service rates low.
(B) It has recently moved to a new area.
(C) It is offering free eye examinations.
(D) It will be equipped with the latest tools.

# House and Office Cleaning

The house and office cleaning division of Kane Upper Town Hotel hires 100 team members who are responsible for keeping clean the public spaces in the building in addition to each of the individual rooms and offices throughout the facility.

- Public spaces, such as restrooms, lobbies, ballrooms, the banquet hall, and other visitors' areas are cleaned every day.
- Individual rooms are cleaned in compliance with guests' schedules. Making a schedule for the rooms is outlined further on Page 10 of this recruit manual.
- Office areas are cleaned on Saturdays. Housekeepers will sweep and wipe floors and throw out the garbage. Team members should water the plants in the offices and arrange the desks.
- The cleaning staff must always be standing by ready for public areas that need prompt attention.

**158.** For whom is the information most likely intended?

(A) Cleaning supply company members
(B) Hotel employees
(C) Travel agents for hotel reservations
(D) Visitors seeking good hotels

**159.** According to the information, how can readers know the housekeeping schedules of the individual rooms?

(A) By referring to a staff training manual
(B) By talking to the service head in the cleaning division
(C) By calling the reception desk of the hotel
(D) By reading a schedule posted in the staff lounge

**160.** How often are the floors of the offices cleaned?

(A) Daily
(B) Weekly
(C) Biweekly
(D) Monthly

**Question 161-164** refer to the following online chat discussion.

| | | |
|---|---|---|
| **Cody Silva** [10:18 A.M.] | | Hello. I want to give you some information regarding yesterday's meeting agenda. Our marketing team suggested that cooling bubble gum would likely be popular in the food market. |
| **Susan Vivianne** [10:19 A.M.] | | I know the reason. People want to feel cool in their mouth after eating something. |
| **Nakata Shunzi** [10:20 A.M.] | | Not to mention the fact that it cleans your teeth. |
| **Cody Silva** [10:21 A.M.] | | Sure. We decided that our company needs to have our own line of special chewing gum with a sugar-free formula. We should get moving fast. |
| **Susan Vivianne** [10:22 A.M.] | | Consumers are becoming more concerned about their health, so how about focusing on using organic ingredients? I can find more information about it for our products. |
| **Cody Silva** [10:23 A.M.] | | That sounds great! Go ahead! |
| **Nakata Shunzi** [10:24 A.M.] | | I like that. But I think we should consider consumer preferences in the flavor. If the taste of the gum is not attractive to prospective clients, the best item we make will just be useless. We need to first conduct market research about consumers' preferred tastes. |
| **Cody Silva** [10:26 A.M.] | | Great. Mr. Nakata, could you set up a meeting with the market research team and public relations team? I want to hear what they have to say. How about Thursday? |
| **Susan Vivianne** [10:27 A.M.] | | Sorry, but I can't make it then. On Thursdays, I always conduct the on-the-job training for new staff. Can we do Wednesday or Friday? |
| **Cody Silva** [10:28 A.M.] | | The end of the week is fine. |
| **Nakata Shunzi** [10:30 A.M.] | | Works for me. I'll also outline the questionnaire for the research on our side. Can any of you guys give me possible questions for the survey? |
| **Cody Silva** [10:31 A.M.] | | Of course. I will. |

**Send**

**161.** What kind of business do the chat participants most likely work at?

(A) A grocery store
(B) A hotel restaurant
(C) A marketing agency
(D) A food manufacturer

**162.** When do the participants plan to meet with the marketing team?

(A) On Tuesday
(B) On Wednesday
(C) On Thursday
(D) On Friday

**163.** At 10:30 A.M., what does Mr. Nakata mean when he says, "Works for me"?

(A) He is able to attend the meeting.
(B) He will talk with researchers right away.
(C) He plans to lead to the on-the-job training.
(D) He wants to make a new product by himself.

**164.** What will Mr. Silva probably do?

(A) Meet the president
(B) Taste some gum flavors
(C) Outline marketing strategies
(D) Prepare some questions

*Go on to the next page*

**Questions 165-168** refer to the following e-mail.

From: Jimmy Khermin

To: Staff, Premium Electronics

Date: Monday, December 7

Subject: Week-long training session

You have already been informed that all staff members of Premium Electronics are required to attend the week-long training session each winter, which focuses on our company's goals and provides you with a chance to get to know other staff members. It can give us a lot of benefits for our business. Our employee surveys show that we have made a major impact on our work productivity and cooperation since starting these sessions five years ago.

The dates of the training session have been posted on our intra-bulletin-board since September, and attendance is required. I would like all of you to get ready for the session by selecting various topics that we can talk about. Staff members at all positions should not hesitate to share their suggestions. What you should do is to e-mail me with "Session Topics" in the subject line. —[1]—. You need to use your own transportation to get to Blue Spruce Park, so please remember to submit a travel reimbursement form before the end of the month. It is recommended that you ride together with others in a group. —[2]—. In addition, there are other means of public transportation available, such as a shuttle bus, subway, and city train, which stop near Blue Spruce Park. —[3]—. Whatever means you choose, please be sure that you get there on time and ready to join us. —[4]—.

Jimmy Khermin

---

**165.** What is the main purpose of the e-mail?

(A) To announce details regarding an annual event
(B) To encourage staff members to volunteer for an event
(C) To advertise a company's latest item at a fair
(D) To publicize new job openings at an electronics company

**166.** How are the employees required to get ready for the event?

(A) By updating personal information
(B) By filling out a questionnaire
(C) By promoting a brand-new item
(D) By preparing discussion topics

**167.** What does Mr. Khermin mention about transportation arrangements?

(A) All expenses will be reimbursed by Premium Electronics.
(B) All employees should take public transportation.
(C) All vehicles are prohibited at the site at certain times.
(D) All staff should get a travel pass from each department.

**168.** In which of the positions marked [1], [2], [3], and [4] does the following sentence best belong?

"There is even a taxi affiliated with our company that provides a huge discounted price for a ride from the office to there."

(A) [1]
(B) [2]
(C) [3]
(D) [4]

Questions 169-172 refer to the following notice.

### SKihut National Archipelago Authority (SNAA)

SKihut National Archipelago includes a main forest, beach areas, and other similar islands. Please be aware that there are some additional tour restrictions during this summer vacation season. If visitors are not accompanied by an authorized guide when they want to take a trip to the islands, they will be restricted from entering these areas. This regulation also applies to those who may want to visit the islands individually by using private boats. These individuals can only see the view of the island from the water and come to anchor on offshore but must not land there.

The SNAA's official cruise tours for visitors to the islands are offered daily throughout the year and move in a cycle with two-hour intervals from 8 A.M. The final tour is available until 4 P.M. except for the winter season from November to February, during which time it can be extended to 6 P.M., depending on weather conditions. Please call +01-319-5225 to make a reservation for the cruise tour. This tour includes some description about the islands' geological and historical features, and attractive aspects of the beautiful view. You can also view a special spot for endangered species by getting an escort from our island rangers.

*Payment and Reservations*

Tours can be conducted with a maximum of 20 participants per group. If the group is smaller than 15, we reserve the right to add other travelers to your tour. You can purchase a ticket at $30 per person for adults and $15 for children. You are asked to pay a deposit of $5 per person in order to hold the reservation. In addition, you can get our special offer when booking it in advance of 6 months. The deposit amount will be credited to your total admission fees. If your group does not show up at the appointed time, the ending time of your trip will remain the same, so as not to disrupt later trips. Any change of other groups' itineraries cannot be allowed.

---

**169.** What is the purpose of the notice?

(A) To update information about a fee
(B) To introduce some attractions
(C) To announce the safety rules about a trip
(D) To inform visitors of the trip policy

**170.** What is implied about visiting SKihut National Archipelago?

(A) Visitors must step into the islands with a guide.
(B) Visitors should comply with their safety rules.
(C) Visitors cannot swim anywhere around the archipelago.
(D) Visitors need to gather groups by themselves.

**171.** What is NOT mentioned about the SNAA?

(A) Night tours can be scheduled.
(B) The capacity of the group is limited.
(C) Early reservations can be discounted.
(D) Tour times are different depending on the season.

**172.** According to the notice, what may happen if a group arrives late for the prearranged trip?

(A) It may be reduced in tour hours.
(B) It may be canceled without any notice.
(C) It may be charged an additional fee.
(D) It may be changed into another ending time.

*Go on to the next page*

# Visiting Hershey County
## Don't miss the chance to experience a fantastic world!

**Chocolate World Tour**

Open daily, 10 A.M.–5 P.M. / $5 admission

The Chocolate World Tour brings you the historical scenes of Hershey County by bike-coaster with a lot of stages and figures.

**Charlie's Chocolate Factory**

Open to the public at no charge, Business Days, noon – 3 P.M.

Constructed by the founder, Mr. John Hershey. Visitors can get a chance to see the chocolate-making procedures and receive some free chocolate items. Guided tours are available for $1 per person.

**Hershey Amusement Park**

Open daily, 9 A.M.–10 P.M. / $10 admission, $40 unlimited pass for the rides.

This amazing theme park is suitable for the whole family. A lot of fantastic rides are available, including roller coasters. Special discounts for the park are given in specific seasons.

**County Chocolate Museum**

Open Tuesday to Sunday, 9 A.M.– 4 P.M. / Free of charge, but donations are welcome.

A variety of impressive chocolates are exhibited in chronological order. Also, the Hershey family's history is played on a big LCD monitor on the ceiling. This museum is located adjacent to the North Gate of the amusement park.

173. What is the purpose of the information?

(A) To describe a list of events
(B) To help visitors to tour certain spots
(C) To give directions to local attractions
(D) To announce some special monuments

174. What is indicated about Hershey Amusement Park?

(A) Its admission fee is not the same year-round.
(B) It varies from the opening time periodically.
(C) It uses a mini-trailer for watching the historical movie.
(D) It is only popular with teenagers and children.

175. According to the information, what do the chocolate factory and the museum have in common?

(A) Both charge no admission fee.
(B) Both require guided tours.
(C) Both show historical events.
(D) Both are located near the shore.

*Go on to the next page*

## CAAA's Twentieth-Annual Athletic Equipment Fair, June 1–10
## Progressive Convention Center, Cleveland, Ohio

The CAAA(Cleveland Area Athletic Association) invites companies to join this fair, which was attended by over 200 businesses last year. This event is related to effective approaches and methods for using the right exercise equipment.

The CAAA is pleased to offer corresponding benefits based on the degree of corporate sponsorship.

(For inquiries, contact Ms. Gloria Sanders at 932-451-3894. To register, e-mail supports@caaa.org.)

▶**Workshop Sponsor — $1,200**
A representative of your company will have a chance to promote your company by speaking as a keynote speaker in one of the workshop sessions.

▶**Stage Sponsor — $2,000**
At each stage displaying equipment, your company's name will be displayed in front of the demonstration booth.

▶**Bag Sponsor — $3,000**
Your company's logo and name will be on fabric tote bags that are distributed to all visitors.

▶**General Program Sponsor — $6,000**
Three executive members of your company will be introduced in a banquet, named "CAAA Night," on the first day of the fair.

From: gloria@caaa.org
To: hsyoon@knetwork.com
Date: May 20
Subject: Thank you

Dear Ms. Yoon,

I would like to show my appreciation for your registration of the Remote Interval Exercise Program as a supporter of the Cleveland Area Athletic Association (CAAA) Fair. Your sponsorship not only enables us to make this event possible, but also stimulates interest in exercise.

Your donation of $2,000 has been credited to our account. In addition, we are attaching your company's name to the demonstration booth at no extra cost. It is a token of our appreciation for the long-standing support of CAAA and its programs. To finalize the promotional materials, please e-mail me your official CI(corporate identity) or BI(business identity) images.

Gloria Sanders
CAAA Fair Coordinator

176. What is the purpose of the flyer?

(A) To announce the success of these successive events
(B) To encourage participants to try out equipment
(C) To promote the benefits of joining an event
(D) To report financial issues to their sponsorship board

177. According to the flyer, when should a call be placed to CAAA's office?

(A) When additional information is needed
(B) When a donation cannot be processed
(C) When participation is required
(D) When a change is made at their level

178. What will happen on June 1?

(A) An athletic game will be started.
(B) A formal gathering will be held.
(C) New board members will be appointed.
(D) Display stages will be set up at the fair.

179. What is suggested about CAAA's event?

(A) It is intended to promote interest in exercise.
(B) It attracts more than 200 companies annually.
(C) It is partially funded by the Cleveland City Council.
(D) It is held at a different location every year.

180. In the e-mail, what is Ms. Yoon asked to do?

(A) Check the amount of supporting budget for taking part in the event
(B) Send an e-mail including the company's logo designs to the fair
(C) Organize an event booth to promote their new items at the fair
(D) Call the customer service center to ask more information about the fair

| To: | berry@linguisticconference.org |
|---|---|
| From: | customerservice@holidaylodge.us |
| Date: | 25 July |
| Re: | Reservation TC1270 |

Dear Dr. Berry,

Thank you for choosing Holiday Lodge Hotel. As requested before, you have made a reservation of 12 rooms for your group. Since you will attend the National Applied Linguistics Forum here this August, you are receiving a special rate of $90 a room per night.

We have you checking in on 3 August, and checking out on 10 August. The room reservations are confirmed under your name. Please be aware of your reservation code, TC1270, which you must use if you need to contact us about these arrangements for any reason.

We are confident that you will enjoy our amazing amenities such as an outdoor pool, a spa, a gym, and a variety of dining options. For a casual dining experience, you may want to try the Romeo's Café terrace, located next to our lobby. If you are interested in dining at Donnatello Restaurant, which was given a 5-star rating from Trip Advisory Guide, we strongly recommend that you make a reservation in advance.

Please let us know if you need more information.

Thank you again for choosing Holiday Lodge Hotel.

Sincerely,

The Holiday Lodge Hotel Staff

To: customerservice@holidaylodge.us

From: berry@linguisticconference.org

Date: 27 July

Re: Reservation TC1270

To Whom It May Concern,

My reservation number is TC1270, and I am writing to correct some errors I noticed in the previous e-mail.

Firstly, the number of reserved rooms is 10, not 12. Also, I will not be arriving until August 4, even though almost all members will get there one day before the conference.

I clearly stated these points on my original reservation request form. Please correct these and contact me in order to confirm that this has been resolved. Thank you in advance for your immediate response to this matter.

Sincerely,

Dr. Bonds Berry

---

**181.** What is the main purpose of the first e-mail?

(A) To confirm the details of a reservation
(B) To notify a customer of a change in hotel price
(C) To explain a variety of amenities
(D) To announce a hotel's temporary construction

**182.** What is suggested about the Donnatello Restaurant?

(A) It was recently opened.
(B) It has been remodeled.
(C) It is usually busy.
(D) It is next to Holiday Lodge Hotel.

**183.** What information in the hotel reservation is wrong?

(A) That Dr. Berry will check in on August 3
(B) That Dr. Berry has organized the forum
(C) That Dr. Berry has paid for all rooms
(D) That Dr. Berry will depart before the conference ends

**184.** What is stated about the hotel reservation?

(A) The reservation code is misprinted.
(B) The number of rooms is not correct.
(C) The attendants for the forum are not enough.
(D) The room rates are different.

**185.** In the second e-mail, the word "matter" in paragraph 3, line 3, is closest in meaning to

(A) situation
(B) substance
(C) material
(D) publication

*Go on to the next page*

### *Athens Gazette*

Local Companies Need More Staff
by Sophia Lauren

Athens (April 10)—It is difficult for us to seek suitable candidates for a position. To make their hiring process easier, some companies make a request to staffing agencies. By finding part-time employees for the peak season or handling the whole application procedure through these agencies, companies save money and time in many ways.

Jane Foster, the general manager of Hellocrew Recruiting, which is one of the oldest staffing agencies in Georgia, said that a number of companies can get an advantage while hiring temporary staff from the agency. "They have a chance to resolve certain hiring matters. Another benefit is that they can train a potential member before they offer him/her full-time employment," Foster said.

To support local companies through this process, we have posted a list of staffing agencies. You can find it on the upper right-hand side of this page at www.athensgazette.com.

## Hellocrew Recruiting
## TEMPORARY EMPLOYEE REQUEST FORM

### Company Information

- **Name:** Brad Triana
- **Field:** Accounting
- **E-mail:** btriana@mscbiz.com

- **Company:** MSC Business Accounting
- **Phone:** 412-237-9400

### Task Information

- **Need number of staff:** minimum 8
- **Expected duration:** 2–3 weeks

- **Opening Position:** office workers

### Specifications:

We have a lot of government-led projects on auditing city councils' accounts in many districts. Because of these projects, we have stored up too many documents and files that we need to arrange. These documents and files should be categorized and scanned more quickly in order to meet a deadline. We are seeking meticulous applicants who are able to follow instructions well.

**How did you find out about us?**
I saw your agency in yesterday's online column in the *Athens Gazette*.

**Thank you for your registration!**
**One of our staffing agents will contact you within 24 hours through e-mail.**

From: Brad Triana <btriana@mscbiz.com>

To: Heather Lowry <hlowry@hellocrew.net>

Subject: Thank You

Date: April 15

Dear Ms. Lowry,

I would like to extend my sincere gratitude for your help. It was my first time working with a staffing agency, so, frankly, I did not have confidence in this process. Because of your agency, we are ready to complete our tasks with the temporary employees you matched with us. You responded to my request form within just three hours and made a list of employees available within just a day! The employees you recommended were really industrious, hardworking, and devoted to our assignments. For that reason, we made a decision to interview two of them for offering them full-time positions.

Best wishes,

Brad Triana

---

**186.** In the article, what advantage is NOT indicated about part-time staff?

(A) Getting specialized and professional support
(B) Saving more than the company's budget planned
(C) Making the recruiting process smoother
(D) Supporting companies in handling some issues

**187.** What is implied about Mr. Triana?

(A) He read Ms. Lauren's article on the Web.
(B) His company is included in the list on the *Athens Gazette*'s page.
(C) His company has worked with Hellocrew Recruiting before.
(D) He did an interview with the *Athens Gazette*.

**188.** In the form, the word "duration" in paragraph 2, line 2, is closest in meaning to

(A) length
(B) strength
(C) growth
(D) path

**189.** What is the main purpose of the e-mail?

(A) To offer both staff members new permanent positions
(B) To confirm a request the sales team made
(C) To express thanks for an issue they dealt with
(D) To complain about some errors in the article

**190.** Who most likely is Ms. Lowry?

(A) A part-timer in the MSC Business Accounting
(B) An official in a city council
(C) A staffing agent at Hellocrew Recruiting
(D) A news writer at the *Athens Gazette*

*Go on to the next page*

## New Local Landmark Construction

At a meeting on Thursday, Hattiesburg officials discussed a local improvement plan that would enable the town to attract more students and visitors. According to Gian Pagnucci, the chair of Hattiesburg College, construction of a multi-complex convention center should be fully considered within both the local council and college's budget. Hence, the city council decided to encourage local companies to join a public bid for this construction project. In addition, local residents are encouraged to submit an entry for a contest to name the center.

Some proposed projects include an outdoor sports park, depending on whether it would be located near the center on Oak Grove Street. According to Mr. Pagnucci, the council will ask all community members to share their ideas. Interested people may bring their opinions to the next weekly meeting on Thursday, 18 June, at 4 P.M. or send an e-mail to the task force team before 22 June. After fully considering extensive opinions from citizens, the planning committee will put forth a final draft to the council for an official discussion. The expected date of the decision is no later than 30 June.

| From: | selindiana@stormmail.com |
|---|---|
| To: | citycouncil@hattiesburg.org |
| Date: | 20 June |
| Subject: | Additional Projects |

Dear Council Official,

I was notified that you are accepting suggestions for the use of the town's budget to build new convention center. Due to another appointment in my schedule, I was not able to attend the weekly meeting for the project, but I would like to express my support for the plan to make our town more attractive. Although the cost of the construction is likely to be reasonable, project planners should fully take into account the effectiveness and proximity to the center, and the benefit of all our community members. This project will be a good source of civic pride and a brand-new landmark where we can enjoy a diversity of activities. Even though it is important for the town's image, its advantages should be evenly distributed among our citizens.

Selin Diana

From: fangyu@solomonunitas.com

To: citycouncil@hattiesburg.org

Date: 21 June

Subject: City Projects

To Whom It May Concern,

I was happy to hear that the new development was decided for our town. Because the town's public facilities are not suitable for a variety of activities for all citizens of all ages, this multi-complex space can give the public many opportunities to enjoy a wide range of events such as NCAA basketball games, local job fairs, and so on. I have just one issue to consider, and it concerns older people.

This project should not just focus on teenagers and young adults. According to the city population distribution data, the elderly form 30 percent of the citizenship in Hattiesburg. Therefore, we should never overlook considering their needs. It would be a remarkable improvement to the town if all of us can enjoy this facility—both young and old—without any inconvenience. Please make sure these benefits are equally shared among all people.

**191.** Why does the town of Hattiesburg need a new project?

(A) The city council canceled a previous project.
(B) The town has raised tax on property.
(C) The area is planning to attract more people.
(D) Citizens have debated a development issue.

**192.** In the article, the phrase "put forth" in paragraph 2, line 6, is closest in meaning to

(A) publish
(B) promote
(C) propose
(D) plant

**193.** When did Ms. Diana have an appointment?

(A) June 18
(B) June 20
(C) June 21
(D) June 30

**194.** What is the second e-mail mainly about?

(A) Celebrating civilian projects
(B) Questioning the directions to the new facility
(C) Complaining about incorrect information
(D) Raising a potential issue

**195.** What will happen by June 30?

(A) A final planning outline will be made with public opinions and officials' research.
(B) The city will have a groundbreaking ceremony for the new multi-complex.
(C) The council will announce a competitive bid for the facility development.
(D) Some citizens will instigate demonstrations against the construction issue.

*Go on to the next page*

From: John Dyson

To: Ben Tannacito

Subject: Trucking Company

Date: March 2

Hello Mr. Tannacito,

I am so glad that you have signed up for deliveries of our furniture — initially a couch for four, a desk in white, two chairs in black, a queen-sized bed — made here at our LINKer Furnishings Factory. I can assure you that you and your customers will be pleased with the products we provide.

Your store is in an area that is new to us, and we are looking forward to delivering our items into a new store. Please let me know if you are interested in this moving service. Our licensed drivers in Stonybrook do not go out to Albany, so a different company should be hired. U-Haul moving company is the best choice that fits your conditions. We would like to work with a company of your choice to keep the service for you as safe as possible.

Sincerely,

John Dyson

## ALTOONA HOME DECO SYSTEM

NEW THIS WEEK!
March 20

### Items from LINKer Furnishings Factory

Dear Customers,

We would like to call your attention to the latest additions to our product lines. You've asked for durable and inexpensive home furniture, and now we're carrying it. We can bring these items directly to you from LINKer Furnishings Factory, located just two hours from here in Buffalo.

- Family-Size Couches
- White Desks with Durable Wood
- Well-Being Black Chairs
- Various Bed Designs and Sizes
- Mobile Closets
- Antibacterial Area Rugs

Next season, we will develop user-friendly office furniture in our Amherst branch. If you have any questions about the items, please feel free to contact linkercustomer@lffactory.com.

# LINKer Furnishings Order Form

**Customer:** ALTOONA HOME DECO SYSTEM
**Order Date:** March 25
**Delivery Date:** April 10

## Delivery Details:

Repeat the initial order with the following changes.
 - No couch for four. (Couch for five needed)
 - Instead of white items, please send me black items.
 - Add one more chair

*P.S. You asked me to let you know if there were any issues with the U-Haul Trucking delivery. The arrival was on time, the driver was friendly, and the items were in good condition.*

**196.** Why did Mr. Dyson send the e-mail?

(A) To advertise new products
(B) To request a delivery estimate
(C) To announce a policy change
(D) To follow up on an order

**197.** Where Is Altoona Home Deco System probably located?

(A) In Stonybrook
(B) In Albany
(C) In Buffalo
(D) In Amherst

**198.** In the notice, what is implied about LINKer Furnishings Factory's products?

(A) They are delivered within just two hours of ordering.
(B) They are likely to best suit small houses.
(C) They are reasonably priced.
(D) They are out of stock because of their popularity.

**199.** What will Altoona Home Deco System probably receive on April 10?

(A) Antibacterial Area Rugs
(B) King-Size Beds
(C) Four Black Chairs
(D) Black Big Desks

**200.** What does Mr. Tannacito indicate in the order form?

(A) He had a good experience with the trucking service.
(B) The U-Haul service has a lot of clients.
(C) He was disappointed with the items he got.
(D) Some wear and tear could be found in the products.

# ACTUAL TEST

## 答對題數表

| | |
|---|---|
| **PART 5** | |
| **PART 6** | |
| **PART 7** | |
| 總題數 | |

**07**

# READING TEST

In the Reading test, you will read a variety of texts and answer several different types of reading comprehension questions. The entire Reading test will last 75 minutes. There are three parts, and directions are given for each part. You are encouraged to answer as many questions as possible within the time allowed.

You must mark your answers on the separate answer sheet. Do not write your answers in your test book.

## PART 5

**Directions:** A word or phrase is missing in each of the sentences below. Four answer choices are given below each sentence. Select the best answer to complete the sentence. Then mark the letter (A), (B), (C), or (D) on your answer sheet.

101. Felix Armstrong, the owner of the Indonesian restaurant, chose to order flatware and other ------- directly from the producer.

(A) supply
(B) supplies
(C) suppliers
(D) supplied

102. Every Monday, we ------- tours of the production facilities to ensure they are in order.

(A) arrive
(B) visit
(C) conduct
(D) inspect

103. Ms. Grant sees to it that she advises the new workers in order to carry out ------- duties efficiently.

(A) they
(B) their
(C) them
(D) theirs

104. Due to the increase in the availability of mobile technology, landlines have become ------- in many domestic homes.

(A) obsolete
(B) extracted
(C) insolent
(D) contemporary

105. The Dart Entertainer Academy holds open auditions every month for those ------- in participating in the annual singing contest.

(A) interest
(B) interested
(C) to interest
(D) interesting

106. Mr. Spencer has received an appreciation plaque at a retirement ceremony for ------- dedication to the company where he has worked for over 25 years.

(A) he
(B) his
(C) him
(D) himself

107. Cox Industries' latest career announcement ------- notes that the managerial position is only accepting current line supervisors.

(A) specify
(B) specific
(C) specifying
(D) specifically

108. The latest novel from Brian Bennett has had positive ------- from the critics.

(A) matters
(B) repairs
(C) reviews
(D) collections

109. Ms. Cunningham was supposed to purchase the tickets to the concert, but she thought that they were too -------.
(A) expense
(B) expensive
(C) expensively
(D) expensiveness

110. The government has urged everyone to renew their annual tax return online -------- to avoid incurring a financial penalty.
(A) early
(B) hardly
(C) enough
(D) usefully

111. At Mason Hospital, all medical records are strictly ------- and can only be released upon permission of the patient.
(A) confiding
(B) confidence
(C) confidential
(D) confidentiality

112. The results from recent client questionnaires ------- in the file attached to this e-mail.
(A) summarizes
(B) summarized
(C) are summarizing
(D) are summarized

113. Under the ------- of Dr. Owen, the Engineering Department of Patel Precision Industries performs a number of material examinations every year.
(A) prediction
(B) indication
(C) completion
(D) supervision

114. The Cornell Ski Resort employed 12 additional safety guards ------- at its Yellowwoods Valley branch during the hectic winter season.
(A) assists
(B) assisted
(C) to assist
(D) have assisted

115. In its latest newspaper advertisement, Prime Bank ------- the general complaint by the public that its interest rates are too high.
(A) tended
(B) refuted
(C) imposed
(D) recuperated

116. The Health Bureau has assured the public that it will expand the number of medical activities ------- in the following year.
(A) distantly
(B) recently
(C) currently
(D) significantly

117. When checking a safety device, please also ensure that the doors and windows are ------- before leaving the office.
(A) security
(B) securely
(C) securing
(D) secured

118. Workers who make use of company vehicles must ------- a legal and up-to-date driver's license.
(A) expel
(B) assign
(C) specify
(D) possess

119. According to a newsletter published today, a significant ------- of employees welcome the chance to feature their newly developed dietary supplement at the upcoming expo.
(A) major
(B) majored
(C) majoring
(D) majority

120. The fire drill will start at 2:00 P.M. in the Minnesota facility, and its manufacturing process cannot recommence ------- it has been finished.
(A) while
(B) until
(C) that
(D) upon

Go on to the next page

121. To prevent any further delays in the delivery process, the production team had to work ------- to fix the broken machines.

(A) swift
(B) swiftly
(C) swiftness
(D) swiftest

122. Kaur Designs ------- staff satisfaction a top priority since its inception 10 years ago.

(A) has considered
(B) will consider
(C) considering
(D) is considered

123. The Walker's Chicken has a number of chain stores ------- Australia and is planning to extend its business abroad.

(A) behind
(B) among
(C) across
(D) despite

124. It is a ------- procedure to delete all confidential files from your computers at the end of the day.

(A) routine
(B) fastened
(C) difficult
(D) mistaken

125. The Adams Hotel installed energy-saving LED lighting ------- all of its rooms last month.

(A) of
(B) on
(C) in
(D) before

126. The employees ------- intend to undergo an interview for transfer have to apply today.

(A) where
(B) who
(C) whose
(D) when

127. The ------- has announced that cameras will be allowed in the courtroom for the first time.

(A) patron
(B) reputation
(C) spokesperson
(D) outcome

128. Train 404 to Minox County departed two hours ------- than expected due to heavy snow in Foxtown.

(A) late
(B) later
(C) latest
(D) lately

129. ------- the battery runs out quicker than expected after being fully charged, contact our authorized service center.

(A) If
(B) So
(C) Even
(D) Such

130. Any inquiries ------- travel expense claims should be sent to the accounts department.

(A) through
(B) according to
(C) related to
(D) upon

**Questions 139-142** refer to the following article.

Canberra (February 22) – Regional airports are planning to ------- the amount of luggage on
**139.**
board the week after next.

Beginning on March 4, the luggage control will be put in force at every airport from Melbourne

to Sydney. "Banning more than two suitcases will help us to better monitor the amount of

luggage used in order to avoid the congestion that occurs ------- the baggage carousels," said
**140.**
Director of Services Dorothy Bailey.

Passengers should pack fewer than two suitcases. -------. Alternatively, they can leave
**141.**
unwanted items in the secure lockers, ------- to hold up to 5kg of luggage.
**142.**

139. (A) propose
(B) relate
(C) enhance
(D) restrict

140. (A) after
(B) among
(C) around
(D) through

141. (A) All extra boxes will be delivered for
free.
(B) Otherwise, they may have to pay extra
per bag.
(C) In fact, they have relaxed the
regulations.
(D) And the passengers are asked to
leave their suitcases in the lockers.

142. (A) equipment
(B) equipped
(C) equip
(D) equips

*Go on to the next page*

Questions 143-146 refer to the following letter.

Dear Mr. Evans,

I appreciate your interest in ------- our marketing department.
                                   **143.**

-------. To apply for a position as a service marketing team member with us, you need to send
**144.**

us your updated résumé, together with a proposal ------- your own marketing approach.
                                                   **145.**

We will be contacting you in two weeks ------- accepting your application to set up an interview
                                         **146.**

from the materials you sent us about your background and career. You are likely to be an ideal

candidate for the position we talked about before.


Best regards,


Anderson Brooks

Marketing Director, Norton Electronics

---

**143.** (A) joining
(B) promoting
(C) evaluating
(D) organizing

**144.** (A) However, I'm afraid we have already
filled the position.
(B) We enjoyed meeting you at your job
interview.
(C) We would be pleased to receive your
application form.
(D) I'm attaching my résumé as
requested.

**145.** (A) describe
(B) describing
(C) described
(D) will describe

**146.** (A) around
(B) until
(C) by
(D) after

# PART 7

**Directions:** In this part you will read a selection of texts, such as magazine and newspaper articles, e-mails, and instant messages. Each text or set of texts is followed by several questions. Select the best answer for each question and mark the letter (A), (B), (C), or (D) on your answer sheet.

**Questions 147-148** refer to the following coupon.

## Limited Offer

***Enjoy Climber Route with your friend for the price of one!***

Present this coupon at the ticket booth and you will receive one more ticket for free when purchasing a full-price adult ticket.

Enjoy the scenery and the refreshments – complimentary food and drink are available at our mountain-top café.
- Cannot be used in conjunction with other coupons
- Expires on 31 December
- Children must be accompanied by their parents

**147.** What is the coupon for?

(A) A sightseeing venue
(B) A cafeteria
(C) A boating site
(D) A sports tournament

**148.** What restriction is placed on the coupon?

(A) It can be used by adults only.
(B) It can be used on weekends.
(C) It cannot be used before 31 December.
(D) It cannot be used with another coupon.

Go on to the next page

## Relocation and Care

When moving animals to a new place, particular care has to be taken to ensure their safe arrival and enhance their ability to fit into their new environment. Always remember they can be very unpredictable. Place them in the designated container, as carrying them without one may allow them to escape. Follow our specific directions on the brochure when relocating animals, as there are a variety of containers for different animals. These leaflets are free and can be found at the cashier.

**149.** Who is the information most likely intended for?

(A) Storekeepers
(B) Animal owners
(C) Container manufacturers
(D) Safety inspectors

**150.** What is available at no cost?

(A) Carriers
(B) Written instructions
(C) Containers
(D) Canned food

**Hawkins Uniforms**
**DELIVERY RECEIPT**

Thank you for your order.

**Order Number:** 452198732
**Date Placed:** June 21
**Date Shipped:** June 25

**Customer Name:** Duncan Restaurant
**Customer Number:** 24

----------------------------------------------------------------

***Item 1:*** Custom-made shirts, logo on the left sleeve
　　　**Color:** Blue / **Size:** Large / **Quantity:** 13

***Item 2:*** Chefs Hats
　　　**Color:** White / **Size:** N/A / **Quantity:** 4

***Item 3:*** Head Scarves
　　　**Color:** Red / **Size:** N/A / **Quantity:** 27

----------------------------------------------------------------

*Visit us online at http://www.hawkinsuniforms.com.*

**151.** How many shirts were ordered?

(A) 24
(B) 13
(C) 4
(D) 27

**152.** What is stated on the receipt?

(A) The order was made online.
(B) Duncan Restaurant is a regular customer.
(C) Thirteen waiters are working at Duncan Restaurant.
(D) The logo of a company appears on the clothes.

| | | |
|---|---|---|
| | | ●▭⊗ |

| | Jeremy Ashton [10:46 A.M.] | Guys, we've got a problem with the dyes again. |
|---|---|---|
| | Nancy Parish [10:46 A.M.] | Not again! What's the problem this time? |
| | Jeremy Ashton [10:47 A.M.] | The 80 purple towels came out in the wrong color. These are more like pink. |
| | Nancy Parish [10:48 A.M.] | That's terrible. We have to deliver all the towels by tomorrow. |
| | Dustin Hyde [10:48 A.M.] | I don't think I have enough time to do it over. Is the rest of the order ready to go out? |
| | Jeremy Ashton [10:49 A.M.] | Yes. All the other colors are ready to go. |
| | Nancy Parish [10:51 A.M.] | Why don't we send them first so that Lisa's team can start preparing for the upcoming event? In the meantime, you can dye the remaining 80 towels again. |
| | Dustin Hyde [10:51 A.M.] | That'd save us some time. But we'll have to check the dye before we rework them. |
| | Nancy Parish [10:52 A.M.] | Sure thing. I'll call Lisa and ask for the color samples. |

**Send**

153. What problem is being discussed?

(A) Some labels were printed incorrectly.
(B) Some dyeing results were unexpected.
(C) An inspector is unavailable.
(D) Some machines are running too slowly.

154. At 10:48 A.M., what does Mr. Hyde imply when he writes, "I don't think I have enough time to do it over"?

(A) The schedule is tight.
(B) They cannot help sending the pink towels.
(C) He doesn't have enough towels to dye again.
(D) The upcoming event should be postponed.

# Reid & Ross Inc. Job Openings

Applications are for the night shift (6:00 P.M. to 5:00 A.M.), unless otherwise stated.

### *Facilities Manager*
Must hold relevant qualifications, in-depth understanding of inventory process, and knowledge of health and safety policies. Also desirable are basic skills in computing and budgeting. Previous experience in mechanical factory work is preferred but not essential.

### *Forklift Truck Technician*
Must be educated to high school level or higher, with two years' experience working in a busy warehouse operating heavy machinery. Must be trained in forklift truck driving. Some day shifts required.

### *Computer Assistant*
Must have a BA degree, with experience of operating SAGE software in an industrial environment. Some day shifts required.

### *Inventory Assistants and Stock Clerks*
Must be conscientious and hard-working. Stock clerks may be required to work the day shift.

Please send résumés to : The Recruitment Manager
Reid & Ross Inc.
472 Southern Lake Drive
Austin, TX 78753

No recruitment agency calls or e-mails.

**155.** What is a requirement for the facilities manager position?

(A) A degree in finance
(B) Knowledge of health and safety policies
(C) Previous experience in conducting inspections
(D) A valid driver's license

**156.** What position does NOT involve day shifts?

(A) Forklift truck technician
(B) Stock clerks
(C) Inventory assistants
(D) Computer assistant

**157.** How will candidates apply for the positions?

(A) By online
(B) By mail
(C) In person
(D) By telephone

***Go on to the next page***

Questions 158-160 refer to the following e-mail.

To : All Staff

From : Elizabeth Webster <Ewebster@gilbertfashion.com>

Re : Spring Collection

Date : December 9

On behalf of the management at Gilbert Fashion, I would like to invite you to a special showing of our new Spring portfolio to be held on December 18 from 4 P.M. to 9 P.M. at Silver Hall. —[1]—. We expect every employee to attend and enjoy a buffet meal on the balcony. —[2]—. There will also be entertainment in the form of Ella Kay and her band.

—[3]—. Please note that although this is a free event to preview our new collection, we need to provide numbers for the caterers, so if you can attend, please give your name to Kate Parry or Henry Rhodes by the end of the week. If you have any tunes that you wish the band to play, we welcome any suggestions. —[4]—.

I look forward to seeing everyone on December 18.

Elizabeth Webster
Human Resources Manager

158. What is the purpose of the e-mail?
   (A) To invite employees to an event
   (B) To ask for volunteers to assist with a party
   (C) To encourage employees to hold their show
   (D) To order food for a celebration

159. What is NOT indicated about the event?
   (A) It is organized by the company.
   (B) It will preview a fashion collection.
   (C) It will feature live music.
   (D) It is held every season.

160. In which of the positions marked [1], [2], [3], and [4] does the following sentence best belong?

   "Simply e-mail me with the song choice or for any further information on the event."

   (A) [1]
   (B) [2]
   (C) [3]
   (D) [4]

ACTUAL TEST 07

PART 7

# Emerald Town of Northern Territory

55 Turner Street
Engawala, Australia 0872

February 11
Mr. Ford Lucas
426 Girraween Road
Palmerston City, Australia 0830

Dear Mr. Lucas,

We have received your application at Emerald Town regarding the position that was advertised last week in the *Darwin Times* for a mining assistant. We are sorry to inform you that this position has already been filled. Nevertheless, we are planning to begin mining in another location in April, and we believe that you would be suitable for this position. With your permission, we would like to keep your details on file. The location is not far from our main production facilities in Darwin, but it will require some travel to Pine Creek, Mataranka, and other areas. Please keep checking our website for any future vacancies that arise with our organization. We wish you luck with your job search.

Kind regards,

Jaxon Bates, Personnel Supervisor

**161.** What is the main purpose of the letter?

(A) To let an applicant know that he failed to meet the qualifications for the position
(B) To ask an applicant for further details of his career
(C) To arrange an interview with an applicant
(D) To inform an applicant that the position he applied for is no longer available

**162.** Where are the main facilities of Emerald Town of Northern Territory located?

(A) In Darwin
(B) In Pine Creek
(C) In Mataranka
(D) In Palmerston City

**163.** What does Mr. Bates suggest that Mr. Lucas do?

(A) Check the website for additional job openings
(B) Send in more information about his qualifications
(C) Contact the main facilities for employment changes
(D) Read the job advertisements in the newspaper

*Go on to the next page*

Questions 164-167 refer to the following text message chain.

| | Morgan Leek<br>[02:32 P.M.] | Hello, James. I saw several flowerpots in your shop yesterday. Where did you get them? |
|---|---|---|
| | James Pipe<br>[02:33 P.M.] | Hello, Morgan. You mean the ones on the table by the window? |
| | Morgan Leek<br>[02:33 P.M.] | Yes. They had a lovely, sweet scent and also looked nice. So, I want to put some of those in my apartment. |
| | James Pipe<br>[02:35 P.M.] | From the garden center on St. George Street, next to Thomas' Bakery. |
| | Morgan Leek<br>[02:36 P.M.] | Oh, I know where the flower shop is. By the way, what are they called? |
| | James Pipe<br>[02:37 P.M.] | It slipped my mind. Anyway, they have a lot of wildflowers and herbs. Just take a closer look and check the scent. |
| | Morgan Leek<br>[02:37 P.M.] | But, I don't know much about wildflowers and herbs. Are they easy to maintain? |
| | James Pipe<br>[02:38 P.M.] | Yes, absolutely. They grow well indoors, and they don't need much water. |
| | Morgan Leek<br>[02:39 P.M.] | That's great! I'm not able to be at home every day. |

Send

**164.** What is mainly being discussed?

(A) Ms. Leek's new apartment
(B) Some plants for the Ms. Leek
(C) A bakery on St. George Street
(D) Sowing some herb seeds

**165.** What does Mr. Pipe suggest that Ms. Leek do?

(A) Stop by the bakery
(B) Meet him at the garden center
(C) Water the flowers every day
(D) Smell the plants

**166.** At 2:37 P.M., why does Mr. Pipe write, "It slipped my mind"?

(A) He doesn't know how much the plants would cost.
(B) He forgot the names of the flowers.
(C) He thinks Ms. Leek cannot take care of the plants.
(D) He doesn't mind how much water they need.

**167.** Why would Ms. Leek find the plants suitable for her?

(A) They are inexpensive.
(B) She is going to grow them outdoors.
(C) The flower shop is located near her apartment.
(D) She doesn't need to water them every day.

# BORDEAUX, FR.

May 2 — Alan Debois, President of the Agricultural Union, is to be awarded the Géant Prize on May 10. —[1]—. This is an annual award to a deserving and active member of the Bordeaux business community, whose achievements have enhanced the region.

As a lifelong farmer, Mr. Debois has a keen interest in the local environment and put forward a proposal to the regional government for the installation of flood barriers to prevent crops and livestock from being affected by annual flooding in Bordeaux. Five years ago, his proposal for flood barriers began to be implemented and the Debois Barriers, as they are known, are now a well-known attraction for tourists. The first set was installed three years ago with a grant from the Environmental Agency. —[2]—. Since then, the barriers have prevented crops from being ruined, saved many cattle from drowning, and raised awareness of the dangers of tidal power. Completed last year in Bordeaux, the barrier installation scheme is now being considered by many coastal regions in France.

—[3]—. This program offers funding for apprenticeships to young adults who want to learn how to become farmers and work on the land. So far, over a hundred people have completed the program and have found employment on farms within the region.

—[4]—. The awards ceremony will take place in the Bordeaux Town Hall from 7 P.M. to 9 P.M. All residents of the town are welcome to attend, and details will be posted on the website, www.bordeaux.fr/awards.

ACTUAL TEST

07

PART

7

**168.** What is the purpose of the article?

(A) To explain why a particular person won a community award
(B) To describe the role of the farming community
(C) To invite the townspeople to a seminar on flood plains
(D) To welcome a new member of the Bordeaux business community

**169.** What is NOT mentioned as a benefit of Dubois Barriers?

(A) Saving the lives of certain livestock
(B) Drawing travelers in Bordeaux
(C) Organizing a recycling program
(D) Raising awareness of tidal power

**170.** When was the Dubois Barrier project completed?

(A) Five years ago
(B) Three years ago
(C) The previous year
(D) On May 10

**171.** In which of the positions marked [1], [2], [3], and [4] does the following sentence best belong?

"In addition, Mr. Debois has also set up the Debois Academy."

(A) [1]
(B) [2]
(C) [3]
(D) [4]

*Go on to the next page*

# PTZ Component Testing

PTZ Component Testing provides a full testing service for all those involved in the radiology industry, as well as hospitals. We offer extensive testing on all equipment using up-to-date machinery. We consider each application individually, tailoring the testing procedure to each specific client. In addition to being a brand-new testing facility, we also provide a mobile service to test the equipment in your workplace.

## Our services:
▶ Analyzing and testing outcomes of new equipment for hospitals and healthcare facilities
▶ Examining reports following testing procedures
▶ Advising and implementing alterations to any equipment offsite or in the facility, if necessary

## Facilities and Personnel

Our main facility is located in Shanghai, China, with supplementary offices in West Java Province and Szechuan. We have links with government-run testing firms globally, which enables us to provide an international service not available anywhere else in the country. Every member of our staff is trained to internationally accepted standards, with an average of 15 years' experience in the testing of radiology equipment.

## Report

Our software provides results in internationally formatted data reports.
Results are printed in hard copy and provided digitally as well.
All information can be accessed on the website using a client-protected coded password.

For more information, contact Vivian Lawson at vivian@ptzcomponents.com.

**172.** The word "tailoring" in paragraph 1, line 3, is closest in meaning to

(A) sewing
(B) adapting
(C) presenting
(D) evaluating

**173.** What service does PTZ Component Testing NOT advertise?

(A) Examining radiology equipment
(B) Providing a mobile service
(C) Inspecting healthcare cleanliness
(D) Analyzing results of some machinery

**174.** According to the advertisement, what makes PTZ Component Testing unique?

(A) It works with similar companies throughout the world.
(B) It is the oldest company in the industry.
(C) Its scientists graduated from internationally renowned universities.
(D) It has a presence in every major city.

**175.** What is indicated about the reports generated by PTZ Component Testing?

(A) They are witnessed by independent experts.
(B) They are available online to the public.
(C) They are presented to customers in two formats.
(D) They can be kept on file for an extra fee.

*Go on to the next page*

From: Nolan Parker <Nparker@toyfactory.com>

To: Khloe Swann <Kswann@toybox.com>

Date: January 25

Subject: Sales update

Attachment: Report-01.xls

Dear Ms. Swann,

I am replying to your inquiry about this month's sales updates. As you can see, I have attached a list of the stock that we sold in December together with a profit and loss spreadsheet. You can see that most of the items sold extremely well. In particular, we sold a record number of the ceramic dolls from Minakawa Inc. The branded stuffed animals from Harpers also continue to be bestsellers, as well as the consoles and electronic games from ELF Ltd. What I find surprising is the lack of sales of the children's wooden building sets. I think the quality was extremely inferior to those of other competitors and we had many complaints that they broke easily. This is shown in the sales figures as refunds.

However, I have sourced a different supplier, so hopefully sales figures for the next few months will reflect this. I am looking forward to meeting you at the annual sales convention next Monday. If you need any further information before then, please let me know.

Sincerely,

Nolan Parker
Sales Manager

From: Khloe Swann <Kswann@toybox.com>

To: Nolan Parker <Nparker@toyfactory.com>

Date: January 26

Subject: Re: Sales update

Dear Mr. Parker,

Thank you for your prompt reply. As you are aware, we have signed a large contract to supply children's toys for the retail stores in Boston and Springfield, both very high-profile areas. From our research, we know that the locals in these areas demand very high-quality merchandise, and they have an even higher than average number of schools and children's clubs. Therefore, I think we should order more stock from Minakawa Inc. Can you supply me with a product list from this company and a contact name and number? I understand the meeting has been rescheduled to Tuesday. Can you confirm this as well?

Khloe Swann
Marketing Manager

**176.** Why did Mr. Parker send the first e-mail?

(A) To provide Ms. Swann with information
(B) To request a list of available playthings
(C) To supply a new date for a meeting
(D) To respond to a proposed change

**177.** According to the first e-mail, what items will be provided by a new supplier?

(A) Electronic games
(B) Stuffed animals
(C) Building sets
(D) Ceramic dolls

**178.** In the second e-mail, the word "locals" in line 3, is closest in meaning to

(A) residents
(B) regions
(C) items
(D) sales

**179.** What is suggested about the ceramic dolls?

(A) They are expected to sell well in the Boston area.
(B) They are not available during the summer season.
(C) They were purchased from Harpers.
(D) Their price has decreased from last month.

**180.** About what do Mr. Parker and Ms. Swann have different information?

(A) The date of a meeting
(B) The contact information for ELF Ltd.
(C) The sales figures for December
(D) The refund details of a client

August 15
## Customer Service Department
## Wells Home Appliances Inc.
22 Saunders Road
San Francisco, CA 94016

To Whom It May Concern,

When my coffee maker (serial code CFM 436) failed to work recently, I took it to the WHA service center in the Morris Shopping Mall, which is listed as one of your repair outlets. I was very annoyed when the shop declined to provide a free repair to my appliance although I have a valid warranty of more than six months. I had to pay for the repairs personally as there are no other local shops listed on your warranty. Here is a list of the charges from the repair center:

### Parts :

| | |
|---|---|
| Filter | $12 |
| Power unit | $17 |
| Labor: $10 per hour | $20 |
| Dispenser nozzle | $21 |
| | |
| **Total** | **$70** |

Please find attached the invoice and my guarantee I received when I bought the coffee maker. If you need any further information, please contact me.

Regards,

Ian Travers
23 Cherrystone Drive
San Jose, CA 95120

# Guarantee

Welcome to your new Wells Coffee Maker. We have been supplying quality kitchen appliances throughout the world for over 30 years, and we pride ourselves on our quality and customer service.

All appliances are manufactured to the highest standards of craftsmanship. We offer a two-year warranty that covers the repair and replacement of your appliance in the event of a malfunction of parts. This warranty covers repairing labor and the replaceable parts only; please be aware that we take no responsibility for the damage to the dispenser nozzle or damage incurred by mishandling.

Attached is a list of authorized repair centers. Should you experience any problems with your new appliance, please take it to one of these WHA service centers for repair together with the original receipt and warranty. These centers have all been approved by Wells for the quality of their service and repairs.

**181.** Why did Mr. Travers write the letter?

(A) To request reimbursement of his expenses
(B) To request a copy of his guarantee
(C) To ask for a replacement for his broken machine
(D) To complain about a mistake on his receipt

**182.** In the letter, the word "declined" in paragraph 1, line 3, is closest in meaning to

(A) descended
(B) rejected
(C) weakened
(D) modified

**183.** What does Mr. Travers mention about the WHA service center?

(A) It offered the service at a reduced rate.
(B) It completed the task quickly.
(C) It carried out unnecessary work.
(D) It is an approved service center.

**184.** What did Wells Home Appliances include with the product warranty?

(A) A customer registration form
(B) A catalog of Wells products
(C) A register of clients
(D) A list of service centers

**185.** What expense amount reported by Mr. Travers will the warranty NOT cover?

(A) $12
(B) $17
(C) $20
(D) $21

# City of Jacksonville
## Council Office: Street Performer Permit Application

The following applicant seeks a license to perform on the streets of Jacksonville as an "artist" and submits the following information as required:

**Artist's Name:**  **Jace Payne**

**Legal Address of Applicant:**  **2194 Richardson Road, Jacksonville**

**Location of performance:**  **Ed Austin Park**

Completed application forms must be accompanied by:

◆ Copy of birth certificate issued by Government Births Bureau
◆ A recording of the applicant playing the relevant instrument or singing
◆ License fee of $30 for each member, item of equipment, and stage
◆ A list of all equipment to be used at the venue
◆ If the music requires an amplifier, please send details of the decibel levels to our noise pollution officer, Mr. Gavin Freeman, to ensure it meets the permitted levels.

The applicant states that the above statement is true and he/she has read and agrees to comply with the provision of Section 44 of the code of the city of Jacksonville as it applies to artists.

**Signature of applicant**  *Jace Payne*
**Date**  *July 24*

---

To: Gavin Freeman <Gfreeman@admin.jacksonville.org>

From: Jace Payne <Jacepayne@bigmail.com>

Date: July 27

Re: Noise permission

Dear Mr. Freeman,

I wish to obtain permission for a street performance to be held at Ed Austin Park from August 1 to 3. I understand that I will need permission to use amplifiers, which are currently capable of emitting 100 decibels maximum. I am planning to use three amplifiers at the event. If you wish to check the noise levels, I'm performing at three venues in the downtown area on weekdays: Marrs Bar, Venure Restaurant, and Streetlife Café. I'll provide free entrance tickets if you want to come along and check that the decibel levels are acceptable.

Regards,

Jace Payne

To: Jace Payne <Jacepayne@bigmail.com>

From: Gavin Freeman <Gfreeman@admin.jacksonville.org>

Date: July 29

Re: Noise Permission

Dear Mr. Payne,

To assess the noise level, I need to operate the measuring equipment on-site. Among the places you've mentioned, Streetlife would work for me. You wrote you are performing on weekdays. When can I come over to see you?

And regarding your application, the person in charge says she hasn't received the recording of your playing yet. If you don't mind, I can record your performance when I visit there to check the amplifiers. Since we don't have much time before August 1, please call me at 500-5157 at your earliest convenience.

Gavin Freeman
Noise Pollution Officer

**186.** What is Mr. Payne applying for?

(A) A permit to sell drinks
(B) A sound check
(C) A safety certificate from the council
(D) A license to perform

**187.** Where will Mr. Freeman most likely see Mr. Payne play?

(A) At a park
(B) At a bar
(C) At a café
(D) At a restaurant

**188.** What required references does Mr. Freeman say Mr. Payne has missed?

(A) A birth certificate
(B) A video clip
(C) A list of equipment
(D) Some money

**189.** What is the purpose of the first e-mail?

(A) To submit an application
(B) To offer directions
(C) To ask for permission to use equipment
(D) To advertise some venues

**190.** What will Mr. Payne most likely use at the event next month?

(A) Electric guitars
(B) Microphone stands
(C) Editing equipment
(D) Loudspeakers

# International Business Newsletter

## MJ Foodville Appoints New Head of Research Team

MJ Foodville (MJF) which has its headquarters in Singapore, has appointed Colton Choi as the new head of its research team. "I am very excited about the new opportunities to open up for me here in Singapore, even though I am sad at having to leave my homeland in Korea," said Mr. Choi in a statement released in the MJF newsletter.

He went on to say that he had been interested in the work done at MJF for many years and is delighted to join the team. His first task once he assumes the position, according to the newsletter, will be to strongly highlight the importance of healthy eating in the Philippines and Indonesia.

Mr. Choi graduated with a master's degree in food and nutrition from the University of London. His previous employment was with Bristol Food Company, where he worked as a research assistant to the company's development director, Julian Baker. He will begin his new role in October at MJF.

---

To: Colton Choi <coltonchoi@gomail.com>

From: Ariana Rose <arianarose@bfc.com>

Date: September 9

Subject: Congratulations

Dear Mr. Choi,

Well done on your new appointment once again. This is an excellent opportunity for you, and I have no doubt that you will make a valuable contribution to the MJ Foodville. When you resigned, I was asked by Mr. Baker to fill in for your position as research assistant. I intend to accept the offer even though I have not given him an answer yet. I have wanted to join the research team since I began working here last year. I extend my heartfelt gratitude to you for putting me forward for the job.

I would very much like to keep in touch and would appreciate your sending me your new address and phone number in Singapore.

Kind regards,

Ariana Rose
Bristol Food Company

To: Ariana Rose <arianarose@bfc.com>

From: Colton Choi <coltonchoi@gomail.com>

Date: September 11

Subject: Re: Congratulations

Dear Ms. Rose,

I'm very pleased to know that you're accepting the offer. Although we had no chance to work on the same team, I heard a lot about you from your manager, Mr. Cox. I'm sure that your experience in the material division would be a great help to the research team. When I nominated you to the position, Mr. Baker readily agreed to give you the opportunity. So, you should return your thanks to Mr. Baker.

I haven't moved to Singapore yet. I found a house to settle in but still don't have a phone number. And my e-mail is to be changed; you can contact me at coltonchoi2793@mjfgroup. com if you need my advice on your new duties that start next month.

Sincerely,

Colton Choi

**191.** Why was the article written?

(A) To announce the appointment of a staff member
(B) To publicize the findings of a questionnaire
(C) To release information about a new product
(D) To inform staff of an upcoming research project

**192.** Where are the headquarters of MJ Foodville located?

(A) Korea
(B) Singapore
(C) Malaysia
(D) Philippines

**193.** What does Ms. Rose ask Mr. Choi to do?

(A) Write a letter of recommendation
(B) Join a research team
(C) Provide contact information
(D) Speak at a meeting

**194.** What is mentioned about Mr. Choi?

(A) He is currently working for MJ Foodville.
(B) He will replace Mr. Cox for the research assistant position.
(C) He recommended Ms. Rose for his previous position.
(D) He decided to stay in his home country.

**195.** What is implied about Ms. Rose?

(A) She is a client of MJ Foodville.
(B) She currently lives in Singapore.
(C) She majored in food and nutrition.
(D) She is currently working for Mr. Cox.

*Go on to the next page*

## *Hatton Business Update*

Trust us for up-to-the-minute news and events

### Information to subscribers:

Requests for subscription renewal are sent automatically one week prior to your current subscription's expiration date, subject to the conditions below. If your subscription finishes prior to a renewal request but you wish to continue to renew your subscription within two months of the actual expiry date, you can purchase any missed issues of the business magazine for 25% off the cover price.

Clients who ask for a renewal or extension prior to April 30 will be offered a 10% reduction on a two-year subscription or a 5% reduction on a 12-month subscription. All online offers cease with the expiration of any subscription, including the search-and-find database, which enables you to browse through the past catalogs of previously published *Hatton Business Update* issues. Visit www.hattononline.com for more information.

---

*Hatton Business Update*

\-\-\-\-\-\-\-\-\-\-\-\-\-\-\-\-\-\-\-\-\-\-\-\-\-\-\-\-\-\-\-\-\-\-\-\-\-\-

Account Number: *34073*

Current Login: *March 6*

Previous Login: *February 27*

\-\-\-\-\-\-\-\-\-\-\-\-\-\-\-\-\-\-\-\-\-\-\-\-\-\-\-\-\-\-\-\-\-\-\-\-\-\-

### *Hatton Business Update* Online Subscription

- **Name:** Austin Crocker
- **Subscription status:** Current subscription expires on March 6.
- **Requested renewal period:** 24 months
- **Payment method:** Bank transfer

Thank you for renewing your *Hatton Business Update* subscription.

**Written by:** Austin Crocker
**Date:** March 6
**Subject:** Subscription Renewal

Dear sir,

I've checked the information about the discount on your website today. I've been very satisfied with your service, so I decided to renew my subscription right away, even though I still have one month left before the expiration date. However, I was surprised to read the message, which states my expiration date is today, March 6. It must be April 6, according to your webpage. Other information on the message seems to be right.

I also checked if I applied for a new subscription instead of renewing it. But it says, "Thank you for renewing your *Hatton Business Update* subscription." Please take care of this issue as soon as possible.

**196.** What is the purpose of the Information?

(A) To announce further discounts on subscriptions
(B) To explain subscription renewal policies
(C) To notify subscribers of changes to online subscriptions
(D) To request that subscribers complete a survey

**197.** In the information, the word "conditions" in paragraph 1, line 2, is closest in meaning to

(A) ends
(B) proposals
(C) terms
(D) names

**198.** What is indicated about *Hatton Business Update*?

(A) Its reporters have won several publishing awards.
(B) Its website provides some information to subscribers.
(C) It published its last issue two months ago.
(D) It recently increased its subscription fees.

**199.** What problem does Mr. Crocker report?

(A) He cannot log on to the website.
(B) He hasn't received any notice about the event.
(C) He got a message with the wrong information.
(D) He wants to get a full refund.

**200.** How much of a discount will Mr. Croker receive?

(A) 5%
(B) 10%
(C) 20%
(D) 25%

# ACTUAL TEST

## 答對題數表

| | |
|---|---|
| **PART 5** | |
| **PART 6** | |
| **PART 7** | |
| 總題數 | |

08

# READING TEST

In the Reading test, you will read a variety of texts and answer several different types of reading comprehension questions. The entire Reading test will last 75 minutes. There are three parts, and directions are given for each part. You are encouraged to answer as many questions as possible within the time allowed.

You must mark your answers on the separate answer sheet. Do not write your answers in your test book.

## PART 5

**Directions:** A word or phrase is missing in each of the sentences below. Four answer choices are given below each sentence. Select the best answer to complete the sentence. Then mark the letter (A), (B), (C), or (D) on your answer sheet.

---

**101.** The nutritional instruction program in Addis Ababa was so ------- that some countries are intending to introduce similar initiatives in their cities.

(A) success
(B) successive
(C) successful
(D) successfully

**102.** Affiliates of Prime.com will now receive unlimited ------- to the organization's exclusive online data pool.

(A) accesses
(B) access
(C) accessing
(D) accessory

**103.** The brochure highlights the sequence of ------- is happening over the two-day event.

(A) that
(B) what
(C) who
(D) when

**104.** Two years ago, Mr. Walker ------- college to join his current company.

(A) leave
(B) left
(C) will leave
(D) was left

**105.** ------- maintenance work on the Kaur Drive, workers at the Mahir Library have to enter via the north entrance to get to work.

(A) Now that
(B) Moreover
(C) Wherever
(D) Because of

**106.** Those who have ------- about their missing baggage have to visit the claim office located next to the luggage carousel.

(A) features
(B) connections
(C) properties
(D) inquiries

**107.** Those who feel dizzy in the heat of the day will realize that the best way to make ------- feel better is to drink some water.

(A) they
(B) them
(C) their
(D) themselves

**108.** The pay increase this year for all employees is the ------- as that incentive last year.

(A) same
(B) repeat
(C) equal
(D) one

109. Farmers in Shamrock are overwhelmed by the enormous demand for ------- organic potato products.

(A) they
(B) themselves
(C) them
(D) their

110. The majority of shoppers at Camden supermarket will readily pay extra for food that is produced -------.

(A) local
(B) locality
(C) locals
(D) locally

111. Although public admission to the Anaheim Society's award ceremony is allowed, the after-party is by ------- only.

(A) collection
(B) invitation
(C) operation
(D) function

112. Company employees have been advised that the new product range's market is highly ------- and will face fierce rivalry from other companies.

(A) competitive
(B) competitors
(C) competition
(D) competitively

113. The customer conference was ------- delayed as the projector had an operational malfunction in the course of the seminar.

(A) enough
(B) many
(C) quite
(D) ever

114. The ------- annual manufacturing costs of the company were estimated to be $12 million as a result of structural renovations.

(A) totaling
(B) totaled
(C) totals
(D) total

115. Visitors ------- to show their passport or photo identification whenever they have to check-in at a hotel.

(A) requests
(B) are requested
(C) to request
(D) requesting

116. The board of directors is considering ------- the headquarters to Vancouver.

(A) to relocate
(B) relocation
(C) relocating
(D) has relocated

117. The Sales Manager, Cody Flynn, insisted that marketing the merchandise ------- online is not a profitable way of attracting young customers.

(A) closely
(B) otherwise
(C) solely
(D) almost

118. Kemp Apparel's second quarter growth rate was higher than originally -------.

(A) anticipates
(B) anticipated
(C) anticipating
(D) anticipation

119. Applicants who passed the initial selection tests for the supervisor position ------- by the company recruiter next week.

(A) will contact
(B) would contact
(C) will be contacted
(D) have been contacted

120. Bainbridge Public Library visitors may check out a total of 5 publications ------- 3 multimedia items per week.

(A) than
(B) just as
(C) so
(D) and

Go on to the next page

121. During their stay, guests have the option of participating in various outdoor activities ------- cycling, fishing, and swimming.
(A) similarly
(B) such as
(C) as far as
(D) likewise

122. Travelers are asked to collect all of their ------- belongings before exiting the train.
(A) personal
(B) accurate
(C) unlimited
(D) believable

123. Changes in LK Telecom's billing policy are ------- determined by how much demand there is.
(A) large
(B) largest
(C) larger
(D) largely

124. The estimate covers all the labor and materials for building a parking ------- on Boulder Road that can accommodate 1,000 vehicles.
(A) structure
(B) structures
(C) structural
(D) structurally

125. Mr. Reynolds should certainly be praised for ------- a welcome reception for the new employees at Orange Software.
(A) correcting
(B) applying
(C) organizing
(D) connecting

126. The retailers on Simpson Street are prohibited from displaying items outside ------- prior consent.
(A) around
(B) without
(C) owing to
(D) as opposed to

127. ------- impresses the board of directors the most is that the White Timber Company has established its presence in the hardwood furniture market.
(A) Nothing
(B) Neither
(C) What
(D) Which

128. While a majority of customers think that the new model is easy to use, those ------- familiar with the original operating system have to look through the user's manual before using the item.
(A) little
(B) none
(C) less
(D) fewer

129. Because of her outstanding performance, Ms. Russell has been ------- to a manager position at Higgins Inc.
(A) promoted
(B) registered
(C) pleased
(D) increased

130. Vending machines containing beverages and snacks are strategically situated ------- the company premises.
(A) between
(B) down
(C) throughout
(D) except

# PART 6

**Directions:** Read the texts that follow. A word, phrase, or sentence is missing in parts of each text. Four answer choices for each question are given below the text. Select the best answer to complete the text. Then mark the letter (A), (B), (C), or (D) on your answer sheet.

Questions 131-134 refer to the following advertisement.

## New Exhibition at Sierra Art Museum

In recent years, Sierra Art Museum has been popular in holding exhibitions on Junk art,

innovative art ------- the great artistic talent shown by famous local artist Diego Harding and his
       **131.**
colleagues.

According to Mr. Harding, his activity would every now and then be termed as "Junk art." -------.
                   **132.**

"Junk art," as his work is called, is once-abandoned items ------- are utilized to come up with a
         **133.**
new creation.

The exhibition will be open to anyone interested from April 1 to June 30. ------, on the evening
           **134.**
of Wednesday, March 23, there will be a reception that will include the staff members of the art

center only. A website is also set up in case someone needs more clarification. The website is

at <u>museum.sierraart.org</u>.

---

**131.** (A) feature
    (B) featured
    (C) featuring
    (D) features

**132.** (A) But the materials for those sculptures are not junk in fact.
    (B) This was once believed to be possible, but Mr. Harding thought otherwise.
    (C) Mr. Harding is now collecting a lot of junk to turn his idea into a reality.
    (D) He came up with the idea of utilizing the things that people throw away every day.

**133.** (A) what
    (B) that
    (C) how
    (D) each

**134.** (A) In addition
    (B) Instead
    (C) Thus
    (D) As a result

*Go on to the next page* ➡

Dear Stellar Store customer,

We appreciate you very much for your interest in joining the Stellar Store Rewards loyalty program. Participating in this program ------- you to enjoy a lot of wonderful rewards. The
**135.**
benefits of being a member of this program are that you will have early ------- about discount
**136.**
deals, access to special exclusive occasions, and the opportunity to be awarded a gift certificate worth $50 for every $400 spent on product purchases.

-------. An individual is only required to submit the enclosed application form to the nearby store,
**137.**
where a membership card can be issued for you. Updates on your account detailing the points you have accumulated and discount coupons you have earned will be provided ------- six weeks
**138.**
after you start using your membership card.

Membership is free and can be canceled at any time. Welcome and start earning your rewards today!

Sincerely,

Amy Henderson

Customer Loyalty Program Director

Enclosure

135. (A) has allowed
(B) is allowing
(C) allowed
(D) will allow

136. (A) performance
(B) evaluation
(C) information
(D) referral

137. (A) Once you cancel, all your coupons will become invalid.
(B) There are no complications in signing up for this program.
(C) You are not on our customer list; however, we will service you as our most important member.
(D) You'll need to visit one of our affiliates to get an application form.

138. (A) within
(B) since
(C) until
(D) due to

## PART 7

**Directions:** In this part you will read a selection of texts, such as magazine and newspaper articles, e-mails, and instant messages. Each text or set of texts is followed by several questions. Select the best answer for each question and mark the letter (A), (B), (C), or (D) on your answer sheet.

**Questions 147-148** refer to the following notice.

Iron Jones Gym is now due for renovation. The gym is to be closed for two weeks in July for building repairs.

The dates below are important:

June 20 – June 30    Renewal of annual membership

July 1 – July 6    Room refurbishment

July 7 – July 14    External window replacement

July 15    Gym reopening

To check our full calendar for the year, go to www.ironjones.com. Membership can be renewed over the telephone. If you are renting sports equipment, the lending period can also be renewed if you'd like. If not, please return the items before June 20. You may reapply for the equipment on July 15. Even if you are renewing a rental agreement, all equipment has to be removed from your previous lockers by June 30, as they will be changed. Anything left in the lockers will be removed after this date. Contact us with any questions at 777-4644 extension 14.

**147.** For whom in the Iron Jones Gym is the notice intended?

(A) Management
(D) Members
(C) Fitness trainers
(D) Gym staff

**148.** How should membership be renewed?

(A) In person
(B) By phone
(C) By e-mail
(D) Through the website

*Go on to the next page*

**Questions 149-150** refer to the following message chain.

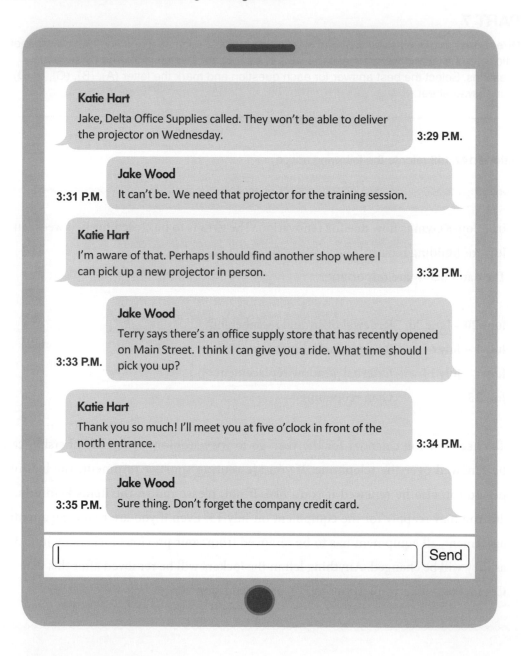

**Katie Hart**
Jake, Delta Office Supplies called. They won't be able to deliver the projector on Wednesday.
3:29 P.M.

**Jake Wood**
3:31 P.M. It can't be. We need that projector for the training session.

**Katie Hart**
I'm aware of that. Perhaps I should find another shop where I can pick up a new projector in person.
3:32 P.M.

**Jake Wood**
3:33 P.M. Terry says there's an office supply store that has recently opened on Main Street. I think I can give you a ride. What time should I pick you up?

**Katie Hart**
Thank you so much! I'll meet you at five o'clock in front of the north entrance.
3:34 P.M.

**Jake Wood**
3:35 P.M. Sure thing. Don't forget the company credit card.

Send

**149.** What problem are the speakers discussing?

(A) The new projector is not working properly.
(B) They cannot attend the workshop on Wednesday.
(C) An order cannot be delivered in time.
(D) Mr. Wood needs a ride to Main Street.

**150.** At 3:31 P.M., what does Mr. Wood mean when he writes, "It can't be"?

(A) He can't find another supplier.
(B) He can't fix the projector.
(C) He can't agree to Ms. Hart's opinion.
(D) He can't accept the failure.

Dear Residents of Henderson,

From August, Sunset Station Dance Hall will become known as the Rainbow Paradise Nightclub. There is a major refurbishment taking place, which will include a new dining area as well as an extension to the dance floor to make it larger. The new owner, Larry Stone, will still maintain the same high quality of food and entertainment that you have been used to in the past. We look forward to seeing you again.

**151.** According to the announcement, what is being changed about the establishment?

(A) Its name
(B) Its location
(C) The menu
(D) The prices

**152.** What is suggested about Mr. Stone?

(A) He plans to change the menu.
(B) He owns other properties in the area.
(C) He used to work in a nightclub.
(D) He plans to extend a dance area.

ACTUAL TEST

08

PART

7

# London Economist
# Business News

September 12, London — Ethan Fletcher, Chief Executive Officer at Filton Heating Components, has announced that the company will be expanding within the country over the next six months. He plans to open stores in Glasgow, Leeds, and London. —[1]—.

Mr. Fletcher admitted that the planned expansion is behind schedule due to complications in the manufacturing plant. He said that the recession "had taken everyone by surprise." Following the installation of new advanced machinery in its production headquarters in Bristol, Mr. Fletcher is confident that the company's expansion will merit the investment. —[2]—.

Filton Heating Components was established by the current CEO's father, who began by recycling metal to make the boiler parts. —[3]—. And it has led to a massive rise in market share for the company over the years.

Next year, the company is hoping to expand into the air conditioning market, and the industry will be closely monitoring its performance. The move will be supplemented by an aggressive advertising and marketing campaign. —[4]—.

**153.** What is suggested about Filton Heating Components?

(A) It has lost significant market share over the years.
(B) Its founder passed the business to his son.
(C) It will expand into the commercial sector.
(D) It closed down its manufacturing plant.

**154.** In which of the positions marked [1], [2], [3], and [4] does the following sentence best belong?

"This recycling initiative led to cheaper components exclusively for the industrial market."

(A) [1]
(B) [2]
(C) [3]
(D) [4]

## Journey in Style through the Highlands with Express Trains

Experience the sights and sounds of a coastal journey along the Highlands route on a three-hour train journey with Express Trains. The 200-kilometer coastal trail encompasses three counties, with beautiful scenery and lush vegetation. Our trip will take you through the high terrain with the option of a tour guide to explain the area. Lunch will be aboard the train passing through the industrial district of the Highlands. Then the journey ends with a visit to a hidden beach where you can see seals and dolphins at play off the coast.

The train leaves the station at 11:30 A.M. from Manchester Station and returns at 2:30 P.M., Mondays to Fridays. Tickets are £40 for adults, £25 for students with valid ID cards, and £20 for children under the age of 12.

For details and a timetable, call
Express Trains
at 0161-334-6259
or
visit our website
at www.expresshighlandstrains.co.uk

**Express Trains Trip**

155. For whom is the brochure most likely intended?

(A) Tour guides
(B) Historians
(C) Train drivers
(D) Tourists

156. The word "hidden" in line 6, is closest in meaning to

(A) restricted
(B) obscure
(C) notorious
(D) crowded

157. How much is the fee for a ten-year-old?

(A) £12
(B) £20
(C) £25
(D) £40

# Melrose Business College

If you are seeking an International Master's Degree in business, then contact the Melrose Business College for details of courses.

The college offers a two-year program, beginning in September, and has a range of courses in international relations and business studies. The courses are taught by reputable faculty members, all of whom have significant hands-on experience in international businesses and trade industries. Together with an innovative exchange program with major companies overseas, this has placed the college in the top three educational establishments in the International Business College rankings.

The application fee is $150 for domestic students and $250 for applicants from abroad. If you quote this advertisement, the price will be halved, as long as you submit the application by the end of June. The application deadline for the upcoming course is July 15. There are also a number of grants and scholarships available. For more information and an application form, visit our website at www.melrosebusiness.edu.

**158.** What is suggested about the International Master's Degree course?

(A) It recently added new faculty members.
(B) It has three enrollment periods.
(C) It has a renowned reputation.
(D) It takes one year to complete.

**159.** According to the advertisement, what is NOT available to students?

(A) An opportunity to work abroad
(B) Access to lecturers with international expertise
(C) The possibility of getting financial assistance
(D) The ability to take courses over the Internet

**160.** What is indicated about the application fee?

(A) It is different for national and international applicants.
(B) It will increase next year.
(C) It must be paid by June 30.
(D) It can be paid online or via credit card.

# Memo

Irvine Hotel

In an effort to try to reduce expenses, the management of the Irvine Hotel will no longer be supplying free toiletries. Guests must specifically ask for them to be supplied, and there is an additional charge. This is part of our cost-cutting initiative. Please make sure that you inform guests of this change when they check in. However, guests can purchase essential toiletries at a reasonable cost from our shop in the foyer. Guests can pre-order well-selected toiletries to await them when they arrive and the cost of these items will be added to the final bill. Please ensure that this message is clearly stated to any person who books over the telephone. We will post notices of this change in every hotel room and also in the lobby so that the message is clear.

**161.** For whom is the memo most likely intended?

(A) Hotel guests
(B) Maintenance staff
(C) Housekeeping staff
(D) Hotel receptionists

**162.** According to the memo, why has a new policy been adopted?

(A) To save the cost of disposable items
(B) To improve training for employees
(C) To use less energy and water
(D) To reduce requests for extra maintenance

**163.** What are hotel employees instructed to do?

(A) Inform guests that toiletries are not complimentary
(B) Charge guests for any water and electricity used
(C) Provide guests with a variety of items at reception
(D) Notify guests of an increase in room rates

*Go on to the next page*

April 30 — Designer Carla Whittle of the Whittle Design Agency has made a donation of half a million pounds to the Soweto Town Direct Disability project. This is a huge boost for the charity as funding for the project has been reduced since last year. "We are truly delighted with Ms. Whittle's contribution," commented David Campbell, the director of the Direct Disability program. —[1]—.

Direct Disability was established a decade ago by local businesspeople to help disabled people to use public facilities. Although it was originally supposed to receive a grant from the government, funding was cut earlier this year due to pressure by the Treasury to reduce public spending. —[2]—. The project now relies upon donations.

Last month, Direct Disability began a fundraising campaign targeting local businesses. "Together with requests for donations, we sent pictures of some facilities we have established," continued Mr. Campbell. —[3]—. One of the installations was fitting a wheelchair ramp to the local library, which is frequented by Ms. Whittle's family. "I had no idea that Ms. Whittle's family used the library until she rang and asked if she could assist in some way," Mr. Campbell said.

Supporters and businesses are delighted with the donation, with local councilor Tom Brady praising the work done by the charity to raise awareness and funding for other projects. Ms. Whittle released a press statement saying, "I have loved the library since I was a child, and although I have now moved abroad, I still have fond memories of it. —[4]—. It is not just about installing access ramps. It means that more local people are now able to access the facilities."

Amy Wellington, Local Contributor

---

**164.** When was the Direct Disability project started?

(A) Two years ago
(B) Three years ago
(C) Five years ago
(D) Ten years ago

**165.** According to the article, why has the project lost funding?

(A) Local businesses refused to help.
(B) Building material costs increased.
(C) The local population had declined.
(D) The government reduced its financial support.

**166.** Who is currently NOT a resident of Soweto Town?

(A) Carla Whittle
(B) David Campbell
(C) Tom Brady
(D) Amy Wellington

**167.** In which of the positions marked [1], [2], [3], and [4] does the following sentence best belong?

"It will certainly help us to install more facilities for disabled people in the community."

(A) [1]
(B) [2]
(C) [3]
(D) [4]

**Questions 168-171** refer to the following e-mail.

To: Chad Rogers <chadrogers@gomail.com>

From: Carrie Slater <carrieslater@widemail.com>

Date: September 5

Subject: Cost Summary

Attachment: estimate_ChadRogers.xls

Dear Mr. Rogers,

I enjoyed meeting with you last week and hearing your ideas for the expansion of your automatic car wash business. As I mentioned, my financial team has been preparing a financial estimate, which is attached to this e-mail.

You said you plan to open business on the site opposite from the Baxter Building to allow a drive-through car wash service. The team has figured the cost of this into the estimate, including an estimate for the renovations and rental that will be required prior to any agreement. I would still recommend the vacant site next to the Prime Building behind Anton Elementary School as a more viable option. As it has already been renovated, this will reduce your costs.

If you want us to carry out the work, we can begin immediately. Please do not hesitate to contact me with any queries. I look forward to hearing from you soon.

Sincerely,

Carrie Slater

**168.** Who most likely is Ms. Slater?

(A) A car wash company owner
(B) A building contractor
(C) A financial consultant
(D) A landscaping professional

**169.** According to the e-mail, what was discussed at last week's meeting?

(A) Designs for a new restaurant
(B) Expansion of a fleet of vehicles
(C) Plans for a business relocation
(D) Potential renovation projects

**170.** What is mentioned as being included in the attachment?

(A) Detailed blueprints
(B) A breakdown of prices
(C) Receipts for renovation materials
(D) Work schedules

**171.** The word "figured" in paragraph 2, line 2, is closest in meaning to

(A) exceeded
(B) discounted
(C) incorporated
(D) transformed

*Go on to the next page*

**Questions 172-175** refer to the following excerpt from an online chat discussion.

| | | |
|---|---|---|
| | **Kayla Maxwell**<br>[10:01 A.M.] | Hello, everyone. I would like to check on the progress of the product development. You are inviting some participants to test the new soap today. Is that correct? |
| | **Jordan Moss**<br>[10:02 A.M.] | But we haven't managed to get enough volunteers yet. Twelve people so far have come forward but we need eight more. |
| | **Erin Parker**<br>[10:02 A.M.] | Then we have no option but to postpone the testing for a few days. |
| | **Kayla Maxwell**<br>[10:03 A.M.] | Can't we just do it with twelve subjects? |
| | **Erin Parker**<br>[10:03 A.M.] | We'd better not. Currently we have only two subjects between the ages of 41 and 50. This can distort the results of the findings. |
| | **Kayla Maxwell**<br>[10:04 A.M.] | There's nothing that we can do if it doesn't work. Can you ensure that the testing is carried out as soon as possible, with the results sent directly to me? I will need some sort of written report by the end of next week. |
| | **Jordan Moss**<br>[10:05 A.M.] | Yes, it was my general plan. I can assure you that you will receive a report by next Friday. |

Send

**172.** What are the speakers mainly discussing?

(A) A recruitment drive
(B) A marketing report
(C) An advertising campaign
(D) A product trial

**173.** What does Ms. Parker tell Ms. Maxwell?

(A) The test has to be delayed.
(B) She'll send a report by the end of the week.
(C) They have to move up the test date.
(D) She'll proceed with the test with 12 people.

**174.** At 10:04 A.M., why does Ms. Maxwell write, "There's nothing that we can do if it doesn't work"?

(A) She doesn't want to volunteer for the test.
(B) She understands why the test has to be postponed.
(C) She can help them gather more participants.
(D) She will work on the research herself.

**175.** What does Mr. Moss say that he will do?

(A) Convince Ms. Parker to reschedule the test
(B) Send the report to Ms. Maxwell by next Friday
(C) Check the release date of the new soap range
(D) Advertise for more people in a newspaper

*Go on to the next page*

To: Philippe D'Anjou <pdanjou@shellie.com>

From: Cassie Swift <cswift@shellie.com>

Date: August 23

Subject: Shellie's products

Philippe,

I wish to draw your attention to negative feedback posted on a number of websites across Asia and Australia in particular about our Shellie range of windbreakers. You should pay particular attention to www.uniquesales.com and www.ratedornot.au. It seems that there are numerous complaints about the quality of the material used for the items. Shellie is going to be featured strongly in our new advertising campaign, so it is imperative that we find out more about the problem. Could you ask your department to look into this matter? At the same time, could your department undertake some further research into the Shellie range to find out if customers have any other concerns? Please make this a priority and report back to me with your findings by the end of next week.

Many thanks for your cooperation,

Cassie

| To: | Cassie Swift <cswift@shellie.com> |
|---|---|
| From: | Philippe D'Anjou <pdanjou@shellie.com> |
| Date: | August 30 |
| Subject: | Re: Shellie's products |

Cassie,

We have investigated the issues that you mentioned in your e-mail dated August 23. We have discovered that there is indeed a global concern about the quality of the material used in the Shellie range. In particular, it seems to be restricted to the all-in-one item, Shellie XK1. Customers are complaining that the material is too thin and prone to ripping. I would ask your manufacturing department to find a solution to this problem.

Additionally, we have found some dissatisfaction with the Shellie YL bra sets. Customers are uncomfortable about the lack of color choice. The website lists any color other than white as out of stock. I will e-mail you with more details by Friday.

The good news is that the level of satisfaction with both the sizing options and the price are very high. Once we sort out the issues raised by our customers, we will be just fine.

Philippe

**176.** Why does Ms. Swift write to Mr. D'Anjou?

(A) To promote two new websites
(B) To complain about the quality of an item
(C) To propose a new advertising campaign
(D) To ask him to research a problem

**177.** In what field does Ms. Swift work?

(A) Manufacturing
(B) Advertising
(C) Customer relations
(D) Product development

**178.** What is NOT stated about Shellie?

(A) Its products are mainly reviewed on two websites.
(B) Its headquarters are in Asia.
(C) It produces women's clothing.
(D) It has a research-related department.

**179.** What does Mr. D'Anjou note about Shellie XK1?

(A) The material is of an inferior quality.
(B) The color choices are not as many as customers want.
(C) The price is too high for the customers.
(D) The item is no longer in fashion.

**180.** In the second e-mail, the word "restricted" in paragraph 1, line 3, is closest in meaning to

(A) reduced
(B) exceptional
(C) limited
(D) confidential

*Go on to the next page*

Questions 181-185 refer to the following article and customer comment.

## Excellence in Technology
## Amanti Boost

### by Alice Cryer, New Delhi News

April 2 — Amanti is renowned for the quality of its mobile technology, and the New Boost mobile phone — due for launch on April 10 — is no exception. It has the capacity to store approximately 3,000 photos and 20 thirty-minute videos at the same time, and in addition, the external memory card provided with it is able to accommodate up to 5,000 tunes.

As an incentive, contract purchasers of the New Boost will receive a free set of state-of-the-art headphones. They were extensively tested by Amanti's research center, and the sound is far superior to the standard earphones supplied with its mobile phones. Moreover, Amanti is offering a new application that will enable users to download music and films faster and cheaper than before.

The New Boost is all new to us. It has a brighter screen as well as a much longer battery life. The New Boost is expected to supersede the company's previous flagship mobile phones and has a bright future ahead.

ACTUAL TEST 08

PART 7

**Feedback** | **Products** | **Services** | **Purchase**

**User Feedback:** Amanti Boost Mobile Phone
**User:** Ranjit Khan, Mumbai
**Posted:** 7:12 P.M. May 23

User rating: ★★★★☆

I really like the New Boost, and I have no regrets about waiting in line to purchase it on the day it was launched. I particularly like the headphones that came free with the phone. I also highly recommend the new application that enables you to download music and films for only 100 rupees a month. At the moment, there aren't many options, though I understand from the company that they will resume adding more contents from May 30.

My only real complaint is the new screen. Although it is brighter and bigger than Amanti's previous models, watching movies is a problem as there is a significant glare.

**181.** What is the purpose of the article?

(A) To announce a company's brand name has been changed
(B) To preview a new mobile device
(C) To explain how to download media onto a memory card
(D) To introduce testimonials from customers

**182.** What is NOT mentioned about the New Boost?

(A) Its larger screen
(B) Its accessories
(C) Its storage capacity
(D) Its carrying case

**183.** When did Mr. Khan most likely purchase his New Boost?

(A) On April 2
(B) On April 10
(C) On May 23
(D) On May 30

**184.** What is indicated about the mobile application?

(A) It is a combined effort between two mobile phone companies.
(B) It is gradually adding more choices to its inventory.
(C) It has been in existence for several years.
(D) It is offered to New Boost purchasers for free.

**185.** What is Mr. Khan's complaint about the screen?

(A) It is too bright.
(B) It is easily damaged.
(C) It doesn't switch to horizontal mode.
(D) It turns off unexpectedly.

*Go on to the next page*

# FASHION SHOW

Kanta Fashion Show was instrumental in revealing a number of innovations in today's fashion. Since last year, designers have been focusing heavily on natural materials.

"The latest designs from fashion houses are an indication of the new trend. If people had not want the designs, they would not have appeared in the show," commented Ms. Grainger, fashion show organizer.

For some companies, including Essie Sew and Laramar, the show gave them the chance to showcase their portfolio for the first time. Another new company, Pantala, revealed a brand-new concept in outerwear, which earned them the coveted Best in Show award, which has been previously won by Mackowns, who have been exhibiting for nearly five years.

Over 10,000 people attended the show at the Downton Hotel, which is located in the center of the town.

## Fashion Review of Pantala
*By Suzy Rees*

Operating for only twelve months, Pantala produces very well-known designs such as the Oasis Collection. Unlike other start-up companies, the organization is unique in not following the traditional designs of the industry.

Personally, I like the Dress Collection, which is a combination of lace, silk, and hemp — not a common choice but one that certainly attracts attention. The dresses come with a free pair of gloves and a handkerchief of the Grace Silver brand.

Their new collection, Autumn Dream, is the only one that uses leather: up to now, the company has only used soft materials. However, one look at their gorgeous jacket with a leather belt, straps, and silk lining will make you notice its quality.

To: Suzy Rees <Suzyrees@fashiontoday.com>

From: Joanne Kay <Joannekay@pantala.com>

Date: May 7

Subject: Upcoming Event

Dear Ms. Rees,

I'm writing to express deep gratitude for your favorable review on our Dress Collection, exhibited at the Kanta Fashion show last month. The show was the second event we've ever participated in, and I'm so glad to know that our collection has drawn much attention from fashion experts so soon.

In particular, I would like to thank you for your warm reviews about Autumn Dream as well as the Dress Collection. And I would like to invite you to our next event at Hummingbird Hotel, which is scheduled to be held on the 11th of next month. This will be the first fashion show hosted by Pantala, featuring the Autumn Dream collection accompanied by several more collections we are launching for the next season.

Thank you in advance for your time and participation.

Joanne Kay
Senior Designer
Pantala Fashion

186. What did Ms. Grainger imply about the fashion designs made of natural materials?

(A) They have been the only clothes on show.
(B) It is hard to design new trends.
(C) Their prices have been falling.
(D) Interest in them has been high.

187. Which company participated in the Kanta Fashion Show last year?

(A) Essie Sew
(B) Laramar
(C) Pantala
(D) Mackowns

188. What is indicated about the first fashion show hosted by Pantala?

(A) It was organized by Ms. Grainger.
(B) The place of the event has not been decided yet
(C) It will be held on June 11.
(D) It will be the second fashion event hosted by Pantala.

189. Which design collection received an award at the show?

(A) Oasis Collection
(B) Spring Collection
(C) Autumn Dream
(D) Grace Silver

190. What does the reviewer suggest about Pantala?

(A) It has been operating for over two years.
(B) It avoids using ideas from other companies.
(C) It has relocated to another location.
(D) It uses only natural materials.

*Go on to the next page*

To: Chloe Page <chloepage@edmonds.com>

From: Kevin Goodwin <kevingoodwin@edmonds.com>

Date: February 17

Subject: Candidate Interview

Attachment: Interview_Schedule.doc

Chloe,

Can I ask a favor of you? Luke Bowden is coming over on Thursday as a prospective candidate for the directorship of the drama school. However, I have double-booked with foreign clients from China at the same time. I cannot reschedule this meeting. Can I swap interview times with you? The original schedule for Mr. Bowden is attached. I hope you can accommodate the changed times.

Mr. Bowden has an impressive résumé, particularly his work with the Oscar Theater, which has been recognized as the top drama teaching academy in the country and is a major rival. I hope he will be a great asset to us. We have also had an excellent reference from Ian Hicks for his outstanding contribution on the board of the Arts and Music Corporation. Mr. Hicks is also coming to join us for lunch.

Thank you,

Kevin Goodwin
Acting Head of Drama
Edmonds Entertainment

## Edmonds Entertainment
### Candidate Interview Schedule

**Candidate Name:** Luke Bowden
**Potential Position:** Director of Drama School
**Interview Date:** February 20

| Meeting | Time | Location |
|---------|------|----------|
| Interview: Chloe Page | 11:00 A.M. – 12:00 P.M. | Building A, Room 205 |
| Lunch with Ian Hicks | 12:20 P.M. – 1:20 P.M. | Building B, Cafeteria |
| Interview: Kevin Goodwin | 1:30 P.M. – 2:30 P.M. | Building A, Room 303 |

**NOTE:** Upon arrival, please show your driver's license to the parking attendant next to the main entrance so that he can check on the necessary information and park your car in a designated area.

| To: | Kevin Goodwin <kevingoodwin@edmonds.com> |
| From: | Chloe Page <chloepage@edmonds.com> |
| Date: | February 17 |
| Subject: | Interview reschedule |

Kevin,

Don't worry about the interview schedule. I'm available on Thursday afternoon. And I also informed Mr. Bowden about the change as soon as I received your e-mail. Upon arrival, he will meet you at Room 303. I have high expectations of him, too. He'd be a great person to work with.

We're going to have lunch together, with Mr. Hicks and Mr. Bowden, right? Then I think Greenwoods restaurant is better than the cafeteria, since this will be the first time for us to meet Mr. Hicks. The restaurant is right next to the company building, so you won't be late for your meeting at 1:30. I'll reserve a table for four.

Good luck with your meeting with the Chinese clients. I'll see you on Thursday.

Chloe Page
General Manager
Edmonds Entertainment

**191.** What is implied about Mr. Bowden?

(A) He has worked for a competitor of Edmonds Entertainment.
(B) He used to work for Edmonds Entertainment many years ago.
(C) He is being recruited for his acting skills.
(D) He has visited Edmonds Entertainment in the past.

**192.** When does Mr. Goodwin indicate he wants to interview Mr. Bowden?

(A) At 11:00 A.M.
(B) At 12:20 P.M.
(C) At 1:30 P.M.
(D) At 2:30 P.M.

**193.** What is Mr. Bowden expected to do?

(A) Leave earlier than originally informed
(B) Book a restaurant
(C) Meet Mr. Hicks at the main entrance
(D) Bring a form of identification

**194.** Who will meet with Mr. Bowden in Room 303?

(A) Ms. Page
(B) Mr. Hicks
(C) Mr. Goodwin
(D) Ms. Oscar

**195.** What will Ms. Page likely to be doing at 1 P.M. on February 20?

(A) Taking a tour of the Edmonds premises
(B) Dining at a nearby restaurant
(C) Having a meeting at the company cafeteria
(D) Interviewing Mr. Bowden

*Go on to the next page*

# Peacock Office Supplies
### *Voted by the Business Times as the best supplier of office supplies!*

To celebrate our 5th anniversary in May, we are offering a special service to all our valued customers. On your request, we will imprint your company and personal information on your purchases, including file folders, envelopes, boxes, whiteboards, and all kinds of ballpoint pens. It is completely free!

Please put a checkmark by the items you want on the ordering form. Also, you'll need to fill in the design layout code, which can be checked on our website. And don't forget to update your customer information so that we can imprint them correctly.

Thank you for choosing Peacock Office Supplies!

---

## Peacock Office Supplies

**Send order to:**
**Name:** Christopher Dixon    **E-mail:** chrisdixon@foxcox.com    **Company:** Fox&Cox Inc.

Please indicate which information you would like to have on your office products and how you want it laid out.

| | File folders | Pens | Business Cards |
|---|---|---|---|
| Company name | ✓ | ✓ | ✓ |
| Company address | | | ✓ |
| Company logo | ✓ | ✓ | ✓ |
| Company website | ✓ | | ✓ |
| Individual name | ✓ | | ✓ |
| Individual phone number | | | ✓ |
| Individual e-mail address | | | ✓ |
| Design layout code | *AD7* | *GK3* | *HL4* |
| Quantity | *20* | *500* | *100* |

After one week of your order being placed, one of our design team members will contact you via e-mail. They will attach a digital copy of the images that you have chosen to go on your office equipment. Please approve these designs or inform us of any changes that you wish to make. We will not go ahead with the order unless we receive confirmation that all images are correct.

Remember to complete the form in its entirety and return it with all the information, including your individual and company details as well as your company logo.

To: Bryan Gibbs <bryangibbs@peakcocksupplies.com>

From: Christopher Dixon <chrisdixon@foxcox.com>

Date: 6 May

Re: Order for Fox & Cox Inc.

Dear Mr. Gibbs,

Having reviewed the information you provided last week, I have decided to change the design layout code of the pens. I would prefer to apply BG33 instead, and add our company website, www.foxcox.com. Once you have made the changes, can you send me the updated version? Everything else is perfect.

Additionally, I am making a presentation at a marketing conference in Berne next month and would like to take some products with the new design with me. Other agencies will be attending, and I want to make an impact. I know your company carries customized corporate items, such as T-shirts, for promotion. Please e-mail me your latest brochure with the prices for these items. In addition, is it possible to add my new choice to this order for one invoice payment, or is it necessary to raise a separate purchase order? Please advise me.

Many thanks.

Christopher Dixon
Marketing Manager
Fox & Cox Inc.

**196.** What is suggested about Peacock Office Supplies?

(A) It will open a new branch in May.
(B) It will host a marketing conference next month.
(C) It doesn't have a team of designers.
(D) It was voted as the best supplier of office products.

**197.** Who submitted the order to Peacock Office Supplies?

(A) A manager at a marketing agency
(B) A logo designer of a design team
(C) An office equipment manufacturer
(D) An editor at the *Business Times*

**198.** What are the customers asked to do to confirm their orders?

(A) Reply to an e-mail
(B) Update their information
(C) Sign an order form
(D) Visit a website

**199.** In the e-mail, what does Mr. Dixon request?

(A) A copy of the invoice for a previous order
(B) A brochure from Peacock Office Supplies
(C) Shipment of his order to Berne
(D) Changes to the quantities of orders he placed

**200.** What is suggested about Mr. Dixon?

(A) He has organized an online meeting.
(B) He is designing a new company's logo.
(C) He produced an innovative advertisement.
(D) He hopes to bring promotional items to a conference.

# ACTUAL TEST

## 答對題數表

| | |
|---|---|
| **PART 5** | |
| **PART 6** | |
| **PART 7** | |
| 總題數 | |

# 09

# READING TEST

In the Reading test, you will read a variety of texts and answer several different types of reading comprehension questions. The entire Reading test will last 75 minutes. There are three parts, and directions are given for each part. You are encouraged to answer as many questions as possible within the time allowed.

You must mark your answers on the separate answer sheet. Do not write your answers in your test book.

## PART 5

**Directions:** A word or phrase is missing in each of the sentences below. Four answer choices are given below each sentence. Select the best answer to complete the sentence. Then mark the letter (A), (B), (C), or (D) on your answer sheet.

101. ------- his one year abroad, Mr. Feltman visited London, Amsterdam, and Brussels.

(A) Behind
(B) During
(C) From
(D) Between

102. Luxembourg Electronics has ------- on a couple of selected brand-name appliances each week.

(A) discount
(B) discounts
(C) discounted
(D) discountable

103. Tacoma Computer's in-store promotion ------- customers a selection of cut-price laptops.

(A) recommends
(B) offers
(C) suggests
(D) instructs

104. Mr. Devlin insisted that in order to meet the deadline, ------- must work extra hours together.

(A) no one
(B) someone
(C) everyone
(D) one another

105. What is notable about the Taipei locality is that travelers will take pleasure in eating ------- yet inexpensive dishes and foodstuff.

(A) delicious
(B) hungry
(C) brief
(D) definite

106. The Experimental Design Company produced a range of clothes using silk and leather in an ------- popular fashion statement.

(A) astonishingly
(B) astonished
(C) astonishment
(D) astonish

107. The customer support team checked your purchase and will immediately inform you ------- the product has been placed for shipment.

(A) but
(B) once
(C) than
(D) so

108. Stock of fresh produce should ------- earlier than the market opening time tomorrow morning.

(A) arrival
(B) arriving
(C) arrive
(D) arrived

**109.** If the fire alarms go off at any time, please contact Mr. Perry in the security office for -------.

(A) assisted
(B) assistant
(C) assistance
(D) assist

**110.** The committee finally chose the design provided by Interlotze Architecture for their new workplace in Moscow following ------- reviews of the six proposals submitted to them.

(A) cares
(B) careful
(C) cared
(D) carefully

**111.** In order for Ines Marketing to keep up with competitors, all its departments have to ------- perform to the highest manufacturing standards.

(A) finely
(B) continually
(C) lately
(D) straightly

**112.** Readers depend upon *Medical Updates Weekly* for ------- information on the latest medical news.

(A) rely
(B) reliable
(C) relying
(D) reliably

**113.** Although she passed the first examination, Ms. Chan failed to get the job as it ------- to someone with better work experience.

(A) gave
(B) has given
(C) was given
(D) will have given

**114.** Only after ------- becomes qualified for the accounting certificate is Omar Jenkins subject to promotion.

(A) he
(B) his
(C) him
(D) himself

**115.** The five fabric conditioners surveyed in the latest ------- were found to have the same effect on clothing.

(A) development
(B) study
(C) history
(D) subject

**116.** The board of directors chose ------- a leading entrepreneur, Simon Rogers, for his outstanding contribution to the organization.

(A) will honor
(B) to honor
(C) would honor
(D) to be honored

**117.** If you have any questions ------- our items or carriage services, please do not hesitate to communicate with John's Floral World.

(A) regard
(B) regards
(C) regarding
(D) regarded

**118.** Because of the complaints filed by foreign clients, Gorden Stanley assured them that he intends to ------- the matter.

(A) go ahead
(B) show up
(C) look into
(D) act out

**119.** The Santiago Photocopier Company has issued a press release, which is targeted at ------- clients to take their old machines in for repair.

(A) encouraging
(B) to encourage
(C) encourage
(D) encourages

**120.** Workers require written ------- from their manager in order to borrow equipment.

(A) authorizes
(B) authorized
(C) authorization
(D) authorize

121. The Talking Leaves Corporation ------- provides customers with the latest information about its organic syrup products.
(A) perfectly
(B) regularly
(C) equally
(D) considerably

122. The following is a list of the conditions that were most commonly ------- by the employees within the company.
(A) stipulating
(B) stipulated
(C) have stipulated
(D) stipulation

123. Mr. Vasquez will open the Pierce mobile phone's production branch ------- it is fully prepared.
(A) as well as
(B) thanks to
(C) due to
(D) as soon as

124. Owing to the recent oil price surge, all production of excessive stocks ------- until further notice.
(A) are deferring
(B) have deferred
(C) have been deferring
(D) will be deferred

125. When it comes to purchases, Townsend Industries assures its customers that they will receive their items ------- two business days.
(A) through
(B) within
(C) around
(D) behind

126. Thanks to the ------- number of foreign customers, Lloyd Bank is fast becoming one of the most promising financial groups.
(A) growing
(B) unknown
(C) costly
(D) closed

127. Perfect for presents, Allan's Premium Coffee Beans are packaged in a ------- colored case.
(A) bright
(B) brightly
(C) brightness
(D) brighten

128. ------- is especially convincing about the proposed rail link is its proximity to the airport.
(A) Which
(B) That
(C) Why
(D) What

129. Without ------- from the author, no part of the article can be used elsewhere.
(A) permission
(B) reluctance
(C) identification
(D) association

130. The Flying Panda Travel Agency, specializing in honeymoon travel packages, is at its ------- between April and June.
(A) busy
(B) busier
(C) busily
(D) busiest

# PART 6

**Directions:** Read the texts that follow. A word, phrase, or sentence is missing in parts of each text. Four answer choices for each question are given below the text. Select the best answer to complete the text. Then mark the letter (A), (B), (C), or (D) on your answer sheet.

**Questions 131-134** refer to the following notice.

The main objective of the Image Nature Stocks publication is to ------- taking photos in the
**131.**
natural surroundings of the wilderness. -------. Apparatus and methods used to capture these
**132.**
images are also discussed in this editorial. Hobbyists and freelance ------- are the ones
**133.**
responsible for submission to this publication, which is issued once every two months.

Snapshots and articles on matters that happened from September are currently being

considered. -------, due to the pressure and the workload that we deal with every day, no
**134.**
feedback is given to individuals who send materials to us. For more information, please visit our

website at www.imagenaturestocks.com.

131. (A) impress
    (B) promote
    (C) impose
    (D) fund

132. (A) This can be a good piece of evidence supporting industrial evolution.
    (B) Those images captured by the space telescope reveal the wonders of outer space.
    (C) Remarkable outdoor scenery and wildlife are the main things concentrated on by this publication.
    (D) We've been looking for feedback from various users who have rated these magazines on our website.

133. (A) professional
    (B) profession
    (C) professionally
    (D) professionals

134. (A) However
    (B) Likewise
    (C) For example
    (D) Therefore

*Go on to the next page*

**To:** Bobby Wright <wbobby@bigmail.com>

**From:** International Association of Miners <admin@associationofminers.com>

**Date:** August 2

**Subject:** Membership information

Dear Mr. Wright,

The International Association of Miners would like to congratulate you on joining our

organization, which ------- the well-being and security of the global mining community by means
      **135.**

of conducting numerous programs and services that address the needs of miners worldwide.

Our ------- mission is to make mining construction better by promoting strict safety measures
   **136.**

in the industry. -------, we offer professionally developed materials for new and experienced
       **137.**

miners on our website, which includes the latest information on the subject of mining rules and

regulations.

-------. We hope to help you to become a better and safer mining expert.
**138.**

Sincerely,

International Association of Miners

---

**135.** (A) supports
    (B) supported
    (C) having supported
    (D) would be supporting

**136.** (A) frequent
    (B) primary
    (C) early
    (D) previous

**137.** (A) However
    (B) By the way
    (C) Furthermore
    (D) As far as I know

**138.** (A) An application for admission is attached to this e-mail.
    (B) This is the first time that we are offering this exceptional opportunity to local miners in Ghana.
    (C) We want you to join our organization in the future, to keep updated with the latest.
    (D) Attached herewith is a document that outlines the advantages of membership.

Questions 139-142 refer to the following article.

Vice president Randolph Ward has unveiled that his ambitious project, Grand Bloom, is expected to be completed in May in Columbia, Missouri. Presently in the finishing stages of construction, the project consists of a brand-named shopping center and leisure complex.

------- will be located on Olson Boulevard.
**139.**

Mr. Ward is organizing a competition to find the best name for the facilities, which will occupy approximately 1,000 square meters and which will have a great ------- of Dawn River.
**140.**

When asked what tips he would give to participants, Mr. Ward commented, "Bear in mind that the premises are surrounded by the river. The successfully-chosen name ------- that." The
**141.**

results will be announced at the end of next month. -------.
**142.**

**139.** (A) Both
(B) Few
(C) Several
(D) Some

**140.** (A) preference
(B) exterior
(C) appearance
(D) view

**141.** (A) reflects
(B) reflected
(C) is reflecting
(D) should reflect

**142.** (A) Mr. Ward is now looking for a site to build this facility.
(B) The prize winner will receive a one-year membership to the complex.
(C) The drawing was held in the new shopping center, and the result was surprising.
(D) The names will be announced at the groundbreaking ceremony.

ACTUAL TEST 09

PART 6

*Go on to the next page*

Questions 143-146 refer to the following e-mail.

**To:** Reginald Reed <reginaldreed@umail.com>

**From:** Aneroid Rental Shop <manager@arentals.com>

**Date:** Wednesday, August 13

**Subject:** Overdue DVD items


Our rental records show that the following items were supposed to be returned to the rental shop

on August 5: *Raining Dark Night* and *An Isolated Island*. Please take ------- back here by the end of
                                                                         **143.**

the week.


-------. However, the items mentioned in the following list are not ------- for the extension: new
**144.**                                                              **145.**

arrivals, overdue items, and those which have been booked by other rental customers.


------- we have sent you this notification as a reminder, please note that it is the customer's
**146.**

responsibility to return or renew our items by the deadline.


Thank you.

143. (A) it
(B) ours
(C) this
(D) them

144. (A) You may not lease, sublicense, rent,
or resell this DVD.
(B) If so, we can renew the due date as
long as they are new arrivals.
(C) Remember that rented DVDs can be
renewed up to seven days by calling
the shop.
(D) It is our responsibility to return the
overdue items.

145. (A) eligible
(B) displayed
(C) finished
(D) capable

146. (A) Except
(B) Although
(C) Likewise
(D) In case

## PART 7

**Directions:** In this part you will read a selection of texts, such as magazine and newspaper articles, e-mails, and instant messages. Each text or set of texts is followed by several questions. Select the best answer for each question and mark the letter (A), (B), (C), or (D) on your answer sheet.

**Questions 147-148** refer to the following information.

# Healing Dream Training Gym
# Uniforms

Newly appointed personal trainers at the Healing Dream Training Gym will be issued with three uniforms that they must wear when training clients. Two are indoor uniforms, and the third is to be kept for outdoor training. These uniforms are free to employees for the mandatory probation period of two months. However, employees who leave within this time will be required to pay for the cost of them. This money will automatically be deducted from the final paycheck as per our terms and conditions of employment. Uniforms must be kept clean at all times; please note that personal trainers have free access to our on-site laundry, which is located in the basement of the building.

**147.** Where would the information most likely be found?

(A) In a travel brochure
(B) In an expense claim
(C) In an employee handbook
(D) In a clothing store

**148.** What is mentioned about the Healing Dream Training Gym?

(A) It only offers indoor training.
(B) It has its own laundry.
(C) It manufactures the uniforms itself.
(D) It is closed for two months of the year.

*Go on to the next page*

# 7th Used Furniture Fair
# with Annual Secondhand Goods Auction

Featuring hundreds of mahogany antique furniture pieces
including chairs, desks, beds, and many more

Saturday, 22 November
32 Reuben Street, Brisbane

Admission: from 11:00 A.M. to 7:00 P.M.
Reception: from 5:00 P.M. to 7:00 P.M.
Auction begins at 7:30 P.M.

Tickets: $5 before 17th November; $7 at the door

For advance tickets, visit our website www.uff.com
or call us at (643) 367-3475.
The ticket price includes the catalog of auction items.

All proceeds of the event go to
Greenslopes Community Hospital.

**149.** What is the purpose of the notice?

(A) To promote the visit of a famous craftsman
(B) To advertise the sale of unique furnishings
(C) To announce the opening of a furniture store
(D) To publicize a community hospital

**150.** What is suggested about the event?

(A) There is an additional fee to attend the reception.
(B) Students receive a special discount.
(C) Antique furniture will be displayed beginning at 7:00 P.M.
(D) Tickets cost less if purchased online.

# Michael's

665 West Broadway
Vancouver, Canada

| February 12 | 4:31 P.M. |
|---|---|
| **Gym Gear** | |
| Sports Direct: jogging pants | 19.99 |
| **General Items** | |
| Brand Zest: boxing gloves and pads | 16.99 |
| Subtotal | 36.98 |
| Tax-8% | 2.96 |
| **Total** | **39.94** |
| Cash tendered | 50.00 |
| Change | 10.06 |

## Returns and Exchanges Policy

Unworn Items may be returned for a refund or exchanged for credit vouchers within 30 days of purchase. These items must be in like-new condition, and the original receipt of purchase must be included. Items purchased on sale cannot be refunded at any time. These items may, however, be exchanged for goods of the same value and must be accompanied by the original receipt.

**151.** What type of store most likely is Michael's?

(A) A souvenir shop
(B) A sports store
(C) A music store
(D) A rental store

**152.** What is true about the store's policy?

(A) All exchanges require an original receipt.
(B) All returned items incur an 8 percent restocking fee.
(C) All purchases must be paid in cash.
(D) All sale items must be in original packaging.

Questions 153-154 refer to the following text message chain.

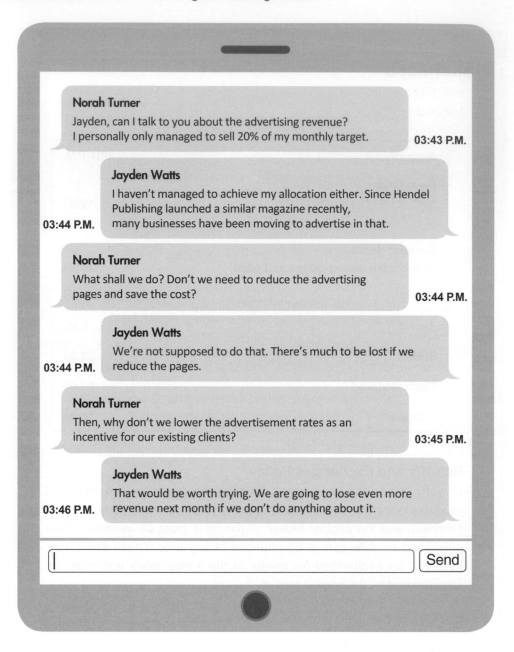

**Norah Turner**

Jayden, can I talk to you about the advertising revenue?
I personally only managed to sell 20% of my monthly target.

03:43 P.M.

**Jayden Watts**

03:44 P.M.

I haven't managed to achieve my allocation either. Since Hendel
Publishing launched a similar magazine recently,
many businesses have been moving to advertise in that.

**Norah Turner**

What shall we do? Don't we need to reduce the advertising
pages and save the cost?

03:44 P.M.

**Jayden Watts**

03:44 P.M.

We're not supposed to do that. There's much to be lost if we
reduce the pages.

**Norah Turner**

Then, why don't we lower the advertisement rates as an
incentive for our existing clients?

03:45 P.M.

**Jayden Watts**

03:46 P.M.

That would be worth trying. We are going to lose even more
revenue next month if we don't do anything about it.

Send

153. What problem is being discussed?

(A) A product's development has been
delayed.
(B) Advertising revenue is falling.
(C) The magazine circulation has been
reduced.
(D) Staff turnover has been increasing.

154. At 3:46 P.M., What does Mr. Watts mean
when he writes, "That would be worth
trying"?

(A) The company shouldn't make any
changes.
(B) He has to cut down the cost by
reducing the pages.
(C) They can offer discounts to current
advertisers.
(D) He wants Ms. Turner to try harder next
month.

## Tapas La Mancha

*Sanchez Pietro, Owner*
*Reviewed by Helene Labore*

**Overall rating: 3 out of 5 stars ★★★☆☆**

**Atmosphere: 3 stars**
Sanchez Pietro refurbished the venue last month. —[1]—. It is spacious inside and has a distinct Spanish theme. However, the noise from the kitchen was loud, and there seemed to be a lack of privacy for couples who were dining.

**Service: 4 stars**
The service was very good with the serving staff extremely polite and efficient. —[2]—. The food arrived quickly and dishes were cleared as soon as we finished our meal.

**Food: 2 stars**
The menu was not very varied and had not really changed from the last time I visited the restaurant, three years ago. —[3]—. I enjoyed the main meal, although the fish was slightly overcooked. The desserts were a big disappointment, as there was little choice and they were tasteless.

**Value : 4 stars**
Although some of the items on the menu are overpriced, on the whole, the meals are relatively inexpensive. —[4]—. The wine list is also very pricey, but the main dishes are true bargains.

**155.** What is the purpose of the information?

(A) To announce the reopening of a restaurant
(B) To summarize the expansion plans of a restaurant
(C) To promote special menus that will be introduced at a restaurant
(D) To assess the quality of a restaurant

**156.** What is suggested about the restaurant?

(A) Its menu items are overall value for money.
(B) It hosts live musical events.
(C) Its menu has significantly changed over these years.
(D) It is located within a city center.

**157.** In which of the positions marked [1], [2], [3], and [4] does the following sentence best belong?

"The portions were small, and the tapas starters were not very tasty."

(A) [1]
(B) [2]
(C) [3]
(D) [4]

*Go on to the next page*

Alltrue Digital Equipment
355 Tree Drive
Sacramento, CA 94203

16 March

Alexander Soskin
2541 Angel Place
Santa Barbara, CA 93109

Dear Mr. Soskin,

We have enclosed the radio that you returned to us for repair. Unfortunately, we are unable to complete the repairs as the fault to the appliance is not covered under our two-year general guarantee.

We have ascertained that the original sound box has been replaced by a component that is not compatible with our brand of audio equipment. Please see the enclosed report from our repair officer for clarification. Our guarantee is also enclosed, which clearly states that should any part be replaced or altered, the work must be carried out by our repair team using our own approved components. The guarantee does not cover unauthorized tampering with the appliance and, therefore, we are unable to repair this appliance under the terms and conditions of the guarantee. If, however, you still wish to have the item repaired, we can do so at a cost of $100.

Many thanks for your cooperation in this matter and for purchasing an item from Alltrue Digital Equipment.

Yours sincerely,

Kevin Constant
Customer Services Manager
Enclosures

---

**158.** What is the main purpose of the letter?

(A) To explain why a request was not fulfilled
(B) To thank a customer for a recent purchase
(C) To request a call back from a repairperson
(D) To request information about digital equipment

**159.** What is NOT included with the letter?

(A) A guarantee
(B) A findings report
(C) A refund
(D) A radio

**160.** What is Mr. Soskin advised to do?

(A) Repair the item himself
(B) Pay for repairs
(C) Purchase an extended warranty
(D) Call an Alltrue Customer Service manager

| | | |
|---|---|---|
| | **Allison Green** [09:43 A.M.] | Good morning, Timothy. I heard you are meeting our Spanish guests when they come on Monday. |
| | **Timothy Moore** [09:43 A.M.] | Hello, Allison. That meeting's giving me a headache. |
| | **Allison Green** [09:44 A.M.] | What's the matter? You speak Spanish pretty well. |
| | **Timothy Moore** [09:45 A.M.] | As a matter of fact, you know I have to prepare for the sales presentation on Tuesday. I just don't have enough time to take care of the Monday meeting. |
| | **Allison Green** [09:46 A.M.] | That must be very hard. Is there anything I can do to help you? |
| | **Timothy Moore** [09:47 A.M.] | Hmm . . . I need to find a caterer to provide lunches and some refreshments. Do you have any suggestions? |
| | **Allison Green** [09:48 A.M.] | I would say Mortime Caterers. They are very reputable, and they provide an excellent lunchtime buffet. Shall I take care of the food service? |
| | **Timothy Moore** [09:49 A.M.] | That would be great. Thank you, Allison. I owe you one. |
| | **Allison Green** [09:50 A.M.] | Don't mention it. I can call them now and see if they are available. |

**Send**

**161.** What will Mr. Moore do on Tuesday?

(A) Visit a restaurant
(B) Prepare for a business trip
(C) Give a presentation
(D) Conduct a job interview

**162.** At 09:44 A.M., what does Ms. Green mean when she writes, "You speak Spanish pretty well"?

(A) She believes Mr. Moore is able to do his job perfectly.
(B) She has a suggestion for Mr. Moore.
(C) She thinks the guests will love Spanish food.
(D) She wants to help Mr. Moore prepare for the Tuesday meeting.

**163.** What does Ms. Green offer to do?

(A) Provide a buffet
(B) Contact a service
(C) Recommend a restaurant
(D) Purchase a new phone

*Go on to the next page*

## Company Library Cards

The Law Society's library system enables members of the business community to use its facilities.

Employees of businesses within the local area will be eligible for a company library card. The cost is just $40 a year, although the fee is waived for charities and nonprofit organizations.

A company library card can be used by local businesses for research purposes, and employees should take responsibility for any books or papers they might borrow. The cardholder is responsible for any fines incurred for late or lost materials.

To apply for a company library card, you must fill out an application form at the library's reception desk. This must be accompanied by a photo identification, a letter confirming your position at your organization, and the fee to join. We will then provide you with a receipt.

If you have any queries, contact us at the main law office at 555-9284.

**164.** What is the purpose of the notice?

(A) To explain a service
(B) To propose an idea
(C) To correct a mistake
(D) To announce an opening

**165.** What is stated about annual fees?

(A) Certain organizations are exempt.
(B) They can be paid by credit card.
(C) They are higher for out-of-town businesses.
(D) They are refunded after a year.

**166.** According to the notice, what must a borrower do if materials are lost?

(A) Waive their membership
(B) Report the loss to their supervisor
(C) Return their company library card
(D) Pay a fine to the library

**167.** What is NOT required at the time of application?

(A) Proof of identity
(B) Payment
(C) Confirmation of employment
(D) A signed contract

# Manager's Behavior

In his new book, *Etiquette in the Workplace*, Manuel Rodriguez gives advice to managers on how to earn and gain respect from employees by behaving in the appropriate manner. —[1]—. Mr. Rodriguez explains that managers who hold a responsible position should conduct themselves in a manner that befits their status, not just in an office environment but in social situations, especially those organized by the company for which they work.

For example, a manager should be in attendance at a social event such as an awards ceremony where other senior employees are invited. This is part of a manager's role. However, a social event such as a sports tournament with more junior members of staff can be avoided. Nevertheless, managers should decline any such invitations with a polite refusal.

—[2]—. A manager should always appear neat and well-groomed. Punctuality is mandatory. When a manager is attending an event arranged by the company, he or she must acknowledge coworkers who are not seen often and ensure that he or she is familiar with their names as a matter of courtesy. Also, it is compulsory for a manager to praise the organizers of events and acknowledge the effort that has gone into making an event successful for all attendees.

Mr. Rodriguez has been writing online for many years and has been recognized as one of the leading authorities on workplace etiquette. —[3]—. He is a regular contributor to television and his book, *Etiquette in the Workplace*, has already sold over 200,000 copies since its publication six months ago, through Mitchell Hamden. —[4]—. It can be ordered online through www.mitchellhamden.com.

**168.** What does the article primarily discuss?

(A) A book about appropriate behavior for managers
(B) A guide to solving improper workplace issues
(C) A leaflet about organizing social events
(D) A brochure about maintaining employment levels

**169.** What is suggested about Mr. Rodriguez?

(A) He has worked for the same company for years.
(B) He is a very successful writer.
(C) He will finish writing his book within six months.
(D) He organizes the company's social events.

**170.** What kind of business does Mitchell Hamden specialize in?

(A) Event organizing
(B) Online design
(C) Employment benefits
(D) Book publishing

**171.** In which of the positions marked [1], [2], [3], and [4] does the following sentence best belong?

"In addition, a good appearance is essential."

(A) [1]
(B) [2]
(C) [3]
(D) [4]

*Go on to the next page*

# Gordon Industries

**To:** All staff
**From:** Grace Elliott
**Date:** June 11
**Re:** Holiday Schedule

Well done for helping Gordon Industries successfully complete its largest contract in the company's nine-year history. As a reward for your hard work, we are organizing a Family Week in the month of July. For one week during the summer vacation, we are holding numerous events to which you and your family are invited free of charge. We hope that the next few years will bring as much success to Gordon Industries, and we are showing our appreciation with the week of events. See below for a day-by-day schedule.

| DATE | EVENT | LOCATION | TIME |
|------|-------|----------|------|
| Monday, July 25 | Water play | Magic Springs Water Park | 11 A.M. to 6 P.M. |
| Tuesday, July 26 | Family picnic | Hot Springs Park Campsite | All Day |
| Wednesday, July 27 | Outdoor activities | Hot Springs Park (See department notice boards for a breakdown of locations) | All day |
| Thursday, July 28 | Field Day (Basketball, Softball, Soccer) | Park Recreation Center | 1 P.M. to 5 P.M. |
| Friday, July 29 | Dance party and children's entertainment | Hot Springs Park Campsite | 3 P.M. to 6 P.M. |

My personal secretary, Amanda Cole, has already booked the children's entertainment and caterers for the event. Before it reaches the fixed number, please call her at extension 256 as soon as possible. There will also be a barbeque party after the sports competition. To sign up for the tournaments, please give your name to Jared Murphy in management support. There will be prizes for the winning teams.

I hope you are all looking forward to the Family Week, as it will be a chance for you to relax and enjoy the company of your family and colleagues. I hope to see everyone there.

Grace Elliott
President
Gordon Industries

**172.** Why was the memo written?

(A) To inform employees of management changes
(B) To introduce a week of family-oriented events
(C) To announce the signing of a major contract
(D) To recruit teams for a sporting event

**173.** How are staff members asked to contact Ms. Cole?

(A) By making a phone call
(B) By registering online
(C) By visiting her office
(D) By sending an e-mail

**174.** When is the barbeque party?

(A) On Monday
(B) On Tuesday
(C) On Wednesday
(D) On Thursday

**175.** What is suggested about Ms. Elliot?

(A) She is the founder of Gordon Industries.
(B) She won't be able to join the Family Week.
(C) She has a nine-year-old son.
(D) She wants to reward her employees with a special event.

*Go on to the next page*

**Supreme Economy News**
**Top Gambling Companies See Expansion in Workforce**

January 7 — Many of the major gambling companies in the Blenheim district have seen a rapid increase in their workforces over the past six months. These are the findings of a report released yesterday from the Conglomeration of Online Casinos. In total, each of the district's top five companies employed 15% more employees compared to the period between July and December last year.

The leading company is Offshore Developments, currently the market leader in the gambling industry. More than 150 staff members were employed at casinos in Blenheim in the latter half of last year. Most of these employees were headhunted from Blake Soft, a small software company specializing in financial program development, which Offshore Developments acquired last June. Two other companies in the industry, Lucky Thistle and Crown Rooms (both specializing in online poker), also joined forces.

The Conglomeration of Online Casinos only takes revenue from gambling establishments in Blenheim into account when publishing its rankings. Each of the top five companies accrued over $1.2 million in annual revenues. Lucky Thistle generated profits of approximately $1.2 million, with Offshore Developments reporting a $1.3 million net profit.

Marcel Prost

# Offshore Developments to Invest in Latest Technology

March 30 — David Carruthers, Chairman of Offshore Developments, is reportedly investing in new software: Marking Up, an online corporate financial program that was tested earlier this year.

This is the first time that Offshore Developments has entered the corporate market. In the past, the company has dealt solely with the individual consumer gambling market. Mark Owen, the business strategy director of Offshore Developments, says, "So that we can develop the technology that will enable corporations to enter the gambling market, we had to hire a number of experts in financial software."

The company has been listed as one of the leading five firms by the Conglomeration of Online Casinos for a number of years, with an average annual profit margin of $1.3 million. This year, the turnover has increased since January with profits of $0.7 million already generated and an additional $4.5 million expected by December.

*G. Harker*

**176.** What is the first article about?

(A) New gambling products released in the marketplace
(B) Marketing methods for gambling firms
(C) Employment growth in large gambling companies
(D) Employee satisfaction in the gambling industry

**177.** In the first article, the word "period" in paragraph 1, line 5, is closest in meaning to

(A) growth
(B) interval
(C) conclusion
(D) exercise

**178.** What is indicated about Offshore Developments?

(A) It is an Internet-based company.
(B) It sells casino supplies.
(C) It has several international offices.
(D) It took over a software company.

**179.** What is suggested about Marking Up?

(A) It is the first product designed by Mr. Carruthers.
(B) Almost two million dollars in sales has already been achieved.
(C) It has been designed for the corporate market.
(D) Customers have criticized it for not being user-friendly.

**180.** How much revenue does Offshore Developments anticipate from January to December?

(A) $1.3 million
(B) $4.5 million
(C) $5.2 million
(D) $6.5 million

*Go on to the next page*

**Questions 181-185** refer to the following e-mail and information.

To: Dieter Van Hugen <dvh@pph.com>

From: Avril Labasse <avrilla@pph.com>

Date: May 12

Subject: Exhibition

Attachment: Minefall Conference Center download

Dear Dieter,

Many thanks for your offer to help with PPH Limited's preparations for the forthcoming Technical Exhibition. This year's show will be from June 21 to 24 and, as in the previous year, the venue will be the Minefall Conference Center. For past exhibitions, I have rented the Benton Room, which allowed us to present our new products and stage a number of seminars. Over the four days, we attracted nearly 1000 people, on average 250 a day. We expect the exhibition to be even bigger this year.

In order to prepare for this eventuality, I would ask you to rent a bigger space. Although the room accommodated all attendees comfortably, the presentation facilities were inadequate. We had to rely upon the center's staff to supply and set up the presentation equipment. Although the feedback was excellent for the most part, a number of attendees complained about the quality of the visual material. This must be rectified this year.

Previously, we held a reception for invited guests in the Manila Suite at the end of the week. This time, we prefer to take them somewhere more upmarket. I suggest either Brown's Restaurant or the Quayside Brasserie to avoid self-catering. Please note, I will make the necessary arrangements and forward the details to you.

Please check the enclosed brochure for the most suitable room for our requirements. As the deadline is only two weeks away, you will need to reserve a suitable room with a deposit as quickly as possible.

Please contact me with any questions or problems that may arise.

Avril Labasse

## Minefall
## CONFERENCE CENTER
*ROOM RENTAL*

**Manila Suite:** This is our biggest room, with daylight ingress to three sides. It is able to accommodate up to 400 guests for any celebration or business event. Catering is supplied by the in-house Minefall Catering Department. Costs begin at $300 for morning or afternoon hire, $500 for the full-day hire. Catering costs are additional.

**The Fortune Room and Day Room:** These are perfect for small private meetings or seminars, with a capacity of 50 people. Equipped for business, these rooms include telephone, computer with Internet access, overhead projector, and dark-colored curtains. Fees for the Fortune Room begin at $200 for a half day and $300 for a full day. The Day Room is slightly larger and has audio facilities. Prices for the Day Room are $220 for a half day and for a $320 full day.

**Sentinel Suite:** Ideal for large-scale presentations, events, and seminars. This room is equipped with a floor-to-ceiling projection screen, stage, lighting, and an all-around sound system. This luxurious suite holds up to 350 guests comfortably. Prices begin at $500 per half day and $700 per day. There Is an added fee for catering services.

**Polar Patio:** Adjacent to the Sentinel Suite, this outdoor venue is available for receptions and refreshments. The cost is $310 for three hours but comes free with the hire of the Sentinel Suite. There Is an added fee for catering services.

181. What most likely was Ms. Labasse's role in last year's exhibition?

(A) She organized PPH Limited's event.
(B) She chose a catering service.
(C) She set up some equipment.
(D) She gave a presentation.

182. How is this year's exhibition expected to be different from last year's?

(A) It will be opened by a celebrity.
(B) It will attract even more visitors.
(C) It will be held at an alternative venue.
(D) It will include additional exhibitors.

183. What problem probably occurred at last year's show?

(A) Some people could not see the presentation screen clearly.
(B) The event location was changed before the exhibition.
(C) The reserved room was too noisy.
(D) A presenter didn't make it in time.

184. Who provided the food services at PPH Limited's reception last year?

(A) Minefall Catering
(B) Polar Patio
(C) Quayside Brasseries
(D) Brown's Restaurant

185. Which space will PPH Limited be likely to reserve this year?

(A) Day Room
(B) Manila Suite
(C) Fortune Room
(D) Sentinel Suite

*Go on to the next page*

## The London branch of Melton Manufacturing is seeking an experienced manager to join the production team!

Melton Manufacturing has been a leading manufacturer and distributor of top-quality automotive parts in the U.K. for half a century. We provide automobile companies both here and abroad with hundreds of car and truck parts.

The production manager will have the responsibility of training and monitoring a production team of 50 full-time staff members as well as many temporary and seasonal workers. The manager is also in charge of the factory environment, ensuring the health and safety of all employees. We are looking for someone with at least four years of relevant experience who has spent one year in the same industry. The successful candidate is expected to work out of hours to oversee deliveries and shipments.

Candidates must be familiar with the production and distribution of materials as well as have a working knowledge of handling requirements. Computer expertise on SPA 43 is also required. Interested parties should send their applications along with a cover letter and references to Tony Beach, Melton Manufacturing, 13 Ryville Crescent, London WR11 4BD.

To: Tony Beach <tonybeach@melton.com>

From: Adam Stern <adamstern@gomail.com>

Date: September 8

Subject: A letter of reference

Attachment: Adam_Stern_Reference.doc

Dear Mr. Beach,

I was surprised by your e-mail. I thought I had enclosed the reference with my résumé; it seems I missed it. I append Mr. Bushell's letter herewith. I'm glad to hear that my résumé is impressive. As to the SPA 43 you inquired about, I qualified for it 5 years ago. I had undertaken an evening course after work for it, and now I am in charge of employee computer training.

Please let me know when I should visit you for an interview. As London is far away from here, I'll need to find a place to stay one night. Again, thank you for considering me for this position.

Sincerely,

Adam Stern

August 27
Mr. Beach
Melton Manufacturing
13 Ryville Crescent
London WR11 4BD

Dear Mr. Beach,

This is a reference for Adam Stern, who is applying for the job of production manager within your organization. I have worked with Mr. Stern for five of his seven years at Packaging Express, where he began as a temporary worker before I took him on full time. Mr. Stern is an extremely competent employee and is currently employed as production supervisor here. He has been particularly instrumental in the implementation and commissioning of new production line equipment that has sped up the production process and reduced wastage.

Mr. Stern is fully qualified for the position advertised and, in addition, has extensive work experience. He has just completed an HNQ in management at Kings Cross College as well as numerous in-house courses.

I have every faith in Mr. Stern's capability for this job, as he has the ability to adapt to any work demands. Please contact me for any further information.


Sincerely,

Trey Bushell
Production Director

**186.** What is suggested about Melton Manufacturing?

(A) It distributes safety equipment.
(B) It offers computer training.
(C) It recently expanded into the U.K.
(D) It specializes in automotive parts.

**187.** According to the job posting, what must the production manager be willing to do?

(A) Handle heavy machinery
(B) Hire team members
(C) Work overtime
(D) Sign a one-year contract

**188.** Why does Mr. Bushell write the letter?

(A) To explain a delay in a shipment
(B) To welcome a new team member
(C) To apply for a new job
(D) To recommend an employee

**189.** What is indicated about Mr. Stern?

(A) He has experience in overseas sales.
(B) He teaches a course at Kings Cross College.
(C) He is skilled in the use of a computer software program.
(D) He is looking for a part-time position at Melton Manufacturing.

**190.** What does Mr. Stern ask Mr. Beach to do?

(A) Visit him at his earliest convenience
(B) Write him a letter of reference
(C) Inform him of a date
(D) Send him an application form

*Go on to the next page*

**Questions 191-195** refer to the following e-mails and form.

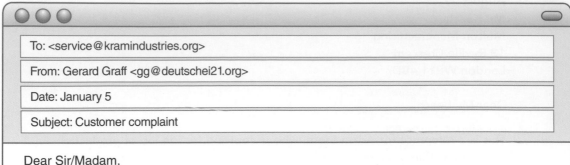

To: <service@kramindustries.org>

From: Gerard Graff <gg@deutschei21.org>

Date: January 5

Subject: Customer complaint

Dear Sir/Madam,

I wish to report a problem with a new wardrobe (catalog number #92). I followed the assembly instructions strictly. However, the wardrobe tilts to one side as the wrong panel was supplied, which is one inch too short. I would like you to replace the panel so that I can reassemble this piece of furniture.

I apologize for the delay in contacting you. I purchased the wardrobe on November 2 but, due to a hospital placement abroad of over two months, I was unable to attempt to assemble the item. I have the packaging in which the item was supplied and can send the receipt issued by your store if necessary.


Sincerely,

Gerard Graff

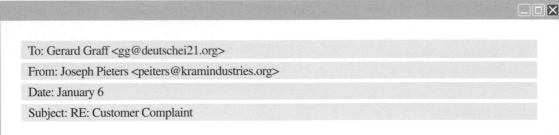

To: Gerard Graff <gg@deutschei21.org>

From: Joseph Pieters <peiters@kramindustries.org>

Date: January 6

Subject: RE: Customer Complaint

Dear Mr. Graff,

Thank you for the e-mail regarding your purchase. We apologize for the difficulties you have had with assembling this item and will send you a replacement part free of charge. We operate a store policy stating that if the item purchased is less than two months old, it can be returned with the original receipt and in its original packaging. For items bought over two months ago, our policy is that they can only be returned if discovered to be damaged at the time of purchase. This necessitates a Faulty Return Form to be completed. This can be found on our website complaints page: www.kramindustries.org/returns. After the form is filled out and submitted, a Merchandise Return Code will be e-mailed to you. For full details on the policies, please see the website.

I hope this is useful information. We would request that you complete a feedback form attached about your experience with the customer service department. Once completed, you will receive a voucher for 15% off your next purchase with our store.

Joseph Pieters
Manager

## Customer Feedback

**Name:** Gerard Graff
**Overall rating:** ★★★★☆ (Good)
**Comments:** I reported a problem with a wardrobe by e-mail, and I received a reply on the following day. I followed the faulty return procedure as informed and got a replacement for the defective part. Thanks to your help, I was able to finish assembling it correctly. However, the illustration on the manual was not very accurate, and I experienced inconvenience in recognizing the problem with the panel. I think that should be corrected as soon as possible. Except for that, I was generally pleased with your service.

**191.** What problem with the product does Mr. Graff report?

(A) A part is defective.
(B) An instruction manual is missing.
(C) The size is wrong for his bedroom.
(D) It is the wrong color.

**192.** What most likely is Mr. Graff's job?

(A) Teaching woodwork
(B) Working within a hospital
(C) Preparing meals
(D) Constructing furniture

**193.** What benefits would Mr. Graff receive from the furniture shop?

(A) A discount coupon
(B) An honorarium
(C) A new piece of furniture
(D) Free delivery

**194.** In the feedback form, the word "recognizing" in line 5, is closest in meaning to

(A) watching
(B) finding
(C) informing
(D) reporting

**195.** According to Mr. Graff, what should be revised?

(A) The assembly instructions
(B) The return code
(C) The website address
(D) The packaging

*Go on to the next page*

## Jason Falls
in the center of Urban Melbourne
business, residential, and commercial space to rent

A contemporary, up-to-date structure surrounded by existing shops and businesses. Close to the train station.
Adjacent to the War Memorial with urban park and sports stadium close by.

**Residential (Floors 2–7):** Two and three-roomed apartments comprising two bathrooms, one en-suite, kitchen-dining room, and living room. For an extra charge, parking is available in the underground car park. Shared rooftop garden as well as on-site laundry facilities.

**Offices (Floor 8–14):** Large and small offices available. Modular layout with open-plan space that can be compartmentalized. Choice of furnishings.

**Commercial (Street level):** Four shop fronts. Retail only, each 500 square meters in floor space. No dining establishments.

**Details on pricing and availability:**
Please direct residential inquiries to Garry Mason, (08) 3014-7610 or residential@jasonfalls.com.au.

Please direct commercial inquiries to Finola Castiel, (08) 3014-7620 or commercial@jasonfalls.com.au.

---

To: Finola Castiel <commercial@jasonfalls.com.au>

From: Thomas Christian <tchristian@christianbrooks.com>

Title: Jason Falls

Date: 10:01, September 2

Dear Ms. Castiel,

My business has recently expanded, and we will be employing new recruits to help with the future workload. We are currently located close to Jason Falls, but there is not enough space for new employees. I would be interested in finding out if the available office space at Jason Falls is sufficient to house 17 staff members, in Administration and Sales. I will need to see the offices for myself sometime next week.

Many thanks.

Thomas Christian

| To: | Elias Innes <e_innes@terralink.org> |
|---|---|
| From: | Finola Castiel <commercial@jasonfalls.com.au> |
| Subject: | Urgent renovation work |
| Date: | 11:30, September 2 |

Dear Mr. Innes,

My colleague Garry Mason referred you to me. I require a quote to remove three internal walls from an office, which are all two meters tall, with one being 20 centimeters thick. The other two are only 15 centimeters wide. These walls were not there originally, but set up by the last tenant's request.

The office is on the twelfth floor of the building, and there's an elevator available. I will need a team of workers who can undertake the work as soon as possible. I have a client who is interested in this office; I think those walls must be removed to accommodate all his staff. I want this renovation work to be done by Sunday.

I hope to hear from you soon.

Regards,

Finola Castiel

**196.** What is indicated about the Jason Falls building?

(A) It is near a train station.
(B) It is far from the War Memorial.
(C) It is on the outskirts of the city.
(D) It is under construction.

**197.** According to the advertisement, what is available to residential tenants for an additional cost?

(A) Cleaning facilities
(B) Underground parking
(C) An extra bedroom
(D) Use of a rooftop garden

**198.** What type of tenant is not allowed to occupy the building?

(A) A law firm
(B) A sales office
(C) A retail store
(D) A restaurant

**199.** What is suggested about Mr. Christian's company?

(A) It is relocating out of Melbourne.
(B) It recently lost some staff.
(C) It has become increasingly successful.
(D) It is changing its main business plans.

**200.** Why does Ms. Castiel want to renovate the office so urgently?

(A) She does not work on Sundays.
(B) A tenant will come to see the property soon.
(C) The walls can be hazardous for the new tenant.
(D) A tenant requests to set up some partitions.

# ACTUAL TEST

## 答對題數表

| | |
|---|---|
| **PART 5** | |
| **PART 6** | |
| **PART 7** | |
| 總題數 | |

# 10

# READING TEST

In the Reading test, you will read a variety of texts and answer several different types of reading comprehension questions. The entire Reading test will last 75 minutes. There are three parts, and directions are given for each part. You are encouraged to answer as many questions as possible within the time allowed.

You must mark your answers on the separate answer sheet. Do not write your answers in your test book.

## PART 5

**Directions:** A word or phrase is missing in each of the sentences below. Four answer choices are given below each sentence. Select the best answer to complete the sentence. Then mark the letter (A), (B), (C), or (D) on your answer sheet.

---

**101.** Dinner will be served by Walsh House ------- Hokuto Grill.

(A) but
(B) nor
(C) and
(D) yet

**102.** Diadora's new running shoe, the Runner Blade, is ------- named for its shape and agility.

(A) suitably
(B) suitable
(C) suitability
(D) suitableness

**103.** ------- in Davison Restaurant, including the expansion of its parking lot, have attracted more customers.

(A) Improved
(B) Improvement
(C) Improvements
(D) Improving

**104.** The Nooseburg Society Association will be in charge of tours of historical sites every day ------- Saturday.

(A) other
(B) except
(C) than
(D) some

**105.** San Marino Steel is now ------- a wide range of steel products for building facilities outside the city.

(A) manufacturer
(B) being manufactured
(C) manufactured
(D) manufacturing

**106.** Ms. Dennings ------- gives a hand to those in charge of the press conferences.

(A) often
(B) early
(C) less
(D) far

**107.** You may answer questions ------- the space provided on the enclosed survey form.

(A) up
(B) out
(C) in
(D) of

**108.** New training methods that could improve productivity -------.

(A) to develop
(B) developing
(C) are being developed
(D) to be developed

**109.** To receive a full refund, please ------- your items in original condition.

(A) returns
(B) returned
(C) return
(D) returning

**110.** Both Saitrich and Petrov electronics companies are financially stronger than many of ------- rival companies.

(A) theirs
(B) they
(C) their
(D) them

**111.** Mr. Vettel broke the record ------- the fastest lap time in the German Grand Prix.

(A) at
(B) within
(C) above
(D) for

**112.** The energy committee has determined that building a roof in a brighter and more reflective blue color will ------- reduce heat, especially in cities.

(A) significantly
(B) extremely
(C) utterly
(D) countlessly

**113.** Ashanti Travel Agency provides the ------- flights available from Tokyo to Beijing and Seoul.

(A) cheapness
(B) cheapen
(C) cheaply
(D) cheapest

**114.** The board of directors ------- approved the plan to make inroads into the overseas market, which was aimed at young adults in Asian countries.

(A) conditions
(B) conditioned
(C) conditional
(D) conditionally

**115.** Publics Dynamics has three facilities with a combined floor space ------- 51,500 square meters.

(A) processing
(B) totaling
(C) finishing
(D) enduring

**116.** When requesting full refunds, customers have to show ------- records including the purchase date.

(A) accurate
(B) delayed
(C) accepting
(D) distant

**117.** Walgreen Alliance deals with a high ------- of claims every day, so it needs capable employees.

(A) set
(B) size
(C) extent
(D) volume

**118.** Recent research findings for Tisler Cookware's new prototype were ------- encouraging.

(A) well
(B) near
(C) freely
(D) very

**119.** ------- several suggestions have been made to improve Manchester City's transportation system, none of them is within budget.

(A) Why
(B) Whether
(C) Although
(D) Unless

**120.** Please check ------- of your order #1282712, which will be shipped by Wednesday.

(A) receipt
(B) receive
(C) received
(D) receiving

**121.** Mr. Shinohara, a plant manager, recently ------- a tour of the facilities for brewing beer for the company's important clients.

(A) conduct
(B) conducted
(C) to conduct
(D) will conduct

**122.** The owner of Hamilton Art Gallery recruits volunteers who enjoy helping ------- with their need for tour guides.

(A) ones
(B) others
(C) any
(D) that

**123.** The board of directors interviewed five top candidates before making the ------- decision about whom to choose as a vice president.

(A) final
(B) finals
(C) finally
(D) finalize

**124.** All fountain pens ------- at Sunday's auction will be open to buyers starting on Saturday at 9:00 A.M.

(A) to be sold
(B) has been sold
(C) is selling
(D) was to sell

**125.** Official ------- is required for all of the airplanes arriving at the airport.

(A) documentation
(B) administration
(C) freight
(D) agency

**126.** As the number of travelers visiting China rises, ------- the demand for tour guides to lead them.

(A) as long as
(B) whereas
(C) so does
(D) as to

**127.** ThermoSafe, a large packaging company, specializes in ------- packaging services for insulated shipping boxes and containers.

(A) absolute
(B) savory
(C) protective
(D) expired

**128.** Neil Berret's new S/S collection features pants in a ------- variety of colors.

(A) wide
(B) width
(C) widen
(D) widely

**129.** Unfortunately, research indicated that the increase in oil prices will ------- economic recovery.

(A) interfere with
(B) correspond to
(C) fall behind
(D) rely on

**130.** All department stores should ------- with regulations regarding sales at special events.

(A) comply
(B) adhere
(C) authorize
(D) follow

## PART 6

**Directions:** Read the texts that follow. A word, phrase, or sentence is missing in parts of each text. Four answer choices for each question are given below the text. Select the best answer to complete the text. Then mark the letter (A), (B), (C), or (D) on your answer sheet.

**Questions 131-134** refer to the following e-mail.

**To:** Maria Gomez <mgomez@samail.com>
**From:** Taylor Fisher <tfisher@lapubliclibrary.com>
**Date:** May 5
**Subject:** Your inquiry

Dear Ms. Gomez,

Thank you for your inquiry about your ------- library book, *The Blossom Girl*. Although the
                                        **131.**
book is now one week overdue, I renewed it through May 12 so that the library will not keep

charging you a late fee.

I did ask my colleagues to check if they could find it on the shelves, just in case someone

could have found or ------- the book. -------.
                        **132.**          **133.**

If you cannot return the book by May 12, we will ------- a new one. In that case, you should
                                                  **134.**
bear the expenses.

Sincerely,

Taylor Fisher
Los Angeles Public Library

131. (A) miss
 (B) to miss
 (C) missing
 (D) missed

132. (A) return
 (B) returned
 (C) be returned
 (D) will return

133. (A) All library patrons are issued a
   membership card.
 (B) You can find the location on our
   website.
 (C) Unfortunately, we failed to find it.
 (D) However, we are closed on Sunday.

134. (A) order
 (B) recognize
 (C) acknowledge
 (D) identify

*Go on to the next page*

**Questions 135-138** refer to the following article.

San Francisco (March 29) — For two weeks only, Starbean will launch a limited edition of

retro packaging for their products, which dates back to thirty years ago, when the brand

------- became popular. This promotion will not apply to Starbean's existing coffee lineup. The
   **135.**

company will be introducing new drinks, including Iced Cinnamon Almond Milk Macchiato,

Coconut Milk Mocha Latte, and Caramel Cocoa Frappuccino, ------- the size compared to the
                                                              **136.**

existing options.

Starbean president Kim Perry says the packaging shows the history of the brand. -------. "We
                                                                                 **137.**

feel this promotion will attract both long-time and new customers," she said. Starbean's retro

packaging products will be available in April. And its new ------- will hit stores in May.
                                                             **138.**

**135.** (A) once
   (B) all
   (C) first
   (D) thus

**136.** (A) double
   (B) doubles
   (C) will double
   (D) doubling

**137.** (A) Market analysts predict that it will
        show disappointing quarterly earnings.
   (B) The price of coffee is expected to
        steadily increase this year.
   (C) That is why Starbean has become so
        popular.
   (D) It also appeals to customers who don't
        have time to enjoy coffee.

**138.** (A) services
   (B) functions
   (C) equipment
   (D) beverages

**To:** All staff

**From:** Accounting Department

**Date:** February 4

**Subject:** Revised Procedures

Please be aware that the reimbursement program for travel expenses has been changed.

-------, the Travel Expense Form was submitted within one month after the trip. Now, employees
**139.**

must submit the form within at least two weeks after traveling. All expenses ------- by the
**140.**

company, providing that they are properly used and have been approved beforehand. Once the

request for travel expenses has been processed, ------- of incurred expenses that have been
**141.**

approved by the company will be sent to the employee. -------. If you need further information,
**142.**

please visit our website at www.tesoro.com/reimbursementprogram.

139. (A) Consequently
(B) Exceedingly
(C) Previously
(D) Eventually

140. (A) pays
(B) paid
(C) have been paying
(D) will be paid

141. (A) notifies
(B) notified
(C) notifying
(D) notification

142. (A) Please e-mail this form to the accounting department.
(B) The company has been encouraging all staff to travel abroad.
(C) The travel expenses will be reimbursed by the proper procedures.
(D) Business trips are restricted due to the financial problems the company has faced.

*Go on to the next page*

---

*www.staplesbestworkplaceaward.com/about*

## About the Award

Organizations with top performance throughout the U.S. give a boost to the country's economy.

Over the years, we've witnessed that ------- success is mostly attributable to having an
                                              **143.**

engaged workforce. Enthusiastic employees tend to have a positive impact on their coworkers.

-------. The Staples Best Workplace Award was ------- fifteen years ago to honor successful
**144.**                                                **145.**

companies whose employees are dedicated to their work. -------, hundreds of organizations
                                                      **146.**

throughout the U.S. have already received the award. If you would like to know about a

complete list of award winners, go to the Recipient page.

---

**143.** (A) his
(B) when
(C) where
(D) their

**144.** (A) Sometimes this can cause customer complaints.
(B) The award ceremony will be held in June.
(C) Only large companies are entitled to receive the prize.
(D) This can be seen in higher productivity.

**145.** (A) established
(B) appealed
(C) asked
(D) inspired

**146.** (A) Now that
(B) On the other hand
(C) Since then
(D) Nevertheless

# PART 7

**Directions:** In this part you will read a selection of texts, such as magazine and newspaper articles, e-mails, and instant messages. Each text or set of texts is followed by several questions. Select the best answer for each question and mark the letter (A), (B), (C), or (D) on your answer sheet.

**Questions 147-148** refer to the following advertisement.

---

## *Nucor Center*

- **More than 40 exciting outdoor sports**
- **More than 50 amazing games with reasonable prices**
- **Special music festival all year round**
- **The country's largest indoor food court**
- **A play area designed only for children under five**

Nucor Center is open throughout the year, Monday through Sunday.

Tickets can be purchased online or at the main gate.

Group discounts apply for groups of 12 or more.

---

**147.** What is being advertised?

(A) A music concert
(B) A competition
(C) An amusement park
(D) A design festival

**148.** Who is eligible for a discount?

(A) People buying tickets as a group
(B) People visiting more than five times a month
(C) People purchasing tickets online
(D) People under five years of age

**Questions 149-150** refer to following information.

## Omnicom S9 Mobile

Thank you for purchasing the Omnicom S9 mobile phone. Your new phone includes state-of-the-art features to make your life more enjoyable. This user manual offers you easy-to-follow instructions for your new mobile phone. If you want to avoid any possibility of damaging your Omnicom S9, please check the list of precautions on page 25 concerning accessories, including battery chargers, phone cases, batteries, and earphones.

**149.** What is the purpose of the information?
- (A) To promote the mobile phone's warranty program
- (B) To offer a discount on electronic devices
- (C) To advise customers to take a look at the manual
- (D) To encourage consumers to buy a new phone

**150.** What is suggested about mobile phone accessories?
- (A) Omnicom S9 includes all of them at no extra cost.
- (B) Using them incorrectly might damage the phone.
- (C) They come with a one-year warranty.
- (D) Authorized dealers can replace the damaged ones with new ones.

Scarlett Portman
51–59 Chester Ave.
Garden City, NY 11530

January 5

Angela West
667 3rd Ave.
Welaka, FL 32193

Dear Ms. West,

I am writing to thank you for your professional reference. I believe that your recommendation letter supporting my application was of great help in securing the position of news interpreter at SBTY.

The experience I have gotten during graduate school, particularly through translating Korean and Japanese into English, made me well suited for this job. Aside from the interpretation, I am now enjoying the challenge of translating medical news program as well.

Again, I really appreciate your help.

Yours sincerely,

Scarlett Portman

ACTUAL TEST

10

PART

7

151. Why did Ms. Portman write the letter?

(A) To approve some information
(B) To express gratitude
(C) To ask for a translation
(D) To offer a position

152. Where does Ms. Portman most likely work?

(A) At a broadcasting network
(B) At a pharmaceutical company
(C) At a language school
(D) At a hospital

Go on to the next page

Questions 153-155 refer to the following e-mail.

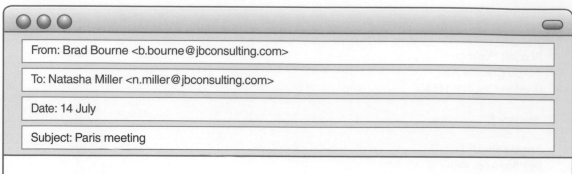

From: Brad Bourne <b.bourne@jbconsulting.com>

To: Natasha Miller <n.miller@jbconsulting.com>

Date: 14 July

Subject: Paris meeting

Hello Natasha,

I'm in Tokyo to supervise the overall inspection process and make sure it is properly carried out, but it's taken longer than I expected. So, I'm going to extend my stay here in Japan for a further two weeks, meaning that I need you to reschedule my appointment on Thursday in Paris.

If you do so, I could prepare for the client meeting with Mr. James next month. And could you send me a copy of the contracts that I drew up? They're probably either in my file cabinet or on my desk. I will not be reachable by phone today. If you need me, please e-mail or message me.

Thank you for your help.

Brad Bourne,
President, Bourne Consulting

**153.** What is the purpose of the e-mail?

(A) To approve a request for an inspection
(B) To summarize a report
(C) To complain about the inspection results
(D) To request assistance in changing a schedule

**154.** Why is Mr. Bourne most likely in Japan?

(A) To open a new facility
(B) To sign a contact
(C) To oversee a project
(D) To interview a candidate

**155.** What is suggested about Mr. James?

(A) He is a factory manager.
(B) He is Ms. Miller's administrative assistant.
(C) He is Mr. Bourne's business client.
(D) He helped Mr. Bourne with the inspection process.

# Aramark Electronics
www.aramarkelectronics.com

Michael Dawson
1C Vestry Road
London, E17 9NH
England

Dear Mr. Dawson,

Thank you for contacting Aramark Electronics for your air-conditioner repair (No. 2912012). To provide the best quality service to our customers, we ask you to take a few minutes to complete the survey. Please send us your completed survey sheet by using the enclosed self-addressed stamped envelope. Thank you for your cooperation.

|  | Strongly Agree | Agree | Disagree | Strongly Disagree |
|---|---|---|---|---|
| Aramark Electronics replied to your request quickly. | X | | | |
| A service technician precisely explained what the problem is. | | X | | |
| Your Aramark Electronics product was immediately repaired and returned. | | | | X |

**Customer Name:** Michael Dawson
**Repair Request Number:** 2912012

**Comments:**
It was better to use Q&A's on your website than to chat with a technician. That's because I could get a quick answer about troubleshooting. The answer written by the technician had detailed information about what to do to solve the problems. My air conditioner, however, was not fixed properly and arrived five days later than the estimated shipping date.

**156.** Why was the letter written to Mr. Dawson?

(A) To complain about what he went through
(B) To announce the recall of defective models
(C) To notify him of policy changes
(D) To get information about customer service

**157.** What does Aramark Electronics offer?

(A) Online assistance
(B) Free shipping
(C) A warranty extension
(D) A troubleshooting manual

**158.** What does Mr. Dawson mention?

(A) The technician perfectly fixed the air conditioner.
(B) The repair took longer than expected.
(C) The air conditioner was defective at the time of purchase.
(D) The manual was difficult to understand.

*Go on to the next page*

Questions 159-160 refer to the following text message chain.

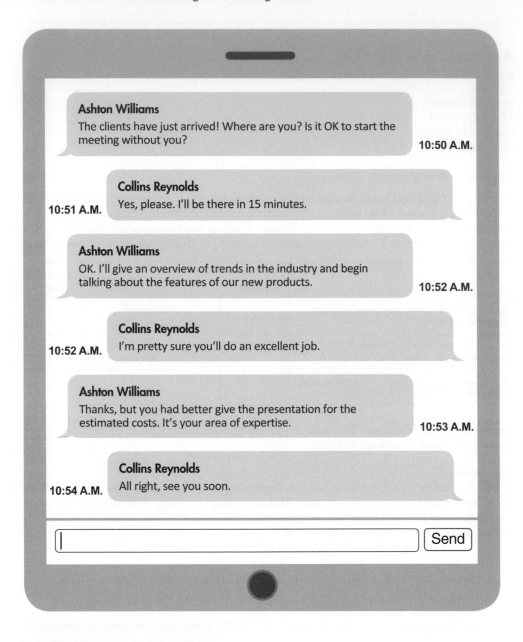

**Ashton Williams**
The clients have just arrived! Where are you? Is it OK to start the meeting without you?
10:50 A.M.

**Collins Reynolds**
10:51 A.M.   Yes, please. I'll be there in 15 minutes.

**Ashton Williams**
OK. I'll give an overview of trends in the industry and begin talking about the features of our new products.
10:52 A.M.

**Collins Reynolds**
10:52 A.M.   I'm pretty sure you'll do an excellent job.

**Ashton Williams**
Thanks, but you had better give the presentation for the estimated costs. It's your area of expertise.
10:53 A.M.

**Collins Reynolds**
10:54 A.M.   All right, see you soon.

Send

159. At 10:51 A.M., what does Mr. Reynolds most likely mean when he writes, "Yes, please"?

(A) He needs more information about the product.
(B) He wants Mr. Williams to stay on schedule.
(C) He wants them to take a fifteen-minute break now.
(D) He recommends that the presentation be delayed.

160. According to Mr. Williams, what is Mr. Reynolds most knowledgeable about?

(A) Manufacturing
(B) Product specification
(C) Marketing strategy
(D) Budgeting

# Business Inside

Lincoln Bookstore recently has acquired the retail space right next to the store's original location at 877 High Road Leytonstone in London. The popular spot will finally launch an expansion project by using the new space. "Since opening our doors five years ago, we have been on the fast track," says Seth Johnson, cofounder and president of Lincoln Bookstore. "We were told that successful stories for offline bookstores are a thing of the past. —[1]—."

Johnson went on to say that the renovated Lincoln Bookstore will be approximately double the size. "The much-anticipated reopening ceremony will be held on November 8," says Johnson. "—[2]—. We're thrilled with the revamped bookstore. —[3]—. It means we could have many books and host various events like book signings. —[4]—."

**161.** What is the purpose of the article?

(A) To introduce a local business owner
(B) To announce changes to a bookstore
(C) To advertise a new book
(D) To promote a book signing event

**162.** Who is Mr. Johnson?

(A) A bookseller
(B) A popular writer
(C) An online book supplier
(D) A real estate agent

**163.** In which of the positions marked [1], [2], [3] and [4] does the following sentence best belong?

"We have proved that the opposite is true."

(A) [1]
(B) [2]
(C) [3]
(D) [4]

ACTUAL TEST **10**

PART **7**

# Manchester Music Festival

Are you interested in participating in one of the famous music festivals as a committed volunteer while enjoying great music? Then, why don't you volunteer at the 25th annual Manchester Music Festival! This year's festival starts from on 1 and runs until August 5 at the Heaton Park in Manchester, and more than 15 professional groups and 25 talented amateur groups — including local favorites Roland Byrd, Jazzmatazz, Acadia Beat — will show off their great performances during the event.

## Volunteers are needed to

- Help with creating, distributing all posters and flyers, and handing out press releases, which starts July 1.

- Greet and interpret for the musicians from July 28 to August 8. All out-of-town musicians will stay at the designated hotel.

- Operate the ticket office and the information desk as well as guide guests to the parking lots during the festival.

To show our appreciation for volunteers' dedication, the rewards are bountiful! Volunteers will receive an official limited-edition Manchester Music Festival T-shirt, VIP invitation to the official after party, a season festival pass, and more.

If you are interested in volunteering, please contact Hilary Roberts at hroberts@ manchestermusicfestival.co.uk by June 15.

---

164. What is indicated about the festival?

(A) It will begin on August 1.
(B) It features various music genres.
(C) It is run by the local government.
(D) It may be postponed due to rain.

165. What is suggested about some of the performers?

(A) They will be donating used musical instruments.
(B) They will be offering autographed CDs.
(C) They will be staying at homes in Manchester.
(D) They will be receiving some interpretation services.

166. What task will NOT be done by volunteers?

(A) Selling tickets for the festival
(B) Transporting musicians to their hotels
(C) Informing visitors of parking locations
(D) Distributing some documents

167. What will volunteers receive for free?

(A) An article of clothing
(B) A voucher for the designated hotel
(C) A ticket for an awards banquet
(D) Food and beverages on festival days

# The Renovation of Marine Park

**By Jack Davenport**

San Diego (April 15) — San Diego's city council has adopted a resolution to renovate Marine Park with unanimous approval. The issue of the renovation project was initially raised three years ago and has been under discussion. After Mayor Natalie Witherspoon took office, the plan was finally approved. She said in an interview, "I told the city that this would be my first act after coming into office, and I plan to fulfill my pledge." —[1]—.

After the park was opened, its two-kilometer trail along the lake became one of the places of interest in San Diego. However, it was not long before residents came to know that the park is not an ideal place for their children. —[2]—.

"We walk the trail on a daily basis, but our kids want to kick a ball around," said city resident Ivanka Aniston. The park is indeed lacking spaces for children to run freely. "We sometimes thought of having lunch at the park, but there are no tables and benches." —[3]—.

As a part of the project, Marine Park will have more green space for outdoor activities. A space will be designed for children to play in safety as well. —[4]—. This was for the convenience of residents who prefer to walk or exercise later in the evening. The renovations will be finished by the end of this year at the latest.

**168.** What is indicated about the park's renovation?

(A) It will end next summer.
(B) Mayor Witherspoon first proposed it.
(C) It will take three years to finish.
(D) All members of the council agreed to it.

**169.** The word "plan" in paragraph 1, line 5, is closest in meaning to

(A) intend
(B) keep
(C) agree
(D) concentrate

**170.** How have residents been using the park?

(A) To eat something
(B) To sell their handmade products
(C) To go for walks
(D) To ride a bicycle

**171.** In which of the positions marked [1], [2], [3], and [4] does the following sentence best belong?

"And the city council has also approved the installation of lampposts along the trail."

(A) [1]
(B) [2]
(C) [3]
(D) [4]

*Go on to the next page*

**Questions 172-175** refer to the following online chat discussion.

| | | |
|---|---|---|
| **Cindy Hilton** [9:45 A.M.] | | I have to arrange transportation from the airport for our annual conference next week. So, I want you to provide me with flight information. As we are holding the conference for the first time, I sincerely hope there aren't any problems during the event. |
| **Mary Kate** [9:46 A.M.] | | I've been waiting for this for a long time. Unfortunately, I forgot to reserve a flight. Will the company reimburse me for the travel expenses if I drive my own car? That's because the flights from San Francisco are full. |
| **Ben Ford** [9:47 A.M.] | | I'll be on Clover Airlines, flight 803 from Dallas to New York at 7:35 A.M. |
| **Cindy Hilton** [9:48 A.M.] | | Oh, that's too bad, Mary. I'll check on that. |
| **Ariana Crawford** [9:49 A.M.] | | All flights from Houston were full as well. So, I have no choice but to take a bus to Philadelphia and then fly to New York, arriving at 7:50 A.M. I managed to get the last ticket. |
| **Cindy Hilton** [9:55 A.M.] | | I've just been told by the finance department that costs of travel by car will not be reimbursed according to the company policy. Why don't you take a train instead? I would appreciate it if you book it immediately and let me know the time of your arrival. |
| **Mary Kate** [9:56 A.M.] | | Sure. |
| **Cindy Hilton** [9:57 A.M.] | | Thank you for the information, Mr. Ford and Ms. Crawford. See you then. |

Send

300

**172.** At 9:46 A.M., what does Ms. Kate most likely mean when she writes, "I've been waiting for this for a long time"?

(A) She is waiting for the details about flight information.
(B) She did not realize flights are fully booked.
(C) She is glad the speakers will finally meet next week.
(D) She has prepared a presentation for the conference.

**173.** At 9:48 A.M., what is Ms. Hilton going to check on?

(A) A flight ticket from San Francisco
(B) The company's reimbursement policy
(C) Ms. Ford's flight information
(D) The start time of the conference

**174.** How will Ms. Kate most likely travel to the annual conference?

(A) By car
(B) By air
(C) By train
(D) By bus

**175.** What is true about the speakers?

(A) They are all flying out of the same city.
(B) They will take the same flight.
(C) They met at the conference last year.
(D) They are all attending a conference in New York.

*Go on to the next page*

# Weekly Business Insight: Trustworthy Brothers

Five years ago, Jay and Gavin Damon set up a company called Trustworthy Brothers, which is truly unique and a game-changing firm in the real estate industry in Barcelona. To renovate older properties, the small firm has much experience working with existing landlords in the city. The brothers have concentrated on an increase in value and rental income potential by effectively evaluating properties and determining what improvements are needed. From building exterior to interior design, Trustworthy Brothers hires skilled and professional laborers to get the project done. Until now, all of their work has been done only in central Barcelona.

One of the local landlords, Jay Manuel, who recently signed a contract with Trustworthy Brothers to renovate his old buildings, said, "Thanks to working with Trustworthy Brothers, I have experienced an increase in tenant demand and rental profits. Furthermore, the renovation has led to cost savings for power and water. Tenants of my building enjoy their leisure time on the new rooftop terrace. I'll definitely recommend Trustworthy Brothers to others."

If you want to contact Trustworthy Brothers, visit their website, trustworthybrothers.com.

From: Michael Keane <mkeane@amail.com>

To: Jay Damon <jdamon@trustworthybrothers.com>

Date: March 24

Subject: New Proposition

Dear Mr. Damon,

I am writing to request a renovation for a building I recently purchased, which is located in a seaside town near Barcelona. I am pretty sure that you would be interested in the renovation project. The building is not currently in good condition because it has been abandoned for several years. So I was able to purchase it at a very low price. The building is, however, very close to a subway station, which I believe is an advantage. I would like to make a request to you to transform my building into a new attractive residence for rent. Please let me know if you are available to talk about it.

Thank you,

Michael Keane

**176.** What does the article NOT indicate about the Trustworthy Brothers?

(A) They have worked in the real estate industry for 10 years.
(B) They improve profits for their clients.
(C) They have worked with landlords in Barcelona.
(D) They employ workers to carry out their plans.

**177.** What is suggested about Mr. Manuel's buildings?

(A) They attract more tenants than before.
(B) They are new buildings.
(C) The rooftop terrace is not open to the tenants.
(D) Mr. Manuel has to pay more for their electricity bills now.

**178.** What does the article indicate potential clients should do?

(A) Ask for an estimate
(B) Visit a website
(C) Negotiate the price
(D) Send a request

**179.** Why was Mr. Keane able to purchase the building at a low price?

(A) It is in a remote area.
(B) It does not have access to a water supply.
(C) It was on sale as a special promotion.
(D) It could not be rented out in its present state.

**180.** How is Mr. Keane's proposal different from typical works for Trustworthy Brothers?

(A) The work would be done outside Barcelona.
(B) Mr. Keane would like to hire a renowned designer.
(C) The fee for the renovation would be paid after the project is finished.
(D) The project should be finished within a strict time limit.

# Penske Books
## Winter Catalog

Dear Customers,

Please enjoy looking over our latest catalog. If you look at the Cookbooks, Food, and Wine section on page 5, you will find some bestsellers that let you know recipes from famous restaurants. Our Travel and Tourism section on page 7 guides you to enjoy your winter vacation wherever you go. For all the latest in the Science Fiction section on page 9, imaginative writers will lead you into the world of fantasy. Highly experienced writers will tell you about the latest trends in the Business and Management section on page 11. You can also see the best-loved books including *Risk Management for Small Businesses*, winner of the Jamison Award (page 13).

Please note that this catalog has only a small number of samples. If you want to see a full list of our titles, go to our website, www.penskebooks.com. For those who live in Pennsylvania, please visit our store for a wealth of additional books that you cannot find on our website.

## Business Perspective
by Yuri Tielemans and Jane Carter

An impressive introduction to business strategy, full of specific cases and entertaining pictures and illustrations to explain key points. The easy-to-follow instructions will give you a better understanding of the business world.

Condition: Very good. $39.95

## Finance Management Analysis
by Thiago Malcom

This book features combining new financial theory with practical examples. Malcom uses real-world scenarios to analyze theoretical principles of finance management. Highly recommended for both businesspeople and students.

Condition: Like new. $25.95.

## Risk Management for Small Businesses
by Alicia Dunst

Essential books for small business owners who take care of high-risk situations effectively. The book contains several interviews with owners running a successful business.

Condition: Fair with some wear to corners and edges. $32.95

## Encyclopedia of Business Marketing
by Anthony Martial

With more than 5,000 definitions of business marketing terms, this book is a must-have item for those who are starting their own business for the first time.

Condition: Good with signs of cover wear. $49.95

---

**181.** Based on the note, what book would Penske Books most likely have in stock?

(A) A biography of a famous musician
(B) A history of Africa
(C) An introduction of the new computer models
(D) An information on top vacation spots in East Asia

**182.** In the note, the word "wealth" in paragraph 2, line 3, is closest in meaning to

(A) value
(B) quality
(C) sense
(D) abundance

**183.** What is suggested about the catalog?

(A) It advertises used books.
(B) It has a complete listing.
(C) It includes mainly academic books.
(D) It is released twice a year.

**184.** Who received an award?

(A) Mr. Tielemans
(B) Mr. Malcom
(C) Ms. Dunst
(D) Mr. Martial

**185.** What feature is NOT mentioned among the descriptions of the books on the catalog page?

(A) Drawings to clarify key points
(B) Interviews with those involved
(C) Examples from real world
(D) Checklists for starting a small company

*Go on to the next page*

**Questions 186-190** refer to the following e-mail, program, and information.

From: James Rodriguez <jrodriguez@ita.com>

To: Brian Mendy <bmendy@altriagroup.com>

Date: December 1

Subject: Invitation for speaker

Dear Mr. Mendy,

I am writing to invite you to be a keynote speaker at the 5th annual Information Technology Association Conference, which is scheduled for May 1-3 in Charlotte, North Carolina. Thousands of business leaders and industry experts will participate in the event, which will be an ideal venue for networking. This conference will be held at the Hyatt Charlotte Hotel, and business leaders will share their insights into the latest trends in the IT industry.

We would appreciate it if you would agree to make a speech on the flexible pricing options you introduced to boost profits for the Internet security program created by the Altria Group. Please let me know your availability.

James Rodriguez
President
Information Technology Association

## Information Technology Association Conference Program

*(May 1 – Schedules)*

| | | |
|---|---|---|
| **8:30 A.M.** | **Visual Communication –** A more effective and better way of communicating as well as saving money and effort <br> Speaker: Elizabeth Cohan, Cofounder of Micron Technology | |
| **9:30 A.M.** | **Revolutionary Change –** The vice president of Supervalu speaks on how her team brought the company back from near bankruptcy and made the company turn a profit through innovative product design <br> Speaker: Anna Kirby, Vice President of Supervalu | |
| **10:30 A.M.** | **Creating a Product –** The secret behind the Altria Group's unique strategy to increase the sales revenues of its computer programs <br> Speaker: Brian Mendy, CEO of Altria Group | |
| **11:30 A.M.** | **Leadership in an IT company –** How to react quickly and efficiently to rapidly changing circumstances <br> Speaker: Laurel Allen, Professor of Charlotte Business School | |
| **12:30 P.M.** | **Lunch** | |

# Information Technology Association Conference

## Registration fees
Information Technology Association members — $1,000
Nonmembers – $1,500

Registration fees include hotel vouchers for use — during the event as well as meals and refreshments. Registration online in advance is required to attend the conference. Presentation videos will be available on our website to all participants the following month.

---

**186.** What is mentioned about the Information Technology Association Conference?

(A) It takes place annually.
(B) An on-site training will be scheduled.
(C) It is a one-day event.
(D) The latest products will be on display.

**187.** When will product pricing most likely be discussed?

(A) At 8:30 A.M.
(B) At 9:30 A.M.
(C) At 10:30 A.M.
(D) At 11:30 A.M.

**188.** What is indicated about Supervalu?

(A) It will merge with a rival company.
(B) It has overcome difficulties.
(C) It has changed the company logo.
(D) It moved its headquarters last year.

**189.** What is a benefit available only to Information Technology Association members?

(A) A private dinner for networking
(B) Free transportation
(C) Upgraded hotel accommodations
(D) Reduced registration fees

**190.** What will Mr. Mendy receive access to in June?

(A) Recordings
(B) Articles
(C) Receipts
(D) Photographs

*Go on to the next page*

# Discount Coupon

### *END-OF-SEASON SALE for One Day Only!*
Wednesday, 2 April

- 20% off one regularly priced item
- 30% off one clearance item

Thousands of items in stock, including coats, shirts, pants, shoes, accessories, and more. We will extend our business hours for this event: 9:00 A.M. – 9:00 P.M.

This coupon is not able to be combined with other promotions. We limit one coupon per customer. Please note that the coupon is not valid on pants. Once the item is purchased, no refunds or exchanges are allowed. Coupon is valid on 2 April only.

**Monstanto**

1040 Grand Concourse

Bronx, NY 10456
Telephone: (718) 681-6000

---

To: Monstanto Employees

From: William Singer, Manager

Date: April 1

Re: Upcoming sale

Today's edition of the *New York Daily* failed to mention that accessories are excluded from the regularly priced items. So, if a customer makes a purchase of the item, please explain the issue and make an apology. And then, please inform the customer of the fact that we'll nevertheless offer 10% discount as a courtesy.

Also, as the promotion has been advertised through all media, more customers are expected to visit our store than usual, especially from 5 P.M. to the closing time. So, we will need more sales associates on duty during that time. Please let me know if you are available for an extra shift.

Thank you.

From: Service Department <service@monstanto.com>

To: Jill Elkins <jelkins@mmail.com>

Date: 2 April, 4:26 P.M.

Subject: Your receipt

Dear Ms. Elkins,

Here is the purchase receipt you recently requested from Monstanto.

| Quantity | Item | Price |
|:---:|:---|:---:|
| 1 | Soft Jacket | $400.00 |
| | 30% promotion discount | -$120.00 |
| | **Item price** | **$280.00** |
| 1 | Ring and necklace set | $160.00 |
| | 10% promotion discount | -$16.00 |
| | **Item price** | **$144.00** |
| 1 | Long denim pants | $28.00 |

**Total** **$452.00**
**Total Saved** **$136.00**

Thank you for shopping at Monstanto.

---

**191.** According to the coupon, what will happen on April 2?

(A) New product line will be unveiled.
(B) The store will remain open longer than usual.
(C) Additional coupons will be handed out in front of the store.
(D) Customers will be able to see a fashion show.

**192.** In the first e-mail, what are sales associates requested to do?

(A) Arrive early to work
(B) Volunteer to work extra hours
(C) Hand out flyers
(D) Take an inventory

**193.** In the first e-mail, the word "advertised" in paragraph 2, line 1, is closest in meaning to

(A) updated
(B) released
(C) attracted
(D) promoted

**194.** What is suggested about Ms. Elkins?

(A) She purchased a clearance item.
(B) She recently moved to Bronx.
(C) She paid for her purchase with a credit card.
(D) She frequently visits Monstanto.

**195.** What did Ms. Elkins probably NOT receive when she purchased the ring and necklace set?

(A) A discount
(B) A gift certificate
(C) An apology
(D) An explanation

*Go on to the next page*

# Student Liaison Officer
## Chicago University

The university is looking for student liaison officers (SLOs) to work in the Student Support Department. The SLOs will meet two times every month to support international students who make up the Student Committee, taking care of services that can assist with various issues including personal problems, academic issues, accommodation, and career advice. The SLOs will also organize monthly meetings in different places on campus to promote a sense of community.

If you are interested, please send us an e-mail at ssd@chiuni.edu.com.

| From: | Bankole Johnson |
|---|---|
| To: | Robert Rivest |
| Date: | February 15 |
| Subject: | Welcome |

Dear Mr. Rivest,

Thank you for accepting our offer for the position of SLO (Student Liaison Officer). There is some paperwork you should complete before your first day of work. Within a week, you will receive a welcome box containing our university's official documents that you need to fill out by the end of this month. This will also let you know the details about your orientation.

Furthermore, we do need an official transcript from your last university. So please send me an official one by the end of this month as well.

Sincerely,

Bankole Johnson
Director of Student Support Department, Chicago University

# San Diego University
# Transcript Request Form

Transcripts will NOT be released if:

   Money is not yet paid to the university.

   There is a hold on your student record.

**Last Name:** Rivest                          **First Name:** Robert

**Degree Obtained:** ☐ Undergraduate          ☑ Graduate (Communication)

**Street Address:** 5801 S Ellis Ave

**Post Code:** 60637          **City:** Chicago          **State:** Illinois

When do you want your transcript proceeded?

☑ Immediately                    ☐ Hold for Final Grades

**Signature:** *Robert Rivest*

---

**196.** What is the purpose of the notice?

(A) To recruit international students for a university

(B) To announce the employment of a new professor

(C) To solicit applications for an open position

(D) To publicize the creation of a new organization

**197.** How frequently does the Student Committee meet with the student liaison officer?

(A) Once a week

(B) Once a month

(C) Twice a week

(D) Twice a month

**198.** What will Mr. Rivest do at Chicago University?

(A) Help relocate the student center

(B) Help all students select appropriate courses

(C) Lead the department of student support

(D) Provide support to international students on campus

**199.** What will Mr. Rivest receive within a week?

(A) A package of documents

(B) A receipt of a payment

(C) A copy of his school transcript

(D) A letter of acceptance

**200.** What is suggested about San Diego University?

(A) It does not have a medical program.

(B) It does not have a graduate course.

(C) It recruits a large number of international students.

(D) It is the last university Mr. Rivest attended.

# Answer Sheet

## ACTUAL TEST 01

### READING SECTION

| | A | B | C | D |
|---|---|---|---|---|
| 101 | Ⓐ | Ⓑ | Ⓒ | Ⓓ |
| 102 | Ⓐ | Ⓑ | Ⓒ | Ⓓ |
| 103 | Ⓐ | Ⓑ | Ⓒ | Ⓓ |
| 104 | Ⓐ | Ⓑ | Ⓒ | Ⓓ |
| 105 | Ⓐ | Ⓑ | Ⓒ | Ⓓ |
| 106 | Ⓐ | Ⓑ | Ⓒ | Ⓓ |
| 107 | Ⓐ | Ⓑ | Ⓒ | Ⓓ |
| 108 | Ⓐ | Ⓑ | Ⓒ | Ⓓ |
| 109 | Ⓐ | Ⓑ | Ⓒ | Ⓓ |
| 110 | Ⓐ | Ⓑ | Ⓒ | Ⓓ |
| 111 | Ⓐ | Ⓑ | Ⓒ | Ⓓ |
| 112 | Ⓐ | Ⓑ | Ⓒ | Ⓓ |
| 113 | Ⓐ | Ⓑ | Ⓒ | Ⓓ |
| 114 | Ⓐ | Ⓑ | Ⓒ | Ⓓ |
| 115 | Ⓐ | Ⓑ | Ⓒ | Ⓓ |
| 116 | Ⓐ | Ⓑ | Ⓒ | Ⓓ |
| 117 | Ⓐ | Ⓑ | Ⓒ | Ⓓ |
| 118 | Ⓐ | Ⓑ | Ⓒ | Ⓓ |
| 119 | Ⓐ | Ⓑ | Ⓒ | Ⓓ |
| 120 | Ⓐ | Ⓑ | Ⓒ | Ⓓ |
| 121 | Ⓐ | Ⓑ | Ⓒ | Ⓓ |
| 122 | Ⓐ | Ⓑ | Ⓒ | Ⓓ |
| 123 | Ⓐ | Ⓑ | Ⓒ | Ⓓ |
| 124 | Ⓐ | Ⓑ | Ⓒ | Ⓓ |
| 125 | Ⓐ | Ⓑ | Ⓒ | Ⓓ |
| 126 | Ⓐ | Ⓑ | Ⓒ | Ⓓ |
| 127 | Ⓐ | Ⓑ | Ⓒ | Ⓓ |
| 128 | Ⓐ | Ⓑ | Ⓒ | Ⓓ |
| 129 | Ⓐ | Ⓑ | Ⓒ | Ⓓ |
| 130 | Ⓐ | Ⓑ | Ⓒ | Ⓓ |
| 131 | Ⓐ | Ⓑ | Ⓒ | Ⓓ |
| 132 | Ⓐ | Ⓑ | Ⓒ | Ⓓ |
| 133 | Ⓐ | Ⓑ | Ⓒ | Ⓓ |
| 134 | Ⓐ | Ⓑ | Ⓒ | Ⓓ |
| 135 | Ⓐ | Ⓑ | Ⓒ | Ⓓ |
| 136 | Ⓐ | Ⓑ | Ⓒ | Ⓓ |
| 137 | Ⓐ | Ⓑ | Ⓒ | Ⓓ |
| 138 | Ⓐ | Ⓑ | Ⓒ | Ⓓ |
| 139 | Ⓐ | Ⓑ | Ⓒ | Ⓓ |
| 140 | Ⓐ | Ⓑ | Ⓒ | Ⓓ |
| 141 | Ⓐ | Ⓑ | Ⓒ | Ⓓ |
| 142 | Ⓐ | Ⓑ | Ⓒ | Ⓓ |
| 143 | Ⓐ | Ⓑ | Ⓒ | Ⓓ |
| 144 | Ⓐ | Ⓑ | Ⓒ | Ⓓ |
| 145 | Ⓐ | Ⓑ | Ⓒ | Ⓓ |
| 146 | Ⓐ | Ⓑ | Ⓒ | Ⓓ |
| 147 | Ⓐ | Ⓑ | Ⓒ | Ⓓ |
| 148 | Ⓐ | Ⓑ | Ⓒ | Ⓓ |
| 149 | Ⓐ | Ⓑ | Ⓒ | Ⓓ |
| 150 | Ⓐ | Ⓑ | Ⓒ | Ⓓ |
| 151 | Ⓐ | Ⓑ | Ⓒ | Ⓓ |
| 152 | Ⓐ | Ⓑ | Ⓒ | Ⓓ |
| 153 | Ⓐ | Ⓑ | Ⓒ | Ⓓ |
| 154 | Ⓐ | Ⓑ | Ⓒ | Ⓓ |
| 155 | Ⓐ | Ⓑ | Ⓒ | Ⓓ |
| 156 | Ⓐ | Ⓑ | Ⓒ | Ⓓ |
| 157 | Ⓐ | Ⓑ | Ⓒ | Ⓓ |
| 158 | Ⓐ | Ⓑ | Ⓒ | Ⓓ |
| 159 | Ⓐ | Ⓑ | Ⓒ | Ⓓ |
| 160 | Ⓐ | Ⓑ | Ⓒ | Ⓓ |
| 161 | Ⓐ | Ⓑ | Ⓒ | Ⓓ |
| 162 | Ⓐ | Ⓑ | Ⓒ | Ⓓ |
| 163 | Ⓐ | Ⓑ | Ⓒ | Ⓓ |
| 164 | Ⓐ | Ⓑ | Ⓒ | Ⓓ |
| 165 | Ⓐ | Ⓑ | Ⓒ | Ⓓ |
| 166 | Ⓐ | Ⓑ | Ⓒ | Ⓓ |
| 167 | Ⓐ | Ⓑ | Ⓒ | Ⓓ |
| 168 | Ⓐ | Ⓑ | Ⓒ | Ⓓ |
| 169 | Ⓐ | Ⓑ | Ⓒ | Ⓓ |
| 170 | Ⓐ | Ⓑ | Ⓒ | Ⓓ |
| 171 | Ⓐ | Ⓑ | Ⓒ | Ⓓ |
| 172 | Ⓐ | Ⓑ | Ⓒ | Ⓓ |
| 173 | Ⓐ | Ⓑ | Ⓒ | Ⓓ |
| 174 | Ⓐ | Ⓑ | Ⓒ | Ⓓ |
| 175 | Ⓐ | Ⓑ | Ⓒ | Ⓓ |
| 176 | Ⓐ | Ⓑ | Ⓒ | Ⓓ |
| 177 | Ⓐ | Ⓑ | Ⓒ | Ⓓ |
| 178 | Ⓐ | Ⓑ | Ⓒ | Ⓓ |
| 179 | Ⓐ | Ⓑ | Ⓒ | Ⓓ |
| 180 | Ⓐ | Ⓑ | Ⓒ | Ⓓ |
| 181 | Ⓐ | Ⓑ | Ⓒ | Ⓓ |
| 182 | Ⓐ | Ⓑ | Ⓒ | Ⓓ |
| 183 | Ⓐ | Ⓑ | Ⓒ | Ⓓ |
| 184 | Ⓐ | Ⓑ | Ⓒ | Ⓓ |
| 185 | Ⓐ | Ⓑ | Ⓒ | Ⓓ |
| 186 | Ⓐ | Ⓑ | Ⓒ | Ⓓ |
| 187 | Ⓐ | Ⓑ | Ⓒ | Ⓓ |
| 188 | Ⓐ | Ⓑ | Ⓒ | Ⓓ |
| 189 | Ⓐ | Ⓑ | Ⓒ | Ⓓ |
| 190 | Ⓐ | Ⓑ | Ⓒ | Ⓓ |
| 191 | Ⓐ | Ⓑ | Ⓒ | Ⓓ |
| 192 | Ⓐ | Ⓑ | Ⓒ | Ⓓ |
| 193 | Ⓐ | Ⓑ | Ⓒ | Ⓓ |
| 194 | Ⓐ | Ⓑ | Ⓒ | Ⓓ |
| 195 | Ⓐ | Ⓑ | Ⓒ | Ⓓ |
| 196 | Ⓐ | Ⓑ | Ⓒ | Ⓓ |
| 197 | Ⓐ | Ⓑ | Ⓒ | Ⓓ |
| 198 | Ⓐ | Ⓑ | Ⓒ | Ⓓ |
| 199 | Ⓐ | Ⓑ | Ⓒ | Ⓓ |
| 200 | Ⓐ | Ⓑ | Ⓒ | Ⓓ |

## ACTUAL TEST 02

### READING SECTION

| | A | B | C | D |
|---|---|---|---|---|
| 101 | Ⓐ | Ⓑ | Ⓒ | Ⓓ |
| 102 | Ⓐ | Ⓑ | Ⓒ | Ⓓ |
| 103 | Ⓐ | Ⓑ | Ⓒ | Ⓓ |
| 104 | Ⓐ | Ⓑ | Ⓒ | Ⓓ |
| 105 | Ⓐ | Ⓑ | Ⓒ | Ⓓ |
| 106 | Ⓐ | Ⓑ | Ⓒ | Ⓓ |
| 107 | Ⓐ | Ⓑ | Ⓒ | Ⓓ |
| 108 | Ⓐ | Ⓑ | Ⓒ | Ⓓ |
| 109 | Ⓐ | Ⓑ | Ⓒ | Ⓓ |
| 110 | Ⓐ | Ⓑ | Ⓒ | Ⓓ |
| 111 | Ⓐ | Ⓑ | Ⓒ | Ⓓ |
| 112 | Ⓐ | Ⓑ | Ⓒ | Ⓓ |
| 113 | Ⓐ | Ⓑ | Ⓒ | Ⓓ |
| 114 | Ⓐ | Ⓑ | Ⓒ | Ⓓ |
| 115 | Ⓐ | Ⓑ | Ⓒ | Ⓓ |
| 116 | Ⓐ | Ⓑ | Ⓒ | Ⓓ |
| 117 | Ⓐ | Ⓑ | Ⓒ | Ⓓ |
| 118 | Ⓐ | Ⓑ | Ⓒ | Ⓓ |
| 119 | Ⓐ | Ⓑ | Ⓒ | Ⓓ |
| 120 | Ⓐ | Ⓑ | Ⓒ | Ⓓ |
| 121 | Ⓐ | Ⓑ | Ⓒ | Ⓓ |
| 122 | Ⓐ | Ⓑ | Ⓒ | Ⓓ |
| 123 | Ⓐ | Ⓑ | Ⓒ | Ⓓ |
| 124 | Ⓐ | Ⓑ | Ⓒ | Ⓓ |
| 125 | Ⓐ | Ⓑ | Ⓒ | Ⓓ |
| 126 | Ⓐ | Ⓑ | Ⓒ | Ⓓ |
| 127 | Ⓐ | Ⓑ | Ⓒ | Ⓓ |
| 128 | Ⓐ | Ⓑ | Ⓒ | Ⓓ |
| 129 | Ⓐ | Ⓑ | Ⓒ | Ⓓ |
| 130 | Ⓐ | Ⓑ | Ⓒ | Ⓓ |
| 131 | Ⓐ | Ⓑ | Ⓒ | Ⓓ |
| 132 | Ⓐ | Ⓑ | Ⓒ | Ⓓ |
| 133 | Ⓐ | Ⓑ | Ⓒ | Ⓓ |
| 134 | Ⓐ | Ⓑ | Ⓒ | Ⓓ |
| 135 | Ⓐ | Ⓑ | Ⓒ | Ⓓ |
| 136 | Ⓐ | Ⓑ | Ⓒ | Ⓓ |
| 137 | Ⓐ | Ⓑ | Ⓒ | Ⓓ |
| 138 | Ⓐ | Ⓑ | Ⓒ | Ⓓ |
| 139 | Ⓐ | Ⓑ | Ⓒ | Ⓓ |
| 140 | Ⓐ | Ⓑ | Ⓒ | Ⓓ |
| 141 | Ⓐ | Ⓑ | Ⓒ | Ⓓ |
| 142 | Ⓐ | Ⓑ | Ⓒ | Ⓓ |
| 143 | Ⓐ | Ⓑ | Ⓒ | Ⓓ |
| 144 | Ⓐ | Ⓑ | Ⓒ | Ⓓ |
| 145 | Ⓐ | Ⓑ | Ⓒ | Ⓓ |
| 146 | Ⓐ | Ⓑ | Ⓒ | Ⓓ |
| 147 | Ⓐ | Ⓑ | Ⓒ | Ⓓ |
| 148 | Ⓐ | Ⓑ | Ⓒ | Ⓓ |
| 149 | Ⓐ | Ⓑ | Ⓒ | Ⓓ |
| 150 | Ⓐ | Ⓑ | Ⓒ | Ⓓ |
| 151 | Ⓐ | Ⓑ | Ⓒ | Ⓓ |
| 152 | Ⓐ | Ⓑ | Ⓒ | Ⓓ |
| 153 | Ⓐ | Ⓑ | Ⓒ | Ⓓ |
| 154 | Ⓐ | Ⓑ | Ⓒ | Ⓓ |
| 155 | Ⓐ | Ⓑ | Ⓒ | Ⓓ |
| 156 | Ⓐ | Ⓑ | Ⓒ | Ⓓ |
| 157 | Ⓐ | Ⓑ | Ⓒ | Ⓓ |
| 158 | Ⓐ | Ⓑ | Ⓒ | Ⓓ |
| 159 | Ⓐ | Ⓑ | Ⓒ | Ⓓ |
| 160 | Ⓐ | Ⓑ | Ⓒ | Ⓓ |
| 161 | Ⓐ | Ⓑ | Ⓒ | Ⓓ |
| 162 | Ⓐ | Ⓑ | Ⓒ | Ⓓ |
| 163 | Ⓐ | Ⓑ | Ⓒ | Ⓓ |
| 164 | Ⓐ | Ⓑ | Ⓒ | Ⓓ |
| 165 | Ⓐ | Ⓑ | Ⓒ | Ⓓ |
| 166 | Ⓐ | Ⓑ | Ⓒ | Ⓓ |
| 167 | Ⓐ | Ⓑ | Ⓒ | Ⓓ |
| 168 | Ⓐ | Ⓑ | Ⓒ | Ⓓ |
| 169 | Ⓐ | Ⓑ | Ⓒ | Ⓓ |
| 170 | Ⓐ | Ⓑ | Ⓒ | Ⓓ |
| 171 | Ⓐ | Ⓑ | Ⓒ | Ⓓ |
| 172 | Ⓐ | Ⓑ | Ⓒ | Ⓓ |
| 173 | Ⓐ | Ⓑ | Ⓒ | Ⓓ |
| 174 | Ⓐ | Ⓑ | Ⓒ | Ⓓ |
| 175 | Ⓐ | Ⓑ | Ⓒ | Ⓓ |
| 176 | Ⓐ | Ⓑ | Ⓒ | Ⓓ |
| 177 | Ⓐ | Ⓑ | Ⓒ | Ⓓ |
| 178 | Ⓐ | Ⓑ | Ⓒ | Ⓓ |
| 179 | Ⓐ | Ⓑ | Ⓒ | Ⓓ |
| 180 | Ⓐ | Ⓑ | Ⓒ | Ⓓ |
| 181 | Ⓐ | Ⓑ | Ⓒ | Ⓓ |
| 182 | Ⓐ | Ⓑ | Ⓒ | Ⓓ |
| 183 | Ⓐ | Ⓑ | Ⓒ | Ⓓ |
| 184 | Ⓐ | Ⓑ | Ⓒ | Ⓓ |
| 185 | Ⓐ | Ⓑ | Ⓒ | Ⓓ |
| 186 | Ⓐ | Ⓑ | Ⓒ | Ⓓ |
| 187 | Ⓐ | Ⓑ | Ⓒ | Ⓓ |
| 188 | Ⓐ | Ⓑ | Ⓒ | Ⓓ |
| 189 | Ⓐ | Ⓑ | Ⓒ | Ⓓ |
| 190 | Ⓐ | Ⓑ | Ⓒ | Ⓓ |
| 191 | Ⓐ | Ⓑ | Ⓒ | Ⓓ |
| 192 | Ⓐ | Ⓑ | Ⓒ | Ⓓ |
| 193 | Ⓐ | Ⓑ | Ⓒ | Ⓓ |
| 194 | Ⓐ | Ⓑ | Ⓒ | Ⓓ |
| 195 | Ⓐ | Ⓑ | Ⓒ | Ⓓ |
| 196 | Ⓐ | Ⓑ | Ⓒ | Ⓓ |
| 197 | Ⓐ | Ⓑ | Ⓒ | Ⓓ |
| 198 | Ⓐ | Ⓑ | Ⓒ | Ⓓ |
| 199 | Ⓐ | Ⓑ | Ⓒ | Ⓓ |
| 200 | Ⓐ | Ⓑ | Ⓒ | Ⓓ |

# Answer Sheet

## ACTUAL TEST 05

### READING SECTION

(Answer grid, questions 101–200, each with options A B C D)

## ACTUAL TEST 06

### READING SECTION

(Answer grid, questions 101–200, each with options A B C D)

# Answer Sheet

## ACTUAL TEST 07

### READING SECTION

| 101 | Ⓐ Ⓑ Ⓒ Ⓓ | 111 | Ⓐ Ⓑ Ⓒ Ⓓ | 121 | Ⓐ Ⓑ Ⓒ Ⓓ | 131 | Ⓐ Ⓑ Ⓒ Ⓓ | 141 | Ⓐ Ⓑ Ⓒ Ⓓ | 151 | Ⓐ Ⓑ Ⓒ Ⓓ | 161 | Ⓐ Ⓑ Ⓒ Ⓓ | 171 | Ⓐ Ⓑ Ⓒ Ⓓ | 181 | Ⓐ Ⓑ Ⓒ Ⓓ | 191 | Ⓐ Ⓑ Ⓒ Ⓓ |
| 102 | Ⓐ Ⓑ Ⓒ Ⓓ | 112 | Ⓐ Ⓑ Ⓒ Ⓓ | 122 | Ⓐ Ⓑ Ⓒ Ⓓ | 132 | Ⓐ Ⓑ Ⓒ Ⓓ | 142 | Ⓐ Ⓑ Ⓒ Ⓓ | 152 | Ⓐ Ⓑ Ⓒ Ⓓ | 162 | Ⓐ Ⓑ Ⓒ Ⓓ | 172 | Ⓐ Ⓑ Ⓒ Ⓓ | 182 | Ⓐ Ⓑ Ⓒ Ⓓ | 192 | Ⓐ Ⓑ Ⓒ Ⓓ |
| 103 | Ⓐ Ⓑ Ⓒ Ⓓ | 113 | Ⓐ Ⓑ Ⓒ Ⓓ | 123 | Ⓐ Ⓑ Ⓒ Ⓓ | 133 | Ⓐ Ⓑ Ⓒ Ⓓ | 143 | Ⓐ Ⓑ Ⓒ Ⓓ | 153 | Ⓐ Ⓑ Ⓒ Ⓓ | 163 | Ⓐ Ⓑ Ⓒ Ⓓ | 173 | Ⓐ Ⓑ Ⓒ Ⓓ | 183 | Ⓐ Ⓑ Ⓒ Ⓓ | 193 | Ⓐ Ⓑ Ⓒ Ⓓ |
| 104 | Ⓐ Ⓑ Ⓒ Ⓓ | 114 | Ⓐ Ⓑ Ⓒ Ⓓ | 124 | Ⓐ Ⓑ Ⓒ Ⓓ | 134 | Ⓐ Ⓑ Ⓒ Ⓓ | 144 | Ⓐ Ⓑ Ⓒ Ⓓ | 154 | Ⓐ Ⓑ Ⓒ Ⓓ | 164 | Ⓐ Ⓑ Ⓒ Ⓓ | 174 | Ⓐ Ⓑ Ⓒ Ⓓ | 184 | Ⓐ Ⓑ Ⓒ Ⓓ | 194 | Ⓐ Ⓑ Ⓒ Ⓓ |
| 105 | Ⓐ Ⓑ Ⓒ Ⓓ | 115 | Ⓐ Ⓑ Ⓒ Ⓓ | 125 | Ⓐ Ⓑ Ⓒ Ⓓ | 135 | Ⓐ Ⓑ Ⓒ Ⓓ | 145 | Ⓐ Ⓑ Ⓒ Ⓓ | 155 | Ⓐ Ⓑ Ⓒ Ⓓ | 165 | Ⓐ Ⓑ Ⓒ Ⓓ | 175 | Ⓐ Ⓑ Ⓒ Ⓓ | 185 | Ⓐ Ⓑ Ⓒ Ⓓ | 195 | Ⓐ Ⓑ Ⓒ Ⓓ |
| 106 | Ⓐ Ⓑ Ⓒ Ⓓ | 116 | Ⓐ Ⓑ Ⓒ Ⓓ | 126 | Ⓐ Ⓑ Ⓒ Ⓓ | 136 | Ⓐ Ⓑ Ⓒ Ⓓ | 146 | Ⓐ Ⓑ Ⓒ Ⓓ | 156 | Ⓐ Ⓑ Ⓒ Ⓓ | 166 | Ⓐ Ⓑ Ⓒ Ⓓ | 176 | Ⓐ Ⓑ Ⓒ Ⓓ | 186 | Ⓐ Ⓑ Ⓒ Ⓓ | 196 | Ⓐ Ⓑ Ⓒ Ⓓ |
| 107 | Ⓐ Ⓑ Ⓒ Ⓓ | 117 | Ⓐ Ⓑ Ⓒ Ⓓ | 127 | Ⓐ Ⓑ Ⓒ Ⓓ | 137 | Ⓐ Ⓑ Ⓒ Ⓓ | 147 | Ⓐ Ⓑ Ⓒ Ⓓ | 157 | Ⓐ Ⓑ Ⓒ Ⓓ | 167 | Ⓐ Ⓑ Ⓒ Ⓓ | 177 | Ⓐ Ⓑ Ⓒ Ⓓ | 187 | Ⓐ Ⓑ Ⓒ Ⓓ | 197 | Ⓐ Ⓑ Ⓒ Ⓓ |
| 108 | Ⓐ Ⓑ Ⓒ Ⓓ | 118 | Ⓐ Ⓑ Ⓒ Ⓓ | 128 | Ⓐ Ⓑ Ⓒ Ⓓ | 138 | Ⓐ Ⓑ Ⓒ Ⓓ | 148 | Ⓐ Ⓑ Ⓒ Ⓓ | 158 | Ⓐ Ⓑ Ⓒ Ⓓ | 168 | Ⓐ Ⓑ Ⓒ Ⓓ | 178 | Ⓐ Ⓑ Ⓒ Ⓓ | 188 | Ⓐ Ⓑ Ⓒ Ⓓ | 198 | Ⓐ Ⓑ Ⓒ Ⓓ |
| 109 | Ⓐ Ⓑ Ⓒ Ⓓ | 119 | Ⓐ Ⓑ Ⓒ Ⓓ | 129 | Ⓐ Ⓑ Ⓒ Ⓓ | 139 | Ⓐ Ⓑ Ⓒ Ⓓ | 149 | Ⓐ Ⓑ Ⓒ Ⓓ | 159 | Ⓐ Ⓑ Ⓒ Ⓓ | 169 | Ⓐ Ⓑ Ⓒ Ⓓ | 179 | Ⓐ Ⓑ Ⓒ Ⓓ | 189 | Ⓐ Ⓑ Ⓒ Ⓓ | 199 | Ⓐ Ⓑ Ⓒ Ⓓ |
| 110 | Ⓐ Ⓑ Ⓒ Ⓓ | 120 | Ⓐ Ⓑ Ⓒ Ⓓ | 130 | Ⓐ Ⓑ Ⓒ Ⓓ | 140 | Ⓐ Ⓑ Ⓒ Ⓓ | 150 | Ⓐ Ⓑ Ⓒ Ⓓ | 160 | Ⓐ Ⓑ Ⓒ Ⓓ | 170 | Ⓐ Ⓑ Ⓒ Ⓓ | 180 | Ⓐ Ⓑ Ⓒ Ⓓ | 190 | Ⓐ Ⓑ Ⓒ Ⓓ | 200 | Ⓐ Ⓑ Ⓒ Ⓓ |

## ACTUAL TEST 08

### READING SECTION

| 101 | Ⓐ Ⓑ Ⓒ Ⓓ | 111 | Ⓐ Ⓑ Ⓒ Ⓓ | 121 | Ⓐ Ⓑ Ⓒ Ⓓ | 131 | Ⓐ Ⓑ Ⓒ Ⓓ | 141 | Ⓐ Ⓑ Ⓒ Ⓓ | 151 | Ⓐ Ⓑ Ⓒ Ⓓ | 161 | Ⓐ Ⓑ Ⓒ Ⓓ | 171 | Ⓐ Ⓑ Ⓒ Ⓓ | 181 | Ⓐ Ⓑ Ⓒ Ⓓ | 191 | Ⓐ Ⓑ Ⓒ Ⓓ |
| 102 | Ⓐ Ⓑ Ⓒ Ⓓ | 112 | Ⓐ Ⓑ Ⓒ Ⓓ | 122 | Ⓐ Ⓑ Ⓒ Ⓓ | 132 | Ⓐ Ⓑ Ⓒ Ⓓ | 142 | Ⓐ Ⓑ Ⓒ Ⓓ | 152 | Ⓐ Ⓑ Ⓒ Ⓓ | 162 | Ⓐ Ⓑ Ⓒ Ⓓ | 172 | Ⓐ Ⓑ Ⓒ Ⓓ | 182 | Ⓐ Ⓑ Ⓒ Ⓓ | 192 | Ⓐ Ⓑ Ⓒ Ⓓ |
| 103 | Ⓐ Ⓑ Ⓒ Ⓓ | 113 | Ⓐ Ⓑ Ⓒ Ⓓ | 123 | Ⓐ Ⓑ Ⓒ Ⓓ | 133 | Ⓐ Ⓑ Ⓒ Ⓓ | 143 | Ⓐ Ⓑ Ⓒ Ⓓ | 153 | Ⓐ Ⓑ Ⓒ Ⓓ | 163 | Ⓐ Ⓑ Ⓒ Ⓓ | 173 | Ⓐ Ⓑ Ⓒ Ⓓ | 183 | Ⓐ Ⓑ Ⓒ Ⓓ | 193 | Ⓐ Ⓑ Ⓒ Ⓓ |
| 104 | Ⓐ Ⓑ Ⓒ Ⓓ | 114 | Ⓐ Ⓑ Ⓒ Ⓓ | 124 | Ⓐ Ⓑ Ⓒ Ⓓ | 134 | Ⓐ Ⓑ Ⓒ Ⓓ | 144 | Ⓐ Ⓑ Ⓒ Ⓓ | 154 | Ⓐ Ⓑ Ⓒ Ⓓ | 164 | Ⓐ Ⓑ Ⓒ Ⓓ | 174 | Ⓐ Ⓑ Ⓒ Ⓓ | 184 | Ⓐ Ⓑ Ⓒ Ⓓ | 194 | Ⓐ Ⓑ Ⓒ Ⓓ |
| 105 | Ⓐ Ⓑ Ⓒ Ⓓ | 115 | Ⓐ Ⓑ Ⓒ Ⓓ | 125 | Ⓐ Ⓑ Ⓒ Ⓓ | 135 | Ⓐ Ⓑ Ⓒ Ⓓ | 145 | Ⓐ Ⓑ Ⓒ Ⓓ | 155 | Ⓐ Ⓑ Ⓒ Ⓓ | 165 | Ⓐ Ⓑ Ⓒ Ⓓ | 175 | Ⓐ Ⓑ Ⓒ Ⓓ | 185 | Ⓐ Ⓑ Ⓒ Ⓓ | 195 | Ⓐ Ⓑ Ⓒ Ⓓ |
| 106 | Ⓐ Ⓑ Ⓒ Ⓓ | 116 | Ⓐ Ⓑ Ⓒ Ⓓ | 126 | Ⓐ Ⓑ Ⓒ Ⓓ | 136 | Ⓐ Ⓑ Ⓒ Ⓓ | 146 | Ⓐ Ⓑ Ⓒ Ⓓ | 156 | Ⓐ Ⓑ Ⓒ Ⓓ | 166 | Ⓐ Ⓑ Ⓒ Ⓓ | 176 | Ⓐ Ⓑ Ⓒ Ⓓ | 186 | Ⓐ Ⓑ Ⓒ Ⓓ | 196 | Ⓐ Ⓑ Ⓒ Ⓓ |
| 107 | Ⓐ Ⓑ Ⓒ Ⓓ | 117 | Ⓐ Ⓑ Ⓒ Ⓓ | 127 | Ⓐ Ⓑ Ⓒ Ⓓ | 137 | Ⓐ Ⓑ Ⓒ Ⓓ | 147 | Ⓐ Ⓑ Ⓒ Ⓓ | 157 | Ⓐ Ⓑ Ⓒ Ⓓ | 167 | Ⓐ Ⓑ Ⓒ Ⓓ | 177 | Ⓐ Ⓑ Ⓒ Ⓓ | 187 | Ⓐ Ⓑ Ⓒ Ⓓ | 197 | Ⓐ Ⓑ Ⓒ Ⓓ |
| 108 | Ⓐ Ⓑ Ⓒ Ⓓ | 118 | Ⓐ Ⓑ Ⓒ Ⓓ | 128 | Ⓐ Ⓑ Ⓒ Ⓓ | 138 | Ⓐ Ⓑ Ⓒ Ⓓ | 148 | Ⓐ Ⓑ Ⓒ Ⓓ | 158 | Ⓐ Ⓑ Ⓒ Ⓓ | 168 | Ⓐ Ⓑ Ⓒ Ⓓ | 178 | Ⓐ Ⓑ Ⓒ Ⓓ | 188 | Ⓐ Ⓑ Ⓒ Ⓓ | 198 | Ⓐ Ⓑ Ⓒ Ⓓ |
| 109 | Ⓐ Ⓑ Ⓒ Ⓓ | 119 | Ⓐ Ⓑ Ⓒ Ⓓ | 129 | Ⓐ Ⓑ Ⓒ Ⓓ | 139 | Ⓐ Ⓑ Ⓒ Ⓓ | 149 | Ⓐ Ⓑ Ⓒ Ⓓ | 159 | Ⓐ Ⓑ Ⓒ Ⓓ | 169 | Ⓐ Ⓑ Ⓒ Ⓓ | 179 | Ⓐ Ⓑ Ⓒ Ⓓ | 189 | Ⓐ Ⓑ Ⓒ Ⓓ | 199 | Ⓐ Ⓑ Ⓒ Ⓓ |
| 110 | Ⓐ Ⓑ Ⓒ Ⓓ | 120 | Ⓐ Ⓑ Ⓒ Ⓓ | 130 | Ⓐ Ⓑ Ⓒ Ⓓ | 140 | Ⓐ Ⓑ Ⓒ Ⓓ | 150 | Ⓐ Ⓑ Ⓒ Ⓓ | 160 | Ⓐ Ⓑ Ⓒ Ⓓ | 170 | Ⓐ Ⓑ Ⓒ Ⓓ | 180 | Ⓐ Ⓑ Ⓒ Ⓓ | 190 | Ⓐ Ⓑ Ⓒ Ⓓ | 200 | Ⓐ Ⓑ Ⓒ Ⓓ |

# Answer Sheet

## ACTUAL TEST 09

### READING SECTION

| | A | B | C | D |
|---|---|---|---|---|
| 101 | Ⓐ | Ⓑ | Ⓒ | Ⓓ |
| 102 | Ⓐ | Ⓑ | Ⓒ | Ⓓ |
| 103 | Ⓐ | Ⓑ | Ⓒ | Ⓓ |
| 104 | Ⓐ | Ⓑ | Ⓒ | Ⓓ |
| 105 | Ⓐ | Ⓑ | Ⓒ | Ⓓ |
| 106 | Ⓐ | Ⓑ | Ⓒ | Ⓓ |
| 107 | Ⓐ | Ⓑ | Ⓒ | Ⓓ |
| 108 | Ⓐ | Ⓑ | Ⓒ | Ⓓ |
| 109 | Ⓐ | Ⓑ | Ⓒ | Ⓓ |
| 110 | Ⓐ | Ⓑ | Ⓒ | Ⓓ |
| 111 | Ⓐ | Ⓑ | Ⓒ | Ⓓ |
| 112 | Ⓐ | Ⓑ | Ⓒ | Ⓓ |
| 113 | Ⓐ | Ⓑ | Ⓒ | Ⓓ |
| 114 | Ⓐ | Ⓑ | Ⓒ | Ⓓ |
| 115 | Ⓐ | Ⓑ | Ⓒ | Ⓓ |
| 116 | Ⓐ | Ⓑ | Ⓒ | Ⓓ |
| 117 | Ⓐ | Ⓑ | Ⓒ | Ⓓ |
| 118 | Ⓐ | Ⓑ | Ⓒ | Ⓓ |
| 119 | Ⓐ | Ⓑ | Ⓒ | Ⓓ |
| 120 | Ⓐ | Ⓑ | Ⓒ | Ⓓ |
| 121 | Ⓐ | Ⓑ | Ⓒ | Ⓓ |
| 122 | Ⓐ | Ⓑ | Ⓒ | Ⓓ |
| 123 | Ⓐ | Ⓑ | Ⓒ | Ⓓ |
| 124 | Ⓐ | Ⓑ | Ⓒ | Ⓓ |
| 125 | Ⓐ | Ⓑ | Ⓒ | Ⓓ |
| 126 | Ⓐ | Ⓑ | Ⓒ | Ⓓ |
| 127 | Ⓐ | Ⓑ | Ⓒ | Ⓓ |
| 128 | Ⓐ | Ⓑ | Ⓒ | Ⓓ |
| 129 | Ⓐ | Ⓑ | Ⓒ | Ⓓ |
| 130 | Ⓐ | Ⓑ | Ⓒ | Ⓓ |
| 131 | Ⓐ | Ⓑ | Ⓒ | Ⓓ |
| 132 | Ⓐ | Ⓑ | Ⓒ | Ⓓ |
| 133 | Ⓐ | Ⓑ | Ⓒ | Ⓓ |
| 134 | Ⓐ | Ⓑ | Ⓒ | Ⓓ |
| 135 | Ⓐ | Ⓑ | Ⓒ | Ⓓ |
| 136 | Ⓐ | Ⓑ | Ⓒ | Ⓓ |
| 137 | Ⓐ | Ⓑ | Ⓒ | Ⓓ |
| 138 | Ⓐ | Ⓑ | Ⓒ | Ⓓ |
| 139 | Ⓐ | Ⓑ | Ⓒ | Ⓓ |
| 140 | Ⓐ | Ⓑ | Ⓒ | Ⓓ |
| 141 | Ⓐ | Ⓑ | Ⓒ | Ⓓ |
| 142 | Ⓐ | Ⓑ | Ⓒ | Ⓓ |
| 143 | Ⓐ | Ⓑ | Ⓒ | Ⓓ |
| 144 | Ⓐ | Ⓑ | Ⓒ | Ⓓ |
| 145 | Ⓐ | Ⓑ | Ⓒ | Ⓓ |
| 146 | Ⓐ | Ⓑ | Ⓒ | Ⓓ |
| 147 | Ⓐ | Ⓑ | Ⓒ | Ⓓ |
| 148 | Ⓐ | Ⓑ | Ⓒ | Ⓓ |
| 149 | Ⓐ | Ⓑ | Ⓒ | Ⓓ |
| 150 | Ⓐ | Ⓑ | Ⓒ | Ⓓ |
| 151 | Ⓐ | Ⓑ | Ⓒ | Ⓓ |
| 152 | Ⓐ | Ⓑ | Ⓒ | Ⓓ |
| 153 | Ⓐ | Ⓑ | Ⓒ | Ⓓ |
| 154 | Ⓐ | Ⓑ | Ⓒ | Ⓓ |
| 155 | Ⓐ | Ⓑ | Ⓒ | Ⓓ |
| 156 | Ⓐ | Ⓑ | Ⓒ | Ⓓ |
| 157 | Ⓐ | Ⓑ | Ⓒ | Ⓓ |
| 158 | Ⓐ | Ⓑ | Ⓒ | Ⓓ |
| 159 | Ⓐ | Ⓑ | Ⓒ | Ⓓ |
| 160 | Ⓐ | Ⓑ | Ⓒ | Ⓓ |
| 161 | Ⓐ | Ⓑ | Ⓒ | Ⓓ |
| 162 | Ⓐ | Ⓑ | Ⓒ | Ⓓ |
| 163 | Ⓐ | Ⓑ | Ⓒ | Ⓓ |
| 164 | Ⓐ | Ⓑ | Ⓒ | Ⓓ |
| 165 | Ⓐ | Ⓑ | Ⓒ | Ⓓ |
| 166 | Ⓐ | Ⓑ | Ⓒ | Ⓓ |
| 167 | Ⓐ | Ⓑ | Ⓒ | Ⓓ |
| 168 | Ⓐ | Ⓑ | Ⓒ | Ⓓ |
| 169 | Ⓐ | Ⓑ | Ⓒ | Ⓓ |
| 170 | Ⓐ | Ⓑ | Ⓒ | Ⓓ |
| 171 | Ⓐ | Ⓑ | Ⓒ | Ⓓ |
| 172 | Ⓐ | Ⓑ | Ⓒ | Ⓓ |
| 173 | Ⓐ | Ⓑ | Ⓒ | Ⓓ |
| 174 | Ⓐ | Ⓑ | Ⓒ | Ⓓ |
| 175 | Ⓐ | Ⓑ | Ⓒ | Ⓓ |
| 176 | Ⓐ | Ⓑ | Ⓒ | Ⓓ |
| 177 | Ⓐ | Ⓑ | Ⓒ | Ⓓ |
| 178 | Ⓐ | Ⓑ | Ⓒ | Ⓓ |
| 179 | Ⓐ | Ⓑ | Ⓒ | Ⓓ |
| 180 | Ⓐ | Ⓑ | Ⓒ | Ⓓ |
| 181 | Ⓐ | Ⓑ | Ⓒ | Ⓓ |
| 182 | Ⓐ | Ⓑ | Ⓒ | Ⓓ |
| 183 | Ⓐ | Ⓑ | Ⓒ | Ⓓ |
| 184 | Ⓐ | Ⓑ | Ⓒ | Ⓓ |
| 185 | Ⓐ | Ⓑ | Ⓒ | Ⓓ |
| 186 | Ⓐ | Ⓑ | Ⓒ | Ⓓ |
| 187 | Ⓐ | Ⓑ | Ⓒ | Ⓓ |
| 188 | Ⓐ | Ⓑ | Ⓒ | Ⓓ |
| 189 | Ⓐ | Ⓑ | Ⓒ | Ⓓ |
| 190 | Ⓐ | Ⓑ | Ⓒ | Ⓓ |
| 191 | Ⓐ | Ⓑ | Ⓒ | Ⓓ |
| 192 | Ⓐ | Ⓑ | Ⓒ | Ⓓ |
| 193 | Ⓐ | Ⓑ | Ⓒ | Ⓓ |
| 194 | Ⓐ | Ⓑ | Ⓒ | Ⓓ |
| 195 | Ⓐ | Ⓑ | Ⓒ | Ⓓ |
| 196 | Ⓐ | Ⓑ | Ⓒ | Ⓓ |
| 197 | Ⓐ | Ⓑ | Ⓒ | Ⓓ |
| 198 | Ⓐ | Ⓑ | Ⓒ | Ⓓ |
| 199 | Ⓐ | Ⓑ | Ⓒ | Ⓓ |
| 200 | Ⓐ | Ⓑ | Ⓒ | Ⓓ |

## ACTUAL TEST 10

### READING SECTION

| | A | B | C | D |
|---|---|---|---|---|
| 101 | Ⓐ | Ⓑ | Ⓒ | Ⓓ |
| 102 | Ⓐ | Ⓑ | Ⓒ | Ⓓ |
| 103 | Ⓐ | Ⓑ | Ⓒ | Ⓓ |
| 104 | Ⓐ | Ⓑ | Ⓒ | Ⓓ |
| 105 | Ⓐ | Ⓑ | Ⓒ | Ⓓ |
| 106 | Ⓐ | Ⓑ | Ⓒ | Ⓓ |
| 107 | Ⓐ | Ⓑ | Ⓒ | Ⓓ |
| 108 | Ⓐ | Ⓑ | Ⓒ | Ⓓ |
| 109 | Ⓐ | Ⓑ | Ⓒ | Ⓓ |
| 110 | Ⓐ | Ⓑ | Ⓒ | Ⓓ |
| 111 | Ⓐ | Ⓑ | Ⓒ | Ⓓ |
| 112 | Ⓐ | Ⓑ | Ⓒ | Ⓓ |
| 113 | Ⓐ | Ⓑ | Ⓒ | Ⓓ |
| 114 | Ⓐ | Ⓑ | Ⓒ | Ⓓ |
| 115 | Ⓐ | Ⓑ | Ⓒ | Ⓓ |
| 116 | Ⓐ | Ⓑ | Ⓒ | Ⓓ |
| 117 | Ⓐ | Ⓑ | Ⓒ | Ⓓ |
| 118 | Ⓐ | Ⓑ | Ⓒ | Ⓓ |
| 119 | Ⓐ | Ⓑ | Ⓒ | Ⓓ |
| 120 | Ⓐ | Ⓑ | Ⓒ | Ⓓ |
| 121 | Ⓐ | Ⓑ | Ⓒ | Ⓓ |
| 122 | Ⓐ | Ⓑ | Ⓒ | Ⓓ |
| 123 | Ⓐ | Ⓑ | Ⓒ | Ⓓ |
| 124 | Ⓐ | Ⓑ | Ⓒ | Ⓓ |
| 125 | Ⓐ | Ⓑ | Ⓒ | Ⓓ |
| 126 | Ⓐ | Ⓑ | Ⓒ | Ⓓ |
| 127 | Ⓐ | Ⓑ | Ⓒ | Ⓓ |
| 128 | Ⓐ | Ⓑ | Ⓒ | Ⓓ |
| 129 | Ⓐ | Ⓑ | Ⓒ | Ⓓ |
| 130 | Ⓐ | Ⓑ | Ⓒ | Ⓓ |
| 131 | Ⓐ | Ⓑ | Ⓒ | Ⓓ |
| 132 | Ⓐ | Ⓑ | Ⓒ | Ⓓ |
| 133 | Ⓐ | Ⓑ | Ⓒ | Ⓓ |
| 134 | Ⓐ | Ⓑ | Ⓒ | Ⓓ |
| 135 | Ⓐ | Ⓑ | Ⓒ | Ⓓ |
| 136 | Ⓐ | Ⓑ | Ⓒ | Ⓓ |
| 137 | Ⓐ | Ⓑ | Ⓒ | Ⓓ |
| 138 | Ⓐ | Ⓑ | Ⓒ | Ⓓ |
| 139 | Ⓐ | Ⓑ | Ⓒ | Ⓓ |
| 140 | Ⓐ | Ⓑ | Ⓒ | Ⓓ |
| 141 | Ⓐ | Ⓑ | Ⓒ | Ⓓ |
| 142 | Ⓐ | Ⓑ | Ⓒ | Ⓓ |
| 143 | Ⓐ | Ⓑ | Ⓒ | Ⓓ |
| 144 | Ⓐ | Ⓑ | Ⓒ | Ⓓ |
| 145 | Ⓐ | Ⓑ | Ⓒ | Ⓓ |
| 146 | Ⓐ | Ⓑ | Ⓒ | Ⓓ |
| 147 | Ⓐ | Ⓑ | Ⓒ | Ⓓ |
| 148 | Ⓐ | Ⓑ | Ⓒ | Ⓓ |
| 149 | Ⓐ | Ⓑ | Ⓒ | Ⓓ |
| 150 | Ⓐ | Ⓑ | Ⓒ | Ⓓ |
| 151 | Ⓐ | Ⓑ | Ⓒ | Ⓓ |
| 152 | Ⓐ | Ⓑ | Ⓒ | Ⓓ |
| 153 | Ⓐ | Ⓑ | Ⓒ | Ⓓ |
| 154 | Ⓐ | Ⓑ | Ⓒ | Ⓓ |
| 155 | Ⓐ | Ⓑ | Ⓒ | Ⓓ |
| 156 | Ⓐ | Ⓑ | Ⓒ | Ⓓ |
| 157 | Ⓐ | Ⓑ | Ⓒ | Ⓓ |
| 158 | Ⓐ | Ⓑ | Ⓒ | Ⓓ |
| 159 | Ⓐ | Ⓑ | Ⓒ | Ⓓ |
| 160 | Ⓐ | Ⓑ | Ⓒ | Ⓓ |
| 161 | Ⓐ | Ⓑ | Ⓒ | Ⓓ |
| 162 | Ⓐ | Ⓑ | Ⓒ | Ⓓ |
| 163 | Ⓐ | Ⓑ | Ⓒ | Ⓓ |
| 164 | Ⓐ | Ⓑ | Ⓒ | Ⓓ |
| 165 | Ⓐ | Ⓑ | Ⓒ | Ⓓ |
| 166 | Ⓐ | Ⓑ | Ⓒ | Ⓓ |
| 167 | Ⓐ | Ⓑ | Ⓒ | Ⓓ |
| 168 | Ⓐ | Ⓑ | Ⓒ | Ⓓ |
| 169 | Ⓐ | Ⓑ | Ⓒ | Ⓓ |
| 170 | Ⓐ | Ⓑ | Ⓒ | Ⓓ |
| 171 | Ⓐ | Ⓑ | Ⓒ | Ⓓ |
| 172 | Ⓐ | Ⓑ | Ⓒ | Ⓓ |
| 173 | Ⓐ | Ⓑ | Ⓒ | Ⓓ |
| 174 | Ⓐ | Ⓑ | Ⓒ | Ⓓ |
| 175 | Ⓐ | Ⓑ | Ⓒ | Ⓓ |
| 176 | Ⓐ | Ⓑ | Ⓒ | Ⓓ |
| 177 | Ⓐ | Ⓑ | Ⓒ | Ⓓ |
| 178 | Ⓐ | Ⓑ | Ⓒ | Ⓓ |
| 179 | Ⓐ | Ⓑ | Ⓒ | Ⓓ |
| 180 | Ⓐ | Ⓑ | Ⓒ | Ⓓ |
| 181 | Ⓐ | Ⓑ | Ⓒ | Ⓓ |
| 182 | Ⓐ | Ⓑ | Ⓒ | Ⓓ |
| 183 | Ⓐ | Ⓑ | Ⓒ | Ⓓ |
| 184 | Ⓐ | Ⓑ | Ⓒ | Ⓓ |
| 185 | Ⓐ | Ⓑ | Ⓒ | Ⓓ |
| 186 | Ⓐ | Ⓑ | Ⓒ | Ⓓ |
| 187 | Ⓐ | Ⓑ | Ⓒ | Ⓓ |
| 188 | Ⓐ | Ⓑ | Ⓒ | Ⓓ |
| 189 | Ⓐ | Ⓑ | Ⓒ | Ⓓ |
| 190 | Ⓐ | Ⓑ | Ⓒ | Ⓓ |
| 191 | Ⓐ | Ⓑ | Ⓒ | Ⓓ |
| 192 | Ⓐ | Ⓑ | Ⓒ | Ⓓ |
| 193 | Ⓐ | Ⓑ | Ⓒ | Ⓓ |
| 194 | Ⓐ | Ⓑ | Ⓒ | Ⓓ |
| 195 | Ⓐ | Ⓑ | Ⓒ | Ⓓ |
| 196 | Ⓐ | Ⓑ | Ⓒ | Ⓓ |
| 197 | Ⓐ | Ⓑ | Ⓒ | Ⓓ |
| 198 | Ⓐ | Ⓑ | Ⓒ | Ⓓ |
| 199 | Ⓐ | Ⓑ | Ⓒ | Ⓓ |
| 200 | Ⓐ | Ⓑ | Ⓒ | Ⓓ |

# ANSWER KEY

## ACTUAL TEST 01

| | | | | |
|---|---|---|---|---|
| 101 (C) | 121 (D) | 141 (B) | 161 (A) | 181 (B) |
| 102 (A) | 122 (B) | 142 (C) | 162 (B) | 182 (D) |
| 103 (C) | 123 (D) | 143 (B) | 163 (D) | 183 (A) |
| 104 (C) | 124 (D) | 144 (C) | 164 (C) | 184 (B) |
| 105 (D) | 125 (C) | 145 (D) | 165 (A) | 185 (C) |
| 106 (A) | 126 (D) | 146 (D) | 166 (A) | 186 (C) |
| 107 (A) | 127 (A) | 147 (D) | 167 (B) | 187 (A) |
| 108 (D) | 128 (C) | 148 (A) | 168 (C) | 188 (B) |
| 109 (A) | 129 (A) | 149 (B) | 169 (D) | 189 (C) |
| 110 (A) | 130 (A) | 150 (C) | 170 (B) | 190 (B) |
| 111 (B) | 131 (A) | 151 (D) | 171 (C) | 191 (D) |
| 112 (C) | 132 (D) | 152 (C) | 172 (B) | 192 (D) |
| 113 (C) | 133 (B) | 153 (B) | 173 (A) | 193 (B) |
| 114 (A) | 134 (C) | 154 (B) | 174 (D) | 194 (C) |
| 115 (B) | 135 (C) | 155 (C) | 175 (C) | 195 (D) |
| 116 (C) | 136 (D) | 156 (D) | 176 (B) | 196 (C) |
| 117 (C) | 137 (A) | 157 (A) | 177 (C) | 197 (D) |
| 118 (B) | 138 (D) | 158 (C) | 178 (A) | 198 (D) |
| 119 (B) | 139 (B) | 159 (A) | 179 (A) | 199 (C) |
| 120 (A) | 140 (C) | 160 (D) | 180 (B) | 200 (A) |

## ACTUAL TEST 02

| | | | | |
|---|---|---|---|---|
| 101 (A) | 121 (D) | 141 (B) | 161 (A) | 181 (D) |
| 102 (B) | 122 (A) | 142 (A) | 162 (B) | 182 (A) |
| 103 (D) | 123 (D) | 143 (A) | 163 (C) | 183 (C) |
| 104 (C) | 124 (A) | 144 (B) | 164 (D) | 184 (B) |
| 105 (D) | 125 (B) | 145 (A) | 165 (C) | 185 (C) |
| 106 (A) | 126 (A) | 146 (D) | 166 (A) | 186 (B) |
| 107 (D) | 127 (B) | 147 (B) | 167 (D) | 187 (A) |
| 108 (C) | 128 (C) | 148 (B) | 168 (B) | 188 (D) |
| 109 (A) | 129 (C) | 149 (A) | 169 (C) | 189 (D) |
| 110 (B) | 130 (A) | 150 (B) | 170 (A) | 190 (B) |
| 111 (C) | 131 (A) | 151 (D) | 171 (B) | 191 (A) |
| 112 (A) | 132 (A) | 152 (C) | 172 (C) | 192 (C) |
| 113 (C) | 133 (B) | 153 (A) | 173 (D) | 193 (B) |
| 114 (A) | 134 (C) | 154 (D) | 174 (B) | 194 (A) |
| 115 (B) | 135 (D) | 155 (B) | 175 (D) | 195 (D) |
| 116 (D) | 136 (C) | 156 (A) | 176 (A) | 196 (C) |
| 117 (D) | 137 (C) | 157 (B) | 177 (C) | 197 (D) |
| 118 (D) | 138 (D) | 158 (C) | 178 (D) | 198 (A) |
| 119 (B) | 139 (C) | 159 (D) | 179 (A) | 199 (B) |
| 120 (C) | 140 (D) | 160 (C) | 180 (D) | 200 (D) |

## ACTUAL TEST 03

| | | | | |
|---|---|---|---|---|
| 101 (B) | 121 (A) | 141 (B) | 161 (B) | 181 (C) |
| 102 (A) | 122 (A) | 142 (D) | 162 (C) | 182 (B) |
| 103 (C) | 123 (C) | 143 (A) | 163 (A) | 183 (D) |
| 104 (D) | 124 (B) | 144 (C) | 164 (C) | 184 (A) |
| 105 (B) | 125 (C) | 145 (C) | 165 (B) | 185 (A) |
| 106 (B) | 126 (D) | 146 (A) | 166 (C) | 186 (C) |
| 107 (B) | 127 (C) | 147 (A) | 167 (D) | 187 (B) |
| 108 (D) | 128 (C) | 148 (A) | 168 (B) | 188 (A) |
| 109 (A) | 129 (D) | 149 (A) | 169 (D) | 189 (D) |
| 110 (C) | 130 (D) | 150 (B) | 170 (C) | 190 (A) |
| 111 (A) | 131 (C) | 151 (B) | 171 (D) | 191 (D) |
| 112 (A) | 132 (B) | 152 (C) | 172 (D) | 192 (C) |
| 113 (D) | 133 (A) | 153 (C) | 173 (A) | 193 (A) |
| 114 (C) | 134 (A) | 154 (D) | 174 (B) | 194 (B) |
| 115 (A) | 135 (A) | 155 (C) | 175 (D) | 195 (A) |
| 116 (D) | 136 (B) | 156 (C) | 176 (D) | 196 (A) |
| 117 (A) | 137 (B) | 157 (B) | 177 (A) | 197 (D) |
| 118 (C) | 138 (A) | 158 (C) | 178 (D) | 198 (D) |
| 119 (C) | 139 (C) | 159 (C) | 179 (D) | 199 (C) |
| 120 (B) | 140 (D) | 160 (A) | 180 (A) | 200 (D) |

## ACTUAL TEST 04

| | | | | |
|---|---|---|---|---|
| 101 (C) | 121 (A) | 141 (A) | 161 (A) | 181 (D) |
| 102 (B) | 122 (A) | 142 (C) | 162 (C) | 182 (C) |
| 103 (B) | 123 (C) | 143 (C) | 163 (B) | 183 (A) |
| 104 (C) | 124 (B) | 144 (A) | 164 (A) | 184 (C) |
| 105 (D) | 125 (B) | 145 (B) | 165 (D) | 185 (B) |
| 106 (B) | 126 (B) | 146 (D) | 166 (B) | 186 (A) |
| 107 (C) | 127 (A) | 147 (A) | 167 (D) | 187 (A) |
| 108 (C) | 128 (C) | 148 (D) | 168 (A) | 188 (B) |
| 109 (C) | 129 (C) | 149 (A) | 169 (A) | 189 (A) |
| 110 (C) | 130 (A) | 150 (C) | 170 (B) | 190 (C) |
| 111 (D) | 131 (A) | 151 (D) | 171 (A) | 191 (A) |
| 112 (B) | 132 (B) | 152 (A) | 172 (D) | 192 (D) |
| 113 (B) | 133 (D) | 153 (C) | 173 (A) | 193 (B) |
| 114 (C) | 134 (D) | 154 (C) | 174 (A) | 194 (B) |
| 115 (C) | 135 (D) | 155 (B) | 175 (C) | 195 (C) |
| 116 (B) | 136 (C) | 156 (B) | 176 (B) | 196 (C) |
| 117 (C) | 137 (A) | 157 (A) | 177 (D) | 197 (A) |
| 118 (C) | 138 (B) | 158 (A) | 178 (A) | 198 (C) |
| 119 (B) | 139 (C) | 159 (D) | 179 (D) | 199 (D) |
| 120 (B) | 140 (A) | 160 (A) | 180 (B) | 200 (A) |

## ACTUAL TEST 05

| | | | | |
|---|---|---|---|---|
| 101 (A) | 121 (D) | 141 (A) | 161 (A) | 181 (C) |
| 102 (C) | 122 (A) | 142 (D) | 162 (A) | 182 (C) |
| 103 (C) | 123 (C) | 143 (D) | 163 (C) | 183 (C) |
| 104 (D) | 124 (D) | 144 (A) | 164 (C) | 184 (C) |
| 105 (D) | 125 (D) | 145 (A) | 165 (D) | 185 (B) |
| 106 (A) | 126 (A) | 146 (C) | 166 (A) | 186 (A) |
| 107 (B) | 127 (D) | 147 (A) | 167 (B) | 187 (C) |
| 108 (A) | 128 (D) | 148 (B) | 168 (D) | 188 (B) |
| 109 (B) | 129 (D) | 149 (B) | 169 (B) | 189 (B) |
| 110 (D) | 130 (A) | 150 (C) | 170 (D) | 190 (A) |
| 111 (D) | 131 (B) | 151 (B) | 171 (B) | 191 (D) |
| 112 (B) | 132 (D) | 152 (A) | 172 (C) | 192 (B) |
| 113 (D) | 133 (B) | 153 (C) | 173 (A) | 193 (B) |
| 114 (A) | 134 (A) | 154 (B) | 174 (C) | 194 (A) |
| 115 (D) | 135 (C) | 155 (D) | 175 (A) | 195 (D) |
| 116 (C) | 136 (A) | 156 (C) | 176 (D) | 196 (B) |
| 117 (A) | 137 (B) | 157 (A) | 177 (A) | 197 (B) |
| 118 (B) | 138 (B) | 158 (C) | 178 (D) | 198 (A) |
| 119 (B) | 139 (D) | 159 (D) | 179 (A) | 199 (B) |
| 120 (A) | 140 (D) | 160 (A) | 180 (D) | 200 (C) |

## ACTUAL TEST 06

| | | | | |
|---|---|---|---|---|
| 101 (B) | 121 (B) | 141 (D) | 161 (D) | 181 (A) |
| 102 (C) | 122 (B) | 142 (A) | 162 (D) | 182 (C) |
| 103 (B) | 123 (D) | 143 (C) | 163 (A) | 183 (A) |
| 104 (B) | 124 (A) | 144 (B) | 164 (D) | 184 (B) |
| 105 (C) | 125 (A) | 145 (D) | 165 (A) | 185 (A) |
| 106 (A) | 126 (D) | 146 (A) | 166 (D) | 186 (A) |
| 107 (C) | 127 (C) | 147 (B) | 167 (A) | 187 (A) |
| 108 (C) | 128 (D) | 148 (A) | 168 (C) | 188 (A) |
| 109 (B) | 129 (C) | 149 (B) | 169 (D) | 189 (C) |
| 110 (C) | 130 (B) | 150 (C) | 170 (A) | 190 (C) |
| 111 (C) | 131 (B) | 151 (C) | 171 (A) | 191 (C) |
| 112 (B) | 132 (D) | 152 (B) | 172 (A) | 192 (C) |
| 113 (C) | 133 (A) | 153 (D) | 173 (B) | 193 (A) |
| 114 (B) | 134 (B) | 154 (B) | 174 (A) | 194 (D) |
| 115 (D) | 135 (A) | 155 (A) | 175 (A) | 195 (A) |
| 116 (C) | 136 (A) | 156 (C) | 176 (C) | 196 (D) |
| 117 (A) | 137 (B) | 157 (A) | 177 (A) | 197 (B) |
| 118 (C) | 138 (A) | 158 (B) | 178 (B) | 198 (C) |
| 119 (D) | 139 (B) | 159 (A) | 179 (A) | 199 (D) |
| 120 (D) | 140 (D) | 160 (B) | 180 (B) | 200 (A) |

## ACTUAL TEST 07

| | | | | |
|---|---|---|---|---|
| 101 (B) | 121 (B) | 141 (B) | 161 (D) | 181 (A) |
| 102 (C) | 122 (A) | 142 (B) | 162 (A) | 182 (B) |
| 103 (B) | 123 (C) | 143 (A) | 163 (A) | 183 (D) |
| 104 (A) | 124 (A) | 144 (C) | 164 (B) | 184 (D) |
| 105 (B) | 125 (C) | 145 (B) | 165 (D) | 185 (D) |
| 106 (B) | 126 (B) | 146 (D) | 166 (B) | 186 (D) |
| 107 (D) | 127 (C) | 147 (A) | 167 (D) | 187 (C) |
| 108 (C) | 128 (B) | 148 (D) | 168 (A) | 188 (B) |
| 109 (B) | 129 (A) | 149 (B) | 169 (C) | 189 (C) |
| 110 (A) | 130 (C) | 150 (B) | 170 (C) | 190 (D) |
| 111 (C) | 131 (C) | 151 (B) | 171 (C) | 191 (A) |
| 112 (D) | 132 (A) | 152 (D) | 172 (B) | 192 (B) |
| 113 (D) | 133 (B) | 153 (B) | 173 (C) | 193 (C) |
| 114 (C) | 134 (C) | 154 (A) | 174 (A) | 194 (C) |
| 115 (B) | 135 (B) | 155 (B) | 175 (C) | 195 (D) |
| 116 (D) | 136 (A) | 156 (C) | 176 (A) | 196 (B) |
| 117 (D) | 137 (D) | 157 (B) | 177 (C) | 197 (C) |
| 118 (D) | 138 (C) | 158 (A) | 178 (A) | 198 (B) |
| 119 (D) | 139 (D) | 159 (D) | 179 (A) | 199 (C) |
| 120 (B) | 140 (C) | 160 (D) | 180 (A) | 200 (B) |

## ACTUAL TEST 08

| | | | | |
|---|---|---|---|---|
| 101 (C) | 121 (B) | 141 (A) | 161 (D) | 181 (B) |
| 102 (B) | 122 (A) | 142 (D) | 162 (A) | 182 (D) |
| 103 (B) | 123 (D) | 143 (B) | 163 (A) | 183 (B) |
| 104 (B) | 124 (A) | 144 (D) | 164 (D) | 184 (B) |
| 105 (D) | 125 (C) | 145 (C) | 165 (D) | 185 (A) |
| 106 (D) | 126 (B) | 146 (A) | 166 (A) | 186 (D) |
| 107 (D) | 127 (C) | 147 (B) | 167 (A) | 187 (D) |
| 108 (A) | 128 (C) | 148 (B) | 168 (B) | 188 (C) |
| 109 (D) | 129 (A) | 149 (C) | 169 (D) | 189 (C) |
| 110 (D) | 130 (C) | 150 (D) | 170 (B) | 190 (B) |
| 111 (B) | 131 (C) | 151 (A) | 171 (C) | 191 (A) |
| 112 (A) | 132 (D) | 152 (D) | 172 (D) | 192 (A) |
| 113 (C) | 133 (B) | 153 (B) | 173 (A) | 193 (D) |
| 114 (D) | 134 (A) | 154 (C) | 174 (B) | 194 (C) |
| 115 (B) | 135 (D) | 155 (D) | 175 (B) | 195 (B) |
| 116 (C) | 136 (C) | 156 (B) | 176 (D) | 196 (D) |
| 117 (C) | 137 (B) | 157 (B) | 177 (A) | 197 (A) |
| 118 (B) | 138 (A) | 158 (C) | 178 (B) | 198 (A) |
| 119 (C) | 139 (B) | 159 (D) | 179 (A) | 199 (B) |
| 120 (D) | 140 (B) | 160 (A) | 180 (C) | 200 (D) |

# 挑戰 NEW TOEIC 新制多益 閱讀滿分

模擬試題1000題

作者 Choi Young Ken | 譯者 蘇裕承 / 關亭薇

解析版

解析本

# 目錄

# ACTUAL TEST
## 1

## PART 5

## 101

All of the new employees receive training packets that ------ details about their duties.

(A) contains
(B) to contain
(C) contain
(D) containing

題型 位置——動詞

翻譯 所有新進員工都會收到訓練資料袋，其中包含載明他們職責的細節。

詞彙 training 訓練
detail 載明細節

關係代名詞是引出形容詞子句的連接詞。連接詞的數量通常比動詞個數少一個，也就是若一句出現兩個動詞，連接詞便只會出現一個。本句中出現了 that，且其前面的主句已經有一個動詞 receive，所以在 that 的子句中應該還需要一個動詞。(B) 和 (D) 為不定詞和動名詞，所以不是解答。

此外，以主格關係代名詞為基準，左邊的先行詞 training packets 和右邊的動詞須在面對複數變化時具一致性。(A) 在動詞加了字尾 s，和複數的先行詞不一致。

和先行詞達成主詞、動詞一致性，且可以放入動詞位置的只剩下 contain，故正確答案為 (C)。

## 102

------- just two miles remaining in the race, Ms. Kaufman had a sizable advantage over the next runner.

(A) With
(B) Though
(C) But
(D) Added

題型 詞彙——介系詞

翻譯 隨著賽程只剩最後兩哩路，考夫曼女士比起下一名跑者，明顯占優勢。

詞彙 remaining 剩下的
sizable 相當大的
advantage 優勢

本題要考形容詞片語。空格後面的 just two miles 為名詞，而 remaining 為分詞作形容詞用，選項中可以和兩者一起使用的只有 with，故正解為 (A)。

★形容詞片語的用法：
with ＋名詞＋ V-ing ／ p.p. ／形容詞（在……的狀態下）。

## 103

Mr. Shaw is not able to participate in the committee convention in Shanghai, so Ms. Jeon will attend in ------ place.

(A) him
(B) he
(C) his
(D) himself

題型 文法——代名詞

翻譯 邵先生無法到上海參加委員大會，所以全女士將代替他出席。

詞彙 participate in 參加
committee 委員
convention 大會
in one's place 代替某人

從空格開始到 place 皆為介系詞 in 的名詞受詞，而可放入 place 前面的，只有所有格人稱代名詞 his，故正解為 (C)。

## 104

The executive director at All Day Department Store is ------ to any changes to the company logo.

(A) eager
(B) interfered
(C) opposed
(D) anxious

**題型** 詞彙──形容詞

**翻譯** 全日百貨公司的執行董事，反對公司商標有任何變動。

**詞彙** executive director 執行董事

各選項的意思如下：(A) eager 熱烈的、迫切希望的；(B) interfered 受妨礙的；(C) opposed 反對的；(D) anxious 覺得不安的。

空格前有 be 動詞 is，後有介系詞 to，所以此題問的是可與這兩者一起使用的形容詞慣用語。選項中只有 opposed 有「be opposed to N」（反對某事）的用法，故正解為 (C)。

★**其他選項的用法：**

be eager for N（渴望得到某物）　　　　be anxious about N（對某事感到不安）
be eager to V（想做某事）　　　　　　be anxious for N / to V（想做某事）
be interfered with N（被某事妨礙）

## 105

The conference center is on Brooklyn Street, ------ across from the new post office.

(A) directs
(B) direct
(C) direction
(D) directly

**題型** 位置──副詞

**翻譯** 會議中心位於布魯克林街，就在新郵局的正對面。

**詞彙** conference center 會議中心

只有副詞才可以用來修飾空格後面的介系詞片語 across from the new post office，故本題正確答案為 (D)。

## 106

------- the rise in steel prices, FTX Builders will most likely revise the bid for the Golden Bridge construction work.

(A) Given
(B) Provided
(C) Namely
(D) Regardless

**題型** 詞彙──介系詞

**翻譯** 有鑑於鋼價上漲，FTX 營造公司極有可能會調整金橋工程的競標金額。

**詞彙** steel 鋼
most likely 極有可能
revise 修改
bid 競標金額
construction work 工程

(A) Given〔介系詞〕考慮到；(B) Provided〔副詞連接詞〕倘若；(C) Namoly〔副詞〕換句話說；(D) Regardless〔副詞〕無論如何。

可放在名詞片語 the rise in steel price 前的詞性為介系詞，選項中只有 Given 的字義與詞性最合適，故正確答案為 (A)。

## 107

**The office complex ------ on the outskirts of the pedestrian shopping area.**

(A) will be built
(B) built
(C) are building
(D) builder

| 題型 | 位置──動詞 |
| 翻譯 | 綜合辦公大樓將蓋在步行購物區外圍。 |
| 詞彙 | office complex 綜合辦公大樓<br>on the outskirts of 在外圍<br>pedestrian 步行的 |

所有句子都需要一個主詞,以及一個動詞來反映出時態與語態。由於句子缺少動詞,選項中可扮演動詞功能者為 (A)、(B)、(C),且因為空格後方沒有名詞作為受詞,所以要選被動態的動詞,故正確答案為 (A)。

**In the past twenty years, clothing designers have become ------ aware of customer needs and preferences.**

(A) increasing
(B) increased
(C) increase
(D) increasingly

| 題型 | 位置──副詞 |
| 翻譯 | 過去二十年來,服裝設計師愈來愈著重顧客需求和喜好。 |
| 詞彙 | clothing 服裝<br>be aware of 注意到<br>preference 喜好 |

在連綴動詞 become 後面,已接著作為補語的形容詞 aware,故此句已為完整的句子,而句子中可有可無的部分為副詞,故應填入 increasingly,本題正確答案為 (D)。

**------- the last four months, Miracle Theater attendance has improved**

significantly.
(A) During
(B) Above
(C) Behind
(D) Into

| 題型 | 位置──介系詞 |
| 翻譯 | 過去四個月內,奇蹟影城的來客數有顯著成長。 |
| 詞彙 | attendance 出席數;來客數<br>improve 成長;進步<br>significantly 顯著地 |

空格後方出現的名詞 the last four months 表示一段期間,而可以和「期間」連用的選項只有介系詞 during,故正確答案為 (A)。

## 110

Temporary workers from Adrian Recruitment Inc. have proven to be highly ------ employees.

(A) competent
(B) competence
(C) competency
(D) competently

題型 位置——形容詞

翻譯 阿德里安人才招募公司的臨時人員，果然都非常有能力。

詞彙 temporary 臨時的
highly 非常地
prove to be 果然是……

可接受空格前 highly 的修飾，並點綴空格後 employees 的詞彙為形容詞 competent（能幹的），所以正確答案為 (A)。

## 111

Revenue from sale of outdoor furniture has been ------- higher than expected over the last six months.

(A) optionally
(B) considerably
(C) eagerly
(D) informatively

題型 詞彙——副詞

翻譯 戶外家具在過去六個月的銷售收益比預期高上許多。

詞彙 revenue 收入
outdoor 戶外的

(A) optionally 隨意地；(B) considerably 相當地；(C) eagerly 熱烈地，熱情地；(D) informatively 資訊豐富地。

句意上，只有 considerably 適合用米強調空格後的比較級，所以正確答案為 (B)。

## 112

Please complete all items on the checklist ------ submitting your entry for the photography contest.

(A) as for
(B) mainly
(C) before
(D) so that

題型 詞彙——介系詞

翻譯 報名參加攝影競賽前，請完成清單上所有事項。

詞彙 complete 完成
checklist 清單
submit 繳交
entry 報名文件
photography 攝影
contest 競賽

(A) as for〔介系詞〕至於；(B) mainly〔副詞〕主要；(C) before〔介系詞、副詞連接詞〕以前；(D) so that〔副詞連接詞〕為了做……。

根據題意，最適合的是 before，以表示在參加攝影競賽「前」，所以正確答案為 (C)。

**113**

Many ------ farmers sell their produce at
Pemberton Green Market.

(A) close
(B) around
(C) local
(D) near

題型 詞彙──形容詞

翻譯 彭柏頓綠色市集裡，有很多當地農民販售自家農產品。

詞彙 produce 農產品

(A) close〔形容詞〕接近的；(B) around〔副詞〕大概、〔介系詞〕在……周圍；(C) local〔形容詞〕當地的、國內的；(D) near〔副詞〕靠近地、〔形容詞〕近的、〔介系詞〕附近。

從句子的脈絡看來，此處應是要表示「當地的」農民，故正確答案為 (C)。

**114**

Owing to predicted bad weather, tomorrow's
outdoor concert has been ------- to next Saturday.

(A) postponed
(B) eliminated
(C) prolonged
(D) implemented

題型 詞彙──動詞

翻譯 因為預期天氣將會變壞，原訂明天舉行的戶外音樂會將延期到下星期六。

詞彙 owing to 因為
predict 預期
bad weather 壞天氣
outdoor 戶外的

(A) postpone 延後、延期；(B) eliminate 除去；(C) prolong 延長；(D) implement 實施。

句意上，適合用於描述天氣不好及調整行程的為 postpone，所以正確答案為 (A)。

**115**

In order to ensure a timely response, please
include your account number on all -------.

(A) are corresponding
(B) correspondence
(C) corresponds
(D) correspond

題型 位置──名詞

翻譯 為確保即時回應，請在所有的信件裡提供您的帳號。

詞彙 in order to V 為了
ensure 確保
timely 即時的
response 回應
include 包含
account number 帳號

在所有選項中，能做介系詞 on 的名詞受詞，又可以被數量形容詞 all 修飾的，為名詞 correspondence（書信往來），所以正確答案為 (B)。

## 116

Lunch will be catered by Welco Café ------ Haqri Grill.

(A) but
(B) nor
(C) and
(D) yet

題型 文法——對等連接詞

翻譯 午餐將由好客咖啡館和哈克里碳烤提供。

詞彙 cater 提供飲食

選項中的四個對等連接詞中，只有 and 在的字義上最為適當，所以正確答案為 (C)。

## 117

Timothy Darlton is highly qualified for the managerial role, ------ requires extensive experience.

(A) whoever
(B) who
(C) which
(D) whatever

題型 文法——關係代名詞

翻譯 提摩西・達爾頓非常適合擔綱管理角色，該職位要有豐富的經驗。

詞彙 qualified 有資格的
managerial 管理的
role 角色
extensive 豐富的、廣泛的
experience 經驗

(A) whoever〔複合關係代名詞〕不論是誰；(B) who〔主格關係代名詞〕；(C) which〔受格關係代名詞〕；(D) whatever〔複合關係代名詞〕不論是什麼。

空格前的 the managerial role 是先行詞，空格後的 requires 則是子句的動詞，所以空格是主格關係代名詞。(A) 和 (D) 為複合關係代名詞，不需要先行詞；(B) 需以人物名詞作為先行詞；(C) which 可以事物或抽象名詞作為先行詞，所以正確答案為 (C)。

## 118

We'd really appreciate your ------ in the Nathan Apartment Complex improvement survey.

(A) participant
(B) participation
(C) participate
(D) participated

題型 位置——名詞

翻譯 我們很感謝您參與改善納森公寓大樓的問卷調查。

詞彙 appreciate 感謝
apartment complex 公寓大樓
survey 問卷調查

所有格人稱代名詞 your 後要接名詞，而 (A) participant（參加者）和 (B) participation（參加）中，最適合句意的是 participation，所以正確答案為 (B)。

**119** --------------------------------------------------------

Mr. Lopez will assist with the manuscript, so it is not necessary to do all the revisions by -------.

(A) yours

(B) yourself

(C) you

(D) your

| | |
|---|---|
| 題型 | 位置——反身代名詞 |
| 翻譯 | 羅培茲先生會協助作業，所以你不需要獨力修改所有手稿。 |
| 詞彙 | assist with 協助<br>manuscript 手稿<br>revision 修改 |

本題為詢問反身代名詞片語 by oneself（獨自；自行）的題型，故答案要選反身代名詞 yourself，本題正確答案為 (B)。

**120** --------------------------------------------------------

Midora Manufacturing reserves the right to delay further deliveries ------ the customer has made all outstanding payments.

(A) until

(B) next

(C) then

(D) later

| | |
|---|---|
| 題型 | 位置——副詞連接詞 |
| 翻譯 | 米多拉製造商保有延後出貨的權利，直到顧客繳交所有未付款項。 |
| 詞彙 | reserve the right to V<br>保留⋯⋯的權利<br>further 之後的<br>delivery 出貨<br>outstanding 未付的 |

(A) until〔介系詞〕〔副詞連接詞〕到⋯⋯；(B) next〔副詞〕接下來、〔形容詞〕下一個的；
(C) then〔副詞〕那時、然後；(D) later〔副詞〕稍後、〔形容詞〕稍晚的、稍後的。

句子中，因為有 reserves 與 has made 共兩個動詞，所以需要一個連接詞。選項中只有 until 可作副詞連接詞使用，故正確答案為 (A)。

**121** --------------------------------------------------------

Blico Marketing Group ------ provides clients with updated information about its services.

(A) equally

(B) perfectly

(C) substantially

(D) regularly

| | |
|---|---|
| 題型 | 詞彙——副詞 |
| 翻譯 | 博立刻行銷集團經常提供客戶旗下最新的服務資訊。 |
| 詞彙 | updated 最新的 |

(A) equally 相同地；(B) perfectly 完美地；(C) substantially 相當地；(D) regularly 定期地。

句子動詞為 provides 且時態為現在式，故可以一起使用的是時間副詞 regularly，本題正確答案為 (D)。

## 122

**Nortize Interiors has quickly gained a ------ for excellence among real estate agents in the city.**

(A) pursuit
(B) reputation
(C) center
(D) design

| | |
|---|---|
| 題型 | 詞彙——名詞 |
| 翻譯 | 諾爾台茲室內設計迅速地在這座城市的房仲業界，建立良好聲譽。 |
| 詞彙 | real estate agent 房屋仲介 |

選項中，只有 reputation 可以和空格後的介系詞 for 連用，並且最符合句意，所以正確答案為 (B)。

## 123

**The board members of Cistal Inc. ------ to make a hiring decision for the executive officer position by the end of next week.**

(A) indicate
(B) allow
(C) assume
(D) expect

| | |
|---|---|
| 題型 | 詞彙——動詞 |
| 翻譯 | 西絲塔公司的董事會預計在下週結束前，決定執行長人選。 |
| 詞彙 | board member 董事會成員 |
| | make a decision 做出決定 |
| | executive officer 執行長 |
| | position 工作職位 |

(A) indicate 表明；(B) allow 允許、同意；(C) assume 推測；(D) expect 期望。

本題選項中，後方可以接不定詞的只有及物動詞 expect，故正確答案為 (D)。

## 124

**Please notify the training session instructor of your anticipated absences ------ different dates can be scheduled.**

(A) ever since
(B) due to
(C) in spite of
(D) so that

| | |
|---|---|
| 題型 | 詞彙——片語 |
| 翻譯 | 務必告知培訓課程講師你預計缺課的時間，如此一來才能安排其他日期受訓。 |
| 詞彙 | notify A of 告知 A |
| | training session 培訓課程 |
| | instructor 講師 |
| | anticipate 預計 |
| | absence 缺課；缺席 |

(A) ever since 自從；(B) due to 因為；(C) in spite of 儘管；(D) so that 如此一來。

(B) 與 (C) 後方應接名詞而非子句，故不是正確答案。只有「so that」能接續「S ＋ can/may/will ＋ V」的句型，且也最符合句意，所以正確答案為 (D)。

## 125

Mr. Miller ------- that only the loan advisors should take part in the meeting on new trends in lending.

(A) specify
(B) to specify
(C) has specified
(D) is specified

題型 位置──動詞

翻譯 米勒先生曾指出，只有融資顧問須參與會議，討論貸款業務的新趨勢。

詞彙 loan advisor 融資顧問
take part in 參與
trend 趨勢 lending 貸款給他人

specify 為及物動詞，後可接續 that 子句，成為「specify that S V」。

(A) 與主詞的單複數變化不一致；(B) 為不定詞，不是動詞，所以不正確。(D) 為被動態。及物動詞以 that 子句作為名詞受詞時，被動句型的結構如下：「It is p.p. that S V」，但本題空格前的主詞為人，而不是「It is p.p.」，故 (D) 也不正確。

因此，型態為主動態，且與主詞的單複數一致的動詞為 has specified，故正確答案為 (C)。

## 126

Employees of Leading-Edge Machinery were amazed to receive an ------ bonus in July.

(A) inexperienced
(B) indefinite
(C) equipped
(D) unexpected

題型 詞彙──形容詞

翻譯 尖端領導機械公司的員工很驚喜，沒想到會在七月收到一筆意外的獎金。

詞彙 be amazed to V 對……感到驚喜

(A) inexperienced 無經驗的；(B) indefinite 無期限的；(C) equipped 裝備的、設置的；(D) unexpected 突然的、意料之外的。

句意上，由於前面有表示驚喜的 were amazed，故此處最適合填入的是 unexpected，正確答案是 (D)。

Ms. Diana must determine ------ or not to submit the proposal to the North American bureau.

(A) whether
(B) neither
(C) either
(D) unless

題型 文法──名詞子句連接詞

翻譯 戴安娜女士必須決定是否要提交企畫書到北美辦公室。

詞彙 determine 決定 submit 提交
proposal 企畫書 bureau 辦公機關

選項中，只有 whether 既可引導名詞子句作為 determine 的受詞，又可與空格後的不定詞連用，故正確答案為 (A)。

whether 是從屬連接詞，但若要表示「是否」的意思，且子句的主詞與主要子句的主詞相同時，子句的動詞可簡化成不定詞。

★下列為 whether 的慣用句型，意思是「是否做……」：
whether to V (or not)
whether or not to V

**128**

Staff members who have not ------ submitted their time sheets must do so by 5:00 P.M. today at the latest.

(A) only
(B) earlier
(C) yet
(D) rather

題型 詞彙——副詞

翻譯 還沒繳交班表的同仁，最晚要在今天下午五點前提交。

詞彙 staff member 同仁
submit 繳交
sheet 班表
at the latest 最晚

動詞為現在完成式時態時，可放在否定詞 not 後面的是 yet，故正確答案為 (C)。

★請熟記下列用法：

have/has not yet p.p.（尚未做……）

**129**

At last month's company banquet, 11 workers were ------ for having served the company for 25 years.

(A) recognized
(B) advocated
(C) resumed
(D) administered

題型 詞彙——動詞

翻譯 上個月的公司餐會上，有 11 名員工因為已經任職 25 年受到表揚。

詞彙 banquet 餐會
serve 任職

(A) recognize 認可、認出；(B) advocate 支持、擁護，(C) resume 恢復、繼續；(D) administer 管理、經營。

(B)、(C) 與 (D) 為被動態時，不與介系詞 for 連用，且不符合句意。而 recognize 既可與介系詞 for 連用，句意又符合，故正確答案為 (A)。

★ recognize 為及物動詞，且有下列慣用法：

recognize sb for sth〔主動態〕（因某事認可某人）
sb be recognized for sth〔被動態〕（某人因為某事被認可）

**130**

Because of its ------ to major tourist attractions, Casey Hotel in Singapore is frequently fully booked.

(A) proximity
(B) exclusion
(C) efficiency
(D) availability

題型 詞彙——名詞

翻譯 新加坡的凱西飯店鄰近主要觀光景點，房間常常預訂一空。

詞彙 tourist attraction 觀光景點

(A) proximity 相近性；(B) exclusion 除外、排除；(C) efficiency 效率；(D) availability 可用性。

(B)、(C) 與 (D) 不與介系詞 to 連用，且不符合句意。只有 proximity 可與空格後的介系詞 to 一起使用，且最適合本題句意，故正確答案為 (A)。

# PART 6

Charles Burrow, founder and president of Burrow's, Crosstown's largest clothing retailer, announced that he **131** $4,000 to the city's new community center. The funds derive from the sale of tickets to a party held last night at his company's **132**. Mr. Burrow will present a check to the center tomorrow at its opening ceremony.

**133** the past thirty years, Mr. Burrow has organized several fundraising events for charitable institutions and community services. **134**.

十字鎮最大的服飾零售業者，也就是布洛斯店的創辦人兼總裁，查爾斯·布洛，宣布將從昨天店裡舉行的晚宴售票所得當中，捐贈四千美元給新設的社區活動中心。布洛先生將在明天活動中心的開幕典禮上捐出支票。

布洛先生過去三十年來，為慈善機構和社區服務舉辦多場募款活動。昨晚的活動是有史以來最成功的一次。

**詞彙** founder 創辦人　president 總裁　retailer 零售業者　community 社區　fund 基金
derive from 從……　present A to B 將 A 送給 B　opening ceremony 開幕典禮
fundraising 募款活動　charitable institution 慈善機構

## 131

(A) will donate
(B) donated
(C) might donate
(D) donating

(A) 將捐贈
(B) 捐贈了
(C) 也許會捐贈
(D) 正在捐贈

**題型** 位置——動詞

因為名詞子句連接詞 that 後面需要一個動詞，所以非動詞的選項 (D) 為錯誤答案。再根據文意判斷，第二句中，布洛先生說明天將捐出 4000 美元的支票，所以較適合填入空格的為未來式的 (A)。

## 132

(A) museum
(B) hotel
(C) residence
(D) store

(A) 博物館
(B) 飯店
(C) 住處
(D) 店鋪

**題型** 詞彙——名詞

文章中提到「十字鎮最大的服飾零售業者」，所以正確答案為 (D)。

## 133

(A) Despite
(B) Over
(C) Between
(D) Beneath

(A) 儘管
(B) 在……期間
(C) 在……之間
(D) 在……之下

**題型 詞彙──介系詞**

空格後出現作為受詞的名詞片語 the past thirty years，表示過去三十年的這段期間，而可以一起連用的介系詞為 over，故正確答案為 (B)。

選項 (A)、(C)、(D) 無法與「期間」連用。

**134** NEW ----------------------------------------

(A) The opening ceremony will begin at 10:00 A.M.

(B) The community center offers classes for adults and children.

(C) Last night's event was the most successful thus far.

(D) Mr. Burrow plans to open a new location in London next year.

(A) 開幕典禮將在早上十點開始。

(B) 社區中心提供成人和小孩的課程。

(C) 昨晚的活動是有史以來最成功的一次。

(D) 布洛先生計劃明年要在倫敦展店。

**題型 填入句子**

從空格前的句子可以看出，布洛先生舉辦了幾次的募款活動，故在文意上最適合與此連接的句子是 (C)。

## 135–138 文章

August 30 — After two years of construction, the largest hotel in Pittsburgh history is almost ready to open. The Rivertop Hotel, on the banks of the Allegherry River, will have 1,500 rooms for visitors. **135**. The first guests will arrive on September 12 as part of a medical technology conference. The project is among four downtown area hotels **136**. According to Kristofer Walsh, president of the Pittsburgh Hotel & Lodging Association, these new developments are a **137**. "We've had a massive influx of visitors over the past few years," said Mr. Walsh. **138**, almost all the hotels in the city are completely full. Clearly, additional hotel rooms are needed.

8 月 30 日──耗時兩年，匹茲堡有史以來最大的飯店即將開張。河頂飯店位於阿勒格尼河河邊，將有 1,500 間客房，還有七間可容納至多 200 人的會議室。第一批賓客將在 9 月 12 日到來，參加醫療科技會議。這項建築計畫是市區四項興建中的其中一項建案。匹茲堡飯店和住宿協會會長克里斯多福．威爾許表示，這些新開發案有其必要。他說：「過去幾年來，遊客大量湧入。」因此，城裡每一間飯店幾乎都爆滿。顯然本市需要更多的飯店房間。

**詞彙** bank 河邊　according to 根據　lodging 住宿　association 協會　massive 大量的
influx 湧入　additional 額外的

**135** NEW ----------------------------------------

(A) It is unclear when it will be ready to accept reservations.

(B) Building renovations will begin next month.

(C) It will also have seven meeting rooms for groups of up to 200 people.

(D) There are multiple companies bidding on the project.

(A) 還不清楚何時開始接受訂房。

(B) 下個月將開始大樓翻新工程。

(C) 還有七間可容納至多 200 人的會議室。

(D) 有很多間公司正在競標這項計畫。

空格前的句子內容提到飯店的特徵為「have 1,500 rooms for visitors」，即能為顧客提供 1,500 間客房，而 (C) 則提及其他特徵，前後語意連貫，故正確答案為 (C)。

---

**136** -------------------------------------------------------------------

(A) to construct

(B) are constructing

(C) were constructed

(D) being constructed

(A) 為了建造

(B) 正在興建

(C) 已完工

(D) 正被興建的

題型 **位置**——分詞片語

先觀察此句的動詞為 is，且句中並未出現連接詞，所以可知 is 為句中唯一的動詞，所以不用考慮 (B) 與 (C)。

各選項的原形動詞 construct，應是要修飾前面的名詞 hotels，成為「hotels that is constructed」，而此處把後方形容詞子句變為分詞片語，省略關係代名詞 that，將 is 改為 being，故變為「hotels being constructed」，正確解答為 (D)。

★形容詞子句變為分詞片語：

1. 刪去關係代名詞

2. 動詞主動語態改為「V-ing」，被動語態改為「being p.p.」，be 動詞則是直接省略

---

**137** -------------------------------------------------------------------

(A) necessity

(B) nuisance

(C) risk

(D) bargain

(A) 必要性

(B) 麻煩事

(C) 風險

(D) 便宜貨

題型 **詞彙**——名詞

根據空格後面的句意，過去幾年湧入大量投宿人潮，可知有額外開發其他飯店的必要，本題正確答案為 (A)。

---

**138** -------------------------------------------------------------------

(A) On the other hand

(B) In other words

(C) In the first place

(D) As a result

(A) 另一方面

(B) 換句話說

(C) 起初

(D) 因此

題型 **詞彙**——副詞

空格前的句子提到湧入大量人潮，且空格後的句子則說城裡每間飯店幾乎都爆滿，兩者具有因果關係，所以答案為 (D)。

## 139–142 電子郵件

| | |
|---|---|
| **To:** Seth Ortega <sortega@xeroxmail.net> | 收件人：塞斯・歐特佳 <sortega@xeroxmail.net> |
| **From:** Jake Morris <jmorris@fubmanufacturing.com> | 寄件人：傑克・默里斯 <jmorris@fubmanufacturing.com> |
| **Date:** May 21 | 日期：5 月 21 日 |
| **Subject:** Factory Manager Position | 主旨：廠長職位 |

Dear Mr. Ortega,

You are officially invited to a second interview. This time, I will be meeting only with the top candidates to determine who is most **139** for the manager position. I believe you possess many of the **140** we are looking for.

I trust that you remain interested in this job opportunity. **141**, would a 3:00 P.M. appointment next Tuesday work for you? Please prepare a proposal that explains how you would increase production at our plant without decreasing quality. **142**.

Jake Morris

敬愛的歐特佳先生，

您正式受邀參加第二階段面試。這次我只會和最優秀的應徵者面談，決定誰最適合這個廠長職位。我們相信您具備多項我們正在尋找的特質。

我相信您仍對這個工作機會感興趣。若是如此，您下週二下午三點方便面試嗎？請您準備一份提案，說明您會如何提升工廠產能，同時無損品質。很期待能聽到您對提升工廠效率的見解。

傑克・默里斯

**詞彙** candidate 應徵者　determine 決定　possess 具備　remain interested in 仍對⋯⋯感興趣
job opportunity 工作機會　appointment 會面約定　work 行得通　proposal 提案
production 產能

**139**
(A) suiting
(B) suitable
(C) suit
(D) suits

(A) 適合的
(B) 適合的
(C) 適合
(D) 適合

**題型** 位置——形容詞

形容詞 suitable（適合的）位在 be 動詞後面，可與 most 結合形成最高級，且可以和介系詞 for 連用，所以答案為 (B)。

**★請記住常用用法：**
**be suitable for . . .**（適合⋯⋯）

**140**
(A) agreements
(B) performances
(C) qualities
(D) promotions

(A) 協議
(B) 表現
(C) 特質
(D) 晉升

根據文章內容，可以知道撰文者為人事專員，而對方因為擁有許多符合該職缺的特質，故被邀請參加二次面試。因此，文意上最適當的選項為 (C)。

**141**----------------------------------------

(A) Despite that         (A) 儘管如此

(B) If so              (B) 若是如此

(C) However         (C) 然而

(D) For example      (D) 舉例來說

題型 **詞彙**──副詞

空格前的句意為推測對方應該仍對該職缺有興趣，而空格後的內容中提及約定時間，所以最適當的選項為 (B)。

**142** NEW ----------------------------------------

(A) I would be happy to write a job reference for you.    (A) 我很樂意為您寫封推薦函。

(B) My assistant will train you in your new duties.    (B) 我的助理會訓練您適應新職務。

(C) I look forward to hearing your vision for an efficient workplace.    (C) 很期待能聽到您對提升工廠效率的見解。

(D) Your new product ideas were especially informative.    (D) 您的新商品構想富含資訊。

題型 **填入句子**

空格前的句子中，請求對方準備一份提案，說明自己如果被賦予工廠管理者的職責，如何在不降低品質的狀況下增加生產量。因此，最符合文意的是 (C)。

## 143–146 文章

| | |
|---|---|
| August 3 | 8月3日 |
| By Chris Garneau | 克里斯·加爾諾撰稿 |
| The Noxville Transportation Committee (NTC) will hold a public meeting at City Hall on Tuesday, August 10, at 6 P.M., to discuss its proposal to extend light rail service to Noxville Industrial Park. | 諾克斯維爾交通委員會將在8月10日週二傍晚6點，於市政廳召開公共會議，討論將輕軌服務，延伸到諾克斯維爾工業園區的提案。 |
| **143**. Residents of the community have complained that the extension will cause too much noise during the rush hours. **144**, the NTC has been researching the possibility of installing noise barriers along the tracks. At the meeting, Alex Khan, chief executive officer of Typhoon Builders, will explain how much noise reduction the NTC can **145** getting with the barriers. A **146** by Mayor Charlie Hoffman will follow. | 路線將穿越住宅區。該社區居民曾抱怨，這會造成尖峰時段過多噪音。對此，委員會研究了沿軌道裝設隔音板的可行性。颱風建設公司的執行長阿歷克斯·柯翰將與會說明，委員會如果裝設隔音板後，預期能降噪音的程度。緊接著會議之後，市長查理·霍夫曼將進行簡報。 |

詞彙 committee 委員會　hold a meeting 召開會議　City Hall 市政廳　extend 延伸　light rail 輕軌
resident 居民　installing 裝設　barrier 隔音板　reduction 降低　anticipate 預期
mayor 市長

**143** NEW ----------------------------------------------------------------

(A) The NTC finished the project ahead of schedule.　　　(A) 交通委員會提前完成了計畫
(B) The rail line will run through a residential area.　　　(B) 路線將穿越住宅區。
(C) The committee chairman will run for mayor　　　(C) 委員會主席明年將參選市長。
election next year.
(D) The NTC has decided to hold monthly meetings.　　　(D) 交通委員會決議每個月召開會議一次。

題型 **填入句子**

空格後面的句子中，提到某事的延長（the extension）造成尖峰時段過多噪音，為當地居民造成
不便。因此，符合文意的是 (B)。

**144** ----------------------------------------------------------------

(A) In addition　　　(A) 此外
(B) In time for　　　(B) 及時趕上
(C) In response　　　(C) 對此
(D) In conclusion　　　(D) 總之

題型 **詞彙——副詞**

空格前的句子中提到居民為噪音提出不滿，而空格後由提到 NTC 正在研究裝設隔音牆的可能
性。由此可知，最適當的詞彙是 In response，故正確答案為 (C)。

**145** ----------------------------------------------------------------

(A) remind　　　(A) 提醒
(B) accept　　　(B) 接受
(C) persuade　　　(C) 說服
(D) anticipate　　　(D) 預期

題型 **詞彙——動詞**

anticipate 可接動名詞作為受詞，又最符合句意，故正確答案為 (D)。

**146** ----------------------------------------------------------------

(A) to present　　　(A) 去呈現
(B) presenter　　　(B) 主持人
(C) presenting　　　(C) 正在簡報的
(D) presentation　　　(D) 簡報

題型 **位置——名詞**

可夾在不定冠詞 A 與介系詞 by 之間的為名詞，所以刪去 (A) 與 (C)。 (B) 雖然也可以放入，但是
by 後面已提及人物，故句意上最合適的為 presentation，本題正確答案為 (D)。

## PART 7

### 147–148 信件

We are aggressively looking for a receptionist for a local law firm in Crimson Shore. Duties include connecting calls, welcoming clients, answering telephones, handling meeting schedules, and sending out the daily e-mail. The qualified applicant should have an outgoing personality and be proficient in document preparation software. A university degree is required. Pay begins at $100 a week. Send your résumé to danielhickman@fairlaw.com.

我們是緋紅海岸當地一家法律事務所，急徵一名接待人員。職務包括轉接電話、接待客戶、接聽電話、安排會議行程，以及寄發每天的電子郵件。應徵者需個性外向，並精通文書處理軟體及擁有大學學歷。每週薪資一百美元起。請將履歷寄到danielhickman@fairlaw.com。

詞彙 aggressively 積極地　receptionist 接待人員　law firm 法律事務所　connect calls 轉接電話
applicant 應徵者　outgoing 外向的　be proficient in 精通　degree 學歷

**What job is most likely available?**

(A) Teller
(B) Lawyer
(C) Supervisor
(D) Assistant

該信件最有可能要招募何種職務？

(A) 出納員
(B) 律師
(C) 管理者
(D) 助理

在第一句「We are aggressively looking for a receptionist for a local law firm」中，提到該地區的法律事務所正在徵求接待人員，故正確答案為 (D)。

**What type of qualification is NOT included as a requirement for the job?**

(A) Accounting
(B) Word processing
(C) Client service
(D) University degree

該職缺不需要何種資格條件？

(A) 會計
(B) 文書處理
(C) 客戶服務
(D) 大學學歷

「proficient in document preparation software」表示需要 (B) 文書處理能力；「Duties include connecting calls, welcoming clients, answering telephones」，表示需要 (C) 客服能力；「A university degree is required.」表示需要 (D) 大學學歷，故沒有包含在文章內的為 (A)。

## 149–150 訊息串

| | |
|---|---|
| **Sylvia Lin** 5:44 P.M.<br>Hi, Jackie. Did you take a look at the photographs of West Third Avenue property? | 希維亞·林〔下午5:44〕：<br>嗨，賈姬。你看過第三西大道那間房子的照片了嗎？ |
| **Jackie McLean** 5:45 P.M.<br>Yes, I did. Considering that many of our designers and editors are working remotely, are all those rooms really needed? | 賈姬·麥克連〔下午5:45〕：<br>有啊。考量到我們很多設計師和編輯都在遠端作業，所有房間真的都會用到嗎？ |
| **Sylvia Lin** 5:47 P.M.<br>As we expand, more people will be working on-site. | 希維亞·林〔下午5:47〕：<br>如果我們擴張營運的話，就會有更多人在那裡工作。 |
| **Jackie McLean** 5:48 P.M.<br>That might not be for some time. | 賈姬·麥克連〔下午5:48〕：<br>短時間內不會吧。 |
| **Sylvia Lin** 5:50 P.M.<br>We need to think of both our immediate and long-term needs. This building provides plenty of room to consider staff expansion. | 希維亞·林〔下午5:50〕：<br>我們必須同時考慮現在和長期需求。那房子裡有足夠的房間，考量之後擴編的話。 |
| **Jackie McLean** 5:52 P.M.<br>That's true. Our needs might change. Particularly when we begin signing agreements with more authors | 賈姬·麥克連〔下午5:52〕：<br>說的也是。我們的需求可能會改變，尤其是和更多作家簽約以後。 |

**詞彙** property 房子；不動產　editor 編輯　remotely 遠端地　on-site 在現場　long-term 長期的
staff expansion 人員擴編　sign an agreement 簽約　author 作家

---

**149**

**What kind of business do the people probably work for?**

(A) A relocation company
(B) A publishing company
(C) A property agency
(D) An exterior design company

這些人可能在什麼公司工作？

(A) 搬家公司
(B) 出版公司
(C) 房仲公司
(D) 外觀設計公司

從下午 5 點 45 分麥克連女士話中提到的「editors」（編輯）和下午 5 點 52 分提到的「signing agreements with more authors」（和更多作家簽約）兩段句子，可以得知正確答案為 (B)。

---

**150** (NEW)

**At 5:52 P.M., what does Ms. McLean most likely mean when she writes, "That's true"?**

(A) A different place should be rented.
(B) A new place will be too expensive.
(C) The property may meet the company's needs in the future.
(D) The property needs overall improvements.

麥克連女士在下午 5:52 的時候寫道：「說的也是」，她最可能的意思是？

(A) 應該租別的地方。
(B) 新地點太貴了。
(C) 新房子可能滿足公司未來的需求。
(D) 新房子需要全面翻修。

下午 5 點 44 分林女士先問麥克連女士是否看過另一間房子的照片，到 5 點 50 分時，她說如果以後招募新人，那間房子能夠提供足夠空間，故麥克連女士回答「That's true.」，指的應是新房子可能滿足公司未來的需求，正確答案為 (C)。

## 151–153 備忘錄

| | |
|---|---|
| **To:** All staff members<br>**From:** Dwight Howard, Director of Operations<br>**Date:** June 5<br>**Subject:** East Wing Closure | 收件人：全體員工<br>寄件人：德懷特·霍華德，營運長<br>日期：6月5日<br>主旨：東側大樓關閉 |

This is to inform you that the east wing of the main office building will be temporarily closed at the end of next week. The maintenance staff will be replacing all ceiling lights in the offices and meeting rooms with high-quality fluorescent lights. Safety regulations stipulate that no staff members be allowed in the area while the work is in progress. The work is due to begin Friday, on June 9, and be finished on Saturday, June 10. The affected offices are 200–262. Staff members in these offices should plan to finish assignments at home or, if necessary, use a temporary work area in another section of the building. To reserve a temporary work area, you may contact Administrative Assistant Michael Kane at extension 242. Please note that temporary work areas are limited and requests must be submitted by 5:00 P.M. on June 7 at the latest.

本信是為通知您，主辦公大樓的東側樓層將在下週末暫時關閉。維修人員將會替換所有辦公室和會議室的天花板照明，換成高品質日光燈。根據安全規定，施工期間禁止任何員工出入。工程將從6月9日週五開始，到6月10日週六結束。受影響的是200號到262號辦公室，這些辦公室員工應規劃在家工作，必要的話，也可使用本建築其他區域的臨時辦公區。若需預訂臨時辦公區，可聯繫行政助理麥可·肯恩，分機為242。請留意臨時辦公區空間有限，最晚必須在6月7日下午五點前提出申請。

**詞彙** wing （建築）側翼　temporarily 暫時地　maintenance 維修　ceiling 天花板
high-quality 高品質的　fluorescent light 日光燈　safety regulation 安全法規
stipulate 規定　be due to V 預計將　assignment 指派的工作
administrative assistant 行政助理　extension 分機　by . . . at the latest 最晚在……前

**151** - - - - - - - - - - - - - - - - - - - - - - - - - - - - - - - - - - - - - - - - - - - - - - - - - - - - - - - -

**What does the memo mainly report?**

(A) Staff members are being relocated to new offices.
(B) Meeting space is being added.
(C) A safety inspection is being conducted.
(D) Office lighting is being upgraded.

**這則備忘錄主要是報告什麼？**

(A) 員工正要搬到新的辦公室。
(B) 將增加會議室空間。
(C) 安檢進行中。
(D) 辦公室照明升級。

從「The maintenance staff will be replacing all ceiling lights in the offices and meeting rooms with high-quality fluorescent lights.」，可以得知備忘錄主要是在告知照明裝備的替換，故正確答案為 (D)。

## 152

| When will the closure begin? | 東側大樓何時開始關閉？ |
|---|---|
| (A) On June 5 | (A) 6 月 5 日 |
| (B) On June 7 | (B) 6 月 7 日 |
| (C) On June 9 | (C) 6 月 9 日 |
| (D) On June 10 | (D) 6 月 10 日 |

從「The work is due to begin Friday, on June 9, and be finished on Saturday, June 10.」中，可以得知關閉期間從 6 月 9 日開始，正確答案為 (C)。

## 153

| What are some staff members asked to do? | 部分員工須做什麼？ |
|---|---|
| (A) Call a manager | (A) 電話連絡經理 |
| (B) Work from home | (B) 在家工作 |
| (C) Vacate the offices | (C) 清空辦公室 |
| (D) Complete work ahead of time | (D) 提前完成工作 |

從「Staff members in these offices should plan to finish assignments at home」中，可以看出受關閉影響的員工需要在家完成工作，故正確答案為 (B)。

## 154–155 電子郵件

**To:** Justin Chu
<jchu@maximummail.com>
**From:** Jimmy Lee
<jlee@exoticdecoration.com>
**Date:** September 11
**Subject:** Late delivery

Dear Mr. Chu,

Thank you for your recent order from Exotic Decoration. Because of a thunderstorm in our area, some of our orders still have not been delivered. Road closures have made it impossible for trucks to pick up products from our storage room, and some of our workers have been unable to commute to work. However, we expect to resume normal operations within 12 hours. Your order should be shipped by the end of the week. The shipping fee on all orders will be free. I sincerely apologize for a delay in shipping.

Best regards,
Jimmy Lee
Customer Relations Manager

---

收件人：賈斯丁・朱
<jchu@maximummail.com>
寄件人：吉米・李
<jlee@exoticdecoration.com>
日期：9月11日
主旨：延遲寄送

親愛的朱先生：

感謝您近期訂購異國裝潢的產品。由於我們地區遭逢雷雨，部分訂購貨品未能寄出。封路使得貨車無法從倉庫取貨，也讓部分員工不能通勤上班。然而，我們希望能在12個小時內恢復正常營運。您訂購的物品將在這週末以前出貨。所有訂單都將免運費。我為延遲出貨誠摯向您致歉。

顧客關係經理
吉米・李 敬上

---

**詞彙** **thunderstorm** 雷雨　**road closure** 封路　**storage room** 倉庫　**commute to work** 通勤上班　**resume** 恢復　**normal operation** 正常營運　**shipping fee** 運費　**sincerely** 誠摯地

## 154

**Why was the order late?**

(A) Payment has still not been received.

(B) Severe weather affected the delivery schedule.

(C) The product that was ordered is not in stock.

(D) The firm used an inaccurate mailing address.

為什麼訂單晚出貨？

(A) 還沒收到付款。

(B) 天氣嚴重影響出貨時程。

(C) 訂購的產品沒有庫存。

(D) 公司寄錯地址。

由「Because of a thunderstorm in our area, some of our orders still have not been delivered.」可知是雷雨影響了貨運，故正確答案為 (B)。

**155**

**What will Mr. Chu receive?**

(A) A discount coupon for his next purchase

(B) A cash refund

(C) Complimentary shipping on his order

(D) A replacement part

朱先生將收到什麼？

(A) 下次購物可用的折價券

(B) 現金退款

(C) 免運費優待

(D) 更換商品

由「The shipping fee on all orders will be free.」可以得知，公司將提供免運以補償顧客，故正確答案為 (C)。

**156–158 電子郵件**

**From:** Tim Daily
<tdaily@sunflower.com>
**To:** Derek Hamilton
<lhamilton@goodcaterer.com>
**Date:** June 12
**Subject:** Re: Floral centerpieces

寄件人：提姆‧戴利
<tdaily@sunflower.com>
收件人：德瑞克‧哈米爾頓
<lhamilton@goodcaterer.com>
日期：6月12日
主旨：關於：檀花

Dear Mr. Hamilton,

This e-mail serves as confirmation of our telephone conversation this morning about your request for 12 flower arrangements for your company awards ceremony. You had asked that they be comparable to the floral centerpieces that we made for your last event. However, my supplier for the rose of Sharon has notified me that, due to a delay at the greenhouses, they won't be available until the end of this month.

Because you need the flower arrangements finished by June 17, I think it would be best to select an alternative flower. I recommend the hollyhock, which is comparable in appearance. Please let me know if this is acceptable by replying to this e-mail. I will then fax you the finished

親愛的哈米爾頓先生：

這封電子郵件是要向您確認今早在電話裡談過的，貴公司頒獎典禮上所需要的12個花卉擺設。您要求這次提供的檀花要比照上次的活動。然而，由於溫室那邊的延誤，木芙蓉的供應商說他們要到本月底才能供貨。

因為您需要所有花卉擺設在6月17日以前完成，我想最好能選擇其他種花替代木芙蓉。我建議外型相似的蜀葵。請回信讓我知道這建議是否可行。我會再傳真最終版合約和價目表給您。如果有

| | |
|---|---|
| agreement and pricing list. If you have any other questions, please contact me at 432-234-2345. | 其他問題，請透過432-234-2345聯絡我。 |
| Thank you, | 感謝您， |
| Tim Daily<br>Manager, Sunflower | 向日葵花店經理<br>提姆·戴利 |

**詞彙** floral centerpiece 檯花（餐桌中央的擺飾）　serve as 作為　flower arrangement 花卉擺設；插花　awards ceremony 頒獎典禮　comparable 相當的　supplier 供應商　greenhouse 溫室　alternative 其他的　appearance 外型　acceptable 可行的　reply to 回覆　agreement 合約

**156** -----------------------------------------------------------------

**What is suggested about Mr. Hamilton?**

(A) He is a friend of Mr. Daily.
(B) He is preparing a private party at his house.
(C) He has asked for a change to his order.
(D) He has used Sunflower's services previously.

下列何者與哈米爾頓先生有關？

(A) 他是戴利先生的朋友。
(B) 他正準備在自宅舉辦私人派對。
(C) 他要求修改訂單。
(D) 他先前用過向日葵花店的服務。

從郵件第一段的「You had asked that they be comparable to the floral centerpieces that we made for your last event.」中，可推測哈米爾頓先生曾與此花店有過生意往來，故正確答案為 (D)。

**157** -----------------------------------------------------------------

**Why does Mr. Daily recommend replacing the rose of Sharon?**

(A) They are out of stock.
(B) They are the wrong size.
(C) They are not cheap.
(D) They are not fresh.

為什麼戴利先生建議替換掉木芙蓉？

(A) 沒有庫存。
(B) 尺寸不對。
(C) 不便宜。
(D) 不新鮮。

從郵件第一段的「However, my supplier for the rose of Sharon has notified me that . . . they won't be available until the end of this month」中，可以知道木芙蓉現在沒有供應，故正確答案為 (A)。

**158** -----------------------------------------------------------------

**What does Mr. Daily ask Mr. Hamilton to do?**

(A) Sign a contract
(B) Talk at the shop
(C) Respond to an e-mail
(D) Send a partial payment

戴利先生要求哈米爾頓先生做什麼事？

(A) 簽約
(B) 到店裡談談
(C) 回覆電子郵件
(D) 支付部分金額

郵件第二段說：「Please let me know if this is acceptable by replying to this e-mail.」，故可知戴利先生要求哈米爾頓先生回覆信件，以確認花卉選擇，故正確答案為 (C)。

## The Museum of Fine Arts

The Museum of Fine Arts will host Ed Harrison on Wednesday, April 5, at 6:00 P.M. Mr. Harrison will talk about his most recent book, *The American Dream's Painting*. Published by Neo Publishing, the volume provides a detailed description of the history of art in North America. The talk is open to the public. No reservation will be taken. Guests must arrive at least half an hour before the start time because seats are limited to 100. For additional information, call 287-333-2422 or go to our website.

## 美術館

艾德‧哈里森受邀在4月5日週三晚上六點,在美術館談他的新書《美國夢之繪》。這本書由新興出版社出版,詳實描述了北美的藝術史。本場講座對外開放。不需要預約座位。由於只有100個座位,請各位賓客在演說開始前提早至少半小時進場。欲知更多資訊,可以來電287-333-2422詢問,或是上官網查詢。

---

**詞彙** **fine art** 美術　**host** 主持　**most recent** 最近的　**volume** 書;冊　**detailed** 詳實的
**description** 描述　**talk** 講座　**be open to** 對……開放　**reservation** 預約
**be limited to** 只有;上限為　**for additional information** 欲知更多資訊

**159** ----------------------------------------------------------------

**Who is Mr. Harrison?**

(A) An author
(B) An artist
(C) A bookstore supervisor
(D) A museum staff member

**哈里森先生是誰?**

(A) 作家
(B) 藝術家
(C) 書店主管
(D) 博物館職員

從第二句「Mr. Harrison will talk about his most recent book, *The American Dream's Painting.*」可以知道,哈里森先生為一名作家,正確答案為 (A)。

**160** ----------------------------------------------------------------

**How should seats for the event be obtained?**

(A) Online
(B) By telephone
(C) By mail
(D) In person

**如何取得講座的席位?**

(A) 上網
(B) 用電話
(C) 寄信
(D) 親自到場

從第六句「Guests must arrive at least half an hour before the start time because seats are limited to 100.」中可知,賓客須提早進場才能確保取得講座的位子,故正確答案為 (D)。

**161–164 文章**

## Expansion Project Moving Forward in Shanghai

July 5 — Roland Technology finished the first stage of its expansion project two weeks ago. Roland Technology, one of the largest manufacturers of components used in computer monitors and projectors, began construction on its three new factories to be built over the next eight years. —[1]—. The first of the factories to be built, in China's Shanghai, is the company's largest factory and will ultimately produce 60% of the company's production quota every year.

The new plant has brought with it a rise in jobs for local citizens. —[2]—. Over 1,500 construction workers were employed to build the large-scale factory and its surrounding structures. Roland Technology President Takahashi Miyuki said, "This is the largest project for our company. When we began construction, we realized that it was going to need plenty of money, resources, and staff. —[3]—.We employed locals to expand the physical plant as well as adding a number of employees to our full time payroll. We hope to do the same thing in Japan. We plan to start building in Tokyo soon."

The company's main office is now located in Tokyo, Japan. Extra factories will be constructed in Roland Technology's other locations, including in Thailand and Korea. While the remaining plants will not be as large as the Shanghai factory, they will still need resources and labor. —[4]—.

## 上海擴建計畫有所進展

7月5日—羅蘭科技兩週前完成第一期擴建計畫。羅蘭科技是電腦螢幕和投影機零組件的製造大廠,目前啟動擴廠計畫,將在未來八年內建設三間新工廠。第一間工廠位於中國上海,是公司旗下最大的工廠,最終產能將達公司年度生產總額的60%。

新工廠為當地市民帶來就業機會。超過1,500名工人受僱來建設這間大型廠房和周邊建築。羅蘭科技的總裁高橋美雪說:「這是公司史上最大的計畫。我們投入建設後,就明白需要大量金錢、資源和人力。我們很高興看到這項計畫對當地勞工的影響。我們聘僱當地人來擴建硬體廠房,也將計多員工轉為全職人員。希望在日本也能比照辦理,很快地,我們就會在東京計劃開始新建設。」

總公司目前設在日本東京。更多工廠會建在羅蘭科技的其他據點,包括泰國和韓國。雖然其餘工廠都不比上海這間來得大,但仍會有資源和人力需求。

---

**詞彙** expansion project 擴建計畫　projector 投影機　production quota 生產總額　surrounding 周邊的　structure 建築　resource 資源　locals 當地人　physical 硬體的　plant 廠房　payroll 職員表;工資表　main office 總公司　labor 人力

**161** - - - - - - - - - - - - - - - - - - - - - - - - - - - - - - - - - - - - - - - - - - - - - - - - - - - - - - - - - - - - - - - - -

**What is mentioned about Roland Technology?**

(A) It produces monitor elements.
(B) It was recently acquired by its competitor.
(C) It is remodeling its company headquarters.
(D) It sells construction materials.

**文中提到羅蘭科技的什麼?**

(A) 生產螢幕元件。
(B) 近期被競爭對手併購。
(C) 總部正在改建。
(D) 販賣建材。

根據第一段第二句的「Roland Technology, one of the largest manufacturers of components used in computer monitors and projectors . . .」,可知羅蘭科技為電腦螢幕與投影機零件的製造廠,故正確答案為 (A)。

**162** - - - - - - - - - - - - - - - - - - - - - - - - - - - - - - - - - - - - - - - - - - - - - - - - - - - - - - -

**What is inferred about the Roland Technology factory in Shanghai?**

(A) It was the third new factory which was built last year.

(B) It is the biggest factory the company has.

(C) It manufactures a quarter of the company's output.

(D) It took over six years to construct.

關於羅蘭科技在上海的工廠，文中可推論出什麼？

(A) 它是去年蓋好的第三間新工廠。

(B) 它是這間公司最大的工廠。

(C) 它的產量是全公司產能的四分之一。

(D) 它耗時六年多才蓋好。

從第一段第三句「The first of the factories to be built, in China's Shanghai, is the company's largest factory and will ultimately produce 60% of the company's production quota every year.」中，可以得知上海的廠房將會是最大的工廠，故正確答案為 (B)。

**163** - - - - - - - - - - - - - - - - - - - - - - - - - - - - - - - - - - - - - - - - - - - - - - - - - - - - - - -

**Where will the next Roland Technology factory be constructed?**

(A) In China

(B) In Thailand

(C) In Korea

(D) In Japan

羅蘭科技的下一間工廠會蓋在哪裡？

(A) 中國

(B) 泰國

(C) 韓國

(D) 日本

從第二段第六句「We hope to do the same thing in Japan.」和第七句「We plan to start building in Tokyo soon.」中，可以得知接下來會在日本建造工廠，故正確答案為 (D)。

**164** (NEW) - - - - - - - - - - - - - - - - - - - - - - - - - - - - - - - - - - - - - - - - - - - - - - - - -

**In which of the positions marked [1], [2], [3] and [4] does the following sentence best belong?**

**"We were delighted to see the influence the project had on local laborers."**

(A) [1]

(B) [2]

(C) [3]

(D) [4]

下列句子最適合出現在 [1]、[2]、[3]、[4] 的哪個位置中？

「我們很高興看到這項計畫對當地勞工的影響。」

(A) [1]

(B) [2]

(C) [3]

(D) [4]

[3] 右側的句子提到聘僱當地人來擴建硬體廠房，可得知題目引用的句子放此最合適，所以答案為 (C)。

## 165–167 文章

Situated on the corner of First Avenue and East Street, Variety opened a decade ago and rapidly became a popular eatery. As its name suggests, Variety features a large collection of dishes prepared with several international recipes. Variety had been closed for two months while undergoing an improvement in management. It reopened its doors two weeks ago. The new chef, Matt Shelian, has made a remarkable menu with an even wider selection of gourmet soups, salads, and delicious entrées. Some of his specialties include excellent seafood dishes, such as the smoked halibut with mango and the shrimp with chili sauce. Please be sure to try the outstanding dessert—caramel apple pie. With so many delicious items to select, Variety is certain to be a new favorite.

多饌飯館坐落在第一大道和東街的交界處。開幕至今已有十載，並迅速累積人氣。店如其名，各種異國料理的餐點是這間店的特色。多饌飯館曾為了改善經營狀況而暫時歇業兩個月，並在兩週前重新開張。新任主廚麥特·薛連推出的菜單讓人驚艷，他推出更多選擇的精緻湯品、沙拉和美味主菜。他的招牌菜包括海鮮盛宴，像是芒果佐煙燻大比目魚和辣醬蝦。也絕對不能錯過出色甜點—焦糖蘋果派。有這麼多美食可供挑選，多饌飯館勢必成為饕客新歡。

**詞彙** decade 十年　eatery 飯館　a large collection of 各種的　reopen 重新開張　remarkable 讓人驚艷的　a selection of 多樣的　gourmet 精緻的　entrée 主菜　specialty 招牌菜　halibut 大比目魚　be certain to V 勢必會……

**165**

**What is the purpose of the article?**

(A) To review a restaurant
(B) To promote a cooking class
(C) To compare two restaurants
(D) To announce a new location

這篇文章目的為何？

(A) 評論一間餐廳
(B) 推廣烹飪課程
(C) 比較兩間餐廳
(D) 宣布搬到新地點

仔細閱讀文章的第一句：「Situated on the corner of First Avenue and East Street, Variety opened a decade ago and rapidly became a popular eatery」及最後兩句「Please be sure to try the outstanding dessert—caramel apple pie. With so many delicious items to select, Variety is certain to be a new favorite.」，可知文章通篇講述「多饌飯館」這間餐廳，故正確答案為 (A)。

**166**

**What is mentioned about Mr. Shelian?**

(A) He is proficient in making seafood dishes.
(B) He uses only local produce.
(C) He has refurbished a restaurant.
(D) He started working at Variety six months ago.

文中提到薛連先生什麼？

(A) 他擅長料理海鮮。
(B) 他只用在地食材。
(C) 他整修了一間餐廳。
(D) 他六個月前開始在多饌飯館工作。

從文章的第四句「Some of his specialties include excellent seafood dishes, such as the smoked halibut with mango and the shrimp with chili sauce.」，其中提到的「seafood」、「halibut」和「shrimp」，皆可知道薛連先生擅長料理海鮮，故本題正確答案為 (A)。

## 167

**What is suggested about the restaurant?**

(A) Its management replaced most of the staff.

(B) It serves an excellent dessert.

(C) Its most popular dish is the halibut.

(D) It has relocated to a new building.

文中提到這間餐廳的什麼資訊?

(A) 管理部門大換員工。

(B) 它的甜點非常出色。

(C) 大比目魚是最受歡迎的菜色。

(D) 店面搬到新的大樓。

文章的第五句「Please be sure to try the outstanding dessert—caramel apple pie.」提到,餐廳的甜點很出色,不容錯過,故可知正確答案為 (B)。

---

**168–171 電子郵件**

**To:** Robert Lim
<rlim@supremetc.co.bb>
**From:** Cynthia Jordan
<cjordan@titangd.co.bb>
**Subject:** Re: Information
**Date:** April 14
**Attachment:** BLS1

收件人:羅伯特·林姆
<rlim@supermetc.co.bb>
寄件人:辛西亞·喬登
<cjordan@titangd.co.bb>
主旨:關於:資訊
日期:4月14日
附件:BLS1

---

Dear Mr. Lim,

I am following up on the Titan Gardening service proposal I sent on 22 March. —[1]—.

We are one of the best in Queensville, and we want to add you to our list of satisfied clients. Our clients include numerous local businesses like hotels, restaurants, and resorts. —[2]—. In the event you overlooked the original proposal, I am attaching it again here.

The proposal is based on the service you asked about, namely the maintenance of the grounds around Supreme Tennis Courts twice a week. —[3]—. If you are interested in more extensive work, such as replacing trees, extra charges would apply.

I'm looking forward to hearing from you. I hope our company will have the chance to be beneficial to you in the future. —[4]—.

Sincerely,
Cynthia Jordan

親愛的林姆先生:

我來信是向您後續詢問,關於我在3月22日寄出的泰坦園藝服務提案。

我們是皇后村最好的廠商,想請您加入成為我們滿意顧客清單上的一員。許多當地企業,像是飯店、餐廳和度假中心都是我們的客戶。如果您上次沒注意到初版提案,我在這封信再次附檔給您。

根據您當初所詢問的服務,也就是超凡網球場一週兩次的場地維護,我們做出這份提案。此外,我們也會持續再次評估您的需求,並且每個月提供您兩次建議。如果你需要其他服務,像是栽種別的樹種,則需要再增加費用。

期待您的回信。我希望我們公司未來能有機會為您服務。

辛西亞·喬登 敬上

---

**詞彙** **follow up on** 後續追蹤　**gardening** 園藝　**proposal** 提案書　**in the event** 如果　**attach** 附加

**168**

Why was the e-mail written?

(A) To schedule a meeting
(B) To explain new prices
(C) To resend a previous estimate
(D) To send in a corrected proposal

為什麼會寫這封電子郵件？

(A) 排定會議
(B) 解釋新的價格
(C) 重寄之前的估價單
(D) 寄出修改過的提案

第二段最後一句說了「In the event you overlooked the original proposal, I am attaching it again here.」，表示怕對方沒看到，所以重寄了提案過去，再從第二段的「If you are interested in more extensive work, such as replacing trees, extra charges would apply.」可以得知，提案內容與價錢相關，故最合適的答案為 (C)。

**169**

What is suggested in the e-mail?

(A) Mr. Lim is a satisfied customer.
(B) Titan Gardening is a new business.
(C) Ms. Jordan had a meeting with Mr. Lim.
(D) Mr. Lim asked Ms. Jordan for some information.

這封電子郵件提到什麼？

(A) 林姆先生這顧客很滿意。
(B) 泰坦園藝是新公司。
(C) 林姆先生和喬登女士開過會。
(D) 林姆先生向喬登女士詢問資訊。

第二段的第一句「The proposal is based on the service you asked about」，可知林姆先生有詢問過喬登女士一些事情，故正確答案為 (D)。

**170**

What type of business does Mr. Lim probably work for?

(A) A hotel
(B) A tennis facility
(C) A restaurant
(D) A gardening center

林姆先生可能從事的行業是？

(A) 飯店業
(B) 網球設施
(C) 餐飲業
(D) 園藝中心

從第二段的第一句「the maintenance of the grounds around Supreme Tennis Courts twice a week」中，可推測林姆先生最可能從事與網球相關的事業，故正確答案為 (B)。

**171** NEW

In which of the positions marked [1], [2], [3] and [4] does the following sentence best belong?

"Additionally, we would reevaluate your requirements on an ongoing basis and relay recommendations to you twice a month."

(A) [1]
(B) [2]
(C) [3]
(D) [4]

下列句子最適合出現在 [1]、[2]、[3]、[4] 的哪個位置中？

「此外，我們也會持續再次評估您的需求，並且每個月提供您兩次建議。」

(A) [1]
(B) [2]
(C) [3]
(D) [4]

[3] 左側的句子提到每週兩次的網球場維護，可知題目引用的句子放此最合適，所以答案為 (C)。

| | | | |
|---|---|---|---|
| **Tyrone Gibson** | 1:32 P.M. | 泰隆・吉布森〔下午1:32〕： | |
| Thank you for participating in the virtual sales meeting this morning. Do you have any other questions? | | 感謝你們參加今天早上的線上業務會議。有其他問題嗎？ | |
| **Judy Chung** | 1:35 P.M. | 茱蒂・鍾〔下午1:35〕： | |
| George and I are not certain about how the new sales territory maps influence established customers. Will the new territories apply exclusively to new customers? | | 喬治和我不太確定，更新銷售區會不會影響到舊客戶。新的銷售區只適用於新客戶嗎？ | |
| **Tyrone Gibson** | 1:37 P.M. | 泰隆・吉布森〔下午1:37〕： | |
| Of course not. The new territories apply to first-time and established customers alike. | | 當然不只。新舊客戶都適用。 | |
| **Judy Chung** | 1:38 P.M. | 茱蒂・鍾〔下午1:38〕： | |
| So, does that mean I will no longer obtain commissions from my French customer, YDV Mechanism? | | 所以這樣的意思是說，我不能再從我的法國客戶YDV機械抽佣金囉？ | |
| **Tyrone Gibson** | 1:39 P.M. | 泰隆・吉布森〔下午1:39〕： | |
| That's right. All established customers in northern France go to George. | | 對，法國北部的舊客戶之後歸給喬治。 | |
| **George Kim** | 1:41 P.M. | 喬治・金〔下午1:41〕： | |
| But why don't I just allow Judy to keep YDV Mechanism? | | 但為什麼我不能讓茱蒂留著她的YDV機械？ | |
| **Tyrone Gibson** | 1:42 P.M. | 泰隆・吉布森〔下午1:42〕： | |
| YDV Mechanism is a big customer. | | YDV機械是大客戶。 | |
| **George Kim** | 1:44 P.M. | 喬治・金〔下午1:44〕： | |
| Yes, but I want to avoid disrupting a productive partnership. Plus, this customer is unimportant to me. | | 是，但我不想中斷這個良好的夥伴關係。而且，這個客戶對我來說並不重要。 | |
| **Tyrone Gibson** | 1:45 P.M. | 泰隆・吉布森〔下午1:45〕： | |
| I don't see it as disrupting, really. However, if you feel strongly about this, George, I might be able to bend the rules if our president approves of it. | | 我不認這會造成中斷。不過，如果喬治你堅持，我也許可以通融，只要總裁同意的話。 | |
| **Judy Chung** | 1:47 P.M. | 茱蒂・鍾〔下午1:47〕： | |
| Why don't I speak to the customer? | | 為什麼不讓我跟客戶說？ | |
| **Tyrone Gibson** | 1:48 P.M. | 泰隆・吉布森〔下午1:48〕： | |
| I don't think that's suitable. | | 我想這不太適當。 | |
| **Judy Chung** | 1:49 P.M. | 茱蒂・鍾〔下午1:49〕： | |
| Understood. | | 了解。 | |
| **George Kim** | 1:49 P.M. | 喬治・金〔下午1:49〕： | |
| All right. We're looking forward to hearing back from you about this matter. | | 好吧。期待知曉您處理的後續消息。 | |

**詞彙** virtual 線上的；虛擬的　**territory** 區域　**established** 已建立的　**commission** 佣金

disrupt 干擾中斷　productive 成效良好的　partnership 夥伴關係　bend the rules 通融
approve of 同意　suitable 適當的

**172** ----------------------------------------

**Who most likely is Mr. Gibson?**

(A) A president

(B) The head of sales

(C) A tour guide

(D) A personnel director

吉布森先生最有可能是？

(A) 總裁

(B) 業務主管

(C) 導遊

(D) 人資經理

下午 1 點 32 分時，吉布森先生說了：「Thank you for participating in the virtual sales meeting this morning」，由於此為上司對下屬的口吻與說詞，故可以知道最合適的答案是 (B)。

**173** ----------------------------------------

**What is inferred about Ms. Chung?**

(A) She has a good rapport with YDV Mechanism.

(B) She is being relocated to an office in France.

(C) She is delighted with the new territory assigned to her.

(D) She did not take part in the sales meeting.

文中提到鍾女士什麼事？

(A) 她和 YDV 機械關係良好。

(B) 她正分派到法國辦公室。

(C) 她對新分配的銷售區感到開心。

(D) 她沒有參加業務會議。

從下午 1 點 41 分金先生說的「But why don't you just allow Judy to keep YDV Mechanism?」與下午 1 點 44 分說的「Yes, but I want to avoid disrupting a productive partnership」，可知金先生不想介入鍾女士與 YDV 機械良好的客戶關係，故可知正確答案為 (A)。

**174** (NEW) ----------------------------------------

**At 1:48 P.M., what does Mr. Gibson most likely mean when he writes, "I don't think that's suitable"?**

(A) He is doubtful that Ms. Chung can meet YDV Mechanism's requirements.

(B) He thinks Ms. Chung has misunderstood.

(C) He would like Ms. Chung to visit France.

(D) He doesn't want Ms. Chung to contact YDV Mechanism regarding this matter.

下午 1:48 時，吉布森先生寫道：「我想這不太適當」，他最可能的意思是？

(A) 他質疑鍾女士能否滿足 YDV 機械的需求。

(B) 他覺得鍾女士誤解了。

(C) 他希望鍾女士拜訪法國。

(D) 他不希望鍾女士就這件事聯繫 YDV 機械。

在吉布森先生說出「我想這不太適當」前，鍾女士曾問：「為什麼不讓我跟客戶說？」，代表吉布森先生的回覆有不希望鍾女士直接聯繫客戶的意思，故答案為 (D)。

**175** ----------------------------------------

**What will probably happen next?**

(A) Ms. Chung will go over the new map of the sales territory.

(B) Ms. Chung will speak with her customer.

(C) Mr. Gibson will call the company's president.

(D) Mr. Kim will accept a job offer from YDV Mechanism.

接下來可能會發生什麼事？

(A) 鍾女士會仔細查看更新的銷售區。

(B) 鍾女士會和客戶談談。

(C) 吉布森先生會致電給總裁。

(D) 金先生會接受 YDV 機械的職缺。

從下午 1 點 45 分吉布森先生說的「However, if you feel strongly about this, George, I might be able to bend the rules if our president approves of it.」中，可以看出他要詢問總裁的意見，故正確答案為 (C)。

## 176–180 電子郵件

**From:** Mary Cho <mcho@dtu.com>
**To:** Peter O'Malley <pomalley@dtu.com>
**Date:** June 3
**Subject:** Worldwide Design Conference

Dear Peter,

Thank you for volunteering to fill in for me at the Worldwide Design Conference in Boston on June 10. I need to stay at the San Francisco main office to meet with some visiting French clients. When I was there last year, I found it extremely worthwhile and was able to make some business contacts with prospective designers.

I've already handled your airplane ticket, hotel, and rental car. These have already been paid for by DTU, and you'll receive $50 a day for meals after you return here. If you decide to take some designers out for dinner, please retain receipts for your records and hand them in to the Accounting Department after you come back for reimbursement.

The timeline for the conference is as follows:

| | |
|---|---|
| Monday | 10 A.M. – 12 P.M. Innovative Graphics |
| | 12 P.M. – 2 P.M. Web Design World and Luncheon |
| | 3 P.M. – 5 P.M. Gigantic Logos 4D |
| Tuesday | The entire day is scheduled for the design exposition |

Best regards,
Mary

寄件人：瑪麗·趙 <mcho@dtu.com>
收件人：彼得·歐馬列 <pomalley@dtu.com>
日期：6月3日
主旨：世界設計大會

親愛的彼得：

感謝你自願代理我於6月10日在波士頓世界設計大會的工作。我需要留在舊金山的總公司和一些從法國來的客戶見面。我去年參加大會，覺得非常值得，而且還可以接觸到有潛力的設計師。

我已經處理好你的機票、飯店住宿和租車。費用已由DTU負擔，等你回來之後，還會收到每天50美元的餐食費補助。如果你打算和設計師一起共進晚餐，記得保留收據紀錄回來報帳，會計部門會再補貼。

大會日程如下：

| | |
|---|---|
| 星期一 | 早上 10 點 – 中午 12 點 創新圖像 |
| | 中午 12 點 – 下午 2 點 網頁設計世界和午餐 |
| | 下午 3 點 – 下午 5 點 4D 大商標 |
| 星期二 | 一日設計大展 |

祝好，
瑪麗

**From:** Peter O'Malley
<pomalley@dtu.com>
**To:** Mary Cho
<mcho@dtu.com>
**Date:** June 10
**Subject:** RE: Worldwide Design Conference

Dear Mary,

I came back from the conference earlier this afternoon. The Monday morning presentation was canceled because the speaker's flight had been delayed. However, the other presentations went smoothly. I heard and experienced many things and will finish a report in two weeks. I really appreciate your giving me the opportunity to represent DTU's advertising department at the conference.

Sincerely,
Peter

寄件人：彼得・歐馬列
<pomalley@dtu.com>
收件人：瑪麗・趙
<mcho@dtu.com>
日期：6 月 10 日
主旨：關於：世界設計大會

親愛的瑪麗：

我今天下午提早離開大會。因為講者的飛機延誤，週一早上的演講取消了。不過，另幾場演講很順利。我增廣見聞許多，會在兩週內寫完報告。真的很感謝您給我機會，讓我在會議上代表 DTU 廣告部門與會。

彼得 敬上

**詞彙** fill in for A 臨時代替 A　**worthwhile** 值得的　**business contacts** 商業接觸　**retain** 保留　**hand in** 繳交　**reimbursement** 報帳　**exposition** 展覽

**176**

**Why did Ms. Cho write an e-mail to Mr. O'Malley?**

(A) To show her gratitude for his suggestion
(B) To give him some information about a business meeting
(C) To check his conference reservation
(D) To issue him a refund

為什麼趙女士要寫電子郵件給歐馬列先生？

(A) 感謝他的建議
(B) 提供一些商務會議的資訊
(C) 確認預訂參與會議
(D) 還款給他

從第一封郵件的「Thank you for volunteering to fill in for me at the Worldwide Design Conference in Boston on June 10.」可知歐馬列先生將代替趙女士參加會議，又從信附贈的大會日程可知道，趙女士是在交代會議的細節資訊給歐馬列先生，故本題正確答案為 (B)。

**177**

**What does Ms. Cho indicate about the conference?**

(A) It is renowned for presentations by leading business owners.
(B) It took place in San Francisco last year for the first time.
(C) It offers opportunities to meet business acquaintances.
(D) It is the best location to meet French businessmen.

趙女士提到大會的什麼事？

(A) 企業領袖的演說讓它聲名大噪。
(B) 它去年首度在舊金山舉行。
(C) 它提供與商務人士交流的機會。
(D) 它是認識法國商人的最佳地點。

從第一封郵件的「When I was there last year, I found it extremely worthwhile and was able to make some business contacts with prospective designers.」中可知，趙女士曾在大會上結識許多設計師，並建立商業往來，故本題正確答案為 (C)。

**178**

**What expenditure will DTU NOT pay for beforehand?**

(A) Food expenses
(B) Hotel charges
(C) Airfare
(D) A car rental charge

**DTU 公司沒有預支的花費是？**

(A) 餐食費
(B) 住宿費
(C) 機票費
(D) 租車費

從第一封郵件的「I've already handled your airplane ticket, hotel, and rental car. These have already been paid for by DTU, and you'll receive $50 a day for meals after you return here.」中，可以得知公司已負擔了機票、飯店與租車費，餐食費則為參加回來後能獲得的費用，故正確答案為 (A)。

**179**

**What presentation was called off at the conference?**

(A) Innovative Graphics
(B) Web Design World
(C) Gigantic Logo 4D
(D) Design Exposition

**大會上哪個演講取消了？**

(A) 創新圖像
(B) 網頁設計世界
(C) 4D 大商標
(D) 設計大展

第二封郵件中，歐馬列先生說：「The Monday morning presentation was canceled because the speaker's flight was delayed.」，表示週一早上的演講因為講者班機延誤而取消，而根據第一封郵件中的日程表，可知此時段的演講為「Innovative Graphics」，故正確解答為 (A)。

**180**

**What department does Mr. O'Malley most likely work for?**

(A) Sales
(B) Advertising
(C) Personnel
(D) Accounting

**歐馬列先生最可能在哪個部門工作？**

(A) 業務部
(B) 廣告部
(C) 人資部
(D) 會計部

從第二封郵件的「I really appreciate your giving me the opportunity to represent DTU's advertising department at the conference.」中，可以知道歐馬列先生代表廣告部出席會議，故最可能在廣告部工作，本題正確答案為 (B)。

## 181–185 電子郵件

**To:** Janice Walker
<jwalker@dailynews.com>
**From:** Rachel Hunter
<rhunter@homedecors.com>
**Date:** May 10

Dear Ms. Walker,

According to our database, your account is overdue at the moment. You have a balance of $735.40 for the work done at your residence. Five workers were at your home to fix the hole in the roof on March 13. An invoice was sent out to you on April 5 and was to be paid by April 23. There is a late fee of $50, but if full payment is made promptly, this late fee will be waived. If you have already submitted payment, contact our main office as soon as possible. Would you please send all correspondence to me because I am monitoring your account?

Thank you.

Sincerely,
Rachel Hunter
Account Manager, Home Decors

---

**To:**
<customerservicerepresentative@homedecors.com>
**From:** Janice Walker
<jwalker@dailynews.com>
**Date:** May 11

To Whom It May Concern,

This is the first notice that I have received regarding this problem. It is possible that you sent the repair invoice to my old address. I moved out of Greenville at the beginning of April. Please either fax a copy of the invoice to me at 432-433-3276 or e-mail it to me at jwalker@dailynews.com. I will send the payment for the full amount as long as I receive the invoice promptly.

Thank you.

Best regards,
Janice Walker

---

收件人：珍妮斯‧沃克
<jwalker@dailynews.com>
寄件人：瑞秋‧杭特
<rhunter@homedecors.com>
日期：5月10日

親愛的沃克女士：

我們資料庫顯示，您的帳戶目前有逾期未繳的狀況——居家維修735.40美元的欠款。3月13日，有五名工人在您家維修屋頂破洞。費用明細已在4月5日寄給您，應於4月23日前繳納。滯納金為50美元，但只要即時全額付款就能免納滯還金。如果您已經付款，請儘快聯絡我們的總公司。由於我正在檢核您的帳戶，可以請您把所有相關信件寄給我嗎？

感謝。

家居裝飾帳戶管理經理
瑞秋‧杭特 敬上

---

收件人：<customerservicerepresentative@homedecors.com>
寄件人：珍妮斯‧沃克
<jwalker@dailynews.com>
日期：5月11日

致相關人士：

這是我第一次收到關於逾期欠款的通知，也許你把維修明細寄到舊地址了。我在今年4月初已經搬離格林維爾市。可以把維修明細傳真到432-433-3276，或是用電子郵件寄給我嗎？我的信箱是jwalker@dailynews.com。一收到明細我即刻就會全額付款。

感謝你。

祝好，
珍妮斯‧沃克

**overdue** 逾期的　　**residence** 住處　　**balance** 欠款，差額　　**late fee** 滯納金
**full payment** 全額繳納　　**promptly** 準時地　　**waive** 撤消　　**as soon as possible** 儘快
**correspondence** 往來信件　　**invoice** 費用清單　　**full amount** 全額　　**relocate** 移居

**181**----------------------------------------------------------------------

**Why did Ms. Hunter send an e-mail to Ms. Walker?**

(A) To notify her of mistakes in an invoice

(B) To ask for an overdue payment

(C) To apologize for an unsatisfactory job

(D) To charge a late fee

為什麼杭特女士要寄電子郵件給沃克女士？

(A) 提醒她費用明細有誤

(B) 要求逾期未繳的款項

(C) 為服務不周道歉

(D) 收取滯納金

從第一封郵件的「According to our database, your account is overdue at the moment. You have a balance of $735.40 for the work done at your residence.」中，可以得知杭特女士致信內容與沃克女士逾期未繳的款項有關，故正確答案為 (B)。

**182**----------------------------------------------------------------------

**What does Ms. Hunter ask Ms. Walker to do?**

(A) Copy a billing statement

(B) Meet the deadline

(C) Check her account

(D) Pay for the invoice in full

杭特女士請沃克女士做什麼？

(A) 影印帳單

(B) 如期繳款

(C) 查看她的帳戶

(D) 繳清費用

杭特女士在信件開頭便提到，沃克女士有逾期未付的費用，且說到「There is a late fee of $50, but if full payment is made promptly, this late fee will be waived.」，表示沃克女士若即時全額付款，可以撤銷滯納金，故杭特女士是在催促沃克女士付清款項，本題正確答案為 (D)。

**183**----------------------------------------------------------------------

**What does Ms. Walker request that customer service do?**

(A) Send a document of her fees by fax

(B) Deposit the payment

(C) Check her current address

(D) Call her right now

沃克女士請客服做什麼？

(A) 傳真繳款文件給她

(B) 繳訂金

(C) 核對她的現址

(D) 馬上打電話給她

從第二封郵件的「Please either fax a copy of the invoice to me at 432-433-3276 or e-mail it to me at jwalker@dailynews.com.」中，可知沃克女士請對方傳真文件給她，故正確答案為 (A)。

**184**----------------------------------------------------------------------

**What is inferred about Ms. Walker?**

(A) She built a new house.

(B) She recently relocated to a new home.

(C) She lost her billing statement.

(D) She went on a business trip in April.

文中提到沃克女士的什麼事？

(A) 她蓋了新房子。

(B) 她搬到新家。

(C) 她弄丟了繳款單。

(D) 她四月出差。

第二封郵件中提到：「It is possible that you sent the repair invoice to my old address. I moved out of Greenville at the beginning of April.」，表示沃克女士四月初就搬家了，故正確答案為 (B)。

**185** ----------------------------------------

What detail did Ms. Walker NOT include in her e-mail?

(A) The former residence
(B) The e-mail address
(C) The name of the account manager
(D) The fax number

沃克女士的電子郵件中沒提到什麼？

(A) 之前的住處
(B) 電子信箱
(C) 帳戶管理經理的名字
(D) 傳真號碼

沃克女士在回信時僅以「To Whom It May Concern」稱呼，並沒有提及他人的名字，所以正確答案為 (C)。

## 186-190 信件

**From:**
<jasonkang@resisdente.com>
**To:**
<bills@planpower.com>
**Date:** June 17
**Subject:** Invoice A893-06

To Whom It May Concern,

Hello, I am writing about my electricity bill for May. The amount due was much higher than I have paid in previous months, which is normally $350. I do not plan on missing the deadline for the payment, but I would like to know why the substantial increase in my bill occurred. If the change is incorrect, I would appreciate an adjustment to my account. I know that my meter is nearly obsolete, so I also wonder if it should be replaced with a new one.

If a technician needs to check it, the best time would be before noon on any weekday. I am at home then and would prefer to be present, if possible, while the work is being done.

With my best regards,
Jason Kang

寄件人：傑森・姜
<jasonkang@resisdente.com>
收件人：帳單管理部門
<bills@planpower.com>
日期：6月17日
主旨：單據A893-06

致相關人士：

哈囉，我來信的目的是為了我五月分的電費帳單，金額比前幾個月多出很多，平常大概都是350美元。我不想錯過繳費期限，但想知道金額為什麼會暴增。如果這是異常變化，我希望帳單可以有所調整。我知道我的電表太老舊，所以我也在考慮是否要替換它。

如果需要技術人員來檢查，週間的每天中午前都可以到府；我會在家，也希望他們作業時我能夠在場。

祝好，
傑森・姜

## Service Technician Log Sheet — New Year Residences

*June 30*

| Technician name | Address of service | Start time | Service |
|---|---|---|---|
| Paula Morreja | 2249 Keystone Blvd. | 10:52 A.M. | Meter repaired |
| Gini Padovani | 2809 Redhill Rd. | 12:38 P.M. | Meter replaced |
| Barak Hilton | 76 Ellington Ave. | 1:40 P.M. | Meter replaced |
| Brad Hopkins | 8100 Saint Rd. | 3:52 P.M. | Meter inspected |

**From:** <bills@planpower.com>
**To:** <jasonkang@resisdente.com>
**Date:** June 30
**Subject:** invoice A893-06

Dear Mr. Kang,

Thank you for contacting Plan Power. I am writing to let you know that the sudden increase in your bill was caused by a faulty meter. The technician who visited your Redhill residence found out that the old device had registered your use of electricity incorrectly.

The device has been replaced, and this type of problem should not take place again. The malfunction affects your bill for May only; the total amount of $127.18 will appear on your next bill. Should you have any questions, please feel free to contact us.

Sincerely,
Mark Dillon
Plan Power Customer Support

## 新年住宅技術人員 工作日誌表

6 月 30 日

| 技術人員姓名 | 服務地址 | 服務時間 | 服務內容 |
|---|---|---|---|
| 寶拉·莫瑞亞 | 鑰石大道 2249 號 | 早上 10:52 | 維修電表 |
| 吉尼·帕多瓦尼 | 紅丘路 2809 號 | 下午 12:38 | 更換電表 |
| 巴拉克·希爾頓 | 艾林頓大道 76 號 | 下午 1:40 | 更換電表 |
| 布萊德·霍布金斯 | 聖人路 8100 號 | 下午 3:52 | 檢查電表 |

寄件人：帳單管理部門
<bills@planpower.com>
收件人：傑森·姜
<jasonkang@resisdente.com>
日期：6月30日
主旨：單據A893-06

親愛的姜先生：

感謝您聯繫「有計畫電力」。這封信是要通知您，您的電費暴增是因為電表出錯。拜訪您紅丘住處的維修人員發現，由於電表老舊，因而錯誤記錄了您的用電狀況。

電表已經換新，日後不會再發生類似問題。機器故障只會影響到您五月的帳單；總金額127.18美元將顯示在您下個月的帳單上。如有其他疑問，也歡迎向我們反應。

有計畫電力客服專員
馬克·迪隆 敬上

---

**詞彙** due 應支付的　miss the deadline 錯過期限　adjustment 調整　meter 電表
if possible 可以的話　log sheet 工作日誌表　inspect 檢查　faulty 故障的　register 記錄
usage 使用量　malfunction 故障

**Why was the first e-mail sent?**

(A) To change a deadline extension
(B) To ask for a receipt
(C) To inquire about the amount
(D) To sign up for online billing

**為什麼會寄第一封電子郵件？**

(A) 展延期限
(B) 要求收據
(C) 詢問金額狀況
(D) 申請網路帳單

從第一封郵件的第三句「I would like to know why the substantial increase in my bill occurred.」，可知姜先生是為了帳單金額的問題寄信，可以得知正確答案為 (C)。

**187**

**What is suggested about Mr. Kang?**

(A) He correctly identified the problem.
(B) He recently moved to a new place.
(C) He has contacted Mr. Dillon several times.
(D) He plans to close his account with Plan Power.

**文中提到姜先生什麼事？**

(A) 他正確地辨認出問題所在。
(B) 他最近搬新家。
(C) 他和迪隆先生接洽多次。
(D) 他想關閉在有計畫電力的帳戶。

從第一封郵件的第五句「I know that my meter is nearly obsolete」和第二封郵件第一段的第二句「The technician who visited your Redhill residence found out that the old device had registered your use of electricity incorrectly.」，可以知道姜先生已猜是電表出問題，檢查結果也符合他的猜測，因此得知正確答案為 (A)。

**188**

**Who visited Mr. Kang's house on June 30?**

(A) Paula Morreja
(B) Gini Padovani
(C) Barak Hilton
(D) Brad Hopkins

**誰在 6 月 30 日到訪姜先生的家？**

(A) 寶拉·莫瑞亞
(B) 吉尼·帕多瓦尼
(C) 巴拉克·希爾頓
(D) 布萊德·霍布金斯

從第二封郵件第一段第二句「The technician who visited your Redhill residence found out that the old device had registered your use of electricity incorrectly.」以及第二段的第一句「The device has been replaced」中，可以得知有維修人員到紅丘路更換電表，而從表格可以看見，曾到紅丘路 2809 號更換電表的人名為「吉尼·帕多瓦尼」，故正確答案為 (B)。

**In the second e-mail, the word "registered" in paragraph 1, line 3, is closest in meaning to**

(A) attended
(B) permitted
(C) recorded
(D) allowed

**第二封電子郵件中，第一段、第三行的「registered」最接近下列哪個意思？**

(A) 出席
(B) 准許
(C) 記錄
(D) 允許

根據文意上，此處應是想表達老舊的電「記錄」了錯誤的使用量，因此正確答案 (C)。

41

**What does Mr. Dillon indicate in his e-mail?**

(A) That the payment is already overdue
(B) That the problem was limited to only one month
(C) That the new service is being provided
(D) That the new meter was ordered

迪隆先生在電子郵件中指出什麼？

(A) 繳費期限已過了
(B) 該問題只發生一個月
(C) 正提供新服務。
(D) 已經下訂新的電表

從第二封郵件第二段的第二句「The malfunction affects your bill for May only.」中可知，故障問題只會影響五月的帳單，故正確答案為 (B)。

**191–195 廣告、電子郵件和簡訊**

## Melody Academy of Music

**32 Saint Street, Seattle, WA 98105**
**www.melody-music.ac**

Melody Academy of Music is delighted to announce its next season of performances — from classical music to jazz, hip hop, and pop.

Please join us to see all that we have to offer! You can buy all kinds of tickets for the entire season or for an individual performance. Tickets can be purchased at half of the original price for Season Ticket buyers.

※ The Mozart Group gives an impressive jazz performance. 18 – 22 March

※ Eugene Ryu performs his award-winning pop songs. One day only — 7 April

※ The Seattle Ensemble plays classical music. 15 – 22 April

※ Catherine Winslet sings while accomplished by live guitar. 23 – 27 April

---

**To:** Jane Austin
**From:** Tylor Yun
**Cc:** Samuel David
**Subject:** Your visit to KG Electronics
**Date:** 29 March

---

Hi Ms. Austin,

On behalf of the personnel department at KG Electronics, I'd like to let you know how happy we are to adopt the personnel management software you will be teaching us about on 21–23 April. As you requested,

## 旋律音樂學院

**98105 華盛頓州西雅圖市聖人街32號**
**www.melody-music.ac**

旋律音樂學院很高興宣布下一季度的表演—包括古典、爵士、嘻哈和流行樂。

歡迎加入我們觀賞所有演出！您可以買下整季所有表演的票，或是針對特定表演購票。購買全季票的聽眾將享原票價的半價優惠。

※ 莫札特團令人印象深刻的爵士樂表演。3月18~22日

※ 歌手尤金·柳的得獎流行音樂表演。只有一天 — 4月7日

※ 西雅圖樂團的古典樂演出。4月15~22日

※ 凱薩琳·溫斯蕾歌唱與現場吉他伴奏。4月23~27日

---

收件人：珍·奧斯丁
寄件人：泰勒·延
副本：山謬·大衛
主旨：KG電子參訪
日期：3月29日

---

奧斯丁女士您好：

謹代表KG電子的人事部門，我們很開心您能在4月21日到23日，蒞臨指導新的人事管理軟體如何使用。我已如您所要求的，備好房間還有必要設備，像是

I reserved the room and necessary devises such as a desktop computer, projector, and microphone. If you need any further assistance with your presentation, do not hesitate to let me know.

As a token of appreciation, Mr. David, our department head, has made special plans to make your visit more memorable. He made a dinner reservation at a very famous Italian restaurant on the first evening of your visit. On the second day of your visit, we will be able to go to see an outstanding performance at the Melody Academy of Music.

Sincerely,
Tylor Yun
KG Electronics

桌電、投影機和麥克風。如果您的簡報還需要進一步協助，不用遲疑，儘管讓我知道。

為了感謝您，我們的部門主管大衛先生已做特殊安排，將令您本次行程更加難忘。在您蒞臨的第一天晚上，他訂好一間相當知名的義大利餐廳的晚餐。第二天，我們可以一起去旋律音樂學院看場出色的演出。

KG 電子
泰勒・延 敬上

## Tylor Yun's phone

*From: Samuel David*

*Received: 8:45 A.M.*

Hi, I just got words from Ms. Austin. Her original flight has been delayed. Therefore, her new arrival time has been changed. However, we're going to still be able to hold the meeting today. She requested that the entertainment be moved to tomorrow, so there is no rush now. If I order the tickets myself rather than have you do it, we can receive a considerable discount. Could you postpone the dinner reservation? If that is not possible, please cancel it. I apologize for the inconvenience this may cause.

## 泰勒・延的手機

*傳訊者：山謬・大衛*

*收訊時間：上午8:45*

嗨，我收到奧斯丁女士的消息。她原來的班機延誤了。所以她抵達的時間有變。不過我們今天的會議還是會舉行。她想把娛樂活動延到明天，這樣行程就不會那麼趕。如果由我來訂票，折扣會比你訂票來得多。可以請你把晚餐的訂位時間延後嗎？如果沒辦法，請把它取消。很抱歉造成你的不便。

**詞彙** award-winning 得獎的　accomplished by 同時有　on behalf of 代表　adopt 採用
as a token of 為了表示……　department head 部門主管　memorable 難忘的
there is no rush 不用趕　considerable 相當多的

**191** --------------------------------------------------------------------

### What is suggested about Melody Academy of Music?

(A) It has an on-site museum.
(B) It is employing a new conductor.
(C) It offers music lessons to young children.
(D) It offers different styles of music performances.

文中提到旋律音樂學院什麼？

(A) 學院現址還有博物館。
(B) 正招聘新的指揮。
(C) 提供小朋友音樂課程。
(D) 有很多不同風格的音樂演出。

從廣告第一段第一句中的「from classical music to jazz, hip hop, and pop.」，可以知道將演出不同風格的音樂，所以正確答案為 (D)。

192

**192** - - - - - - - - - - - - - - - - - - - - - - - - - - - - - - - - - - - - - - - - - - - - - - - -

**How much discount will Season Ticket buyers get?**

(A) 20%

(B) 30%

(C) 40%

(D) 50%

買全季票的觀眾可以拿到多少折扣？

(A) 20%

(B) 30%

(C) 40%

(D) 50%

廣告第一段的最後一句「Tickets can be purchased at half of the original price for Season Ticket buyers.」，表示購買全季票的人能以半價購買門票，故正確答案為 (D)。

**193** - - - - - - - - - - - - - - - - - - - - - - - - - - - - - - - - - - - - - - - - - - - - - - - -

**What is Ms. Austin scheduled to do during her visit?**

(A) Revise legal documents

(B) Demonstrate how to use some software

(C) Repair presentation equipment

(D) Conduct a survey

奧斯丁女士訪問期間要做什麼？

(A) 修改法律文件

(B) 展示如何使用某種軟體

(C) 修理簡報設備

(D) 進行調查

電子郵件第一段的第一句提及：「I'd like to let you know how happy we are to adopt the personnel management software you will be teaching us about on 21–23 April.」，表示奧斯丁女士將拜訪公司，並進行軟體使用方法的教學，所以正確答案為 (B)。

**194** - - - - - - - - - - - - - - - - - - - - - - - - - - - - - - - - - - - - - - - - - - - - - - - -

**What performance was Ms. Austin originally scheduled to attend?**

(A) The Mozart Group

(B) Eugene Ryu

(C) The Seattle Ensemble

(D) Catherine Winslet

奧斯丁女士本來會觀賞的表演是？

(A) 莫札特團

(B) 尤金·柳的演出

(C) 西雅圖樂團

(D) 凱薩琳·溫斯蕾的演出

從郵件第一段的第一句「you will be teaching us about on 21–23 April」中，可以得知奧斯丁女士將在 4 月 21 日至 23 日前往進行教學，且第二段的最後一句也提到「On the second day of your visit, we will be able to go to see an outstanding performance at the Melody Academy of Music.」，表示他們將在奧斯丁女士來訪的第二天（22 日）前往觀賞演出。

再對照廣告第二段的第三點「The Seattle Ensemble plays classical music. 15–22 April」，可以得知 4 月 22 日只有西雅圖樂團有演出，故正確答案為 (C)。

**195** - - - - - - - - - - - - - - - - - - - - - - - - - - - - - - - - - - - - - - - - - - - - - - - -

**What is Mr. Yun asked to do?**

(A) Make a flight reservation

(B) Set a meeting time

(C) Train new employees

(D) Call off a meal reservation

延先生被要求做什麼？

(A) 訂機位

(B) 安排會議時間

(C) 訓練新進員工

(D) 取消晚餐訂位

從簡訊的最後一句「Could you postpone the dinner reservation? If that is not possible, please cancel it.」中，可知大衛先生請延先生延後或取消晚餐訂位，故正確答案為 (D)。

## OHQ Containers
## Mobile Refrigerated Storage Units

OHQ Containers provides refrigerated storage units to restaurants, cafés, grocery stores, and other businesses that are currently looking for cold-storage solutions.

**All the units below include :**
1. Lockable door latches, non-slip flooring, and interior fluorescent light fixtures
2. A 20-metre power cable

**Service for your business :**
Our delivery service is available to any location in Scotland. All the units are available for short-term, monthly, or annual lease.

**Our storage options are:**

| Unit | Door Type | Length (metres) | Floor Space (square metres) | Internal Capacity (cubic metres) |
|---|---|---|---|---|
| Economy | Single | 3.0m | 7.5m$^2$ | 18.75m$^3$ |
| Standard | Double | 6.0m | 15.0m$^2$ | 37.5m$^3$ |
| Supreme | Double | 9.0m | 22.5m$^2$ | 56.25m$^3$ |
| Supreme Plus | Plus Double | 12.0m | 30.0m$^2$ | 75.0m$^3$ |

Should you need any help with making a decision, our outstanding customer service representatives will recommend the ideal storage solution for you. For further information, please visit http://www.OHQ.com.

## OHQ 冷凍櫃
## 行動冷凍櫃

OHQ貨櫃提供行動冷凍櫃給餐廳、咖啡廳、雜貨店和其他需要冷藏空間的行業。

**所有的冷凍櫃都包括：**
1. 可上鎖的門扣、止滑地墊、內部日光燈照明裝置
2. 20公尺長的電纜線

**商家服務：**
冷凍櫃可達蘇格蘭的任何地點。
所有型號都可以短租、月租或年租。

**可供選擇的型號：**

| 類型 | 門型 | 長度 (公尺) | 地面空間 (平方公尺) | 內部容量 (立方公尺) |
|---|---|---|---|---|
| 經濟型 | 單門 | 3.0公尺 | 7.5平方公尺 | 18.75立方公尺 |
| 標準型 | 雙門 | 6.0公尺 | 15.0平方公尺 | 37.5立方公尺 |
| 超級型 | 雙門 | 9.0公尺 | 22.5平方公尺 | 56.25立方公尺 |
| 加大超級型 | 加大雙門 | 12.0公尺 | 30.0平方公尺 | 75.0立方公尺 |

如果對於決定型號需要任何協助，我們出色的客服專員會向您建議最適合的方案。欲查詢更多資訊，可上官網 http://www.OHQ.com。

**OHQ Containers—Customer Inquiry Form**
**Name:** Aiden Park
**Business:** Park's café
**E-mail:**
<parkscafé@plantomorrow.com>
**Date:** Oct. 14

Hello, I was told about your company from my friend, Bill Folder, who is currently using one of your units for his own business. I am also the owner of a restaurant, and our freezer can no longer accommodate our food storage needs. Thus, we require an OHQ unit that can be placed near the back entrance of the building. We don't need a lot of extra storage space, but we do need a unit with double doors so we can easily load everything in and out. Please tell me which unit you recommend and also the possible date of delivery. Also, I was wondering if your units are equipped with a digital temperature display. We need to be able to closely monitor the temperature at all times.

Thank you.

OHQ 冷凍櫃—客戶詢問表單
姓名：艾登・帕克
商家：帕克咖啡
電子信箱：
<parkscafé@plantomorrow.com>
日期：10月14日

哈囉，我的朋友比爾・佛德向我介紹貴公司。他的店正在使用貴公司的冷凍櫃。我也是餐廳老闆，而我們的冷凍庫容量，已經冰不下需要的食材了。所以我們需要一個可放在大樓後門旁的OHQ冷凍櫃。容量不需要額外加大，但需要雙門，好方便補貨和取貨。請您推薦我哪個型號合適，並告知可能送達的日期。另外，我也想知道冷凍櫃有沒有溫度顯示的數位面板，我們需要隨時嚴密監控溫度。

感謝。

## Customer Review

I have been using OHQ Containers for about four months now, and I am fully contented with my choice. And I was pleased to have my first month's rental fee waived thanks to OHQ's refer-a-friend programme, which allowed my friend and me to receive a free month's rental each. I started with a smaller 37.5 cubic-metre storage unit, but it became clear this month that I would need something one size bigger to serve the increasing guests. The day after I called OHQ, a company representative delivered a new unit that meets my needs perfectly. I highly recommend OHQ Containers to everyone that is in need of efficient cold storage for their business.

Aiden Park, Owner, Park's Café

## 顧客評論

我使用OHQ冷凍櫃大概四個月了，讓我十分滿意。我也很高興可以享有第一個月免租費的好友推薦專案，讓我和朋友都享受到免租費一個月的優惠。我一開始用的冷凍櫃是37.5立方公尺的容量，不過這一個月下來，很明顯我需要更大尺寸的冷凍櫃，以服務增加的顧客。我打電話給OHQ的隔天，公司專員便送來了新冷凍櫃，完美符合我的需求。大家如果需要營業用、而且好用的冷凍設備，我非常推薦OHQ冷凍櫃。

帕克咖啡老闆艾登・帕克

---

詞彙 **mobile** 行動的 **refrigerated** 冷藏的 **cold-storage** 冷藏空間 **latch** 門扣 **non-slip** 止滑的 **flooring** 地墊 **fluorescent light fixture** 日光燈照明裝置 **power cable** 電纜線 **short-term** 短期的 **lease** 租約 **freezer** 冷藏庫 **accommodate** 容納 **be equipped with** 配備有 **monitor** 監控 **at all times** 隨時 **be contented with** 滿意 **rental fee** 租金 **waive** 減免 **refer-a-friend programme** 好友推薦專案（**programme**為英式拼法；**program**則為美式拼法） **meet one's needs** 符合需求 **efficient** 效率高的

**196**

| | |
|---|---|
| **What information about OHQ Containers is NOT given in the advertisement?** | **OHQ 冷凍櫃的廣告沒提到什麼資訊？** |
| (A) The total number of doors | (A) 門的數量 |
| (B) The type of lighting | (B) 照明類型 |
| (C) The range of temperature settings | (C) 溫度的設置範圍 |
| (D) The size of the interior space | (D) 冷凍櫃容量 |

根據廣告提供的資訊，(A) 門的數量可從表格的「Door Type」得知；(B) 照明類型可從第二段第二句的「interior fluorescent light fixtures」得知；(D) 冷凍櫃容量可從「Floor Space」與「Internal Capacity」得知，故只有溫度設置範圍無從知曉，本題答案為 (C)。

**197**

| | |
|---|---|
| **What is indicated about Mr. Park?** | **文中提到帕克先生什麼？** |
| (A) He used to be a coworker of Mr. Folder. | (A) 他曾是佛德先生的同事。 |
| (B) He supports the local community. | (B) 他支持當地社區。 |
| (C) He plans to switch to a new delivery company. | (C) 他想轉業開配送公司。 |
| (D) He got a discount from OHQ Containers. | (D) 他拿到 OHQ 冷凍櫃的折扣。 |

從評論第二句的「And I was pleased to have my first month's rental fee waived」、「receive a free month's rental」，可推測帕克先生與朋友都獲得一個月租金減免，所以正確答案為 (D)。

**198**

| | |
|---|---|
| **What is suggested about Park's Café?** | **文中提到帕克咖啡什麼？** |
| (A) It features organic produce. | (A) 特色是使用有機食材。 |
| (B) It is located near OHQ Containers. | (B) 位於 OHQ 公司附近。 |
| (C) It plans to extend its business hours. | (C) 想要延長營業時間。 |
| (D) Its business continues to grow. | (D) 生意蒸蒸日上。 |

從評論第三句中的「increasing guests」可以得知帕克咖啡的客人增加，故正確答案為 (D)。

**199**

| | |
|---|---|
| **Which unit is Mr. Park currently using?** | **帕克先生現在使用的冷凍櫃是哪款？** |
| (A) Economy | (A) 經濟型 |
| (B) Standard | (B) 標準型 |
| (C) Supreme | (C) 超級型 |
| (D) Supreme Plus | (D) 加大超級型 |

評論的第三句提到：「I started with a smaller 37.5 cubic-metre storage unit, but it became clear this month that I would need something one size bigger to serve the increasing guests.」，帕克先生一開始使用的冷凍櫃容量為 37.5 立方公尺，對照表格為標準型，但他之後換成了大一個尺寸的機型，因此推測應為超級型，故正確答案為 (C)。

## 200

**In the review, the word "contented" in line 1, is closest in meaning to**

(A) pleased

(B) angry

(C) dismayed

(D) astonished

在顧客評論中，第一行的「contented」，最接近下列哪個意思？

(A) 滿意的

(B) 生氣的

(C) 沮喪的

(D) 驚訝的

根據評論第一句前半，帕克先生已使用 OHQ 產品四個月，且評論最後他說：「I highly recommend OHQ Containers to everyone」，表示他對產品感到滿意，故正確答案為 (A)。

# ACTUAL TEST
# 2

# PART 5

## 101

**Salespeople at Cedarville Grocery Store receive extra pay when ------ work extended hours.**

(A) they
(B) their
(C) them
(D) theirs

**題型** 文法──代名詞

**翻譯** 西達韋爾雜貨店的銷售人員在他們加班時，會領到加班費。

**詞彙** salespeople 銷售人員
grocery store 雜貨店
work extended hours 加班

空格左邊為副詞子句連接詞 when，右邊為子句的動詞 work，故空格應為一個可以代入主詞位置的主格人稱代名詞，所以正確答案為 (A)。

(B) 為所有格人稱代名詞，如果要成為正確答案，空格後面應出現名詞。(C) 為受格人稱代名詞，但空格是主詞位置。(D) 為所有格代名詞，雖然可以代入主詞位置，但是不符合本句的句意。

## 102

**Ms. Juntasa has been ------ recommended by her former employers.**

(A) high
(B) highly
(C) higher
(D) highest

**題型** 位置──副詞

**翻譯** 洪塔沙女士的前雇主們大力推薦她。

**詞彙** former 之前的
employer 雇主

空格左邊為 be 動詞的現在完成式 has been，右邊為過去分詞 recommended，由此可知此句為被動式。動詞為被動式時，可以放入 be 動詞與過去分詞之間的是副詞。(B) highly 為副詞，意思是程度上「非常」，與本題句意相符，故本題正確答案為 (B)。

(A) 可當作形容詞或副詞使用，但作為副詞時，字義通常為高度上的「高高地」，如形容鳥飛得高時說的「birds fly high」，故與本題句意不符；(C) 為 high 的比較級，而 (D) 為 high 的最高級，因為本題並未出現需要比較的對象，所以皆無法代入空格。

## 103

**The use of high-quality but ------ mechanical components resulted in a decline in costs for Mr. David's factory.**

(A) unhappy
(B) incomplete
(C) unaware
(D) inexpensive

**題型** 詞彙──形容詞

**翻譯** 大衛先生的工廠使用高品質又不貴的機械元件，降低了成本。

**詞彙** high-quality 高品質的
component 元件
A result in B A 造成 B
decline 降低

(A) unhappy 不滿意的、不開心的；(B) incomplete 不完整的；(C) unaware 不知道的；(D) inexpensive 廉價的、不貴的。

從句意來看，對等連接詞 but 前後應為帶有相反意味的字，故前為 high-quality，後應為 inexpensive，表示雖然品質高，但價錢不高，故答案為 (D)。

(B) 不符句意；(A) 後頭應接介系詞 with，形成形容詞片語；(C) 後頭則應接介系詞 of，組成形容詞片語。

##  104

The publishing conference has been rescheduled ------ tomorrow due to the worsening weather conditions.

(A) in
(B) by
(C) for
(D) out

| 題型 | 詞彙──介系詞 |
| 翻譯 | 由於天氣情況惡化，出版會議改為明天召開。 |
| 詞彙 | worsening 惡化的 |
| | weather conditions 天氣狀況 |

因為選項 (A)、(B)、(D) 完全無法與 reschedule 連用，故正確答案為 (C)。

★「reschedule」為及物動詞，有以下常見用法：
reschedule A for B〔主動態〕（重新將 A 的行程安排為 B）
A be rescheduled for B〔被動態〕（A 的行程被重新安排為 B）

## 105

Alpha Tech's most recent software makes it ------ than ever for publishers to create newspapers.

(A) easy
(B) ease
(C) easily
(D) easier

| 題型 | 位置──形容詞（比較級） |
| 翻譯 | 阿爾發科技的最新軟體，讓出版社發行報紙比起以往更加容易。 |
| 詞彙 | publisher 出版社 |

本題解題重點在空格後方，由於 than ever 前一定要放比較級，故正確答案為 (D)。

★使役句中，使用虛受詞（it）與真受詞的正確用法如下：
make it Adj. (for N) to V

##  106

A limited ------ of time for questions will be provided subsequent to Mr. Yamaguchi's talk.

(A) amount
(B) number
(C) value
(D) record

| 題型 | 詞彙──名詞 |
| 翻譯 | 山口先生演講後將會限時開放問答。 |
| 詞彙 | subsequent to . . . 在……之後 |

(A) amount（時間、金額等的）量；(B) number 數；(C) value 值、價值；(D) record 紀錄。

因為空格後之介系詞 of 的名詞受詞為 time，所以正確答案為 (A)。

## 107

**Customers ------ purchase merchandise from Easy-To-Go.com typically receive their orders within three business days.**

(A) whomever
(B) whom
(C) whose
(D) who

題型 **文法——關係代名詞**

翻譯 從 Easy-To-Go.com 買東西的顧客，通常會在三個工作天內拿到訂購商品。

詞彙 **merchandise** 商品
**typically** 通常

空格左側出現的先行詞 customers 為人物名詞，而空格右側緊接著出現動詞 purchase，所以答案要選能作為主格關係代名詞的 who，正確答案為 (D)。

(A) whomever 為複合關係代名詞，其意思已經包含了先行詞，所以後方不應出現受詞 merchandise；(B) whom 為受格關係代名詞，雖然與作為先行詞的人物名詞一致，但是後方同樣不應出現受詞；(C) whose 為所有格關係代名詞，空格右側應出現的是「名詞＋動詞」的結構。

## 108

**The ------ of this training session is to provide business owners with the tools to make informed decisions.**

(A) guide
(B) experience
(C) objective
(D) solution

題型 **詞彙——名詞**

翻譯 這個培訓課程的目標，是讓企業主有辦法做出明智的決定。

詞彙 **training session** 培訓課程
**informed** 明智的；見多識廣的
**make a decision** 做出決定

(A) guide 導覽員；(B) experience 經驗、經歷；(C) objective 目標；(D) solution 解決方法。

solution 後接介系詞 to 表示某事物的解決辦法，如「solution to the problem」，且無法與「is to V」連用。從句意來判斷，可直接選出正確答案為 (C)。

★建議直接將句型背起來，以便日後輕鬆解開題目：
**the solution to N**（某事的解決辦法）
**the objective of sth is to V**（某物的目的是做……）

## 109

**Ms. Lee is ------ responsible for supervising quality assurance procedures at the Hawksdale facility.**

(A) primarily
(B) nearly
(C) slowly
(D) previously

題型 **詞彙——副詞**

翻譯 李女士主要負責監督霍克斯戴爾工廠的品管過程。

詞彙 **supervise** 監督
**assurance** 保證
**procedure** 過程
**facility** 工廠；(有特定用途的)場所

(A) primarily 主要地；(B) nearly 幾乎；(C) slowly 緩慢地；(D) previously 以前。

此題依句意判斷，適合與形容詞片語「be responsible for」（負責）一起使用的為 primarily，故本題正確答案為 (A)。

## 110

------- for the Valleywood Photography Contest must be received by May 25.

(A) Being entered
(B) Entries
(C) Enters
(D) Entered

| 題型 | 位置——名詞 |
| --- | --- |
| 翻譯 | 谷林攝影大賽的參賽收件到 5 月 25 日截止。 |

先判斷句子中動詞為被動式 must be received，主詞為空格至 contest 的部分，再觀察「for the Valleywood Photography Contest」就算刪除，整句也符合文法，故此應做修飾空格用，且空格應填入名詞。

就算將 (A) 視為動名詞句型，代入主詞的位置，也無法與句中的動詞連用，故 (A) 非正解。(B) 為名詞 entry 的複數型，意思是「參賽作品」或「參賽者」，為合適答案。(C) 為動詞第三人稱，(D) 為過去分詞或過去式，皆無法代入空格。本題正確答案為 (B)。

## 111

Riley Textile Corporation reported a 10 percent rise ------ profits last year.

(A) off
(B) at
(C) in
(D) up

| 題型 | 詞彙——介系詞 |
| --- | --- |
| 翻譯 | 芮莉織品企業報告公司去年在收益方面成長了 10%。 |
| 詞彙 | textile 織品<br>corporation 企業，公司 |

可以和名詞 rise（增加；上升）連用的介系詞為 in，故正確答案為 (C)。

★請熟記下列用法：
a rise in sth（在某事上的增加、上升）。

## 112

Because of the decrease in the cost of materials, the price of Supreme Laboratory's cutting-edge microscope will be lower than -------.

(A) anticipated
(B) organized
(C) experimented
(D) inclined

| 題型 | 詞彙——動詞 |
| --- | --- |
| 翻譯 | 因為材料成本降低，極優實驗室尖端的顯微鏡價格將比預期來得低。 |
| 詞彙 | laboratory 實驗室（可簡稱為 lab）<br>cutting-edge 尖端的；劃時代的<br>microscope 顯微鏡 |

(A) anticipate 預期、期待；(B) organize 整理、準備；(C) experiment 實驗；(D) incline 傾向。

此題只要知道單字的意思即可解出，表示價格低於「預期」為最合理的說法，故正確答案為 (A)。

(C) 為不及物動詞，應與介系詞 with 連用。(D) 為及物動詞。通常以被動「be inclined to V」（有……的傾向）出現。

★請記住此題的用法：
比較級＋ than anticipated（比預期中的更……）

**113**

Admission to the Maxwell Botanical Garden will be free every Thursday from 10 A.M. to 2 P.M. ------ the spring.

(A) beneath
(B) throughout
(C) without
(D) down

| 題型 | 詞彙──介系詞 |
| --- | --- |
| 翻譯 | 馬克思威爾植物園整個春季,每週四早上十點到下午兩點都可免費入園。 |
| 詞彙 | admission to . . . 進入…… |
| | botanical garden 植物園 |
| | free 免費的 |

(A) beneath 在某物下面(有表面接觸);(B) throughout(一段期間)自始至終;(範圍/場所)整體;(C) without 無、缺少;(D) down(方向)往下。

throughout 與空格後表示一段期間的名詞 spring 相關,且較符合句意,故正確答案為 (B)。

**114**

All staff members who ------- drilling equipment must wear safety goggles.

(A) operate
(B) operates
(C) operating
(D) is operated

| 題型 | 位置──動詞 |
| --- | --- |
| 翻譯 | 所有操作鑽孔設備的員工都必須穿戴護目鏡。 |
| 詞彙 | staff member 員工 |
| | drilling equipment 鑽孔設備 |
| | wear 戴;穿 |
| | safety goggles 護目鏡 |

看到先行詞 All staff members 加上主格關係代名詞 who,就要知道後面要接動詞,且先行詞與動詞的單複數一致。

(C) 為現在分詞或動名詞,所以不是答案。此題中先行詞為複數名詞,與 (B) 的單數動詞不一致,所以 (B) 不是答案。(D) operate 一字可同時作為不及物動詞或及物動詞使用,但是空格後面出現名詞受詞 drilling equipment,故 operate 在此句為及物動詞且應為主動式,被動式的 (D) 不是答案。

(A) 既為主動式,又和先行詞的單複數一致,故正確答案為 (A)。

**115**

A replacement key for your car may be ordered directly from our dealership, ------ you demonstrate proof of ownership.

(A) as though
(B) provided that
(C) regardless of
(D) instead of

| 題型 | 詞彙──副詞連接詞 |
| --- | --- |
| 翻譯 | 只要您證明車輛的所有權,就可以和我們經銷商直接訂購新鑰匙。 |
| 詞彙 | replacement 替代品 |
| | dealership 經銷商 |
| | demonstrate 出示 |
| | proof 證明 |
| | ownership 所有權 |

(A) as though 好像;(B) provided that 只要、如果;(C) regardless of 不管;(D) instead of 反而、代替。

連接詞個數會比動詞個數少一個。本題出現的動詞有主要子句的 may be ordered 與從屬子句的 demonstrate 兩個,所以空格應代入連接詞。

(C) 與 (D) 為介系詞，所以無法代入空格。(A) 與 (B) 為副詞子句連接詞，皆可填入空格，但是最符合句意的是 provided that，故正確答案為 (B)。

**116** --------

We encouraged guests to leave ------- for improving the service at our airline.

(A) suggest
(B) suggested
(C) suggesting
(D) suggestions

| 題型 | 位置——名詞 |
| 翻譯 | 我們鼓勵賓客留下建議，讓我們可以改進飛航服務。 |

leave 可同時當作不及物動詞與及物動詞使用，本題的 leave 解釋為「留下」，是及物動詞，後方接名詞 suggestions 為「留下建議」之意，故正確答案為 (D)。

**117** --------

An uncommonly large number of employees in the Accounting Department retired last year, leaving 13 positions -------.

(A) dedicated
(B) hollow
(C) invalid
(D) vacant

| 題型 | 詞彙——形容詞 |
| 翻譯 | 會計部門去年不尋常地有大量員工退休，釋出了 13 個空缺。 |
| 詞彙 | uncommonly 不尋常地<br>accounting 會計 |

(A) dedicated 奉獻的；(B) hollow（內部）空的、空虛的；(C) invalid 無效的；(D) vacant（空間、工作）空缺的。本題根據字義即可選出正確答案為 (D)。

**118** --------

Kane's in Denversville is a full-service photography studio ------ in family portraits.

(A) specialist
(B) specially
(C) specialize
(D) specializing

| 題型 | 位置——現在分詞 |
| 翻譯 | 肯恩家是一間位於丹佛斯維爾、提供全面服務的攝影工作室，特別擅長拍攝家族照。 |
| 詞彙 | full-service 全面服務<br>photography studio 攝影工作室<br>portrait 人像照片；肖像畫 |

從句子結構判斷，前方已出現一個 be 動詞 is，且沒有連接詞，所以不該再出現別的動詞，故 (C) 不是正確答案；(B) 為副詞，與本題句意也不符，故也不正確。

(A) 為名詞，雖然可以和空格後的介系詞 in 連用，意為「（某領域）專家」，但此句已有名詞 photography studio 作為主詞補語，來解釋 Kane's 這個主詞，空格若要再填入一個名詞，兩者之間應要有對等連接詞 and，故 (A) 不是正確答案。

(D) 為現在分詞，可以和空格後的介系詞 in 連用，並修飾前面的名詞，故正確答案為 (D)。

★請熟記此用法：
specialize in . . .（擅長……）

## 119

**Larkhill Health Center is always ------ to consider the certified specialists who are interested in joining our organization.**

(A) possible
(B) willing
(C) necessary
(D) useful

| 題型 | 詞彙——形容詞 |
| --- | --- |
| 翻譯 | 雲雀丘健康中心向來都樂意請有證照的專業人員加入我們工作團隊。 |
| 詞彙 | certified 有證照的<br>specialist 專業人員 |

(A) possible 可能的；(B) willing 樂意的、自發的；(C) necessary 需要的；(D) useful 有用的、有幫助的。

雖然 (A) 與 (C) 可以和空格後的不定式連用，句意也相符，但是這種用法一定要用於虛主詞 it 開頭的句型。

(D) 因為不符合句意，所以不是正確答案。(B) 的前方可為人物、公司或團體等名詞，後方也可使用不定式，故正確答案為 (B)。

★虛主詞「it」開頭的句型，如：
It is possible to V（做某事是可能的）
It is necessary to V（做某事是必須的）

★請熟記下列用法：
sb be willing to V（某人樂意做……）」

## 120

**Government ------ on the import of construction materials were temporarily lifted so as to meet increasing demand.**

(A) authorities
(B) treatments
(C) restrictions
(D) supplies

| 題型 | 詞彙——名詞 |
| --- | --- |
| 翻譯 | 為因應需求增加，政府暫時取消了建材進口量的限制。 |
| 詞彙 | import 進口<br>construction materials 建材<br>temporarily 暫時地<br>so as to V 為了……<br>demand 需求 |

(C) restrictions 指政府下令造成的限制、規定時，多為複數型，單數型則泛指限制，後方接著介系詞 on 時表示在某方面的限制。本題正確答案為 (C)。

(A) authorities 專指具有公權力的政府機關時必為複數型，而為單數 authority 時則可泛指權威或掌權者。(B) 意為治療、對待或待遇，與本題不符。(D) 意為必需品或供給，不符合題目。

★請熟記下列用法：
restrictions on . . .（在……的限制）
impose/place/put restrictions（施加限制）
tighten restrictions（加強限制）
ease restrictions（放寬限制）
lift restrictions（取消限制）

**121** ----------------------------------------

**Spring Deli's fruit and vegetable tray is popular now that it is appealing and ------ priced.**

(A) afford
(B) afforded
(C) affordable
(D) affordably

題型 位置──副詞

翻譯 春天小館的蔬果盤現在非常流行，既討喜、價格也實惠。

詞彙 tray 淺盤；托盤
now that 因為；既然
appealing 吸引人的
price 為某物定價

因為有對等連接詞 and，當左側的 appealing 為形容詞時，右側應也為形容詞。又因空格已出現過去分詞 priced 來扮演形容詞，故空格內要填入可發揮修飾作用的副詞 affordably，所以答案為 (D)。

(A) afford〔及物動詞〕有可做……的經濟能力；(C) affordable〔形容詞〕便宜的，經濟能力可負擔的；(B) afforded 為過去分詞或過去式，並非副詞。上述選項皆無法代入空格，故不是正確答案。

★請熟記下列用法：

at an affordable price（買得起的價格）　　reasonably priced（價格合理的）
affordably/modestly priced（價格低廉的）　realistically priced（價格實際的）

**122** ----------------------------------------

**Mr. Davidson volunteered to help at the reception desk ------ he has not ever worked directly with clients.**

(A) even though
(B) or
(C) until
(D) so that

題型 詞彙──連接詞

翻譯 雖然戴維森先生沒有直接面對顧客的經驗，他仍自願在服務台幫忙。

詞彙 volunteer to V 自願……
reception desk 服務台
client 顧客

(A) even though〔副詞連接詞〕雖然；(B) or〔對等連接詞〕或者、否則；(C) until〔副詞連接詞〕〔介系詞〕直到；(D) so that〔副詞連接詞〕以便。

句子中共有兩個動詞 volunteered 和 has not ever worked，故空格為應代入連接詞的位置。選項 (A) 到 (D) 中，既可當做連接詞又符合句意的是 even though，所以正確答案為 (A)。

**123** ----------------------------------------

**Smith's Plumbing has eight company-owned trucks, four of ------ are currently in the auto repair shop.**

(A) whose
(B) other
(C) whom
(D) which

題型 文法──關係代名詞

翻譯 史密斯水電公司總共有八輛卡車，其中四輛目前在維修廠。

詞彙 company-owned 公司擁有的
currently 目前
auto repair shop 汽車維修廠（auto 有一意思為 automobile 汽車的簡寫）

本題要考的為下列特定句型：**先行詞＋逗號＋部分（數字）＋ of ＋ whom/which ＋動詞**。

根據先行詞，使用不同的受格關係代名詞。若先行詞為人物，則使用 whom；若為事物或抽象名詞，則使用 which。

此題中先行詞為「eight company-owned trucks」，為事物名詞，故後方使用 which，且這個 which 指的就是前方的先行詞（公司的八輛卡車），而「four of which」指的是八輛卡車中的四輛，因此正確答案為 (D)。

**124**

Hampton Accounting has ------ costs by restricting international travel and encouraging the use of online video conferencing.

(A) reduced
(B) stated
(C) qualified
(D) examined

| 題型 | 詞彙——動詞 |
| --- | --- |
| 翻譯 | 漢普頓會計公司限制國外出差，並鼓勵使用線上視訊會議，減少了公司開銷。 |
| 詞彙 | restrict 限制<br>video conferencing 視訊會議 |

(A) reduce 減少、降低（量、程度、金額）；(B) state 聲明、陳述；(C) qualify 賦予資格；(D) examine 檢測、檢查。

選項中只有及物動詞 reduce 可與名詞受詞 costs 連用並符合句意，故正確答案為 (A)。

★**請熟記下列用法：**
reduce costs/expenses/expenditures（減少成本、費用、經費）
increase costs/expenses/expenditures（增加成本、費用、經費）

**125**

Dawson Corporation announced in a press conference that it is planning to expand ------ Europe.

(A) of
(B) into
(C) around
(D) at

| 題型 | 詞彙——介系詞 |
| --- | --- |
| 翻譯 | 道森企業在記者會中宣布，它計劃拓展進歐洲。 |
| 詞彙 | corporation 企業；公司<br>press conference 記者會 |

expand（擴張）可同時作為不及物動詞與及物動詞使用。當作不及物動詞時與介系詞 into 連用，故正確答案為 (B)。

★**介系詞 into 可以和帶有「變化」之意的動詞與名詞一起使用**

## 126

As ------ a month has passed since the products were sent, we should ask the delivery company for an update.

(A) nearly
(B) immediately
(C) partially
(D) thoroughly

| 題型 | 詞彙——副詞 |
|---|---|
| 翻譯 | 產品寄出幾乎有一個月了，我們應該追問貨運公司進度。 |
| 詞彙 | ask A for B 向 A 詢問 B；向 A 要求 B<br>delivery company 貨運公司 |

(A) nearly 幾乎；(B) immediately 立刻；(C) partially 部分地、偏頗地；(D) thoroughly 徹底地、完全地。

由於空格後出現 a month，故此處要選適合與數字相關用語連用者 nearly，故正確答案為 (A)。

## 127

Seeking new sources of revenue, many local orchards ------ catering to tourists in the past five years.

(A) to begin
(B) have begun
(C) will have begun
(D) will begin

| 題型 | 位置——動詞 |
|---|---|
| 翻譯 | 為了開拓財源，五年來很多當地果園已開始迎合觀光客的需求。 |
| 詞彙 | sources of revenue 財源<br>orchard 果園<br>cater to . . . 迎合……的需求 |

首先注意句子中沒有動詞，故空格內填入的一定為動詞。再看到句中出現的時間副詞為「in the past five years」，表示發生在過去的一段時間內，所以應使用現在完成式的 have begun，故正確答案為 (B)。

★請熟記下列的時間副詞句型，且注意此時動詞的時態為現在完成式：
in/for/over/during/within the past/last . . .（在過去的〔一段時間內〕）

## 128

Meteorologists forecast three ------- days of rain, which should provide a welcome relief from the unseasonable heat.

(A) sensitive
(B) refreshed
(C) consecutive
(D) deliberate

| 題型 | 詞彙——形容詞 |
|---|---|
| 翻譯 | 氣象專家預測接連三天都會下雨，可紓解這季節反常的炎熱。 |
| 詞彙 | meteorologist 氣象專家<br>forecast 預測（經濟、天氣）<br>relief 舒緩效果<br>unseasonable 不合季節的 |

(A) sensitive 敏感的；(B) refreshed 恢復精神的；(C) consecutive 連續的；(D) deliberate 故意的。

根據字義即可選出空格應填入 consecutive，且此字可與空格前的基數（three）連用，故正確答案為 (C)。

★**請熟記下列用法：**

基數（two、three......）＋ consecutive ＋複數名詞（接連幾個......）

序數（second、third......）＋ consecutive ＋單數名詞（連續的第......）

**129**

Caribbean Bay Hotel's kitchen is open 24 hours a day, making sure that you have the dining service you need ------ you desire it.

(A) wherever

(B) even if

(C) whenever

(D) in order that

題型 **文法──複合關係副詞**

翻譯 加勒比海灣飯店的廚房全天無休，確保您在任何時間想要用餐，都能享用到餐飲服務。

(A) wherever〔複合關係副詞〕不論何處；(B) even if〔副詞連接詞〕即使；(C) whenever〔複合關係副詞〕不論何時；(D) in order that〔副詞連接詞〕為了要......。

選項 (A) 到 (D) 皆可用於副詞子句，但是符合空格前、後句意者為 whenever，故正確答案為 (C)。

**130**

Jacob Lee told his manager about the complaints from overseas clients, and she promised to ------ the problem.

(A) look into

(B) pick up

(C) show up

(D) turn off

題型 **詞彙──片語**

翻譯 雅各・李向經理報告海外顧客的客訴，經理她承諾會調查相關問題。

(A) look into 調查；(B) pick up 撿起、接走（人）、學會、得到（疾病）；(C) show up 登場、參加；(D) turn off 關閉。

本題考的是片語的意思，此題只有 look into 既可與後面的名詞 problem 連用，又符合句意，故正確答案為 (A)。

# PART 6

**131–134 資訊**

Hightech staff members who have been working full time for more than two years are **131** to apply for internal transfers and job advancement opportunities within the firm. **132**. Those interested will be considered together with external **133**. Staff members who have essential qualifications to fill the open positions will be given **134** if outside recruitment isn't considered to be in the company's best interest.

高科技公司工作超過兩年的全職員工，都有資格申請內部轉調或晉升的機會。有意願者應該先和主管面談，並且將和外部應徵者一起競爭。如果外部招募不符合公司最佳利益，具備完整資格的內部員工將獲優先考慮。

**詞彙** staff member 員工　work full time 全職　apply for 申請　internal 內部的　transfer 轉調
job advancement 晉升　within the firm 公司內部　external 外部的　qualification 資格條件
open position 職缺　recruitment 招募

**131** -----------------------------------------------------------------------

(A) eligible
(B) collaborative
(C) exclusive
(D) prominent

(A) 符合資格的
(R) 合作的
(C) 排外的
(D) 重要的

**題型 詞彙——形容詞**

空格內只有填入 eligible 才符合句意，且只有 eligible 可與不定詞 to 一起出現，意思為「有資格去做某事」，故正確答案為 (A)。

其餘的 (B) 到 (D) 無法和不定詞 to 連用，而且也與句意不符。

**132** NEW -----------------------------------------------------------------------

(A) Staff members who wish to apply should first meet with their managers.
(B) Actually, all staff members are required to report their work hours daily.
(C) For instance, a competitive benefit package is given to full-time workers.
(D) We are delighted to welcome new staff members to our Hightech team.

(A) 有意願者應該先和主管面談。
(B) 其實，每個員工每天都需要回報工時。
(C) 舉例來說，給予全職員工更優勢的福利方案。
(D) 我們很高興歡迎高科技公司團隊的新進員工。

**題型 填入句子**

空格前的句子提到「staff members who have been working full time for more than two years」，而空格後的句子僅以省略代稱「Those interested」（有意願者），代表空格處應先提及過公司內部那些有意願的職員，故正確答案為 (A)。

## 133

(A) factors
(B) candidates
(C) occupations
(D) suppliers

(A) 因素
(B) 應徵者
(C) 職業
(D) 供應商

題型 **詞彙——名詞**

第一句中提到可應徵職缺的對象為公司工作兩年以上的全職員工,而最後一句中提及「outside recruitment」,故空格處應提及的是外部應徵者,答案為 (B)。

## 134

(A) preferring
(B) preferred
(C) preference
(D) prefer

(A) 偏好的
(B) 更合意的
(C) 優先權
(D) 更喜歡

題型 **位置——名詞**

此題空格應填入名詞,指給予內部員工的東西,故正確答案為 (C)。

★授與動詞 give 的句型如下:
give sb sth〔主動態〕
sb be given sth〔被動態〕

## 135–138 文章

The Michael Theater will be extending its run of Shining Stars, a play by Justine Kay. Due to an unexpected rise in **135** for the tickets, the last performance will now occur on March 18. The move comes as something of a surprise, considering the **136** reviews written by critics after the show's opening on February 2. **137**. However, the show has abruptly become popular among younger people, most of whom get their news through the Internet. They are **138** interested in the play's exploration of economic issues and career choices.

麥可劇場將會加演賈絲汀·凱依的戲劇《群星閃耀》的場次。門票需求的增加超乎預期,最後一場演出如今將在 3 月 18 日登場。之所以加演也是意外,因為 2 月 2 日的開幕場演出飽受評論家的批評,起初門票銷售表現並不好。不過,演出突然在年輕人之間大受歡迎,他們大多都是在網路得知演出訊息。他們對劇中探索經濟議題和職涯選擇的部分,明顯很感興趣。

詞彙 **come as something of a surprise** 形容某事的發生令人意外 **critic** 評論家 **abruptly** 突然 **exploration** 探索 **economic** 經濟的

**135**

(A) demanded
(B) demanding
(C) to demand
(D) demand

(A) 被需求的
(B) 苛求的
(C) 有所要求
(D) 需求

**題型** 位置——名詞

可夾在介系詞 in 與 for 中間的應該為名詞，此處只有 demand 適合填入，故正確答案為 (D)。

**136**

(A) brilliant
(B) deep
(C) harsh
(D) prompt

(A) 傑出的
(B) 深的
(C) 嚴厲的
(D) 敏捷的

**題型** 詞彙——形容詞

此題須根據空格上下文判斷。空格前指出演出加場令人意外，空格後說考慮到評論家給的評價，代表評論家給的評價並不好，才會顯得加場這件事情令人意外，故本題應填入 harsh，正確答案為 (C)。

**137** (NEW)

(A) Actors from the show are local residents.
(D) The premlere was attended by local business leaders.
(C) The initial box office sales had also been weak.
(D) Moreover, the theater company has been around for several years.

(A) 全部的演員都是當地居民。
(B) 當地企業領袖來觀賞首演。
(C) 起初門票銷售表現也不好。
(D) 不只如此，劇院公司在此已經很多年了。

**題型** 填入句子

however（然而）前後的兩句通常意思相反，故只要知道 however 後句的意思就能推測前句的內容。後句表示演出突然在年輕人間大受歡迎，所以 however 前句應與受歡迎相反，故最適合填入 (C)。

**138**

(A) apparent
(B) more apparent
(C) apparentness
(D) apparently

(A) 明顯的
(B) 更明顯的
(C) 顯著性
(D) 明顯地

**題型** 位置——副詞

副詞為句子中可有可無的存在，就算刪去副詞也不影響句意。本句就算刪除空格也是正確的句子，故空格填入的應為副詞 apparently，正確答案為 (D)。

On April 5, Emerson Radio will celebrate its twenty-fifth anniversary. That's a quarter of a century of stimulating **139**. Over the years, we **140** our listeners breaking news, thought-provoking stories, and popular music throughout the world. Now, we encourage you to celebrate with us during an open house from 7:00 P.M. to 9:00 P.M. on April 5 at our Charles Avenue studio. Take a tour and see some of the behind-the-scenes magic. Watch a demonstration of our digital audio equipment. **141**. The open house is free, but registration is required. We hope you can join us for this **142** event.

艾默生廣播將在 4 月 5 日慶祝 25 週年，這是長達四分之一個世紀且具啟發性的廣播服務。過去幾年來，我們持續提供聽眾即時新聞、發人深思的故事，還有來自全球的流行音樂。現在，我們希望您也來共襄盛舉，一起在 4 月 5 日晚上 7 點到 9 點，前往位於查爾斯大道的錄音室，參觀開放的錄音室並一窺幕後魔法。觀看我們的數位錄音設備，還可以和幾位您所喜愛的廣播員見面。參訪完全免費但需要報名。我們希望您可以參加這特別的活動。

**詞彙** anniversary 週年紀念日　stimulating 具啟發性的　breaking news 即時新聞　thought-provoking 發人深思的　throughout the world 全球　open house 開放日　take a tour 參觀　behind-the-scenes 幕後秘辛　demonstration 展示　registration 報名

**139** --------------------------------------------------------

(A) concerts
(B) development
(C) programming
(D) discussions

(A) 演奏會
(B) 發展
(C)（電視，廣播）節目
(D) 討論

**題型** 詞彙——名詞

從第一句中的艾默生廣播與空格後的下一句中提到即時新聞、故事與音樂，可知空格應填入 programming，正確答案為 (C)。

**140** --------------------------------------------------------

(A) offers
(B) will offer
(C) offering
(D) have offered

(A) 提供
(B) 將會提供
(C) 正在提供
(D) 已提供

**題型** 位置——動詞

從空格前方的「Over the years」可知道，動詞應為現在完成式，表達數年間不斷提供聽眾服務，故正確答案為 (D)。

現在完成式時態的意義為「過去發生的行為一直持續到現在」。

**141** [NEW] --------------------------------------------------

(A) We hope to merge with another local radio station in the coming year.
(B) You can also meet some of your favorite broadcasters.
(C) This is the second event in our April schedule.
(D) This station continues to be an essential part of your neighborhood.

(A) 我們希望在明年和當地另一間廣播電台合併。
(B) 還可以和幾位你所喜愛的廣播員見面。
(C) 這是四月分行程的第二個活動。
(D) 電台會持續成為您鄰里重要的一份子。

**題型 填入句子**

空格前面的兩個句子提到，參觀時可以看到錄音室裡的狀況，並觀看設備展示，所以此處應是承接上兩句，講述參加活動的好處，故正確答案應為 (B)。

**142**

(A) special
(B) specialize
(C) specially
(D) specialization

(A) 特別的
(B) 專攻
(C) 特別地
(D) 專門化

**題型 位置——形容詞**

此處應選能修飾名詞 event 的形容詞，故正確答案為 (A)。

## 143–146 電子郵件

**To:** David Kim <dkim@eleganthotel.com>
**From:** Albert Lee <alee@eleganthotel.com>
**Date:** 22 June
**Subject:** Good Afternoon

Dear David,
I was recently notified of your upcoming **143**. Though the new position as general manager in our New York location formally **144** on 1 August, I wanted to offer my best wishes to you now.

The transition can be **145**, so please don't hesitate to contact me if you need any assistance. Your performance as assistant general manager at the Elegant Hotel here in Singapore has been outstanding. **146**.

Congratulations!

Sincerely,
Albert Lee

收件人：大衛·金 <dkim@eleganthotel.com>
寄件人：艾柏特·李 <alee@eleganthotel.com>
日期：6 月 22 日
主旨：午安

親愛的大衛：

我最近接獲你即將晉升的通知。雖然紐約部門的總經理職位正式上任日是 8 月 1 日，我還是想要現在獻上最好的祝福。

職位變動可能頗具挑戰性，所以如果需要任何協助請儘管告訴我。你在新加坡優雅飯店擔任協理時表現一向傑出。我有信心你可以勝任新職務。

恭喜！

艾柏特·李 敬上

**詞彙 notify** 通知 **upcoming** 即將到來的 **general manager** 總經理 **location** 據點 **best wishes** 最好的祝福 **transition** 變動 **don't hesitate to V** 立刻……（多用於書信中）**assistance** 協助 **performance**（工作）表現 **assistant general manager** 協理

**143**

(A) promotion
(B) award
(C) event
(D) trip

(A) 晉升
(B) 獎賞
(C) 事件
(D) 旅行

全文第一句提及「new position」（新職位）與「general manager」（總經理），最後一句又提到前一個職位為「assistant general manager」（協理），故可知道收信人應是得到升職，正確答案為 (A)。

**144** ----------------------------------------

(A) began
(B) begins
(C) could begin
(D) has begun

(A) 開始了
(B) 開始
(C) 可能開始
(D) 已開始

題型 **位置**——動詞

電子郵件撰寫的日期為 6 月 22 日，而升職後正式上班的日期為 8 月 1 日，故空格中可填入未來式，且由於簡單現在式也可用來表示「確定的計畫和安排」，所以也可填入簡單現在式，故本題正確答案為 (B)。

★**簡單現在式的使用時機：**
1. 敘述當下發生的事件
2. 永久成立的事實、習慣或反覆發生的事
3. 請求和提供指示
4. 表示確定好的計劃和安排

**145** ----------------------------------------

(A) challenging
(B) challenges
(C) challenge
(D) challenged

(A) 富有挑戰性的
(B) 挑戰
(C) 挑戰
(D) 受到挑戰的

題型 **位置**——形容詞

此題考的是 challenging 與 challenged 的字義差別，前者形容「事情」具挑戰性，後者形容「人」感覺受到挑戰，故正確答案為 (A)。

★**其餘相似的形容詞組舉例：**
**bored**（感到無聊的）vs **boring**（令人乏味的）　　**pleased**（滿意的）vs **pleasing**（令人滿意的）
**frightened**（受驚的）vs **frightening**（令人驚恐的）　　**worried**（擔心的）vs **worrying**（令人擔憂的）

**146** (NEW) ----------------------------------------

(A) The New York hotel is bigger and has additional amenities.
(B) I'm presently interviewing candidates for all the positions.
(C) In the meantime, inquire about staff member discounts at the hotel.
(D) I am confident that you will succeed in your new role.

(A) 紐約飯店更大，而且有更多設施。
(B) 我目前在面試各項職缺的應徵者。
(C) 在此期間，向同事詢問旅館折扣。
(D) 我有信心你可以勝任新職務。

題型 **填入句子**

空格前面的句子提到，收信人先前也有良好的工作表現，故在文意上適合填入的句子為 (D)。

**147–148 簡訊**

| | |
|---|---|
| **From:** Montera Hassan<br>**To:** Grace Kim | 傳訊者：蒙特拉·哈珊<br>收訊者：葛瑞絲·金 |
| Grace, my smartphone battery is almost dead. I think I left my power cord at the office.<br><br>Would you please call my customer and tell him I'll be roughly 20 minutes late? I'm heading back to the office to get the cord right now. | 葛瑞絲，我智慧型手機電池的電快用光了。我想我把充電線放在辦公室。<br><br>可以請你幫我打電話給客戶，告訴他我會晚大概20分鐘到嗎？我現在趕回去辦公室拿充電線。 |

**詞彙** battery is dead 電池電量耗盡　power cord 充電線　roughly 大概　head back to 趕回……

**147**

**Why did Mr. Hassan send a message to Ms. Kim?**

(A) To inquire whether she found his power cord
(B) To ask that she contact a customer
(C) To remind her to recharge a battery
(D) To check the location of an accounting division

**為什麼哈珊先生寄簡訊給金女士？**

(A) 詢問她有沒有找到他的充電線
(B) 請她聯絡客戶
(C) 提醒她更替電池充電
(D) 確認會計部門的位置

文章中提到：「Would you please call my customer and tell him I'll be roughly 20 minutes late?」，由此可知，哈珊先生請求金女士幫忙聯絡客戶，故正確答案為 (B)。

**148**

**What will Mr. Hassan probably do next?**

(A) Find his computer
(B) Return to his office
(C) Purchase a power cord
(D) Contact the technical support department

**哈珊先生接下來可能會做什麼？**

(A) 找他的電腦
(B) 回到辦公室
(C) 買新的充電線
(D) 聯絡技術支援部門

文章中提到：「I'm heading back to the office to get the cord right now.」，由此可知，哈珊先生接下來要做的事情應是「回到辦公室」，故正確答案為 (B)。

Dayton Café owner, Brandon Ehret, has signed a lease for a second restaurant at 623 Smithon Avenue.

The building, close to Rolling Concert Hall, previously housed a branch of Carol Financial Group. Mr. Ehret's most recent venture, to be called Tiara Snacks, will begin service on August 1. At first, however, the small restaurant will be open only during the evening hours. The idea is to build a customer base, particularly among concertgoers, prior to adding a lunch service. Mr. Ehret's original restaurant, Dayton Café, is located on First Street, near the Winning Grocery Store bus stop. Executive Chef Jessica Choi will supervise the two locations.

戴頓咖啡店老闆布蘭登‧艾瑞特，在史米森大道623號上簽下了第二間餐廳的租約。

該建築鄰近滾石演奏廳，前身是卡羅金融集團的分部。艾瑞特先生最近的創業——皇冠小吃，將在8月1日開始營業。不過營運初期只會在傍晚營業，目的是要在開始提供午餐前建立顧客群，尤其鎖定演奏廳的觀眾。艾瑞特先生的第一間餐廳戴頓咖啡店，位在第一街上，就在公車站牌「勝利雜貨店」旁邊。主廚潔西卡‧崔將督管這兩間店。

**詞彙** **lease** 租約　**be close to** 鄰近　**house** 為……提供空間　**branch** 分部；分公司　**venture** （風險高的）商業活動　**build a customer base** 建立客群　**concertgoer** 演奏廳的常客　**original** 原先的；最早的　**executive chef** 主廚　**supervise** 監督管理

**What is the article about?**

(A) The opening of a new restaurant
(B) An outstanding real estate agent
(C) A change in prices
(D) A restaurant's relocation

這篇文章是有關於什麼？

(A) 一間新餐廳開張
(B) 一名傑出的房地產仲介
(C) 價格變動
(D) 餐廳位置搬遷

文章第一句提到：「Dayton Café owner, Brandon Ehret, has signed a lease for a second restaurant at 623 Smithon Avenue.」，由此可知這篇文章講述的應是一間新餐廳的開張，故正確答案為 (A)。

**What is suggested about Tiara Snacks?**

(A) It is situated adjacent to a public transportation route.
(B) It is expected to receive business from concert patrons.
(C) It is supposed to start serving lunch on August 1.
(D) It is Mr. Ehret's third restaurant.

文中提到關於皇冠小吃什麼事？

(A) 它鄰近公共運輸路線。
(B) 它預期能吸引演奏廳的觀眾。
(C) 它會從 8 月 1 日開始供應午餐。
(D) 它是艾瑞特先生的第三間餐廳。

文章中提到：「The idea is to build a customer base, particularly among concertgoers, prior to adding a lunch service.」，由此可知只在傍晚時間提供服務是為了吸引演奏廳的常客，故正確答案為 (B)。

## 151-153 信件

**From:** Alex Baldwin
**To:** Garrison Builders employees
**Date:** 15 June
**Subject:** All-staff meeting

To all of the employees,

Next Monday, 29 June, we will have a guest speaker at our all-staff meeting in room 304. Dee Ihibramvich is a senior architect at the Extraordinary Firm in Bern, where she has worked for the last ten years. She led the design project of Bern's Bundle House as well as the Titan Skyscraper in Rome. These two buildings received international awards for their innovative designs.

Before making a name for herself in Europe, Ms. Ihibramvich spent six years in San Francisco at the Dynamic Architect Organization (DAO). It was at the DAO that I had the opportunity to cooperate with her on many projects. Ms. Ihibramvich will be here in London for two weeks and has consented to deliver a speech at our meeting about many of her internationally admired design projects.

All employees are required to participate.

---

寄件人：阿歷克斯・包德溫
收件人：葛瑞森建築全體員工
日期：6月15日
主旨：全員大會

致全體員工，

下週一6月29日，將有客座講者蒞臨我們在304號會議室舉辦的員工大會。迪・伊希布拉姆維奇是非凡公司在瑞士伯恩的資深建築師，她在當地已工作十年之久。她領導了伯恩住宅區，以及羅馬泰坦摩天大樓的設計專案。兩項專案都因為創新設計取得國際獎項肯定。

伊希布拉姆維奇女士在歐洲闖出名堂之前，曾在舊金山的動感建築組織（DAO）待過六年。也就是在DAO中，我才有機會和她合作多項計畫。伊希布拉姆維奇女士會在倫敦待兩個星期，並答應要來我們會議上演講，談談她多項深受國際推崇的建築計畫。

所有員工都必須參加。

---

**詞彙** all-staff meeting 全員大會　senior architect 資深建築師　as well as 以及　innovative 創新的　make a name for oneself 闖出名堂　cooperate with 與……合作　consent to V 答應要……　deliver a speech 演講　admired 被推崇的

**151** ------

**Why was the memo written?**

(A) To announce a plan to open another satellite branch
(B) To employ a new employee
(C) To suggest a construction project
(D) To introduce an architect's accomplishments

為什麼會有這篇備忘錄？

(A) 宣布開分公司的計畫
(B) 聘用新員工
(C) 提出建設計畫
(D) 介紹一名建築師的成就

文章中提到：「She led the design project of Bern's Bundle House as well as the Titan Skyscraper in Rome. These two buildings received international awards for their innovative designs.」，由此可以得知伊希布拉姆維奇女士過去的經歷與獲獎紀錄，故正確答案為 (D)。

## What does Mr. Baldwin suggest about Ms. Ihibramvich?

(A) She will lead a design project for his company.
(B) She intends to open her own business.
(C) She is a former coworker of his.
(D) She is relocating to a new city.

關於伊希布拉姆維奇女士，包德溫先生說了什麼？

(A) 她將為他的公司主導一個設計專案。
(B) 她打算開創自己的事業。
(C) 她之前是他的同事。
(D) 她要搬到新城市。

仔細查看寄件人「From」的部分，可知此為包德溫先生所寫，而內容中提到：「It was at the DAO that I had the opportunity to cooperate with her on many projects.」，由此可知，包德溫先生和伊希布拉姆維奇女士曾為同事，故正確答案為 (C)。

## Where is Garrison Builders located?

(A) In London
(B) In San Francisco
(C) In Rome
(D) In Bern

葛瑞森建築位於哪裡？

(A) 倫敦
(B) 舊金山
(C) 羅馬
(D) 伯恩

先看到信件收件人為葛瑞森建築的全體員工，再從內容第二段最後一句得知，演講者將到訪倫敦（will be here in London），此處重點在於「here」一字，代表寫信者以自身角度出發，告訴員工們演講者將來此處，因此可知道公司就位於倫敦，故正確答案為 (A)。

## 154–155 訊息串

| | |
|---|---|
| **Edwin Chung**    3:24 P.M.<br>Jasmine sent you an e-mail with the sales figures two hours ago. She's been wondering if she could hear back from you. | 愛德溫・鍾〔下午3:24〕：<br>茉莉兩小時前發給你一封有銷售數字的電子郵件，她想知道你是否會回信。 |
| **Jim Carter**    3:25 P.M.<br>I'm not at my desk. Don't you think she's concerned because the figures are lower than expected? | 金・卡特〔下午3:25〕：<br>我不在位子上。你不覺得她會這麼關心這件事，是因為成果不如預期嗎？ |
| **Edwin Chung**    3:26 P.M.<br>Maybe. | 愛德溫・鍾〔下午3:26〕：<br>可能吧。 |
| **Jim Carter**    3:27 P.M.<br>I was called away to inspect the packaging machine. It's not working properly. | 金・卡特〔下午3:27〕：<br>我被叫去檢查包裝機，它無法正常運作。 |
| **Edwin Chung**    3:28 P.M.<br>Should I call a repair person? | 愛德溫・鍾〔下午3:28〕：<br>需要我叫維修人員嗎？ |
| **Jim Carter**    3:30 P.M.<br>I'm hoping to take care of it myself. Why don't you set up a conference call for Tuesday morning? The team will have to talk about the report. | 金・卡特〔下午3:30〕：<br>我想自己處理就好。你何不在週二早上安排電話會議？團隊需要談談這份報告。 |

| Edwin Chung | 3:30 P.M. | 愛德溫‧鍾〔下午3:30〕： |
|---|---|---|
| I will do that. | | 好的。 |

**詞彙** sales figures 銷售數字　hear from sb （透過電話、信件）接到某人的消息　concerned 抱持關心的
call away 叫走　packaging machine 包裝機　not work properly 無法正常運作
repair person 維修人員　set up 安排準備　conference call 電話會議

## 154 NEW

**At 3:25 P.M., what does Mr. Carter probably mean when he writes, "I'm not at my desk"?**

(A) He got off work early.
(B) He will miss a deadline.
(C) He is stopping by Mr. Chung's office.
(D) He cannot reply to Jasmine.

下午 3:25 的時候，卡特先生寫道：「我不在位子上」，他最可能的意思是？

(A) 他早退。
(B) 他將錯過截止日期。
(C) 他將順道拜訪鍾先生的辦公室。
(D) 他沒辦法回覆茉莉。

從下午 3 點 27 分卡特先生的訊息：「I was called away to inspect the packing machine.」，可知道卡特先生離開座位無法回覆，故正確答案為 (D)。

## 155

**What is Mr. Chung requested to do?**

(A) Go over documents
(B) Arrange a meeting
(C) Check travel plans
(D) Fix some devices

鍾先生被要求做什麼？

(A) 查閱文件
(B) 安排一個會議
(C) 確認旅遊計畫
(D) 修理一些裝置

3 點 30 分時卡特先生提議「set up conference call」，表示要安排電話會議，而鍾先生隨即答應，所以可知鍾先生被要求安排會議，故正確答案為 (B)。

## 156–158 信件

### Rachel Artwork Museum

15 March
Ms. Jennifer Baek

Dear Ms. Baek,

As a Rachel Artwork Museum member, you will shortly be able to make use of our special appreciation deals. —[1]—. From 1 to 28 April, members will receive an additional 30 percent discount on all gift shop products. Members will also be offered a free beverage with their meal in the on-site café. Furthermore, people who become new members no later than 28 April will be offered a 15 percent membership fee discount. —[2]—.

### 瑞秋美術館

3月15日
珍妮佛‧拜克女士

親愛的拜克女士：

您是瑞秋美術館的會員，不久後將能享有特別優惠。從4月1日到28日，會員在紀念禮品店將享額外七折的商品折扣，在館內咖啡店裡用餐還可享一杯免費飲料。此外在4月28日以前，加入會員的入會費將打八五折。所以邀請您的親朋好友和同事，到我們官網上登記成為會員。

So invite your family members, friends, and colleagues to go to our website and register.

—[3]—. The formerly closed fourth-floor galleries, which feature sculptures and paintings by ancient Persian artists, will be open to all visitors until 7:30 P.M. every Tuesday of this month. Images of select artwork from these galleries can be seen on our Web page. —[4]—. We look forward to seeing you soon.

Sincerely,
Justine Liu
Director of Membership Management

4月來逛美術館還有一個好康。四樓為古波斯藝術家之雕塑和繪畫的特色展區，原先是關閉的，但從這個月的每週二開始，將全面對外開放到晚間7:30。該展區嚴選的圖片影像也能在官網上看到。我們期待您大駕光臨。

會員管理部主任
賈絲汀・劉 敬上

> 詞彙 **appreciation deal** 特別優惠　**register** 登錄　**gallery**（藝術品）展區　**ancient** 古老的
> **sculpture** 雕塑　**be open to** 對……開放

**156**----------------------------------------------------------------

**What is mentioned about the Rachel Artwork Museum?**

(A) It has a place to eat.
(B) It will be closed down for one month.
(C) It will have photos on exhibit.
(D) It has a workshop for art courses.

文中提到關於瑞秋美術館什麼事？

(A) 有吃飯的地方。
(B) 將會關閉一個月。
(C) 將舉行照片展。
(D) 有舉辦藝術課程的工作坊。

信件第一段第三句提到：「Members will also be offered a free beverage with their meal in the on-site café.」，由此可知博物館內設有餐廳，故正確答案為 (A)。

**157**----------------------------------------------------------------

**What will be different on Tuesdays?**

(A) Admission to the museum will be free.
(B) Extra galleries will be open.
(C) Operating hours at the restaurant will be extended.
(D) People will buy some Persian artwork.

週二將有什麼地方不同以往？

(A) 入館免費。
(B) 額外開放其他展覽區。
(C) 餐廳營業時間延長。
(D) 大家會選購波斯藝術品。

信件中提到：「The formerly closed fourth-floor galleries . . . will be open to all visitors until 7:30 P.M. every Tuesday of this month.」，由此可知每週二將額外開放展區，故正確答案為 (B)。

**158** NEW -----

**In which of the positions marked [1], [2], [3], and [4] does the following sentence best belong?**

**"April is a great time to come by the museum for another reason."**

(A) [1]
(B) [2]
(C) [3]
(D) [4]

下列句子最適合出現在 [1]、[2]、[3]、[4] 的哪個位置中？

「4 月來逛美術館還有一個好康。」

(A) [1]
(B) [2]
(C) [3]
(D) [4]

信件第一段講述的是會員優惠，第二段 [3] 號之後的句子則指出原先關閉的展區會在每週二開放，可把看作此時參訪美術館的另一個理由（another reason），因此題目中的句子應放於此處最為合適，正確答案為 (C)。

### 159–160 告示

| Notice | 告示 |
|---|---|
| September 8 — An article about the upcoming remodeling projects in the public library network, published in our September 7 edition, incorrectly listed the closure date of the library's Kirkstein and Dodgeville branches as October 15. However, according to the library's spokesperson, only the Kirkstein branch will be closed from October 15 through November 20. The Dodgeville branch will keep operating as normal until the Kirkstein branch reopens on November 21. From that date, the Dodgeville branch will be closed until December 25. Please go to the library's website for further information. We sincerely apologize for any inconvenience our mistake may have caused. | 9月8日──本報於9月7日當期公告關於公共圖書館將進行分館整修計畫的文章，誤把克爾克絲坦和道奇維爾分館的休館日期寫為10月15日。然而據圖書館發言人表示，只有克爾克絲坦分館會從10月15日開始休館到11月20日。道奇維爾分館將如常運作，直到克爾克絲坦分館11月21日重新開放後，才會開始休館到12月25日。欲知詳細資訊，請上圖書館官方網站。若我們的錯誤造成任何不便，誠摯向您道歉。 |

**詞彙** remodeling 整修　list 列出　closure 關閉　spokesperson 發言人
from A through B 從 A 到 B　as normal 一如往常　for further information 欲知詳細資訊

**159** -----

**Where would this notice probably be found?**

(A) In a library's yearly report
(B) On a schedule of gatherings
(C) In a remodeling plan
(D) In a local newspaper

哪裡比較有可能看到這項告示？

(A) 在圖書館的年度報告上
(B) 在聚會的行程表上
(C) 在整修平面圖上
(D) 在當地報紙上

從告示第一句「An article . . . published in our September 7 edition」中，可以知道此文章應刊於報紙上。另外也可以從出刊日期發現，此文章標為 9 月 8 日發行，內容又說 9 月 7 日也有發行，因此推測應該比較像是報紙的發行頻率，故正確答案為 (D)。

**When will the Dodgeville branch close for the renovation project?**

(A) On October 15
(B) On November 20
(C) On November 21
(D) On December 25

道奇維爾分館將從什麼時候開始休館，以進行翻修工程？

(A) 10 月 15 日
(B) 11 月 20 日
(C) 11 月 21 日
(D) 12 月 25 日

從告示中的「The Dodgeville branch will keep operating as normal until the Kirkstein branch reopens on November 21. From that date, the Dodgeville branch will be closed . . .」，可知 11 月 21 日克爾克斯坦分館開放，故換道奇維爾分館休館，本題正確答案為 (C)。

### 161–164 文章

| Farther Rider is gone! | 馳遠騎士車款將停售！ |
|---|---|
| By Jamal Lopez | 賈邁爾·羅培茲撰文 |

On Tuesday, Typhoon Motors, the producer currently manufacturing Farther Rider motorcycles, announced a delay in the launch of the new Fast DM model. Industry rivals responded in surprise at the news. —[1]—. And Farther Rider motorcycle enthusiasts went to its website to express bewilderment with Typhoon Motors for calling off May's eagerly awaited release.

颱風汽車，也就是馳遠騎士車款目前的製造商，週二宣布將延後發布新的快速DM車款。同業得知消息紛紛表示驚訝。喜好馳遠騎士車款的熱情用戶也湧上官網，針對颱風汽車取消眾所期盼的五月新款發表，紛紛表示不解。

It appears the determination to equip the Fast DM with a hybrid system, which uses gasoline and electric power alike, is to blame. Typhoon Motors admits that the current prototype was rejected due to its huge dimensions and heavy weight. This design of the power system would have needed a larger motorbike body than planned. They had concerns about the durability of its exterior. —[2]—.

之所以下此決定，似乎是因為他們決意要在快速DM車款加裝油電混合動力系統，才會導致問題發生。颱風汽車坦承，現階段的系統原型尺寸大又笨重，因此遭到淘汰。這種動力系統的設計，需要一個比預期來得更大的車體。他們對系統外部的耐受度也有疑慮。

Besides the design difficulties, the Farther Rider plant, having been equipped to manufacture previous models, is not ready for production of the Fast DM hybrid. —[3]—. New machines will need to be purchased, and the assembly line will have to be reconfigured.

不只是設計困難，颱風汽車車廠的設備都是用來生產以前的型號，目前也沒有準備好生產快速DM油電混合動力車。工廠需要採購新機械設備，產線也需要重新配置。

Two years ago, Typhoon Motors was widely complimented by motorcycle fans after it intervened to save Farther Rider from going bankrupt. What a difference two years has made? —[4]—.

颱風汽車兩年前力挽馳遠車款，助其擺脫破產命運，受到車迷的大力讚揚。這兩年間改變了什麼？而現在開始，他們得再次贏回顧客的信譽。

詞彙 rival 對手　motorcycle = motorbike 機車；摩托車　enthusiast 熱情用戶；愛好者
bewilderment 不解；困惑　eagerly awaited 眾所期盼的　release 發表；上市　prototype 原型
durability 耐受度　reconfigure 重新配置　intervene 干預　go bankrupt 破產
outfit 為……提供設備

**161**

---

**What is suggested about Typhoon Motors?**

(A) It owns the Farther Rider motorbike brand.
(B) It intends to sell a model at a discounted price.
(C) It is relocating its main office.
(D) It will introduce a new motorbike in May.

文中提到關於颱風汽車什麼事？

(A) 擁有馳遠騎士車款品牌。
(B) 有意要以折扣價格販售一個車款。
(C) 正在搬遷總公司。
(D) 五月會發布新款摩托車。

從文章第一段第一句：「Typhoon Motors, the producer currently manufacturing Farther Rider motorcycles」，便可以知道颱風汽車擁有馳遠騎士車款，故正確答案為 (A)。

**162**

---

**What is NOT mentioned as a difficulty with the power system?**

(A) It weighs a lot.
(B) It isn't cheap.
(C) It isn't strong.
(D) It is too big.

下列何者關於動力系統的缺點，並沒有在文中提到？

(A) 它很重。
(B) 它不便宜。
(C) 它不夠堅固。
(D) 它太大了。

第二段第二句說道：「Typhoon Motors admits that the current prototype was rejected due to its huge dimensions and heavy weight.」，表示動力系統過大且過重，此處便提及了 (A) 與 (D)。從第二段最後一句的「They had concerns about the durability of its exterior.」則得知 (C) 動力系統堅固性的問題。

(B) 在文章中完全未提及，故正確答案為 (B)。

**163**

---

**Why will the factory be remodeled?**

(A) It does not conform to a new regulation.
(B) It has not been updated in over two decades.
(C) It had been outfitted to produce older models.
(D) It is so small that it cannot produce two models at the same time.

為什麼工廠需要改建？

(A) 它不符合新規定。
(B) 它已超過 20 年沒有更新了。
(C) 它有的是生產舊型號的設備。
(D) 它太小了，沒辦法同時生產兩種型號。

從第三段第一句「the Farther Rider plant, having been equipped to manufacture previous models, is not ready for production of the Fast DM hybrid.」，可以知道工廠的設備適合生產之前的型號，故正確答案為 (C)。

In which of the positions marked [1], [2], [3], and [4] does the following sentence best belong?

"From now on, they will have to bring back the goodwill of these prospective customers."

(A) [1]
(B) [2]
(C) [3]
(D) [4]

下列句子最適合出現在 [1]、[2]、[3]、[4] 的哪個位置中？

「而現在開始，他們得再次贏回顧客的信譽。」

(A) [1]
(B) [2]
(C) [3]
(D) [4]

從文章第一段最後一句可知，有大量的客戶湧入網站表示不滿，最後一段則是說明颱風汽車曾如何贏得顧客喜愛，代表現在公司必須設法再次奪回信賴，故題目引述的句子應放於 [4] 最適合，故正確答案為 (D)。

---

**165–168 文章**

## Hair Style Salon

9 August — Hair Style Salon had an impressive grand opening earlier last week. Owner and hair stylist Arthur Lee mentioned that the event was well attended, and many appointments in the salon have been reserved during the past week. James Morgan, who came by the salon for the first time yesterday, said that he is not surprised that Hair Style Salon is already popular. "It offers quality cuts," he said, "And it's within walking distance because it's situated on the same street where I and many people in the commercial area work."

In fact, Hair Style Salon is situated on crowded Madison Avenue, down the street from Darlington University. "I selected Madison Avenue as a result of its proximity to the campus, and I want to appeal to university students and faculty members," said Lee at the salon opening.

Another new client mentioned that the rates for the salon's services and hair care items were not that expensive. "I was happy to find a good hair salon that is affordably priced," said Michelle Lin, a satisfied customer. "I will absolutely be returning."

Please don't hesitate to call 031-532-4343 or visit www.hairstylesalon.com for additional information or to set up an appointment.

## 美髮造型沙龍

8月9日——美髮造型沙龍在上週初風光開幕。店長兼髮型設計師的亞瑟·李表示，開幕活動的出席很踴躍，過去一週以來也有很多人預約。昨天首次到沙龍的詹姆士·摩根說，他對這間店已廣受歡迎並不感到意外。「剪髮品質很好，」他說，「走路過來也很近，和我還有很多人工作的繁忙商業區在同一條街上。」

的確，從達靈頓大學往下走，美髮造型沙龍位於人來人往的麥迪遜大道上。「我選擇麥迪遜大道，就是因為它鄰近校園，而我想吸引大學生和教職員前來。」李先生在開幕式上表示。

另一名新顧客提到，沙龍服務和美髮保養產品的費用都不算貴。「我很高興可以找到一間價位負擔得起的好髮廊，」對服務相當滿意的顧客米雪兒·林說，「我絕對還會再來。」

欲知更多資訊或預約，請儘速致電031-532-4343或上官網www.hairstylesalon.com。

**詞彙** grand opening 盛大開幕活動　be well attended 出席踴躍的
within walking distance 在走路能到的距離　commercial area 商業區　as a result of 因為
proximity 鄰近性　appeal to 吸引　faculty member 教職員　affordably priced 價格可負擔的
don't hesitate to V 盡速……　set up an appointment 預約時間

**165**

**What is the purpose of the article?**

(A) To inform people of the relocation of a business
(B) To encourage hair stylists to attend an event
(C) To introduce the neighborhood to a new business
(D) To notify students of a special discount

這篇文章的目的為何？

(A) 宣告店家搬家的消息
(B) 鼓勵髮型師參加某個活動
(C) 介紹臨近地區有一間新店開張
(D) 告知學生優惠訊息

從第一段的「Hair Style Salon had an impressive grand opening earlier last week.」可以得知，
這篇文章公告新理髮店開張的訊息，故正確答案為 (C)。

**166**

**What is mentioned about Mr. Morgan?**

(A) He works on Madison Avenue.
(B) He owns the Hair Style Salon.
(C) He participated in the salon's grand opening.
(D) He made an appointment through the Internet.

文中提到摩根先生什麼事？

(A) 他在麥迪遜大道上工作。
(B) 他是美髮造型沙龍的所有人。
(C) 他參與了這間沙龍的盛大開幕式。
(D) 他透過網路預約剪髮。

從摩根先生所說的「it's situated on the same street where I and many people in the commercial
area work.」，以及「Hair Style Salon is situated on crowded Madison Avenue」，可以知道摩
根先生就在摩迪遜大道上班，故正確答案為 (A)。

**167**

**Why did Mr. Lee select a particular site for his business?**

(A) There is no competition in the community.
(B) There are many parking garages nearby.
(C) The rent is much lower than other locations.
(D) It is adjacent to a university.

李先生為什麼替他的店選擇這個地點？

(A) 這個社區沒有其他競爭對手。
(B) 這附近有很多停車場。
(C) 這裡租金比其他地點便宜許多。
(D) 這裡鄰近一間大學。

從第二段「I selected Madison Avenue as a result of its proximity to the campus, and I want to
appeal to university students and faculty members」中，可知李先生看準大道鄰近校園，想吸
引學生與教職員，才選擇此處開店，故正確答案為 (D)。

**168**

**What is suggested about Hair Style Salon?**

(A) It is looking for a new stylist.
(B) It sells hair products at a reasonable price.
(C) It offers a discount to new customers.
(D) It provides complimentary hair care vouchers.

文中提到關於美髮造型沙龍什麼事？

(A) 正在招募新的髮型師。
(B) 販售價格合理的美髮用品。
(C) 新顧客可享優惠。
(D) 提供免費美髮護理。

從第三段的「the rates for the salon's services and hair care items were not that expensive.」
可以看出店內沙龍服務與頭髮保養產品都不貴，故正確答案為 (B)。

## *Company World* Subscribers!

Right now, you can register to receive personalized e-mails every Wednesday morning with the latest in business and financial news. You can get the same exhaustive coverage you expect from *Company World* magazine each month without having to wait for 30 days. Select your favorites from a comprehensive list of topics and receive various fascinating articles on those topics every week. This service is available exclusively to subscribers of *Company World*.

It's simple to get started. Just go to www.companyworld.com. Click Sign Up for Personalized E-mails, provide your e-mail address, and select your preferences for the service, knowing that you can change them whenever necessary. You can also keep having access to subscription information online.

## 《企業世界》的訂戶！

即刻開始，只要註冊就能在每週三早上收到客製化的電子郵件，提供您最新的商業和財經新聞，還可以得到《企業世界》雜誌月刊每個月的詳盡報導，而不需要再等30天。廣泛的主題任君隨喜好挑選，每週都可以就相關主題收到好文章。這項服務只提供給《企業世界》的訂戶。

要啟用服務很簡單。只要上www.companyworld.com，點選「加入客製化電子郵件」，提供您的電子郵件信箱和選擇服務偏好，您可以隨時依需求更改，也可持續得知相關訂閱資訊。

**詞彙** subscriber 訂戶　register 註冊　personalized 客製化的　latest 最新的　exhaustive 詳盡的　coverage 報導　comprehensive 廣泛的　fascinating 吸引人的　exclusively 獨家地　sign up for 加入；報名　preference 偏好

 169

**What is being advertised?**

(A) A discussion with a financial specialist
(B) A method of paying bills through the website
(C) A weekly online newsletter
(D) A class in corporate investment

這則廣告是在宣傳什麼？

(A) 和財經專家的討論會
(B) 網路付款的方式
(C) 每週電子報
(D) 企業投資課程

廣告第一段第一句便開門見山說出主旨：「Right now, you can register to receive personalized e-mails every Wednesday morning with the latest in business and financial news.」，故可知道本篇在宣傳電子報，正確答案為 (C)。

 170

**What is suggested about the service?**

(A) It is designed for subscribers of a publication.
(B) It will be available 30 days from now.
(C) It is already popular with business owners.
(D) It is the third in a series of the latest services being offered.

文中談到關於這項服務什麼事？

(A) 它是設計給某個刊物的訂戶。
(B) 從現在起 30 天都有效。
(C) 在企業主之間已經很流行。
(D) 這是最新服務系列中的第三項服務。

廣告第一段最後一句說道：「This service is available exclusively to subscribers of *Company World*.」，表示電子報紙提供給《企業世界》的訂戶，故正確答案為 (A)。

**171**

What are interested people asked to do in order to receive the service?

(A) Send in an application
(B) Register online
(C) Make a call
(D) Mail a request

感興趣的人要怎麼做才可以取得服務？

(A) 寄出申請
(B) 上網註冊
(C) 打電話
(D) 寄信請求

從第二段的「Just go to www.companyworld.com. Click Sign Up for Personalized E-mails . . . 」，可知只要上網註冊便可訂閱電子報，故正確答案為 (B)。

## 172–175 訊息串

| | |
|---|---|
| **Dominic Flores** 2:26 P.M.<br>Ms. Han, it looks like there will be a storm tomorrow, so the roof work on your hospital's new east wing will need to be postponed. | 多明尼克・佛羅雷斯〔下午2:26〕：<br>韓女士，看來明天會有暴風雨，所以您醫院新東側建築的屋頂工程需要延後。 |
| **Sooji Han** 2:27 P.M.<br>Does that mean no work all day? | 秀智・韓〔下午2:27〕：<br>意思是說整天都停工嗎？ |
| **Dominic Flores** 2:27 P.M.<br>Absolutely not! My employees can help Tony Lim's workers fix the support beams inside the old building. | 多明尼克・佛羅雷斯〔下午2:27〕：<br>當然不是！我的員工會協助湯尼・琳姆先生的工人維修老舊建築的樑架。 |
| **Sooji Han** 2:28 P.M.<br>How long will it take to fix them? | 秀智・韓〔下午2:28〕：<br>還需要多久才會修好？ |
| **Dominic Flores** 2:28 P.M.<br>Let me find out. | 多明尼克・佛羅雷斯〔下午2:28〕：<br>我確認一下。 |
| **Dominic Flores** 2:29 P.M.<br>Tony, how close are you to completing your project? | 多明尼克・佛羅雷斯〔下午2:29〕：<br>湯尼，你的工作進度如何？ |
| **Tony Lim** 2:31 P.M.<br>Everything was fine until this morning, when the structural engineer visited with some updates. We'll be working overtime for the next ten days. | 湯尼・琳姆〔下午2:31〕：<br>到今天早上為止一切都很順利，但結構工程師有來看翻修狀況後，我看接下來十天還得加班趕工。 |
| **Dominic Flores** 2:32 P.M.<br>What do you think about my employees assisting you tomorrow? | 多明尼克・佛羅雷斯〔下午2:32〕：<br>我的員工明天去幫你的話，你覺得怎麼樣？ |
| **Tony Lim** 2:33 P.M.<br>That's terrific! Then, we could maybe finish in three days. | 湯尼・琳姆〔下午2:33〕：<br>太棒了！這樣的話大概可以三天內完工吧。 |

| | | | |
|---|---|---|---|
| **Sooji Han** | 2:35 P.M. | 秀智·韓〔下午2:35〕： | |

**Sooji Han** 2:35 P.M.
So, will your employees require access to the old building?

**Dominic Flores** 2:36 P.M.
For tomorrow, yes. Would it be all right for them to park their vehicles in front of the old building?

**Sooji Han** 2:38 P.M.
Of course. There should be sufficient places near the main entrance. And could you please tell them not to drive their cars on the lawn?

秀智·韓〔下午2:35〕：
所以您的員工會需要進到舊大樓嗎？

多明尼克·佛羅雷斯〔下午2:36〕：
明天的話，要。車停在舊大樓門口可以嗎？

秀智·韓〔下午2:38〕：
當然。大門附近的空間應該很夠。可以麻煩您提醒他們，車不要壓到草坪嗎？

**詞彙** postpone 延後　support beam 支撐樑　structural engineer 結構工程師
inclement（天氣）惡劣的

**172**----------------------------------------------------------------

**What does Mr. Flores indicate will disrupt work tomorrow?**

(A) A defective machine
(B) Late shipping
(C) Inclement weather conditions
(D) A shortage of employees

佛羅雷斯先生指出，什麼會中斷明天的工程？

(A) 有問題的機械
(B) 延後到貨
(C) 惡劣的天氣條件
(D) 缺工

下午 2 點 26 分時佛羅雷斯先生提到：「it looks like there will be a storm tomorrow, so the roof work on your hospital's new east wing will need to be postponed.」由此可知，因為天氣惡化導致工程延期，故正確答案為 (C)。

**173** NEW ----------------------------------------------------------

**At 2:31 P.M., what does Mr. Lim most likely mean when he writes, "We'll be working overtime for the next ten days"?**

(A) His workers have not been arriving at work on time.
(B) His workers' plan is to get off work early on Thursday.
(C) His workers are needed at two separate work areas.
(D) His workers' construction project was made more challenging.

下午 2 點 31 分時，當琳姆先生寫道：「我看接下來十天還得加班趕工」，他最可能的意思是？

(A) 他的工人最近都沒有準時抵達。
(B) 他的工人計劃要在週四提早下班。
(C) 有兩個不同的工地需要用到他的工人。
(D) 他的工人在建案裡將面臨更多挑戰。

就在前一句中，琳姆先生說：「Everything was fine until this morning」，由此可知工程現在出現了困難挑戰，導致必須加班趕工，故正確答案為 (D)。

## 174

**Who most likely is Ms. Han?**

(A) A gardening designer
(B) A hospital manager
(C) A transportation supervisor
(D) A construction materials supplier

**韓女士的職業最有可能是？**

(A) 園藝設計師
(B) 醫院經理
(C) 運輸業主管
(D) 建材供應商

下午 2 點 26 分時佛羅雷斯先生提到：「the roof work on your hospital's new east wing」，
且由韓女士緊接著回覆，代表韓女士應為醫院相關人員，所以正確答案為 (B)。

## 175

**What is one thing Mr. Flores inquires about?**

(A) The building entrance for their use
(B) Directions to the newest building
(C) Suggestions for the structure's new wing
(D) Permission to park

**佛羅雷斯先生問了什麼事？**

(A) 建築大門能否讓他們使用
(B) 到最新大樓的路徑
(C) 給予新蓋側翼大樓的建議
(D) 停車許可

下午 2 點 36 分佛羅雷斯先生說：「Would it be all right for them to park their vehicles in front of
the old building?」，詢問是否可以停車，故正確答案為 (D)。

## 176–180 電子郵件

**From:** Deborah Wing
**To:** Tim Anthony
**Subject:** Retirement banquet
**Date:** May 9

寄件人：黛柏拉・溫
收件人：提姆・安束尼
主旨：退休餐會
日期：5月9日

Dear Tim,

As you know, I am on the committee in charge of planning Mr. Dalton's retirement banquet. We want to include a slideshow presentation using photographs taken during diverse corporate events held over the past ten years, and we're seeking someone who wants to create the slideshow for us.

I remember your telling me that you studied photography in college, so I was wondering if you would be interested in doing this. If you accept, I can send an e-mail within three days requesting pictures from those who have them and then get them to you at your earliest convenience. Your assistance would be greatly appreciated. I'm certain Mr. Dalton together with the remainder of the team, would enjoy the show!

Sincerely,
Deborah

親愛的提姆：

你知道，我是籌備道爾頓先生退休餐會的委員會成員。我們想要用過去十年，在各種企業活動所拍攝的照片做成投影片，目前正在找人製作。

我記得你跟我說過，你在大學主修攝影，所以我想問看看你有沒有興趣做這件事。如果你答應的話，我會在三天內再發一封信，請同仁提供照片，並儘早搜集給你讓你方便作業。感謝你的協助，我很確定，道爾頓先生和團隊裡的其他人，都會很享受這部影片。

黛柏拉 敬上

| From: Tim Anthony | 寄件人：提姆·安東尼 |
| To: Deborah Wing | 收件人：黛柏拉·溫 |
| Subject: RE: Retirement banquet | 主旨：關於：退休餐會 |
| Date: May 10 | 日期：5月10日 |

| Dear Deborah, | 親愛的黛柏拉： |
|---|---|
| I would like to create the slideshow for Mr. Dalton's retirement banquet. I think we both agree that he's been a great supervisor here. However, I don't think I'm the best person for doing that. I took pictures at one event, but, in fact, I majored in journalism in college. There's a woman whom I want to recommend for creating the slideshow. Her name is Catherine Heinz. I believe she may be interested in doing it. I know she previously created a slideshow for a training session. If Ms. Heinz can't do it for the event, please contact me and I'll recommend another person to you. | 我很樂意製作道爾頓先生退休餐會上的投影片。我們都同意他是一位很棒的主管。不過，我並不是最適合做這件事情的人。我確實在一場活動上負責攝影，但事實上，我大學主修新聞。我想推薦你一位適合做投影片的人選，她叫做凱薩琳·海因茲。我相信她會有興趣。據我了解，她之前做過培訓課程的投影片。假如海因茲女士這次不能幫忙，請聯絡我，我到時候再向妳推薦其他人。 |
| Sincerely,<br>Tim | 提姆 敬上 |

詞彙 **as you know** 如你所知　**committee** 委員會　**in charge of** 負責　**retirement banquet** 退休餐會　**slideshow** 投影片　**at your earliest convenience** 在您方便時儘早　**major in** 主修

**How do Ms. Wing and Mr. Anthony most likely know each other?**

(A) They work for the same company.
(B) They attended the same university.
(C) They live in the same apartment complex.
(D) They collaborated on a special project.

溫女士和安東尼先生最有可能是怎樣認識彼此的？

(A) 他們在同一間公司工作。
(B) 他們上同一間大學。
(C) 他們住在同一個公寓大樓裡。
(D) 他們合作過某個特殊專案。

從第二封郵件中的「I think we both agree that he's been a great supervisor here.」，可以推測溫女士與安東尼先生應為同事，故正確答案為 (A)。

**What does Ms. Wing offer to do?**

(A) Order invitations to a retirement banquet
(B) Make a copy of materials for a training session
(C) Gather pictures from employees
(D) Participate in an upcoming show

溫女士主動提議要做什麼？

(A) 整理退休餐會的邀請函
(B) 為培訓課程影印資料
(C) 從同仁那裡搜集照片
(D) 參加之後的演出

溫女士在第一封郵件中說：「I can send an e-mail within three days requesting pictures from those who have them and then get them to you」，表示自己可以幫忙搜集照片，故正確答案為 (C)。

**178**

**Why does Mr. Anthony say that he studied journalism?**

(A) He'd like to relocate to another position.

(B) Ms. Wing needs assistance with an article.

(C) Ms. Wing asked him to confirm his qualifications.

(D) He'd like to correct a misunderstanding.

為什麼安東尼先生提到他學的是新聞？

(A) 他想要調到另一個職位。

(B) 溫女士需要人寫篇文章。

(C) 溫女士請他確認他自己的資格。

(D) 他想要澄清一個誤會。

溫女士先在郵件中寫道「I remember your telling me that you studied photography in college」，針對此事，安東尼以「but, in fact, I majored in journalism in college」回覆，故可以得知，溫女士記錯安東尼先生的主修科目，而他想要更正這件事，故正確答案為 (D)。

**179**

**What does Mr. Anthony indicate about Ms. Heinz?**

(A) She is more experienced with an assignment than he is.

(B) She is more flexible about a schedule than he is.

(C) She will replace Mr. Dalton after he leaves the company.

(D) She has a university degree in journalism.

安東尼先生提到關於海因茲女士什麼事？

(A) 她在這件事（製作投影片）上比他更有經驗。

(B) 她在時間安排上比他更有彈性。

(C) 她將接任道爾頓先生離職後的職位。

(D) 她有新聞系畢業的大學學歷。

安東尼先生先推薦了海因茲女士，並說：「I know she previously created a slideshow for a training session.」，表示海因茲女士有製作投影片的經驗，故正確答案為 (A)。

**180**

**Why might Ms. Wing contact Mr. Anthony again?**

(A) He sets up Ms. Heinz's schedule.

(B) He can enroll her in training sessions.

(C) He takes photographs at all of the company events.

(D) He can recommend other people to assist her.

溫女士為什麼還有可能會再次聯絡安東尼先生？

(A) 他負責安排海因茲女士的行程。

(B) 他可以為她報名培訓課程。

(C) 他在公司全部的活動裡都負責拍照。

(D) 他可以推薦其他人來提供協助。

根據安東尼先生撰寫的郵件，其中說道：「If Ms. Heinz can't do it for the event, please contact me and I'll recommend another person to you.」，表示若他推薦的人無法幫忙，溫女士可再連絡他，他會再推薦其他人，故正確答案為 (D)。

## Innovation Centre

Overlooking the shore, Innovation Centre combines a relaxing resort with the services to fulfill your business needs. In addition to 10 meeting rooms for large conferences, the Opal Room and Sapphire Room provide the perfect solution for small groups of a maximum of 10 people.

Innovation Centre has both a formal dining room and a more comfortable eatery. One-, two-, and three-bedroom suites have high-speed Internet access, fax machines, and coffee makers. Guests can also make use of the indoor and outdoor swimming pools. For more information, contact Randy Frederick at 424-2769 or randyfrederick@innovationcentre.com.

---

**TO:** Cameron Gee <camerongee@bronzejournal.com>
**FROM:** Randy Frederick <randyfrederick@innovationcentre.com>
**DATE:** March 21
**SUBJECT:** Reservation

---

Dear Ms. Gee,

Thank you for your partial deposit of $300.00 for a one-bedroom suite for June 12 and June 13. We have reserved the Opal Room for your event on June 13, but we'll need a total deposit of $500.00 by April 1 to put it on hold for you.

Please let us know what equipment you will need for your presentation so that we can prepare the conference room for you beforehand.

Moreover, to talk about the luncheon for your group, you must contact our catering manager, Lilly Pontiac, at 424-4327, extension 22.

Sincerely,
Randy Frederick
Reservations Manager, Innovation Centre

## 創新中心

眺望海岸美景,創新中心結合休閒場所和您所需的商業服務。不但有10間大型會議廳,蛋白石會議室和藍寶石會議室也能提供給10人以下的小團體使用。

創新中心有正式的晚宴廳,也有更加舒適的餐館。單人、雙人或三人套房均配備高速網路、傳真機和咖啡機。賓客也能使用室內和室外的游泳池。欲知更多資訊,請聯絡蘭迪・弗瑞德瑞克,電話424-2769或是電子郵件randyfrederick@innovationcentre.com。

---

收件人:卡麥隆・杰 <camerongee@bronzejournal.com>
寄件人:蘭迪・弗瑞德瑞克 <randyfrederick@innovationcentre.com>
日期:3月21日
主旨:訂房

---

親愛的杰女士:

感謝您預訂6月12日和13日的單人套房,並支付300美元的部分訂金。我們已為您13日的活動訂了蛋白石會議室,不過我們需要您在4月1日以前支付總共500美元的訂金,才能為您保留房間。

請告訴我們您的簡報需要什麼設備,我們可以提前為您準備會議室。

此外,關於您團隊的午餐會,您需要聯絡我們的外燴經理莉莉・彭提亞克,她的電話是424-4327分機22。

創新中心訂房經理
蘭迪・弗瑞德瑞克 敬上

---

**詞彙** in addition to 除了……(還有)　eatery 餐館　suite 套房　high-speed 高速的　deposit 訂金
beforehand 提前　luncheon 午餐會　catering 外燴　extension 分機

**181**

**Who is the advertisement probably intended for?**

(A) Family members
(B) Hotel supervisors
(C) New employees
(D) Business specialists

這個廣告的目標對象可能為何？

(A) 家庭成員
(B) 飯店主管
(C) 新進員工
(D) 商務專業人士

從廣告中的「Innovation Centre combines a relaxing resort with the services to fulfill your business needs.」，可以知道這則廣告的主打客群為商務人士，故正確答案為 (D)。

**182**

**What is NOT mentioned as a feature of the Innovation Centre?**

(A) A fitness facility
(B) Restaurants
(C) An indoor pool
(D) In-room fax machines

廣告中沒有提及創新中心的哪一項特色？

(A) 健身場所
(B) 餐廳
(C) 室內游泳池
(D) 套房內的傳真機

廣告的第二段說到「Innovation Centre has both a formal dining room and a more comfortable eatery.」、「fax machines」、「indoor and outdoor swimming pools」，依序提及選項 (B)、(D) 與 (C)，但是並未提到健身場所，故本題答案為 (A)。

**183**

**What is indicated about Ms. Gee?**

(A) She is the CEO of a large company.
(B) She has stayed at the Innovation Centre before.
(C) She assumed the responsibility for a presentation.
(D) She received a discounted rate for the conference space.

文中提到杰女士的什麼事？

(A) 她是一間大公司的執行長。
(B) 她之前住過創新中心。
(C) 她負責某項簡報。
(D) 她用優惠價格訂到會議室。

從寫給杰女士的信件中，可以看到：「Please let us know what equipment you will need for your presentation . . .」，故可推測杰女士將會進行簡報，本題正確答案為 (C)。

**184**

**What is suggested about Ms. Gee's event?**

(A) Full payment for the conference space has been made.
(B) Ten or fewer people will participate.
(C) Attendees will be offered a discount on rooms.
(D) It will be held on April 1.

文中提到關於杰女士的活動什麼事？

(A) 會議室所需款項已經結清。
(B) 參加人數不多於十人。
(C) 參與者將享有住房優惠。
(D) 將在 4 月 1 日舉行。

從廣告中的「the Opal Room and Sapphire Room provide the perfect solution for small groups of a maximum of ten people」，與信件中的「We have reserved the Opal Room for your event on June 13」，可以得知因為杰女士借用的會議室最多只能容納十人，故會議參加人數最多只有十位，正確答案為 (B)。

## 185

**What will Ms. Gee ask Ms. Pontiac to do?**

(A) Cancel a reservation
(B) Review her presentation
(C) Prepare a food service
(D) Make a payment

杰女士將會對彭提亞克女士要求什麼？

(A) 取消訂房
(B) 檢閱她的簡報
(C) 準備餐點服務
(D) 付款

從信件最後的「Moreover, to talk about the luncheon for your group, you must contact our catering manager, Lilly Pontiac」中，可知關於準備午餐會的事項，杰女士需要聯絡彭提亞克女士，故本題正確答案為 (C)。

**186–190 網頁、電子郵件和表格**

| BROWSE | ORDER | HOME | GALLERY | CONTACT |
|---|---|---|---|---|

### Middletown Office Furniture

Welcome to our Web page! Look around our inventory to visualize workspaces that are stylish and useful. We have been serving Richmond Cape for more than a decade, and you can rely on our high-quality office furniture to satisfy your needs. We provide the following deals at all times:
- Complimentary shipping and handling for new customers
- Significant discounts to schools and nonprofit organizations (Contact us for further information)

| 瀏覽 | 訂購 | 首頁 | 商品展示 | 連絡我們 |
|---|---|---|---|---|

### 米德爾敦辦公家具行

歡迎來到我們的網站！瀏覽我們的商品清單，想像辦公區可以如此時尚便利。我們在里奇蒙海岬服務超過十年，您可以信賴我們，高品質辦公家具肯定能滿足您的需求。
我們隨時提供下列交易方式：
- 新客戶享有免費送貨到府和包裝服務
- 學校和非營利組織享有大折扣（請聯絡我們獲取更多資訊）

**From:** James Harley
<jharley@standardlawfirm.co>
**To:** Lemington Chen
<lchen@standardlawfirm.co>
**Date:** 15 April
**Subject:** Office furniture upgrade

Hello Mr. Chen,

I've completed some research and would like to recommend that we choose Middletown Office Furniture for the desks and other items for our office remodeling. Although we've never bought from them before, they provided references that offered excellent recommendations.

寄件人：詹姆斯‧哈雷
<jharley@standardlawfirm.co>
收件人：雷明頓‧陳
<lchen@standardlawfirm.co>
日期：4月15日
主旨：辦公家具升級

陳先生您好：

我研究了一陣子，想建議我們選擇米德爾敦辦公家具行，來選購辦公室裝修後的辦公桌和家具。雖說我們從來沒向這間家具行採購過東西，但他們的參考資料已經提供了很好的建議。

I think we should decide on a larger desk type for our main workspace (15 desks), with corresponding filing cabinets and bookshelves. For the support team and interns who work upstairs, I recommend a simpler desk style.

If you approve of these recommendations, I'd like to place the order as soon as possible so that the products will be shipped while almost all of our employees are away at the meeting in New York.

However, our work areas will seem quite dirty because we will clear out the old furniture and wait for the arrival of the new products.

Please inform me what you think of the plan I have summarized above.

James

---

**Order Number:** F2465Z
**Contact:** James Harley (067) 523-4352
**Delivery to:** Standard Law Firm, 252 Square Street, San Francisco, CA 94108
**Delivery Date & Time:** 8–9 August, 11:00–18:00

| Quantity | Item Code | Description |
|---|---|---|
| 15 | CDF4524 | Dayton Office Desks |
| 15 | FCT1275 | Prime Filing Cabinets, light brown |
| 6 | AA2042 | Crystal Bookshelves, light brown |
| 7 | GE3182 | Versatile Desks |

**Note:** Due to demand, we are out of ITEM AA2042 at our Casey Town store. These products will be shipped to your office directly from our production site, so they will be delivered into San Francisco from Charleston rather than from Casey Town. This might delay the delivery by two or three days. Every effort will be made to have the entire order shipped on the same day.

---

我們得決定一下，我覺得主辦公室要用比較大的辦公桌型（15張桌子），還有符合該款式的檔案櫃和書架。至於在樓上工作的客服團隊和實習生，我建議用比較簡單的桌款。

如果您接受我的建議，我想儘快下訂單，這樣家具就能到貨，此時剛好大多數同仁都出差到紐約開會。

不過，這樣辦公區就會看起來很髒亂，畢竟我們還要把舊家具清空，等新家具來才行。

再請您告訴我，您對上述總結建議的看法。

詹姆斯

---

訂單號碼：F2465Z
聯絡人：詹姆斯‧哈雷(067)523-4352
寄件地址：94108加州舊金山市方形街252號，標準法律事務所
寄件日期和時間：8月8到9日，11點到晚上6點間

| 數量 | 商品代碼 | 商品描述 |
|---|---|---|
| 15 | CDF4524 | 戴頓辦公桌 |
| 15 | FCT1275 | 一流檔案櫃，淺褐色 |
| 6 | AA2042 | 水晶書架，淺褐色 |
| 7 | GE3182 | 多功能辦公桌 |

注意：由於AA2042商品的需求過多，我們位於凱西鎮的店面目前缺貨。這些商品將會直接從工廠送到您的辦公室，所以會從查爾斯敦運送到舊金山，而非由凱西鎮寄送。有可能會延後兩到三天才會送達，我們會盡力讓整筆訂單在同一天出貨。

---

**詞彙** visualize 想像　complimentary shipping 免費運貨　nonprofit organization 非營利組織
reference 參考資料　workspace = work area 辦公室　corresponding 一致的
filing cabinet 檔案櫃　place the order 下訂單　clear out 清空　production site 工廠
every effort will be made 盡全力　alleviate 減輕

**186**

**What is suggested about Middletown Office Furniture?**

(A) It offers free interior design services.

(B) It provides special discounts to educational organizations.

(C) It has recently expanded its type of products.

(D) It has just opened a satellite branch.

文中提到關於米德爾敦辦公家具行什麼事？

(A) 提供免費室內裝潢服務。

(B) 對教育機構提供特別優惠。

(C) 最近拓展新產品。

(D) 近期開設分店。

根據網頁內容中的「Significant discounts to schools and nonprofit organizations」，學校為教育機構，應享有優惠，所以正確答案為 (B)。

---

**187**

**What is most likely true about Standard Law Firm's furniture order?**

(A) It will be shipped free of charge.

(B) It includes a product which is no longer manufactured.

(C) It was placed too late for shipment in August.

(D) It includes a style selected by the support team.

關於標準法律事務所的訂單，下列描述何者最可能為真？

(A) 免運費。

(B) 裡面有已經停產的產品。

(C) 訂單已趕不上八月的配送。

(D) 其中包括客服團隊所挑選的型號。

從第一篇的網頁內容中，可以得知「Complimentary shipping and handling for new customers」，表示新客戶可以免付運費與包裝費。再根據電子郵件上說的「Although we've never bought from them before」，表示事務所之前不曾向家具行購買物品，故可推測事務所作為新客戶，應可享受免運費的優惠，故正確答案為 (A)。

---

**188**

**Why does Mr. Harley want to schedule a delivery during the particular period?**

(A) He will receive an extra discount.

(B) He requires some furniture for an important conference.

(C) He needs additional time to shop for the new furniture.

(D) He would like to alleviate inconvenience for colleagues.

為什麼哈雷先生想要在特定時間內讓商品送達？

(A) 他可以拿到額外折扣。

(B) 有場重要的會議需要這些辦公家具。

(C) 他需要額外的時間來選購新家具。

(D) 他想要減輕同仁的不便。

從電子郵件第三段的「I'd like to place the order as soon as possible so that the products will be shipped while almost all of our employees are away at the meeting in New York.」，可以得知哈雷先生希望家具在員工出差期間送達，推測最可能的原因是不想造成同仁的麻煩，故正確答案為 (D)。

**189**

----

**What product will probably be placed upstairs at Standard Law Firm?**

(A) Dayton Office Desks
(B) Prime Filing Cabinets
(C) Crystal Bookshelves
(D) Versatile Desks

哪個產品可能會被放在標準法律事務所的二樓？

(A) 戴頓辦公桌
(B) 一流檔案櫃
(C) 水晶書架
(D) 多功能辦公桌

從郵件第二段的「For the support team and interns who work upstairs, I recommend a simpler desk style.」可以知道，樓上最可能放置的桌子，且是簡單的款式，參照表格上的桌款，只有「Dayton Office Desks」和「Versatile Desks」，前者更加專業，應是給主辦公室使用的桌型，故本題正確答案為 (D)。

**190**

----

**According to the form, where is the furniture made?**

(A) San Francisco
(B) Charleston
(C) New York
(D) Casey Town

根據表格，家具都在哪裡生產？

(A) 舊金山
(B) 查爾斯敦
(C) 紐約
(D) 凱西鎮

表格下方提到：「These products will be shipped to your office directly from our production site, so they will be delivered . . . from Charleston」，表示直接從工廠出貨，且出貨地點為查爾斯敦，故可知工廠就位於查爾斯敦，本題正確答案為 (B)。

**191–195 電子郵件、菜單和意見卡**

**From:** Nathan Jerome <njerome@happydiningarea.com>
**To:** John McNeil <jmcneil@happydiningarea.com>
**Date:** Tuesday, July 11
**Subject:** Menu tasting

寄件人：納森·傑若米 <njerome@happydiningarea.com>
收件人：約翰·麥可尼爾 <jmcneil@happydiningarea.com>
日期：7月11日，週二
主旨：試菜活動

Hello Mr. McNeil,

It's hard to believe that Ms. Theresa will be here in only two weeks! Since her review will be published in the local newspaper, why don't we make sure that our selections are reflective of the best of the Happy Dining Area? To get advice on the menu we'll be serving her, I've determined we should host a special menu-tasting event on Thursday of next week.

I have several recommendations for what we can serve at the menu tasting. What about arranging a satisfying fish dish? Maybe our baked sea bream would be a good choice.

麥可尼爾先生您好，

令人難以置信，距離德瑞莎女士到訪不到兩週了！既然她的評論會在當地報紙上登出，我們何不精選菜色，呈現「幸福餐廳」最好的一面？為了得到當天菜單的建議，我決定在下週四舉行一場特別的試菜活動。

對於試菜活動要提供的菜色，我有幾個建議。何不安排一道令人滿意的魚肉料理？或許烤海鯛魚是不錯

89

On the other hand, I insist on providing the new special pizzas we intend to release on our regular menu. Of course, that is assuming construction of the brick oven is finished by that time. Additionally, I think we can serve a minimum of two of our fruit desserts that are popular at all times. However, I have complete confidence in you, as head chef, to finalize the menu choices.

Finally, I want to provide our menu-tasting patrons with an opportunity to visit the kitchen while they are here. Please inform me of what you think about this and how best to prepare for it.

Thank you.
Sincerely,
Nathan

的選擇。另外，我堅持一定要呈獻新的特製披薩，也就是我們打算在平時菜單上推出的那款。當然，前提是到時候磚窯已經蓋好。還有，我想我們可以提供至少兩道總是廣受歡迎的水果甜點。不過我有信心，身為主廚的你，一定能把最終的菜單確定下來。

最後，我想要讓來參與試菜活動的客人，能有機會現場參觀廚房。請告訴我你的看法，還有怎麼準備最好。

感謝。
納森 敬上

## Happy Dining Area Tasting Menu

### Thursday, July 20

Baked sea bream in garlic sauce
Beef steak with cucumber salad
Roasted chicken with chili sauce
Cheesecake with walnuts
All of the steamed shellfish in a broccoli soup
Smoked salmon with mashed potato

## 幸福餐廳試菜活動菜單

### 7月20日週四

蒜醬烤海鯛
牛排佐小黃瓜沙拉
辣醬烤雞
胡桃起司蛋糕
蒸鮮貝花椰菜濃湯
燻鮭魚佐馬鈴薯泥

## Tasting Feedback Card

**Name:** Jessie Jackson

Please remark on your tasting experience at the Happy Dining Area.

I was pleased by the gentle sweetness of the cucumber dish; the sauce was a little sour for my taste, though. The sea bream, on the other hand, surpassed all my expectations. The roasted chicken was tender, yet overall it was not tasty. Concerning the dessert, it was very delicious, although a bit dry. I was very impressed by the useful design of your kitchen. I look forward to tasting the new brick-oven pizzas when they're released. I'm disappointed that you couldn't offer them today.

## 試菜活動意見卡

姓名：潔西·傑克森

請留下您參加幸福餐廳試菜活動的心得。

我很滿意小黃瓜料理溫和的甜味，不過醬汁對我來說有點酸；海鯛則是好得超乎預期；烤雞很嫩，不過整體來說不太好吃；甜點很美味但有點乾。貴餐廳廚房的實用設計讓我印象深刻。我很期待能吃到之後新推出的窯烤披薩。很遺憾今天沒辦法品嘗到。

**詞彙** tasting 試菜　vegetarian 素食的；素食者　a minimum of 最少　patron 客人　sea bream 海鯛　garlic 蒜　cucumber 小黃瓜　roasted 烤的　walnut 胡桃　steamed 蒸的　broccoli 花椰菜　smoked salmon 燻鮭魚　mashed potato 馬鈴薯泥　on the other hand 則是；另一方面　surpass one's expectations 超乎預期　be impressed with 對……印象深刻

**191** --------

**Why is the menu tasting being conducted?**

(A) To prepare for a visit from a restaurant reviewer

(B) To choose dishes to enter in a cooking competition

(C) To assess a chef who is applying for a job

(D) To select dishes to add to the daily menu

為什麼要舉辦這場試菜活動？

(A) 為美食評論家的到來做準備

(B) 為了選出參賽用的菜色

(C) 為了測試主廚應徵者的實力

(D) 為了選出平日菜單要新增的菜色

郵件第一段提到的「Ms. Theresa will be here」且「her review will be published in the local newspaper」故可知道德瑞莎女士應為美食評論家，且她即將造訪餐廳。

隨後在同一段落還提到「I've determined we should host a special menu-tasting event on Thursday of next week.」，表示因為有她的到來，才想要舉辦試菜活動，故正確答案為 (A)。

**192** --------

**In the e-mail, the word "satisfying" in paragraph 2, line 2, is closest in meaning to**

(A) deep

(B) plentiful

(C) gratifying

(D) creative

電子郵件第二段、第二行中的「satisfying」最接近下列哪個意思？

(A) 深的

(B) 豐富的

(C) 令人心滿意足的

(D) 有創意的

郵件第一段提到美食評論家的到訪，故第二段說「What about arranging a satisfying fish dish?」，最可能是要做出使評論家「滿意的」魚肉料理，故可推論正確答案為 (C)。

**193** --------

**What is mentioned about the tasting menu?**

(A) It lists dishes that were provided free of charge.

(B) It includes a dish suggested by Mr. Jerome.

(C) It was served to patrons in the eatery's kitchen.

(D) It isn't available every weekday.

文中提到關於試菜活動的菜單什麼事？

(A) 列舉了免費供應的菜色。

(B) 包括傑若米先生所推薦的菜色。

(C) 在餐廳廚房裡供客人享用。

(D) 平常日都沒有供應。

從郵件中的「Maybe our baked sea bream would be a good choice.」，可知傑若米先生提議了鯛魚料理。再從菜單中的「Baked sea bream in garlic sauce」和意見卡中提到的「The sea bream, on the other hand, surpassed all my expectations.」，可看出試菜活動上的確供應了他推薦的鯛魚料理，故正確答案為 (B)。

**194** --------

**What menu item was probably Ms. Jackson's favorite?**

(A) The sea bream

(B) The soup

(C) The cucumber

(D) The chicken

傑克森女士可能最喜歡哪一道料理？

(A) 海鯛

(B) 湯品

(C) 小黃瓜

(C) 雞肉

透過意見卡上的「The sea bream, on the other hand, surpassed all my expectations.」，便可知道傑克森女士最喜歡的料理為海鯛，正確答案為 (A)。

**195** - - - - - - - - - - - - - - - - - - - - - - - - - - - - - - - - - - - - - - - - - - - - - - - - - - - - - - - - - -

**What is indicated about the brick oven?**

(A) It is extremely big for the kitchen.
(B) It has to be fixed.
(C) It didn't pass a safety inspection.
(D) It is still being constructed.

文中提到磚窯什麼？

(A) 對廚房來說太大了。
(B) 需要修理。
(C) 沒有通過安檢。
(D) 還在興建。

從郵件中的「Of course, that is assuming construction on the brick oven is finished by that time.」，與意見卡上的「I look forward to tasting the new brick-oven pizzas when they're released.」可以推測，因為磚窯尚未完工，傑克森女士沒能嚐到披薩，故正確答案為 (D)。

## 196–200 電子郵件、傳單和簡訊

**To:** Students
**From:** Jamal Crawford
**Subject:** Presenter series
**Date:** May 5

Dear students,

There's good news! Ms. Ito Hirosa has agreed to attend our Presenter Series this summer. As part of your student internship responsibilities, you will have to prepare her lodging here at the university for August 19–21 and get the relevant document completed and approved so that Ms. Ito can receive her honorarium. Also, please reserve a room for her presentation. I suggest the Dynasty Auditorium because it can accommodate the most people, but any other presentation room in the business building would be fine as well.

Additionally, if Ms. Ito provides her summary, you will have to design a leaflet and post it in the common areas throughout the building. I believe you will be able to assign the job duties among the six of you without any problems.

Thanks!

Dr. Crawford
Professor, Dickson School of Business

收件人：學生
寄件人：賈麥爾·克勞佛
主旨：系列講座
日期：5月5日

各位學生：

好消息！伊藤恕沙女士同意在這個夏天出席系列講座。身為實習學生的你們要負責安排她在8月19到21日在校期間的住宿，完成相關文件的核准，讓她順利拿到酬金。也要預約好她簡報所需的場所。我建議朝代演講廳不錯，可以容納最多人，不過，商院大樓裡的其他簡報廳也都可以。

另外，如果伊藤女士提供摘要，請你們設計傳單，並張貼在全商院大樓的公共區域。我想你們六位能妥善分工而沒有任何問題。

感謝！

迪克森商學院
克勞佛教授

## Dickson School of Business

### Presenter Series featuring

Ms. Ito Hirosa
Vice President, Tokyo Investment, Japan
Establishing Different Finance Relationships
August 20, 6:00 P.M.
True-Blue Room

In the past two decades, numerous financial organizations have limited lending to minimize their risk. This policy, however, leads to unfavorable market conditions. How can banks reduce their risk while still offering ideal funding opportunities to business owners? One possible solution that is becoming popular is "Alternative Finance." I will give an abstract of "Alternative Finance," share some persuasive materials gathered by researchers at Tokyo Investment and Dickson School of Business, and talk about how this worldwide banking change can revive our field.

**From:** Jim Curry
**To:** Lisa Presley
**Received:** May 16, 7:00 P.M.

Lisa, I'm in the media room about to print the leaflet you created, and I've noticed a mistake. Ms. Ito's bio was partially omitted from the leaflet! Could you please correct the leaflet promptly and resend it to me? The media room is closing in 20 minutes, and Dr. Crawford emphasized that the leaflets must be posted no later than tonight.

## 迪克森商學院

### 特色系列講座

伊藤恕沙女士
日本東京投資副社長
建立不同的金融關係
8月20日，晚上六點
純藍演講廳

過去二十幾年來，很多金融機構都藉由有限的放貸，來讓風險極小化。這項措施卻帶來不利的市場條件。銀行要如何降低風險，又同時提供資金機會給企業老闆？一項可能的方案愈來愈流行，也就是「替代性金融」。我將會概述何謂「替代性金融」、分享從東京投資還有迪克森商學院取得的可信資料，並談談這個全球性的銀行變革，如何振興金融領域。

傳訊者：吉姆・何瑞
收訊者：麗莎・普萊斯利
收訊時間：5月16日晚上7點

麗莎，我目前在多媒體室準備要印妳做好的傳單，但我發現有錯誤。伊藤女士的介紹有部分缺漏！可否請妳儘快改好重傳給我？多媒體室20分鐘後就要關了，但克勞佛教授強調最晚今天晚上要貼出傳單。

---

**詞彙** internship 實習　lodging 住宿　honorarium 酬金　leaflet 傳單
financial organization 金融機構　unfavorable 不利的　abstract 概述　persuasive 可信的
revive 振興　bio 人物介紹（為 biography 的縮寫）　partially 一部分　omit 缺漏
no later than 不遲於

**(196)**

**What is suggested about the True-Blue Room?**

(A) It is not situated in the business building.
(B) It is the place for all events in the Presenter Series.
(C) It is smaller than the Dynasty Auditorium.
(D) It is made available on August 21.

文中提到關於純藍演講廳什麼事？

(A) 不在商院大樓裡。
(B) 是整場系列講座都要使用的房間。
(C) 比朝代演講廳來得小。
(D) 8 月 21 日那天可供使用。

第一封郵件提到：「I suggest the Dynasty Auditorium because it can accommodate the most people」，可知朝代演講廳是最大的，間接可推知其他演講廳都比較小，故正確答案為 (C)。

(A) 郵件最後有說「any other presentation room in the business building would be fine as well」，表示演講可以舉辦在商院大樓的其他演講廳，而傳單上標示演講地點於純藍演講廳，故可知道純藍演講廳就在商院大樓裡。

(B) 從傳單上只能知道這是系列講座的其中一個，且辦在純藍演講廳，但並沒有說系列講座全都使用此房間。

(C) 從傳單上只能知道 8 月 20 日會在此舉辦講座，並不知道場地其他日期是否可供使用。

**197** ----------------------------------------------------------------------

**In the e-mail, the word "problems" in paragraph 2, line 3, is closest in meaning to**

(A) declarations
(B) inquiries
(C) shipments
(D) conflicts

電子郵件中第二段、第三行的「problems」，最接近下列哪個意思？

(A) 聲明
(B) 詢問
(C) 運貨
(D) 衝突

解讀全句即可知道，克勞佛教授希望他們能自行分配，六個人順利合作完成工作，故此處的 problems 最接近的意思應為 (D)。

**198** ----------------------------------------------------------------------

**What is the topic of Ms. Ito's presentation?**

(A) The most recent trend in banking
(B) A job opening in finance
(C) Unique methods of collecting materials
(D) Biographies of experienced business owners

伊藤女士演講的主題是什麼？

(A) 銀行業務的最新趨勢
(B) 新的金融職缺
(C) 獨特的找資料方法
(D) 資深企業主的傳記

從傳單上最後一句的「talk about how this worldwide banking change can revive our field」可以知道，伊藤女士將在演講中介紹可以振興金融業的新趨勢，故正確答案是 (A)。

**199** ----------------------------------------------------------------------

**What difficulty does Mr. Curry mention?**

(A) A number has been incorrectly marked.
(B) The leaflet is missing some details.
(C) The leaflet will not be posted online.
(D) The room booked for the presentation is not open.

柯瑞先生提到什麼困難？

(A) 數字寫錯了。
(B) 傳單缺少一些細節。
(C) 傳單將不會張貼上網。
(D) 準備用來簡報的會議室沒有開放使用。

從第二封信件的「Ms. Ito's bio was partially omitted from the leaflet!」中，可以發現傳單上缺漏了一些伊藤女士的介紹資料，故正確答案為 (B)。

**200** ------------------------------------------------------------

**Who most likely is Ms. Presley?**

(A) A repair person in the media room

(B) A secretary to Ms. Ito

(C) A speaker from the Presenter Series

(D) A student at Dickson School of Business

普萊斯利女士最有可能的身分是？

(A) 多媒體室的維修人員

(B) 伊藤女士的祕書

(C) 系列講座的其中一位講者

(D) 迪克森商學院的學生

從第一封信件中最後一句可知道，總共有六位商學院的實習生要協助承辦這項活動，再從全信內容可知，職務包含安排住宿、準備文件、設計張貼傳單以及借用演講廳，而第三封信件要求普萊斯利女士修改傳單，故可知道她應為實習生之一，正確答案為 (D)。

# ACTUAL TEST

# 3

## PART 5

**101**

------- the heavy snow this morning, the company picnic will proceed as planned.

(A) Due to
(B) Despite
(C) Because of
(D) Regarding

| 題型 | 詞彙——介系詞 |
| --- | --- |
| 翻譯 | 儘管早上下了大雪，公司野餐行程照舊。 |
| 詞彙 | proceed as planned 照計畫進行 |

本題四個選項都以介系詞作結，後方接續的皆為名詞，故應從字義判斷。後半句表示公司野餐將照常舉行，前半句則表示今早下了大雪，所以表達相反內容的「儘管」為正確答案，故答案為 (B)。

**102**

The school ------- was an alumnus of the school, so he is very popular with the students.

(A) principal
(B) principles
(C) principals
(D) principle

| 題型 | 詞彙——名詞 |
| --- | --- |
| 翻譯 | 校長是這間學校的校友，所以很受學生歡迎。 |
| 詞彙 | principal〔名詞〕校長；〔形容詞〕最重要的 |
| | principle 原則 |
| | alumni 校友 |

此題即使不知道 alumnus 的意思，也可從後句的 he 知道，空格應填入具有「人物」意思的單數名詞，故正確答案為 (A)。

**103**

In his report, Young-Ho pointed ------- several mistakes that had been made by the developers when building the new Civic Center.

(A) over
(B) under
(C) out
(D) from

| 題型 | 詞彙——片語 |
| --- | --- |
| 翻譯 | 永浩在報告中指出，開發商在建設新市政中心時的許多缺失。 |
| 詞彙 | point out 指出 |
| | developer 開發商 |
| | civic 市政的 |

本題只有 (C) 能和空格前的 point 成為片語，故正確答案為 (C)。

**104**

If Marsha ------- in charge of the project, we probably would have had more success.

(A) has been
(B) is
(C) was not
(D) had been

| 題型 | 文法——假設語氣 |
| --- | --- |
| 翻譯 | 如果當初是由瑪莎負責這項計畫，我們也許會更成功。 |
| 詞彙 | be charge in 負責 |

本題要考的是與過去事實相反的假設句型，主句出現「would have ＋過去分詞」，故條件子句的動詞時應為過去完成式，正確答案為 (D)。

★請熟記假設語氣文法（其中 S1 為子句主詞，S2 為主句主詞）：
If S1 V-ed（過去式）, S2 would/might/could /should V（與現在事實相反）
If S1 had p.p.（過去完成式）, S2 would/might/could /should have p.p.（與過去事實相反）

**105**

John was disappointed because, out of all the reports, the director singled out ------- as needing more work.

(A) he
(B) his
(C) him
(D) himself

| 題型 | 文法——所有格代名詞 |
| --- | --- |
| 翻譯 | 約翰感到沮喪，因為主任在所有提交的報告中挑出他的報告仍需加強。 |
| 詞彙 | single out 挑出 |

介系詞後方可使用受格、所有格代名詞，以及反身代名詞。句意上，此處填入 his report 較為適當，故具有此涵義的選項中即為答案，正確答案為 (B)。

★所有格代名詞：
I → mine（我的）　　　　　　we → ours（我們的）
you → yours（你的）　　　　　you → yours（你們的）
he → his（他的）　　　　　　they → theirs（他們的）
she → hers（她的）

**106**

After the last class, Mr. Morris had each of the students ------- the test from last year before taking the final exam.

(A) will review
(B) review
(C) was reviewed
(D) to review

| 題型 | 文法——使役動詞 |
| --- | --- |
| 翻譯 | 最後一堂課後，摩里斯先生讓每位學生在期末考前複習去年度的考題。 |

此處為老師讓學生複習考題，應用原形動詞，故正確答案為 (B)。

★使役動詞的用法如下：
make/let/have sb/sth V （使某人或某物去⋯⋯）
make/let/have sb/sth p.p. （使某人或某物被⋯⋯）

## 107

**The team's performance on the assignment was ------- poor, so two of the team members were fired yesterday.**

(A) unaccepted

(B) unacceptably

(C) unaccepting

(D) unacceptable

題型 位置──副詞

翻譯 團隊在這次任務的表現差得讓人無法接受,所以其中兩人昨天被開除了。

詞彙 assignment 任務

本題要選能可以修飾形容詞 poor 的副詞 unacceptably,以表示「令人無法接受地」糟糕,故正確答案為 (B)。

**------- we work all weekend, we will not likely be able to have the presentation slides completed by Monday morning.**

(A) Even so

(B) Evenly

(C) Eventually

(D) Even if

題型 位置──副詞子句連接詞

翻譯 就算我們趕工整個週末,也不太可能在週一一早上前完成簡報投影片。

詞彙 presentation slide 簡報投影片

本題的句子中,出現 work 與 be 動詞,因為分別位於兩個子句中,所以本題少一個連接詞,應在空格中代入連接詞。(A)、(B) 與 (C) 為副詞,所以不是答案,正確答案為 (D)。

副詞子句連接詞 Even if 與 Even though(就算……)常常為正確答案,請務必熟記。

## 109

**The company gala was in full -------, and all of the employees seemed to be having a fantastic time.**

(A) swing

(B) team

(C) moon

(D) party

題型 詞彙──片語

翻譯 公司晚宴熱烈進行,似乎所有員工都玩得很開心。

詞彙 gala 晚宴
in full swing 熱烈進行,如火如荼

選項中只有 swing 可填入句中,形成常用片語「in full swing」,並帶有「熱烈進行」的意思,故本題正確答案為 (A)。

**110**

The team leader asked ------- all employees do an exceptional job on the project, as the client is an important one for the company.

(A) what
(B) to
(C) that
(D) where

題型 **文法**——關係代名詞

翻譯 團隊主管要求所有員工為了這項專案全力以赴，因為這次的顧客對公司來說很重要。

詞彙 exceptional 傑出的

當前面出現意為邀請、要求或提議的動詞時，後面 that 子句中的 should 常常被省略，但後方動詞仍需呈現原形。正確答案為 (C)。

★請熟記下列句型：
S1 ＋邀請、要求、提議、命令動詞＋ that ＋ S2 ＋（should）V

**111**

Five of the new hires, in fact all those hired by the Marketing Department, performed beyond expectations last quarter, but the other three new employees -------.

(A) did not
(B) do not
(C) did
(D) will not

題型 **文法**——時態

翻譯 其中五位新進員工—事實上是行銷部門的所有新人，在上一季的表現超乎預期；不過，另外三人卻沒有如此表現。

詞彙 new hire 新進員工
beyond expectations 超乎預期
quarter 季度

因為主要子句的動詞 performed 為過去式，所以正確答案為時態相同的 (A)。

**112**

It is ------- for each member of the sales team to expect large bonuses this year because company profits increased so much.

(A) reasonable
(B) reasoned
(C) reasonableness
(D) reason

題型 **詞彙**——形容詞

翻譯 銷售團隊裡每個人今年都期待豐厚的年終獎金，這很合理，因為今年公司獲利很多。

詞彙 bonus 獎金
profit 獲利

本題的 It 為虛主詞，真主詞是後方的不定詞片語 to expect large bonuses this year，所以空格要填入形容詞 reasonable，代表期待豐厚年終獎金是很「合理的」，故正確答案為 (A)。

**113**

The passenger was advised to ------- to the check-in counter to have a boarding pass issued.

(A) returned
(B) returning
(C) returns
(D) return

題型 文法──動詞

翻譯 乘客接獲建議,請他返回登機櫃檯辦理登機證。

詞彙 counter 櫃台
boarding pass 登機證
issue 發行

被動式後面經常出現介系詞、不定詞或副詞,請務必熟記。本題從空格前方出現的 to 可判斷應填入原形動詞,所以答案為 (D)。

**114**

------- this morning, he would have been able to participate in our strategy meeting.

(A) Simon did arrive
(B) Simon will arrive
(C) Had Simon arrived
(D) Simon is arriving

題型 文法──假設語氣

翻譯 如果西蒙早上有到的話,就能參與我們的策略會議。

詞彙 participate in 參與
strategy 策略

本題重點為假設語氣,(A)、(B) 與 (D) 若代入空格,整句會缺少連接詞且不符句意,而 (C) Had Simon arrived 其實是將 If Simon had arrived 倒裝並省略 If 的用法,故本題正確答案為 (C)。

★假設語氣:

假設語氣的過去完成式句型為:

If S1 had p.p., S2 would have p.p.

省略倒裝句型會將 If 省略,並把原本在主詞後面的 had 放到最前面,變成:
Had S1 p.p., S2 would have p.p.

**115**

After a couple of slow years for our company, our sales really ------- last year.

(A) took off
(B) fell down
(C) took on
(D) outran

題型 詞彙──片語

翻譯 業績慘澹了幾年,本公司銷售總算在去年揚升。

詞彙 slow year 業績慘澹的年

(A) take off 上升、起飛;(B) fall down 下降、墜落;(C) take on 接受、承擔;(D) outrun 勝過。

在句意上,銷售額「上升」較符合脈絡,所以正確答案為 (A)。

**116**

------, Nathan submitted the report in time for the meeting, even though he was sick all week.

(A) Undeniably
(B) Rarely
(C) Absolutely
(D) Surprisingly

| 題型 | 詞彙——副詞 |
|---|---|
| 翻譯 | 雖然納森一整週都在生病，他仍及時提交會議報告，令人大感意外。 |
| 詞彙 | in time 及時 |

(A) undeniably 不可否認地；(B) rarely 罕見地；(C) absolutely 絕對地；(D) surprisingly 令人意外地。

在選出能整句修飾的副詞前，要先看懂空格以外的文意。後句提到，雖然生病一週，但還是能提交報告，故空格中填入「令人意外地」較適合，正確答案為 (D)。

**117**

According to Jason, the projector still has ------- the problems that were mentioned by the mechanic last week.

(A) both of
(B) every
(C) either
(D) seen

| 題型 | 詞彙——名詞 |
|---|---|
| 翻譯 | 根據傑森的說法，就像技工在上週所反應的，投影機還是有兩個問題。 |
| 詞彙 | projector 投影機<br>mechanic 技工 |

因為空格後面出現複數名詞 the problems，且在句意上表示「兩個」問題皆還存在最為合適，故正確答案為 (A)。

「both of the N」、「both the N」兩種用法皆可以使用。

**118**

The guest speaker ------- next Monday, so please reach out to him this week to confirm his travel schedule.

(A) has arrived
(B) arrive
(C) is arriving
(D) is arrived

| 題型 | 文法——現在進行式 |
|---|---|
| 翻譯 | 客座講者下週會來，請在這週和他聯繫以確認行程。 |
| 詞彙 | guest speaker 客座講者<br>reach out to sb 和某人聯繫 |

從空格後方出現的 next Monday 可知此句有未來的意涵，所以正確答案為 (C)。

★現在進行式可用於：
1. 談論「此刻進行的動作」
2. 談論「這段時間正在發生的事情」（不一定是說話時進行的動作）
3. 表示「正在變化的情形」
4. 談論「未來已計畫好或正要開始發生的事情」

**119**

The president of the company was excited to have negotiated such a ------- deal, so he let all of the employees go home early yesterday.

(A) terrify
(B) terribly
(C) terrific
(D) terrified

題型 詞彙──形容詞
翻譯 公司總裁很興奮他談成一筆很棒的交易，所以他昨天讓所有員工提早下班。
詞彙 president 總裁
negotiate 談判
deal 交易

(A) terrify〔動詞〕使⋯⋯害怕；(B) terribly〔副詞〕很糟地；(C) terrific〔形容詞〕很棒的；(D) terrified〔形容詞〕感到害怕的。

先判斷空格應填入可修飾名詞 deal 的形容詞，故 (A)、(B) 不是答案，再從字義判斷最適合填入的為「terrific」，因此正確答案為 (C)。

**120**

Even though Rachel ------- with the company for very long, she is already thinking of moving on to another job.

(A) weren't
(B) hasn't been
(C) could be
(D) will be

題型 文法──現在完成式
翻譯 雖然瑞秋在公司待得不久，但她已經在考慮換工作。
詞彙 move on to another job 換工作

本題主要從句意上判斷空格處的動詞時態。因為後句為現在進行式，所以空格所屬的子句內容應是從過去一直進行到現在的事件或狀態，因此正確答案是使用現在完成式的 (B)。

**121**

It was strange that Takashi was late to the meeting because ------- he is extremely punctual.

(A) usually
(B) eventually
(C) more
(D) seldom

題型 詞彙──副詞
翻譯 隆史這麼晚來開會很奇怪，因為他通常非常準時。
詞彙 punctual 準時的

此處的副詞放在主詞 he 與 be 動詞 is 前面，有強調的意思，而根據句意，填入 usually 表示隆史「通常」會準時到，因此顯得他遲到很奇怪，故正確答案為 (A)。

## 122

CraneSteel is committed to ------- the highest levels of customer service and is dedicated to its philosophy of social and environmental responsibility.

(A) providing
(B) provision
(C) provided
(D) provide

| 題型 | 文法——介系詞 |
| --- | --- |

**翻譯** 起重鋼鐵致力於提供最高品質的顧客服務，也矢志貫徹兼顧社會和環保責任的經營哲學。

**詞彙** be committed to / be dedicated to 致力於
philosophy 哲學
environmental responsibility 環保責任

此處需多留意 be committed to 的介系詞 to，後面可以出現動名詞或名詞，並非不定詞的 to。此句想在 committed to 後接動詞 provide，故要變成動名詞 providing，正確答案為 (A)。

## 123

When Janet announced that she will ------- in May, nobody was surprised, given her age and poor health.

(A) have retired
(B) be retired
(C) retire
(D) retires

| 題型 | 文法——原形動詞 |
| --- | --- |

**翻譯** 考量珍妮特的年紀和不佳的健康狀況，當她宣布五月退休時，沒有人感到驚訝。

**詞彙** given (that) 考量，因為

助動詞 will 後面出現的動詞應為動詞原形。動詞 retire 為不及物動詞，所以使用被動式的 (B) 不是答案，因此正確答案是動詞原形 (C)。

## 124

As ------- earlier, we do not intend to talk about issues that we have already covered in previous meetings.

(A) discuss
(B) discussed
(C) discussing
(D) discussion

| 題型 | 文法—— as |
| --- | --- |

**翻譯** 如同先前所討論的，我們不打算再討論之前幾次會議中談過的議題。

**詞彙** cover 涉及

as 可作為關係代名詞，表示「如同、好像」，引導非限定性形容詞子句，修飾後面整個主要子句。此句原應為分開的兩個句子：「We discussed something earlier.」與「We do not . . . meetings.」，此處以 as 連結，而成了「As discussed earlier, we . . . meetings.」，故正確答案為 (B)。

as 後面如果接續名詞，意思就會變成表達資格的「身為……」，與此處的 discussion 不符，所以 (D) 不是正確答案。

**125**

-------, our weekly staff meetings have been very productive, so let's continue to keep up the good work.

(A) This Wednesday
(B) Always
(C) Of late
(D) Soon

| 題型 | 詞彙──副詞 |
| --- | --- |
| 翻譯 | 最近我們的員工週會非常有成效，所以讓我們繼續保持。 |
| 詞彙 | productive 有成效的；多產的 keep up the good work 繼續保持 |

本題關鍵為現在完成式動詞 have been，故得知空格填入的副詞應具有表示一段時間的意思，所以正確答案為 (C)。

**126**

------- of the companies is focusing on teamwork, diversity, and trust in this year's workshop.

(A) Every
(B) Many
(C) Much
(D) Each

| 題型 | 文法──動詞單複數 |
| --- | --- |
| 翻譯 | 今年的研討會裡，每間公司都專注於團隊合作、多元性和互信。 |
| 詞彙 | diversity 多元性 |

(A) 後面應緊接可數名詞的單數型，(B) 應與複數動詞連用，而 (C) 則應與不可數名詞連用，所以正確答案應為 (D)。

★請熟記此句型：
**each/one of the ＋複數名詞＋單數動詞**
each 或 one 代表每一個或其中一個，所以搭配的動詞為單數

**127**

Interviews ------- all day Thursday in the second-floor conference room.

(A) conduct
(B) have conducted
(C) will be conducted
(D) are conducting

| 題型 | 文法──動詞被動式 |
| --- | --- |
| 翻譯 | 週四一整天，二樓的會議室都將舉行面試。 |

空格為代入主要動詞的位置，但是後面沒有出現受詞，所以應填入被動式，本題正確答案為 (C)。

其餘選項皆為主動式，所以不是正確答案。

**128**

Makoto has been with the company more than twice ------- any of the other employees, so she is the best person to answer any questions you may have.

(A) as far as
(B) in comparison to
(C) as long as
(D) relative to

題型 文法——比較級

翻譯 真琴在公司待的時間是其他人的兩倍久，所以如果你有任何問題，問她最合適。

從句意上看來，應出現次數、時間相關的用語，此處的 twice as long as 表示她待在公司的時間是其他人的兩倍長，故正確答案為 (C)。

★比較級有一句型為：

表示倍數的數詞（如 twice、three times、four times 等）＋ as much/many as（有……倍多）

**129**

It is truly ------- that Pro Consulting was not chosen to undertake the advertising campaign, but Amway Design Co. will do just as good a job.

(A) regrets
(B) regretting
(C) to regret
(D) regrettable

題型 詞彙——形容詞

翻譯 真的非常遺憾的，專業諮詢公司沒有中選接下這次的廣告活動，但安路設計公司也一樣會做得很好。

詞彙 undertake 承接

be 動詞後面應出現形容詞才是正確句型，同時根據句意判斷，空格處填入 regrettable 較為適當，故正確答案為 (D)。

**130**

Mr. Simpson was a horrible -------, so none of the executives had any intention of hiring him.

(A) interviewer
(B) interviewed
(C) interview
(D) interviewee

題型 詞彙　名詞

翻譯 辛普森先生是個很糟的應徵者，所以行政主管中沒人有意錄用他。

詞彙 executive 行政主管
intention 意願

根據句意可判斷，空格應代入名詞補語作為主詞，所以人物名詞 (A) 或 (D) 為正確答案，其中
(A) interviewer 為面試官，(D) interviewee 為應徵者，故正確答案為 (D)。

## PART 6

**131–134 電子郵件**

| | |
|---|---|
| **From:** Gordon Iwatani<br><gordoniwatani@fastermail.com><br>**To:** Recruit Manager<br><recruit4@mtlanguage.com><br>**Date:** April 14<br>**Subject:** Re: Japanese language teacher | 寄件人：岩谷高登<br><gordoniwatani@fastermail.com><br>收件人：人資經理<br><recruit4@mtlanguage.com><br>日期：4月14日<br>主旨：關於：日語老師 |

Dear Sir:

I am writing in response to a notice I saw that said your language school is seeking a Japanese instructor. As **131** be clear from my credentials, which I have attached to this e-mail, I spent most of the last decade as a Japanese language teacher in China, **132** almost eight years as an instructor at the most prestigious language school in Shanghai.

In addition to my work experience and academic qualifications, I enjoy a number of hobbies, which you may find interesting. I have spent most of my life playing the violin, and I currently play in an **133** orchestra. I also have a black belt in judo and enjoy going on long runs and cycling in my free time. I have a bright personality and adjust well to new environments. **134**. Please let me know if I can provide you with more information.

Sincerely yours,
Gordon Iwatani

您好：

我看到貴語言中心在找日語教師，所以來信詢問。從我隨信附上的資歷應該可以得知，我有八年在上海最有聲望的語言學校教書，之後十年至今則多在中國擔任日語老師。

除了我的工作經驗和學歷，我也有很多嗜好，也許會讓您感興趣。我學了大半輩子的小提琴，現在在一個業餘交響樂團演奏。我是柔道黑帶高手，有空的時候，也喜歡長跑和騎自行車。我個性陽光，面對新環境也能調適得很好。感謝您費時考慮我的應徵申請。如果需要我提供更多資訊，也請讓我知道。

岩谷高登 敬上

**詞彙 in response to** 回應……　**seek** 尋找　**instructor** 教師　**credential** 資歷　**attach** 附上
**decade** 十年　**prestigious** 有聲望的　**bright personality** 陽光的個性　**adjust to** 適應
**environment** 環境

**131** - - - - - - - - - - - - - - - - - - - - - - - - - - - - - - - - - - - - - - - - - - - - - - - - - - - - - - - - - - - - - - - - - - - - - - - - - - - - - - - - - - - - - - - - -

| | |
|---|---|
| (A) can | (A) 可以 |
| (B) would | (B) 會是 |
| (C) should | (C) 應該 |
| (D) was | (D) 曾是 |

**題型 詞彙──助動詞**

從前後文可推測，此句應該是想表達，從資歷中可看出他具有教學經驗，故正確答案為 (C)。

## 132

(A) I spent
(B) having spent
(C) will spend
(D) be spending

(A) 我花費了
(B) 已花費了
(C) 將花費
(D) 正在花費

題型 **文法**——分詞片語

此處因逗號前後為主詞相同的子句，故將後句主詞省略、主動動詞改為 -ing 形式，即分詞構句的型態。而又因為後句描述的時間點早於前句，為了與前句使用的過去式區隔，此處便須使用過去完成式 had p.p.，過去完成式助動詞改為 -ing 則成為「having p.p.」，故本題正確答案為 (B)。

## 133

(A) amateur
(B) ordinary
(C) emerging
(D) odd

(A) 業餘的
(B) 尋常的
(C) 新興的
(D) 奇特的

題型 **詞彙**——形容詞

本題詢問修飾名詞 orchestra 的形容詞詞彙。根據內容脈絡，此處為描述個人興趣，前文表示自己會拉奏小提琴，故此處最可能指有加入業餘交響樂團，故正確答案為 (A)。

## 134 [NEW]

(A) I appreciate your time in considering my application.
(B) I look forward to meeting you tomorrow.
(C) I graduated from high school in Tokyo.
(D) I very much look forward to meeting my new students tomorrow.

(A) 感謝您費時考慮我的應徵申請。
(B) 期待明天和您相見。
(C) 我畢業於東京的高中。
(D) 我很期待明天見到新學生。

題型 **填入句子**

本篇文章為提交履歷表的電子郵件，而空格出現在結尾問候的部分，所以向對方表達感謝的句子較適當，正確答案為 (A)。

### 135–138 電子郵件

| To: slivingston@kmail.net<br>From: marsvideos@mars.com<br>Subject: Your order | 收件人：slivingston@kmail.net<br>寄件人：marsvideos@mars.com<br>主旨：您的訂購 |
| --- | --- |
| Dear sir,<br><br>We are in receipt of your e-mail regarding the products you purchased from Mars Videos **135** July. Unfortunately, we have not yet been able to locate the shipment. | 您好：<br><br>我們已經收到您所寄的電子郵件，是關於您在七月從火星影視購買的商品。很抱歉，我們目前沒辦法確認商品送到哪裡。 |

Based on our records, you purchased four Blu-ray discs and two DVDs amounting to a total of $83. Factoring in shipping costs, this amount __136__ to a total order of $97. __137__.

We would suggest that you do one of the following things. (1) If you hold tight and wait just a little bit longer, you may receive the products. We have seen instances where bad weather or other mishaps created delays in shipments. (2) If you would not like to wait, we can cancel the order now and provide a full __138__.

Yours sincerely,
Kyle Johnson
Customer Services Manager

根據我們的紀錄，您購買了四片藍光和兩張DVD，總額是美金83元。加上運費整筆訂單則為97元。我們的紀錄顯示，已經在7月17日從您的信用卡扣款。

我們向您建議兩個方式。（1）如果您願意再等候，就有可能會收到商品。確實有前例是因為天氣不佳，或其他意外導致延後到貨。（2）如果您不想等候，我們可以馬上取消訂單，並予以全額退款。

客服部經理
凱爾·強森 敬上

**詞彙** in receipt of . . . 收到……　locate 確定……的位置　shipment 運送　based on . . . 根據……　factor . . . in 加上……　hold tight 等候　mishap 意外　charge . . . 向……收費

**135**------------------------------------------------

(A) in
(B) on
(C) when
(D) or

(A) 在……期間
(B) 在……時候
(C) 當
(D) 或

**題型** 詞彙——介系詞

在月份前面加上 in 表示「在……月」，所以正確答案為 (A)。

**136**------------------------------------------------

(A) increase
(B) increased
(C) will increase
(D) has been increasing

(A) 增加
(B) 增加到
(C) 將增加
(D) 一直以來在增長

**題型** 位置——主要動詞

空格中應該填入主要動詞，且主詞為單數。雖然 (B)、(C)、(D) 都可以填入，但是價格已經訂好了，所以使用過去式最適當，故正確答案為 (B)。

(D) 因為是從過去一直進行到現在的意思，所以不是正確選項。

**137** NEW ------------------------------------------

(A) You are a valued customer, and we will ship your products today.
(B) Our records show we charged your credit card for this amount on July 17.
(C) Please let us know what you think of this policy.
(D) We will go ahead and charge your credit card for the total amount.

(A) 您是很寶貴的顧客，我們今天就會出貨。
(B) 我們的紀錄顯示，已經在7月17日從您的信用卡扣款。
(C) 您不妨提供對於公司政策的意見。
(D) 我們將繼續進行，並從您的信用卡扣款總額。

題型 填入句子

前文中，經理已說明費用細項，故此處句子最可能也與費用相關。又從後文可知，顧客若是不願等待延誤送達的商品，店家可以取消訂單並退款，故此處應是告知已經以信用卡向顧客收費，故正確答案為 (B)。

## 138

(A) refund
(B) shipment
(C) order
(D) apology

(A) 退款
(B) 運送
(C) 訂單
(D) 道歉

題型 詞彙——名詞

由於空格出現在取消訂單的相關句子中，所以表示全額退款的「full refund」為最佳答案，本題正解為 (A)。

## 139–142 通知

Attention employees:

I have received several complaints regarding usage of the employee break room. This notice serves as a reminder of the rules we all must follow.

First, please remember to wash, dry, and put away in its appropriate place any plate, bowl, cup, or utensil that you've used. This should be done immediately after **139**.

Second, there have been complaints about smoking in the break room. As you all know, we have a strict policy against smoking in the building. If you want to smoke, you **140** to do so in the designated smoking area on the back patio or elsewhere outside the building.

Finally, please do not take food that is not yours. All food kept in the refrigerator should be properly **141** with the owner's name. Take only food that is yours. **142**.

Grace Ikawa
Manager

各位員工請注意：

我已經接到很多關於員工休息室使用的抱怨。本通知提醒大家遵守以下規則。

首先，請記得使用過後，馬上把杯盤、碗和餐具，洗淨、擦乾並且物歸原位。

再者，也有人反應休息室有人抽菸。如你們所知，公司嚴格規定不能在建築物裡面抽菸。如果你想抽菸，需要在特定吸菸區，像是後方露臺或是公司外面。

最後，請不要拿走別人的食物。冰箱內所有食物都應該確實貼上持有人的標籤。你只能取用自己的食物。維持舒適的休息室環境供大家使用，是很重要的事。

經理
井川葛瑞絲

詞彙 usage 使用　break room 休息室　serve as 作為　reminder 提醒　strict 嚴格的
against 反對　designated 指定的，特定的　patio 露臺

**139**

(A) be used            (A) 被使用
(B) using              (B) 正在用
(C) use                 (C) 使用
(D) to use            (D) 去用

題型 **位置——名詞**

根據文意，此處應是表示「使用後」，請注意 (C) use 此處為名詞，故放於介系詞 after 後面也不需要變成動名詞，故正確答案為 (C)。

**140**

(A) would request     (A) 會要求
(B) requested        (B) 要求過
(C) will request      (C) 將要求
(D) are requested    (D) 被要求

題型 **位置——主要動詞**

空格出現於描述一般規定的句子中，應使用現在式，並因文意為要求對方，而此處前方主詞為被要求的人物 you，所以搭配動詞要使用現在被動型，正確答案為 (D)。

**141**

(A) labeling          (A) 正在貼標籤
(B) labeled           (B) 被貼標籤
(C) label             (C) 貼標籤
(D) to label          (D) 去貼標籤

題型 **文法——過去分詞**

空格應填入表示被動的過去分詞，故正確答案為 (B)。

**142** (NEW)

(A) We will be holding tomorrow's staff meeting in the break room.
(B) We will be shutting down the break room beginning next week.
(C) Let us all enjoy the food in the refrigerator together.
(D) It is important that we keep the break room a pleasant place to use.

(A) 我們明天將在休息室開會。
(B) 下週開始我們會關閉休息室。
(C) 讓大家一起共享冰箱裡的所有食物。
(D) 維持舒適的休息室環境供大家使用，是很重要的事。

題型 **填入句子**

整篇公告主題環繞著員工休息室的環境維護，故最後以維持環境很重要作為結束最為適當，正確答案為 (D)。

## 143–146 評論

Maya Gordon's new guide to doing business in the Middle East is an interesting and comprehensive journey through the Middle Eastern business world.

In this book, readers are provided **143** a unique yet clear understanding of what the business culture is like in several key Middle Eastern countries. Among the many topics covered by Professor Gordon are essential ones like proper greeting etiquette, proper etiquette during business meals, the use of business cards, and the intricacies of negotiating with Middle Eastern counterparts.

If you are just getting acquainted with the business scene in the Middle East, this book is **144** reading. No other guide delves into so many critical aspects of Middle Eastern business conduct in such depth and with such detail. **145** , Professor Gordon has organized her book by business center (including Dubai, Qatar, and Abu Dhabi), allowing readers to focus on the specific area they are interested in. **146** .

Once you have read *Doing Business the Middle Eastern Way*, you will have no trouble conducting yourself appropriately in the Middle East.

瑪雅·高登的中東新生意指南，綜覽了中東的商業界，既全面也很有意思。

這本書針對幾個中東關鍵國家的商業文化，提供讀者獨特卻清楚的見解。高登教授所著墨的多項主題都很重要，像是適當的招呼禮儀、商務餐敘的用餐禮儀、名片的使用，還有和中東企業磋商的複雜細節。

如果您只是剛開始了解中東的商業界生態，這本書是必讀之作。它深度鑽研中東商業實務許多重要面向，非常詳盡，無人能出其右。不僅如此，高登博士也按照重要商務核心（包括杜拜、卡達和阿布達比）疏理這本書，方便讀者聚焦自己有興趣的區域。其中關於杜拜的章節格外有趣。

只要您讀過《學中東人做生意》，置身中東也可應付自如。

**詞彙** comprehensive 全面的　kcy 關鍵的　cover 著墨　etiquette 禮儀　business card 名片　intricacy 複雜的事物　counterpart 同行；相對應者　be acquainted with . . . 剛開始了解……　delve into 深度鑽研　aspect 面向　conduct 實務　conduct oneself 舉止得體　lukewarm 冷淡的

**143** ----------------------------------------------------------------

(A) with
(B) on
(C) in
(D) at

(A) 以
(B) 在……之上
(C) 在……裡面
(D) 在……地方

**題型** 位置——介系詞

「provide sb with sth」為固定用法，故正確答案為 (A)。

★「provide」的用法有兩種，如下：

provide sb with sth
provide sth to sb

## 144

(A) absolute
(B) ridiculous
(C) compulsory
(D) confident

(A) 完全的
(B) 荒謬的
(C) 必須做的
(D) 自信的

**題型** 詞彙——形容詞

本段後文提到「No other guide delves into so many critical aspects of Middle Eastern business conduct in such depth and with such detail.」，可知此書飽含中東商業實務的詳細解說，故可推測此書對剛接觸中東商業的人來說，是本必讀、必備的書籍，故本題正確答案為 (C)。

**145**

(A) By comparison
(B) Unfortunately
(C) Moreover
(D) As a result

(A) 相比之下
(B) 遺憾地
(C) 不僅如此
(D) 結果是

**題型** 詞彙——副詞

空格前文描述書籍內容詳細、面向多元，後文則描寫書籍內容的編排方式，可推測此處的副詞應具有補充的意涵，故本題正確答案為 (C)。

**146** NEW

(A) The chapter on Dubai is particularly enjoyable.
(B) Professor Gordon has also written on Asia.
(C) This guide is not as interesting as some of the others on the market.
(D) Book critics have been lukewarm on the book.

(A) 其中關於杜拜的章節格外有趣。
(B) 高登教授對亞洲也有所著墨。
(C) 這本指南和某些市面上的書相形之下顯得較無趣。
(D) 書評對本書的反應冷淡。

**題型** 填入句子

前句中提到，書籍內容按照商務核心城市編排，並說讀者可以聚焦感興趣的區域，故此處最可能向讀者推薦書中的某個章節，所以正確答案為 (A)。

# PART 7

**147–148 訂購單**

| | |
|---|---|
| **MEGA DEPOT, INC.**<br><br>Taking care of all of your home and office needs<br><br>Contents:<br># 2 color ink cartridges<br># 1 black and white ink cartridge<br># 10 packs of letter-size paper (50 sheets each)<br># 1 postcard for re-orders<br><br>Use the enclosed postcard when re-ordering these products.<br><br>If you would like to speak to a customer service representative, call 301-555-1999 Mon.–Fri. 10 A.M. to 6 P.M.<br><br>NOT FOR CONSUMPTION | **巨得寶股份有限公司**<br><br>滿足您家居和辦公需求<br><br>產品內容：<br># 彩色墨水匣兩盒<br># 黑白墨水匣一盒<br># 標準紙張（每包50張）10包<br># 供再次訂購使用之明信片一張<br><br>如需再次下訂產品，請使用隨信附上的明信片。<br><br>如欲和客服人員聯繫，請在週一到週五早上10點到下午6點間，撥打301-555-1999。<br><br>產品不可食用 |

 詞彙 take care of one's needs 滿足某人的需求　content 內容　ink cartridge 墨水匣　re-order 再訂購　enclosed 隨函附上的　representative 代表人員　consumption 食用

 **147**

---

**What most likely is the reason for buying these products?**

(A) To print documents
(B) To place an order for supplies
(C) To write letters
(D) To create artwork

**最可能購買這些產品的原因是？**

(A) 列印文件
(B) 訂購日用品
(C) 寫信
(D) 從事藝術創作

訂購單上的墨水匣、紙張與明信片和印刷最為相關，故正確答案為 (A)。

**148**

---

**What is true about the order form?**

(A) It warns people not to eat the product.
(B) It includes a receipt for the product.
(C) It does not describe the contents of the order.
(D) It provides an address for the store.

**關於這張訂購單，何者為真？**

(A) 警告民眾產品不能吃。
(B) 隨產品附上收據。
(C) 沒有描述訂購的內容。
(D) 有提供店址。

最下方的「NOT FOR CONSUMPTION」表示「不可食用」，故正確答案為 (A)。

| | |
|---|---|
| **Jane Smith** 3:34 P.M.<br>Hi, Mr. Austin. Are you at baggage claim? | 珍・史密斯〔下午3:34〕：<br>嗨，奧斯丁先生。你在提領行李區嗎？ |
| **Miles Austin** 3:38 P.M.<br>Ms. Smith? I'm through customs with my luggage, and I'm at the East Gate. Are you around here? | 邁爾斯・奧斯丁〔下午3:38〕：<br>史密斯女士？我拿著行李正在過海關，我在東門。妳在附近嗎？ |
| **Jane Smith** 3:39 P.M.<br>I just got here, so sorry! There was a mechanical problem, so my train was delayed. I'm on my way downstairs now. | 珍・史密斯〔下午3:39〕：<br>很抱歉，我才剛到！我的火車因為機械故障延誤了。我正準備下樓。 |
| **Miles Austin** 3:41 P.M.<br>Oh, OK. No problem. I can come your way. But what are you wearing? | 邁爾斯・奧斯丁〔下午3:41〕：<br>喔，好的。沒問題，我可以去找妳。但妳穿什麼？ |
| **Jane Smith** 3:43 P.M.<br>Blue dress, heels, and a black purse. I'm also carrying a fashion magazine. | 珍・史密斯〔下午3:43〕：<br>藍色洋裝、高跟鞋和黑包包。我手上還拿著一本時尚雜誌。 |
| **Miles Austin** 3:44 P.M.<br>Understood. I'll see you in front of the customs. | 邁爾斯・奧斯丁〔下午3:44〕：<br>了解。出關那裡見。 |

**詞彙** baggage claim 提領行李區　customs 海關　mechanical 機械的　come one's way 去找某人

**149** ------------------------------------------------

**What is suggested about Mr. Austin and Ms. Smith?**

(A) They have never met before.

(B) They have a meeting tomorrow.

(C) They both took trains.

(D) Jane Smith has just bought a magazine.

文中提到關於奧斯丁先生和史密斯女士什麼事？

(A) 他們素未謀面。

(B) 他們明天要開會。

(C) 他們都搭火車。

(D) 珍・史密斯剛買了一本雜誌。

本題要使用刪去法。(B) 為無法確定的內容；(C) 從開頭奧斯丁先生說的「I'm through customs with my luggage」看來，他應是搭乘飛機前來；(D) 只能知道史密斯小姐手上拿著雜誌，無法確定是否是剛剛買的；所以本題最合理的答案應為 (A)。

**150** ------------------------------------------------

**Where is Mr. Austin waiting?**

(A) At a magazine stand

(B) At the customs

(C) On a train

(D) Upstairs

奧斯丁先生在哪裡等？

(A) 在雜誌攤旁邊

(B) 在海關前

(C) 火車上

(D) 樓梯上來的地方

根據最後的「I'll see you in front of the customs.」可知，奧斯丁先生會在海關處等史密斯女士，故正確答案為 (B)。

**151** NEW

**At 3:44 P.M., why does Mr. Austin say, "Understood"?**

(A) He just saw Ms. Smith.
(B) He'll be able to recognize Ms. Smith.
(C) He is also chairing the meeting.
(D) He does not want to be late.

下午 3:44 時，為什麼奧斯丁先生說：「了解」？

(A) 他剛見到史密斯女士。
(B) 他可以認出史密斯女士。
(C) 他也要主持會議。
(D) 他不想遲到。

題目引用句子的意圖，可以在前、後句中找到關鍵線索。前句中，史密斯女士向他說明自己的衣著，故此處奧斯丁先生說的「了解」，應代表他能根據這些描述找到史密斯，故正確答案為 (B)。

---

## 152–154 部落格

**February 24**

We moved ahead another 25 km on our trek today. My feet are killing me. —[1]—. I really should not have worn my new boots. My knees are a little sore, too, but all in all it was a good day. We got off to a bit of a slow start by sleeping in. Keiko was on alarm duty, so that one is on her! All downhill after that, though. The view was unbelievable. We took tons of photos. I can't wait to show them to you when we're back. —[2]—. We even saw a snow leopard! Those are extremely rare and almost impossible to actually see live. It was hard to see it amidst all the snow—it came into view for about three seconds. It looked beautiful. Keiko missed it— sweet revenge for failing to wake us up in time for the sunrise, ha ha! —[3]—.

**February 26**

Sorry for not checking in yesterday. It rained all day, and there wasn't much interesting news to tell you. We found a quaint little café and just spent the entire day there. The staff was giving us dirty looks, but they never actually asked us to leave. —[4]—. Well, tomorrow's the last day. I'm really looking forward to seeing all of you the day after!

**2月24日**

我們今天又跋涉前進了25公里。我的腳折磨死我了，我真不該穿我的新靴子。膝蓋也有點痠，不過總體來說今天還是很不錯。起步慢了，因為睡得有點晚。京子負責叫我們起床，所以是她的錯！雖然之後就順利多了。風景美得難以置信。我們拍了超多照片。我等不及回去秀給你們看啦。我們還看到雪豹！牠們非常非常稀有，幾乎不可能親眼目睹。到處都雪，很難從中看出牠來──大概只有三秒鐘看得見。牠很漂亮，京子就錯過了──誰叫她沒叫醒我們，害我們錯過日出，這是甜蜜的復仇，哈哈！

**2月26日**

抱歉昨天沒有看部落格。整天都在下雨，也沒什麼有趣的事可以跟你們說。我們找到一間別致的小咖啡店，整天都待在那裡。店員看我們不爽，但也沒有真的來趕我們走。我們最後只能消磨時間、聊天、吃東西和玩遊戲。明天就是最後一天了。真想在後天趕快見到你們。

---

**詞彙** sore 痠痛的　all in all 總體來說　get off 起步　sleep in 睡到很晚才起床
on alarm duty 負責叫起床　all downhill 全為下坡路，引申為順利　tons of 非常多的
snow leopard 雪豹　amidst . . . 在……之中　come into view 進入視線　in time 及時
quaint 別致的　give sb dirty looks 看某人不爽

**152** ----------------------------------------

**How are the two people most likely traveling?**　　　這兩人最可能用什麼方式旅行？

(A) On roller skates　　　　　　(A) 溜冰鞋

(B) By motorcycle　　　　　　　(B) 摩托車

(C) On foot　　　　　　　　　　(C) 步行

(D) By plane　　　　　　　　　　(D) 搭飛機

文章一開始提到：「My feet are killing me. I really should not have worn my new boots. My knees are a little sore, too, but all in all it was a good day.」，表示因為穿了新鞋導致腳痛，由此可見，兩人應是徒步旅行，故正確答案為 (C)。

**153** ----------------------------------------

**On what date will the blogger return?**　　　這名部落客哪天回家？

(A) March 2　　　　　　　　　　(A) 3 月 2 日

(B) March 1　　　　　　　　　　(B) 3 月 1 日

(C) February 28　　　　　　　　(C) 2 月 28 日

(D) February 27　　　　　　　　(D) 2 月 27 日

最後一天的日記為 2 月 26 日，且說了「Well, tomorrow's the last day. I'm really looking forward to seeing all of you the day after!」，其中後句的「the day after」和前句的「tomorrow」要看在一起，所以就是指「the day after tomorrow」（後天）的意思，可以注意這樣的省略用法。本題正確答案為 (C)。

**154** **NEW** ----------------------------------------

**In which of the positions marked [1], [2], [3], and [4] does the following phrase belong?**　　　下列句子最適合出現在 [1]、[2]、[3]、[4] 的哪個位置中？

**"We ended up just lounging around all day, talking, eating, and playing games."**　　　「我們最後只能消磨時間、聊天、吃東西和玩遊戲。」

(A) [1]　　　　　　　　　　　　(A) [1]

(B) [2]　　　　　　　　　　　　(B) [2]

(C) [3]　　　　　　　　　　　　(C) [3]

(D) [4]　　　　　　　　　　　　(D) [4]

本題為填入句子的題型，應先分析題目的句子。根據 [4] 前面的內容，可以得知 2 月 26 日因為下雨，他們整天待在咖啡廳，而題目的句子解釋了他們在咖啡廳裡做的事情，故可推測此句最適合放於 [4]，正確答案為 (D)。

155–156 表單

## NON-DELIVERY FORM

**Date:** 5/16        **Time:** 11:08 A.M.
**Delivery person:** Sam

**Package number:** 3494-836636-92
**From:** General Office Supplies

**Reason for non-delivery**
   Item too big □
   Resident not home to sign for delivery ☑

   **Notes:** Item sent by express delivery

**Options:**

(A) Dial 1-800-555-2215 toll free 24 hours a day to reach
     our automated service.
     You will need to have the package number.

(B) Dial 1-401-555-2216 during office hours (9 A.M.–
     5:30 P.M., closed on Sundays.)

*Remember:* *We will keep the package for only five days*
*from the date of failed delivery, after which it will be*
*returned to the sender.*

---

## 寄件未達表單

日期：5月16日    時間：早上11:08
送貨員：山姆

包裹號碼：3494-836636-92
寄件者：大眾辦公用品

寄件未達原因：
   商品太大 □
   住戶不在家未簽收 ☑

   備註：此為快遞件

選項：

(A) 撥打1-800-555-2215 24小時免
     付費電話，使用我們的自動化服
     務。您需要提供包裹號碼。

(B) 在上班時間（早上9點到下午
     5:30，週日休息）撥打1-401-
     555-2216。

*提醒：寄件失敗後我們只會保管貨*
*品五天，之後將會退還給寄件人。*

---

**詞彙** non-delivery 寄件未達   resident 住戶   express delivery 快遞   toll free 免費
automated 自動化的   sender 寄件人

**155**

**Who filled out this form?**

(A) The sender
(B) An automated service
(C) A courier
(D) The resident

是誰填寫了這張表單？

(A) 寄件者
(B) 自動化服務
(C) 快遞員
(D) 住戶

此表單說明了包裹寄送失敗的原因與處理辦法等等，故最可能為快遞員填寫，正確答案為 (C)。

**156**

**What will happen after five days?**

(A) Sam will come back with the package.
(B) The resident will call the delivery company.
(C) The item will be sent back.
(D) The resident will come home.

五天後會發生什麼事？

(A) 送貨員山姆會帶著包裹再次前來。
(B) 住戶會打電話給快遞公司。
(C) 包裹將被退還。
(D) 住戶會回家。

根據「Remember: We will keep the package for only five days from the date of failed delivery, after which it will be returned to the sender.」可以得知，包裹只能保管五天，之後會歸還給寄件人，故正確答案為 (C)。

## 157–158 信件

| | |
|---|---|
| Zebra Car Rental<br>1154 West Avenue<br>San Francisco, CA 85445 | 斑馬租車服務<br>85445加州舊金山<br>西大道115號 |

Dear customers,

Due to the increasing demands for our cars and vans, Zebra Car Rental is expanding its operations. This will involve a new front yard plus office and warehouse extensions, which will enable us to stock and store more cars and vans.

These changes will take place next month. Especially, we will be closing the warehouse from 8 to 11 of November. However, you can still see a list of our available vehicles for rent online. Please use this website to book a test drive at www.zebracars.com during this period. We hope that you have a good winter and look forward to greeting you at our new facilities in December.

Chris Murphy
General Manager, Zebra Car Rental

親愛的顧客：

由於小客車和廂型車的需求與日俱增，斑馬租車公司將擴大營運，包括增建前院、辦公室和倉庫擴建，可供我們停放更多車輛。

下個月就會開始動工。特別提醒，11月8日到11日間倉庫將會關閉。不過您還是能在網路上看到租車清單。這段期間請用www.zebracars.com預約試乘。我們祝福您冬天愉快，也很期待在12月，用嶄新設備歡迎您大駕光臨。

克里斯·墨菲
斑馬租車服務總經理

**詞彙** expand 擴大　operation 營運　front yard 前院　extension 擴建　stock 儲藏　store 儲存　take place 發生　test drive 試乘

 **157**

**What is the main purpose of this letter?**

(A) To advise on new prices
(B) To announce renovations
(C) To introduce a website
(D) To offer discounts

這封信的目的為何？

(A) 針對新價格給予建議
(B) 宣布要整建
(C) 介紹官網
(D) 提供折扣

在第一段在提到「Zebra Car Rental is expanding its operations」後說明增建的細節，包含「a new front yard plus office and warehouse extensions」，故可知道這封信件主要告知了租車公司將要整建一事，本題答案為 (B)。

**What is stated about the company?**

(A) It has reduced its stock.
(B) It sells items from around the world.
(C) It allows customers to reserve test drives.
(D) It will be closed throughout the winter.

**文中提到關於這間公司什麼事？**

(A) 將減少停放車輛。
(B) 販售來自全球的商品。
(C) 允許顧客預約試乘。
(D) 整個冬天都將關閉。

「We will be closing the warehouse from 8 to 11 of November. However, you can still see a list of our available vehicles for rent online.」中提到，雖然 11 月 8 日至 11 日倉庫不會開放，但是顧客可在線上瀏覽可供出租的車輛，且還說了：「Please use this website to book a test drive at www.zebracars.com during this period.」，表示在倉庫不開放的期間仍可線上預約試乘，所以正確答案為 (C)。

## 159–160 網路聊天室

| | |
|---|---|
| **Tyler Wood**    5:10 P.M.<br>It's incredible! I love the updated graphics. Much better than the last one. | 泰勒・伍德〔下午5:10〕：<br>好棒！我喜歡新的畫面，比上一版好多了。 |
| **Sarah Brooks**    5:11 P.M.<br>Are you kidding? For $95, they'd better come up with better quality than that. | 莎拉・布魯克斯〔下午5:11〕：<br>你在開玩笑嗎？花了95美元應該要有更好的質感才對。 |
| **Tyler Wood**    5:11 P.M.<br>It is a bit expensive, I know. But I'm sure you were blown away by the soundtrack. | 泰勒・伍德〔下午5:11〕：<br>我知道是有點貴。但我確定配樂好聽到爆炸。 |
| **Gavin Ward**    5:12 P.M.<br>Totally! The music was really great. Didn't you think so, Sarah? | 蓋文・華德〔下午5:12〕：<br>完全同意。音樂真的很棒！莎拉，妳不覺得嗎？ |
| **Sarah Brooks**    5:14 P.M.<br>Well, I wouldn't say "blown away", but it was alright. The thing I did like was the character voice acting. They really stepped it up on that one. It annoys me when a good story just crumbles under terrible performances. Speaking of which, the story was pretty good, too. | 莎拉・布魯克斯〔下午5:14〕：<br>嗯，我不會說「好聽到爆炸」，但是還行。我喜歡的是聲優的演出。他們真的有更上一層樓。故事好但表現爛真的很惱人。說到這個，這故事也很棒。 |
| **Gavin Ward**    5:15 P.M.<br>Ha ha, I think she might finally be caving, Tyler! | 蓋文・華德〔下午5:15〕：<br>哈哈，我想她終於淪陷了，泰勒！ |
| **Tyler Wood**    5:16 P.M.<br>About time. Superior graphics, music, and story—with a solid 80 hours of entertainment, including all of the extra missions. What more can you ask for? | 泰勒・伍德〔下午5:16〕：<br>也該是時候了。絕佳的畫面、音樂和故事情節——80個小時的充實娛樂，還有所有的支線任務。還能再要求什麼？ |

**詞彙** graphics 畫面；圖像　are you kidding? 你在開玩笑嗎　come up with 呈現
be blown away 感到十分驚豔　character 角色　step it up 更上一層樓；更好　crumble 崩壞
cave 妥協　about time 該是時候了　solid 連續的

121

**159** ----

**What is the conversation most likely about?**

(A) A musical
(B) A movie
(C) A video game
(D) A book

**這最有可能是關於什麼的對話？**

(A) 一部音樂劇
(B) 一部電影
(C) 一個電玩遊戲
(D) 一本書

對話中出現「updated graphics」、「The music was really great」、「the character voice acting」以及最後的「a solid 80 hours of entertainment, including all of the extra missions.」，可知道此娛樂包含影像、音樂、聲優演出、長達 80 小時還有任務，故最可能為電玩遊戲，本題正確答案為 (C)。

**160** [NEW] ----

**At 5:14 P.M., what does Sarah Brooks mean when she writes, "They really stepped it up"?**

(A) The company did a good job.
(B) The participants walked away.
(C) The users went upstairs.
(D) The performers stopped acting.

**下午 5:14 時，莎拉·布魯克斯寫道：「他們真的有更上一層樓」，她的意思為何？**

(A) 他們公司做得好。
(B) 參加者離開了。
(C) 使用者上樓了。
(D) 表演者停止演出了。

前文華德先生說電玩的音樂好聽，布魯克斯女士則覺得還好，表示自己更喜歡聲優的演出，並說出：「They really stepped it up on that one.」，故可知這應是在稱讚遊戲中的元素，故最符合文意的為 (A)。

**161–163 文章**

Yesterday, both the governor and the state attorney general joined hands in urging for changes to what they called a "broken" public education system in the state. Governor Wayne Johnson and Attorney General Vicki Perez spoke at length about the issue when it was brought up during a debate on education held at Silver Town City Hall yesterday. It was the first time this state has seen the governor and the state attorney general make such a joint statement.

The problems discussed by Mr. Johnson and Ms. Perez can be easily summarized into three key points, which were:

1. The quality of teachers has deteriorated significantly in public schools across the state. Mr. Johnson and Ms. Perez noted the reason for this being that budget cutbacks had been made, which led to teacher salaries steadily decreasing in recent years.

2. Standardized test scores for students across the state have also been steadily decreasing in recent years. The average scores in the state are now below average when compared to other states across the country.

昨天，州長和州檢察長共同敦促，要為他們口中「崩壞的」公共教育體制帶來改變。昨天在銀鎮市政廳舉辦了教育議題的辯論會，州長韋恩·強森和州檢察長維琪·培瑞茲議論許久，這也是兩人首度在該州做出聯合聲明。

強森先生和培瑞茲女士討論的問題，可以總結為以下三點：

1. 州立學校內教師的品質明顯惡化。兩人指出原因在於預算縮減，導致近年來教師薪資逐步地下滑。

2. 近年來學生考試成績也逐漸下降，與其他州相比，已低於平均值。

3. The curriculum for middle and high school students has not changed sufficiently over the past decade to keep up with changes being made in other states. Students who have not been exposed to evolved curriculums have been struggling in college when studying with students from schools in other states. The problem starts early on in each student's education and is a fundamental one, Mr. Johnson and Ms. Perez said.

The State Ministry of Education has yet to issue an official response to the statement made by Mr. Johnson and Ms. Perez.

3. 國高中學生的課程在過去十年來,不像其他州的課程充分與時俱進。該州的畢業生沒有接觸到改進後的課程,在大學就學時和其他州的學生競爭就比較辛苦。兩人都指出這是根本問題,在教育學生的早期階段就已經存在。

針對兩人的聲明,州教育部目前沒有做出正式回應。

---

**詞彙** governor 州長　attorney general 檢察長　join hands in V-ing 聯手……　urge for 敦促　at length 許久　be brought up 被提起　make a statement 做出聲明　joint 聯合的　key point 要點　deteriorate 惡化　note 指出　budget 預算　cutback 縮減　steadily 逐步地　standardized 標準化的　compared to . . . 與……相比　curriculum 課程　keep up with changes 與時俱進　be exposed to 接觸　evolved 改進的　fundamental 根本的　issue a response 做出回應

---

**161**

**What was NOT mentioned about yesterday's statement?**

(A) It was about issues with the school system.

(B) Mr. Johnson and Ms. Perez are from different states.

(C) Three key Issues were discussed.

(D) The State Ministry of Education did not respond.

昨天的聲明中,沒有提到什麼?

(A) 它和學校體制的議題有關。

(B) 強森先生和培瑞茲女士來自不同州。

(C) 討論了三個關鍵議題。

(D) 州教育部沒有回應。

(A) 可從第一段的「a "broken" public education system in the state」得知;(C) 可從第二段的「The problems discussed . . . can be easily summarized into three key points」得知;(D) 則可從最後的「The State Ministry of Education has yet to issue an official response」得知,故只有 (B) 未被提及,本題正確答案為 (B)。

---

**162**

**What is one of Mr. Johnson and Ms. Perez's main points?**

(A) The state has too many schools.

(B) Students have been doing better in college.

(C) The quality of teachers is lower than it used to be.

(D) The students are unhappy with the new policy.

下列何者為強森先生和培瑞茲女士的主張?

(A) 該州學校太多了。

(B) 學生在大學的表現更好。

(C) 教師的品質比以前差。

(D) 學生對新政策感到不滿。

從第一個要點指出的內容:「The quality of teachers has deteriorated significantly in public schools across the state.」可以得知,教師的素質較以前低落,故正確答案為 (C)。

## 163

**According to the two officials, what has caused a change in teacher quality?**

(A) Teacher salaries are decreasing.
(B) Many teachers are moving to other states.
(C) The teachers are not happy with the schools.
(D) It is the Ministry of Education's fault.

根據這兩個官員的說法，什麼改變了教師的品質？

(A) 教師薪資正在減少。
(B) 教師外流到其他州。
(C) 教師對學校感到不滿。
(D) 是教育部的錯。

根據第一個要點中的「the reason for this being that budget cutbacks had been made, which led to teacher salaries steadily decreasing in recent years.」，預算縮減造成教師薪資下滑，教師的品質也逐漸惡化，故正確答案為 (A)。

### 164–167 通知

Sunny Shiny Daycare Center has been caring for children for more than thirty years. Our reputation continues to grow as the center that provides quality learning and playtime in a warm, friendly, and safe environment for children.

We would like to announce the opening of our newest daycare center next month, right here in Orange County. It is planned to be our largest center yet, able to accommodate up to 50 children. Of course, the newest center will have all of the fun-filled game centers and facilities that parents are used to seeing, including a fortress playground, swimming pool, and state-of-the-art computer corner.

We will be holding an open house from January 27 to 31 next year, and all interested parents are invited to join us for a full tour of our facilities and an open dialogue with our award-winning staff. Please don't hesitate to bring your children with you so that they can truly take a "full" tour by immersing themselves in a number of fun activities that will give them a taste of what life at the center would be like every day.

We hope to see all of you in January. If you would like more information, please call 201-555-8765 or e-mail us at sunnyshiny@mnet.org.

At Sunny Shiny, you are always in good hands.

Lucy Mason
Managing Director
Sunny Shiny Daycare Center

日光閃閃日托中心照顧兒童已超過30年之久。我們提供溫暖、友善又安全的環境，給予兒童高品質的學習和休閒時光，不斷累積良好聲譽。

我們在此宣布，下個月將在橘郡開設新的日托中心。它將是我們歷來最大的中心，最多可以容納50名孩童。最新的日托中心當然會有樂趣十足的遊戲中心和相關設施，誠如家長所熟悉的，像是城堡遊樂場、游泳池、最先進的電腦中心。

我們將在明年1月27日到31日開放參觀，完整導覽院內設施，歡迎感興趣的家長前來，和本中心曾獲獎的員工對話。儘管帶著貴子弟一起來，「全面」體驗各種有趣的活動，感受未來在我們中心的每一天日常。

我們希望會在一月見到您。欲知更多資訊，可以撥打201-555-8765或是寫信到sunnyshiny@mnet.org詢問。

日光閃閃給您最全面的照護。

日光閃閃日托中心總經理
露西‧梅森

**詞彙** daycare 日間照顧　quality 高品質的　accommodate 容納　fun-filled 樂趣十足的
facility 設施　fortress 城堡　playground 遊樂場　state-of-the-art 先進的　corner 中心
open house 參觀日　don't hesitate to V 別猶豫　immerse oneself in sth 沉浸於某事
give sb a taste 讓某人體驗　be in good hands 被好好照顧

**164**

| | |
|---|---|
| **What is NOT a purpose of the notice?** | 何者並非這篇通知的目的？ |
| (A) To announce the opening of a new daycare center | (A) 宣布新的日托中心要開幕 |
| (B) To inform parents about an open house | (B) 告知家長參觀日的活動 |
| (C) To discuss the history of Sunny Shiny | (C) 討論日光閃閃日托中心的沿革 |
| (D) To provide contact information to parents | (D) 給予家長聯繫方式 |

「We would like to announce the opening of our newest daycare center next month, right here in Orange County.」點出 (A) 日托中心的開幕，並於下文中提及 (B) 參觀日：「We will be holding an open house from January 27 to 31 next year」，以及 (D) 聯繫方式：「If you would like more information, please call 201-555-8765 or e-mail us at sunnyshiny@mnet.org.」，故可知道未提及的只有中心沿革，本題正確答案為 (C)。

**165**

| | |
|---|---|
| **What is a feature of Sunny Shiny Daycare Center?** | 日光閃閃日托中心有什麼特色？ |
| (A) A tennis court | (A) 網球場 |
| (B) A swimming pool | (D) 游泳池 |
| (C) A rock-climbing wall | (C) 攀岩牆 |
| (D) A water slide | (D) 滑水道 |

根據「the newest center will have all of the fun-filled game centers and facilities」、「including a fortress playground, swimming pool, and state-of-the-art computer corner.」可知，日托中心有遊樂場、泳池與電腦中心，故正確答案為 (B)。

**166**

| | |
|---|---|
| **How long will the open house last?** | 參觀日會持續幾天？ |
| (A) 2 days | (A) 2 天 |
| (B) 4 days | (B) 4 天 |
| (C) 5 days | (C) 5 天 |
| (D) 6 days | (D) 6 天 |

根據「We will be holding an open house from January 27 to 31 next year」，可以得知參觀日為期五天，故正確答案為 (C)。

**Why might some people call Sunny Shiny?**
(A) To talk to their award-winning staff
(B) To buy tickets to the swimming pool
(C) To make a reservation for the open house
(D) To ask for more information

為什麼有些人可能會打電話給日光閃閃日托中心？
(A) 想和曾獲獎的員工對話
(B) 想要買游泳池的門票
(C) 預約參加參觀日活動
(D) 詢問更多資訊

根據「If you would like more information, please call 201-555-8765 or e-mail us at sunnyshiny@mnet.org.」可以得知，想知道更多資訊的人可以打電話給日托中心，故正確答案為 (D)。

### 168–171 新聞快報

Devastating wildfires spread throughout California today, causing enormous damage to homes and farmland. —[1]—. Reports show that five people were injured, with hundreds more people having to abandon their residences as fires spread as wide as 8 kilometers and slowly moved towards the city of Los Angeles. David Meyer, Chief Firefighter in the suburb of Annandale, said that this year's fires may be the worst he's seen in his long and storied career, but that his team of firefighters is up to the challenge. "Just the sheer speed with which the fire spread was unbelievable," he said. —[2]—. "My guys have really been battling out there, and we still have a ways to go." —[3]—.

It is not clear how these fires got started. It is usually the case, though, that wildfires are the product of human negligence, such as a careless cigarette or unattended campfire, or of natural causes, such as lightning hitting a dry patch of wood or grass.

—[4]—. Last year, parts of Northern California suffered heavy losses following almost two weeks of rampant forest fires, which ultimately caused injury to three people. Two years ago, the same area saw fires injure 40 people.

今天毀滅性的野火肆虐加州，造成住宅和農地大規模毀損。報導指出火災蔓延了8公里，並朝洛杉磯市方向持續緩慢延燒，數以百計的民眾被迫遠離家園，且造成五人受傷。安嫩代爾郊區的消防隊長大衛・梅耶爾表示，這是他長年服役以來所見過最糟的火災，但消防隊已經準備好因應挑戰。「火災蔓延速度快得難以置信。」他說，「消防隊已經奮戰一段時間了，但距離全面撲滅還有一段路。」

目前還不清楚起火原因。雖然通常是因為人為疏失，像是亂丟菸蒂、無人看管的營火，或是天災所引起，好比閃電打到乾柴或草堆。

加州歷年來都會發生野火災情。去年部分北加州地區為延燒將近兩週的猖獗森林大火所苦，火災最終造成三人受傷。同一地區兩年前也發生火災，造成40人受傷。

**詞彙** devastating 毀滅性的　wildfire 野火　enormous 大規模的　farmland 農地
be injured 受傷　residence 家園　suburb 郊區　long and storied 歷時長的　be up to 準備好
sheer speed 高速　have a ways to go （離成功）有一段距離　negligence 疏失
careless 隨便的　unattended 無人看管的　natural cause 天災；自然因素　lightning 閃電
patch 堆　suffer 受……所苦　heavy loss 嚴重損失　rampant 猖獗的

**168** ----------------------------------------

To whom is Mr. Meyer most likely referring in his comment?

(A) His friends
(B) Other firefighters
(C) His classmates
(D) His sons

梅耶爾先生發言中所提到的人最可能是誰？

(A) 他的朋友
(B) 其他的消防員
(C) 他的同學
(D) 他的兒子

從「David Meyer, Chief Firefighter in the suburb of Annandale」可知梅耶爾先生為地區消防隊長，故當他說：「My guys have really been battling out there, and we still have a ways to go.」，其中的「My guys」最可能為他手下的消防隊員，故正確答案為 (B)。

**169** ----------------------------------------

Which cause of wildfires is NOT mentioned in the bulletin?

(A) Failure to extinguish a campfire
(B) Carelessly dropping a cigarette
(C) Lightning striking dry grass
(D) Someone intentionally starting a fire

新聞快報中沒有提到哪個造成野火的原因？

(A) 沒能撲滅營火
(B) 亂丟菸蒂
(C) 閃電打到乾草
(D) 人為縱火

第二段寫了：「wildfires are the product of human negligence」，並舉出「a careless cigarette」和「unattended campfire」兩個例子，同時提到天災如「lightning hitting a dry patch of wood or grass」也是野火生成的可能原因；上述依序提及 (B)、(A) 與 (C)，故本題正確答案為 (D)。

**170** ----------------------------------------

According to the bulletin, how many people have been injured in wildfires over the last 3 years?

(A) Forty
(B) Forty-five
(C) Forty-eight
(D) Forty-three

根據新聞快報，過去三年來有多少人因為野火而受傷？

(A) 40
(B) 45
(C) 48
(D) 43

第一段提到「Reports show that five people were injured」，表示今年的大火造成五人受傷，而最後一段則說到「Last year . . . two weeks of rampant forest fires . . . caused injury to three people.」，可知去年受傷人數是三人，再由之後的「Two years ago, the same area saw fires injure 40 people.」知道兩年前受傷人數為 40 人，三者相加為 48 人，故正確答案為 (C)。

In which of the positions marked [1], [2], [3] and [4] does the following sentence belong?

"Wildfires have been an annual tradition in California."

(A) [1]
(B) [2]
(C) [3]
(D) [4]

下列句子最適合出現在 [1]、[2]、[3]、[4] 的哪個位置中？

「加州歷年來都會發生野火災情。」

(A) [1]
(B) [2]
(C) [3]
(D) [4]

本題為填入句子的題型，應先分析題目的句子。題目的句子點出關鍵字「annual」，表示野火成為每年都會發生的災禍，故可推測後文也應與火災時間點有關。[4] 後文出現「Last year」與「Two years ago」，故題目句子最適合填放在此處，本題正確答案為 (D)。

### 172–175 訊息

Please be advised that our annual company workshop will take place this year on Saturday, April 30. I know many of you will be disappointed that we are holding the workshop on a weekend, but we really had no choice this year. You will be happy to know, however, that all employees may choose any day the week after the workshop to leave work at lunchtime, except Thursday.

Each of you will have received a copy of a report this morning. We ask that you read each of the case studies contained in the report carefully prior to the workshop. Also, this year, we are asking each of the supervisors of the five departments to prepare and give a 10-minute presentation. The presentation should cover the strategies discussed during last year's workshop and how they were implemented throughout the past year.

We will be having a special guest join us this year. Joan Mitchell, whom you all know for having just recently won the Businessperson of the Year Award, will be joining us in the morning to talk about marketing tips that have helped her during her career and to lead group bonding sessions. While you enjoy your lunch, I will be presenting on client management, followed by the presentations from each of the department supervisors.

We are planning to have light cocktails and snacks available at the end of the workshop for those of you who do not need to rush home.

Thanks,
Gregory A. Manning
Manager

請留意，公司年度研討會今年將在4月30日週六舉行。我知道很多人對於要在週末舉行研討會感到失望，但今年真的別無選擇。不過，想必您也會很開心得知，所有員工都可以在研討會結束後的下一週，選擇任一天的中午過後進行補休，除了週四以外。

各位今天早上將會收到一份報告副本。我們請您務必在參加研討會前，仔細讀過報告中所提到的每項個案研究。今年我們也將要求五個部門的主管準備10分鐘的簡報。其中必須提到去年研討會所討論過的各項策略，和它們在過去一年來落實的成效如何。

今年將有位特別來賓。眾所皆知最近才榮獲年度最佳商務人士獎的瓊安‧米契爾，將會在早上進行演講，分享她從業以來受用的市場策略，以及帶領「團隊凝聚」場次。每位主管報告後，我會在各位享用午餐時，簡報顧客關係管理的情形。

研討會的尾聲，我們也準備了簡單的雞尾酒和小餐點，給不趕著回家的各位享用。

感謝，
經理 格里高利‧A‧曼寧

**詞彙** annual 年度的　workshop 研討會　take place 舉行　case study 個案研究
prior to . . . 在……前　supervisor 主管　cover 提到　implement 落實
group bonding 團隊凝聚　rush home 趕著回家

**172**

**What is Mr. Manning's main purpose for writing this message?**

(A) To prepare cocktails and snacks for staff
(B) To introduce Joan Mitchell to everyone
(C) To ask supervisors to prepare presentations
(D) To give information about an annual event

曼寧先生寫這封訊息的目的為何？

(A) 為員工準備雞尾酒和小點心
(B) 介紹瓊安·米契爾給大家
(C) 請主管準備簡報
(D) 提供年度活動的有關資訊

文章的目的通常出現在一開始的部分。根據「Please be advised that our annual company workshop will take place this year on Saturday, April 30.」可以得知，此則訊息目的是提供公司年度研討會活動的資訊，故正確答案為 (D)。

**173**

**What is NOT true about this year's annual workshop?**

(A) It is again scheduled to be held on a Saturday.
(B) There will be refreshments for the employees at the end.
(C) Client management will be discussed at the workshop.
(D) A guest speaker will join in the morning.

關於今年度的研討會，何者有誤？

(A) 再度在週六舉辦。
(B) 結束前會提供茶點。
(C) 會討論顧客關係管理的情形。
(D) 早上將有客座講者。

(B) 在最後一段的「light cocktails and snacks available」出現；(C) 在第二段的「I will be presenting on client management」出現；(D) 在第三段出現：「We will be having a special guest join us this year. Joan Mitchell . . . will be joining us in the morning」，故這些選項皆不是答案。

而根據「I know many of you will be disappointed that we are holding the workshop on a weekend, but we really had no choice this year.」，可知公司因為別無選擇才將研討會訂於週末，故本題答案為 (A)。

**174**

**In total, how many minutes will the supervisor presentations take?**

(A) 10 minutes
(B) 25 minutes
(C) 30 minutes
(D) 50 minutes

所有的主管簡報總共會花多少分鐘？

(A) 10 分鐘
(B) 25 分鐘
(C) 30 分鐘
(D) 50 分鐘

根據「Also, this year, we are asking each of the supervisors of the five departments to prepare and give a 10-minute presentation.」，五名主管各自準備十分鐘的報告，所以共需花費 50 分鐘，本題正確答案為 (D)。

**What is suggested about Joan Mitchell?**

(A) She is a department supervisor.
(B) She was at the annual workshop last year.
(C) She will be presenting during lunch.
(D) She has been successful in the industry.

文中提到關於瓊安‧米契爾什麼事？

(A) 她是一名部門主管。
(B) 她去年有來參加年度研討會。
(C) 她會在午餐時簡報。
(D) 她是業界成功人士。

根據第三段的第一句：「Joan Mitchell, whom you all know for having just recently won the Businessperson of the Year Award」，可以得知她獲得了年度最佳商務人士獎，應為業界成功人士，故正確答案為 (D)。

## 176–180 電子郵件

| | |
|---|---|
| **To:** evanmoss@linkup.com<br>**From:** justinduncan@comwire.com<br>**Date:** September 14<br>**Subject:** Bank account transfers | 收件人：evanmoss@linkup.com<br>寄件人：justinduncan@comwire.com<br>日期：9月14日<br>主旨：銀行帳戶移轉 |

Dear Mr. Moss,

Before I temporarily relocated to Hawaii, I asked Linkup Bank to transfer my bank account to the branch here on the island. Although I intended to be here for six months, I have completed my research and will be returning home. Can you now transfer my account back to my initial branch, as from today, September 14? When I return, I would also like to apply for a mortgage. I would appreciate some advice on the most suitable mortgage. I have tried to access the home buying page on your website. However, there is a message that says it is being upgraded at present.

Many thanks for your help.
Yours faithfully,
Justin Duncan

親愛的摩斯先生：

在我暫時調往夏威夷以前，曾經請聯上銀行把我的銀行帳戶轉移到夏威夷的分行。雖然原訂計畫是我會在這裡待上六個月，不過我已經完成研究準備回家。您能在今天，也就是9月14日，再把我的帳戶轉回開戶的銀行嗎？等我回去，我也想申請不動產抵押貸款。如果您能給我最適合的建議，我會很感激。我嘗試上您們官網看購屋的頁面。不過上面提到網頁目前還在更新當中。

非常感謝您的協助。
賈斯丁‧鄧肯 敬上

**To:** justinduncan@comwire.com
**From:** evanmoss@linkup.com
**Date:** September 15
**Subject:** Your e-mail message

Dear Mr. Duncan,

Thank you for your e-mail message yesterday. Please note that your bank account has now been restored to the original branch as you requested. Secondly, we will need to discuss your financial circumstances before we can offer you a mortgage. There are many factors to take into consideration including your income, monthly outgoings and existing loans. May I suggest that you make an appointment to see the mortgage advisor regarding this matter at the Bradford branch when you have a convenient time? Lastly, I must apologize for the error on the website. We are currently upgrading the system and have had to take the page you are seeking off-line until the upgrades have been completed. We hope it will be operational within two days.

Kind regards,
Evan Moss
Customer Service Representative

---

收件人：justinduncan@comwire.com
寄件人：evanmoss@linkup.com
日期：9月15日
主旨：您的電子郵件訊息

親愛的鄧肯先生：

感謝您昨天的來信。請留意，您的帳戶已經如您所需，回歸到原先的銀行分行了。再者，在提供您不動產抵押貸款前，我們必須先討論您的財務狀況。您的收入、月開銷和目前所負擔的貸款，都必須列入考量。我想向您建議，如果時間允許的話，是否可以和布拉福分行專職不動產抵押貸款的專員，約時間討論相關事宜？最後，關於官網的問題，我必須和您致歉。系統目前正在更新，不得不把您所查詢的頁面暫時撤下，等到更新完成後會再重新上線。我們希望網頁可以在兩天內回復運作。

祝好，
客服代表
伊凡・摩斯

---

**詞彙** relocate 調職　transfer 轉移　Initial 原先的　mortgage 不動產抵押貸款　at present 現在
restore 回歸　financial circumstances 財務狀況　take sth into consideration 將某事列入考量
outgoings 開銷　operational 運作的

**176**

**What is the purpose of the first e-mail?**

(A) To complain about a transaction
(B) To close an account in Bradford
(C) To transfer money to a third branch
(D) To change an arrangement with a bank

第一封電子郵件的目的為何？

(A) 抱怨某筆交易
(B) 關閉在布拉福分行的帳戶
(C) 將錢轉給第三方分行
(D) 和銀行修改個人設定

第一則電子郵件提到「I asked Linkup Bank to transfer my bank account to the branch here on the island. . . . Can you now transfer my account back to my initial branch, as from today, September 14?」，表示一開始因為外派，要求銀行將帳戶轉往分行，現在希望再轉回原行，故正確答案為 (D)。

**What most likely is true of Mr. Duncan?**

(A) His permanent residence is in Bradford.
(B) His transfer to Hawaii was for a year.
(C) He is renting an apartment.
(D) He had previously worked for Linkup.

關於鄧肯先生，何者最可能為真？

(A) 他的永久居留地在布拉福。
(B) 他轉調夏威夷為期一年。
(C) 他正在租一間公寓。
(D) 他曾在聯上銀行工作。

第一則電子郵件中，鄧肯先生解釋因為結束外派，即將回家，故要求將銀行帳戶從分行轉回原行時，說了「Can you now transfer my account back to my initial branch?」，並表示結束外派回來之後，想要申請貸款。

第二則郵件則說了「Please note that your bank account has now been restored to the original branch as you requested.」，表示帳戶已回到原行，並針對貸款回覆道：「May I suggest that you make an appointment to see the mortgage advisor regarding this matter at the Bradford branch when you have a convenient time?」，建議鄧肯先生到時與布拉福分行的專員討論諮詢，綜合上述可知「initial branch」與「original branch」指的都是「Bradford branch」，故可推測鄧肯先生的原居住地應為「Bradford」，故正確答案為 (A)。

## 178

**What does Mr. Moss suggest that Mr. Duncan should do?**

(A) Call the Hawaii branch for advice
(B) Contact the IT department for help
(C) Close his account
(D) Meet with one of the bank's lending officers

摩斯先生建議鄧肯先生怎麼做？

(A) 電洽夏威夷分行請求建議
(B) 聯繫資訊部門請求協助
(C) 關閉他的帳戶
(D) 和銀行的貸款專員見面

根據「May I suggest that you make an appointment to see the mortgage advisor regarding this matter at the Bradford branch when you have a convenient time?」可知，摩斯先生建議鄧肯先生於方便的時間前往布拉福分行，並向此處的專員諮詢貸款事宜，故正確答案為 (D)。

## 179

**What is NOT mentioned as a factor that Mr. Duncan should consider in deciding on a mortgage?**

(A) His monthly expenditure
(B) The amount of his salary
(C) The number of existing loans he may have
(D) The length of time he would need to repay

鄧肯先生申請不動產抵押貸款，何者不必列入考量？

(A) 他的月開銷
(B) 他的薪水
(C) 他現在有的貸款金額
(D) 他還款時間會為期多久

從回信中的「There are many factors to take into consideration including your income, monthly outgoings and existing loans.」，可以得知銀行客服人員摩斯女士告訴了鄧肯先生，貸款前須考慮所得、支出與既有貸款狀況，因此未被提及的只有 (D)，故本題正確答案為 (D)。

**180**

In the second e-mail, the word "matter" in line 6, is closest in meaning to

(A) concern
(B) substance
(C) result
(D) oversight

在第二封電子郵件，第六行的「matter」，最接近下列哪個意思？

(A) 關心的事
(B) 物質
(C) 結果
(D) 疏忽

該句「May I suggest that you make an appointment to see the mortgage advisor regarding this matter . . .」中的「matter」意思為「事件」、「問題」，故選項中最接近的為 (A)。

## 181–185 廣告和電子郵件

### Sale of the year! DON'T MISS OUT!

You all know it's sale season, and Brady's Bargain Bin is having the biggest sale of them all! You have to see it to believe it! Here are just a few of our bargain deals:

- 50% off our entire line of TVs, featuring the most popular brands in today's market. We have all kinds, from hand-held portable TVs to mega screen monsters, all for half off! Whatever kind of TV you are looking for, look no further than Brady's.

- Sampson washer/dryers for only $1000. Sound too good to be true? These popular products usually sell for up to $2500, but we're selling them for less than half that price! We have all of the latest models, and we'll even ship them right to your front door free of charge!

- Top-end cameras and camcorders up to 75% off! That's right—75%! All of our stock of recording devices needs to go, which is music to your ears. What's more—if you buy one of our cameras or camcorders, we'll throw in a black canvas bag you can carry it around in.

So hurry on down to Brady's Bargain Bin. These deals will only last for five more days!

### 年度特賣！不容錯過！

您熟悉的特賣季來了，貝萊迪特賣區將舉辦超級大拍賣！眼見為憑！這裡提供幾項優惠商品：

- 各式名牌電視通通五折，不管是可攜式電視還是超大螢幕，一律半價！不論您在找什麼型號，千萬不要錯過貝萊迪。

- 山普森洗／烘衣機只要1000美元。好得不像真的吧？市售價通常高達2500美元，我們這邊居然半價不到！這裡有最新型號，甚至免運費送貨到府。

- 頂級相機與可攜式攝影機下殺至2.5折！沒錯—2.5折！攝錄器材庫存大出清，何其悅耳的好消息。更讚的是，任購一台相機或攝影機，隨機附贈黑色帆布攝影包，方便您外出攜帶使用。

火速趕來貝萊迪特賣區一探究竟。特價只會再持續五天！

**From:** hjjang@kmail.net
**To:** jameskim@vogmail.com
**Subject:** Bought a camcorder!

Hey James,

I just got back from Brady's Bargain Bin. The crowd was unbelievable. I'm not going to visit there again anytime soon!

The camcorders they had left were definitely not top-end—even mid-range is a stretch. The prices were pretty cheap, though. I ended up buying the Morson camcorder, which they were selling for $150. I know the reviews say the Kell camcorder is of higher quality, but I had one before, and it barely lasted me two years before breaking apart—definitely not worth the price, which is more than double that of the Morson. For the tripod, I bought the one that comes with the Kell instead of the matching of one for the Morson. That one looks much better than the one for the Morson.

Anyway, I look forward to seeing you soon.
Best,
Hyuk-Joon Jang

寄件人：hjjang@kmail.net
收件人：jameskim@vogmail.com
主旨：買了一台攝影機！

嘿，詹姆斯：

我剛從貝萊迪特賣區回來，人多得難以置信。短期內我不想再去那裡逛了。

他們剩下的攝影機實在不是最頂級的，要我說是中等還嫌太誇張。雖說是很便宜，我最後買了摩森牌攝影機，售價150美元。我知道柯爾牌的品質評價最好，不過我之前用過，勉強撐了兩年就解體了—它幾乎是摩森牌的兩倍貴，完全不值那個價。至於腳架，我買了柯爾牌隨附的而不是摩森牌搭配的，畢竟它看起來好太多了。

總之，期待很快見到你。
祝好，
張赫俊

---

**詞彙** miss out 錯過　bargain 特賣品　deal 交易　entire 全部的　half off 半價
look no further than sth 不要錯過某事；只看眼前的某事即可　the latest 最新的
free of charge 免費　top-end 頂級的　stock 庫存　music to ears 悅耳的消息　throw in 附贈
hurry on 火速趕往　mid-range 中等　stretch 誇大；離譜　tripod 腳架

**181**

### Which of the following is true?

(A) The sale will only last for one more week.
(B) Most of the televisions at Brady's are on sale.
(C) The largest discount mentioned in the ad is for cameras.
(D) Products not mentioned in the ad are not for sale.

### 下列何者為真？

(A) 特賣會只會再持續一週。
(B) 貝萊迪大部分的電視都在特價。
(C) 廣告中提到的最大折扣商品是相機。
(D) 廣告中沒提到的商品都沒有特價。

由於廣告的最後一部份提到：「Top-end cameras and camcorders up to 75% off!」，可知相機與攝影機享有 2.5 折，比起其他 5 折或折價的商品，是有最多折扣的，故正確答案為 (C)。

(B) 從廣告中的「50% off our entire line of TVs」可知，全部的電視都在特價，並非只有大部分特價。

---

## 182

**Which sale products also come with free shipping?**　哪些特賣商品免費送貨到府？

(A) Televisions　　　　　　　　　　　(A) 電視

(B) Washers　　　　　　　　　　　　(B) 洗衣機

(C) Camcorders　　　　　　　　　　(C) 攝影機

(D) Roller skates　　　　　　　　　　(D) 直排輪

廣告中提到洗／烘衣機時，說道：「We have all of the latest models, and we'll even ship them right to your front door free of charge!」，故可知洗／烘衣機享有免費配送服務，正確答案為 (B)。

---

## 183

**How much will the black canvas camera bag cost?**　黑色帆布攝影包要價多少？

(A) $1,000　　　　　　　　　　　　　(A) 1000 美元

(B) 75% off of the normal price　　　　(B) 平常價格的 2.5 折

(C) 50% off of the normal price　　　　(C) 平常價格的 5 折

(D) Nothing　　　　　　　　　　　　(D) 不用錢

廣告在提到相機的部份說了「if you buy one of our cameras or camcorders, we'll throw in a black canvas bag」，故可知布包為附贈品，故本題正確答案為 (D)。

---

## 184

**Why was Brady's Bargain Bin so crowded?**　為什麼貝萊迪特賣區擠滿了人？

(A) There is a sale at Brady's Bargain Bin.　(A) 那裡有特賣會。

(B) The store has just recently opened.　　(B) 店最近才開張。

(C) People came out to see Mr. Jang.　　(C) 大家想看張先生。

(D) The store will close soon.　　　　　(D) 店很快就要關了。

第一則內容為貝萊迪特賣區的促銷活動廣告，且電子郵件上也說：「I just got back from Brady's Bargain Bin. The crowd was unbelievable.」，表示在特賣會見識到大批人潮，故可推測是特賣活動引來人潮，正確答案為 (A)。

---

## 185

**Which of the following is NOT true?**　下列何者為非？

(A) Mr. Jang has never owned a Kell camcorder.　(A) 張先生從未擁有柯爾牌攝影機。

(B) Camcorders and tripods are sold separately.　(B) 攝影機和腳架被分開來賣。

(C) Kell camcorders are more expensive than the Morson brand.　(C) 柯爾牌攝影機比摩森牌來得貴。

(D) Mr. Jang bought the Morson camcorder.　(D) 張先生買了摩森牌攝影機。

---

電子郵件最後一部份提到「I know the reviews say the Kell camcorder is of higher quality, but I had one before . . .」，由此可知張先生曾經擁有過柯爾牌的攝影機，故選項 (A) 為錯誤敘述，本題答案為 (A)。

(B) 郵件中，張先生提及自己買了摩森牌攝影機與柯爾牌腳架，故知道這兩項商品為分開出售；(C) 從「Kell camcorder is . . . definitely not worth the price, which is more than double that of the Morson.」可知，柯爾牌攝影機價格約為摩森牌的兩倍；(D) 可從「I ended up buying the Morson camcorder」得知。

## 186–190 通知、履歷和電子郵件

### Seeking a General Sales Manager

A leading electronics retail chain is looking to hire a bright, diligent, and motivated person to take the position of General Sales Manager, a role that will have the person be in charge of all 22 of our stores throughout Asia. The successful candidate should have a degree from a prominent business school, as well as at least six years of comparable managerial experience, ideally in the electronics retail industry. We primarily sell high-end electronics, so the successful candidate will be someone who is willing and able to grow the market for such products in the Asian region. Candidates must have a valid driver's license and have some experience living in more than one country, as the position will require quite a bit of travel. For anyone interested in the position, please send your résumé (with photograph) and a list of references to mlinton@kmail.com by no later than March 31.

### 誠徵銷售總經理

電子零售連鎖業者領導品牌想要找一位聰明、勤奮、積極的人，接任銷售總經理職位，掌管全亞洲22家分店。合適的應徵者需有著名商學院學歷，且有六年以上類似職務的管理經驗，以電子零售業為佳。我們主要販售尖端電子設備，所以應徵者必須有意願、有能力在亞洲地區，讓產品的市場有所成長。由於該職務不時需要出差，應徵者需持有有效的汽車駕照，並有一國以上的他國居住經驗。有興趣應徵者，請在3月31日前，將您的履歷（附照片）和相關推薦人名單寄到 mlinton@kmail.com。

**Name:** Daniel Shin
**Date of Birth:** November 5, 1981
**Place of Birth:** Seoul, Korea
**Nationality:** American
**E-mail:** dshin@kmail.com

**Education**

| | |
|---|---|
| 1993–1997: | Andover High School |
| 1997–2001: | Harvard University (BA) |
| 2006–2008: | Brussels Business School (MBA) |

**Work Experience**

| | |
|---|---|
| 1995–1997: | Andover Deli (Stockroom) |
| 1998–1999: | Sandwich Center (Waiter) |

姓名：丹尼爾‧申
生日：1981年11月5日
出生地：南韓首爾
國籍：美國
E-mail：dshin@kmail.com

學歷

| | |
|---|---|
| 1993–1997 | 安多弗高中 |
| 1997–2001 | 哈佛大學（學士） |
| 2006–2008 | 布魯塞爾商學院（商管碩士） |

工作經歷

| | |
|---|---|
| 1995–1997 | 安多弗餐館（倉管） |
| 1998–1999 | 三明治中心（服務生） |

| | | | |
|---|---|---|---|
| 1999–2001: | Pierre Valentine's (Waiter) | 1999–2001 | 皮耶・瓦倫丁的店（服務生） |
| 2009–2010: | Xenith Electronics (Assistant Manager, Hong Kong) | 2009–2010 | 珊尼斯電子（副理，香港） |
| 2010–2012: | Steinway Electronics (Retail Manager, Singapore) | 2010–2012 | 史坦威電子（零售經理，新加坡） |
| 2012–present: | Self-employed | 2012–現在 | 自營業 |

**Other**

I hold a valid driver's license, and I am fluent in Mandarin and Korean.

其他

我持有有效駕照，中文和韓文也很流利。

---

**To:** Gregory Smith
**From:** Matt Linton
**Subject:** Re: General Sales Manager (3 attachments)
**Date:** March 18

收件人：格里高利・史密斯
寄件人：麥特・林頓
主旨：關於：銷售總經理（3個附件）
日期：3月18日

---

Greg,

Thanks again for the wonderful dinner last night. Please also thank Julie and let her know how much I enjoyed the evening!

Anyway, did you have a chance to look at the latest applications for GSM that I sent you this morning? I've attached them here again in case you haven't had time. We have three new candidates. I know we still have some time, but take a look at this Daniel Shin fellow. He looks like he might be perfect for the job. Yes, he's short of one of the requirements from the ad, but he's got everything else and more, right?

The one thing that concerns me is his most recent experience. Self-employed? That has to mean something else. Let's bring him in for an interview and ask him about it. What do you think?

Best,
Matt

格瑞格：

再次感謝昨天美好的晚餐，也幫我向茱莉道謝，告訴她我當晚有多愉快！

對了，你看過今天早上寄給你的資料嗎？關於最近幾位應徵銷售總經理職缺的。怕你先前沒有時間看，我在這封信再次附檔給你。我們有三名新的應徵者，雖然還有時間決定，但你不妨看一下其中一位丹尼爾・申。他看起來很適合這份工作，雖然他有一個條件不符合人事廣告的需求，但他符合其餘的要求，甚至比那更好，對吧？

其中讓我很關切的一點，是他最近期的工作經驗。自營業？應該別有所指。我想讓他來面試，談談這個部分。你覺得呢？

祝好，
麥特

---

**詞彙** leading 領導業界的　electronics 電子業　retail chain 零售連鎖業者　bright 正向的
diligent 勤奮的　in charge of 負責掌管　degree 學歷　prominent 著名的　comparable 類似的
high-end 尖端的　valid 有效的　driver's license 駕照　résumé 履歷　reference 推薦人
no later than 在（一段時間）之前　nationality 國籍　stockroom 倉庫　self-employed 自營業的
attach 附（檔案）　concern 使⋯⋯關切

**186** ---------------------------------------------------------------

**Which of the following is NOT a requirement for applicants?**

(A) A photograph
(B) Relevant work experience
(C) Fluency in Mandarin
(D) A list of references

下列何者並非應徵條件？

(A) 照片
(B) 相關工作經驗
(C) 流利的中文能力
(D) 推薦人名單

第一則內容的最後一句提到：「For anyone interested in the position, please send your résumé (with photograph) and a list of references to mlinton@kmail.com by no later than March 31.」，說明應徵者需附上履歷、照片以及推薦人，但未提及中文能力，故本題正確答案為 (C)。

**187** ---------------------------------------------------------------

**Which requirement is NOT met by Mr. Shin?**

(A) He has only lived in one country.
(B) He does not have six years' managerial experience.
(C) He does not have a driver's license.
(D) He does not have a business degree.

申先生的哪項條件不符？

(A) 他只有住過一個國家。
(B) 他沒有六年的管理經驗。
(C) 他沒有駕照。
(D) 他沒有商學院學歷。

(A) 履歷表上的「工作經歷」顯示申先生曾在香港與新加坡生活過；(C) 履歷表上的「其他」項目提到擁有駕照一事；(D) 履歷表的「學歷」提到「Brussels Business School」，故申先生故有商學院學歷。綜合上述可知，申先生缺乏的是管理經驗，故本題答案為 (B)。

**188** ---------------------------------------------------------------

**What appears to be true about Mr. Linton?**

(A) He thinks highly of Daniel Shin.
(B) He has not yet met Julie.
(C) He is Greg's boss.
(D) He is from Korea.

關於林頓先生，何者為真？

(A) 他很看好丹尼爾·申。
(B) 他沒和茱莉見過面。
(C) 他是格瑞格的上司。
(D) 他來自韓國。

先找出林頓先生為電子郵件的寄件人，再從信件內容中的「. . . take a look at this Daniel Shin fellow. He looks like he might be perfect for the job.」可知，林頓先生認為申先生可能適合該職位，故本題正確答案為 (A)。

**189** ---------------------------------------------------------------

**Why did Mr. Linton attach the applications to his e-mail?**

(A) He forgot to send them to Mr. Smith this morning.
(B) He wants Mr. Smith to show them to Julie.
(C) Mr. Shin's résumé does not include a photo.
(D) He thinks Mr. Smith may not have seen them.

為什麼林頓先生要在電子郵件裡面附加檔案？

(A) 他今天早上忘記一併寄給史密斯先生。
(B) 他想要讓史密斯先生把資料給朱莉看。
(C) 申先生的履歷沒有附照片。
(D) 他覺得史密斯先生可能還沒看過資料。

郵件中提到「. . . did you have a chance to look at the latest applications for GSM that I sent you this morning? I've attached them here again in case you haven't had time.」，可知林頓先生認為史密斯先生可能還未看過資料，故在信件中再次附上，因此本題正確答案為 (D)。

**What does GSM most likely stand for?**

(A) General Sales Manager
(B) Greg's Sales Memo
(C) Global Sales Mechanism
(D) General Staff Management

**GSM 最有可能的意思是？**

(A) 銷售總經理
(B) 格瑞格的銷售備忘錄
(C) 全球行銷機制
(D) 人事總管理

郵件中說到「applications for GSM」，故可推測 GSM 最可能是徵才廣告標題中的「General Sales Manager」，本題正確答案為 (A)。

## 191-195 文章和電子郵件

### More Improvement Ahead

At Wednesday's city council meeting, the Manchester City Council unanimously voted to explore options for more renovations to be conducted on city infrastructure. According to Michael Mann, the City Treasurer, the recent renovation of the Manchester Public Library surprisingly came in significantly below budget. Council members, therefore, decided to put together a short list of other improvement projects that could be completed with the excess funds.

The most well-received suggestions include adding a wheelchair ramp to Manchester Community Center, replacing broken streetlamps in downtown Manchester, and repairing the parking areas in Manchester Park. According to Mr. Mann, the council has decided to open the decision up to public opinion. Those interested in putting forth their ideas may do so at the next council meeting on Wednesday, April 22 at 5 P.M. or can send an e-mail to City Hall by no later than April 29. After April 29, the city planning committee will put before the council a final list for discussion. A final decision is expected shortly thereafter.

### 更多整建計畫

曼徹斯特市市議會在週三的會上一致通過，以研擬方案來整治市區的基礎建設。根據市府財政局長麥克·曼恩的說明，最近正在整建的曼徹斯特公共圖書館，其花費出乎意料地遠低於預算，所以市議員決定整理一份短清單，將剩餘經費挹注在其他改善計畫上。

目前最多人提出的建議包括：增設曼徹斯特社區中心的無障礙坡道、更換曼徹斯特市中心壞掉的路燈，以及整修曼徹斯特公園的停車場。曼恩先生表示，市議會決定要再諮詢民意。想進一步表達意見的民眾，可在下週三4月22日下午五點出席議會會議，或者在4月29日前寫電子郵件到市府信箱。市政規畫委員會將在4月29日後彙整一份最終清單，呈報給議會討論。議會將在短期內做出決議。

---

**From:** sshort@hostmail.com
**To:** citycouncil@manchester.org
**Date:** April 24
**Subject:** Improvement projects

**寄件人：** sshort@hostmail.com
**收件人：** citycouncil@manchester.org
**日期：** 4月24日
**主旨：** 整建計畫

---

Dear City Council Members,

I understand that you are accepting suggestions for improvement projects to city facilities. I had a doctor's

親愛的市議員：

我知道針對市區設施的整建計畫，市議會正在做詢意見。我當天預約了看

appointment, so I was not able to attend the council meeting on Wednesday, but I wanted to express my strong support for replacing broken streetlamps in the downtown area. I work downtown, and when I get off work late, I've noticed that quite a number of streetlamps are in need of replacement. The dark streets are actually a bit frightening. Brightening the streets again should bring more people downtown and reduce crime. This will benefit all of the residents of Manchester. I hope that you will choose this project.

Susan Short

診，因此不克出席週三的議會，但我想表達我強烈支持替換市中心壞掉的路燈。我在市中心工作，下班時間較晚的時候，我注意到很多路燈需要換了。街道很暗確實有些恐怖。讓街道更明亮，可以吸引更多人來市區，也能減低犯罪發生。這對曼徹斯特的全體市民都好。希望您會選擇這項計畫。

蘇珊·秀特

---

**From:** mchoi@hostmail.com
**To:** citycouncil@manchester.org
**Date:** April 27
**Subject:** City projects

寄件人：mchoi@hostmail.com
收件人：citycouncil@manchester.org
日期：4月27日
主旨：市政計畫

---

To Whom It May Concern,

Finally, a renovation project that was actually completed under budget. Although the public library mostly to be young adults and parents with young children that go to the library. I was hoping we could use the leftover funds on a project that would benefit the senior citizens of Manchester.

The community center is where most older citizens gather, and it is a crime that there are no wheelchair ramps at the entrance to the center. Many of the citizens that frequent the center are in need of wheelchair assistance and have difficulty or need assistance from others just in order to get into the building. Choosing this as the improvement project would really be applauded by people who didn't feel they gained much from the renovation of the library. It is important that the chosen project benefit the entire Manchester community. Thank you for your attention.

Milton Choi

此致有關人士：

總算有項整建計畫在預算內完成。雖然曼徹斯特公共圖書館向所有人開放，不分老少都可以去使用，但還是年輕人和帶著小孩的父母居多。我希望我們可以把剩下的預算，用來照顧曼徹斯特的年長市民。

社區中心是最多年長市民聚集的地方，入口處卻沒有無障礙坡道，這跟犯罪沒有兩樣。很多去那裡的人都需要使用輪椅，他們經常遇到困難，或必須仰賴他人協助才能進到裡面。選擇這項整建計畫，肯定能讓沒有感受到圖書館整建好處的市民大為讚賞。做出能嘉惠曼徹斯特整體社區的計畫很重要。感謝您的關心。

米爾頓·崔

---

**詞彙** city council 市議會　unanimously 意見一致地　conduct 進行　infrastructure 基礎建設　treasurer 財政局長　put a list 列出清單　excess fund 過多的經費　ramp 坡道　put forth 表達　committee 委員會　discussion 討論　thereafter 那之後　facility 設施　doctor's appointment 約診　get off work 下班　people of all ages 各年齡的人們　leftover 剩餘的　applaud 讚賞

**191**

**Why does the city of Manchester have funds available?**

(A) The city council raised taxes last year.
(B) It received a generous donation.
(C) It canceled a renovation project.
(D) Its previous project cost less than expected.

為什麼曼徹斯特市有預算可用？

(A) 市議會去年加重課稅。
(B) 它接獲鉅額捐款。
(C) 它取消了一項整建計畫。
(D) 上一個計畫的開銷比預期來得少。

根據第一篇的文章內的「the recent renovation of the Manchester Public Library surprisingly came in significantly below budget」可知，由於整修圖書館的花費低於預期，故有了多餘的經費能進行其他項目的整建，故本題正確答案為 (D)。

**192**

**In the article, the phrase "put before" in paragraph 2, line 7, is closest in meaning to**

(A) move fast
(B) do first
(C) provide to
(D) place on top

文章中第二段、第七行的「put before」最接近下列哪個意思？

(A) 快點移動
(B) 首先做
(C) 提供給
(D) 置於最上方

原句為：「After April 29, the city planning committee will put before the council a final list for discussion.」，表示委員會將彙整最終清單，並交給議會討論，故從前後文能夠推敲此處應有「提交」之意，故正確答案為 (C)。

另外，「put sth before sb」即有正式地提交意見、提案給某人考慮的意思。

**193**

**When did Ms. Short have a doctor's appointment?**

(A) April 22
(B) April 24
(C) April 27
(D) April 29

秀特女士預約什麼時候看診？

(A) 4 月 22 日
(B) 4 月 24 日
(C) 4 月 27 日
(D) 4 月 29 日

根據秀特女士撰寫的電子郵件，其中說到「I had a doctor's appointment, so I was not able to attend the council meeting on Wednesday」，再對照第一篇文章最後的「the next council meeting on Wednesday, April 22 at 5 P.M.」可以得知，會議將在 4 月 22 日舉行，而秀特女士當天有預約看診故無法與會，所以正確答案為 (A)。

**What does Mr. Choi mention in his e-mail about Manchester Public Library?**

(A) It hasn't been renovated for years.

(B) It is used mainly by young citizens.

(C) It has many good programs for senior citizens.

(D) It is in need of further renovations.

崔先生在電子郵件中提到關於曼徹斯特公共圖書館什麼事？

(A) 已多年未整修。

(B) 主要是年輕市民在用。

(C) 提供給年長者很多好課程。

(D) 需要更多整修。

崔先生撰寫的電子郵件在第二句便提到：「it tends mostly to be young adults and parents with young children that go to the library.」，前往圖書館的族群多為年輕人，所以本題正確答案為 (B)。

**On what point would Mr. Choi and Ms. Short most likely agree?**

(A) The chosen project should be beneficial to the entire community.

(B) The city should save the extra funds instead of doing a project.

(C) The city council should push back the deadline for receiving public opinions.

(D) The downtown streetlamps are not really in need of replacement.

看起來，崔先生和秀特女士都同意的論點為何？

(A) 選定的計畫要對社區整體有幫助。

(B) 市府應該要省下多出的經費，而不是執行計畫。

(C) 市議會應該延後徵詢民意的截止日期。

(D) 市中心的路燈不是真的需要替換。

秀特女士在郵件倒數第二句說了「This will benefit all of the residents of Manchester.」，崔先生也在同樣在郵件倒數第二句提到「It is important that the chosen project benefit the entire Manchester community.」，可見兩人都認為整建計畫需造福全社區，故本題正確答案為 (A)。

(B) 申先生建議裝設無障礙坡道，秀特女士則建議更換路燈，兩人並未提及省下經費一事；(C) 全文未提及此事；(D) 根據秀特女士，「quite a number of streetlamps are in need of replacement」，故路燈確實需要更換。

## 196–200 文章和電子郵件

Over the past two days, our two local high schools (Grand Park and Fontana) came together to put on a joint fundraising festival to help raise funds for those affected by the recent devastating earthquake that left more than 30,000 people homeless in Ridgewood.

Never before in our community have the two schools joined together to hold a charity event, and it was a smashing success! The schools were able to raise more than $150,000 to help the disaster victims. Mayor Jeremy Irons graciously accepted the money, thanking

過去兩天，當地的兩間高中（大園和方塔納）聯合舉辦了募款活動，協助募款給最近受到毀滅性的大地震影響，而無家可歸的三萬多名里奇伍德的居民。

本社區兩間學校先前從未聯手舉辦慈善活動，這次卻非常成功！學校為受災戶募款超過15萬美元。市長傑瑞米‧艾隆斯心懷感激收下捐款，向所有參與活動的學校成員致謝，並承諾會把所有捐款拿來替災民蓋新家。

each member of the two schools who participated in the event, and he promised that the entire amount would go towards constructing new homes for the victims of the earthquake.

Those who attended the two-day festival will have a few memories they will never forget. Groups of students put on quite a show on the stage at Fontana High School, consisting of unforgettable song and dance performances, comedy skits, and dramatic plays. Each performance was done by a group intentionally composed of students from both schools. This was to symbolize the need for all of us to join together in times of difficulty. There was also a basketball tournament that took place at Grand Park High School on Sunday. Non-student members of our community were also free to take part in the tournament, and everyone said they had a blast.

For the most popular event at the festival, however, the karaoke singing competition on the second day. Contestants were staff and students from each school. One of the students from Fontana High School, Mark Saint, ultimately won the competition, and from the sounds of the cheering, you could tell it wasn't close. When speaking at the closing of the festival on Sunday evening, Mayor Irons emphasized how proud he was of the entire Ridgewood community. This paper would also like to thank everyone involved for providing a ray of hope during what would otherwise be a dark time.

---

參加這兩天活動的人，肯定留下了難以忘懷的回憶。學生團體在方塔納高中的舞台上表現精采，帶來難忘的歌舞表演、喜劇小品和戲劇。每項演出都是特地由兩校同學所共同參與，象徵人溺己溺、共體時艱的精神。週日在大園高中也舉辦了籃球聯賽。不是學生的社區民眾也開放參加。每個人都說自己玩得很盡興。

然而，最受歡迎的活動莫過於第二天的卡拉OK大賽。參賽者是兩間學校的教職員和學生。方塔納高中的同學馬克·聖特最終勝出，從歡呼的聲響，就能得知比數懸殊。週日傍晚活動閉幕式上，市長艾隆斯強調，他為里奇伍德全體市民感到很驕傲。這篇文章也感謝所有與會者，在他人深陷黑暗時，不吝給予希望之光。

---

**From:** Jeremy Irons
**To:** pjones@fontana.co.edu;
mthacher@grandpark.co.edu
**Subject:** Thank you so much!
**Date:** Tuesday, October 1

---

Dear Priscilla and Mary,

I wanted to thank both of you again for your incredible efforts and success this past weekend. You have brought so much joy to our community by collaborating on this amazing event. Please take a moment during your next school day to pass on my appreciation to everyone who took part.

---

寄件人：傑瑞米·艾隆斯
收件人：pjones@fontana.co.edu;
mthacher@grandpark.co.edu
主旨：非常感謝！
日期：10月1日，週二

---

親愛的普莉西雅和瑪麗：

我想再次感謝兩位的驚人付出，上個週末很成功。兩位合作的精彩活動，為社區帶來很多歡樂。也請兩位找一天上學日，抽空幫我向所有參與者再次傳達感謝之意。

Unfortunately, all-day meetings kept me from joining in the festivities on Saturday, but I was told it was a lot of fun—I heard great things about the display of world foods even though I missed it. That was truly a great idea!

I know Sunday was wonderful because I was there to take it all in. Mary, that Mark is quite a talent. Maybe we will see him on television someday! He could make a good musician, and a proud alumnus of Grand Park High School. Anyway, again, my heart-felt congratulations. On behalf of Ridgewood, I thank both of you.

Jeremy Irons, Mayor

---

**From:** marksaint@kmail.net
**To:** judithsaint@kmail.net
**Subject:** I Won!

---

Hi Mom,

Guess what? I won! I still can't believe it. I was pretty nervous up there. Once I got going, though, I was able to relax a bit. I sang *Imagine* by John Lennon, and I think it was a good choice.

The guys and I are going to go out to celebrate while the feeling is still fresh. We might be a little bit late, so don't wait up. Don't worry—I'll be home before 11.

Love,
Mark

---

很遺憾整天的公務會議，讓我沒能參與週六的活動。不過我聽說非常好玩──各國美食展據說很棒。雖然我錯過了，但這真是很棒的創意！

週日好極了，這我就知道了，因為我有幸共襄盛舉。瑪麗，那位馬克真是個人才。也許有一天我們會在電視上看到他！他會成為很好的音樂人，也會是大園高中的傑出校友。總之，我衷心祝福。我也代表里奇伍德向兩位致謝。

市長傑瑞米·艾隆斯

---

寄件人：marksaint@kmail.net
收件人：judithsaint@kmail.net
主旨：我贏了！

---

嗨，媽媽：

猜得到嗎？我贏了！我還是沒有辦法相信。我上場時很緊張。不過，比賽一開始我就放鬆了一點。我唱的是約翰藍儂的《想像》，我想這是個好的選擇。

我和大家想趁著開心的感覺還在去外面慶祝一下。可能會比較晚回家，就不要等我了。不要擔心，我11點前會到家。

愛妳，
馬克

---

**詞彙** put on 舉辦　fundraising 募款的　charity event 慈善活動　smashing 極好的　graciously 感激地　put on a show 帶來表演　consist of 由……組成　intentionally 特意地　join together in times of difficulty 共體時艱　tournament 聯賽　take place 發生　take part in 參加　have a blast 玩得盡興　contestant 參賽者　a ray of hope 希望之光　effort 付出　collaborate 合作　all-day 整天的　alumnus 校友　heart-felt 衷心的　wait up 等待而不睡

**196** -------------------------------------------------------------------------

**In the first e-mail, the phrase "took part" in paragraph 1, line 3, is closest in meaning to**

(A) attended
(B) enjoyed
(C) achieved
(D) completed

在第一封電子郵件中，第一段、第三行的「took part」最接近下列哪個意思？

(A) 參與
(B) 享受
(C) 獲得
(D) 完成

原句「Please take a moment during your next school day to pass on my appreciation to everyone who took part.」表示要向參加活動的人致上感謝，選項中只有 attend 同樣表達參與、出席活動，故本題正確答案為 (A)。

**197** -------------------------------------------------------------------------

**Which of the following happened first?**

(A) The mayor, Mr. Irons, attends the fundraiser.
(B) The local residents take part in the basketball tournament.
(C) Mark Saint sings "Imagine" in the singing contest.
(D) A variety of world foods are displayed in the festival.

下列哪件事情最先發生？

(A) 市長艾隆斯先生出席募款活動。
(B) 當地居民參加籃球聯賽。
(C) 馬克‧聖特在歌唱比賽裡唱《想像》。
(D) 活動上展示各國料理。

(A) 根據第一封郵件的「Unfortunately, all-day meetings kept me from joining in the festivities on Saturday」與「I know Sunday was wonderful because I was there to take it all in」可以得知，市長未出席週六的活動，只參加了週日的，所以本選項描述的事件為週日發生。

(B) 從文章的「There was also a basketball tournament that took place at Grand Park High School on Sunday」可知，籃球聯賽在週日舉行；(C) 從「the karaoke singing competition on the second day」中，可以得知歌唱比賽也在週日舉行。

(D) 第一封郵件中，市長曾說：「Unfortunately, all-day meetings kept me from joining in the festivities on Saturday, but ... I heard great things about the display of world foods」，表示各國美食展發生在週六。由於 (A)、(B) 與 (C) 皆為週日的活動，本題正確答案為 (D)。

**198** -------------------------------------------------------------------------

**On what day did the event begin?**

(A) Tuesday
(B) Monday
(C) Sunday
(D) Saturday

活動從哪一天開始？

(A) 週二
(B) 週一
(C) 週日
(D) 週六

在市長撰寫的郵件中提到：「I wanted to thank both of you again for your incredible efforts and success this past weekend.」並在接下來的內容提及週六、週日舉辦的活動，故正確答案為 (D)。

**According to the article, what mistake did Mr. Irons make?**

(A) He thought they had raised only $100,000.

(B) He wasn't able to attend the event on Saturday.

(C) He thought Mark Saint attended Grand Park High School.

(D) He addressed his e-mail to Judith Saint.

根據文章，艾隆斯先生搞錯了什麼？

(A) 他以為募款只募了 10 萬。

(B) 他週六沒辦法參加活動。

(C) 他以為馬克·聖特是大園高中的學生。

(D) 他把電子郵件寄給了茱蒂絲·聖特。

艾隆斯在郵件中提到：「He could make a good musician, and a proud alumnus of Grand Park High School.」，代表他認為馬克是大園高中的學生，但是根據文章報導中的「One of the students from Fontana High School, Mark Saint」，馬克其實是方塔納高中的學生，所以本題答案為 (C)。

**In the second e-mail, what is implied about Mark?**

(A) He is disappointed about not winning the contest.

(B) He was on a TV program.

(C) He has sung "Imagine" before in other contests.

(D) He went out with his friends after the festival.

第二封電子郵件提到了馬克什麼事？

(A) 他很失望輸掉了比賽。

(B) 他上了電視節目。

(C) 他之前曾在其他比賽中唱過《想像》。

(D) 活動後他和朋友外出。

在郵件中馬克寫道：「The guys and I are going to go out to celebrate」，表示他和朋友一起出去慶祝贏得歌唱比賽，由此可知本題正確答案為 (D)。

# ACTUAL TEST
# 4

## PART 5

**101**

Because the regular building inspection will be conducted, please use the side ------ to the main lobby for next week.

(A) entering
(B) entered
(C) entrance
(D) to enter

題型 位置──名詞
翻譯 因為要進行例行性的大樓安全檢查，下週請從側門進入大廳。
詞彙 regular 例行的
inspection 檢查

先注意只有名詞可當作及物動詞 use 的受詞，並可受形容詞 side 修飾，故只有 entrance 符合文意，正確答案為 (C)。

**102**

National Council of Teachers and Education states that all in-state instructors are dedicated to ------ their students from in-school violence.

(A) save
(B) saving
(C) saved
(D) safety

題型 位置──動名詞
翻譯 全國教師教育協會表示，州內所有教員都必須致力於保護學生免於校園暴力。
詞彙 council 協會
state 表示
sb be dedicated to sth
某人致力於某事
violence 暴力

be dedicated to 中，「to」為介系詞，故空格處的動詞應加上「-ing」，正確答案為 (B)。

★請熟記下列兩用法，都是「某人致力於某事」的意思：
sb dedicate oneself to sth
sb be dedicated to sth

**103**

The marketing department must ------ reliable information to other companies for securing the copyrights they have reserved in their book publishing sector.

(A) influence
(B) provide
(C) register
(D) remain

題型 詞彙──動詞
翻譯 行銷部門必須提供可靠的資訊給其他公司，以保障他們在出版部門所保留的版權。
詞彙 reliable 可靠的
secure 保障
copyright 版權
publishing 出版

(A) influence 造成影響；(B) provide 提供；(C) register 登錄；(D) remain 剩下。根據題目，此處句意應為「提供」可靠資訊，故正確答案為 (B)。

## 104

**All the employees must follow the current workplace policies ------ otherwise directed from the manager on-site.**

(A) below
(B) either
(C) unless
(D) while

| | |
|---|---|
| 題型 | **詞彙**──連接詞 |
| 翻譯 | 除非管理者在現場給予其他指示，否則所有員工都必須遵守目前工作場所規定。 |
| 詞彙 | **workplace** 工作場所<br>**policy** 規定<br>**direct** 給予指示<br>**on-site** 在場的 |

(A) below〔介系詞〕〔副詞〕在下；(B) either〔副詞〕也；〔形容詞〕其中一個的、〔連接詞〕或者；(C) unless〔連接詞〕除非；(D) while〔連接詞〕正當、儘管、然而。

本題只要知道四個選項的意思即可作答。句意上，此處應是「除非」獲得指示，否則應該遵守規定，故正確答案為 (C)。

## 105

**If you have any problems with the purchased items, please contact the technical support team and tell them the current conditions -------.**

(A) most precise
(B) precise
(C) more precise
(D) precisely

| | |
|---|---|
| 題型 | **位置**──副詞 |
| 翻譯 | 如果您所購買的商品發生任何問題，請和技術支援團隊聯繫並確切告知現況。 |
| 詞彙 | **purchased** 購買的<br>**technical** 技術的<br>**current** 當前的　**condition** 狀況 |

觀察題目可知，即使沒有空格，此句也已是完整的結構，所以空格並非必要的要素，故知道此處應填入的是副詞，正確答案為 (D)。

## 106

**Applicants who have more than 5 years of experience in marketing will ------ the opportunity to be promoted to a managerial position.**

(A) give
(B) be given
(C) be giving
(D) have given

| | |
|---|---|
| 題型 | **文法**──被動 |
| 翻譯 | 有五年以上行銷資歷的申請者，將給予機會晉升到主管職。 |
| 詞彙 | **applicant** 申請者<br>**opportunity** 機會<br>**promote** 升職<br>**managerial** 管理的 |

動詞 give 後面需要接續兩個受詞，結構如「give sb sth」；如果加入介系詞，則為「give sth to sb」。

因為空格後面只出現 opportunity 一個受詞，故此處應用被動，表示申請者「被給予」機會，故正確答案為 (B)。

**A marketing director at Samhwa Electronics carefully reviewed the terms of contracts with the huge ------ company, Whale Co., known as the leading enterprise in Canada.**

(A) distribute
(B) is distributed
(C) distribution
(D) distributes

| 題型 | 位置——名詞 |
|---|---|
| 翻譯 | 三華電子的行銷經理細心檢閱和加拿大龍頭企業—威爾物流公司所簽訂的合約條款。 |
| 詞彙 | term 條款<br>contract 合約<br>leading enterprise 龍頭企業 |

名詞 company 前可以代入形容詞、分詞,或代入名詞形成複合名詞,選項中除了 distribution 之外,其他皆為動詞,故正確答案為 (C)。

**Ms. Watson submitted two proposals to encourage employees of Allo-Plus Batteries to create a good working environment, but the management declined to accept -------.**

(A) fewer
(B) one another
(C) either
(D) much

| 題型 | 文法——代名詞 |
|---|---|
| 翻譯 | 華森女士提出兩個方案來鼓勵加把勁電池的員工,以創造良好的工作環境,但都被管理部門婉拒。 |
| 詞彙 | proposal 方案<br>decline 拒絕 |

從句意判讀,女子提出兩個方案,但兩個都被拒絕了,而 either 意為「兩者之間無論哪一個」,故最適合填入空格內,表示兩個方案無論哪個都被拒絕了,故正確答案為 (C)。

(B) one another 是相互代名詞,用在三個以上的人或物,表示其中「兩兩彼此……」的意思。

**109** ----------------------------------------

**Standard Property Realty has benefited financially ------ the well-prepared contract with the worldwide development company.**

(A) about
(B) as
(C) from
(D) for

| 題型 | 文法——介系詞 |
|---|---|
| 翻譯 | 標準不動產公司和一家環球發展公司簽訂了完善的契約,從中獲利良多。 |
| 詞彙 | benefit 獲利<br>financially 財務上地<br>well-prepared 完善的 |

不及物動詞 benefit 有「獲得利益」的意思,故後接介系詞 from 可說明「從何處」獲利,故本題正確答案為 (C)。

注意表示「得到」、「獲得」某物的動詞常常與介系詞 from 一起使用。

**110**

In order to increase sales figures, employees at Mobby Telecoms ------ to work overtime until they recover the former amounts.

(A) to agree
(B) agreeing
(C) have agreed
(D) agreement

| 題型 | 位置──動詞 |
|---|---|
| 翻譯 | 為了增加銷售額，摩比通訊的員工已經同意加班，直到回復到之前的銷售量。 |
| 詞彙 | sales 銷售<br>figures 數字<br>work overtime 加班<br>former 之前的 |

分析句子結構後可知，句中沒有出現動詞，所以空格處應填入動詞 have agreed，注意此處使用現在完成式是為了要強調動作「已經完成」的狀態。本題正確答案為 (C)。

**111**

------- who purchased the brand-new smartphone T-Star 7 in advance online can receive a refund in full if the model is sold out in the early stage.

(A) They
(B) Them
(C) Which
(D) Those

| 題型 | 文法──代名詞 |
|---|---|
| 翻譯 | 如果第一批全新智慧型手機 T 星 7 提早完售的話，那些上網預購的顧客可以取得全額退款。 |
| 詞彙 | brand-new 全新的<br>in advance 提早<br>refund 退款<br>sell out 完售<br>in the early stage 初期 |

空格後方有關係代名詞 who，代表此處應填入的是先行詞。指示代名詞 Those 本來就有「那些人」的意思，此處代入主詞位置，成為「Those who . . .」，意為「那些……的人」，在句意上為最適合的答案，故正確答案為 (D)。

注意在此用法下，those 後方常會有修飾用的關係代名詞 who、分詞 V-ing 或 V-ed 或介系詞片語「with . . .」。

**112**

Over the past seven years, Xvid Clip Productions ------ the rules about reserving the right to protect its own contents.

(A) set
(B) has set
(C) will be setting
(D) to set

| 題型 | 文法──動詞 |
|---|---|
| 翻譯 | Xvid 影像製作公司在過去七年來，已經制定規則以保留自製內容的權利。 |
| 詞彙 | reserve 保留<br>content 內容 |

本題為時態題型，解題關鍵在句內的「時間修飾語」。因為句子缺少動詞，所以空格應填入動詞，故刪去 (D)。再透過「Over the past seven years」可知道，動詞時態應為現在完成式，以表示動作事件從過去持續到現在，故正確答案為 (B)。

**113**

The total damage caused by inside information leakage is ------ to billions of dollars, which is likely to be a third of annual revenue.

(A) profitable
(B) equivalent
(C) considerate
(D) preventable

| 題型 | 詞彙——形容詞 |
| --- | --- |
| 翻譯 | 內部資料外洩所造成的損害,總額相當於數十億美元,約是年營收的三分之一。 |
| 詞彙 | leakage 外洩<br>a third of 三分之一<br>revenue 收益 |

(A) profitable 有益的;(B) equivalent 相等的;(C) considerate 貼心的;(D) preventable 可預防的。

四個形容詞中,可表示「等同於」的只有 equivalent,故正確答案為 (B)。

**114**

The candidates have stated that they accept their respective ------ for their promotions to Lecovo Technology's overseas branches.

(A) venues
(B) registration
(C) nominations
(D) suspension

| 題型 | 詞彙——名詞 |
| --- | --- |
| 翻譯 | 應徵者均表示,可以接受提名指派到樂可沃科技的海外分公司,作為晉升獎勵。 |
| 詞彙 | candidate 應徵者<br>respective 分別的 |

(A) venue 現場、場所;(B) registration 登錄;(C) nomination 提名、候選人;(D) suspension 暫停。

空格處與後方的「to Lecovo Technology's overseas branches」連在一起,可看為是 promotions(晉升獎勵),故應選 nominations 最為合適,表示應徵者覺得被「提名」到海外公司這件事,是具有獎勵意義的事情,故本題正確答案為 (C)。

**115**

Our county offers you exceptional and fantastic attractions such as Sea Land, Character World, and Fun Driving Park, ------ that you have a memorable vacation.

(A) ensure
(B) ensures
(C) ensuring
(D) ensured

| 題型 | 文法——分詞片語 |
| --- | --- |
| 翻譯 | 我們縣有超棒絕佳的景點,像是海洋大地、人物世界和趣味駕駛公園,保證您有個難忘的假期。 |
| 詞彙 | exceptional 超棒的<br>attraction 觀光景點 |

本題為分詞片語,若前後兩句主詞相同,則省略一個,後方的主動動詞改為「V-ing」,若為被動動詞則改為「V-ed」。

此句因為 offer 跟 ensure 主詞皆為 Our county,因此將後方 ensure 改為 ensuring,故正確答案為 (C)。

**116** - - - - - - - - - - - - - - - - - - - - - - - - - - - - - - - - - - - - -

**Employees who have not yet enrolled in the on-the-job training should submit their applications -------.**

(A) previously
(B) immediately
(C) closely
(D) roughly

| 題型 | 詞彙——副詞 |
|---|---|
| 翻譯 | 還沒報名在職訓練的員工應該立刻提出申請。 |
| 詞彙 | enroll in 報名<br>on-the-job training 在職訓練<br>submit 提出<br>application 申請 |

(A) previously 以前；(B) immediately 立刻；(C) closely 仔細地；(D) roughly 大致地。

本句為要求尚未報名活動的人「立刻」提出申請，故空格處應填入 immediately，正確答案為 (B)。

本題也可以從各副詞的文法、字義解題。(A) previously 多搭配過去時態；(C) closely 多與 check（檢查）、look into（調查）等單字一起使用；(D) roughly 則常接續數字，表示粗估的數量。

**117** - - - - - - - - - - - - - - - - - - - - - - - - - - - - - - - - - - - - -

**Economic analysts have devised three ------ approaches to the current problems related to the long-term financial downfall.**

(A) difference
(B) differ
(C) different
(D) differently

| 題型 | 位置——形容詞 |
|---|---|
| 翻譯 | 經濟分析師想出三個不同的方法，來因應當前有關經濟長期不振的問題。 |
| 詞彙 | analyst 分析師<br>devise 構思<br>approach 方法<br>downfall 衰頹 |

空格位於名詞 approach 前，故應代入形容詞 different，本題正確答案為 (C)。

**118** - - - - - - - - - - - - - - - - - - - - - - - - - - - - - - - - - - - - -

**In an effort ------ sales of newly released items in an e-commerce market, the company has suggested doing viral marketing by using various SNS channels.**

(A) increase
(B) increasing
(C) to increase
(D) increasingly

| 題型 | 位置——不定詞 |
|---|---|
| 翻譯 | 為了增加新品在電子商務市場上的銷售，這間公司建議經由多個社群媒體，進行病毒式行銷。 |
| 詞彙 | in an effort to V 為了……（而努力）<br>e-commerce 電子商務<br>viral 病毒的<br>SNS = Social Network Site<br>社群媒體網站 |

全句句意為努力達成某件未來發生的事，故分詞 increasing 與不定詞 to increase 中，要選擇不定詞，本題正確答案為 (C)。

「in an effort to V」為常用用法，建議直接記起來。

## 119

Those who get a refund in full should first contact the sales manager ------ they want to receive it by check.

(A) then
(B) if
(C) despite
(D) shortly

| 題型 | 詞彙──連接詞 |
| --- | --- |
| 翻譯 | 接受全額退費的消費者若欲接受支票退費，必須先聯繫銷售經理。 |
| 詞彙 | check 支票 |

(A) then〔副詞〕當時；(B) if〔連接詞〕如果；(C) despite〔介系詞〕儘管如此；(D) shortly〔副詞〕立即。

選項中只有 if 是可以連結主詞與動詞的連接詞，且句意上也最合適，故本題正確答案為 (B)。

------- you find any errors in those articles for the next issue, please report them directly to the chief editor before publishing them.

(A) Had
(B) Should
(C) Were
(D) Have

| 題型 | 文法──假設語氣 |
| --- | --- |
| 翻譯 | 倘若您發現下一期的文章有任何錯誤，請趕在出版前直接向主編反應。 |
| 詞彙 | issue 一期（刊物）<br>directly 直接<br>chief editor 主編 |

本題考的是作為情態助動詞的 should，此時意思為「萬一」、「如果」，是語氣較強的假設，可直接取代 if 引導後方條件句，故正確答案為 (B)。

## 121

We are sorry to inform you that we cannot use the photo that was sent ------ the application in the mail package.

(A) along with
(B) in addition
(C) on account
(D) instead

| 題型 | 詞彙──介系詞 |
| --- | --- |
| 翻譯 | 抱歉通知您，我們無法使用您在信件中和申請書一起寄來的照片。 |
| 詞彙 | inform 通知<br>mail package 信件 |

選項中，只有 along with 可以直接和名詞連用，且句意上也最適合，故正確答案為 (A)。

★**本題其餘三個選項若要和名詞連用，應如下：**
in addition to N（除……之外）
on account of N（因為）
instead of N（替代）

**122**

Each division and executive at Hans Corporation has a framework document that contains the ------ of responsibilities and accountabilities for each position.

(A) statement
(B) department
(C) increment
(D) enforcement

| 題型 | 詞彙──名詞 |
|---|---|
| 翻譯 | 漢斯企業裡的每個部門和主管都有一套文件架構，其中包括一份正式聲明，寫到每一項職務的責任和擔當。 |
| 詞彙 | division 部門<br>executive 執行團隊<br>framework 架構<br>accountability 責任，擔當<br>position 職位 |

(A) statement 聲明、對帳單、陳述書；(B) department 部門；(C) increment 增加；
(D) enforcement 施行。

上述名詞選項中，含有文書類意思的為 statement，故正確答案為 (A)。

**123**

Giant Mall has newly developed the rapid order processing system to ------ shipping to customers.

(A) obtain
(B) reduce
(C) expedite
(D) increase

| 題型 | 詞彙──動詞 |
|---|---|
| 翻譯 | 巨人商城開發了最新的快速交易處理系統，以便加快出貨給顧客。 |
| 詞彙 | rapid 快速的 |

(A) obtain 獲得；(B) reduce 減少；(C) expedite 迅速執行；(D) increase 使增加。

從題目可知「最新的交易系統」與「出貨給顧客」兩件事情，新系統能夠做的事情一定是有利於顧客的，因此只有填入 expedite 並解釋為「系統可迅速出貨」才符合文意，故正確答案為 (C)。

**124**

------ the firefighters arrive at the scene of the crime, the building will have been totally destroyed by an arsonist.

(A) Because
(B) By the time
(C) In spite of
(D) Furthermore

| 題型 | 詞彙──連接詞 |
|---|---|
| 翻譯 | 消防員趕到縱火的犯罪現場前，大樓將已完全燒毀。 |
| 詞彙 | scene 現場<br>crime 犯罪<br>arsonist 縱火犯 |

(B) by the time〔連接詞〕等到……時；(C) in spite of〔連接詞〕儘管；(D) furthermore〔副詞〕此外。

首先觀察前句的動詞時態為現在式 arrive，而後句為未來完成式 will have been，再根據句意知道，此處的連接詞應和時間有關，為時間副詞子句連接詞，故正確答案為 (B)。

★ **By the time** 是在前後事件發生具「時間差異」時使用，且主要子句的時態常以「完成式」出現，表示「等 A 發生時，B 早已發生了」，較常見以下兩種用法：

By the time S V, S will have p.p.

By the time S V-ed, S had p.p.

**125**

His comments on the article that dealt with the environmental issues ------ the need for the conservation of our ecological environment.

(A) acquire

(B) emphasize

(C) customize

(D) sophisticate

| 題型 | 詞彙——動詞 |
| --- | --- |
| 翻譯 | 針對那篇討論環保議題的文章，他在評論中強調保護生態環境的必要。 |
| 詞彙 | deal with 討論<br>environmental 環境的<br>issue 議題<br>conservation 保護<br>ecological 生態的 |

(A) acquire 得到；(B) emphasize 強調；(C) customize 訂製；(D) sophisticate 老練世故地行事。上述四個動詞選項中，可與主詞 His comments 連用的動詞只有 emphasize，故正確答案為 (B)。

**126**

Last year, New York Modern Art Supplies was relocated to Macy Avenue beyond 42th Street ------ its previous store.

(A) on

(B) from

(C) with

(D) about

| 題型 | 詞彙——介系詞 |
| --- | --- |
| 翻譯 | 去年，紐約現代藝術用品公司從之前的店面搬到比第 42 街更遠的梅西大道上。 |
| 詞彙 | relocate 搬遷<br>beyond 超過<br>previous 之前的 |

(A) on 可用來表示時間點或場所；(B) from 可表示出發點或地點；(C) with 表示道具、方法或對象；(D) about 則出現在前後文相關時。

從 relocate 和 previous store 可知道，此處的介系詞應要具「從某處往另一處」的空間改變的意涵，故選項中只有 from 合適，正確答案為 (B)。

**127**

Our goal is to attract ------ sensitive customers to the item design when they consider purchasing something.

(A) highly

(B) properly

(C) much

(D) far

| 題型 | 詞彙——副詞 |
| --- | --- |
| 翻譯 | 我們的目標是要吸引購物時，對產品設計抱有高敏感度的顧客。 |
| 詞彙 | sensitive 敏感的 |

(A) highly 非常；(B) properly 合適地；(C) much 十分；(D) far 遙遠地、久遠地。

從句意上來看，此處應是要表示「非常」敏感的顧客；much 後應接比較級，才具有強調的意思，而 highly 則可以直接修飾形容詞，故本題正確答案為 (A)。

**128** ----------------------------------------

Many salespeople were disappointed because the sales figures were ------ lower than they expected.

(A) significance
(B) significant
(C) significantly
(D) more significant

| 題型 | 位置——副詞 |
| --- | --- |
| 翻譯 | 很多業務都很失望，因為銷售數字顯著地低於預期。 |
| 詞彙 | salesperson 業務<br>disappoint 失望<br>sales figure 銷售數字 |

本句即使沒有空格也已經是完整的句子，故空格應填入的是修飾用的副詞，正確答案為 (C)。

**129** ----------------------------------------

Before installing the security program on your computer, please delete the former version of any antivirus software as ------as possible.

(A) quicken
(B) quick
(C) quickly
(D) quicker

| 題型 | 文法——比較級 |
| --- | --- |
| 翻譯 | 在你的電腦上安裝安全軟體之前，最好儘快刪掉任何之前安裝的防毒軟體。 |
| 詞彙 | antivirus 防電腦病毒的 |

「as . . . as possible」表示「儘可能……」，其中可代入形容詞或副詞。此題這個片語是在修飾動詞 delete，表示要儘快刪除，故片語中間填入的應為副詞，正確答案為 (C)。

**130** ----------------------------------------

Giantbook Publishing provided Mr. Dany with a full refund ------ there was a trivial printing error on the cover page.

(A) although
(B) as though
(C) whether
(D) if

| 題型 | 詞彙——連接詞 |
| --- | --- |
| 翻譯 | 雖然只是封面上一個很小的印刷失誤，巨書出版仍給予丹尼先生全額退費。 |
| 詞彙 | trivial 微小的<br>cover page 封面 |

(A) although 雖然；(B) as though 就像……一樣；(C) whether 是否；(D) if 如果。從字義上看，空格處最適合填入的是 although，故本題正確答案為 (A)。

## PART 6

| EGE buys FilaGas | 艾克隆海灣能源收購斐樂瓦斯 |
|---|---|
| Exron Gulf Energy announced this morning that it had acquired FilaGas in an effort to gain entry **131** the Permian Basin oil field. EGE spokesperson Jarvis Meeks said they wanted to take advantage of FilaGas' firm foothold in the recently discovered oil-rich area, given FilaGas already operates half a dozen drilling concessions in the basin. **132**. | 艾克隆海灣能源今早宣布收購斐樂瓦斯，以便取得二疊紀盆地油田的開採權。公司發言人賈維斯·密克斯說，他們想要妥善利用斐樂瓦斯在新發現的產油區所建立的穩定基礎，斐樂瓦斯在當地已經有六座鑽油井，而且六座都全力運作。 |
| Ray Littman, an expert in the energy sector, predicts that the acquisition will make EGE the leader in oil exploration in the Permian Basin, head and shoulders above its **133**. EGE's early move also saved the oil giant millions of dollars, as the cost of buying land in the area continues to skyrocket. **134**, land prices per acre in the Delaware field rose from $14,516 to $49,000 in just two years. | 能源領域的專家瑞·利特曼，預測這波收購將讓艾克隆海灣能源擠下其他競爭者，成為二疊紀盆地石油勘探的龍頭公司。由於當地的地價持續飆漲，這次的快動作也讓這個石油巨人省下數百萬美元的土地購買費用。事實上，只不過在過去兩年內，德拉瓦區的地價就從每英畝14,516美元，飆漲到49,000美元。 |

**詞彙** **acquire** 收購　**entry** 進入權　**basin** 盆地　**spokesperson** 發言人　**take advantage of** 利用　**foothold** 穩定基礎　**oil-rich** 產油豐富的　**given (that)** 考慮到　**drilling** 鑽挖　**concession** 許可權　**sector** 領域　**exploration** 勘探　**head and shoulders above sb** 遠遠強過某人　**giant** 產業龍頭　**skyrocket** 飆升　**acre** 英畝　**at full capacity** 全力（運作）

**131** -----------------------------------------------------------

(A) into
(B) with
(C) for
(D) of

(A) 進到
(B) 伴隨
(C) 為了
(D) 屬於

**題型** **詞彙——介系詞**

此題只要看 entry 和後方的地點，即可知道此處介系詞應和 entry 一致，帶有「進入」的意涵，以表示某地的進入權，故正確答案為 (A)。

**132** NEW -----------------------------------------------------

(A) FilaGas is still considering the offer.
(B) All six are drilling at full capacity.
(C) EGE will acquire more companies soon.
(D) The purchase cost is higher than EGE expected.

(A) 斐樂瓦斯還在考慮這項提議。
(B) 六座都全力運作。
(C) 艾克隆海灣能源很快會收購更多公司。
(D) 收購案花的錢比預期來得高。

**題型 填入句子**

前文「FilaGas already operates half a dozen drilling concessions in the basin」若從字面上直翻，意思是斐樂瓦斯已經讓盆地裡六個鑽油井的許可權生效，言下之意即為在當地已有六座鑽油井，故空格處應接續鑽油井的話題，因此最合適的答案為 (B)。

**133** ----------------------------------------

(A) buyers
(B) observers
(C) investors
(D) competitors

(A) 買家
(B) 觀望者
(C) 投資者
(D) 競爭者

**題型 詞彙——名詞**

即使不確定片語「head and shoulders above . . .」的意思，也可從「the acquisition will make EGE the leader in oil exploration」知道，收購後能源公司將成為產業的領頭羊，無人能出其右，故在 above 後應填入 competitors，表示超越競爭者。本題正確答案為 (D)。

**134** ----------------------------------------

(A) In this instance
(B) After all
(C) Despite this
(D) As a matter of fact

(A) 這個案例中
(B) 畢竟
(C) 儘管如此
(D) 事實上

**題型 詞彙——連接副詞**

前句最後提到「the cost of buying land in the area continues to skyrocket」，表示土地成本持續飆升，此句後方又以實際數字解釋上升趨勢，故此處的連接副詞應具有「進一步說明」的意味，故要選 As a matter of fact，本題正確答案為 (D)。

## 135–138 通知

We highly recommend early bookings as flights to the remote Finnish village of Ivalo are very limited. Thomson Airways offers **135** flights to Ivalo direct from the U.K. The rest of the year, one can take Finnair flights from Helsinki. In case you choose to cancel a flight reservation, Thomson requires a seven-day notice, while Finnair only asks for three for your ticket **136** in full. Both airlines serve meals and drinks to first-class travelers for the **137** of the flight. **138**.

因為到芬蘭偏鄉伊瓦洛的航班非常有限，我們強烈建議提早訂票。湯森航空提供從英國直飛伊瓦洛的季節性航班。其餘月分只能搭乘芬蘭國內線，從赫爾辛基前往當地。如果您要取消訂位，湯森航空須預留七天通知期，而芬蘭航空只要求三天，就能給與您的機票全額退費。兩家航空公司的頭等艙旅客在飛行期間，都有提供餐點和飲料。經濟艙則沒有提供這項服務。

**詞彙** booking 預定　flight 航班　remote 偏遠的　in case 萬一，如果　reservation 預約
notice 通知

**135** ----------------------------------------------------------------

(A) season
(B) seasons
(C) seasoning
(D) seasonal

(A) 季節
(B) 四季
(C) 調味
(D) 季節性的

**題型 位置——形容詞**

空格位於名詞 flights 前，故應填入可修飾名詞的形容詞 seasonal，正確答案為 (D)。

**136** ----------------------------------------------------------------

(A) are refunding
(B) will be refunded
(C) to be refunded
(D) had been refunding

(A) 正在給與退款
(B) 將被退款
(C) 能被退款
(D) 過往一直在退款

**題型 文法——不定詞**

以連接詞 while 開始的子句擁有完整的主詞與動詞，且此處沒有其他連接詞，所以不能再代入其他動詞，因此能選的只有 to be refunded，正確答案為 (C)。

**137** ----------------------------------------------------------------

(A) length
(B) degree
(C) site
(D) month

(A) 期間
(B) 度數
(C) 地點
(D) 月分

**題型 詞彙——名詞**

上述四個名詞中，只有 length 適合與表示期間的介系詞 for 及名詞 flight 連用，意為「在飛行期間」，故正確答案為 (A)。

**138** (NEW) ----------------------------------------------------------------

(A) Frequent flyers to Ivalo can fly year-round via Thomson Airways.
(B) This service does not apply to those in the economy class.
(C) Flights to and from Ivalo can be canceled without prior notice.
(D) We recommend morning flights so that they serve meals to all passengers.

(A) 經常來往伊瓦洛的乘客，整年都可以透過湯森航空前往當地。
(B) 經濟艙則沒有提供這項服務。
(C) 如果要取消往返伊瓦洛的機票，不需要提前通知。
(D) 我們建議搭早班飛機，因為機上將提供所有乘客餐點。

**題型 填入句子**

前一句「Both airlines serve meals and drinks to first-class travelers」的重點為餐飲服務以及頭等艙旅客，故此處應接續服務的主題，進階比較頭等艙與其他艙別，故正確答案為 (B)。

**139–142 通知**

## Industrial Park Gets Go-ahead

Drastic changes **139** to the residents of Fairbank. On Monday, a real estate developer, Ultima Holdings, announced that its 30-acre Industrial and Technology Park has been given the go-ahead by the Fairbank Town Council. **140**. The park will include the construction of several high-rise office buildings as well as manufacturing and warehouse facilities. **141** of the acreage will also be devoted to recreational purposes, such as a golf course and a driving range. Most local residents protested during talks on the proposed development, **142** it as a future source of noise, traffic, and pollution.

## 工業園區獲得許可

白岸鎮的居民即將遭逢劇變。地產開發商天涯海角控股，於週一宣布白岸鎮議會已經給予許可，讓他們建設佔地30英畝的工業科技園區。許可案在6月2日週一宣布通過。園區內將建設幾座摩天辦公大樓、工廠和倉儲設施。部分土地也將作為娛樂用途，像是高爾夫球場和練習場。大多數居民在會議間都反對這項提議的開發案，認為它將帶來噪音、交通和汙染問題。

**詞彙** drastic 劇烈的　resident 居民　real estate 房地產　developer 開發商　industrial 工業的
go-ahead 許可　high-rise 高聳的　manufacturing 製造的　acreage （以英畝丈量的）土地
be devoted to . . . 被用於……　recreational 娛樂的　course 球場
driving range 高爾夫球練習場

**139** --------------------------------------------------

(A) will have come　　　　　　　　　　(A) 將已來到
(B) came　　　　　　　　　　　　　　 (B) 已經來到
(C) are coming　　　　　　　　　　　 (C) 正在到來
(D) comes　　　　　　　　　　　　　 (D) 到來

**題型 文法——** 時態

閱讀完整篇文章便可知道，工業園區確定進行開發，但是工程尚未開始，故「drastic changes」尚未產生，因此 (B) 過去式不正確，且因為主詞為複數，所以 (D) 也不正確。

(A) 未來完成式，代表事件從過去一直持續至未來，但是「drastic changes」應該是從現在持續至未來，而 (C) 現在進行式除了用在表示動作進行，也能表示談論未來，故正確答案為 (C)。

**★未來完成式**
句型：will have p.p.
使用時機：動作開始於過去，現在還沒完成，將在未來的某時刻完成
常見搭配片語：by then（到那時）、by that time（到那時）、by the end of the year（今年年底）

**140** (NEW) --------------------------------------------------

(A) The approval was announced on Monday, June 2.　　(A) 許可案在6月2日週一宣布通過。
(B) The plan will be welcomed by the town's members.　　(B) 鎮民將會歡迎這項計畫。
(C) Residents and developers both await the council's decision.　　(C) 居民和開發商都在等議會的決議。
(D) Nonetheless, Ultima Holdings withdrew its plans to develop.　　(D) 然而，天涯海角控股撤回了開發計畫。

題型 填入句子

前句提到，議會於週一給予建設許可，若此處提出準確批准日期為「6月2日」，與前文文意連貫，故正確答案為 (A)。

(B) 從後文的「Most local residents protested」可知多數居民並不贊成此計畫；(C) 前文提及議會已給予開發商許可；(D) 後文詳述開發計畫的細節，看不出有撤回計畫的打算。

**141** ----------------------------------------------------------------

(A) Some
(B) Many
(C) One
(D) Few

(A) 有些
(B) 很多
(C) 一個
(D) 很少

題型 位置——代名詞

此處前句以「The park will include . . .」說明園區內在商業相關建設的規畫，而後文則轉為談論娛樂相關設施，故可知此處適合以「Some of the . . .」表示「某部分的」土地規畫，因此正確答案為 (A)。

**142** ----------------------------------------------------------------

(A) see
(B) sees
(C) seeing
(D) seen

(A) 認為
(B) 認為
(C) 他們把……認為
(D) 被認為

題型 文法——分詞片語

從整句看來，此句逗號前後的兩個動作 protest 與 see，主詞皆為 Most local residents，故可以省略兩句間的連接詞、加上逗號，並將主動態的 see 改為 seeing，使後句成為分詞片語。本題正確答案為 (C)。

## 143–146 信件

July 12
Ms. Amanda Pickwick
Origami Paper Company
278 East Road
Teaneck, NJ 07666

7月12日
阿曼達·皮克維克女士
摺紙紙張公司
07666 紐澤西州提內克市
東路278號

Thank you for your inquiry about purchasing four bottles of Iron Gall Ink from Collins Supply Company. We are happy to inform you that we have the ink in stock and can ship it to you if you fill in the enclosed order form today. **143** . As you are a regular customer of more than two years now, we are also pleased to provide you with a 5 percent discount on this and other **144** orders. **145** ,

感謝您來信詢問購買四瓶柯林斯供應商鐵膽墨水。我們很高興知會您本店還有庫存，只要您今天填寫好隨信附上的訂購表單，我們就能出貨。預期您將在五到七個工作天內收到商品。由於您是常客，兩年多來經常購買我們商品，您這次以及

you can earn store credits with every purchase. When you have **146** store credits, you can use these to purchase other products. This is our way of thanking you for your continued patronage.

Sincerely,
Dave Earnshaw
Customer Relations Manager
Enclosure: #Order Form.pdf

未來的交易都將享有5%的折扣。此外您每一次的購買，都會得到商家點數，累積的點數可以用來兌換其他商品。這是我們感謝您經常光顧的一份心意。

顧客關係經理
戴夫·恩蕭 敬上
附檔：訂單表格.pdf

**詞彙** inquiry〔名詞〕詢問　in stock 有庫存　ship 出貨　fill in 填寫　enclosed 隨信附上的
regular customer 常客　patronage 光顧　calligraphy 書法　package 包裝
business day 工作天

---

**143** NEW

(A) You may want to choose it from our online catalog of calligraphy inks.
(B) However, we will ask you to return the product in its original package.
(C) You can expect that you can receive your order within 5–7 business days.
(D) Unfortunately, we have no records of any order of Iron Gall Ink.

(A) 您或許會想要從我們的線上墨水型錄選購商品。
(B) 不過，我們會要求您以原包裝退貨。
(C) 預期您將在五到七個工作天內收到商品。
(D) 很遺憾，我們沒有任何和鐵膽墨水有關的訂購紀錄。

**題型 填入句子**

空格的前一句提到「we have the ink in stock and can ship it to you if you fill in the enclosed order form today」，可知只要填寫訂購單，公司就會配送貨品，因此空格處應針對訂購後配送流程進行說明，故正確答案為 (C)。

---

**144**

(A) upcoming
(B) preceding
(C) preliminary
(D) sequential

(A) 即將來臨的
(B) 先前的
(C) 初步的
(D) 按順序發生的

**題型 詞彙──形容詞**

此句「we are also pleased to provide you with a 5 percent discount on this and other . . . orders」，表示將為客戶此次的訂單提供折扣，後並說到 other 故最可能表示的是其他「將來的」訂單，正確答案為 (A)。

---

**145**

(A) However
(B) In addition
(C) Nonetheless
(D) Of course

(A) 然而
(B) 此外
(C) 雖然
(D) 當然

163

前句提及折扣優惠，後句則說到點數累積相關內容，故此處的連接副詞應帶有「額外說明」之意，選項中只有 In addition 適合，所以正確答案為 (B)。

**146**--------------------------------------------------------------------------------

(A) accumulates  　　　　　　　　　　　　(A) 累積

(B) accumulating  　　　　　　　　　　　(B) 正在累積

(C) to accumulate  　　　　　　　　　　　(C) 去累積

(D) accumulated  　　　　　　　　　　　　(D) 累積到

題型 **文法**──動詞

此句已經有了 have 故後續只能接 to V，變成「have to V」（必須），或是接 p.p. 變成現在完成式，而根據後文，此處應是使用現在完成式，表示累積點數後便可使用，故正確答案為 (D)。

# PART 7

## 147–148 告示

The Oregon Prime Association (OPA) is opening a local chapter in Eugene in October. This organization will be gathered on every Friday at the Culpepper, 305 Washington Drive, at 8:00 P.M. It is open to the public at any time.

If you are interested in this and want to use public transportation, Eugene Red Bus leads to the site, two blocks away, at the corner of James Boulevard and Fleming Avenue. If you plan to drive yourself, the parking lot, Hopkins Park, is free for all citizens after 7 P.M.

We have a lot of topics for next year's events for our community, so we hope you will be about to join our activities together. For more information about topics and presenters, visit our website at www.opaeugene.org.

奧勒岡首席協會十月將在尤金市開設分會。該組織將在每週五晚間八點舉行聚會，地址是華盛頓大道305號的科爾佩珀。不論何時，都會對外開放。

如果您有興趣，且打算搭乘公共運輸工具前往的話，尤金市紅巴士會停靠在詹姆斯大街和佛萊明大道的轉角，距離這裡兩個街區的站牌。如果您打算自行開車前往，霍普金斯停車場在晚間七點過後，開放市民免費停車。

明年的聚會我們會討論很多有關社區的話題，所以我們希望您能一起加入活動。如果想要了解更多關於主題和講者的資訊，可以上官網www.opaeugene.org查詢。

## 147

**Where would the notice more likely be posted?**

(A) At a community center
(B) At a parking lot
(C) At a local restaurant
(D) At a residential hotel

這則告示最可能貼在哪裡？

(A) 社區中心
(B) 停車場
(C) 當地餐廳
(D) 當地旅舍

本文是有關社區活動聚會的告示，所以最適合張貼在社區中心，故正確答案為 (A)。

## 148

**According to the notice, what is available on the online homepage?**

(A) Some videos regarding local promotion
(B) Procedures about local parking
(C) Documents for the registration
(D) Some details about the meeting

根據這則告示，該協會網頁能找到什麼資訊？

(A) 推廣當地的影片
(B) 當地停車的流程
(C) 報名用的文件
(D) 和聚會有關的一些細節

根據最後一句：「For more information about topics and presenters」，可以得知網頁上會刊登聚會相關的額外資訊，故正確答案為 (D)。

Sigma Network Corporation: 2018 Biennial Event!
Thank you for your interest in the COD Network
Conference at Sigma Network Corp.
Please complete the request form below.

## 2018 COD Network Conference

Millennium Hotel St. Louis
Conference Registration Form
October 10 –14, 2018

| **Name Badge and Mailing Information** |
| (use a separate form for each person) |

Name _____ (for POD database)

Badge Name _____ (this name will appear on your name badge)

Title _____

Department/Unit _____

Institution/Organization _____

Mailing Address

City _____ State/Prov. _____ Postal Code _____

Work Phone _____ Fax _____ E-mail _____

## Conference Registration

| | Early Bird (postmarked by 9/21) | Regular (postmarked after 9/21) | On-site | Registration Amount Enclosed |
|---|---|---|---|---|
| **Member** (must have paid 2018–2019 dues) | $180 | $220 | $240 | $_____ |
| **Non-member** (includes 1 year membership) | $255 | $295 | $315 | $_____ |
| **Student or Retired** | $130 | $160 | $180 | $_____ |
| **One Day Only** ___Thurs ___Fri ___Sat | $130 | $140 | $150 | $_____ |

** If you need to get a temporary parking permit during the conference, please stop by our reception desk and pick it up from our personnel for the event.

西格瑪通信公司：2018年雙年活動！
感謝您有興趣參加西格瑪通信公司舉行的COD網路會議。
請填寫以下的申請表格。

## 2018 年 COD 網路會議
### 會議報名表

聖路易千禧飯店
2018年10月10日到14日

| 名牌和郵遞資訊（每人須分開填寫表格） |
| --- |

姓名_____（作為POD資料庫建檔使用）

名牌_____（將顯示於您的名牌上）

職稱_____

部門／單位_____

機構／組織_____

郵寄地址_____

城市____州／省____郵遞區號____

辦公電話_____傳真_____

電子郵件信箱_____

## 會議登記

| | 早鳥（郵戳早於9月21日） | 一般（郵戳晚於9月21日） | 現場登記 | 報名金額總計 |
|---|---|---|---|---|
| **會員**（須已繳交2018–2019兩年年費） | $180 | $220 | $240 | $____ |
| **非會員**（包括一年期會員） | $255 | $295 | $315 | $____ |
| **學生或退休人士** | $130 | $160 | $180 | $____ |
| **只參加一天** ___週四 ___週五 ___週六 | $130 | $140 | $150 | $____ |

＊＊如果您在會議期間需要臨時停車證，請前往接待處找我們的會議人員索取。

詞彙 **badge** 名牌　**postmark** 郵戳　**due** 會費　**temporary** 臨時的　**personnel** 人員

**149**

**What is implied about the 2018 COD Conference?**

(A) It offers in-advance payers some discounts.
(B) Its members should register for participation online.
(C) It provides the conference with just regular members.
(D) It has been held in St. Louis once a year.

文中提到關於 **2018 COD** 會議什麼事？

(A) 給予提前報名付款的人折扣。
(B) 會員必須在線上登記參加。
(C) 只讓一般會員參加會議。
(D) 一年一度在聖路易舉辦。

從表格中可看到，早鳥票價為 180 美元，比一般定價的 220 美元與現場價的 240 美元都要便宜，故可知早報名的人可獲得折扣，正確答案為 (A)。

**150**

**What will Sigma Network staff do?**

(A) E-mail potential clients their conference details
(B) Accept participants' papers for the conference
(C) Deliver short-term parking permits to attendees
(D) Organize and designate the conference rooms

西格瑪通信公司的員工會做什麼事？

(A) 寄電子郵件給潛在客戶，提供會議的詳細資料
(B) 接受與會者的開會文件
(C) 給與參加者臨時停車證
(D) 安排指定會議室

從前後文可知，最後一句「pick it up from our personnel for the event」中的 it 即為前句的 a temporary parking permit，所以會議人員會發放臨時停車證給與會人員，正確答案為 (C)。

**151–152 電子郵件**

| | |
|---|---|
| **To:** Sales Associates<br>**From:** Richard Steve, General Manager<br>**Date:** October 10<br>**Subject:** Urgent Issue | 收件人：業務專員<br>寄件人：李察·史帝夫總經理<br>日期：10月10日<br>主旨：緊急狀況 |
| Dear Sales Associates,<br><br>Our advertisement in the recent issue of *Cal-State Post* has some errors. It indicates that our date for the half-price sale is November 11 instead of November 1. Although a correction of the error appears in the next month's issue of paper copies, our customers cannot be aware of this error on the Web. Therefore, if they ask whether it is November 1 or November 11 for the sale, first apologize for this inconvenience and then offer them a coupon for 10% off any item they want to buy, at both off-line stores and online ones. If consumers have more questions about it, please direct them to the floor manager. Thank you for your understanding.<br><br>Richard Steve,<br>General Manager, Kingswhite Clothing | 親愛的業務專員：<br><br>我們在最近一期《加州時報》的廣告有誤，將半價特賣會的日期寫成11月11日，而不是11月1日。雖然下個月出刊的紙本會予以更正，但網路上的顧客不會發現這個錯誤。因此，如果他們詢問到底特賣會是在1日還是11日，務必先向顧客表示，我們為帶來的不便深感歉意，並提供他們九折折價券，任何商品不分線上或實體商店，都可使用這張折價卷。如果消費者有更多疑問，請直接轉接給樓層經理處理。感謝您的諒解。<br><br>白王服飾總經理<br>李察·史帝夫 |

詞彙 issue 一期　correction 更正　paper copy 紙本　inconvenience 不便　forward 轉接（電話）

**151**

---

**What is stated about *Cal-State Post*?**

(A) It publishes articles and advertisements every week.

(B) It posted an apology for the error of their promotion date.

(C) It attached a discount coupon on the page of Kingswhite's advertisement.

(D) It misprinted the date of Kingswhite Clothing's sale.

文中提到關於《加州時報》什麼事？

(A) 每週都發行文章和廣告。

(B) 已經為寫錯促銷日期刊出道歉聲明。

(C) 在白王服飾的廣告上附上折價券。

(D) 把白王服飾特賣的日期給印錯了。

從郵件的寄件人可知，這應是白王服飾的公司內部通知，而郵件第一句也點出「Our advertisement in the recent issue of Cal-State Post has some errors. It indicates that our date for the half-price sale is November 11 instead of November 1.」，故可知報紙上誤植服飾特賣的日期，本題正確答案即 (D)。

**152**

---

**What does Mr. Steve require the associates to do?**

(A) Advise customers to discuss extra issues with a supervisor

(B) Tell customers about problems with an item's malfunction

(C) Explain the reason why they made a mistake

(D) Send the correction of the misprinted date to the magazine

史帝夫先生要專員做什麼？

(A) 如顧客有其他疑問，建議他們和主管討論

(B) 告訴顧客某項產品有何不良

(C) 解釋為何出錯

(D) 寄給雜誌修正過後的日期

根據「If consumers have more questions about it, please direct them to the floor manager」，史帝夫先生囑咐業務專員，若顧客有疑問，可轉交給樓層經理處理，故正確答案為 (A)。

153–155 信件

| ANNUAL SPRING MEETING | | 年度春季會議 |
| --- | --- | --- |

**Central Pennsylvania University**     **Mellon Board Room**
**April 13, 2018**                                    **9:00 – 12:00**

**8:30 – 9:00**     Registration & Breakfast

**9:00 – 10:30**   Panel Discussion: Expanding the Teacher
                          Toolbox

Peggy Daniel, Director, Intercultural Communication
Center, & Rebecca Oreto, Associate Professor, Carnegie
University
  *Technology in your hands: using creative materials and
  building academic fluency*

Steve Lin, English Language Program Coordinator,
Chatham University
  *Highlighting some collaborative group activities in a
  "Glee" syllabus*

Jane Piadget, ESL Teacher & ELL Coordinator, Franklin
Regional School District
  *Teacher Technology Tips–Using Puzzlelet.com and
  Mobile Devices*

Christopher Pierce, Instructor, Pittsburgh City
University, English Language Institute
  *Using Jigsaw Puzzle to generate and share vocabulary
  activities*

**10:30 – 11:15**   Interest Groups Gathering Sessions &
                          Networking

**11:15 – 12:00**   General Business Meeting and Elections

**Free to members of Three Rivers TESOL**
**$5.00 for non-members**

Map: http://www.cpu.edu/campusmap/
Directions: http://www.cpu.edu/about/directions.cfm
Parking at the Terrace Parking Lot

Special thanks to Central Pennsylvania University for
hosting our 2018 Spring Meeting!

---

**年度春季會議**

中央賓州大學　梅隆董事會會議室
2018年4月13日　9:00–12:00

8:30–9:00報到＆早餐

9:00–10:30分組座談：擴充教師的
工具箱

- 跨文化傳播中心主任，珮姬‧丹尼爾＆卡內基大學副教授，瑞貝卡‧奧瑞圖〈科技自在手中：運用創意素材及創建知識暢通性〉

- 查塔姆大學英文學程幹事，史帝夫‧林〈團康活動重點初探：以《歡樂合唱團》課程規畫為例〉

- 法蘭克林地區學校，英語為第二外語教學教師＆英語學習課程幹事，珍‧皮亞傑〈教學科技訣竅：使用Puzzlelet.com和行動裝置〉

- 匹茲堡市立大學英語所講師，克里斯多福‧皮爾斯〈運用拼圖來引導、共享詞彙練習活動〉

10:30–11:15團體討論＆人脈拓展

11:15–12:00全體商務大會和選舉

三河英語教學的會員免費
非會員5元

校園地圖：http://www.cpu.edu./campusmap/
怎麼抵達：http://www.cpu.edu/about/directions.cfm
請將車輛停在露天平台停車場

感謝中央賓州大學提供場地舉行2018年春季會議！

---

**詞彙** panel 小組　toolbox 工具箱　intercultural 跨文化的　material 素材　syllabus 課程規畫
jigsaw 拼圖　generate 產生　networking 商業社交

**153**

---

**For whom is the workshop most likely intended?**

(A) Human resources experts
(B) Business analysts
(C) Educational graduate students
(D) New employees at local colleges

這場研討會主要訴求對象是誰？

(A) 人資專家
(B) 商業分析師
(C) 教育研究所學生
(D) 當地大學的新進員工

從「the Teacher Toolbox」、「group activities」、「Teacher Technology Tips」和「vocabulary activities」等關鍵字，可以知道會議上發表的主題皆與教育及教師有關，故判斷會議最可能的受眾為教育相關學系的學生，因此正確答案為 (C)。

**154**

---

**Whose topic involves web-based learning?**

(A) Ms. Daniel
(B) Mr. Lin
(C) Ms. Piadget
(D) Mr. Pierce

誰的主題有談到線上學習？

(A) 丹尼爾女士
(B) 林先生
(C) 皮亞傑女士
(D) 皮爾斯先生

從發表主題來看，「Teacher Technology Tips–Using Puzzlelet.com and Mobile Devices」中，因為出現網址，故最可能和線上學習有關，正確答案為 (C)。

**155**

---

**What is NOT indicated about the workshop?**

(A) It is a half-day event.
(B) It includes free lunch.
(C) It introduces new items.
(D) It may require a fee to attend.

關於這個研討會，何者為非？

(A) 是個為期半天的活動。
(B) 提供免費午餐。
(C) 引介新教學方法。
(D) 可能需要參加費。

議程中未提及午餐資訊，故本題答案為 (B)。

(A) 從時間規畫來看，會議只到中午 12 點，故為半天活動；(C) 從座談主題「Expanding the Teacher Toolbox」即可知會議是在介紹新的教學方法；(D) 從下方的「$5.00 for non-members」可知，非會員須繳交 5 美元的費用。

**156–157 訊息串**

| | | |
|---|---|---|
| **Michelle Lia** 　　　　　　　　　11:01 A.M. <br> Hi, Mr. Miller. I'm at the restaurant, Garcia's. I need to arrange the tables of dessert for the afternoon wedding banquet. But, the door is locked and I left my key at home. | 米雪兒‧萊亞〔上午11:01〕： <br> 嗨！米勒先生。我已到「賈西亞的家」餐廳。我需要安排下午結婚宴會的甜點桌。不過門鎖上了，我又把鑰匙放在家裡。 |
| **Sean Miller** 　　　　　　　　　11:03 A.M. <br> Ms. Savova isn't there? She usually goes to the restaurant early to get the event ready. | 尚恩‧米勒〔上午11:03〕： <br> 薩摩瓦女士不在那嗎？她通常都會提前到餐廳準備活動。 |

| | |
|---|---|
| **Michelle Lia** 11:04 A.M.<br>I see. It doesn't make sense. You are in late today, right? | 米雪兒・萊亞〔上午11:04〕：<br>我知道，這才奇怪呀。你今天會晚到，是嗎？ |
| **Sean Miller** 11:05 A.M.<br>Yes, I am. Now I'm on my way to a meeting with other clients, but I'm 20 minutes early, so I have time to stop by and let you in. | 尚恩・米勒〔上午11:05〕：<br>對，我現在在路上，要去和其他客戶開會，但我有提早20分出發，所以有時間過去一趟讓妳進去。 |
| **Michelle Lia** 11:07 A.M.<br>Thank you so much! I'll wait at the terrace next to the main lobby. | 米雪兒・萊亞〔上午11:07〕：<br>非常感謝你！我在大廳旁的露台那邊等。 |

**詞彙** arrange the table 擺設餐桌　on one's way to . . . 在前往……的路上

 **156** ----------------------------------------

**Who most likely is Mr. Miller?**

(A) A café waiter
(B) A restaurant manager
(C) A café cashier
(D) A restaurant chef

米勒先生最有可能是？

(A) 咖啡店服務生
(B) 餐廳經理
(C) 咖啡店收銀員
(D) 餐廳主廚

萊亞女士一開始說了：「I'm at the restaurant Garcia's.」、「the door is locked and I left my key at home」，表示人到餐廳卻沒有鑰匙無法進去，而米勒先生最後回道：「I have time to stop by and let you in」，表示他能讓萊亞女士進餐廳，代表他是有餐廳鑰匙的人，故他最可能是餐廳主管，最適合的答案為 (B)。

 **157** NEW ----------------------------------------

**At 11:04 A.M., what does Ms. Lia most likely mean when she writes, "It doesn't make sense"?**

(A) Her peer doesn't show up in advance.
(B) She does not understand what Mr. Miller said.
(C) The situation is unsuitable for the event.
(D) Event attendees are already there.

上午 11:04 時，萊亞女士寫道：「這才奇怪呀」，她最可能的意思是？

(A) 她的同事沒有提前到。
(B) 她不懂米勒先生在說什麼。
(C) 情況不適合舉辦活動。
(D) 參加活動的人已經到場。

根據前一句「She usually goes to the restaurant early to get the event ready.」，可知薩摩瓦女士原本都會提前抵達餐廳，故此時萊亞女士如此回應，最可能代表薩摩瓦女士今天不如往常，沒有提前到達，故正確答案為 (A)。

| | |
|---|---|
| **From:** Nancy Haywood<br>**To:** All staff<br>**Date:** June 30<br>**Subject:** Updated Information – Parking | 寄件人：南茜‧海伍德<br>收件人：全體同仁<br>日期：6月30日<br>主旨：更新停車資訊 |

Dear colleagues,

Please be aware that there are some changes about using the parking lot. You cannot park your vehicles in the Sutton Hall parking lot from July 10 through July 15 because it will be under construction. —[1]—. The expected date of reopening is scheduled for Monday, July 16, but is subject to change. —[2]—. Employees are encouraged to use public transportation and discuss temporary teleworking with your managers. Please note that all costs spent using other means of transportation or parking sites (e.g., Stapleton Parking Area) will be fully reimbursed at the beginning of August. —[3]—.

Also, please note that two additional spaces will be made in the parking lot as soon as the work has been completed. —[4]—. These places will be designated through a drawing to interested full-time staff members. If you want to join the lottery, please contact me via e-mail at n.haywood@suttoncorp.com as soon as possible. Thank you.

Nancy Haywood

親愛的同事：

請留意使用停車場的方式有一些改變。因為索頓大廳停車場進行工程，所以從7月10日到15日，你們不能把車停在那裡。停車場地面要加防水層，還要增建安全圍籬。預計要到7月16日週一才會重新開放，但也會再變動。建議同仁使用公共運輸工具，或者和主管討論暫時在家工作。請留意，使用其他交通工具或者其他的停車場（像是斯泰普頓停車區），都將在八月初給予全額補助。

另外也請注意，等到整修完畢後，停車場會多出兩個停車位，是專門規劃給有需要的全職員工，以抽籤方式選出。如果想要參加抽籤，請儘快用電子郵件n.haywood@suttoncorp.com聯絡我。謝謝。

南茜‧海伍德

**詞彙** **parking lot** 停車場　**be subject to** （可能）受……影響　**public transportation** 公共運輸工具　**teleworking** 遠端辦公　**means** 方法　**reimburse** 報銷，補償　**designate** 指派　**drawing** 抽籤　**lottery** 抽籤；樂透

**158**

**According to the e-mail, what should employees talk with their supervisors about?**

(A) The possibility of working remotely
(B) The best alternative parking spaces near the company
(C) How to participate in the parking space lottery
(D) The amount of reimbursed expenses they can get

根據這封電子郵件，員工應和主管討論什麼事情？

(A) 遠距離工作的可能性
(B) 公司附近最適合的替代停車場
(C) 如何參加抽籤抽停車位
(D) 可以獲得補助的金額多寡

根據「Employees are encouraged to . . . discuss temporary teleworking with your mangers」，若想遠端辦公，員工可與主管討論，故正確答案為 (A)。

**159**

| What is implied about the Stapleton Parking Area? | 文中提到關於斯泰普頓停車區什麼事？ |
|---|---|
| (A) It will be closed on Sundays. | (A) 週日不開放。 |
| (B) It has the latest equipment. | (B) 設備最先進。 |
| (C) It was recently expanded. | (C) 最近剛增建。 |
| (D) It charges drivers for its use. | (D) 駕駛人使用需付費。 |

根據「all costs spent using . . . parking sites (e.g., Stapleton Parking Area) will be fully reimbursed」，使用斯泰普頓停車區的費用可申請補報銷，因此可推測此停車場會收取提車費，故正確答案為 (D)。

**160** (NEW)

| In which of the positions marked [1], [2], [3], and [4] does the following sentence best belong? | 下列句子最適合出現在 [1]、[2]、[3]、[4] 的哪個位置中？ |
|---|---|
| "The surface will be waterproofed, and safety fences will be constructed." | 「停車場地面要加防水層，還要增建安全圍籬。」 |
| (A) [1] | (A) [1] |
| (B) [2] | (B) [2] |
| (C) [3] | (C) [3] |
| (D) [4] | (D) [4] |

題目給的句子在說明停車場將增建的設施，故所屬段落應與工程內容，[1] 後接續工程持續時間，為最合適的位置，其他 [2] 與 [3] 前後討論的是員工的應對方法，[4] 是工程後新車位的抽籤，都與題目句子關係較小，故本題正確答案為 (A)。

## 161–164 網路討論區

| Chris Paul | 3:30 P.M. | 克里斯·保羅〔下午3:30〕： |
|---|---|---|
| Jim and I are grabbing an early meal after work around 4:00. Anyone want to join us? | | 金和我工作完要早點出去吃飯，大概四點吧。有人要加入嗎？ |
| **Jeremy Lavine** | 3:31 P.M. | 傑瑞米·拉文〔下午3:31〕： |
| Maybe. I still have something more to do on a report for my boss. Where are you going? | | 大概吧。我還有報告要交給老闆。你們要去哪？ |
| **Chris Paul** | 3:32 P.M. | 克里斯·保羅〔下午3:32〕： |
| We're thinking of going to the Mexican bar on Washington Avenue. It's called TACO Ring. | | 我們考慮要去華盛頓大道的墨西哥酒吧，叫做塔可圈的那家。 |
| **Danny Rivera** | 3:33 P.M. | 丹尼·李維拉〔下午3:33〕： |
| Oh, you are unlucky! That place closed last week. | | 喔，你們有點衰！那間店上週收起來了。 |
| **Chris Paul** | 3:34 P.M. | 克里斯·保羅〔下午3:34〕： |
| Really? That's too bad. I heard there are a variety of great things to eat there. | | 真的嗎？真不巧，我聽說那裡東西還蠻多不錯吃的。 |

| | |
|---|---|
| **Danny Rivera** 3:35 P.M.<br>How about Romeo Pizzeria near Carnegie Street? They have a lot of delicious dishes and snacks on Tuesdays. | 丹尼・李維拉〔下午3:35〕：<br>卡內基街附近的羅密歐披薩店怎麼樣？週二的菜色好吃、點心也不賴。 |
| **Chris Paul** 3:37 P.M.<br>That sounds great. Does anyone want to go there with us? | 克里斯・保羅〔下午3:37〕：<br>聽起來還不錯。有人要跟我們去嗎？ |
| **Jeremy Lavine** 3:38 P.M.<br>OK. But I won't be able to get there until around five, I guess. | 傑瑞米・拉文〔下午3:38〕：<br>可以。但我猜我五點前到不了。 |
| **Brad Triana** 3:39 P.M.<br>It will be great for me. Lavine, I just sent you the modified reporting documents. | 布萊德・崔安那〔下午3:39〕：<br>對我來說是好消息，拉文，我剛剛把改完的報告寄給你了。 |

**詞彙** grab a meal 吃飯

**161**

**What are the chat participants discussing?**　對話成員在討論什麼？

(A) The place to go for dinner　(A) 要去哪裡吃晚餐
(B) The meeting for a weekly sales report　(B) 每週銷售報告的會議
(C) The menu at TACO Ring eatery　(C) 塔可圈餐館的菜單
(D) The introduction of new members to others　(D) 介紹新成員給大家

從「grabbing an early meal」、「bar」、「pizzeria」和「delicious dished and snack」等關鍵詞可知，整篇對話內容與下午要吃的食物及餐廳有關，故正確答案為 (A)。

**162**

**What information does Mr. Rivera provide about TACO Ring?**　關於塔可圈，李維拉先生提供了什麼資訊？

(A) The taste of the food is not good.　(A) 食物不好吃。
(B) The menu is very diverse.　(B) 菜色很多元。
(C) The restaurant has gone out of business.　(C) 餐廳不再營業了。
(D) They are gathered there for a meeting.　(D) 他們要到那裡開會。

李維拉先生在下午 3 點 33 分說了「That place closed last week.」，由此可知，塔可圈已從上週開始停業，故正確答案為 (C)。

**163** NEW

**At 3:34 P.M., why most likely does Mr. Paul write, "That's too bad"?**

(A) He cannot go with his colleagues for dinner.
(B) He wanted to eat at TACO Ring.
(C) He has a lot of things to report to his boss.
(D) He has had a delicious meal at TACO Ring.

下午3:34，為何保羅先生寫道：「真不巧」？

(A) 他無法和同事一起出去吃晚餐。
(B) 他想去塔可圈吃飯。
(C) 他還有很多事得報告老闆。
(D) 他在塔可圈吃過好吃的菜。

前文中，保羅先生先說：「We're thinking of going to the Mexican bar on Washington Avenue. It's called TACO Ring.」，他提議去塔可圈餐廳用餐，而李維拉先生則說：「That place closed last week.」，表示塔可圈已歇業，故此處保羅先生所謂的「That's too bad.」最可能代表他原想去該處用餐，故正確答案為 (B)。

**164**

**What does Mr. Lavine decide to do?**

(A) Join his coworkers for a meal
(B) Request a food delivery
(C) Work overtime on a task
(D) Look for another cafeteria

拉文先生決定做什麼？

(A) 加入同事吃晚餐的行列
(B) 請人外送
(C) 加班來完成工作
(D) 考慮其他自助餐廳

拉文先生最後說：「OK. But I won't be able to get there till around five, I guess.」，表示他可以和同事們一起享用晚餐，但是下午五點後才能抵達，故正確答案為 (A)。

**165–168 通知**

## Pennwholeissue Co.

### We value your opinion!

The Pennwholeissue Corporation has been conducting open polls of the public about current issues for over two decades. All of our questions are based on phone interviews with adults, who are eighteen years of age or older living in our designated polling areas. To ensure the same opportunity for participation for these adults, potential respondents are chosen by a computer at random.

To find information on what people think about recent world issues, please visit our Latest Poll Issues tab on our website. New polls are created weekly, and all of them are saved and accessible through the Internet. If you want to find polls by subject, use the sorting tools for a specific topic or Subject on the banner on the right. Should you want to copy the tables, graphs, charts, or other graphics

## 全賓州議題公司

### 你的意見，我們重視！

全賓州議題公司過去二十年來，持續針對當前議題進行民調。我們所有的問題都是透過電話訪問，訪問住在特定民調區域，18歲以上的成年人。為了確保每個人公平參與的機會，均由電腦隨機抽選受測者。

想知道民眾對於當今全球議題怎麼想，可以到我們官網的「最新民調議題」查詢。每週都會舉行新的民調，資料都會在網路上存檔並且公開。如果您想要根據主題查詢民調，使用篩選工具找尋特定主題，也能使用頁面橫幅右方的「主題」。如果您想使用全賓州議題公司所製作的表格、圖表、曲線圖或是其他

made by Pennwholeissue, click the Contact Us banner and request them through our Permission Division. You can easily find the information about an easy-to-use online manual form with specifications about how and where to use them. Usually, we can respond to your request within 24 hours after you submit it.

圖像，請點選「聯絡我們」，並詢問我們的授權部門。您也可以很輕鬆地在網站找到好用的線上手冊的資訊，關於如何使用和在哪裡使用也有詳細說明。填單繳交後，我們通常會在24小時內回覆您。

**詞彙** poll 民調　be based on 根據　designated 特定的　potential 可能的　respondent 回覆者 at random 隨機　accessible 可取得的　sorting tool 篩選工具　easy-to-use 好用的 manual 手冊　specification 詳細說明

**165** ------------------------------------------------------------

**What is NOT mentioned about poll participants?**

(A) They are interviewed via the phone.
(B) They are randomly selected.
(C) They should be adults.
(D) They should be interviewed in a group.

關於民調參與者，文中沒有提到什麼？

(A) 他們經由電話訪問。
(B) 他們被隨機抽選。
(C) 他們必須是成年人。
(D) 他們應該參與團體訪問。

本題解題重點在第一段。從「All of our questions are based on phone interviews with adults, who are eighteen years of age or older」可知道民調使用 (A) 電話進行，且受訪者需為滿 18 歲的 (C) 成年人，再從「potential respondents are chosen by a computer at random」可以得知，受訪者採 (B) 隨機抽選。根據上述，文中未提及的只有團體訪問一事，故本題答案為 (D)。

**166** ------------------------------------------------------------

**What is indicated about Pennwholeissue Co.?**

(A) It publishes books about world-historical issues.
(B) It posts new poll results on the Web every week.
(C) It is seeking new employees for Web management.
(D) It has more branches in other locations.

文中提到關於全賓州議題公司什麼事？

(A) 它出版和世界歷史議題有關的書籍。
(B) 它每週都會在網站上公布新民調。
(C) 它想聘人來管理網頁。
(D) 它有其他分店。

根據第二段的「New polls are created weekly, and all of them are saved and accessible through the Internet.」，可知每週都會舉行新的投票，且會在網路上公布結果，故正確答案為 (B)。

**167** ------------------------------------------------------------

**How can readers be permitted to get graphics?**

(A) By submitting a paper form
(B) By calling a Web master
(C) By sending a request letter
(D) By contacting them on the Web site

讀者要怎麼樣取得圖片使用許可？

(A) 繳交紙本表格
(B) 打電話詢問網頁專家
(C) 透過信件提出要求
(D) 透過網站聯繫

根據第二段的「Should you want to copy ... graphics made by Pennwholeissue, click the Contact Us banner and request them through our Permission Division」部分，可知若讀者想要圖片，可點擊網站上的橫幅廣告，並詢問公司的授權部門，故正確答案為應為 (D)。

The word "current" in paragraph 1, line 2, is closest in meaning to

(A) contemporary
(B) tentative
(C) momentous
(D) appropriate

第一段、第二行中的「current」，最接近下列哪個意思？

(A) 當代的
(B) 暫時性的
(C) 重大的
(D) 適當的

原文中使用的是 current issue，又說要進行民調，故可知道此處的「current」應和「最近的、當前的」有關，選項中字義最相近的為 contemporary，故正確答案為 (A)。

## 169–171 廣告

<table>
<tr><td>

### Need to take a break?

**Come along on the Rocky Mountains Trip!**

**with Bluespruce's Tips for "Best Southwest Vacation!"**
**Bluespruce Co. Offers:**

The Great Outdoors!

See incredible views of oak groves and valleys along the ranges while you breathe fresh mountain air. Over 20 km of off-road hiking and riding a cable car to the mountain top, which is offered for an additional fee, is prepared for you. Travel along this beautiful ridge on your own or with a trained guide. The Extreme Sports Activities program allows you to enjoy a variety of sports such as rock-climbing, white-water rafting, and so on. Indoor Unity Day is also provided by having a barbeque party, Bingo game, and live music performance in our condominium. If you want to join us in this group, we offer a special price based on the number of participants in our events. Should you have more questions about our activities and costs, do not hesitate to contact us at 750-8103.

</td><td>

### 想要休息嗎？

來場洛磯山脈之旅吧！

藍雲杉公司給您「最好的西南部假期」！

藍雲杉公司提供：

最好的戶外活動！

呼吸山中的新鮮空氣，享受群山間像樹林和山谷交織，令人難以置信的美景。加價還能享受超過20公里的越野腳踏車之旅，還能搭乘纜車到達山頂。無論是要自行延著美麗的山脊旅行，還是要找經驗豐富的嚮導陪同都行。我們的「極限運動課程」讓您也能體驗各式各樣的運動，像是攀岩、泛舟等等。在我們的大樓內也提供室內團康活動「室內團聚日」，包括烤肉派對、賓果遊戲或現場音樂表演。如果您想要入團共襄盛舉，我們會根據參加人數提供不同的價格優惠。如果還有其他關於活動和費用的問題，不用遲疑，馬上打電話到750-8103。

</td></tr>
</table>

**詞彙** **oak** 橡樹　**grove** 樹林　**valley** 山谷　**off-road** 越野的　**cable car** 纜車　**ridge** 山脊　**trained** 受訓練的　**rafting** 泛舟　**condominium** 大樓

**What most likely is Bluespruce?**　　　藍雲杉最可能是什麼公司？

(A) A travel agency　　　　　　　　(A) 旅行社

(B) A national park　　　　　　　　(B) 國家公園

(C) A recreational area　　　　　　(C) 遊樂區

(D) A sports complex　　　　　　　(D) 運動中心

從第三句的「a trained guide」、第四句的「program」與倒數第二句的「If you want to join us in this group, we offer a special price based on the number of participants in our events.」可知，藍雲杉公司有專業導遊，並有許多種類的行程，且收費按參加人數調整，故最可能為旅行社，本題答案為 (A)。

## 170

**What is indicated about the Rocky Mountains?**　文中提到關於洛磯山脈什麼事？

(A) They include a variety of waterfalls and lakes.　(A) 那裡有各種瀑布和湖泊。

(B) They are located in the Southwest.　(B) 位於西南方。

(C) They have a lot of complimentary activities.　(C) 贈送很多活動。

(D) They require visitors to get a license for activities.　(D) 參加活動需要證照。

根據「Come along on the Rocky Mountain Trip! with Bluespruce's Tips for "Best Southwest Vacation!"」可知，洛磯山脈應位於西南部，故本題正確答案為 (B)。

**What is offered at an extra cost?**　　需要額外花費的是什麼？

(A) A cable car　　　　　　　　(A) 纜車

(B) A Bingo game　　　　　　　(B) 賓果遊戲

(C) Live entertainment　　　　　(C) 現場娛樂表演

(D) A rock-climbing activity　　　(D) 攀岩活動

廣告第二句中提到：「biking and riding a cable car to the mountain top」、「an additional fee」，故可知腳踏車與纜車都需要額外收費，正確答案為 (A)。

**172–175 備忘錄**

## Hopkins Apparel

Weekly Reports about Management Status, April 7–11
Assigned: Jose Mackerry, Project Manager

This week's achievements:

* Talked with five manufacturing companies in Hochimin, Vietnam, with experience of making handbags. —[1]—. Gave them our brand-new bag designs and asked questions about minimum order amount, costs of production, and shipping and processing time. —[2]—.

* According to initial data about contacted manufacturers, Staple Industries is the most suitable for our needs in terms of time and cost. —[3]—. In addition, Jim Bommer, an account manager, called me first. He was very passionate and professional, and gave us immediate answers to all our requests. I strongly believe that Staple Industries could have a good relationship with us in this business.

* The other companies we contacted were unable to accept our schedule or meet our pricing requirements. —[4]—. Therefore, we do not need to consider them.

Plans for the week of April 15–20

==========[an intentionally blank page] ===========

## 霍普金斯服飾

管理週報，4月7日到11日
報告人：專案經理荷西·馬克力

本週成就：

＊和越南胡志明市五家有相關經驗製造商，討論手提包的事宜。提供他們新包包的設計，並詢問最低訂購量、製造成本、出貨和物流時間。

＊經初步了解各家廠商，史泰博製造最符合我們對時間和成本的需求。這間公司太小，不能滿足產量，但願意配合增僱員工來完成工作。此外，是客戶經理吉姆·布默先和我聯繫。他非常熱情，而且也很專業，對於我們的需求即時給予答覆。我深信，史泰博製造在這筆生意中，可以和我們合作得很好。

＊其他聯繫過的公司都不能配合我們的時間安排和定價要求，所以我們不需再多加考慮。

4月15日到20日的計畫

[此頁刻意留白]

---

**詞彙** **apparel** 服飾　**manufacture** 製造　**minimum** 最少的　**processing time** 物流時間
**intentionally** 刻意地　**blank** 空白的

**172**

----

**What is suggested about Hopkins Apparel?**

(A) It has a branch in Vietnam.
(B) It plans to acquire other companies.
(C) Its project manager will retire soon.
(D) It is planning to introduce some new items.

文中提到關於霍普金斯服飾什麼事？

(A) 在越南有分店。
(B) 計劃要收購其他公司。
(C) 專案經理快要退休了。
(D) 計劃發布新品。

從第一點的「Gave them our brand-new bag designs」可知，公司給了製造商新包包的設計，還討論了最低訂購量、成本、出貨等事宜，故公司最可能正計劃發布新產品，本題正確答案為(D)。

---

**According to the report, what did Mr. Mackerry do during the week of April 7?**

(A) He chose the best partner possible.
(B) He got a permit to make a product.
(C) He called a shipping company for negotiation.
(D) He held training sessions for new recruits.

根據報告，馬克力先生在 4 月 7 日這週做了什麼事情？

(A) 他挑選可能是最好的合作夥伴。
(B) 他獲得製造產品的許可。
(C) 他和航運公司進行磋商。
(D) 他為新進員工舉行訓練課程。

根據第二點：「Staple Industries is the most suitable for our needs in terms of time and cost.」，馬克力先生挑選出最適合的合作商，故正確答案為 (A)。

---

## 174

**What is mentioned about Mr. Bommer?**

(A) He is willing to work with Hopkins Apparel.
(B) He needs more information about new bags.
(C) He has worked as a project manager at Hopkins Apparel.
(D) He wanted to meet Mr. Mackerry for pricing negotiation.

文中提到關於布默先生什麼事？

(A) 他很樂意和霍普金斯服飾合作。
(B) 他需要更多和新包包有關的資訊。
(C) 他曾在霍普金斯服飾擔任專案經理。
(D) 他想和馬克力先生見面協商定價的事。

第二點提到「Jim Bommer」，並說：「He was very passionate and professional, and gave us immediate answers to all our requests.」，故可知布默先生為人熱情且即時回覆問題，應有意願與霍普金斯服飾公司合作，故正確答案為 (A)。

## 175

(NEW)

---

**In which of the positions [1], [2], [3], and [4] does the following sentence best belong?**

**"The company is too small to produce our request, but it is willing to hire additional employees to carry out the work."**

(A) [1]
(B) [2]
(C) [3]
(D) [4]

下列句子最適合出現在 [1]、[2]、[3]、[4] 的哪個位置中？

「這間公司太小，不能滿足產量，但願意配合增僱員工來完成工作。」

(A) [1]
(B) [2]
(C) [3]
(D) [4]

題目引述的句子為特定公司的描述，故適合放在講述某公司的段落。第二點主要講述「Staple Industries」，且在 [3] 後使用了「In addition」（此外），並在後文繼續描述該公司的某人物，故可知句子應最適合填入此處，正確答案為 (C)。

## 176–180 電子郵件

**To:** Steve Jack
<stevejack@fastmail.com>
**From:** John Dewy
<jdewy@aaco.com>

Dear Mr. Jack,

Your application for the managerial position of the Accounting Department at Arizonas Accounting Co. has been carefully reviewed by our department. This year's application process was highly competitive, and we were able to offer a position to only two of those who applied. Based on their recommendation, I regret to inform you that we cannot act favorably on your application and go with you at this time.

If you wish further information regarding this action, please feel free to contact the recruiting division of the Human Resources Department.

Recruiting Office

Telephone: (480) 965-3344
e-mail: recruit@aaco.com
URL: http://recruit.aaco.com/manger-apply

If you wish to be considered for other positions at Arizonas Accounting Co., more information and Web links are available at http://www.aaco.com/departments.

We thank you for your interest in Arizonas Accounting Co. and wish you success in your future endeavors.

Sincerely,
John Dewy
Arizonas Accounting Co.

---

收件人：史帝夫・傑克
<stevejack@fastmail.com>
寄件人：約翰・杜威
<jdewy@aaco.com>

親愛的傑克先生：

您應徵亞歷桑納會計事務所會計部門經理一職的履歷資料，已由我們的部門仔細審查過了。今年度的徵選過程高度競爭，從眾多應徵者中我們只能選出兩人。根據部門建議，很遺憾通知您，我們這次不能如您所願地通過您的申請。

關於這項決定，如果您想了解更多，請您聯繫人資部門的招募處。

人事辦公室

電話：(480)965-3344
信箱：recruit@aaco.com
網址：http://recruit.aaco.com/manger-apply

如果您還考慮亞歷桑納會計事務所的其他職務，也可以在http://www.aaco.com/departments找到更多連結和資訊。

感謝您對亞歷桑納會計事務所的熱忱，也祝福您未來求職順利。

亞歷桑納會計事務所
約翰・杜威 敬上

**To:** John Dewy
<jdewy@aaco.com>
**From:** Steve Jack
<stevejack@fastmail.com>

Dear, Mr. Dewy,

I am writing this e-mail inquiring about your e-mail. I am sorry to hear that the position I applied for was not given to me, but thank you for informing me so kindly. However, I wonder what other departments are dealing with monetary issues at your company. Because I majored in business at the University of Arizona, I can handle any other matters related to accounts, budgets, and distribution management. Would it be possible for me to apply for these relevant positions in your company during this season? If so, please let me know at your earliest convenience.

By chance, the duties that I currently perform for SYSMATIC Ltd. are exactly the same as the responsibilities mentioned above. So, I would like to know very quickly about other job openings at Arizonas Accounting Co.

I look forward to becoming a valuable member of Arizonas Accounting Co.

Regards,
Steve Jack

收件人：約翰‧杜威
<jdewy@aaco.com>
寄件人：史帝夫‧傑克
<stevejack@fastmail.com>

親愛的杜威先生：

我來信是想詢問您上一封的電子郵件。很遺憾聽到我沒有獲取該職位，但謝謝您友善地告訴我這件事。不過，我想了解貴公司哪些部門也處理金融業務。我在亞歷桑納大學主修商學系，能應對不論會計、預算或是物流管理有關的業務。不知道有沒有可能，讓我在這一季應徵貴公司這些相關職位呢？如果可以的話，請儘早讓我知道。

我目前在「體系公司」所負責的工作，湊巧也和上述職務完全一致。所以我希望能儘快知道，亞歷桑納會計事務所其他相關職缺。

我非常期待可以成為貴公司的有力員工。

祝好，
史帝夫‧傑克

---

**詞彙** managerial 管理的　accounting 會計的　act on sth 根據某事行動　go with sb 同意某人的意見
endeavor 努力　monetary 金融的　relevant 相關的　at one's earliest convenience 儘早
by chance 碰巧　opening 職缺

 **176** - - - - - - - - - - - - - - - - - - - - - - - - - - - - - - - - - - - - - - - - - - - - - - - - - - - - - - - - - - -

**For what kind of company does Mr. Dewy most likely work?**

(A) A law firm
(B) A financial business
(C) A publishing company
(D) A governmental office

杜威先生最可能在什麼公司上班？

(A) 法律事務所
(B) 金融業務
(C) 出版公司
(D) 政府機關

根據第一封郵件的信尾簽名：「John Dewy, Arizonas Accounting Co.」，可知杜威先生隸屬於會計事務所，故選項中最適合作為答案的為 (B)。

## 177

**In the first e-mail, what is the recipient NOT asked to do for more information?**

(A) Send an e-mail to the personnel division
(B) Click some links on the Web
(C) Call the company directly
(D) Post questions on the Web

在第一封電子郵件中，收件人如欲獲得更多資訊，不需要做哪件事？

(A) 寄電子郵件給人事處
(B) 點選網站上的一些連結
(C) 直接打電話到公司
(D) 到網站上張貼疑問

第一封信件的第二至四段皆與聯絡方式有關。先從「please feel free to contact the recruiting division of the human resources department」得知，收件人可與人事處聯絡，且下方提供了電話、電子信箱以及網址，故可知三種管道皆開放聯絡，此處提及了選項 (A) 與 (C)。再從第四段的「more information and Web links are available at http://www.aaco.com/departments.」，可知點選網站也是一種方式。

綜合上述，郵件中未提到的只有 (D)，故本題答案為 (D)。

## 178

**What is suggested about Arizonas Accounting Co.?**

(A) It had a lot of remarkable candidates.
(B) It has entered into a partnership with SYSMATIC.
(C) It has increased its sales figures in distribution.
(D) It employed a lot of new employees for the assembly lines.

文中提到關於亞歷桑納會計事務所什麼事？

(A) 有很多優秀的人上門應徵。
(B) 和體系公司有合夥關係。
(C) 在物流方面的銷售額有成長。
(D) 為生產線聘僱了很多新進員工。

根據第一封郵件的「This year's application process was highly competitive」可以得知，今年應徵者的競爭激烈，故正確答案為 (A)。

## 179

**Why was the second e-mail written?**

(A) To advertise the applicant's merits to the manager
(B) To negotiate further conditions for the position
(C) To recommend a suitable person for a position
(D) To ask whether other related positions are available

為什麼會寫第二封電子郵件？

(A) 應徵者向經理宣傳自身的優點
(B) 協商該職位的後續情況
(C) 替某職位推薦適合人選
(D) 詢問是否有其他相關職缺

根據第二封郵件第一段最後：「Would it be possible for me to apply for these relevant positions in your company during this season?」，可知應徵者想知道是否有其他適合自己的職缺，故寫了郵件過去，本題正確答案為 (D)。

**What most likely is NOT indicated about Mr. Jack?**

(A) He has a bachelor's degree.
(B) He studied business law in college.
(C) He can do various monetary tasks.
(D) He wants to transfer to a new company.

關於傑克先生，何者為非？

(A) 他有大學學歷。
(B) 他在大學學過商業法。
(C) 他能處理多項金融業務。
(D) 他想要換公司。

本題的解題重點皆在第二封郵件。從第一段的「I majored in business at the University of Arizona」中，可知 (A) 傑克先生具大學學歷，而透過「I can handle any other matters related to accounts, budgets, and distribution management.」，可知 (C) 他能夠處理金融相關業務。

此外，他最後提到：「I currently perform for SYSMATIC Ltd.」卻又說「I look forward to becoming a valuable member of Arizonas Accounting Co.」，表示他目前任職於另一公司，但期望進入會計事務所工作，代表他有離職意願，所以 (D) 也是正確的敘述

綜合上述，選項中未提及的只有 (B)，故本題答案為 (B)。

### 181–185 目錄與電子郵件

| Issue 100, June<br>Table of Contents | 六月號，第 100 期<br>目錄 |
|---|---|
| **Monthly Cover: 100th Issue Anniversary** | **月刊封面：慶祝發行第100期** |
| P. 01–10 ·······················Top Chefs | 第1到10頁……頂尖主廚 |
| P. 15 ······················· Recipe Index | 第15頁……食譜索引 |
| **P. 16 – Artichokes, Globe** | **第16頁—球狀洋薊** |
| Artichoke and ricotta salad with tomato and rosemary vinaigrette<br>Chickpea, fennel and artichoke salad with lemon and date dressing<br>Linguine with fresh tomatoes and artichokes<br>Zesty rice salad with preserved lemon, artichokes, and asparagus | 洋薊和乳清起司沙拉佐番茄與迷迭香醋油醬<br>鷹嘴豆、茴香、洋薊沙拉佐檸檬椰棗醬汁<br>義大利細扁麵佐新鮮番茄與洋薊<br>香米沙拉醃製檸檬、洋薊和蘆筍 |
| **P. 20 – Bacon** | **第20頁—培根** |
| Chicken supreme with beans and lemon<br>Crispy eggs with bacon and lentils<br>Filet mignon with duck liver pâté and red wine sauce<br>Potato, broad bean, and crispy bacon salad with mint dressing<br>Roman-style lamb cutlets<br>Sautéed Brussels sprouts with bacon and almonds | 嫩雞佐豆子與檸檬<br>脆蛋佐培根和扁豆<br>菲力牛排佐鴨肝醬與紅酒醬<br>馬鈴薯、蠶豆和香脆培根沙拉佐薄荷醬<br>羅馬風味羊排<br>培根杏仁炒抱子甘藍 |

## P. 30 – Beef

Baked beef kofta with paneer
Beef and caramelized shallot pies with cauliflower tops
Beef and yellow split pea salad with pumpkin seed dressing
Beef olives with cherry tomatoes

## P. 35 ·················································Winners' Recipes

## P. 36 – Sweety & Breeze Pudding

Experience the soft and sweet texture of food with good flavor!

## P. 38 – Oriental Balsamic Salad

Tropical fruit salad has a variety of tasteful ingredients you would not expect.

---

**From:** jdoris@royalrecipe.com
**To:** t-daven@lycoos.com
**Date:** 20 May
**Subject:** Contest Winning

Dear Mr. Daven,

I am happy to inform you that your entry of Daven's Sweety & Breeze-to-Make Pudding is the winner of our contest. Your innovative recipe will be published in the June issue of our magazine. However, the title may be shortened by our editors due to limited space in the column of the Winner's Recipes section.

Before we publish your recipe in our magazine, I would like to ask some additional information. In the recipe you submitted, honey could be used instead of sugar as a sweetener. Could you tell me how much honey is used in comparison with using sugar? Is there any other replacement if there is no honey at home? In addition, the recipe shows that the pudding should be frozen in the freezer before eating. What is the minimum amount of time and proper degree for freezing it? Thank you for giving us this information.

It is also usual for us to include a picture of the author when we publish a recipe. Please attach a clear half-length photograph of you in your reply e-mail to this.

Thank you,
Jane Doris

---

第30頁—牛肉

南亞牛肉丸佐凝乳起司
牛肉、焦烤紅蔥派綴花椰菜
牛肉、黃豌豆沙拉佐南瓜子醬
橄欖牛肉捲佐櫻桃番茄

第35頁……冠軍菜單

第36頁—蜜糖微風布丁

體驗食物軟嫩甜蜜的口感和好味道！

第38頁—東方義大利紅酒醋沙拉

熱帶水果沙拉有多種你意想不到的美味食材。

---

寄件人：jdoris@royalrecipe.com
收件人：t-daven@lycoos.com
日期：5月20日
主旨：獲獎事宜

親愛的戴文先生：

很高興通知您，您的參賽甜點「蜜糖微風特製布丁」贏得我們的比賽。您的創意食譜將會在六月號的雜誌登出。不過，因為「冠軍菜單」的專欄空間有限，菜單名稱可能會被編輯稍微縮短。

雜誌登出您的食譜前，我想向您詢問其他資訊。您的食譜當中提到，可以用蜂蜜替代糖來帶出甜味。可以請您告訴我，如果不用糖，改用蜂蜜需要的量是多少嗎？如果家裡沒有蜂蜜，還能用什麼替代？此外，菜單中提到，布丁在吃之前要先冷凍。最短需要冷凍多久的時間？最合適的溫度是多少？謝謝您提供這些資訊。

刊登食譜的時候，我們通常也會登出作者的照片。請您回覆這封信時，也附上一張您清楚的半身照。

謝謝您，
珍・朵麗絲

詞彙 innovative 創新的　column 專欄　in comparison with sth 與某事相比　attach 附上
half-length 半身的

**Why was the e-mail sent to Mr. Daven?**

(A) To point out errors in his submission
(B) To encourage him to register for a cooking class
(C) To tell him about the winning process
(D) To discuss the publication of a recipe

為什麼要寄電子郵件給戴文先生？

(A) 指出提交內容有錯誤
(B) 鼓勵他報名烹飪課程
(C) 告訴他贏得比賽的過程
(D) 討論食譜刊登的事

根據信件開頭部分的「Your innovative recipe will be published in the June issue of our magazine.」可以得知，此封郵件是為了通知戴文先生，他的食譜將被刊登在六月號的雜誌，故正確答案為 (D)。

**In the e-mail, the word "entry" in paragraph 1, line 1, is closest in meaning to**

(A) front of building
(B) new staff member
(C) contest submission
(D) lowest degree

電子郵件中第一段、第一行的「entry」最接近下列哪個意思？

(A) 建築正面
(B) 新進員工
(C) 申請參加比賽
(D) 最低度數

原句「your entry . . . is the winner of our contest」，表示他的「entry」贏得了比賽，故此字義最可能與「參賽作品」相關，所以最適當的答案為 (C)。

**What does Ms. Dorris NOT ask Mr. Daven to provide?**

(A) A modified recipe title
(B) An amount of an ingredient
(C) A length of time for a process
(D) A photograph of himself

朵麗絲女士沒有要求戴文先生提供什麼？

(A) 改完的食譜名稱
(B) 某樣食材的量
(C) 某項過程的時間長短
(D) 他的照片

(B) 第二段的「Could you tell me how much honey is used in comparison with using sugar?」即是在詢問蜂蜜的確切用量；(C) 同段下兩句的「What is the minimum amount of time . . . for freezing it?」詢問冷藏的時間；(D) 最後一段的「Please attach a clear half-length photograph of you」則要求提供照片。

綜合上述可知，(A) 並沒有被提及到，且郵件中說的是「the title may be shortened by our editors」，表示菜單名稱會由編輯縮短，故本題正確答案為 (A)。

184

On what page does Mr. Daven's recipe appear? | 戴文先生的食譜將在哪一頁刊出？

(A) 16 | (A) 16
(B) 20 | (B) 20
(C) 36 | (C) 36
(D) 38 | (D) 38

郵件開頭便提到「Daven's Sweety & Breeze-to-Make Pudding」，故可知這就是食譜的名稱，再回頭對照目錄，可找到「P. 36–Sweety & Breeze Pudding」，故食譜刊登在第 36 頁，本題正確答案為 (C)。

**185**

What can be inferred about the recipes? | 文中提到關於食譜什麼事？

(A) The artichoke is cooked with lamb cutlet. | (A) 洋薊和羊排一同烹煮。
(B) The Oriental Balsamic Salad has a sweet flavor. | (B) 東方義大利紅酒醋沙拉有甜味。
(C) A key to making pudding is the place it is cooked. | (C) 做布丁的關鍵是製作的地點。
(D) All of the recipes are made by head chefs. | (D) 所有的食譜都是主廚做的。

本題不一定得知道每道菜式與食材的名稱，只要會對照即可。

(A) 在第 18 頁洋薊相關的菜單中沒有出現羊排；(C) 從郵件中的「the recipe shows that the pudding should be frozen in the freezer before eating」，可知布丁在吃前要冷凍，故關鍵應該是溫度調節；(D) 從目錄中無法得知此事。

目錄在「Oriental Balsamic Salad」的項目有寫到「Tropical fruit salad」，故可知沙拉上有熱帶水果，而水果應具甜味，故本題正確答案為 (B)。

### 186–190 網頁、清單和文章

**Event Name:** Long-Night-Summer Song Festival
**Location:** Daytona Beach, Florida
**Dates:** 1–14 August
**Contact:** Sabrina Anne:
sanne@musicsurvival.com

活動名稱：漫漫夏夜音樂節
地點：戴通納海灘，佛州
日期：8月1日到14日
聯絡人：莎柏琳娜・安：
sanne@musicsurvival.com

**About:**

This annual event, in its fifth anniversary, brings in over 100 solo and group contestants from around the southeastern area of the United States of America. In particular, there are a lot of competitive and competent applicants in diverse fields of music. In addition, Music Survival, an organizer of this event, expects that more than 2,000 audience members will be gathered in Daytona Beach, Florida, which is nearly double that of

關於這項活動：

這項年度盛事已經是第五度舉辦，帶來100組來自美國東南部各地，單人或團體的參賽者。特別的是，參賽者來自各類音樂領域，都很有競爭力和能力。不只這樣，活動主辦方「生存音樂」預期，佛州戴通納海灘將聚集超過2,000名聽眾，比去年多出一倍。這項比賽儼然成為佛

the previous year. This contest has become one of the largest beach events in Florida. Daytona Beach, one of the longest sandy beaches in Florida, is located about one hour from Orlando. During this week, the city of Daytona holds the 40th World Grand Prix Championship, which is internationally recognized in car-racing sports. Visitors can get a chance to attend these fantastic events for free, with just $5 for parking.

州最大規模的海灘活動。戴通納海灘是佛州最長的沙灘之一，距離奧蘭多市約一個小時的車程。戴通納市將在這週舉辦第40屆國際賽車大獎世界冠軍賽，這是全球賽車的運動盛會。遊客可以免費參加這項很棒的活動，停車費只需要五元。

## The Winners of the Fifth Annual Long-Night-Summer Song Festival

[Solo Section]

| Placement | Name | State | 曲目 |
|---|---|---|---|
| 1st Prize | Ashton Jane | Alabama | Cooling Summer Night |
| 2nd Prize | Justin Moore | Georgia | The End of the Moon |
| 3rd Prize | Simon Rick | North Carolina | Mixed Bowl in the World |
| 4th Prize | Tyler Smith | Florida | Catcher in the Lie |

[Group Section]

| Placement | Name | State | 曲目 |
|---|---|---|---|
| 1st Prize | Tina Band | Tennessee | Don't Bully the Rustic |
| 2nd Prize | South Life | South Carolina | Never Stop Exploring |

## 第五屆漫漫夏夜音樂節優勝者

單人組

| 名次 | 姓名 | 州 | 曲目 |
|---|---|---|---|
| 第一名 | 艾希頓·珍 | 阿拉巴馬 | 〈涼爽夏夜〉 |
| 第二名 | 賈斯丁·摩爾 | 喬治亞 | 〈月球盡頭〉 |
| 第三名 | 西蒙·瑞克 | 北卡羅來納 | 〈世界的攪拌碗〉 |
| 第四名 | 泰勒·史密斯 | 佛羅里達 | 〈謊言捕手〉 |

團體組

| 名次 | 姓名 | 州 | 曲目 |
|---|---|---|---|
| 第一名 | 蒂娜樂團 | 田納西 | 〈不要霸凌鄉下人〉 |
| 第二名 | 南方生活 | 南卡羅來納 | 〈從不停止探險〉 |

## What's New in Northeast Florida?

By Donald Scott

The annual Long-Night-Summer Song Festival took place last week, and it was the perfect way to say farewell to the hot summer season. Because of the beautiful weather, the number of visitors was over double that of the preceding years, even more than the host anticipated.

The contest drew music artists for both the solo and group sections. They introduced themselves to visitors by stimulating their emotions with their great voices. All people on the Daytona Beach fully shared their emotion. I strongly believe that this is the reason why we consider music as one of the composite arts. A feast of songs made the festival more and more exciting and helped everyone to relax.

## 佛州東北有什麼新鮮事？

唐納·史考特撰文

上週才結束的一年一度的漫漫夏夜音樂節，是告別炎熱夏季的最好方式。由於天氣很棒，訪客超乎主辦單位預期，比去年多出一倍以上。

競賽吸引了個人樂手和音樂團體，他們用美妙的聲音和激昂的情感，向遊客介紹自己，他們的情感渲染了整個戴通納海灘。我深信這也是為什麼，我們認為音樂是一種綜合藝術。歌曲饗宴讓音樂節更加好玩，也讓每個人都能放輕鬆。

As a result of this contest, Ashton Jane, with the amusing song, Cooling Summer Night, won the first prize in the solo section, and Tina Band from Tennessee did it in the group section with Don't Bully the Rustic, which deals with anti-social issues. The winning process consisted of both judges and audience members at the rate of fifty-fifty voting.

With the success of this festival, John McKayne, the state governor of Florida, announced that the Department of Culture in Florida will expand the scale of this event all over the country in the near future. By doing so, the state intends to advertise its region to all citizens as one of the most prosperous culture states in the U.S.

競賽的結果，由艾希頓‧珍的好玩曲目〈涼爽夏夜〉拿下單人組冠軍。來自田納西州的蒂娜樂團則是用〈不要霸凌鄉下人〉，一首處理反社會議題的曲目，奪下團體組之冠。評分過程不只有評審給分，觀眾評分也占了其中的一半。

由於音樂節大獲成功，佛州州長約翰‧麥凱因宣布，佛州文化部將在不久的將來，把音樂節的規模擴大到全國。這樣一來，佛州就能向全美國人民行銷佛州特色，推廣佛州所擁有的豐富文化。

---

**詞彙** competent 有能力的　say farewell 道別　preceding 之前的　host 主辦單位　anticipate 預期
anti-social 反社會的　in the near future 不久的將來

---

**186**

**What is indicated about contestants?**

(A) They are from a certain group of states.
(B) They are all professional musicians.
(C) They are requested to register early.
(D) They are all in-state residents.

文中提到關於參賽者什麼事？

(A) 他們來自不同的州。
(B) 他們都是專業音樂人。
(C) 他們被要求要提早報名。
(D) 他們都是佛州的居民。

根據網頁內容中的「contestants from around the southeastern area of the United States of America」可以得知，參賽者皆來自美國東南部地區，故正確答案為 (A)。

---

**187**

**What is indicated about this year's event?**

(A) It is the largest festival ever.
(B) It costs $5 per person to join.
(C) It took place in Daytona Beach for the first time.
(D) It was the last event be held.

文中提到今年漫漫夏夜音樂節什麼事？

(A) 是歷年來最大。
(B) 活動入場費每人五美元。
(C) 首度在戴通納海灘舉辦。
(D) 這是最後一次舉辦該活動了。

網頁內容中已提及「This contest has become one of the largest beach events in Florida.」，表示音樂節是佛羅里達州規模最大的海灘活動；再根據報導文章中的第一段：「the number of visitors was over double that of the preceding years, even more than the host anticipated」，得知參觀人數超過往年的兩倍，甚至超過主辦單位預期，所以可推測今年的音樂節是最成功的一次，故正確答案為 (A)。

(B) 網頁最後一句寫道：「Visitors can get a chance to attend these fantastic events for free」，表示可免費進場；(C) 往年的舉辦地點並無法從文中得知；(D) 從報導文章的最後一段：「the Department of Culture in Florida will expand the scale of this event all over the country in the near future」，可知音樂節將推及全國，故今年不會是最後一次舉辦。

**Who is the second prize winner in solo category?**

(A) Ashton Jane
(B) Justin Moore
(C) Tyler Smith
(D) South Life

誰是單人組的第二名？

(A) 艾希頓‧珍
(B) 賈斯丁‧摩爾
(C) 泰勒‧史密斯
(D) 南方生活

對照清單可知，單人組第二名為「Justin Moore」，故正確答案為 (B)。

189

**What does Mr. McKayne intend to do?**

(A) He will develop the event into a nationwide event.
(B) He will never accept the following events.
(C) He will run for election to the National Assembly.
(D) He will change the event into a charitable one.

麥凱因先生想要做什麼？

(A) 他將把活動發展成全國性的活動。
(B) 他不會接受後續活動。
(C) 他打算要參選國會議員。
(D) 他要把活動轉型為慈善活動。

根據報導文章的最後一段：「John McKayne . . . announced that the Department of Culture in Florida will expand the scale of this event all over the country」，麥凱因先生預計將音樂節推廣成全國性的活動，故本題正確答案為 (A)。

190

**Which song was performed by an in-state participant?**

(A) Cooling Summer Night
(B) Mixed Bowl in the World
(C) Catcher in the Lie
(D) Never Stop Exploring

哪首曲目是由當地參賽者所演出？

(A) 〈涼爽夏夜〉
(B) 〈世界的攪拌碗〉
(C) 〈謊言捕手〉
(D) 〈從不停止探險〉

「in-state」在文中代表「佛羅里達州」，故參照得獎者名單，可知來自佛羅里達州的歌手為「Tyler Smith」，參賽曲目則為「Catcher in the Lie」，故本題正確答案為 (C)。

**191–195 資訊、電子郵件和停車證**

## Borough of Ebensburg

### Continuing Education Classes – June

Continuing education classes are open to all residents in the Borough of Ebensburg aged 19 and over. Classes are held at Mount Aloysius College unless otherwise notified. For the registration process, please see page 4 of this brochure. There is more detailed information about tuition, fees, and payment options.

## 艾本斯堡區

### 進修教育課程—六月

所有艾本斯堡區的居民，只要年滿19歲都能參加進修教育課程。除非另外通知上課地點，否則都在蒙特阿洛伊修斯學院開課。註冊方式詳參本手冊第四頁，也有更多學雜費和付費選項的詳細資訊。

| How to Start Your Own Business | |
| --- | --- |
| Mondays, 1 P.M. – 3 P.M. | Sutton Hall, Room 101 |
| Instructor : M. Judies, Co-chair of Indiana Retailer Association | |

| Taking a Photo — Easy and Fun Photography World! | |
| --- | --- |
| Tuesdays, 2 P.M. – 5 P.M. | Stapleton Library, Room 202 |
| Instructor : S. Kenneth, Manager of Narin-Arto Pictures | |

| Become a Real Estate Agent — Preparation for the License Test | |
| --- | --- |
| Wednesdays, 1 P.M. – 4 P.M. | Leonard Hall, Room 305 |
| Instructor : K. Peter, President of Jack's Realty Firm | |

| To Make Your Car Perfect! — Self-Care Tips | |
| --- | --- |
| Thursdays, 3 P.M. – 6 P.M. | Lael Auto Lab, Monroeville Campus |
| Instructor : T. Schenider, Mechanic of Heinz Auto Parts, PA | |

| 如何創業？ | |
| --- | --- |
| 週一下午1點到3點 | 索頓大廳101室 |
| 講師：印第安納零售公會聯合主席，M·茱蒂斯 | |

| 拍張照—簡單又愉快的攝影世界！ | |
| --- | --- |
| 週二下午2點到5點 | 斯泰普頓圖書館202室 |
| 講師：納林歐德攝影公司經理，S·肯尼斯 | |

| 成為一名不動產仲介—準備考證照 | |
| --- | --- |
| 週三下午1點到4點 | 里昂納德大廳305室 |
| 講師：傑克房地產公司總裁，K·彼得 | |

| 讓你的車超完美—自助保養祕訣 | |
| --- | --- |
| 週四下午3點到6點 | 蒙洛維爾校區萊澳汽車實驗室 |
| 講師：宥州海因茲汽車零件技師，T·史耐德 | |

---

**TO :** Gloria Park (and 12 others)
**FROM :** Jerry Gebhard
<jgebhard@ebensburg.gov>
**SUBJECT :** [URGENT] Class Canceled
**DATE :** June 19

---

To All Class Participants:

Ms. Judies asked me to let every student know the class has been canceled due to an important issue she should attend to, so it will be rescheduled soon. Once we know the date and time, we will inform you of it via e-mail and send a new parking permit too, because your current permit is no longer valid. Sorry for this inconvenience.

Regards,
Jerry Gebhard
Manager, the Department of Local Welfare, Borough of Ebensburg
Telephone: 743-8917

---

收件人：葛洛麗亞·帕克（和其他12人）
寄件人：傑瑞·葛博哈德
<jgebhard@ebensburg.gov>
主旨：（緊急）課程取消
日期：6月19日

---

此致所有學員：

茱蒂斯女士請我通知各位，因為她要處理一件重要的事情，課程必須取消，很快會再擇日安排補課。一旦我們知道日期和時間，會儘快透過電子郵件通知你們，並給與新的停車許可證，畢竟到時候現有的這張就會失效。抱歉造成不便。

祝好，
艾本斯堡區地方福利部經理
傑瑞·葛博哈德
電話：743–8917

| Mount Aloysius College Facility Division<br>TEMPORARY ONE DAY PASS<br>FOR TODAY ONLY | 蒙特阿洛伊修斯學院分部<br>單日臨時通行證<br>僅限當天 |
|---|---|
| **SOUTH BLUE LOT**<br><br>**Valid Date:** June 22<br><br>**Time Stamp:** 1:30 P.M.<br><br>* Please display this permit on the front window of your vehicle so it is visible from the outside. | 南方藍停車場<br><br>有效日期：6月22日<br><br>時間戳章：下午1:30<br><br>＊ 請將此許可張貼於前座車窗上，以供外部人員辨識。 |

**詞彙** borough 行政區　continuing education 進修教育　tuition 學費　retailer 零售商
attend to 處理　permit 許可證　valid 有效的

---

 **191**

**Who most likely is T. Schenider?**

(A) A repairman
(B) A council member
(C) A local business owner
(D) An association chair

**T·史耐德先生最有可能是？**

(A) 維修人員
(B) 市議員
(C) 當地商家老闆
(D) 公會主席

根據表格最後：「T. Schenider, Mechanic of Heinz Auto Parts, PA」，可以得知史耐德先生最可能從事汽車、器械相關的工作，故本題答案應選 (A)。

---

**192**

**What is NOT indicated about participants in the continuing education classes?**

(A) They live in the Borough of Ebensburg.
(B) They paid class tuition and fees.
(C) They should be at least 19 years old.
(D) They graduated from Mt. Aloysius College.

**關於進修教育課程參加者，文中沒有提到什麼事？**

(A) 他們住在艾本斯堡區。
(B) 他們要繳交學雜費。
(C) 他們最少要滿 19 歲。
(D) 他們從蒙特阿洛伊修斯學院畢業。

第一篇資訊已提到「Continuing education classes are open to all residents in the Borough of Ebensburg aged 19 and over.」，故可知課程參加者須為年滿 19 歲的艾本斯堡區居民，符合 (A) 與 (C)，同段後文也提到學雜費相關的資訊，故符合 (B)。

而根據「Classes are held at Mount Aloysius College」，只能得知課程會在該學院舉辦，並未提及參加課程者必須是該校畢業生，故本題正確答案為 (D)。

**193** ----------------------------------------

**What is Ms. Park most likely interested in?** 　帕克女士對什麼可能最感興趣？

(A) Real estate 　　　　　　　　　　　　(A) 不動產
(B) Owning a business 　　　　　　　　(B) 創業
(C) Photography 　　　　　　　　　　　(C) 攝影
(D) Car maintenance 　　　　　　　　　(D) 維修汽車

先觀察帕克女士為郵件的收件人，且根據該郵件內容，可知帕克女士參加了茱蒂斯女士的課程，再對照表格可知，她的講座題為「How to Start Your Own Business」，是在講授創業的方法，故帕克女士最可能對創業有興趣，正確答案為 (B)。

**194** ----------------------------------------

**In the e-mail, the phrase "attend to" in line 2, is closest in meaning to** 　電子郵件中，第二行的「attend to」，最接近下列哪個意思？

(A) participate in 　　　　　　　　　　(A) 參加
(B) take care of 　　　　　　　　　　　(B) 處理
(C) bring up 　　　　　　　　　　　　 (C) 提到
(D) sing up for 　　　　　　　　　　　(D) 報名

attend 為及物動詞時，字義較近 participate in（參加）；而當作不及物動詞時，意思則與 take care of（處理）、deal with（處理）較為相似。

「due to an important issue she should attend to」從句意解釋應是「因為她需處理一件重要的事情」，故 attend to 在此可看作「處理」的意思，本題正確答案為 (B)。

**195** ----------------------------------------

**On what date will the rescheduled class take place?** 　補課改到哪一天？

(A) June 20 　　　　　　　　　　　　　(A) 6 月 20 日
(B) June 21 　　　　　　　　　　　　　(B) 6 月 21 日
(C) June 22 　　　　　　　　　　　　　(C) 6 月 22 日
(D) June 23 　　　　　　　　　　　　　(D) 6 月 23 日

本題要對照郵件與停車證。從郵件上的「Once we know the date and time, we will inform you of it. . . . and send a new parking permit too」，表示補課日期確定後會再告知，並同時寄發停車證；再從停車證上的有效日期 6 月 22 日可知，補課就是在該日進行，故正確答案為 (C)。

## Richmond Daily Post

**In Brief 17 March**

As reported earlier this year, Giant Hawk Grocery is going to open its additional distribution center. Completion of construction was delayed for a time because there were some problems with the ground conditions at the site. However, these matters have been completely resolved and the 20,000-square-meter area will be fully operational starting on April 5, when the opening ceremony is held with numerous citizens.

The warehouse has a special section with state-of-the-art equipment to wrap up packages with a vacuum pack system. In addition, other equipment can keep foods frozen or cool by applying quick-cooling technology.

The new distribution center is expected to create more than 200 new jobs, according to Chuck Conrad, General Manager of Operations. Due to the size and scope of the work, a variety of new employees will be needed from loaders and drivers to office clerks.

---

**TO:** Chuck Conrad <chuck@gianthawk.co.ca>
**FROM:** Mallory Blaniar <mblaniar@gianthawk.co.ca>
**SUBJECT:** Notification Company
**DATE:** 20 April

---

Dear Conrad,

Thanks for inviting me to the grand opening at the beginning of this month. It's unbelievable that I have seen such a well-organized event. We should get Mr. Andrew something to show our appreciation for preparing it.

I think that it is time to choose a company that sends automatic notifications to employees' cell phones. This service would enable us to deliver messages to our staff promptly and prevent some mistakes. I have the contact information of a company working with customer service at Sending to You. I guess that this is a good company, but Unitas Notification also looks great, and its monthly fees are lower than the former.

---

## 李奇蒙日報

**3月17日新聞速報**

如同今年初的消息，巨鷹百貨即將開幕新的物流中心。由於地基的建設問題，造成了工程完工時間延誤。不過，相關問題已經完全解決，而佔地2,000平方公尺的新區域，將從4月5日全面啟用，並舉行盛大開幕儀式，多位市民都能前來參與。

倉庫特別配備最先進的機器，使用真空系統進行包裝。另外也有設備運用快速冷藏科技，能迅速將食品冷藏冷凍。

營運長查克‧康洛德表示，新的物流中心估計將創造超過200個工作機會。因應工作規模和領域，將釋出各種職缺，從上貨員、駕駛到公司職員都有。

---

**收件人：**查克‧康洛德 <chuck@gianthawk.co.ca>
**寄件人：**馬洛妮‧布藍尼爾 <mblaniar@gianthawk.co.ca>
**主旨：**簡訊公司
**日期：**4月20日

---

親愛的康洛德：

感謝您邀請我參加這個月初的盛大開幕式。沒想到我能見證這麼好的活動安排。我想應該準備一些東西，向籌備活動的安德魯先生表達我們的謝意。

我想是時候找間可以自動發送提醒訊息到員工手機的公司。這樣的服務可以發送即時訊息給我們的員工，也可以避免出錯。我有一間提供這種顧客服務的公司「為你傳達」的聯絡方式。我想這間應該不錯，但是「全體通知」看起來也不差，月租費也相較便宜。

| | |
|---|---|
| Anyway, I attached the information for both companies to help you decide. Please let me know what you think.<br><br>Regards,<br>Mallory Blaniar | 總之，我把兩間公司的資訊附給您，再由您決定。再請您告訴我您的想法。<br><br>祝好，<br>馬洛妮·布藍尼爾 |

## UNITAS NOTIFICATIONS

2:20 P.M.

To Giant Hawk Employees,

The frozen-item deliveries expected to arrive on Monday will not arrive until Wednesday. Employees who had volunteered to work overtime on Monday and Tuesday night at the Richmond Distribution Center will not be needed. However, we will need help for the overnight shift on Wednesday night. If you are willing to work additional hours at that time, please contact Sue Trinity in the Personnel Division.

## 全體通知

下午2:20

此致巨鷹百貨全體員工：

原訂要在週一送到的冷凍配送，將在週三才會送到。所以本來在週一和二晚上自願加班的李奇蒙物流中心的員工就不需要來了。不過，週三晚上我們會需要大夜班的人力。有意願在該時段加班的同事，請聯絡人事部的蘇·崔納提。

**詞彙** in brief 新聞速報；簡而言之　at the site 現場　operational 運作的　state-of-the-art 先進的　wrap up 包裝　vacuum 真空　promptly 準時地

**196** ---------------------------------------------------------------

**What is the purpose of the article?**

(A) To introduce a start-up venture
(B) To report on a business index
(C) To provide information on a new local issue
(D) To demonstrate the latest equipment

這篇文章的目的為何？

(A) 介紹一個新創產業
(B) 報告一項商業指標
(C) 提供一項在地議題的訊息
(D) 展示最先進的設備

文章刊登在「Richmond Daily Post」，表示為李奇蒙地區的日報，且文章第一句便說明了主旨：「Giant Hawk Grocery is going to open its additional distribution center.」，並通篇介紹巨鷹百貨，從完工消息、佔地、開幕、倉庫、提供職缺等皆有所提及，故可知道這篇文章在宣傳李奇蒙地區第一家百貨的開幕消息，正確答案為 (C)。

**197** ---------------------------------------------------------------

**What is most likely true about the Richmond Distribution Center?**

(A) Its opening ceremony was very impressive.
(B) Mr. Conrad will soon be retired from the site.
(C) Ms. Blaniar is one of the volunteer workers.
(D) Some technical issues took place.

關於李奇蒙物流中心，何者最可能為真？

(A) 開幕式讓人印象深刻。
(B) 康洛德先生很快就會從那裡退休。
(C) 布藍尼爾女士是其中一名自願加班的人。
(D) 發生了一些技術問題。

文章第一段的最後即寫道：「the opening ceremony is held with numerous citizens」，表示商店曾舉行開幕典禮，故可推測郵件內第二句：「It's unbelievable that I have seen such a well-organized event.」，其中的「event」指的就是開幕典禮，且寄件人表示活動籌備得相當好，故本題正確答案為 (A)。

## 198

**What is the e-mail mainly about?**

(A) Celebrating the opening ceremony
(B) Organizing the upcoming event
(C) Helping choose a company
(D) Breaking off a business connection

該封電子郵件的主旨為何？

(A) 慶祝開幕式
(B) 準備即將到來的活動
(C) 協助選擇一家廠商
(D) 打斷商業合作關係

本題詢問郵件的目的，注意不能被第一個段落的內容誤導，應先掌握整體脈絡後再進行解題。

從篇幅的分配可知，郵件內容著重在第二段，且在段落第一句表明：「I think that it is time to choose a company that sends automatic notifications to employees' cell phones.」，表示要選定能發送簡訊的公司，並在後文提供相關廠商的資訊，故本題正確答案為 (C)。

## 199

**What company was selected by Mr. Chuck?**

(A) The company that Ms. Blaniar works with
(B) The company that employees want to join
(C) The company that operates an overnight service
(D) The company that is cheaper than another

查克先生選了哪間公司？

(A) 布藍尼爾女士工作的公司
(B) 員工想去的公司
(C) 在大夜班營運的公司
(D) 比起另一家廠商更便宜的公司

根據訊息可以得知，「全體通知」公司最後被選為合作業者，負責對員工發送通知訊息。而再回看郵件內容，其中提到：「Unitas Notification also looks great, and their monthly fees are lower than the former」，可以得知這間公司的優勢在於費用較為低廉，故本題最適合的答案為 (D)。

## 200

**What does the message ask the employees wishing to work extra to do?**

(A) Contact the human resources department
(B) Work for another distribution center
(C) Go to the warehouse from Tuesday
(D) Reply to the message within a day

簡訊中，要求有意願加班的員工去做什麼？

(A) 聯絡人資部門
(B) 到另一間物流中心工作
(C) 從週二開始到倉庫工作
(D) 一天內回覆訊息

從訊息的最後一句：「If you are willing to work additional hours at that time, please contact Sue Trinity in the Personnel Division.」，可知有意加班的人可與人事部聯絡，故正確答案為 (A)。`

# ACTUAL TEST
## 5

### 101

**Mr. Robertson was concerned that the suggested hotel was not ------- enough to the airport.**

(A) close
(B) closer
(C) closest
(D) closely

| 題型 | 位置——形容詞 |
| --- | --- |
| 翻譯 | 羅伯森先生很擔心,人家推薦他的旅館距離機場不夠近。 |
| 詞彙 | be concerned 擔心 |

本題要考的是「be 動詞＋形容詞＋ enough」的用法,意思是「足夠……」,如選項 (A) 代入句子內,成為「not close enough」,即描述了旅館「不夠近」的狀態。另外,本題因為沒有出現可比較的對象,所以不適用比較級與最高級,故本題正確答案為 (A)。

### 102

**The University of Texas at Arlington provides residents ------- various recreational programs.**

(A) for
(B) at
(C) with
(D) as

| 題型 | 位置——介系詞 |
| --- | --- |
| 翻譯 | 阿靈頓的德州大學提供給居民各式娛樂課程。 |
| 詞彙 | residents 居民 |
| | recreational 娛樂的 |

本題重點是動詞 provide,固定用法為「provide A with B」或「provide B for A」,皆表示向 A 提供 B,另外使用動詞 offer 寫為「offer A B」,也是同樣的意思;本題正確答案為 (C)。

### 103

**Office supplies should be ------- only for business-related purposes.**

(A) purchase
(B) purchases
(C) purchased
(D) purchasing

| 題型 | 位置——動詞 |
| --- | --- |
| 翻譯 | 辦公用品的購買必須要基於工作用途。 |
| 詞彙 | office supply 辦公用品 |

本題詢問的是辦公用品 office supplies 與購買 purchase 之間的關係。purchase 除了是動詞購買之外,也可以當作名詞使用,但本句不在此例。

作為動詞使用時,因為句子內已經有 be 動詞,空格中不可代入一般動詞,故先剔除 (A) 與 (B)。又因為辦公用品無法主動購買自己,所以本句應使用被動式,表示「用品被購買」,故正確答案為 (C)。

**104**

In order to stick to the ------- of Omega Fashions, buyers ought to present a valid receipt when getting a refund.

(A) product
(B) sales
(C) manual
(D) policy

題型 詞彙——名詞

翻譯 為了遵守歐米茄時尚的規定，顧客要退款時需出示有效收據。

詞彙 stick to 遵守
valid 有效的

本句應為遵守退貨「規定」的意思，所以空格處最適合填入 policy，正確答案為 (D)。

★意為「遵守」的詞彙有：comply with、stick to、adhere to、follow、observe；這些動詞後面常接續的受詞有：regulation、standard、policy、deadline。

**105**

Anyone attending the mountain climbing activity has to prepare proper -------.

(A) equip
(B) equipped
(C) equipping
(D) equipment

題型 位置——名詞

翻譯 任何參加登山活動的人都需要準備合適的裝備。

詞彙 proper 合適的

proper 是形容詞，而只有名詞 equipment 既可被形容詞修飾，又可扮演及物動詞 prepare 的受詞，因此本題正確答案為 (D)。

**106**

The state-of-the-art program will ------- reduce the amount of time it takes to meet the deadline.

(A) significantly
(B) recently
(C) inappropriately
(D) approximately

題型 詞彙——副詞

翻譯 最先進的軟體能趕在截止日前，大幅減少所需時間。

詞彙 meet the deadline 趕上截止日

本題詢問的是可以修飾動詞 reduce 並符合句意的選項，而根據句意，此處應該是想表示「大幅地」，故正確答案為 (A)。

**107**

Promising candidates should possess a license to operate ------- bulldozers and excavators.

(A) either
(B) both
(C) during
(D) after

題型 詞彙——連接詞

翻譯 有希望錄取的應徵者都要有推土機和挖土機駕照。

詞彙 promising 有希望的
possess 擁有
bulldozer 推土機
excavator 挖土機

199

本題要考的是為對等連接名詞的 both，用法為「both A and B」，指「A 和 B 都……」，所以正確答案為 (B)。

注意當 (A) 作為對等連接詞時，後面應出現的不是 and 而是 or，表示為「either A or B」，指「不是 A 就是 B」。

**108**

We are scheduled to ------- the final results of the survey conducted last week with our customers on our website.

(A) share
(B) split
(C) ask
(D) improve

| 題型 | 詞彙——動詞 |
| --- | --- |
| 翻譯 | 我們預計在官網上和顧客分享上週民調的結果。 |
| 詞彙 | conduct 進行<br>split 隔開 |

本題的解題關鍵在於「with our customers」，應找出符合「與顧客一起做某事」的情境的選項，因此最適合填入 share，表示與顧客「分享」結果，故正確答案為 (A)。

**109**

The department of human resources replaced its chairs with ------- ones to decrease noise in the office.

(A) lightly
(B) lighter
(C) lightest
(D) lightness

| 題型 | 位置——形容詞 |
| --- | --- |
| 翻譯 | 人資部門把椅子換成比較輕的，來減少辦公室噪音。 |

只有形容詞可放在代名詞 ones 前面並修飾該代名詞。本句出現明確的比較對象，所以使用比較級最為合適，正確答案為 (B)。

(A) 為副詞無法代入；(C) 此為最高級，要空格前出現定冠詞 the 才可填入；(D) 為名詞，但此處無法形成複合名詞，字義也與句意不符。

**110**

The schedule for the conference call has been changed, so those involved will attend on Monday -------.

(A) alike
(B) yet
(C) likewise
(D) instead

| 題型 | 詞彙——副詞 |
| --- | --- |
| 翻譯 | 電話會議改時間了，所有與會者改成下週一參加。 |
| 詞彙 | conference call 電話會議 |

(A) alike 相似的；(B) yet 尚未；(C) likewise 相似地；(D) instead 取而代之。

本句前面提到行程出現變更，而後面則接續替代方案，所以應是表示與會者不會在原時間參加會議，「取而代之」，改在下週一開會，因此本題最適合的答案為 (D)。

## 111

------- of Mr. Anderson's telephone messages is to be left with his secretary while he has a meeting with his clients.

(A) Everyone
(B) Other
(C) All
(D) Each

| 題型 | 位置──代名詞 |
|---|---|
| 翻譯 | 安德森先生和客戶開會時，收到的每一封簡訊都會轉給他的祕書。 |

先判斷此句從開頭到 messages 皆為主詞，且由於動詞為單數 is，故此處主詞也為單數。(A) 字義與句意不符；(B) 為形容詞，後方無法接續 of；(C) 作為代名詞時，表複數的名詞，與此處不符，故可知本題正確答案為 (D)。

★熟記此用法：
each of the . . .（每一個……）

## 112

Given the nature of the meeting, formal attire is considered -------.

(A) useful
(B) appropriate
(C) affirmative
(D) indicative

| 題型 | 詞彙──形容詞 |
|---|---|
| 翻譯 | 考量會議的性質，穿著正式服裝才合適。 |
| 詞彙 | given 考量到<br>nature 特性<br>formal attire 正式服裝 |

(A) useful 有用的；(B) appropriate 合適的；(C) affirmative 肯定的；(D) indicative 顯眼的。

本題的句子中提到參加會議與正式服裝，故空格應代入字義為「合適的」的形容詞，因此正確答案為 (B)。

## 113

General Electronics plans to start a new business that ------- its customers to access more information.

(A) enabled
(B) enable
(C) has enabled
(D) will enable

| 題型 | 文法──時態 |
|---|---|
| 翻譯 | 大眾電子打算要開始新業務，將使顧客可以獲得更多資訊。 |
| 詞彙 | access 獲得 |

關係代名詞 that 前的先行詞 a new business 為單數，(B) 為主詞是複數時使用的動詞，所以答案可先排除 (B)。依照題意，公司計劃將開始新的業務，「未來」才能提供服務，故本題應使用未來式，正確答案為 (D)。

## 114

The managers at Lion Autos award a prize to employees who continuously ------- their expectations.

(A) exceed
(B) command
(C) desire
(D) suggest

| 題型 | 詞彙——動詞 |
|---|---|
| 翻譯 | 獅子汽車的經理頒獎給表現頻頻超乎預期的員工。 |
| 詞彙 | award a prize 頒獎 |

(A) exceed 超出；(B) command 指揮；(C) desire 想要；(D) suggest 建議、暗示。

本題以受詞 their expectations 作為線索，找出適合的動詞即可。「exceed one's expectations」是使用於狀況超乎期待時的片語，因此本題正確答案為 (A)。

★熟記下列「expectation」相關用法：
meet/fulfill one's expectation（符合某人的期待）
fail to meet/fulfill one's expectation（未符合某人的期待）
exceed one's expectation（超出某人的期待）

## 115

The recently released film by Astro Enterprises has received customer reviews and ratings that are ------- positive.

(A) except
(B) exception
(C) exceptional
(D) exceptionally

| 題型 | 位置——副詞 |
|---|---|
| 翻譯 | 星星娛樂公司最近發行的影片，獲得的觀眾評價和評分特別地好。 |
| 詞彙 | rating 評分<br>except 除了……之外<br>exceptional 傑出的 |

空格後為形容詞 positive，故可知此處應填入能修飾形容詞的副詞 exceptionally，本題正確答案為 (D)。

At Berkshire Hardaway, managers of each department are chosen based on their expertise and experience in a ------- area.

(A) granted
(B) provided
(C) particular
(D) substantial

| 題型 | 詞彙——形容詞 |
|---|---|
| 翻譯 | 在博克夏爾哈德威公司,各部門的經理都是基於特定領域的專業和經驗才能當上主管。 |
| 翻譯 | expertise 專業知識 |

(A) granted 承認的、准許的；(B) provided 提供的；(C) particular 特定的；(D) substantial 可觀的。

觀察空格前為不定冠詞 a，後為名詞 area，故空格應填入形容詞，本題只有 (C) 的字義適合與 area 搭配，解釋成「特定領域」，故正確答案為 (C)。

**117**

Valuable, fragile or perishable items would be much more expensive to ship ------- they need greater care.

(A) because
(B) nevertheless
(C) however
(D) even

題型 **位置**──連接詞

翻譯 昂貴、易碎或易腐壞物品的運費特別貴，因為它們需要更小心搬運。

詞彙 perishable 易腐壞的

觀察句子中有動詞 be 和 need，故中間需要一個連接詞才能使句子成立，所以空格處應填入連接詞 because，其他的選項皆為副詞，故本題正確答案為 (A)。

**118**

McKain and Mae is a full-service law firm that can help clients with a ------- of specialized legal needs.

(A) kind
(B) range
(C) way
(D) direction

題型 **詞彙**──名詞

翻譯 麥肯和梅是間提供全方位服務的法律事務所，給予有各式特殊需求的顧客法律協助。

詞彙 full-service 全方位服務
law firm 法律事務所

一般將「wide range of」的意思記做「各式各樣的」，實際上去掉 wide，僅出現「a range of」時，意思也是「各種的」，故本題正確答案為 (B)。

★熟記下列用法：
a (wide) range of（各式各樣的）

**119**

The newest version of our computer program for business expenses, ------- contains various functions, is relatively easy to use.

(A) it
(B) which
(C) whose
(D) those

題型 **位置**──關係代名詞

翻譯 最新版的營業支出軟體擁有多項功能，使用起來相對簡單。

從選項應可知道，本題要考的是關係代名詞。根據句意，從空格處到 functions 是在修飾說明前方的 computer program，表示「軟體有很多功能」，由於先行詞為事物，且子句前後各出現一個逗號，故此處應使用的關代為「which」，本題正確答案為 (B)。

注意本題的先行詞並非離關代最近的 business expenses。

**120**

------- you encounter any problems regarding assembly or operation, please call our customer service center.

(A) If
(B) Whether
(C) As
(D) Nor

題型 詞彙──連接詞

翻譯 如果您在安裝或操作時發現問題,請聯繫我們的客服中心。

詞彙 assembly 安裝
operation 操作

逗號前是條件,而後是與該條件相關的解決方法,所以本句應出現連接詞 If,表示「如果」前句發生,則後句發生,故正確答案為 (A)。

請注意,當逗號後面出現祈使句時,最前面的空格填入 If、When 以及不定詞的題型相當常見。

★以下為祈使句的用法:
1. 用來提供建議、勸告、命令、指示、鼓勵或祝賀
2. 祈使句的動詞要使用原形動詞
3. 祈使句常省略主詞 you;在句首或句尾加上 please 會更有禮貌,放在句尾時,前面要用逗號隔開。

**121**

The following document details the statistics the government will need for its ------- of next year's budget.

(A) analyze
(B) analyzes
(C) to analyze
(D) analysis

題型 位置──名詞

翻譯 下列文件詳細記錄了,政府用來分析明年度預算所需的統計資料。

詞彙 detail 詳細記錄
statistics 統計資料

空格前方為所有格 its,後方則接續介系詞,選項中只有 (D) 名詞可被所有格修飾,故此處只能填入 analysis,正確答案為 (D)。

**122**

------- a lot of people in Salt Lake City showed interest in the lifelong education program, none have yet enrolled.

(A) Even though
(B) As though
(C) However
(D) Likewise

題型 詞彙──連接詞

翻譯 即便有很多鹽湖城居民對終生學習課程表示興趣,卻沒有人註冊報名。

詞彙 show interest 表示出興趣
lifelong education 終生學習
enroll 報名

(A) Even though〔連接詞〕即使;(B) As though〔連接詞〕彷彿;(C) However〔副詞〕但是;(D) Likewise〔副詞〕同樣地。

前句表示居民有興趣,後句卻說沒有人報名,由此可見,兩個子句的內容為相反狀況,故最適合填入可連接對立內容的 Even though,正確答案為 (A)。

## 123

**Sales in North America are expected ------- most of the company's profits.**

(A) generate
(B) generated
(C) to generate
(D) will generate

題型 **位置**——不定詞

翻譯 北美區的業務預期將創造公司絕大部分的收益。

expect 本身就有期待、預料的意思，「expect a baby」則是指有孕在身。「be expected to V」放在此句的意思是「被預計會……」，用在題中意思即為，業務成效被預計會創造收益，故正確答案為 (C)。

## 124

**Lawyers process a sizable number of cases at the same time ------- strict time limits.**

(A) near
(B) toward
(C) following
(D) within

題型 **詞彙**——介系詞

翻譯 律師在非常有限的期間內，同時處理了大量案件。

根據題意，空格中應填入表示特定「期限」的介系詞，故正確答案為 (D)。

## 125

**The feasibility for the construction of the new museum is heavily ------- upon the city authorities' ability to pass the budget.**

(A) depend
(B) depended
(C) dependable
(D) dependent

題型 **位置**——形容詞

翻譯 新博物館建設能否順利進行，高度取決於市府是否通過預算。

詞彙 **feasibility** 順利進行
**heavily** 極度地
**city authorities** 市政府

「depend (up)on」為動詞片語，意思是「取決於……」，而由於本題前方出現 be 動詞，故片語可變化為「be dependent (up)on」或「be depending (up)on」。選項中沒有出現 depending，故正確答案為 (D)。

**126** ----------------------------------------

To prevent dairy and other ------- products from going bad, all trucks for Andy's food delivery service company are refrigerated.

(A) perishable
(B) pervasive
(C) adverse
(D) solid

| 題型 | 詞彙——形容詞 |
| --- | --- |
| 翻譯 | 為避免乳製品或其他易腐敗的產品壞掉,安迪食品運送公司的貨車都有冷藏功能。 |
| 詞彙 | dairy 乳製的 <br> be refrigerated 冷藏的 |

(A) perishable 易腐敗的;(B) pervasive 瀰漫的;(C) adverse 有害的;(D) solid 固體的、堅固的、可信的。

對等連接詞 and 前後應為同等的內容,選項中與 dairy 性質最相關的為 perishable,代表乳製品與車上其他產品都有易腐壞的特性,故正確答案為 (A)。

**127** ----------------------------------------

The Ministry of Finance reported that many small and medium-sized businesses are ------- strapped during their first year of business.

(A) finance
(B) financial
(C) financing
(D) financially

| 題型 | 位置——副詞 |
| --- | --- |
| 翻譯 | 財政部報告指出,很多中小企業第一年經營時財務上都會資金緊縮。 |
| 詞彙 | small and medium-sized businesses 中小企業 <br> be strapped 缺錢的 |

選項中只有副詞可夾在被動式的 be 動詞與 p.p. 之間,並修飾後方 p.p.,故本題正確答案為 (D)。

**128** ----------------------------------------

Mr. Nakamoto recommends that travel expense reports be submitted ------- after employees return from their trip.

(A) measurably
(B) vaguely
(C) uniquely
(D) promptly

| 題型 | 詞彙——副詞 |
| --- | --- |
| 翻譯 | 中本先生建議,員工出差回來後便立即提交差旅支出報告。 |
| 詞彙 | travel expense report 差旅費報告 |

(A) measurably 顯著地;(B) vaguely 模糊地;(C) uniquely 獨特地;(D) promptly 立即、準時地。

本題空格後為時間相關的連接詞 after,故空格處填入的應是可修飾時間用語的副詞,並從句意判斷,應帶有「立即」的意思,故本題正確答案為 (D)。

以往考題中,也曾在作為介系詞的 before 或 after 前面,出現過字義相同的 just、right、shortly、immediately,表示「在某事前/後立刻……」。

**129**

**After careful -------, we decided to move to a larger location to accommodate more tourists.**

(A) deliberate
(B) deliberated
(C) deliberately
(D) deliberation

| 題型 | 位置——名詞 |
| 翻譯 | 經過審慎考慮，我們決定搬到更大的地點來接納更多旅客。 |

(A) deliberate〔動詞〕慎重考慮、〔形容詞〕故意的、慎重的、緩慢的；(D) deliberation〔名詞〕考慮；討論。

空格前的形容詞 careful 只能修飾名詞，故此處應填入 deliberation，正確答案為 (D)。

**130**

**With her outstanding performance, Ms. Ashley has already ------- herself from her colleagues.**

(A) differentiated
(B) designated
(C) featured
(D) performed

| 題型 | 位置——形容詞 |
| 翻譯 | 艾許利女士的傑出表現，讓她在同事中出類拔萃。 |
| 詞彙 | outstanding 傑出的 performance 表現 colleague 同事 |

(A) differentiate 使……產生不同、區別；(B) designate 指定；(C) feature 以……為特色；(D) perform 演出。

「differentiated oneself from B」意思是「使自己不同於 B」，而根據句意，此處應是說明女子憑著好表現，讓自己和同事有所區別、從其中脫穎而出的意思，故最適合填入的答案為 (A)。

## PART 6

**131-134 電子郵件**

**To:** Brian Nixon
<bnixon@futuresky.co.au>
**From:** Jessica Hepburn
<jhepburn@cardinalfargo.org.au>

---

Dear Mr. Nixon,

We have received your application for a photographer at Cardinal Fargo Studio. The **131** is still available. **132**.

I was quite **133** with your previous experience of working at other major studios, so you must be accustomed to some of the job duties we require. **134**, our main business would be quite different from what you have done before, so you need to spend some time getting to know about this. I have scheduled a job interview for 15 September at 10:00 A.M. To confirm the schedule, please call my office at (01) 444-0125. I am looking forward to seeing you soon.

Sincerely,
Jessica Hepburn, Personnel Manager
Cardinal Fargo Studio

收件人：布萊恩‧尼克森
<bnixon@futuresky.co.au>
寄件人：潔西卡‧赫本
<jhepburn@cardinalfargo.org.au>

---

親愛的尼克森先生：

我們已收到您應徵鮮紅法戈工作室攝影師一職的申請。職缺目前依然開著，如果您對該職位還有興趣，下一階段將進行個人面試。

您在多間大型工作室豐富的工作經驗讓我印象深刻，所以您必然很熟悉我們所要求的某些工作內容。不過，我們的主要業務會和您之前做過的很不同，所以您會需要花些時間了解。我在9月15日的上午10點安排了面試。如果想要確認面試時間，可以撥打(01)444-0125聯絡我的辦公室。希望能很快跟您見面。

鮮紅法戈工作室人事經理
潔西卡‧赫本 敬上

---

**詞彙** be accustomed to V-ing 熟悉做……　job duty 工作內容　look forward to V-ing 期待……
reimbursement 核銷

**131** - - - - - - - - - - - - - - - - - - - - - - - - - - - - - - - - - - - - - - - - - - - - - -

(A) document
(B) position
(C) operation
(D) appointment

(A) 文件
(B) 職缺
(C) 手術
(D) 約會

**題型** 詞彙——名詞

前面出現「your application for a photographer」，所以此句應該延續告知該職位的相關訊息，故正確答案為 (B)。

**132** [NEW] ----------------------------------------

(A) Could you give us additional information regarding reimbursement?

(B) To be specific, do you have any experience in designing unique styles?

(C) Directions to the room for the interview can be found on our website.

(D) If you are still interested in this job, an individual interview is the next step.

(A) 可以請您給我們關於核銷的額外資訊嗎？

(B) 更精確地問，不知道您有沒有設計獨特風格的相關經驗？

(C) 可以在官網上找到前往面試地點的資訊。

(D) 如果您對該職位還有興趣，下一階段將進行個人面試。

**題型 填入句子**

空格前文表示收到應徵履歷，並確認尚有職缺，後段則詳細說明工作內容並在「I have scheduled a job interview for 15 September at 10:00 A.M.」，提及面試安排，故此處的句子應和職位、面試相關，正確答案為 (D)。

**133** ----------------------------------------

(A) impress

(B) impressed

(C) impressive

(D) impression

(A) 使……有印象

(B) 感到印象深刻

(C) 令人印象深刻的

(D) 印象

**題型 文法——動詞**

當表示某人對某事印象深刻，使用「sb be impressed with/by」，而表示某事或某人令人印象深刻，則是「sth/sb be impressive」。本句為人事經理對應徵者履歷感到印象深刻，故正確答案為 (B)。

**134** ----------------------------------------

(A) However

(B) Therefore

(C) Consequently

(D) Moreover

(A) 不過

(B) 因此

(C) 因此

(D) 此外

**題型 詞彙——副詞**

前一句中提到：「you must be accustomed to some of the job duties we require」，猜測應徵者應對一些工作內容感到熟悉，後句卻說：「our main business would be quite different from what you have done before」，表示職務會和以往不同，故空格內應填入具有「相反」字義的 However，正確答案為 (A)。

## 135–138 信件

April 20

Leonardo Cruise
111342 Main Street Kroger, CA 91101

Dear Mr. Cruise,

We are delighted to inform you of the fact that Kroger Recycling Program will start in our area on May 1. Residents who would like **135** in the program will be offered a blue container with wheels. To **136** a container, please call 800-111-1217.

As scheduled, the program will take place once a week instead of twice a week. **137**, this will reduce greenhouse gas emissions and provide us with a better environment.

If you need further information, such as a list of recyclable materials and maps, visit our website at www.krogerrecycling.com. **138**.

Sincerely,

Dwayne Damon, General Manager
Kroger Recycling Program

---

4月20日

李奧納多·克魯斯
91101 加州克羅格市主街111342號

親愛的克魯斯先生：

我們很高興通知您，克羅格回收計畫將從5月1日開始在我們地區實施。我們將提供一個有輪的藍色回收箱，給有意參與計畫的住戶。如欲索取回收箱，請聯絡800-111-1217。

如同先前所規劃的，這項計畫一週進行一次，而非一週兩次。因此，這項計畫將有效降低溫室氣體排放，並讓我們擁有一個更好的環境。

如果您需要更多資訊，像是可回收物品的清單或地圖，可以上我們官網www.krogerrecycling.com查詢。我們希望您能參與這項重要計畫。

克羅格回收計畫總經理
德偉恩·戴蒙 敬上

**詞彙** as scheduled 按照事先約定的時間　take place 進行　greenhouse gas 溫室氣體　emissions 排放

**135**
(A) participate
(B) participated
(C) to participate
(D) participating

(A) 參與
(B) 參與過
(C) 去參與
(D) 正在參與

**題型 文法——動詞**

「would like to V」意近「want to V」，為「想要」的意思，故此處要填入 (C)。

**136**
(A) request
(B) reinvent
(C) review
(D) remove

(A) 要求
(B) 改造
(C) 複習
(D) 移開

210

題型 **詞彙**——動詞

前句說：「Residents who would like to participate in the program will be offered a blue container with wheels.」，表示會為參加活動的居民提供回收箱，故後句故撥打電話「索取」的句意應較為適當，正確答案為 (A)。

**137** -----------------------------------------------------------

(A) However

(B) Consequently

(C) Meanwhile

(D) On the other hand

(A) 然而

(B) 因此

(C) 同時

(D) 另一方面

題型 **詞彙**——副詞

前句提到會減少資源回收計畫的實施時間，後句則說明此計畫可能帶來的正面影響，兩句間具有因果關係，因此此處填入 Consequently 最適當，正確答案為 (B)。

**138** (NEW) -----------------------------------------------------------

(A) The program has raised significant funds thanks to generous donors.

(B) We hope that you take part in this important program.

(C) You will get the blue container within 10 days.

(D) Please make sure that you do not put fragile materials in your container

(A) 多虧民眾慷慨捐款，這個計畫募得大量資金。

(B) 我們希望您能參與這項重要計畫。

(C) 您將在十天內拿到藍色回收箱。

(D) 請你確保不會在回收箱內放置易碎物品。

題型 **填入句子**

前句提到，想知道更多資訊可以瀏覽官網，故此處是在鼓勵有興趣的人加入回收計畫，最符合段落脈絡，正確答案為 (B)。

## 139–142 文章

City Mayor Alexandra Smith made the announcement that Robin Williams Tunnel **139** to better accommodate larger trucks. Drivers using the tunnel have increased significantly over the last few years due to the growth of freight transportations in this area. It is expected to take approximately ten months to finish this expansion project. **140**.

Jacksonville Road, which runs **141** the tunnel, is to be closed and traffic congestion between Amitiel and Hennatown will increase during that time. " **142**, it is the only possible option we could have," said mayor Smith.

市長亞歷山卓拉·史密斯宣布，羅賓威廉斯隧道將要進行擴建，方便大型載貨卡車通行。過去幾年來，因為當地貨運運輸的成長，使用隧道的駕駛也明顯增加。擴建計畫完工預計大約要10個月。經過精確的測量後，時間從原來估計的18個月縮短了。

沿著隧道的傑克森韋爾路將會封閉，在這段期間，阿米提爾和黑娜敦之間的交通將會更堵塞。「很遺憾，這是唯一可能的選擇。」市長史密斯說。

**詞彙** city mayor 市長　make an announcement 宣布　accommodate 容納
freight transportation 貨運運輸　traffic congestion 交通堵塞

211

(A) expand
(B) to expand
(C) was expanded
(D) will be expanded

(A) 擴建
(B) 去擴建
(C) 已被擴建
(D) 將被擴建

**題型 文法──動詞**

that 子句出現主詞,故空格應填入動詞。因此,首先可將 (B) 不定詞排除。因為隧道不可能自行擴張,所以使用主動式的 (A) 也可排除,且主詞為第三人稱單數,(A) 與主詞的單複數不符。

剩下的兩個被動式選項中,可以從時態進行選擇。由於工程尚未開始,所以過去式並不正確,故正確答案為 (D)。

**140** [NEW]

(A) Robin Williams Tunnel was completed one hundred years ago.
(B) Those living in Amitiel have complained about traffic jams.
(C) Freight service companies hope to recruit graduates from Hennatown University.
(D) The provisional estimate of eighteen months has been reduced as a result of accurate measurement.

(A) 羅賓威廉斯隧道一百年前就已經蓋好了。
(B) 住在阿米提爾的人長久以來都對塞車抱有不滿。
(C) 貨運公司希望能招聘黑娜敦大學的畢業生。
(D) 經過精確的測量後,時間從原來估計的 18 個月縮短了。

**題型 填入句子**

因為空格後直接開啟新的段落,故此處應代入與前句有關的內容。前一句提到:「It is expected to take approximately ten months to finish this expansion project.」,表示預計要花費十個月才竣工,故此句提及「工程歷時」相關的內容最為適當,正確答案為 (D)。

**141**

(A) along
(B) next
(C) while
(D) over

(A) 沿著
(B) 下一個的
(C) 當……的時候
(D) 在……之上

**題型 詞彙──介系詞**

由於空格後接續名詞,判斷應是介系詞,故可先刪除 (B) 與 (C),再從字義辨別 (A) 與 (D)。run over 是「溢出」的意思,但此句應是要說「道路在隧道中延伸」,故選有「沿著……」之意的 along 最適合,正確答案為 (A)。

**142**

(A) Surprisingly
(B) Accordingly
(C) Therefore
(D) Unfortunately

(A) 令人驚訝地
(B) 相應地
(C) 因此
(D) 遺憾地

**題型** 詞彙——副詞

前句提到可能會出現交通壅塞，空格後句又說「這是唯一的方法」，故空格處應有表示無奈的詞，選項中只有 Unfortunately 最合適，故正確答案為 (D)。

## 143–146 電子郵件

**To:** Sarah O'Connor
<sarah_oconnor@pinghwacorp.com>
**From:** Jim Lennon
<jim_lennon@ams.com>
**Date:** November 11
**Subject:** AMS
**Attachment:** AMS Brochure

Dear Ms. Sarah O'Connor,

We would like to express our gratitude for your inquiry on AMS. Our most advanced software program has helped a great number of companies streamline their performance appraisal process, **143** time and money.

We would recommend that you **144** the attached file. It contains information about five top-notch companies taking advantage of AMS. As you are aware, the ability to browse through evaluation sheets based on ratings has been exceptionally helpful to them. **145**, they can easily find all candidates who are eligible for promotion with our software program. In addition, after the entire digital sorting process is done, there is no paper clutter. **146**.

If you have any questions regarding this, please let me know.

Sincerely,
Jim Lennon
AMS Marketing Manager

---

收件人：莎拉·歐康諾
<sarah_oconnor@pinghwacorp.com>
寄件人：金·藍儂
<jim_lennon@ams.com>
日期：11月11日
主旨：AMS
附件：AMS小冊

小冊親愛的莎拉·歐康諾女士：

感謝您向AMS詢價。我們最先進的軟體程式，已協助大量企業提高評鑑程序的效率，省時又省錢。

我們建議您詳讀附檔，其中包含五間頂尖企業善用AMS而得利的資訊。如您所知，用排名來瀏覽績效表單的功能，對這幾家企業來說特別有幫助。因此藉由我們的軟體，他們可以輕易找到所有適合升遷的候選人。此外，所有分類過程數據化後，也不會有公文凌亂的情形。所有的表單在電腦化的資料庫中都整理得井然有序。

如果您還有其他相關問題，請讓我知道。

AMS行銷經理
金·藍儂 敬上

**詞彙** brochure 小冊子　inquiry 詢問　streamline 使簡化　appraisal 評鑑　top-notch 頂尖的
browse through 瀏覽　evaluation sheet 績效表單　exceptionally 特別地
be eligible for 有資格　clutter 凌亂

## 143

(A) save

(B) saves

(C) saved

(D) saving

(A) 節省

(B) 節省

(C) 節省了

(D) 節省

題型 **文法**──動詞

由於前面已出現 has helped，在沒有連接詞的狀態下，此處的動詞不可以一般的型態出現，故可先刪除 (A) 與 (B)。本句說明軟體能夠省時與省錢，故此處應是省略連接詞 and、加上逗號，並將主動動詞 save 改為 saving，正確答案為 (D)。

**144**

(A) review

(B) make

(C) prepare

(D) throw

(A) 仔細審閱

(B) 做

(C) 準備

(D) 丟

題型 **詞彙**──動詞

本題選出最符合句意的字彙即可。寄件者請收件者詳讀附檔，因為檔案內的資料與收件者的詢問相關，故正確答案為 (A)。

**145**

(A) As a result

(B) As long as

(C) In the meantime

(D) In keeping with

(A) 因此

(B) 只要

(C) 同時

(D) 與……一致

題型 **詞彙**──片語

前句說明軟體可協助公司績效評鑑，空格後則表示，公司能輕易 ] 找出適合升遷的候選人，故空格處應承接上句，表示「藉著軟體的協助」，才能輕鬆選出有資格的晉升者，正確答案為 (A)。

另外，本題的空格為副詞的位置，而 (B) 是連接詞，(D) 則為介系詞，所以在詞性上就不適合。

**146** NEW

(A) Our software will be updated next week.

(B) It will be a difficult task for you to sift through qualified candidates for promotion.

(C) All the sheets are well organized in the computerized database.

(D) Candidates should have at least 3 years of experience in a related field.

(A) 我們的軟體下週將會更新。

(B) 要從符合資格的人選當中選出晉升者，對你來說是個艱難的任務。

(C) 所有的表單在電腦化的資料庫中都整理得井然有序。

(D) 應徵者至少要有相關領域三年的工作經驗。

題型 **填入句子**

此句應與前句有關聯。前句提到，軟體能將分類過程數據化，減少紙本凌亂狀況，所以此句應延續「電子化的益處」說明，故選擇有提到電腦化的 (C) 最適當，正確答案為 (C)。

**147–148 簡訊**

| | |
|---|---|
| Dear Mr. Hughes, | 親愛的休斯先生： |
| This is a reminder from Golden State DVD Rental Service that DVDs that have been checked out in your name are due on December 15. Please return them to the location that you visited or any branch location by that date to avoid fees for overdue rentals. | 黃金州DVD出租服務提醒您，以您的名義租借的DVD將在12月15日到期。請在這個日期以前，到您租借的地點或是其他分店歸還DVD，以免被徵收逾期費用。 |
| Golden State DVD Rental Service Staff | 黃金州DVD出租服務員工 |
| (This is an automated message, do not reply to this text. If you have any questions with regard to this, please call our service representative in the main office at 211-232-0104.) | （這是自動寄發的訊息，請不要回覆。假如您有任何相關疑問，請撥打總部客服專線211-232-0104，由客服代表為您服務） |

**詞彙** due 應給的　branch 分店　overdue 逾期的　rental 租金　automated 自動的
with regard to . . . 與……相關

 **147**

**Why did Mr. Hughes receive the text message?**

(A) Because the items that he borrowed should be turned in soon

(B) Because he should pay late fees by December 15

(C) Because the items he requested are already sold out

(D) Because his membership card is set to expire on December 15

休斯先生為什麼收到簡訊？

(A) 因為他借的東西需要儘快歸還

(B) 因為他在 12 月 15 日前要繳交逾期費用

(C) 因為他要求的商品已經售罄

(D) 因為他的會員卡將在 12 月 15 日到期

從第一段第二行的「DVDs that have been checked out in your name are due on December 15」中，可知休斯先生租借的物品即將到期，故此簡訊是在提醒歸還，正確答案為 (A)。

 **148**

**According to the text message, what could Mr. Hughes do if he has any questions?**

(A) Visit the rental service company's website

(B) Speak with a service representative

(C) Send a text message to a service representative

(D) Go to any branch location of the rental service

根據簡訊，如果休斯先生有疑問應該怎麼做？

(A) 瀏覽出租店的網站

(B) 和客服代表聯繫

(C) 傳簡訊給客服代表

(D) 去出租服務的任何一家分店

最後一句是本題的解題線索。「If you have any questions with regard to this, please call our service representative」說到，若有問題可打電話聯繫客服，故正確答案為 (B)。

## 149–150 電子郵件

| | |
|---|---|
| **From:** Tom Affleck <affleck@valerofurniture.com> **To:** Scarlett Lawrence <lawrence@smail.com> **Date:** March 11 **Subject:** Shipping delay | 寄件人：湯姆・艾佛列克 <affleck@valerofurniture.com> 收件人：史嘉莉・勞倫斯 <lawrence@smail.com> 日期：3月11日 主旨：延遲寄送 |

---

Dear Ms. Lawrence,

Thank you for your recent purchase from Valero Furniture. Some of the items have yet to be shipped owing to the heavy snow in our area. Closures on the roads have also made it harder for items to be delivered from our warehouse. To make matters worse, the snow has caused power failures in our region. We, however, promise that we will get back to normal within 12 hours. Thus, your order will be shipped no later than Wednesday. The shipping fee on all affected orders will be fully refunded. We do apologize for any inconvenience this may cause you.

Sincerely,
Tom Affleck
Customer Service Manager

親愛的勞倫斯女士：

感謝您近期在瓦萊羅家具購買商品。由於我們地區下大雪，部分訂購貨品未能寄出。封路使得倉庫出貨更加困難。更糟的是，大雪造成我們地區停電。但我們承諾會在12個小時內回復正常運作。因此您的訂單最晚會在週三前出貨。受影響訂單的運費將會全額退費。很抱歉可能對您造成不便。

客服經理
湯姆・艾佛列克 敬上

---

**詞彙** owing to 由於　closure 封閉　to make matters worse 更糟的是
get back to normal 回復正常　no later than . . . 不遲於　shipping fee 運費

**Why was the e-mail written?**

(A) To give an update on the weather conditions
(B) To inform Ms. Lawrence of a late shipment
(C) To advertise furniture
(D) To report that some roads have been closed

寫這封電子郵件的目的是？

(A) 更新氣候狀況
(B) 告知勞倫斯女士寄送延遲
(C) 廣告家具
(D) 報告部分道路封閉

從第二句的「owing to the heavy snow」可以得知，大雪使運送發生延遲，故可知正確答案為 (B)。

**What will Ms. Lawrence receive?**

(A) A confirmation e-mail
(B) A discount voucher for a future purchase
(C) Free shipping on her order
(D) An additional new product

勞倫斯女士將收到什麼？

(A) 一封確認的電子郵件
(B) 一張家具的優惠券
(C) 她的訂單免運費
(D) 額外贈送一樣新品

從倒數第二句的「The shipping fee on all affected orders will be fully refunded.」可知，公司為受影響的訂單客戶退還運費，故女子不用為訂單支付運費，正確答案為 (C)。

## 151–152 告示

| New Rules for Trash Collection | 收垃圾的新規定 |

Krudenwald City will set a limit on the number of trash bins, which starts on April 25. Therefore, residents can now put no more than three trash bins outside for each curbside pickup, even though the monthly fee for trash collection is still unchanged. The sum of all trash bins should not exceed 100 liters in size.

City officials said that encouraging residents to take advantage of the city's free collection and recycling services for metal, plastic, and paper is part of the city's efforts to reduce the cost of trash collection. This will decrease landfill dumping fees as well.

克魯登華德市將從4月25日開始限制垃圾桶數量。每個月的垃圾清潔費沒有改變，但之後每一次垃圾車來，居民拿來丟的垃圾量不得超過三桶。總容量不得超過100公升。

市府官員表示，此舉能鼓勵居民利用市區免費的回收站，以及金屬、塑膠還有紙張的回收服務，為市府推廣降低收垃圾成本盡一份力。同時也能減少垃圾掩埋的花費。

**詞彙** trash bin 垃圾桶　curbside 路邊　pickup 小貨車　curbside pickup 垃圾子母車
monthly fee 月費　exceed 超過　landfill 垃圾掩埋　dumping 丟棄

**151**

What is the purpose of the notice?

(A) To provide a new service
(B) To announce a policy change
(C) To complain about recycling fees
(D) To recommend a landfill site

這篇告示的目的為何？

(A) 提供一項新服務
(B) 宣布一個規定異動
(C) 抱怨回收費
(D) 推薦一個掩埋場

第一句「Krudenwald City will set a limit on the number of trash bins, which starts on April 25.」提到，從 4 月 25 日開始將限制垃圾桶的數量，接著繼續針對費用、容量的異動描述，因此正確答案為 (B)。

**152**

According to the notice, what can residents use free of charge?

(A) A recycling service
(B) A trash collection service
(C) A trash bin
(D) A landfill site

根據告示，居民可以免費使用的服務是什麼？

(A) 回收服務
(B) 幫忙收垃圾的服務
(C) 垃圾桶
(D) 掩埋場

第二段中提到「encouraging residents to take advantage of the city's free collection and recycling services」，表示鼓勵居民使用免費的回收站與回收服務，故正確答案為 (A)。

另外，可從第一段的中提到的「the monthly fee for trash collection is still unchanged」得知，收垃圾的月費仍然不變，所以不是免費服務，故 (B) 不正確。

## MEMO

**To:** All employees
**From:** Christian Diesel, Director of Operations
**Date:** Thursday, July 28
**Subject:** West Wing Closure

The west wing of the building will be closed in the first week of August. The maintenance department will be in charge of replacing all the chairs and desks with environmentally friendly ones. According to the safety regulations, the site is off-limits to all employees while the maintenance staff is at work. The replacement schedule will start on Tuesday, August 1, and it will be finished on Saturday, August 5.

The affected offices are 1201–1235. Employees involved should work at home or, if necessary, a temporary workspace can be prepared for them in another part of the building. You may call administrative assistant Natalie Johansson at extension 51 to request a temporary workspace. Please note that we have limited temporary workspaces, which will be provided on a first-come, first-served basis. Thank you for your cooperation.

## 備忘錄

**此致：**所有員工
**來自：**克里斯提安·迪索營運長
**日期：**7月28日，週四
**主旨：**西翼大樓關閉

西翼大樓將會在8月第一週關閉。維修部門會負責把所有桌椅，替換成更環保的材質。依照安全規則，維修人員施工期間，所有員工均禁止進入。更換作業將從8月1日週二開始，並會在8月5日週六結束。

受到影響的辦公室是1201至1235號辦公室，相關員工可以在家辦公，或如果有必要的話，公司也可以在大樓內準備另一間臨時辦公區，供員工使用。您可以透過分機51，向行政助理娜塔莉·喬韓森提出需求。請留意臨時辦公區空間有限，將優先提供給先行申請的人。感謝您的配合。

 **詞彙** be in charge of 負責　environmentally friendly 環保的　off-limits 禁止進入的
if necessary 如果必要的話　administrative 行政的　extension 分機
on a first-come, first-served basis 先到者先得

**153**

**What is the reason for the closure of the west wing?**

(A) A regular inspection will be taking place.
(B) The headquarters will be moved to a different location.
(C) Office furniture will be replaced.
(D) Space for meetings will be added.

為什麼西翼大樓會關閉？

(A) 要實施例行性檢查。
(B) 總部要搬到其他地點。
(C) 要更換辦公家具。
(D) 要增設會議空間。

從第二句：「The maintenance department will be in charge of replacing all the chairs and desks with environmentally friendly ones.」，可知道封鎖大樓西翼是為了將桌椅換成環保材質。(C) 將 desks 與 chairs 合稱為 office furniture，符合文意，故正確答案為 (C)。

**154** - - - - - - - - - - - - - - - - - - - - - - - - - - - - - - - - - - - - - - - - - - - - -

Which of the following offices will be temporarily unavailable?

(A) 1200
(B) 1224
(C) 1236
(D) 1240

以下哪間辦公室將暫時無法使用？

(A) 1200
(B) 1224
(C) 1236
(D) 1240

第二段開頭提及受影響的辦公室：「The affected offices are 1201–1235.」，故只要從選項中找出在這段序號內的辦公室即可，正確答案為 (B)。

**155** - - - - - - - - - - - - - - - - - - - - - - - - - - - - - - - - - - - - - - - - - - - - -

What should employees do if they would like to request a temporary workspace?

(A) Contact their supervisor
(B) Write an e-mail to Mr. Diesel
(C) Apply online
(D) Call Ms. Johansson

如果員工欲申請臨時辦公區，應該怎麼做？

(A) 聯繫主管
(B) 寫電子郵件給迪索先生
(C) 線上申請
(D) 打電話給喬韓森女士

第二段提到，如果辦公室無法使用，可選擇在家上班，也可以使用臨時辦公室，並說：「You may call administrative assistant Natalie Johansson at extension 51 to request a temporary workspace.」，表示要透過電話向喬韓森助理申請，故正確答案為 (D)。

## 156–158 電子郵件

**From:** Angelina Grant
<agrant@lowecatering.com>
**To:** James Hardy
<jhardy@uig.com>
**Date:** June 11
**Subject:** Catering service

寄件人：安潔莉娜·格蘭特
<agrant@lowecatering.com>
收件人：詹姆斯·哈迪
<jhardy@uig.com>
日期：6月11日
主旨：外燴服務

Dear Mr. Hardy,

This e-mail is to confirm your telephone conversation yesterday with respect to your request for a catering service for the annual corporate conference. My understanding is that it should be similar to what you requested for last year's conference. Unfortunately, my food supplier has notified me of the fact that due to a shortage of beef, they are unable to provide it until next week. As you will hold the conference on June 15, I think it would be necessary to choose a different type of meat. I recommend chicken, which could be ready in time. So, if this is acceptable, please let me know by responding

親愛的哈迪先生：

這封電子郵件是要和您確認，您昨天在電話中為貴公司年度會議提出餐飲服務的需求。我的理解是，餐食服務的菜色應該要和去年的會議類似。但很遺憾，我的食物供應商通知我目前牛肉缺貨，到下週前都沒有辦法供貨。由於會議將在6月15日舉行，我想有必要選擇其他種類的肉品。我建議選雞肉，比較能趕上時間。所以如果這項建議可行，請直接回信告訴我。只要您同意

directly to this e-mail. Once you agree to the alternative, I will send you the contract and estimate sheet. If you need more information, please call me at 514-212-0114.

Thank you,
Angelina Grant, Manager
Lowe Catering Service

替代方案，我會寄合約和估價單給您。如果您需要更多資訊，可以透過514-212-0114聯絡我。

感謝，
羅威餐飲服務經理
安潔莉娜‧格蘭特

**詞彙** with respect to 關於　catering service 外燴服務　shortage 缺貨
hold the conference 舉行會議　be ready in time 即時準備好　alternative 替代方案
estimate sheet 估價單

**156** -------------------------------------------------------------------------

**What is suggested about Mr. Hardy?**

(A) He is Ms. Grant's colleague.
(B) He is planning a dinner party for his friends.
(C) He has requested a service from Lowe Catering Service before.
(D) He has asked for a change to a service.

文中提到關於哈迪先生什麼事？

(A) 他是格蘭特女士的同事。
(B) 他要為朋友準備晚宴。
(C) 他先前曾向羅威餐飲服務提出需求。
(D) 他要求更換服務內容。

第二句提到「My understanding is that it should be similar to what you requested for last year's conference.」，表示今年的餐飲菜色要與去年相似，由此可知，哈迪先生曾經光顧過羅威餐飲服務，故正確答案為 (C)。

**157** -------------------------------------------------------------------------

**Why does Ms. Grant recommend replacing the food item?**

(A) It is out of stock.
(B) It is very expensive.
(C) It lacks freshness.
(D) It doesn't taste good.

為什麼格蘭特女士建議更換餐點內容？

(A) 它沒有貨了。
(B) 它非常貴。
(C) 它不新鮮。
(D) 它不好吃。

第三句提到「due to a shortage of beef, they are unable to provide it until next week」，表示因為牛肉庫存不足，直到下週都無法供貨，意即目前沒有該項食材，故正確答案為 (A)。

**158** -------------------------------------------------------------------------

**What does Ms. Grant ask Mr. Hardy to do next?**

(A) Send a contract
(B) Call her immediately
(C) Reply to an e-mail
(D) Cancel a meeting

格蘭特女士要求哈迪先生接下來做什麼？

(A) 寄合約
(B) 馬上打電話給她
(C) 回覆電子郵件
(D) 取消會議

注意本題關鍵在倒數第三句，而不是最後一句。根據「So, if this is acceptable, please let me know by responding directly to this e-mail.」，如果哈迪先生同意替代方案，需要回覆電子郵件給格蘭特女士，所以正確答案為 (C)。

(A) 寄送合約的人是格蘭特女士；(B) 格蘭特女士只請哈迪先生在需要更多資訊時打給她，並沒有要求；(D) 沒有提及此事。

### 159–160 訊息串

| | |
|---|---|
| **Seneca Co. Agent** 5:15 P.M.<br>Hello, this is Seneca Co. Service Center. What's your problem? | 聖內嘉公司專員〔下午5:15〕：<br>聖內嘉公司客訊中心您好。請問您遇到什麼問題？ |
| **Martin Ford** 5:15 P.M.<br>I am having trouble with updating the newest version of software for my desktop. | 馬丁‧福特〔下午5:15〕：<br>我的桌機無法更新最新版本的軟體。 |
| **Seneca Co. Agent** 5:16 P.M.<br>What kind of desktop do you have? | 聖內嘉公司專員〔下午5:16〕：<br>請問您的桌機型號是？ |
| **Martin Ford** 5:17 P.M.<br>It's an XPS 8910. In order to download the software, I have to enter the correct serial number, but I can't find it. | 馬丁‧福特〔下午5:17〕：<br>是 XPS 8910。下載軟體要正確的序號，但我找不到。 |
| **Seneca Co. Agent** 5:18 P.M.<br>Here's how to find the serial number on your product. It is printed near the barcode on your product packaging. | 聖內嘉公司專員〔下午5:18〕：<br>要找到產品序號，它就印在產品包裝的條碼旁邊。 |
| **Seneca Co. Agent** 5:18 P.M.<br>It could be too small to read, so take a photo of the number with your mobile phone, then zoom in. | 聖內嘉公司專員〔下午5:18〕：<br>可能字太小不好看清楚，所以請用手機拍照，然後再放大。 |
| **Martin Ford** 5:19 P.M.<br>Yes, there is a ten-digit number on it. Is that it? | 馬丁‧福特〔下午5:19〕：<br>好，那裡有一組十碼數字。就是它嗎？ |
| **Seneca Co. Agent** 5:20 P.M.<br>Yes, that's right. Is there anything else that I could do to help you? | 聖內嘉公司專員〔下午5:20〕：<br>是的，沒錯。還有什麼可以幫助您的嗎？ |
| **Martin Ford** 5:20 P.M.<br>No. Thank you so much. | 馬丁‧福特〔下午5:20〕：<br>沒有。非常感謝您。 |

**詞彙** serial number 序號　barcode 條碼　product packaging 產品包裝　zoom in 放大　digit 位數

**159**

**What is Mr. Ford trying to do?**

(A) Find his password
(B) Create an account
(C) Buy a computer
(D) Download software

福特先生想做什麼？

(A) 找到密碼
(B) 申請帳號
(C) 買台電腦
(D) 下載軟體

福特先生在下午 5 點 15 分時説了：「I am having trouble with updating the newest version of software for my desktop.」，又在 5 點 17 分提到「In order to download the software」，表示他想要下載軟體為電腦升級，但卻遇到困難，故正確答案為 (D)。

 **160** **NEW** --------------------------------------------------

**At 5:19 P.M. what does Mr. Ford most likely mean when he writes, "Is that it"?**

(A) He wanted to check what he was looking for.
(B) He didn't understand the agent's idea.
(C) He has not used the online service before.
(D) He wanted to end the online chat.

下午 5:19 時，福特先生寫道：「就是它嗎」，他最可能的意思是？

(A) 他想確定找到的是不是對的東西。
(B) 他不了解專員的想法。
(C) 他從未用過線上服務。
(D) 他想要結束線上聊天

5 點 18 分時，公司專員教導福特先生尋找下載用的序號，故此時福特先生説的「Is that it?」應該是在確認自己找到的是否為正確序號，正確答案是 (A)。

---

### 161–163 電子郵件

**From:** Bradley Cooper
[bcooper@sysco.com]
**To:** Robert Gosling
[rgosling@sysco.com]
**Date:** January 4
**Subject:** Donation program

寄件人：布萊德利·庫柏
[bcooper@sysco.com]
收件人：羅伯特·葛斯林
[rgosling@sysco.com]
日期：1月4日
主旨：捐款計畫

---

Dear Mr. Gosling,

I have looked into the documents you gave with regard to Sysco's new donation program. —[1]—. At the next department meeting, you should share the information in the documents with our members. —[2]—. Moreover, I will encourage them to check the list of recommended organizations and participate in the program by selecting at least one of these to donate to before the program starts in February. —[3]—.

Please give me a call at your earliest convenience to discuss some issues about the program. —[4]—. Thank you in advance for your cooperation.

Sincerely,
Bradley Cooper
The Department of Human Resources

親愛的葛斯林先生：

關於西斯科的新捐款計畫，我仔細看過您提供的文件。您需要在下一次的部門會議，和我們同仁分享這份文件裡的訊息。此外，我會鼓勵他們看看推薦的組織名單，並在二月計畫開始前，請他們挑選其中至少一家來捐款。這還會花上幾週才能做決定。

請儘早打給我討論這項計畫的內容。在此先感謝您的配合。

人資部門
布萊德利·庫柏 敬上

---

**詞彙** **look into** 仔細看　**at one's earliest convenience** 在某人方便時儘早

**161** - - - - - - - - - - - - - - - - - - - - - - - - - - - - - - - - - - - - - - - - - - - - - - - - - - - - - - - - - - - - - - - - - - - - - - - - -

**What does Mr. Cooper want Mr. Gosling to do?**　　庫柏先生想要葛斯林先生做什麼？

(A) Discuss details about the program　　　　(A) 討論計畫的細節

(B) Make a donation to some organizations　　(B) 捐款給某些組織

(C) Reschedule a department meeting　　　　(C) 重新安排部門會議的時間

(D) Create a donation program　　　　　　(D) 發想一個捐款計畫

在郵件第一段前面，庫柏先生便説：「At the next department meeting, you should share the information in the documents with our members.」，要求葛斯林先生向同事分享資訊，且在第二段第一句，他又提到：「Please give me a call at your earliest convenience to discuss some issues about the program.」，表示想要討論計畫的內容，故正確答案為 (A)。

另外，(B) 是庫柏先生想要求同事做的事；(C) 未提及此事；(D)「Sysco's new donation program.」即為捐款計畫，不須再發想。

**162** - - - - - - - - - - - - - - - - - - - - - - - - - - - - - - - - - - - - - - - - - - - - - - - - - - - - - - - - - - - - - - - - - - - - - - - - -

**What is suggested about Sysco's new donation program?**　　文中提到關於西斯科的新捐款計畫什麼事？

(A) It is scheduled to go into effect in February.　　(A) 計畫將在二月生效。

(B) It is limited only to employees.　　　　　(B) 只限員工參與。

(C) It is held twice a year.　　　　　　　　(C) 每年舉辦兩次。

(D) It allows for employees to choose only one organization.　　(D) 員工只許選一家組織捐款。

根據第一段的第二句：「the program starts in February」，可知捐款計畫將在二月開始，故正確答案為 (A)。

(B) 參與對象與 (C) 舉辦次數的內容無法在文中找到線索，(D) 則可從「selecting at least one of these to donate」得知，員工可選擇至少一家組織捐款。

**163** (NEW) - - - - - - - - - - - - - - - - - - - - - - - - - - - - - - - - - - - - - - - - - - - - - - - - - - - - - - - - - - - - - - - - - - - -

**In which of the positions marked [1], [2], [3], and [4] does the following sentence best belong?**　　下列句子最適合出現在 [1]、[2]、[3]、[4] 的哪個位置中？

**"This will take several weeks to decide."**　　「這還會花上幾週才能做決定。」

(A) [1]　　　　　　　　　　　　　　　(A) [1]

(B) [2]　　　　　　　　　　　　　　　(B) [2]

(C) [3]　　　　　　　　　　　　　　　(C) [3]

(D) [4]　　　　　　　　　　　　　　　(D) [4]

題目引述的句子與「做決定」相關，故只要找出郵件中相似主題的段落即可。[3] 前句提到，庫伯先生要讓同事挑選至少一家組織捐款，所以將句子填入此處，可沿續句意，表示挑選的過程會花費幾週的時間，故正確答案為 (C)。

| | |
|---|---|
| May 1<br>Ryan Eastwood<br>Pinewood Apartment #1299<br>Orange County, California 562 | 5月1日<br>萊恩・伊斯伍德<br>562加州橘郡松木公寓1299號 |

Dear Mr. Eastwood,

Your Pinewood rental apartment is subject to a regular maintenance assessment. We are scheduled to visit on Tuesday, May 15, at 2:00 P.M. What we request is that tenants be present. Please let us know a time that works for you if this time is inconvenient for you. —[1]—.

During the assessment, we check several important items to make sure that they are working properly, which include appliances, the gas line, and plumbing. —[2]—.

According to our check-up lists, the interior of your apartment has not been painted for five years. If you want your house to be repainted, our maintenance staff will handle the task. We will make the utmost effort to finish the work in a timely fashion. —[3]—. We have a range of colors for painting, and you can see them by visiting our website at www.pinewood.com/colorsforpaint. —[4]—. Finally, our records indicate that the furniture in your house was fully replaced last year, so the replacement is not available at this time.

If you have any questions, please call me anytime.

Best Regards,
Chris Hemsworth
Office Manager

親愛的伊斯伍德先生：

您所租的松木公寓將實施例行性的維修評估。我們計畫在5月15日週二的下午兩點拜訪您。我們要求住戶必須在場。如果時間不便的話，還請您讓我們知道適合的時間。

評估過程中，我們會檢查多項重點項目，包括家電、瓦斯或水管管線，確認它們運作無虞。如有需要，就會進行維修工作。

根據我們的檢查清單，您的公寓內部已經五年沒有粉刷了。如果您想要重新粉刷，我們的維修人員也能處理。我們會盡全力以最有效率的方式完工。我們有很多顏色的油漆可供選擇，您可以造訪我們的官網www.pinewood.com/colorsforpaint查看。最後，我們的紀錄也指出，您去年才全面更換房裡的家具，所以現階段還不需要更換家具。

如果您有任何問題，請隨時跟我聯絡。

祝好，
辦公室主任
克里斯・漢斯沃

詞彙 **be subject to** 承受　**maintenance** 維修　**assessment** 評估　**tenant** 住戶、租客
**present** 在場的　**appliances** 家電用品　**plumbing** 水管管線
**make the utmost effort to V** 盡全力去……　**in a timely fashion** 有效率地

**164**

**Why was the letter sent to Mr. Eastwood?**

(A) To provide him with information on a rental promotion
(B) To notify him of a late payment
(C) To inform him of upcoming check-ups
(D) To suggest an annual event in an apartment

為什麼要寄這封信給伊斯伍德先生？

(A) 提供他租屋促銷的資訊
(B) 通知他帳款遲交
(C) 通知他之後要來檢查
(D) 建議公寓裡辦一項年度活動

信件開頭便寫表示要進行維修評估，且使用「scheduled to」，表示「計劃」在某時間拜訪，故最符合文意的選項為 (C)。

(A) 租屋資訊、(B) 拖欠費用以及 (D) 年度活動，皆沒有出現在文章中。

---

**165** --------------------------------------------------------------------------

**What is Mr. Eastwood asked to do on the afternoon of May 15?**

(A) Visit a Website
(B) Choose paint colors
(C) Reply to an e-mail
(D) Stay at home

伊斯伍德先生在 5 月 15 日下午被要求做什麼？

(A) 查看網頁
(B) 選擇油漆顏色
(C) 回覆電子郵件
(D) 待在家裡

第一段說到 5 月 15 日會進行維修評估，又說「What we request is that tenants be present.」，要求評估時住戶也在場，故最符合文意的選項為 (D)。

---

**166** --------------------------------------------------------------------------

**What home improvement work is Mr. Eastwood currently eligible for?**

(A) Painting a house
(B) Changing to new appliances
(C) Fixing doors
(D) Replacing furniture

哪一種家居改善方式，目前適合伊斯伍德先生？

(A) 粉刷房子
(B) 換家電
(C) 修理門
(D) 換家具

根據最後一段第一句：「According to our check-up lists, the interior of your apartment has not been painted for five years.」，可知公寓內已五年未粉刷，且後文也說，若有需要，可以幫忙處理，故正確答案為 (A)。

(B) 第二段只說會檢查家電是否能正常運作，並未提到要換新；(C) 未在文中提及；(D) 最後一段的最後一句提到，去年已經更換過家具，所以這次不會處理家具。

---

**167** (NEW) --------------------------------------------------------------------

**In which of the positions marked [1], [2], [3], and [4] does the following sentence best belong?**

**"If necessary, maintenance work will be performed."**

(A) [1]
(B) [2]
(C) [3]
(D) [4]

下列句子最適合出現在 [1]、[2]、[3]、[4] 的哪個位置中？

「如有需要，就會進行維修工作。」

(A) [1]
(B) [2]
(C) [3]
(D) [4]

題目引述的句子與「物品維修」有關，且應該是先經過檢查，才發現需要維修的狀況，故應選出內容相似的段落。[2] 的前句提到「we check several important items」，表示將檢查多個項目，包含家電、瓦斯、水管管線等，將句子接續此處，意即檢查後若有需要，會進行維修，故為適當的位置，本題正確答案為 (B)。

[3] 前面已經提到「If you want your house to be repainted, our maintenance staff will handle the task.」，故放於此處會造成句意重複，所以並不適合。

**168–171 表格**

| Moonlight Questionnaire | 月光問卷 |
|---|---|
| Thank you for participating in the preview of the film tentatively named Moonlight. As the film is in its final stages, it would be a great help for the final editing if you could give us your opinions about the film. Please take a few minutes to answer to the following questions. | 感謝您參加電影《月光（暫名）》的試片。由於本片正在最後收尾階段，如果您願意分享意見，將對本片最後剪輯有莫大幫助。請花幾分鐘回答下列問題。 |
| **Name:** Rachel Jane<br>**Address:** 2885 Sanford Avenue Grandville 28912 | 姓名：瑞秋‧珍<br>地址：28912格蘭維爾，桑福德大道2885號 |
| **What was your impression of this film?** | 您對這部片的印象是？ |
| I loved it! I enjoyed watching the same characters and scenes that I had imagined when reading the original novel a few years ago. It was a perfect adaptation of the novel. | 我好愛！我好喜歡裡面的角色與場景，跟我幾年前讀原著小說所想像的一模一樣。改編得很完美。 |
| **How about the sound quality? Please elaborate.** | 音質如何？請詳細說明。 |
| It was very clear. Especially, I loved its soundtrack. In general, there was no part where I could hardly understand the dialogue. | 非常清楚。我尤其喜歡原創配樂。總的來說，整部片裡沒有一句對白是我聽不懂的。 |
| **If there are any parts that seem too long, please elaborate on this.** | 如果有太冗長的橋段，請詳細說明。 |
| It seemed that this film was a bit longer than any other films that I have ever seen. However, all scenes were necessary for its storyline and flowed together smoothly. I would personally recommend not making any cuts. | 這部片確實比我看過的片子都要來得長一些。不過每個場景，對故事走向來說有它的必要，進行得也很流暢。我會建議不要再多作刪減。 |
| **Do you have any other comments?** | 有其他的建議嗎？ |
| Emma Aniston and James Niro gave quite excellent performances. I have never paid attention to Jessica Watson before. This time, she was amazing, and I hope she wins an award for this film. Just one thing I would like to mention is that what she wore in the movie didn't seem true to the original. The film is set in the mid-1880s. I think she should have worn something historically accurate. | 艾瑪‧阿尼斯頓和詹姆斯‧尼洛演得超棒。我先前從沒注意過潔西卡‧華森。這次她的演出很驚人，我希望她能因為這部片得獎。只有一件事是我想提的，她在電影中穿得服裝和原著中的不像。電影背景設定在1880年代中期。我覺得她應該穿著更貼近歷史的服裝。 |

**詞彙** tentatively 暫時地 in final stages 收尾階段 adaptation 改編 elaborate 詳細說明 storyline 故事走向 cut 刪減 true to the original 忠於原著 be set in 設定在……年代 mid- （某年代的）中期 accurate 正確的

**168** ------------------------------------------------------------

| | |
|---|---|
| **To whom was the questionnaire given?** | 這份問卷是給哪些人填的？ |
| (A) Professional writers | (A) 職業作家 |
| (B) Acting class members | (B) 演員訓練班學員 |
| (C) Directors in the film industry | (C) 影視產業導演 |
| (D) Audience members at a film screening | (D) 試映會的觀眾 |

從問卷第一句的「Thank you for participating in the preview of the film」，可知在為對方參加電影試映會表示感謝，且第一段的最後還請對方填寫電影相關的資料，故可以知道，這份問卷是給參加電影試映會的觀眾填寫，正確答案是 (D)。

**169** ------------------------------------------------------------

| | |
|---|---|
| **What is indicated about *Moonlight*?** | 文中提到關於《月光》什麼事？ |
| (A) It has a relatively short running time. | (A) 片長相對短。 |
| (B) It is based on a book. | (B) 根據一本書改編。 |
| (C) It is filmed in a documentary style. | (C) 用紀錄片風格拍攝。 |
| (D) It was completed a few years ago. | (D) 幾年前已經完成。 |

根據問卷第一題的回答，最後一句寫到「a perfect adaptation of the novel」，由此可知，這部電影是以小說為基礎改編，因此正確答案為 (B)。

(A) 從第三題回答的第一句：「this film was a bit longer than any other films that I have ever seen」，可知電影偏長；(C) 未曾提及此事；(D) 從問卷說明裡的「As the film is in its final stages」，可知電影還在編輯，尚未完成。

**170** ------------------------------------------------------------

| | |
|---|---|
| **What can be inferred about Ms. Watson?** | 從文中可以推論關於華森女士什麼事？ |
| (A) She recently starred in several films. | (A) 她最近演出多部電影。 |
| (B) She dropped out of the film. | (B) 她退出這部電影的演出。 |
| (C) She was participating in the preview of the film. | (C) 她參加了試映會。 |
| (D) She had an impressive performance in the film. | (D) 她在電影中的表演讓人印象深刻。 |

問卷的最後一題中說道：「I have never paid attention to Jessica Watson before. This time, she was amazing, and I hope she wins an award for this film.」，表示以前未注意到這位演員，但她在這部電影中表現十分傑出，甚至希望她因此得獎，故可推測演員華森女士發揮了令人印象深刻的演技，正確答案為 (D)。

**171** ------------------------------------------------------------

| | |
|---|---|
| **What does Ms. Jane recommend?** | 珍女士建議什麼？ |
| (A) Enabling the dialogue to be understood more easily | (A) 讓對話更好理解 |
| (B) Making clothing more authentic | (B) 讓服裝更寫實 |
| (C) Including more soundtracks | (C) 加入更多電影配樂 |
| (D) Shortening the film | (D) 縮短電影 |

本題要從問卷的最後一題找出正確答案。裡頭提到：「what she wore in the movie didn't seem true to the original」，表示演員在電影中的服裝並未忠於原著，並說道「she should have worn something historically accurate」，認為演員應穿著更符合歷史的服裝，由此可知，本題正確答案為 (B)。

(A) 第二題回答中的「there was no part where I could hardly understand the dialogue」即說明臺詞並沒有艱澀難懂的部分；(C) 未提及此事；(D) 雖有提到電影偏長，但也說了「I would personally recommend not making any cuts.」，表示認為沒有縮短的必要。

## 172–175 網路討論區

| | |
|---|---|
| **Sandra Lopez** 9:02 A.M.<br>Good morning. The board of directors approved our company's merger at the December meeting. I would like to know what you heard from the managers' meeting at the headquarters. | 珊德拉・羅培茲〔上午9:02〕：<br>早。董事在12月的董事會議上批准了我們公司的合併案。我想知道你們在總部的經理會議上，聽說了些什麼？ |
| **Kate Lively** 9:03 A.M.<br>At first, it caused a lot of confusion, but everything is restored to normal now. People seem to know what is going to happen. | 凱特・萊芙莉〔上午9:03〕：<br>起先是一陣大混亂，但現在所有事情都已經回歸正軌。大家似乎知道接下來的狀況。 |
| **Cameron Winslet** 9:03 A.M.<br>Employees here are convinced that the merger will lead to changes in personnel. Everybody is expressing concerns about any moves in February. That's because it is our busiest time of the year. When are we going to get detailed information on this? | 喀麥隆・溫斯雷〔上午9:03〕：<br>這裡的員工認為合併將造成人事動盪。所有人都很關心二月的任何動靜，畢竟那是一年最忙的時候。什麼時候可以知道詳情呢？ |
| **Cate Adams** 9:05 A.M.<br>I am not in the right position to answer these questions without knowing more information from the head office. | 凱特・亞當斯〔上午9:05〕：<br>沒從總公司那裡知道更多訊息以前，我不適合回答這些問題。 |
| **Sandra Lopez** 9:07 A.M.<br>I'll keep working on this. I will get more information before long. In February when the four of us meet together, I will make a report. | 珊德拉・羅培茲〔上午9:07〕：<br>我會持續追蹤這件事，儘快了解更多。等到二月我們四個見面時，再向各位報告。 |
| **Cameron Winslet** 9:08 A.M.<br>It seems that some of our employees will move boxes in March. | 喀麥隆・溫斯雷〔上午9:08〕：<br>聽起來，有些同仁可能在三月面臨調動？ |
| **Sandra Lopez** 9:09 A.M.<br>It could be possible. The personnel department is still figuring out which offices will receive employees from the other teams. | 珊德拉・羅培茲〔上午9:09〕：<br>的確有可能。人事部門還在安排，看哪些部門將吸收其他團隊的人。 |
| **Cate Adams** 9:10 A.M.<br>There must be plenty of decisions to be made. | 凱特・亞當斯〔上午9:10〕：<br>一定還有很多事要決定。 |

**詞彙** board of directors 董事　merger 合併　be restored to normal 回歸正軌　changes in personnel 人事動盪　not in the right position to V 不適合去……　before long 儘快 reshuffle 崗位調整

## 172

**Why did Ms. Lopez start an online chat with the managers?**

(A) To cancel a meeting
(B) To announce an upcoming merger
(C) To gather some opinions
(D) To change the date of the relocation

為什麼羅培茲女士和經理線上討論此事？

(A) 取消會議
(B) 告知未來合併事宜
(C) 收集意見
(D) 擇期搬遷

羅培茲女士在 9 點 2 分時說道：「I would like to know what you heard from the managers' meeting」，表示想了解經理會議的內容，故可知最適合的答案為 (C)。

另外，(A) 與 (D) 皆未在文中提及；(B) 合併一事是在董事會議上公布的。

## 173 (NEW)

**At 9:07 A.M., what does Ms. Lopez most likely mean when she writes, "I'll keep working on this"?**

(A) She is trying to get an update.
(B) Employees increased substantially last year.
(C) The headquarters will be moved in February.
(D) She is making an effort to get back to normal.

早上 9 點 7 分時，羅培茲女士寫道：「我會持續追蹤這件事」，她最可能的意思是？

(A) 她嘗試要取得最新狀況。
(D) 去年員工人數大增。
(C) 總部將在二月遷址。
(D) 她努力要讓一切回歸正常。

題目引用的句子出現前，溫斯雷先生表示想知道合併案的詳情，但亞當斯女士並未回答，故此處羅培茲女士說的「I'll keep working on this.」，應是代表會繼續關注此事以獲得資訊，因此正確答案為 (A)。

## 174

**When will the managers receive the updated information?**

(A) In December
(B) In January
(C) In February
(D) In March

經理們何時可以得知更新的資訊？

(A) 12 月
(B) 1 月
(C) 2 月
(D) 3 月

羅培茲女士在 9 點 7 分時說：「In February when the four of us meet together, I will make a report.」，表示會在四人二月見面時告知訊息，由此可知，正確答案為 (C)。

## 175

**What is the personnel department expected to do?**

(A) Reshuffle some employees
(B) Provide employees with office supplies
(C) Introduce new employees
(D) Replace the old personnel system

人事部門預計會做什麼？

(A) 人事洗牌
(B) 提供員工辦公用品
(C) 引介新員工
(D) 重整人事制度

根據9點9分時羅培茲女士的回覆：「The personnel department is still figuring out which offices will receive employees from the other teams.」，人事部門在安排部門間的人員調動，故本題正確答案為 (A)。

## 176–180 信件和電子郵件

| | |
|---|---|
| ### Statewide Insurance Co. | ### 國廣保險公司 |
| 848 Main Street, Fresno, CA 93721-2760 | 93721-2760 加州佛雷斯諾市大街848號 |
| April 8<br>George Hanks<br>2451 Inyo Street, Fresno, CA 93721 | 4月8日<br>喬治·漢克斯<br>93721加州佛雷斯諾市音約街2451號 |
| Dear Mr. Hanks, | 親愛的漢克斯先生： |
| Thank you for applying for the position of junior associate with Statewide Insurance Co. We regret to inform you that we decided to select another applicant after much consideration. However, we were very impressed by not only what you have done in the past few years, but also the knowledge and expertise you showed when you are interviewed. Therefore, we would like to offer you a vacant position that we believe suits you. | 感謝您申請國廣保險公司初級助理的職位。很遺憾通知您，經過多番思慮，我們選擇了另一名應徵者加入我們。但我們對您印象深刻，不只因為您近年的成就，還有您面試時所表現的知識和專業。因此，我們想要提供您一個相當適合您的職缺。 |
| The position that we offer you is a part-time job, unlike the one you applied for. The working hours are from 2 P.M. to 6 P.M. on Tuesday and Thursday, and 3 P.M. to 7 P.M. on Monday, Wednesday, and Friday. Your primary responsibilities will be gathering and analyzing information and data, providing potential clients with tailor-made plans, and planning insurance products. | 這是一份兼職工作，和您原先申請的有別。工時是每週二和週四的下午兩點到六點，以及週一、三、五的下午三點到七點。您的主要職責會是蒐集並分析資料和數據，向潛在客戶提供客製化的提案，並規劃保險產品。 |
| If you are interested in this position, feel free to call me at 515-217-0121 or email me at markchan@statewideinsurance.com. | 如果您對這個職位有興趣，儘管打電話給我，號碼是515-217-0121或是來信到markchan@statewideinsurance.com。 |
| **From:** George Hanks [ghanks@atmail.com]<br>**To:** Mark Chan [markchan@statewideinsurance.com]<br>**Date:** April 10<br>**Subject:** Re: Your letter | 寄件人：喬治·漢克斯 [ghanks@atmail.com]<br>收件人：馬克·陳 [markchan@statewideinsurance.com]<br>日期：4月10日<br>主旨：關於：您的來信 |

Dear Mr. Chan,

Thank you for your letter in which you offered me a job. I am very delighted to join Statewide Insurance Co. I am wondering, however, if the company could adjust my business hours.

At the interview session, I mentioned that I have been working as a volunteer with the International Insurance Society (IIS). There could be a scheduling conflict on Monday and Tuesday since I am now working for the organization Monday and Tuesday from 9 A.M. to 3 P.M. So, I would really appreciate it if your company would allow me to work from 4 P.M. to 8 P.M. on Monday and Tuesday.

I am looking forward to hearing from you soon.
Best wishes,
George Hanks

親愛的陳先生：

謝謝您來信提供我工作。我很高興可以加入國廣保險公司。但我在想貴公司能不能調整我的工作時間。

我在面試時曾經提到，我至今都在國際保險協會(IIS)擔任志工。由於我目前在那裡的排班是週一和二的早上九點到下午三點，這會和您安排的週一、周二時間有衝突。如果貴公司可以為我將週一和二的班，調整為下午四點到晚上八點，我會非常感謝。

期待您的回覆。
祝好，
喬治・漢克斯

**詞彙** insurance 保險　Junior associate 初級助理　regret to 遺憾要做……
potential clients 潛在客戶　tailor-made 客製化的　adjust 調整　business hour 工作時間

 **176** ------------------------------------------------

**For what kind of company does Mr. Chan most likely work?**

(A) A law firm
(B) An auto manufacturer
(C) A publisher
(D) An insurance company

陳先生最可能是在什麼公司上班？

(A) 法律事務所
(B) 汽車製造業
(C) 出版商
(D) 保險公司

信件第一行中便出現公司名稱「Statewide Insurance Co.」，且第二段的最後也提到：「Your primary responsibilities will be. . . planning insurance products.」，直接表示應徵者將負責保險相關的業務，故正確答案為 (D)。

**177** ------------------------------------------------

**In the letter, the word "select" in paragraph 1, line 2, is closest in meaning to**

(A) go with
(B) receive
(C) depend on
(D) account for

在信件中，第一段、第二行的「select」，最接近下列哪個意思？

(A) 選擇
(B) 接受
(C) 依賴
(D) 對……負責

信件開頭向收件者前來應徵表示感謝，但又說到「遺憾」、「另一位應徵者」、「多番思慮」等字眼，故此處的動詞 select 應是「選擇」的意思，表示選擇、錄取了其他的應徵者，故正確答案為 (A)。

## 178

**What is mentioned about Mr. Chan's company?**

(A) It has joined with the International Insurance Society.
(B) It recently signed a great number of clients.
(C) It has never hired full-time employees before.
(D) It offers an insurance planning service.

文中提到關於陳先生的公司什麼事？

(A) 和國際保險協會合夥。
(B) 最近和大量客戶簽約。
(C) 以前從未僱用全職員工。
(D) 提供保險規劃服務。

從陳先生感謝漢克斯先生應徵職缺，可知道陳先生任職於國廣保險公司，並可推測保險公司主要業務即在於提供保險規畫。除此之外，信件第二段透露公司某職缺的內容，並提到：「providing potential clients with tailor-made plans, and planning insurance products」，表示要對潛在客戶提供客製化的提案，並規劃保險產品，故可知道本題正確答案為 (D)。

(A) 從電子郵件可知，世界保險協會是漢克斯先生擔任志工的地方，而 (B) 與 (C) 則是皆未在文中提及。

## 179

**Why was the e-mail written?**

(A) To ask for a change of working hours
(B) To make inquiries about benefits for employees
(C) To recommend someone else qualified for the position
(D) To request a pay increase

為什麼要寫這封電子郵件？

(A) 詢問能否更改工作時間
(B) 詢問員工福利
(C) 推薦其他勝任這個職缺的人選
(D) 要求加薪

寄送郵件的目的可以從第二句得知，由於漢克斯先生寫道：「I am wondering, however, if the company could adjust my business hours.」，且第二段整段也說明時間安排，故可知調整工作時間為郵件重點，正確答案為 (A)。

## 180

**What most likely will NOT be a responsibility Mr. Hanks takes at Mr. Chan's company?**

(A) Collecting materials
(B) Counseling customers
(C) Introducing products
(D) Interviewing job applicants

下列何者最不可能是漢克斯先生在陳先生公司裡，所要負責的職務？

(A) 蒐集資料
(B) 向客戶提出建議
(C) 介紹產品
(D) 面試應徵者

根據信件第二段：「Your primary responsibilities will be gathering and analyzing information and data, providing potential clients with tailor-made plans, and planning insurance products.」，漢克斯先生將要負責的職務有資料與數據的蒐集與分析、對潛在客戶提供客製化計畫與保險商品規劃，正好依序符合選項 (A)、(B) 與 (C)，且並沒有提到面試應徵者，故本題的答案為 (D)。

## New York Media Corporation Research and Development Team

Annual Performance Appraisal Report

**Name:** Kim Barrymore
**Title:** Research Associate

Please write all major events and projects in which you took part this year.

1. Offered four-week course of media law for students at New York University majoring in mass communication (February 2–28)

2. Represented Research and Development Team at the 10th anniversary of News Media Conference, New York City (March 2–3)

3. Acted as a guest speaker, "*Current Status of Internet Media*" at the World Journalism Forum, London, England (May 12–15)

4. Carried out a research project on a new wave of Internet broadcasting (January — November). Study submitted to *Broadcasting Trade Journal*, accepted for publication.

5. Led public tours of new headquarters at New York Media Corporation (December).

## NY Media's Kim Barrymore Receives Award

by David Stewart, JSP Journalist

December 17—Kim Barrymore from New York Media Corp. has been named Journalist of the Year for her research project on a new wave of Internet broadcasting.

Margot Green, editor-in-chief of New York Media Corp., mentioned that it is unusual for the award to be given to a researcher. She went on to say, "It is attributable to Barrymore's hard work and dedication. And we're very delighted to have her on our team."

Ms. Barrymore joined New York Media Corp. 10 years ago after earning a doctorate degree in mass communication from New York University. She received her undergraduate education at Brooklyn Latin School in New York.

The award ceremony will be held on 23 December at the New York Conference Center.

## 紐約媒體企業 研發團隊

年度績效考核報告

姓名：金・巴利摩
職稱：研究員

請寫下所有您在今年所參與的重要活動和計畫：

1. 紐約大學，指導大眾傳播科系的學生四週的媒體法規課程（2月2日至28日）

2. 紐約，第10屆新聞媒體會議，研發團隊代表（3月2日至3日）

3. 英國倫敦，世界新聞論壇，「網路媒體的現況」客座講者（5月12日至15日）

4. 執行一項網路傳播新潮流的研究計畫（1月至11月）。研究獲登《傳播業期刊》。

5. 多次帶領紐約媒體企業新總部的公眾導覽（12月）

## 來自紐約媒體的金・巴利摩獲獎

JSP 記者 大衛・史都華撰文

12月17日—紐約媒體企業的金・巴利摩，以她研究網路傳播新潮流的計畫，獲頒年度傑出記者獎。

紐約媒體的主編瑪格特・格林表示，這個獎很少頒給研究者。她說：「這歸功於金・巴利摩的勤奮和奉獻。我們非常欣喜有她在我們團隊裡。」

巴利摩女士十年前取得紐約大學大眾傳播的博士學位後，便來到紐約媒體企業就職。而她大學讀的是紐約的布魯克林拉丁學院。

頒獎典禮將在12月23日於紐約會議中心舉行。

詞彙 performance appraisal report 績效考核報告　research associate 研究員　mass communication 大眾傳播　guest speaker 客座講者　current status 現況　carry out 執行　wave 潮流　editor-in-chief 主編　be attributable to 歸功於　dedication 奉獻　earn a doctorate degree 取得博士學位

**181**

---

**According to the report, why did Ms. Barrymore go to England?**

(A) To report a case

(B) To study mass media

(C) To deliver a speech

(D) To tour a new research facility

根據報告，為什麼巴利摩女士要去英國？

(A) 報告案例

(B) 研讀大眾傳播

(C) 發表演說

(D) 導覽新的研究場所

從報告的第三點，可以看到「Acted as a guest speaker . . . at the World Journalism Forum, London, England」，故可知巴利摩女士前往英國擔任論壇的講者，故正確答案為 (C)。

**182**

---

**What does the report suggest happened at New York Media Corp. in December?**

(A) An international forum was held.

(B) New courses for university students were given.

(C) A new head office was opened.

(D) The cost for public tours decreased.

從報告中可以得知，紐約媒體企業 12 月發生了什麼事？

(A) 舉行了一場國際論壇。

(B) 為大學生開設了新課程。

(C) 開設新的總部。

(D) 公眾導覽的支出減少了。

本題為「換句話說」的題型。報告的第五點寫道：「Led public tours of new headquarters at New York Media Corporation」，表示巴利摩女士 12 月時，多次帶領新總部的導覽活動，故此時公司發生的事件應是「開設新總部」一事。

因為後方敘述不符，本題不能看到「public tour」這個詞彙就馬上選 (D)，而「headquarters」意近於「head office」，故本題正確答案為 (C)。

**183**

---

**Where most likely did Ms. Barrymore's article first appear?**

(A) A magazine published by New York University

(B) On the website of New York Media Corporation

(C) In an industry publication

(D) In a scientific journal

巴利摩女士的文章最有可能在哪裡首次刊登？

(A) 紐約大學的雜誌

(B) 紐約媒體企業的網站

(C) 一份業界刊物

(D) 一本科學期刊

報告的第四點提到「Study submitted to *Broadcasting Trade Journal*, accepted for publication」，表示將研究送交給《傳播業期刊》，且文章獲得刊登，故這份期刊應是文章首次刊登處。選項中最符合的為點出業界刊物的 (C)，故正確答案為 (C)。

**184** ----------------------------------------

**What does Ms. Green imply about the Journalist of the Year award?**

(A) It offers both a medal and prize money.

(B) It is presented by New York Media Corp.

(C) It is rarely presented to a researcher.

(D) It is only for New York residents.

針對年度傑出記者獎，格林女士暗示什麼？

(A) 有提供獎牌和獎金。

(B) 由紐約媒體企業所頒發。

(C) 不常頒給研究者。

(D) 只會頒給紐約居民。

先找出「格林女士」為報導文章第二段提到的「Margot Green, editor-in-chief of New York Media Corp.」，代表格林女士是紐約媒體的主編，再從她說的「it is unusual for the award to be given to a researcher」可知，年度傑出記者獎鮮少頒發給研究者，故正確答案為 (C)。

**185** ----------------------------------------

**What is mentioned about the News Media Conference?**

(A) It is usually organized by the government.

(B) It was not held for the first time this year.

(C) It gives university students complimentary tickets.

(D) It is held every two years.

文中提到關於新聞媒體會議什麼事？

(A) 通常由政府主辦。

(B) 這不是今年第一次舉辦。

(C) 提供大學生免費門票。

(D) 每兩年舉辦一次。

報告第一點寫到「the 10th anniversary of News Media Conference」，故媒體會議今年為第十次舉辦，因此正確答案為 (B)。

### 186–190 文章、資訊和表格

<table>
<tr><td>

## Honeywell International's Offices to Be Relocated

March 1 — Honeywell International is scheduled to move its offices in Sydney, Melbourne, and Brisbane into company-owned properties. The significant increase in rental costs forced the company to make such a decision.

"We came to realize that building our own offices would result in saving money in many ways," said Elizabeth Lohan, Honeywell International's general director. She also mentioned that sharing space with other businesses has caused discomfort and inconvenience when doing businesses. Construction of its headquarters in Sydney, which began two years ago, will finally be finished this month.

Construction of the other branch offices in Melbourne and Brisbane will be finished in one year, and then employees will be moved accordingly.

</td><td>

## 漢尼威國際辦公室即將搬遷

3月1日—漢尼威國際計劃將其位於雪梨、墨爾本和布里斯本的辦公室，搬到公司名下的大樓內。租金飛漲迫使公司做出這項決定。

「我們注意到，自己的辦公室自己蓋，可以從很多方面把錢省下來。」漢尼威國際總經理伊莉莎白・蘿涵說。她也提到和其他企業共享辦公空間，會在辦公時造成困擾與不便。設在雪梨的總部於兩年前開始建設，終於將在這個月落成。

墨爾本和布里斯本的分公司建設計劃將在一年內完成，屆時員工也會搬過去。

</td></tr>
</table>

A representative of the company said that its entire workforce, which totaled approximately 1,000 employees last year, will be relocated to the new buildings no later than July.

一名公司代表表示，全體員工（去年估計約有1,000人）最晚將在七月以前，全數搬入新大樓。

## TIAA Relocation Services

We will handle everything for you. TIAA makes your move easier.

A relocation consulting service will be provided free of charge. Our consultant will visit your office or your home to give an estimate for the move. We will send you a written estimate by e-mail within two to three days after the visit.

Whenever you need us during the move, we will always be there for you.

- Do you need help packing? Our team members can help you with anything.

- Do you want to move any classified materials? We will arrange a schedule with your security staff to make sure that confidential files and documents are monitored without interruption.

- Do you need some space to hold your belongings? Our strictly-controlled warehouse is prepared for you.

We will fulfill our tasks. We will do our best to make all items neatly arranged.

## TIAA 搬家服務

通通由我們為您打點。TIAA讓您搬家更輕鬆。

免費的搬家諮詢服務。我們顧問會親訪您的辦公室或住家，並對搬家進行估價。寫好的估價單會在諮詢後的兩到三天內，用電子郵件寄給您。

不論您什麼時候需要搬家，我們都準備好為您服務。

- 您需要打包嗎？我們人員全都可以幫忙。

- 您需要搬移機密資料嗎？我們會和您的安全人員一起安排行程，確保機密文件和檔案都在監督之下搬運不被干擾。

- 您需要空間保存私人物品嗎？我們準備好嚴密管理的倉庫等您到來。

我們使命必達。盡我們所能讓一切物品整整齊齊。

## TIAA Relocation Services Estimate Sheet

Please complete the following request form to schedule a visit for an accurate estimate.

| Company Name : Honeywell International | Name of contact person : Elizabeth Lohan |
|---|---|
| Telephone number : 128-01-2821169 | E-mail : el0800@atmail.co.au |
| Pick-up address : 680 George Street, Sydney | Delivery address: 458 Harris Street, Sydney |
| Pick-up date : April 3 | Delivery date : April 3 |

Preferred date and time for an estimate: March 3, 10:00 A.M.

## TIAA 搬家服務估價單

請完成下列需求表格，以便安排現場精準估價。

| 公司名稱： 漢尼威國際 | 聯絡人姓名： 伊莉莎白·蘿涵 |
|---|---|
| 電話號碼： 128-01-2821169 | 信箱： el0800@atmail.co.au |
| 載貨地址： 雪梨喬治街 680 號 | 寄送地址： 雪梨哈里斯街 458 號 |
| 載貨日期： 4月3日 | 寄送日期： 4月3日 |

偏好的估價日期和時間：3月3日早上10點

**詞彙** property 房產　rental costs 租金支出　come to realize 注意到；終於意識到
result in . . . 帶來……的結果　in many ways 很多方面　general director 總經理
do business 辦公　give an estimate 進行估價　classified 機密的　confidential 機密的
interruption 干擾　belongings 私人物品　strictly-controlled 嚴密監控的
fulfill one's task 達成使命　do one's best 竭盡所能　(be) neatly arranged 整齊排放

**186**

In the article, the word "forced" in paragraph 1, line 2, is closest in meaning to

(A) compelled
(B) acted quickly
(C) broke down
(D) made a difference

在文章中，第一段、第二行的「forced」最接近下列哪個意思？

(A) 迫使
(B) 迅速做出反應
(C) 壞了
(D) 做出改變

此句説到「The significant increase in rental costs forced the company to make such a decision.」，其中提到「租金飆漲」、「公司下決定」，且從前句知道，公司的部分辦公室即將搬遷，故此處 force 最可能是「強迫」的意思，表示租金飆漲迫使辦公室搬遷，故正確答案為 (A)。

★熟記下列用法：
force/compel sb to V（強迫某人去做某事）
sb be forced/compelled to V（某人被迫得做某事）

**187**

What is inferred about Ms. Lohan?

(A) She was promoted to general director this year.
(B) She has worked for Honeywell International for five years.
(C) She will move to the new headquarters in April.
(D) She works in Honeywell International's Brisbane office.

文中提到蘿涵女士什麼事？

(A) 她今年升為總經理。
(B) 她在漢尼威國際工作五年了。
(C) 她會在四月搬到新總部去。
(D) 她在漢尼威國際布里斯本分公司工作。

蘿涵女士在文章與估價單上皆有出現。文章第一段即説到公司將雪梨、墨爾本及布里斯本的辦公室遷入名下的大樓，第二段則提到：「Construction of its headquarters in Sydney, which began two years ago, will finally be finished this month.」，表示在雪梨的總部大樓本月即將完工，故屆時雪梨的辦公室應會遷進去。

再從搬家公司估價單上聯絡人姓名的「Elizabeth Lohan」可知，蘿涵女士需要搬家服務，故她應是要搬往總部大樓的人員之一，本題正確答案為 (C)。

(A) 僅知蘿涵女士為總經理，但文中未提及何時晉升的；(B) 文中並未提及此事；(D) 從估價單上的地址來看，她是在雪梨而非布里斯本工作。

**What kind of service does TIAA offer?**

(A) Constructing buildings
(B) Transporting sensitive items
(C) Maintaining computer systems
(D) Strengthening security

**TIAA 提供什麼服務？**

(A) 建設大樓
(B) 搬運敏感物件
(C) 維護電腦系統
(D) 強化保全

TIAA 為搬家服務業者。公司資訊的第二點也寫到「classified materials」、「confidential files and documents」等字詞，故可知該公司也負責運送機密文件，因此本題正確答案為 (B)。

**What is implied about the Harris Street location?**

(A) It will accommodate nearly 1,000 employees.
(B) It was constructed in approximately two years.
(C) It has recently been remodeled.
(D) It is now rented by other firms.

**文中提到哈里斯街地點什麼事？**

(A) 將要容納近 1,000 名員工。
(B) 花了大約兩年來建設。
(C) 最近才整修。
(D) 現在也有其他公司租用。

文章第二段的最後一行提到：「Construction of its headquarters in Sydney, which began two years ago, will finally be finished this month.」，表示歷時兩年建設的雪梨總部大樓將在 3 月完工，而且根據估價單，總經理蘿涵女士預計 4 月就要搬到哈里斯街，故可推測哈里斯街就是這棟大樓的所在處，正確答案為 (B)。

(A) 文章內容是說等在雪梨、墨爾本與布里斯本的大樓都蓋好後，1,000 名員工會依照原本的辦公室位置，分配到三棟大樓中，所以哈里斯街的大樓只會容納原本就在雪梨辦公的員工。

**What will most likely happen on March 3?**

(A) A TIAA employee will visit George Street.
(B) Items will be properly arranged.
(C) Ms. Lohan will check an e-mail to review an estimate.
(D) Classified documents will be moved.

**在 3 月 3 日這天最有可能發生什麼事？**

(A) 一名 TIAA 的員工會拜訪喬治街。
(B) 東西都會被整理好。
(C) 蘿涵女士會收電子郵件查閱估價單。
(D) 機密文件會被移動。

根據估價單上的最後一行，漢尼威國際偏好 TIAA 在 3 月 3 日前來估價。由於搬家公司應是要在載貨地點估價，故參照表格中的載貨地址，可知搬家公司會前往雪梨喬治街 680 號，正確答案為 (A)。

| Home | Events | Location | Contact Us |
|---|---|---|---|

**Event Name:** International Sand Sculpture Festival
**Location:** Haulover Beach, Miami
**Date:** 28–29 July
**Contact:** Denzel Freeman:
dfreeman@hauloverbeach.com

### About:

The oldest and largest sand sculpture contest in Miami, which brings in over 50 master contestants from all over the world creating sculptures from 10,000 tons of sand. The festival marks the 7th anniversary this year. Last year alone, more than 20,000 visitors went to the Haulover Beach International Sand Sculpture Festival, which has become one of the largest beach events in Miami. In addition to the contest, the two-day festival features live music and sand workshops for children. When darkness falls, the sculptures will appear in a different light. Even though the event is free for all, $5 for parking will be charged.

| 首頁 | 活動 | 地點 | 聯絡我們 |
|---|---|---|---|

活動名稱：國際沙雕節

地點：邁阿密樂華海灘
日期：7月28日、29日
聯絡人：丹佐・費里曼
dfreeman@hauloverbeach.com

關於：

邁阿密歷史最悠久、規模最大的沙雕競賽，50名以上來自世界各地的大師齊聚競爭，用一萬噸的沙創造作品。今年已經是第七屆了。光是去年就有超過兩萬名遊客來到樂華海灘國際沙雕節，也成為邁阿密最大型海灘活動其中一項盛事。除了競賽，兩天的節慶期間也有特色現場音樂表演和兒童沙雕工作坊。當夜幕低垂，沙雕也會搭配不同燈光呈現。沙雕節雖然免費入場，但會收取五元的停車費。

## Winners of the 7th International Sand Sculpture Festival

| Placement | Name | Title of Piece |
|---|---|---|
| First Place | Humphrey Washington, England | Dinosaurs |
| Second Place | Jack Nicholson, Canada | Spaceships |
| Third Place | Johnny Spacey, U.S. | Castle |
| Fourth Place | Russel Pitt, Denmark | Pirates and Princesses |
| Fifth Place | Lonardo Travolta, Argentina | *Sea Creatures* |

## 第七屆國際沙雕節得獎者

| 名次 | 姓名 | 作品名稱 |
|---|---|---|
| 第一名 | 韓福瑞・華盛頓，英國 | 恐龍 |
| 第二名 | 傑克・尼可森，加拿大 | 太空船 |
| 第三名 | 強尼・史派西，美國 | 城堡 |
| 第四名 | 盧梭・皮特，丹麥 | 海盜和公主 |
| 第五名 | 羅納度・特拉維塔，阿根廷 | 海怪 |

## WHAT'S NEW IN MIAMI

By Christian Winslet

(1 August) — The 7th International Sand Sculpture Festival was held last weekend and was the best way to enjoy the summer. Due to the exceptionally fantastic weather, the event attracted more visitors than last year. This year, there was a competition for solo masters. They created eye-catching sand creatures and turned mere sand and water into genuine art. Masters depicted everything from sea creatures to castles and even spaceships in a somewhat exaggerated way.

Humphrey Washington from England beat three-time champion Jack Nicholson from Canada with his "Dinosaur" sculpture, which dazzled the judges with its absolute artistic realism. All the sculptures were attractive, but my personal favorite was "Pirates and Princesses," which vividly expressed comic gestures through the characters' arms and faces.

Children could participate in the sand class led by sand sculpting experts who were not participating in the contest. Live music pleased visitors' ears as well. This must be the perfect way to enjoy the hottest season.

## 邁阿密新鮮事

克莉斯汀‧溫斯雷撰文

（8月1日）—第七屆國際沙雕節於上週末舉辦，是享受夏日的最佳選擇。因為天氣超級好，參加人數比去年還多。今年有沙雕大師單人賽。參賽者的沙灘創作很吸睛，他們將普通的沙子和水變成真正的藝術。不論是海怪、城堡，甚至是有些誇張的太空船，都是大師描繪的鉅作。

來自英國的韓福瑞‧華盛頓，靠著作品「恐龍」的高超藝術寫實風格，讓評審眼睛一亮，擊敗了奪過三次冠軍、來自加拿大的傑克‧尼可森。所有作品都很吸引人，不過我個人最喜歡的是「海盜和公主」，角色的肢體和表情栩栩如生，別有一番風味。

兒童也可以參加沙雕課，由沒有參賽的沙雕專家領班授課。現場音樂表演也讓遊客一飽耳福。這真是最炎熱季節的最佳享受。

**詞彙** mark 紀念　eye-catching 吸睛的　genuine 真正的　depict 描繪　somewhat 有些
exaggerated 誇張的　beat 擊敗　dazzle 讓人眼睛一亮　comic gestures 有趣的姿勢

**What is mentioned about the contestants?**

(A) They are all amateurs.
(B) They have an acquaintance with Mr. Freeman.
(C) They had to sign up online in advance for the event.
(D) They are from various countries.

**文中提到參賽者什麼事？**

(A) 都是業餘人士。
(B) 認識費里曼先生。
(C) 活動前必須先在網路上報名。
(D) 來自不同的國家。

(B) 與 (C) 皆未在文中提及。透過網頁內容開頭的「master contestants」可推測參賽者不是業餘人士，故 (A) 也不正確；同句後方描述「from all over the world」，表示參賽者來自世界各地，因此本題正確答案為 (D)。

## 192

**In the article, the word "attracted" in paragraph 1, line 3, is closest in meaning to**

(A) moved

(B) drew

(C) won

(D) participated

在文章中，第一段、第三行的「attracted」，最接近下列哪個意思？

(A) 感動

(B) 招徠

(C) 贏得

(D) 參與

此句全句為「Due to the exceptionally fantastic weather, the event attracted more visitors than last year.」，其中提到「極好的天氣」、「活動」與「比去年更多的遊客」，故可推測，此處的 attracted 應為「吸引、招徠」，以解釋在好天氣下活動「招徠」許多遊客，故本題最合適選項 (B)。

## 193

**What is indicated about this year's event?**

(A) It cost 5 dollars to attend.

(B) It had over 20,000 visitors.

(C) It took place at Haulover Beach for the first time.

(D) It had adult-only programs.

文中提到今年活動的什麼事？

(A) 參加要花五美元。

(B) 有超過兩萬名遊客。

(C) 首度在樂華海灘舉辦。

(D) 有僅限大人參加的活動。

本題的解題線索大部分都在網頁內容中。中間提到：「Last year alone, more than 20,000 visitors ...」，表示去年就有超過兩萬名遊客，而報導文章中，則又說「the event attracted more visitors than last year」，意即今年遊客人數比去年更多，由此可以推測出正確答案為 (B)。

(A) 網頁最後的「the event is free for all」，參加費用為免費，五美元是停車費用；(C) 根據網頁第二句：「The festival marks the 7th anniversary this year.」，今年已為第七屆；(D) 有「sand workshops for children」，是給兒童的沙雕工作坊，但無法知道是否有僅限大人參加的活動。

## 194

**What is indicated about Mr. Nicholson?**

(A) He has won the contest before.

(B) He has led a sand class.

(C) He just moved to Canada.

(D) He is a member of a national team.

文中提到尼克森先生什麼事？

(A) 他之前曾贏過比賽。

(B) 他曾教過沙雕課。

(C) 他剛搬到加拿大。

(D) 他是國家代表隊成員。

從報導文章第二段第一行的「three-time champion Jack Nicholson」，可以知道尼克森先生曾獲得三次優勝，正確答案為 (A)。

## 195

**Whose sculpture did Ms. Winslet like the most?**

(A) Mr. Washington's
(B) Mr. Nicholson's
(C) Mr. Spacey's
(D) Mr. Pitt's

溫絲雷女士最喜歡誰的沙雕？

(A) 華盛頓先生的
(B) 尼可森先生的
(C) 史派西先生的
(D) 皮特先生的

溫斯雷女士在她撰寫的報導文章中說到「my personal favorite was "Pirates and Princesses"」，在對照得獎清單可知，此為皮特先生的作品，故正確答案為 (D)。

**196–200 小冊子、時間表和電子郵件**

## International Financial Investment Forum

Nairobi Conference Center, Kenya
Thursday, November 8

The 1st International Financial Investment Forum in Kenya will be a venue for discussing the current state of financial investment industry. Africa is one of the fastest growing markets in the world. The tourism and building infrastructure have brought a huge influx of money into Africa. World-renowned presenters will bring their expertise, passion, and enthusiasm to their session and share their insights on various issues. To participate in the forum, all involved are required to have their names registered. Anyone who would like to attend, please feel free to visit our website at www.ifif.org and fill in the sign-up form. No participation fee is charged.

Please note that applications for participants will be accepted entirely on a first-come, first-served basis because of the limited number of seats.

| Time | Presenter | Title |
|---|---|---|
| 9:00 A.M. | Keira Jane | Current Status of Africa |
| 10:30 A.M. | Catherine Jones | Economic and Market Outlooks in Africa |
| 12:00 P.M. | Lunch Break | |
| 1:00 P.M. | Clive Gibson | Strategic Investment |
| 2:00 P.M. | George Bloom | Quality Decision-Making Process |
| 3:00 P.M. | Sandra Ryan | *Risk Management* |

## 國際金融投資論壇

奈洛比會議中心，肯亞
11月8日週四

肯亞第一屆國際金融投資論壇將討論目前金融投資界的局勢。非洲是世界上其中一個快速成長的市場。觀光業和基礎建設帶動大量資金湧入非洲。揚名世界的講者將在這場論壇，展現他們的專業知識、熱情還有熱忱，並分享對於各類議題的洞見。如欲參加論壇者都須以姓名報名。有興趣參加者，歡迎上官網www.ifif.org查詢，並填寫報名表。入場完全免費。

請留意因為座位有限，與會申請將完全採取優先報名，優先入場的機制。

| 時間 | 講者 | 主題 |
|---|---|---|
| 上午 9:00 | 凱拉·珍 | 非洲現況 |
| 上午 10:30 | 凱薩琳·瓊斯 | 非洲經濟與市場展望 |
| 中午 12:00 | 午餐休息 | |
| 下午 1:00 | 克里夫·吉普森 | 策略性投資 |
| 下午 2:00 | 喬治·布魯 | 高品質決策過程 |
| 下午 3:00 | 珊德拉·萊恩 | 風險管理 |

**From:** Sandra Ryan
<sryan@ryaninvestmentgroup.com>
**To:** Megan Diaz
<mdiaz@ifif.org>
**Subject:** November Forum
**Date:** September 15

Dear Ms. Diaz,

Thank you for giving me the opportunity to be a part of this meaningful forum. First of all, I have to say that the international forum will have a great impact on the industry in Africa, which needs more investment across the board.

I have received the full schedule of presentations. Unfortunately, I have an important commitment in Kenya after the lunch break, so I have to leave the venue by 11:00 at the latest. The schedule indicated that I am the last presenter. Although I already reported the issue to the organizing committee, I want to get a definite answer. So if it is possible to change my presentation schedule, please send me a revised schedule and distribute it to everyone.

Thank you.

Sincerely,
Sandra Ryan
Ryan Investment Group

---

寄件人：珊德拉・萊恩
<sryan@ryaninvestmentgroup.com>
收件人：梅根・迪亞茲
<mdiaz@ifif.org>
主旨：11月的論壇
日期：9月15日

親愛的迪亞茲女士：

感謝您給我機會參加這麼有意義的論壇。首先，這個國際論壇將對非洲的產業帶來很大的影響，這裡需要來自全方位更多的投資挹注。

我已接到所有講座的行程了。但很遺憾在午餐休息時間後，我在肯亞有個重要的任務，所以我最晚必須在11點離開會場。行程表上顯示我是最後一名講者。雖然我已經向籌辦委員會反應過這個問題，但我想要一個明確答案。如果可以重新安排我的演講時間，請寄給我一份修改後的行程表，也麻煩將它寄給大家。

感謝。

萊恩投資集團
珊德拉・萊恩 敬上

---

**詞彙** venue 發生場所　infrastructure 基礎建設　influx 湧進　world-renowned 揚名世界的　share one's insights on sth 分享對於某事的洞見　register 報名　outlook 展望　strategic 策略性的　have an impact on sth 對某事物產生影響　across the board 全面　commitment 任務　committee 委員會　distribute 分送

**196**

**What are participants required to do?**

(A) Arrive at the event site 30 minutes early
(B) Register online
(C) Receive name cards
(D) Take a designated seat

**參加者需要做什麼？**

(A) 提前 30 分鐘到場。
(B) 線上報名
(C) 取得名牌
(D) 按指定座位入座

在第一篇文章第一段的最後部分提到，想要參加的人必須「visit our website at www.ifif.org and fill in the sign-up form」，告知需在官方網站上填寫報名表，故正確答案為 (B)。

## 197

**Who will make a speech on economic forecasts?**

(A) Keira Jane
(B) Catherine Jones
(C) Clive Gibson
(D) George Bloom

誰將發表預測經濟的演說？

(A) 凱拉·珍
(B) 凱薩琳·瓊斯
(C) 克里夫·吉普森
(D) 喬治·布魯

forecast 的字義為「預測」，故表格中最符合的演說主題為「Economic and Market Outlooks in Africa」，且講者為「Catherine Jones」，正確答案為 (B)。

## 198

**When will Ms. Ryan probably speak at the forum if it is rescheduled?**

(A) 9:00 A.M.
(B) 12:00 A.M.
(C) 2:00 P.M.
(D) 3:00 P.M.

如果萊恩女士的講座重新安排，可能的時間是？

(A) 上午 9:00
(B) 中午 12:00
(C) 下午 2:00
(D) 下午 3:00

萊恩女士在郵件第二段提到「I have to leave the venue by 11:00 at the latest」，表示最晚得在上午 11 點前離開活動現場，故她的演講應移到上午 9 點進行，正確答案為 (A)。

## 199

**What is indicated about Ms. Ryan?**

(A) She has to go to the airport after her presentation.
(B) She has an appointment during the forum.
(C) She changed her topic before the event.
(D) She is a member of the organizing committee.

文中提到萊恩女士什麼事？

(A) 她演講完就必須趕到機場。
(B) 她在論壇期間有其他任務。
(C) 她在活動前更改題目。
(D) 她是籌辦委員會的一員。

從郵件的第二段：「I have an important commitment in Kenya after the lunch break」，可知萊恩女士在午餐後有重要的約會，(B) 將 commitment 改為字義相似的 appointment，故正確答案為 (B)。

## 200

**What does Ms. Ryan request that Ms. Diaz do?**

(A) Extend the registration date
(B) Get approval from the hotel
(C) Update an event document
(D) Change a location

萊恩女士要求迪亞茲女士做什麼？

(A) 延後報名日期
(B) 取得飯店的同意
(C) 更新活動文件
(D) 換地點

從郵件最後的部分可以找到本題的答案。萊恩女士在郵件最末寫了：「if it is possible to change my presentation schedule, please send me a revised schedule」，故可知她要求收件人迪亞茲女士更改論壇日程，故正確答案為 (C)。

# ACTUAL TEST

# 6

## PART 5

**101**

As one of the company's events, GLK-Auto provides complimentary auto parts to ------ loyal customers.

(A) they
(B) their
(C) them
(D) theirs

題型 位置──代名詞

翻譯 GLK 汽車在活動中贈送汽車零件給他們的忠誠顧客。

詞彙 complimentary 免費的
loyal customer 忠誠顧客

由於介系詞 to 後面的名詞子句出現 loyal customers，故可知空格處應填入可修飾名詞的所有格，正確答案為 (B)。

**102**

Taking advantage of Power-Shoulder to ------ goods can prevent people from getting injured on their shoulders.

(A) achieve
(B) cause
(C) lift
(D) culminate

題型 詞彙──動詞

翻譯 藉由「強力肩膀」的幫助，人們得以避免抬貨時傷到肩膀。

詞彙 take advantage of 利用
goods 貨品

(A) achieve 達成；(B) cause 導致；(C) lift 舉起；(D) culminate 以……告終。

可以和受詞 goods 一起使用的動作為「舉起」，故正確答案為 (C)。請注意，culminate 為不及物動詞，後面無法直接接續名詞。

**103**

Some ------ coast communities are totally dependent on the shipping and fishing industry to earn a living.

(A) locate
(B) local
(C) location
(D) locals

題型 位置──形容詞

翻譯 一些沿岸社區的當地居民，完全仰賴船運和漁業維持生計。

詞彙 coast 海岸
be dependent on 仰賴
earn a living 維持生計

空格後方為名詞，前方則是數量形容詞 some，故此處應代入可以修飾名詞的形容詞 local，正確答案為 (B)。

**104**

Ruby's Friday restaurant is always ------ to provide exceptional dishes to our customers by hiring professional chefs.

(A) delicious
(B) ready
(C) experienced
(D) complicated

| 題型 | 詞彙——形容詞 |
|---|---|
| 翻譯 | 露比的星期五餐廳聘僱專業廚師，總是準備好獻上極佳的菜色給顧客。 |
| 詞彙 | exceptional 極佳的 |

根據句意，此處應是想表示餐廳「準備」好要提供佳餚，因此空格填入 ready 最為適當，故正確答案為 (B)。

**105**

If you have a problem with the item, please return it to the nearest store ------ seven days of the purchase to get a refund.

(A) until
(B) out of
(C) within
(D) from

| 題型 | 詞彙—— 介系詞 |
|---|---|
| 翻譯 | 如果產品有問題，請在購買七天內前往最近的店家退款。 |

空格後的 seven days 為表示「期間」的名詞，故空格內填入具有「在……之內」意思的介系詞 within 最適當，正確答案為 (C)。

(A) until 為表示「時間點」的介系詞或連接詞，故不是正確答案；(B) out of 為表示場所或帶有中斷意義的介系詞；(D) from 為表示開始時間點或出發時間點的介系詞，以上三個選項皆不是正確答案。

**106**

A ------ of products targeted for the winter season has been gradually piled into stockrooms in Portland stores.

(A) series
(B) lack
(C) frequency
(D) length

| 題型 | 詞彙——名詞 |
|---|---|
| 翻譯 | 針對冬季推出的系列商品，漸漸堆積在波特蘭店的倉庫裡。 |
| 詞彙 | target 針對<br>pile 堆積<br>stockroom 倉庫 |

此處表示「一系列的」產品最為適當，故正確答案為 (A)。

★記住下列表示用法：

many（許多的）
a number of（一些的）
a selection of（一些的；精選的）
a series of（一些的；一系列的）

a collection of（一些的；一批的；收藏的）
a variety of（各式各樣的）
a diversity of（各式各樣的）

## 107

According to the monthly financial report, these results of increasing loans on properties accord ------ with predictions in the popular magazine, *Jerry's Economy.*

(A) newly
(B) lately
(C) closely
(D) drastically

題型 詞彙──副詞

翻譯 根據財務月報,增加的房地產貸款額度和受歡迎雜誌《傑瑞經濟》的預測密切一致。

「accord with」的意思是「與……一致;與……符合」,所以表示與預測「密切地」吻合最為適當,故正確答案為 (C)。

另外,lately 及 recently 常與過去式或現在完成式使用,而像 drastically 這樣帶有「大幅」之意的副詞,則常用來修飾表示「增加」或「減少」的動詞。

**108**

A policy without any discussion among the management should not ------ the decision-making process regarding expanding their branches internationally.

(A) act
(B) remind
(C) influence
(D) confess

題型 詞彙──動詞

翻譯 主管之間未經討論的政策,不應該影響增設國際分部的決策過程。

詞彙 decision-making 決策的
expand 增設

(A) act 行動;實施;(B) remind 提醒;(C) influence 影響;(D) confess 懺悔、告白。根據本題句意,此處應表示尚未被討論的政策不該「影響」決策,故空格處填入 influence 最適當,正確答案為 (C)。

**109**

Premium Ltd. has made an extensive ------ to its assembly line to increase its productivity, which had caused a lot of mechanical problems.

(A) modifying
(B) modification
(C) modify
(D) to modify

題型 位置──名詞

翻譯 優質有限公司為了增加產能大規模改進裝配線,它先前造成很多機械故障。

詞彙 extensive 大規模的
assembly line 裝配線

先觀察到空格前方有冠詞「an」及形容詞 extensive,故此處填入名詞最適當,正確答案為 (B)。

另外,(A) modifying 為及物動詞加上 -ing 形成的動名詞,後方需出現受詞;(C) 為動詞原形;(D) 為不定詞。

## 110

**Mr. Terry has sent the loan application to several banks for securing funds displayed on the proof of bank statement ------ to purchase a new house in Austin, Texas.**

(A) require
(B) will require
(C) required
(D) requiring

| 題型 | 文法——分詞 |
| --- | --- |
| 翻譯 | 泰瑞先生向數間銀行提出貸款申請，以獲得買德州奧斯丁新房時，所需的銀行財力證明上有充裕資金。 |
| 詞彙 | secure 獲得<br>proof of bank statement 銀行財力證明 |

因為句子沒有連接詞，且已經出現動詞 has sent，如果要代入 (A) 或 (B) 等動詞，就必須要有連接詞，所以可以先排除這兩個選項。

(C) 過去分詞與 (D) 現在分詞中，bank statement 為動作 require（要求）的承受對象，也就是財力證明為「被要求」的物品，而過去分詞具有「被動意義」，故空格處填入過去分詞較為適當，本題正確答案為 (C)。

## 111

**Ms. Yoon has started the research project on second language writers by -------, but recently asked peers to help with collecting reliable data.**

(A) her
(B) hers
(C) herself
(D) she

| 題型 | 文法—— 反身代名詞 |
| --- | --- |
| 翻譯 | 尹女士起先是靠自己開始研究雙語作家的計畫，但最近開始請同儕幫忙蒐集可信的資料。 |
| 詞彙 | peer 同僚 |

因為空格在介系詞 by 的後面，故可先刪去為主格的 (D) she。而根據句意，此時應是說尹女士「靠自己」進行研究，而「by ＋反身代名詞」具有「獨自」、「憑己之力」的意思，最符合本題句意，故正確答案為 (C)。

★下列用法皆表示「獨自」：
by oneself
on one's own
alone

## 112

**------- this year's annual profits are lower than expected, the management at Johnny Index Distributions is not willing to approve employees' annual pay raise.**

(A) Owing to
(B) Given that
(C) With regard to
(D) In case of

| 題型 | 詞彙——片語 |
| --- | --- |
| 翻譯 | 考量今年的年度獲益低於預期，「強尼指標物流公司」的管理階層不想給員工年度加薪。 |
| 詞彙 | pay raise 加薪 |

空格後面出現主詞 this year's annual profits 與動詞 are，而逗號後面又出現另一組主詞與動詞，故本句還需要一個連接詞。選項中，唯一的連接詞片語為 Given that，其餘皆為介系詞片語，所以正確答案為 (B)。

另外，(A)、(C) 與 (D) 後方都要加名詞才能使用。

★請記住下列片語：
owing to N（由於……）
with regards to N（關於……）
in case of N（如果……）

 **113** ----------------------------------------------------------------

**The Maxi Department Store has attracted a lot of people due to its ------ to many urban transportation.**

(A) arena
(B) field
(C) proximity
(D) width

| 題型 | 詞彙──名詞 |
| --- | --- |

翻譯 馬克西百貨公司鄰近多個都市交通要點，靠著地緣之便吸引了很多人來。

詞彙 urban 都市的
transportation 交通運輸

(A) arena 競技場；(B) field 田地、領域；(C) proximity 鄰近性；(D) width 寬度、幅度。根據句意，此處應是表示百貨公司因與交通運輸的「鄰近性」而引來顧客，故正確答案為 (C)。

**114** ----------------------------------------------------------------

**------- advance ticket sales number more than three thousand, Penn Entertainment uses its main auditorium at Kovalchick Convention Center in Flint City.**

(A) Whether
(B) If
(C) That
(D) Despite

| 題型 | 詞彙──連接詞 |
| --- | --- |

翻譯 如果預購票售出超過三千張，賓州娛樂就會啟用位於弗林特市柯瓦爾奇客會議中心的大禮堂。

詞彙 advance ticket 預購票
number 到達（……的數值）

空格後的 number 為動詞，因此本句有兩組的主詞與動詞，故句中還缺一個連接詞。(D) Despite 為介系詞，可先刪去。(A)、(B) 與 (C) 皆為連接詞，而逗號前為副詞的位置，所以空格應代入的是「副詞連接詞」，且根據句意，此處應是說「如果」票賣得多則啟用場地，故本題正確答案為 (B)。

(A) Whether 可使用於名詞子句與副詞子句，但是使用於副詞子句時，一定會和 or 一起出現，表示「不管是……（或是）……」；(C) that 為用於名詞子句與形容詞子句的連接詞。

**115** ----

**Candidates are ------ to submit their portfolios to apply for the position at Alex Cooper Appliances.**

(A) will ask
(B) asks
(C) asking
(D) asked

**題型** 文法──被動

**翻譯** 亞歷克斯庫柏電器行職缺的應徵者被要求提交作品集。

根據句意，此處應是表示職缺應徵者「被要求」繳交作品集，空格前已有 are，後也有不定詞 to submit，故空格應填入 asked，正確答案為 (D)。

**116** ----

**The award committee of Selex Security Service nominated the top 10 employees ------- are entitled to get the Employee of the Year Award at its 20th anniversary banquet.**

(A) those
(B) anyone
(C) who
(D) which

**題型** 文法──關係代名詞

**翻譯** 塞雷克斯保全服務公司的頒獎委員會提名十位頂尖員工，他們將在二十週年餐會上獲頒年度最佳員工。

**詞彙** be entitled to 有……資格
banquet 餐會

觀察選項可知本題要考的是關係代名詞。(A) 與 (B) 為代名詞，無法代入空格，又因為空格前的先行詞為人物名詞 employees，故此處要使用 who，以引導後方用來修飾員工的形容詞子句，正確答案為 (C)。

**117** ----

**The newly installed program for the staff payroll system will be operational ------ on Friday, March 17, unless otherwise directed by a general manager.**

(A) beginning
(B) to begin
(C) will begin
(D) beginner

**題型** 位置──介系詞

**翻譯** 最新安裝的員工薪資帳冊軟體將從 3 月 17 日週五開始運作，除非總經理另外給予指示。

**詞彙** payroll 薪資帳冊

beginning on 後接時間，代表某事「從某時間開始」，意思近似介系詞 from，本題正確答案為 (A)。

## 118

**As of next year, UPT Electronics ------ its branches into other countries, especially Eastern Asia, for diverse businesses.**

(A) have expanded
(B) are expanding
(C) will expand
(D) is expanded

| 題型 | 文法──動詞 |
| --- | --- |
| 翻譯 | UPT 電子明年將到其他國家拓展分公司,特別是東亞,開拓不同業務。 |
| 詞彙 | as of . . . 自……開始 |

本句主詞為專有名詞且為單數,所以動詞應使用單數型動詞,故可先刪除 (A) 與 (B),又因為空格後面出現受詞 its branches,故可知本句為主動式,正確答案為 (C)。

★動詞題型可依照下列順序選出正確答案:
1. 有無主要動詞
2. 主詞與動詞的單複數是否一致
3. 句中動詞是否為被動式
4. 動詞是否符合句中時態

## 119

**You can easily find the Stapleton Library, which is located slightly ------ the Oak Grove on the IUP Campus.**

(A) over
(B) among
(C) between
(D) past

| 題型 | 詞彙──介系詞 |
| --- | --- |
| 翻譯 | 要找到斯泰普頓圖書館並不難,它就在賓州印第安納大學校園內,過了橡樹林一點點後。 |

(A) over 為表示「在期間之內;在空間之上」的介系詞;(B) among 表示「在(三個以上的名詞)之間」,與複數名詞連用;(C) between 應與「A and B」的結構或兩個場所連用,表示「在(兩個名詞)之間」,同與複數名詞連用;(D) past 意為「經過某時間點或地點」。

上述選項中,可以和「場所」一起使用的為 (A) 與 (D),但是圖書館不會在某個空間之上,故 over 並不適用,所以空格處應填入 past,正確答案為 (D)。

## 120

**If you purchase the latest items from Savannah Electronics, please thoroughly ------ the manual that comes with the item.**

(A) program
(B) gather
(C) direct
(D) review

| 題型 | 詞彙──動詞 |
| --- | --- |
| 翻譯 | 如果您在沙瓦納電器行買了最新產品,請務必完整詳讀所附的產品說明書。 |

選項中只有 review 適合受副詞 thoroughly 修飾並與 the manual 連用,表示完整詳讀説明書,故本題正確答案為 (D)。

**121**

Whenever ------ with prospective clients, please keep in mind that you should tell them about approaching special offers such as online discounts.

(A) to speak
(B) speaking
(C) spoke
(D) spoken

題型 位置——現在分詞

翻譯 每當與潛在客戶談話時，務必記得要告訴他們近期內會推出的優惠方案，像是線上折扣。

詞彙 prospective 潛在的
approaching 將推出的

Whenever 為連接詞，可引導分詞子句，分詞子句中若動詞為主動，則應將動詞改為現在分詞的「V-ing」形式，此時整個子句便成了分詞片語，如同此處用來表示條件的「Whenever speaking . . . clients」，故本題正確答案為 (B)。

**122**

Recruitment experts will help to distinguish a ------ candidate from other applicants by using tools for assessment of aptitude.

(A) selling
(B) promising
(C) reminding
(D) proposing

題型 詞彙——分詞

翻譯 人資專家運用職能評估工具，就能分辨應徵者是否有潛力。

詞彙 assessment 評估
aptitude 才能

此題是將動詞改為分詞，作為形容詞使用。根據句意，空格中的字義應與應徵者的性質相關，故填入 promising 最為適當，正確答案為 (B)。

**123**

Montgomery Corp. is ------ to confirm that they achieve a diversity of positive results from distribution, exclusive sales, and service sectors.

(A) pleasure
(B) please
(C) pleasing
(D) pleased

題型 位置——分詞

翻譯 蒙哥馬企業欣喜證實了，他們在物流、專賣和服務部門，取得多樣正向成果。

本題要考的是固定用法「sb be pleased to V」，表示某人很高興地去做某事，故正確答案為 (D)。

★記住以下用法：
sb be pleased to V（某人很高興地去做某事）
sb be pleased with N （某人因某物而開心）

**124**

Working as a senior manager at Punxtwaney City Museum two years ago, Mr. McNab has ------ been in charge of directing main exhibitions.

(A) since
(B) yet
(C) ever
(D) too

題型 文法——副詞

翻譯 麥卡納柏先生兩年前開始在龐蘇托尼市立博物館擔任資深經理，自此負責督導多項重要展覽。

(A) since 的意思為「自……以來」，可作為介系詞、連接詞與副詞使用，放在現在完成式的句子時，則表示持續的狀態。此句表示「從擔任經理以來」，便一直負責監督展覽，故本題正確答案為 (A)。

(B) yet 為副詞時的意思是「尚未」；當作同等連接詞時則為「然而」；當作副詞時，常與否定句或不定詞連用。(C) ever 的意思為「時常」、「不論何時」，使用時常常需要代入 hardly ever、if ever、ever since、比較級＋ than ever 或最高級＋ ever。(D) too 放在句尾時，代表「也」的意思，而用來修飾形容詞或副詞時，則帶有「非常」的意思。

**125**

Premier Investment Co. was forcibly operating inefficient production lines at a deficit, which might be damaging the company's ------ for maintaining its rank in the financial world.

(A) reputation
(B) negotiation
(C) consideration
(D) rotation

題型 詞彙——名詞

翻譯 優質投資公司面臨赤字，還是硬撐著效率不彰的生產線，這可能不利保持他們公司在金融圈的聲望。

詞彙 forcibly 被迫
deficit 赤字；虧損
production line 生產線
rank 等級

(A) reputation 聲望；(B) negotiation 協商；(C) consideration 考慮；(D) rotation 迴轉。

根據句意，此處應是表示損害公司「名聲」的意思，故空格填入 reputation 最為合適，正確答案為 (A)。

**126**

After parliament members reach an agreement to the amendments, the new regulations will be fully understandable to ------ concerned about the election.

(A) each other
(B) whatever
(C) anything
(D) everyone

題型 詞彙——代名詞

翻譯 國會議員對修正案達成共識後，這項新規定將讓每個關心選舉的人都能夠了解透徹。

詞彙 parliament 國會
reach an agreement 達成共識
amendment 修正
regulation 規定，條例

從句意來看，規定應是讓「人」能夠了解，所以空格處要填入與人物相關的代名詞。(A) each other 應使用於描述「兩者之間」的情境，然而本句並未明確表示事件涉及的人數，所以此選項無法成為答案。(B) whatever 是事物的代名詞，(C) anything 的字義則代表「任何事物」，所以皆不適合。選項中只有 everyone 適合填入空格處，故正確答案為 (D)。

**127**

------- all the prerequisite courses have been finished, the graduate students should prepare for their comprehensive written and oral test.

(A) While
(B) So that
(C) As soon as
(D) In that

題型 **詞彙**——連接詞
翻譯 研究生修完所有必修課，就可以準備資格考和口試。
詞彙 prerequisite 必修的
oral test 口試

(A) While 在……期間、相反地；(B) So that 為了；(C) As soon as 一……就；(D) In that 以……方面來説。

本題四個選項皆為副詞連接詞。根據字義，填入 as soon as 即表示必修課一被修完，學生就能準備口試，在句意上最為合適，故正確答案為 (C)。

另外，so that 與 in that 皆不可放在句子開頭。

**128**

The board of directors has already recognized ------- of the issue when all sales figures started to take a downward curve in the budget report.

(A) specifically
(B) specify
(C) specific
(D) specifics

題型 **位置**——名詞
翻譯 當預算報告顯示所有的銷售數字開始有下滑趨勢，董事會就已意識到這個問題的詳細情形。
詞彙 take a downward curve 呈下滑趨勢

及物動詞 has recognized 的主動式後面應出現受詞，故可先刪去 (A) 副詞與 (B) 動詞。(C) specific 作為形容詞時，字義為「具體的」，當成名詞使用時，意思是「詳細項目」，特別注意作為名詞時為可數名詞，所以應有冠詞、所有格等限定詞，或是改為複數字尾「-s」，由於此處前方沒有限定詞，故應改為複數型 specifics，本題正確答案為 (D)。

**129**

Once you submit the application for the position, you are ------ to hear the interview schedule from the Personnel Division.

(A) limited
(B) sought
(C) bound
(D) covered

題型 **詞彙**——動詞
翻譯 一旦您應徵該職位，就會知道人資部門的面試安排日程。
詞彙 be bound to V 必然會……

255

本題建議直接將固定用法 be bound to V 背起來。根據句意，此處應表示應徵後「就會」聽聞面試安排，故正確答案為 (C)。

★請熟記下列表示「將會」的用法：
be expected／set／bound／supposed／going to V

**130** ----------------------------------------------------------------------------------------------------

**If the item you purchased had been damaged, you ------ to return it to a nearby store for exchange.**

(A) would have been opted
(B) would have opted
(C) has opted
(D) is being opted

| 題型 | 文法──動詞 |
| 翻譯 | 如果您買的商品有瑕疵，您大可選擇到附近的店面換貨。 |
| 詞彙 | opt 選擇 |

先觀察子句中的主詞為空格前方的 you，所以可先刪除單數動詞的 (C) 與 (D)。(A) 與 (B) 依序為被動與主動，動詞 opt 意為「選擇」，為人主動進行的動作，故此處使用主動即可，正確答案為 (B)。

## PART 6

### 131–134 電子郵件

**To:** Brad Triana
**From:** John Fontainne
**Date:** 17 March
**Subject:** A request for advice about theater renovation

Dear Mr. Triana,

We have spent a lot of time dealing with the recommendations you gave at the last meeting. Above all, we **131** a wide black curtain that blocks the noise from the outside of the stage. For testing its degree of blocking, our worker stood **132** near the stage, and we couldn't hear any sound during pre-practice. We also have plans to comply with your recommendations to expand the control console, enabling experienced staff to work closely together. **133**.

We are pleased **134** your useful and informative guidelines and look forward to meeting you next time.

Sincerely,
John Fontainne

收件人：布萊德·崔安納
寄件人：約翰·馮丹
日期：3月17日
主旨：請給予劇院整修建議

親愛的崔安納先生：

我們花了很多時間消化您上次在會議裡的建議。最重要的是，我們買了一個又寬又大的黑布幕，可以用來隔絕舞台外的噪音。為了測試減噪程度，我們的同仁站得離舞台很近，我們排練時也聽不到任何聲音。我們目前也規劃採納您的建議，擴大控制台讓經驗豐富的同仁可以更密切合作。這會讓燈光和音效的操作比以往更有效率。

我們很開心能有您實用又完整的指示，期待下次再見。

約翰·馮丹 敬上

**詞彙** above all 最重要的　pre-practice 排練　comply with 依從　control console 控制台
informative 資訊豐富的　guideline 指示

**131**- - - - - - - - - - - - - - - - - - - - - - - - - - - - - - - - - - - - - - - - - - - - - - - - - - - - - - - -

(A) purchase
(B) purchased
(C) will purchase
(D) are purchasing

(A) 購買
(B) 購買了
(C) 將購買
(D) 正在購買

**題型 文法──動詞**

本題考的是動詞時態，如果句中沒有出現時間修飾語，則可透過前後句的脈絡解題。前一句使用過去完成式，提到花了許多時間消化建議，並按照建議購買黑布幕。

從句意來看，購買布幕為已完成的事項，所以使用過去時態 purchased 最為適當。且從時態來看，因為先消化建議再購買布幕，故先發生的事情使用過去完成式，後發生的使用簡單過去式，本題正確答案為 (B)。

(A) shortly
(B) hardly
(C) only
(D) rather

(A) 不久
(B) 幾乎不
(C) 只有
(D) 相當

題型 **詞彙──副詞**

根據句意，此處應表示工人「相當」靠近舞台，故選項中最合適的為 rather，正確答案為 (D)。

**133** NEW

(A) This can enable us to manage our lighting and sounds more effectively than before.
(B) The prior curtain is too thin to screen noise from the outside.
(C) There is only one improvement we made among your recommendations.
(D) We want to increase the number of ticket sales for the next performance.

(A) 這會讓燈光和音效的操作比以往更有效率。
(B) 之前的布幕太薄擋不住外來噪音。
(C) 您的建議裡，我們只採納了其中一項予以改進。
(D) 我們想要增加下一場表演的售票量。

題型 **填入句子**

填入句子的題型應先解讀前後句，再選出選項中最符合脈絡者，可特別關注指示詞（代名詞）與連接詞（連接副詞），並判斷前後文的關係。

前句提到擴大控制台，可以「enabling experienced staff to work closely together」，讓同事間更緊密合作，因此可判斷後方接續的句子應和控制台擴大、同事合作有關，故最適合的答案為 (A)。

**134**

(A) to
(B) with
(C) for
(D) on

(A) 去
(B) 有
(C) 為了
(D) 在……之上

題型 **詞彙──介系詞**

本題考的是固定用法「be pleased with N」，意思為「因某事感到高興、滿意」，在此解釋為因對方給予的指示而感到高興，故正確答案為 (B)。

**135–138 文章**

| *Indiana Tribune* – Business Briefing | 《印第安納論壇》—企業簡報 |
|---|---|
| Clarion (20 October) – Tyler Srinogil has been promoted to the chief editor of the *Indiana Tribune*. The board of directors **135** his promotion on Friday. **136** . As of next month, he will supervise the featured columns and inserted images. **137** , he will manage the overall operations for IndianaTribune. com, the company's online website. Tyler Srinogil is an industrious staff member **138** the improvement of IndianaTribune.com last year. | 克拉里翁（10月20日）—泰勒·史里諾吉爾晉升為《印第安納論壇》的總編輯。董事會已在週五確認了他的升遷。泰勒·史里諾吉爾兩年來擔任助理編輯。於是他將從下個月開始管理專欄和圖片。此外，他也會管理公司官網IndianaTribune. com的整體營運。泰勒·史里諾吉爾是名勤奮的員工，他去年對IndianaTribune. com的改進有所貢獻。 |

**詞彙** tribune 論壇　column 專欄　industrious 勤奮的

**135** -------------------------------------------------

| | |
|---|---|
| (A) confirmed | (A) 確認了 |
| (B) indicated | (B) 已指出 |
| (C) provided | (C) 提供了 |
| (D) rewarded | (D) 獎勵了 |

**題型 詞彙——動詞**

根據第一句的「Tyler Srinogil has been promoted to the chief editor of the *Indiana Tribune*.」，表示史里諾吉爾先生受到升遷，故此句應是承接上句，表達董事會「確認了」某人的升遷訊息，故空格處要填入 confirmed，正確答案為 (A)。

**136** (NEW) -------------------------------------------------

| | |
|---|---|
| (A) Tyler Srinogil has served as assistant editor for two years. | (A) 泰勒·史里諾吉爾兩年來擔任助理編輯。 |
| (B) The chief editor position will stay open until filled. | (B) 總編輯的職缺會空出來，直到有人補上。 |
| (C) The *Indiana Tribune* has just leased a new building space downtown. | (C) 《印第安納論壇》近來在市中心租了新辦公空間。 |
| (D) The management is offering him a new position as the webmaster. | (D) 管理部門給他一個網頁管理的新職務。 |

**題型 填入句子**

本題可使用刪去法。空格處前句提到史里諾吉爾先生獲得升遷，後句則提到他往後的工作內容，故此處簡介他過往的職務，符合前後脈絡，正確答案為 (A)。

(B) 總編輯就是史里諾吉爾先生，此職缺並沒有空出；(C) 文中並未提及此事；(D) 雖然後文也說到會管理官網，但因後句先提到他的職務為專欄及圖片管理，網頁管理是更後面才提到的主題，故此內容不適合接於此處。

**137**

(A) However
(B) In addition
(C) Meanwhile
(D) For instance

(A) 然而
(B) 此外
(C) 同時
(D) 舉例來說

題型 **詞彙**——連接副詞

前句說到史里諾吉爾先生將負責監督專欄及圖片，後句又說網頁也在職務範圍內，故此處應填入有「補充說明」的意思的副詞，故正確答案為 (B)。

**138**

(A) who contributed to
(B) that contributes to
(C) whose contributes to
(D) contributing

(A) 他對……有所貢獻
(B) 它導致……
(C) 他的貢獻對……
(D) 貢獻

題型 **文法**——動詞

先觀察空格為名詞受詞，由於 contribute 為不及物動詞，所以應該變成片語「contribute to」才能接續名詞，故 (D) 分詞 contributing 應改成 contributing to 才正確。(C) 中的「whose」為所有格，後面應該接續名詞，而不是動詞。

由於主詞為人物，且句子最後出現 last year（去年），故使用人物關係代名詞 who 與過去式 contributed to 最正確，本題答案為 (A)。

## 139–142 資訊

Thank you for your order from Elliezon.com. We sincerely hope that you are content with the quality of our products. If you are not **139**, you can return and refund the products with the original receipts and boxes you received within 10 days of the delivery date. In order to get a refund, you should complete the form in the box and sent it to us with the items. All merchandise **140** in the original packaging. **141**. This is because a credit card cancellation takes more time than a cash transaction. We appreciate your business and hope that you will continue to **142** with us.

感謝您在Elliezon.com下訂單。我們誠摯希望您滿意我們的產品品質。如果您不滿意，可以持原收據和外包裝在到貨的十天內退貨並取得退款。要取得退款，您需要填寫箱子內的表單，並將它和商品一起寄還給我們。所有商品都應該以原包裝運送。退款過程會花上一到兩週。因為取消信用卡交易會比現金來得久。感謝您的購買，也希望您會繼續購買我們的商品。

詞彙 **merchandise** 產品　**transaction** 交易

260

**139**

| | |
|---|---|
| (A) satisfying | (A) 令人滿意的 |
| (B) satisfied | (B) 感到滿意的 |
| (C) satisfy | (C) 使滿意 |
| (D) satisfaction | (D) 滿足 |

題型 **文法**──分詞形容詞

空格前有 be 動詞，故此處不能再填入動詞，(C) 不正確；而填入名詞 satisfaction 語意不通，故 (D) 也不正確。在 (A)、(B) 兩個分詞中，人物主詞為感受情感的「對象」，所以正確答案為 (B)。

★ **V-ed 與 V-ing：**
描述某人的感覺、表情，要用「V-ed」形式；描述引起這種感覺的人物、環境、事件時則使用「V-ing」形式。

**140**

| | |
|---|---|
| (A) will ship | (A) 將運送 |
| (B) have been shipped | (B) 已經被運送 |
| (C) are shipping | (C) 正在運送 |
| (D) should be shipped | (D) 應該被運送 |

題型 **文法**──動詞

先觀察本句主詞為不可數名詞 merchandise，視為單數，故動詞也應為單數動詞。(B) 與 (C) 皆是複數型動詞，所以不正確。而因為空格後面沒有受詞，所以本句動詞應為被動式，故要選 should be shipped，正確答案為 (D)。

**141** (NEW)

| | |
|---|---|
| (A) We extend an apology for the inconvenience. | (A) 我們對造成不便致歉。 |
| (B) The items you ordered are out of stock. | (B) 您所訂購的商品目前沒有存貨。 |
| (C) We have confidence in the quality of all the items. | (C) 我們對所有商品的品質很有信心。 |
| (D) It takes one or two weeks to process the refund. | (D) 退款過程會花上一到兩週。 |

題型 **填入句子**

後句接續了「This is because . . .」在解釋空格處內容的原因，故只要找出與後句有因果關係的句子即可。後句提到某事的原因在於比起現金交易，取消信用卡交易將花費更多時間，故空格處應填入與退款、時間相關的內容，因此正確答案為 (D)。

**142**

| | |
|---|---|
| (A) shop | (A) 購物 |
| (B) learn | (B) 學習 |
| (C) place | (C) 放置 |
| (D) compile | (D) 匯編 |

題型 **詞彙**──動詞

根據句意，此處應表示希望對方會繼續和自己「交易」，故選項中最適合填入 shop，正確答案為 (A)。

261

After three years of __143__ growth, Korean smartphone retailer SLP is planning to expand its business into the U.S. and Canada. __144__. On November 11, SLP's CEO, Jeremy Kim, announced that the company intends to open more than 100 branches in North America. __145__, SLP is looking for passionate individuals with an adventurous spirit and dedication to customer service to become franchise owners. Future __146__ are advised to contact Christine Jung at +82-2-333-8282.

經過三年穩定成長，韓國手機零售商SLP正規劃將業務擴展到美國和加拿大。該公司在亞洲區已有很多營業店面。SLP執行長傑瑞米‧金在11月11日宣布，公司有意在北美開超過100家分店。因此，SLP正在徵求有熱情、具冒險精神、為顧客服務熱忱的人成為分店長。如欲應徵者，請您聯絡克莉絲汀‧鐘，電話是+82-2-333-8282。

**詞彙** franchise 經銷權　domestic economy 國內經濟

**143** --------------------------------------------------

(A) appropriate
(B) advisable
(C) steady
(D) beneficent

(A) 適當的
(B) 可取的
(C) 穩定的
(D) 行善的

**題型** 詞彙──形容詞

根據後句提到的擴展業務範圍，此處應使用正面的形容詞，表示公司三年來良好的、穩定的成長，故選項中最適合填入 steady，正確答案為 (C)。

**144** (NEW) --------------------------------------------------

(A) The U.S. needs to attract more smartphone users for boosting its domestic economy.
(B) The company has already operated many stores in Asian areas.
(C) SLP is recognized worldwide in the smartphone field.
(D) The weather in Korea is similar to eastern America in many ways.

(A) 美國需要吸引更多智慧型手機使用者，以活絡其國內經濟。
(B) 該公司在亞洲區已有很多營業店面。
(C) SLP 在智慧型手機領域享有全球知名度。
(D) 韓國的天氣和美國東部有很多相似之處。

**題型** 填入句子

前一句提到，韓國公司計劃進入北美洲市場，而空格的下一句提到，公司預計設立百間北美分處，所以空格處應和海外擴張相關。

(B) 提到公司已在亞洲區擁有多家公司，最適合承接後句將到美洲設立據點的內容，故正確答案為 (B)。

**145**  ----------------------------------------

| | |
|---|---|
| (A) Moreover | (A) 並且 |
| (B) Nonetheless | (B) 雖然 |
| (C) However | (C) 然而 |
| (D) Therefore | (D) 因此 |

題型 **詞彙**──連接副詞

前句提及在北美設立分公司，後面則提到正尋找經營者，因為設了分公司，故需要經營者，兩者間具有因果關係，故此處使用表示結果的 Therefore 最適合，正確答案為 (D)。

**146** ----------------------------------------

| | |
|---|---|
| (A) candidates | (A) 應徵者 |
| (B) residents | (B) 居民 |
| (C) experts | (C) 專家 |
| (D) architects | (D) 建築師 |

題型 **詞彙**──名詞

綜合全文，此處應表示之後的「應徵者」可以聯絡公司，故正確答案為 (A)。

## PART 7

| | |
|---|---|
| **Posting Item:** XA-360 Deer Power Lawn Mower<br>**Price:** $700<br>**Location:** Fairfax, VA<br><br>**Item Description:**<br>Bought at LEX store a year ago. Paid $1000 for it. Had a two-year warranty. Fuel box is not working and should be replaced by the buyer.<br><br>In good condition. (No image available)<br><br>The price is fixed. (Not negotiable)<br><br>If you have any questions about the item, please feel free to contact me. (fairJohn@horrisnet.com) | 張貼物品：XA–360鹿力割草機<br>價格：700美元<br>地點：維吉尼亞州費爾法克斯郡<br><br>物品描述：<br>一年前在LEX店家以1000元購入。兩年保固。燃料箱故障，買家須自行更換。<br><br>狀況良好。（未附圖）。<br><br>不二價。（不可議價）。<br><br>如果您對商品有任何問題，請儘管和我聯繫（fairJohn@horrisnet.com）。 |

**詞彙** lawn 草坪　mower 割草機　warranty 保固

**147** - - - - - - - - - - - - - - - - - - - - - - - - - - - - - - - - - - - - - - - - - - - - - - - - - - - - - - - - - - - - - - - - - - - -

**What is NOT indicated about the lawn mower?**　文中沒有提到割草機什麼事？

(A) A part should be purchased.　(A) 有一零件需要購買。
(B) A manual is included.　(B) 有附上說明書。
(C) The price cannot be changed.　(C) 價格不能更動。
(D) It is a pre-owned item.　(D) 是二手商品。

可先從「Bought at LEX store a year ago.」知道產品為一年前購入，故現已是二手商品，
(D) 正確。再從「Fuel box is not working and should be replaced by the buyer.」可知燃料箱需
要更換，(A) 正確；且「The price is fixed. (Not negotiable)」提到價格不可議，故 (C) 也正確。
文中沒有提到說明書，故本題答案為 (B)。

**148** - - - - - - - - - - - - - - - - - - - - - - - - - - - - - - - - - - - - - - - - - - - - - - - - - - - - - - - - - - - - - - - - - - - -

**What is the seller likely to do?**　賣家可能會做什麼？

(A) Respond to an inquiry　(A) 回覆詢問
(B) Extend the warranty　(B) 展延保固
(C) Attach some pictures via e-mail　(C) 透過電子郵件附上照片
(D) Send the item to a buyer directly　(D) 直接把商品寄給買家

廣告最後有留下聯絡方式，且寫了歡迎提問，故賣家最可能會回覆詢問，正確答案為 (A)。

**149–151 資訊**

Johnstown City has planned to recruit a new financial planner in order to replace Mr. Kevin Davis, who has lately expressed his intent to retire. Mr. Davis will hand over his responsibilities on October 31 after holding the role for fourteen years. —[1]—.

The city finance director reports to the city manager and is in charge of supervising the monetary issues of the city. —[2]—. This position is a complex one, requiring the ability to enhance or put into effect a huge range of policies and steps to support the city's aims and to organize and keep the entire city's financial records.

"The new planner will have a lot of things to do," said city manager Cindy Fetterman. "The prospective staff member must have extensive experience managing the finances of an organization or a company."

According to Ms. Fetterman, the application screening period will begin soon, and interviews for the position begin in early September. —[3]—. The new employee will be confirmed at the end of October. —[4]—.

約漢斯敦市計劃要僱用新的財務規畫師，來接替最近有意退休的凱文‧戴維斯先生。戴維斯先生職掌14年，將在10月31日移交他的職務。

市府財政局長的職責是向市執行官報告，並負責管理城市的金融事宜。職務複雜，需要能改進、落實面向廣泛的政策，更要能進一步協助達成市鎮目標，也要安排、維持全市的財政紀錄。

「新的財務規畫師有很多事情要做，」市執行官辛蒂‧菲特曼說，「我們期望的同仁需要有在機構或公司內管理財務的豐富經驗。」

菲特曼女士表示，很快就會開始篩選應徵申請，並在九月初進行面試。8月20日以後收到的應徵資料將不予考慮。新人員的人選將在十月底確認。

**詞彙** hand over 交出　hold the role 擔任職務　monetary 金融的　financial records 財政紀錄　screening period 篩選期

 **149**

**What is the information mainly about?**

(A) Johnstown City has a plan to rebuild the city hall.

(B) There is a job opening for a city position in finance.

(C) The city's financial issues have not yet been resolved for two consecutive years.

(D) To celebrate Mr. Davis's retirement, city officials organized a banquet.

這篇文的主要資訊為何？

(A) 約漢斯敦市規劃重建市鎮廳。

(B) 市府開出財政相關的職缺。

(C) 市府的財政問題接連兩年都沒辦法解決。

(D) 為了慶祝戴維斯先生退休，市府官員辦了餐會。

段落重點通常會出現在開頭。本篇第一句即提到某市將僱用新的財務規畫師，後文依序也提到職務範圍、對應徵者的期許，以及應徵流程，故正確答案為 (B)。

## 150

**According to the information, what is required for the position?**

(A) A master's degree in finance
(B) A willingness to work on weekends
(C) A capacity for finance-related issues
(D) Moving to Johnstown City

根據文中資訊，這個職位有什麼條件？

(A) 財經碩士學位
(B) 願意在週末上班
(C) 處理財政事務的能力
(D) 搬到約漢斯敦市

根據第三段的引言：「The prospective staff member must have extensive experience managing the finances of an organization or a company.」，可知應徵者需具有處理財務的經驗，故選項中最相符的為 (C)。

## 151 NEW

**In which of the positions marked [1], [2], [3] and [4] does the following sentence best belong?**

**"Applications received after August 20 cannot be considered."**

(A) [1]
(B) [2]
(C) [3]
(D) [4]

下列句子最適合出現在 [1]、[2]、[3]、[4] 的哪個位置中？

「8 月 20 日以後收到的應徵資料將不予考慮。」

(A) [1]
(B) [2]
(C) [3]
(D) [4]

題目引述的句子明示應徵申請表的提交時間，故最適合放在與應徵流程相關的段落，[3] 的前句提到會在九月初進行面試，故申請表繳交時間應寫在此處，補充說明面試前的紙本程序，本題正確答案為 (C)。

### 152–153 文章

Bremerton, March 6 — Bremerton has recently invited local property developers to bid for constructing a business complex on a 30,000-square-meter area in the northern area of the town.

The business complex will be built near 81 Penn Highway, on the site that used to be an industrial complex that formerly included Waxon Generator, Bill's Auto Parts, and Ulus Steel Manufacturing. The new buildings will be equipped with the latest energy- and water-saving systems. The town also plans to erect a small residential section near the area within three years.

"We are pleased about this opportunity to bring new business to our town," said Mayor Gilford Hubric. "The business complex will be located in the best area, adjacent to a national main highway and many popular

布雷默頓，3月6日—布雷默頓近來為了在北區興建佔地三萬平方公尺的商業區，邀請當地的房地產開發商參與競標。

新的商業區將蓋在81號賓州公路旁邊，該址原是包括華克森發電、比爾汽車零件、烏利斯製鋼的工業區。新建物將配備最新的節能省水系統。該鎮也計畫三年內在附近設立小型住宅區。

「我們很高興有這個機會，為鎮上帶來新商機。」鎮長吉爾福德·胡布里克說，「新的商業區將坐落在最好的地區，鄰近全國主要幹道和很多有名的住宿地點。」他也提到等

accommodations." He also mentioned that the space will be distributed among occupants based on their needs after the first blueprint is designed.

Most of these activities in Bremerton have been prompted by the recent expansion of the local sports complex in the Millner neighborhood.

到初步藍圖設計出來，會再根據廠商需求分配空間。

布雷默頓近來多項建設都是受到鄰近地區米爾納的綜合運動場擴建工程所推動的。

**詞彙** bid 競標　business complex 商業區　erect 設立　residential 居住的
be adjacent to 鄰近　occupant 占用者；居住者　blueprint 藍圖　prompt 促成

**152**

**What is suggested about the northern area of Bremerton?**

(A) It is close to the sports complex.
(B) A variety of metal products were made there.
(C) It is currently a residential area.
(D) Its population has suddenly increased.

文中提到布雷默頓的北區什麼事？

(A) 距離綜合運動場很近。
(B) 曾生產多種金屬製品。
(C) 而今是住宅區。
(D) 近來人口暴增。

文章第一段提到布雷默頓北區興建商業區，第二段又說了：「The business complex will be built . . . on the site that used to be an industrial complex」，且提到 Generator（電力）、Auto Parts（汽車零件）、Steel Manufacturing（製鋼）等公司名稱，故可推測出該園區以前專門生產金屬製品，本題答案為 (B)。

**153**

**What characteristic of the business complex is NOT mentioned?**

(A) Its location near a major highway
(B) Its proximity to hotels
(C) Its energy-efficient structure
(D) Its country-operated area

文中沒有提到商業區有何種特色？

(A) 鄰近全國主要幹道
(B) 距離飯店很近
(C) 節能設備
(D) 公營區域

根據第三段中的「The business complex will be . . . adjacent to a national main highway and many popular accommodations」，可看出商業區將靠近主要幹道以及知名住宿地點，故 (A) 與 (B) 有在文中提及。

另外則可從第二段中間部分的「The new buildings will be equipped with the latest energy- and water-saving systems.」看出商業區配有節能設施，故 (C) 也有提及。綜合上述，本題正確答案為 (D)。

ACTUAL TEST 6 PART 7 中譯＋解析

267

| Jane Palmer | 09:12 A.M. |
|---|---|
| David, I have a question about the changes you asked me to make to the floor plans for the shopping mall. | |

| David Hauer | 09:13 A.M. |
|---|---|
| Of course, What's up? | |

| Jane Palmer | 09:14 A.M. |
|---|---|
| Are you asking me to e-mail you the entire pages or just page 3, the one in error? | |

| David Hauer | 09:16 A.M. |
|---|---|
| I can't have access to my e-mail account now. The Internet service is temporarily disconnected here. | |

| Jane Palmer | 09:16 A.M. |
|---|---|
| I can wait, I think. You don't meet with the clients until tomorrow. | |

| David Hauer | 09:17 A.M. |
|---|---|
| Why wait? Can you fax page 3 to me? | |

| Jane Palmer | 09:18 A.M. |
|---|---|
| Sure. What's the number? | |

| David Hauer | 09:19 A.M. |
|---|---|
| 705-3583. | |

| Jane Palmer | 09:25 A.M. |
|---|---|
| OK. It's done. If you don't receive it, I can send it again. | |

| David Hauer | 09:27 A.M. |
|---|---|
| Here. I got it. Thanks! | |

珍·帕默〔上午09:12〕：
大衛，你要求我修改的購物中心樓層規畫，我有一個問題。

大衛·浩爾〔上午09:13〕：
好的，怎麼了？

珍·帕默〔上午09:14〕：
你是要我寄全部頁數給你，還是只要出錯的第三頁就好？

大衛·浩爾〔上午09:16〕：
我現在沒辦法連到信箱看。這裡暫時沒有網路服務。

珍·帕默〔上午09:16〕：
我想我可以等。你明天才要見客戶吧？

大衛·浩爾〔上午09:17〕：
為什麼要等？妳可以傳真第三頁給我嗎？

珍·帕默〔上午09:18〕：
當然。傳真號碼是？

大衛·浩爾〔上午09:19〕：
705-3583。

珍·帕默〔上午09:25〕：
沒問題，傳好了。如果沒收到，我再傳一次。

大衛·浩爾〔上午09:27〕：
有了。收到了，感謝！

**154**

**Who most likely is Ms. Palmer?**

(A) A computer programmer
(B) An architect
(C) An attorney
(D) An Internet service manager

帕默女士最有可能是？

(A) 程式設計師
(B) 建築師
(C) 律師
(D) 網路服務經理

從帕默女士第一句話可知，帕默女士被要求繪製樓層規畫圖，所以她最可能為一名建築師，正確答案為 (B)。

**155** (NEW) - - - - - - - - - - - - - - - - - - - - - - - - - - - - - - - - - - - - - - - - - - - - - - - - - - - - - - - - - - - -

**At 9:17 A.M., what does Mr. Hauer most likely mean when he writes, "Why wait"?**

(A) He wants to get the paper now.
(B) He thinks he had better postpone the meeting.
(C) He asks about the Internet connection.
(D) He needs to download the form.

上午 9:17 時，當浩爾先生寫道：「為什麼要等」，他最可能的意思是？

(A) 他現在就想收到文件。
(B) 他認為最好延後會議。
(C) 他詢問網路連線。
(D) 他需要下載表格。

浩爾先生先前說到自己暫時無法連接網路，並在之後提及此句話，且請對方傳真第三頁過來，故可推測他是因為想快點收到文件，才會要求對方在網路不通的狀況下使用傳真，故正確答案 (A)。

---

### 156–157 信件

| Shirley Eye Care | 雪麗眼睛保健 |
|---|---|
| #203, 151 Fleming Avenue<br>Bayside, NY 11361<br>March 17 | 11361紐約州貝塞區弗萊明大街151號203室<br>3月17日 |
| Heather Lory | 海瑟·洛瑞 |
| #403 West Gate Apartments<br>333 Lancaster Boulevard<br>Bayside, NY 11361 | 11361紐約州貝賽區蘭卡斯特大道333號<br>西門公寓403室 |
| At Shirley Eye Care, it is our priority to continuously provide the best service for you. Starting on August 1, all payments will not be made at the time of service but must be paid within 15 business days. Enclosed you will find the details about the reason why we changed the billing policy. | 持續提供您最好的服務，是雪麗眼睛保健的首要之事。從8月1日起，服務完不再需要馬上付費，而是可以在15個工作天內付款。您可以在隨函附上的詳細說明中，了解我們改變付費方式的原因。 |
| The new policy enables us to continue to offer the best eye care service to you and your family without any rate increases in the upcoming 2 years. If you have more questions about this payment policy, please call our client account manager, Kevin Loyce, at 715-6534. | 新規定讓我們可以繼續提供您和家人最好的眼睛保健服務，未來兩年內也不會調整價格。如果您對新的付費規定有更多疑問，可以聯絡我們的客戶經理凱文·羅伊斯，電話是715-6534。 |
| Sincerely,<br>Jane Shirley<br>Enclosure | 珍·雪麗 敬上<br>附件 |

**詞彙** enclosed 附函　billing policy 收費方式

**What is the purpose of this letter?**

(A) To recruit licensed nurses

(B) To publicize a clinic's service

(C) To inform a customer of a policy change

(D) To make a correction to a billing statement

這封信的目的為何？

(A) 聘僱有執照的護理師

(B) 宣傳診所的一項服務

(C) 告訴客戶一項規定異動

(D) 修正帳單明細

信件第一段便提及付款方式的變動，且最後一句也直接點出「the reason why we changed the billing policy」，故可知這封信的目的是告知政策異動，正確答案為 (C)。

**What is suggested about Shirley Eye Care?**

(A) It makes an effort to keep service rates low.

(B) It has recently moved to a new area.

(C) It is offering free eye examinations.

(D) It will be equipped with the latest tools.

文中提到雪麗眼睛保健什麼事？

(A) 努力維持低收費。

(B) 最近搬到新地區。

(C) 提供免費的視力檢查。

(D) 配備最先進的設備。

根據第二段第一句的「to continue to offer the best eye care . . . without any rate increases in the upcoming 2 years」，可知近兩年都不會調漲價格，故正確答案為 (A)。

**158–160 資訊**

| House and Office Cleaning | 住房和辦公室清潔 |
|---|---|
| The house and office cleaning division of Kane Upper Town Hotel hires 100 team members who are responsible for keeping clean the public spaces in the building in addition to each of the individual rooms and offices throughout the facility. | 肯恩上城鎮飯店的住房和辦公室清潔部門聘用100人加入團隊，負責大樓公共空間及所有客房與辦公室整潔。 |

• Public spaces, such as restrooms, lobbies, ballrooms, the banquet hall, and other visitors' areas are cleaned every day.

• Individual rooms are cleaned in compliance with guests' schedules. Making a schedule for the rooms is outlined further on Page 10 of this recruit manual.

• Office areas are cleaned on Saturdays. Housekeepers will sweep and wipe floors and throw out the garbage. Team members should water the plants in the offices and arrange the desks.

• The cleaning staff must always be standing by ready for public areas that need prompt attention.

- 每天打掃公共區域，像是廁所、大廳、舞廳、宴會廳，和其他訪客使用區域。

- 依據房客時間表打掃客房。如何安排客房時間表，概述在招募手冊第10頁。

- 每週六打掃辦公區域。清潔人員會掃地拖地並清空垃圾筒，也為辦公室植栽澆水和整理桌面。

- 打掃人員必須隨時在需要及時留意的公共區域附近待命。

**詞彙** ballroom 舞廳　banquet 宴會　in compliance with 依據　outline 概述　arrange 整理　stand by 待命

**158**

**For whom is the information most likely intended?**

(A) Cleaning supply company members
(B) Hotel employees
(C) Travel agents for hotel reservations
(D) Visitors seeking good hotels

這些資訊最可能是要給誰看的？

(A) 清潔公司員工
(B) 旅館員工
(C) 負責訂房的旅行社員工
(D) 想找好飯店的遊客

段落第一句提到，飯店僱了一百名員工負責清潔，且分點列出打掃公共區域、打掃客房等職責，故可推測出這篇文章的公告對象為飯店員工，正確答案為 (B)。

 **159**

**According to the information, how can readers know the housekeeping schedules of the individual rooms?**

(A) By referring to a staff training manual
(B) By talking to the service head in the cleaning division
(C) By calling the reception desk of the hotel
(D) By reading a schedule posted in the staff lounge

根據文中資訊，讀者要如何得知客房的清理時間表？

(A) 參考員工訓練手冊
(B) 詢問清潔部門長官
(C) 致電飯店接待處
(D) 看員工休息室張貼的行程表

第一點寫道：「Making a schedule for the rooms is outlined further on Page 10 of this recruit manual.」，可從此句看出此篇文章是摘錄自招募手冊，且安排客房時間表的方式要參照手冊得知，故正確答案為 (A)。

**160**

**How often are the floors of the offices cleaned?**

(A) Daily
(B) Weekly
(C) Biweekly
(D) Monthly

辦公室的地板多久清掃一次？

(A) 每天
(B) 每週
(C) 每雙週
(D) 每個月

從第三點中的「Office areas are cleaned on Saturdays」可知，辦公室是每週六清掃，故正確答案為 (B)。

### 161–164 網路討論區

| | |
|---|---|
| **Cody Silva** 10:18 A.M.<br>Hello. I want to give you some information regarding yesterday's meeting agenda. Our marketing team suggested that cooling bubble gum would likely be popular in the food market. | 寇帝‧席爾瓦〔上午10:18〕：<br>哈囉。我想給你們昨天會議流程的資訊。我們行銷團隊提議，清爽泡泡糖可能會在零食市場上受到歡迎。 |
| **Susan Vivianne** 10:19 A.M.<br>I know the reason. People want to feel cool in their mouth after eating something. | 蘇珊‧薇薇安〔上午10:19〕：<br>我知道原因。人們吃完東西後，會希望口腔內感覺清爽。 |

| | | |
|---|---|---|
| **Nakata Shunzi** | 10:20 A.M. | 中田俊二〔上午10:20〕： |
| Not to mention the fact that it cleans your teeth. | | 別忘了它還能清潔牙齒。 |
| **Cody Silva** | 10:21 A.M. | 寇帝・席爾瓦〔上午10:21〕： |
| Sure. We decided that our company needs to have our own line of special chewing gum with a sugar-free formula. We should get moving fast. | | 沒錯。我們公司決定，要有自己的產線生產無糖配方的特製口香糖。我們必須加快腳步。 |
| **Susan Vivianne** | 10:22 A.M. | 蘇珊・薇薇安〔上午10:22〕： |
| Consumers are becoming more concerned about their health, so how about focusing on using organic ingredients? I can find more information about it for our products. | | 消費者愈來愈注重健康，不如我們強調使用有機原料怎麼樣？我可以為產品找出更多關於有機原料的資訊。 |
| **Cody Silva** | 10:23 A.M. | 寇帝・席爾瓦〔上午10:23〕： |
| That sounds great! Go ahead! | | 聽起來很好！就這麼做！ |
| **Nakata Shunzi** | 10:24 A.M. | 中田俊二〔上午10:24〕： |
| I like that. But I think we should consider consumer preferences in the flavor. If the taste of the gum is not attractive to prospective clients, the best item we make will just be useless. We need to first conduct market research about consumers' preferred tastes. | | 我喜歡這個想法。不過，我想也要考慮消費者的口味偏好。如果口香糖的口味不能吸引潛在消費者，我們產品做得再好也沒用。我們得先針對消費者喜歡的口味進行市場研究。 |
| **Cody Silva** | 10:26 A.M. | 寇帝・席爾瓦〔上午10:26〕： |
| Great. Mr. Nakata, could you set up a meeting with the market research team and public relations team? I want to hear what they have to say. How about Thursday? | | 好。山田先生，可以請你安排和市場研究團隊與公關團隊開會嗎？我想聽聽他們怎麼說。週四怎麼樣？ |
| **Susan Vivianne** | 10:27 A.M. | 蘇珊・薇薇安〔上午10:27〕： |
| Sorry, but I can't make it then. On Thursdays, I always conduct the on-the-job training for new staff. Can we do Wednesday or Friday? | | 抱歉，那個時間我不行。週四我都得為新進員工進行在職訓練。週三或五可以嗎？ |
| **Cody Silva** | 10:28 A.M. | 寇帝・席爾瓦〔上午10:28〕： |
| The end of the week is fine. | | 週五可以。 |
| **Nakata Shunzi** | 10:30 A.M. | 中田俊二〔上午10:30〕： |
| Works for me. I'll also outline the questionnaire for the research on our side. Can any of you guys give me possible questions for the survey? | | 我也可以。我也會擬好我們的問卷大綱，供研究使用。你們之中有誰可以給我一些問卷可用的問題嗎？ |
| **Cody Silva** | 10:31 A.M. | 寇帝・席爾瓦〔上午10:31〕： |
| Of course. I will. | | 當然。我再給你。 |

**詞彙** **agenda** 議程　**bubble gum** 泡泡糖　**not to mention** 更別說　**public relations** 公關
**on-the-job training** 在職訓練

**161** ----------------------------------------

**What kind of business do the chat participants most likely work at?**

(A) A grocery store
(B) A hotel restaurant
(C) A marketing agency
(D) A food manufacturer

對話成員最有可能是哪一種企業的員工？

(A) 雜貨店
(B) 餐旅業
(C) 行銷代理商
(D) 食品製造商

根據開頭席爾瓦先生提議的產品「cooling bubble gum」，以及在 10 點 21 分時他說的：「We decided that our company needs to have our own line of special chewing gum with a sugar-free formula.」，表示公司決定有自己的口香糖產線，可推知對話成員的工作應為食品製造相關，故正確答案為 (D)。

 **162** ----------------------------------------

**When do the participants plan to meet with the marketing team?**

(A) On Tuesday
(B) On Wednesday
(C) On Thursday
(D) On Friday

對話成員打算什麼時候和行銷團隊見面？

(A) 週二
(B) 週三
(C) 週四
(D) 週五

10 點 26 分時席爾瓦先生先提議與行銷團隊開會，隨後薇薇安女士表示要週三或五才有空，而他則在 10 點 28 分時回覆了「The end of the week is fine.」，一週中最後的工作日即為週五，故會議應是週五舉行，正確答案為 (D)。

 **163** (NEW) ----------------------------------------

**At 10:30 A.M., what does Mr. Nakata mean when he says, "Works for me"?**

(A) He is able to attend the meeting.
(B) He will talk with researchers right away.
(C) He plans to lead to the on-the-job training.
(D) He wants to make a new product by himself.

早上 10：30 時，當中田先生寫道：「我也可以」，他最可能的意思是？

(A) 他可以出席會議。
(B) 他會馬上和研究者談。
(C) 他計劃要主導在職訓練。
(D) 他想要自己做新產品。

上句中席爾瓦先生贊成週五舉行會議，故中田先生此句回覆應是代表週五的時間他可以參加，所以正確答案為 (A)。

 **164** ----------------------------------------

**What will Mr. Silva probably do?**

(A) Meet the president
(B) Taste some gum flavors
(C) Outline marketing strategies
(D) Prepare some questions

席爾瓦先生可能會怎麼做？

(A) 和總裁見面
(B) 試吃一些口香糖的口味
(C) 概述行銷策略
(D) 準備一些問題

10 點 30 分時中田先生請成員們提供問卷問題，席爾瓦先生給予肯定回覆，表示他會準備問題，故正確答案為 (D)。

**From:** Jimmy Khermin
**To:** Staff, Premium Electronics
**Date:** Monday, December 7
**Subject:** Week-long training session

You have already been informed that all staff members of Premium Electronics are required to attend the week-long training session each winter, which focuses on our company's goals and provides you with a chance to get to know other staff members. It can give us a lot of benefits for our business. Our employee surveys show that we have made a major impact on our work productivity and cooperation since starting these sessions five years ago.

The dates of the training session have been posted on our intra-bulletin-board since September, and attendance is required. I would like all of you to get ready for the session by selecting various topics that we can talk about. Staff members at all positions should not hesitate to share their suggestions. What you should do is to e-mail me with "Session Topics" in the subject line. —[1]—. You need to use your own transportation to get to Blue Spruce Park, so please remember to submit a travel reimbursement form before the end of the month. It is recommended that you ride together with others in a group. —[2]—. In addition, there are other means of public transportation available, such as a shuttle bus, subway, and city train, which stop near Blue Spruce Park. —[3]—. Whatever means you choose, please be sure that you get there on time and ready to join us. —[4]—.

Jimmy Khermin

寄件人：吉米‧赫爾明
收件人：優質電子員工
日期：12月7日，週一
主旨：一週培訓課程

您應該已接獲通知，所有優質電子的員工都需要參加為期一週的冬季培訓課程，課程聚焦在更明確了解公司目標，同時也能認識其他同仁。對我們的公司有非常多好處。員工問卷顯示，自從五年前開始培訓課程，對我們公司的工作產能和同仁間的合作都有了很大的影響。

訓練課程的日期自九月起就發布於內部布告欄，大家都必須參加。我希望您們都能準備好各式各樣的主題到課程上討論。所有同仁都可以盡情分享建議。您要做的只是回信給我，主旨請寫「課程主題」。您得自行前往藍雲杉公園，所以請記得這個月底前填寫交通費的差旅核銷單。也建議您可以團體共乘前往。此外，也有很多大眾運輸工具可以搭乘，像是接駁公車、地鐵、市營火車，會停在藍雲杉公園附近。從辦公室到那裡甚至有和公司合作的計程車行，提供非常優惠的折扣。不管您選擇什麼方式前往，請確保能準時到達，而且準備好加入我們。

吉米‧赫爾明

**詞彙** **week-long** 為期一週的　**intra-bulletin-board** 內部布告欄　**reimbursement** 核銷單
**shuttle bus** 接駁公車　**be affiliated with** 隸屬於

----------------------------------------------------------------------

**What is the main purpose of the e-mail?**

(A) To announce details regarding an annual event
(B) To encourage staff members to volunteer for an event
(C) To advertise a company's latest item at a fair
(D) To publicize new job openings at an electronics company

這封電子郵件的目的為何？

(A) 宣布一項年度活動的細節
(B) 鼓勵同仁當某個活動的志工
(C) 在商展上推廣公司的最新產品
(D) 公告電子公司開出的新職缺

郵件第一句表示收件者應已接獲通知，並説：「all staff members . . . are required to attend the week-long training session each winter」，表示收件者要參加每年冬天舉辦的、為期一週的培訓課程，且第二段詳細説明了課程準備、核銷方式、交通方式等，故可知郵件的目的是傳達公司的年度活動，正確答案為 (A)。

**166** ----------------------------------------------------------------

**How are the employees required to get ready for the event?**

(A) By updating personal information
(B) By filling out a questionnaire
(C) By promoting a brand-new item
(D) By preparing discussion topics

員工需要為活動準備好什麼？

(A) 更新個人資訊
(B) 填寫問卷
(C) 推銷全新產品
(D) 準備討論題目

根據第二段第二句的「I would like all of you to get ready for the session by selecting various topics that we can talk about」，收件者需要準備主題好在研習課程上討論，故正確答案為 (D)。

**167** ----------------------------------------------------------------

**What does Mr. Khermin mention about transportation arrangements?**

(A) All expenses will be reimbursed by Premium Electronics.
(B) All employees should take public transportation.
(C) All vehicles are prohibited at the site at certain times.
(D) All staff should get a travel pass from each department.

關於交通安排，赫爾明先生怎麼說？

(A) 優質電子會補貼所有開銷。
(B) 所有員工都需要搭乘大眾運輸工具。
(C) 該地點在特定時間內完全不能通車。
(D) 每個員工都需要從各部門取得通行證。

根據第二段的「so please remember to submit a travel reimbursement form before the end of the month.」部分，可以得知交通費用可以全額報銷，故正確答案為 (A)。

**168** NEW ---------------------------------------------------------

**In which of the positions marked [1], [2], [3], and [4] does the following sentence best belong?**

**"There is even a taxi affiliated with our company that provides a huge discounted price for a ride from the office to there."**

(A) [1]
(B) [2]
(C) [3]
(D) [4]

下列句子最適合出現在 [1]、[2]、[3]、[4] 的哪個位置中？

「從辦公室到那裡甚至有和公司合作的計程車行，提供非常優惠的折扣。」

(A) [1]
(B) [2]
(C) [3]
(D) [4]

題目引述的句子提到「There is even a taxi」，故可推測前文應該提及其他交通方式。郵件第二段的後半部分中説了的「there are other means of public transportation available」，並提到接駁車、地鐵等大眾運輸，故句子應接於此句後方，表示「甚至有和公司合作的計程車行」可以使用，故句子適合填入 [3]，正確答案為 (C)。

## SKihut National Archipelago Authority (SNAA)

SKihut National Archipelago includes a main forest, beach areas, and other similar islands. Please be aware that there are some additional tour restrictions during this summer vacation season. If visitors are not accompanied by an authorized guide when they want to take a trip to the islands, they will be restricted from entering these areas. This regulation also applies to those who may want to visit the islands individually by using private boats. These individuals can only see the view of the island from the water and come to anchor on offshore but must not land there.

The SNAA's official cruise tours for visitors to the islands are offered daily throughout the year and move in a cycle with two-hour intervals from 8 A.M. The final tour is available until 4 P.M. except for the winter season from November to February, during which time it can be extended to 6 P.M., depending on weather conditions. Please call +01-319-5225 to make a reservation for the cruise tour. This tour includes some description about the islands' geological and historical features, and attractive aspects of the beautiful view. You can also view a special spot for endangered species by getting an escort from our island rangers.

### Payment and Reservations

Tours can be conducted with a maximum of 20 participants per group. If the group is smaller than 15, we reserve the right to add other travelers to your tour. You can purchase a ticket at $30 per person for adults and $15 for children. You are asked to pay a deposit of $5 per person in order to hold the reservation. In addition, you can get our special offer when booking it in advance of 6 months. The deposit amount will be credited to your total admission fees. If your group does not show up at the appointed time, the ending time of your trip will remain the same, so as not to disrupt later trips. Any change of other groups' itineraries cannot be allowed.

## 滑雪屋國家群島管理處（SNAA）

滑雪屋國家群島主要有一片森林、還有海灘地區和其他類似島嶼。請注意在這次夏天的度假季中有新的旅遊限制。遊客來到島上旅遊，如果沒有核准的嚮導隨行的話，將被限制出入這些區域。這項規定也同樣適用於自行以私人船隻前往群島的遊客。他們只許從海上欣賞島上風景，停在近海處，但不准登島。

由SNAA管理處主辦的巡航之旅提供遊客全年服務，從每天上午八點開始，每隔兩小時有一個船班，直到下午四點的末班船為止。但冬季從十一月到二月，將根據天氣狀況延長到下午六點。請來電+01-319-5225預約航遊。該行程包含島嶼地質和歷史特色的解說，也能欣賞美麗風景的迷人風貌。您也可以申請島上管理員的陪同，參觀瀕危物種群聚的特別景點。

### 付款和預約

該行程每團最多能容納20人。如果人數少於15人，我們保有在行程裡安排加入其他旅客的權利。成人票為每人30美元，小孩則是15美元。為保留預約，您需要支付5美元的保證金。此外，如果提前六個月訂票將享有特別優惠。保證金將計入入場費的總金額當中。如果您的團體沒有按預約時間準時到場，旅程結束的時間仍不會改變，以免影響後續行程。我們嚴禁更改其他團體的行程。

---

**詞彙** archipelago 群島　endangered species 瀕危物種　escort 陪同　deposit 保證金　disrupt 干擾

**169**

**What is the purpose of the notice?**

(A) To update information about a fee
(B) To introduce some attractions
(C) To announce the safety rules about a trip
(D) To inform visitors of the trip policy

這則公告的目的為何？

(A) 更新某個費用的資訊
(B) 介紹一些景點
(C) 宣布旅程的安全規定
(D) 知會遊客旅遊規定

開頭的第二句便提到「Please be aware that there are some additional tour restrictions during this summer vacation season」，提到暑假期間有額外限制，並在後文說明遊客若無嚮導隨行則無法登陸島嶼，故可知這篇文章的目的是在告知遊客觀光規定，正確答案為 (D)。

**170**

**What is implied about visiting SKihut National Archipelago?**

(A) Visitors must step into the islands with a guide.
(B) Visitors should comply with their safety rules.
(C) Visitors cannot swim anywhere around the archipelago.
(D) Visitors need to gather groups by themselves.

文中提到關於參觀滑雪屋國家群島什麼事？

(A) 遊客登島需要嚮導陪同。
(B) 遊客須遵守安全規定。
(C) 遊客在群島周圍任何地方都不許游泳。
(D) 遊客需要自己組團遊玩。

從第一段第三句的「If visitors are not accompanied by an authorized guide . . . they will be restricted from entering these areas」可以知道，遊客若沒有合格的嚮導隨行，就無法入島觀光，故正確答案為 (A)。

**171**

**What is NOT mentioned about the SNAA?**

(A) Night tours can be scheduled.
(B) The capacity of the group Is limited.
(C) Early reservations can be discounted.
(D) Tour times are different depending on the season.

文中沒有提到 SNAA 什麼事？

(A) 可以安排夜間行程。
(B) 團體人數受到限制。
(C) 早鳥預約享有優惠。
(D) 船班班數根據季節有所不同。

最後一段說明付款與預約，其中說到「with a maximum of 20 participants per group」，表示團體最多 20 人，所以有提及 (B)。再從「you can get our special offer when booking it in advance of 6 months」可知 (C) 早鳥預約優惠。

而從第二段的「The final tour is available until 4 P.M. except for the winter season」，可以得知冬季的船班時間不同，也提及了 (D)。綜合上述，本題正確答案為 (A)。

**172**

**According to the notice, what may happen if a group arrives late for the prearranged trip?**

(A) It may be reduced in tour hours.
(B) It may be canceled without any notice.
(C) It may be charged an additional fee.
(D) It may be changed into another ending time.

根據公告，如果團體在已安排好的行程中遲到，會發生什麼事？

(A) 旅遊行程時間將減少。
(B) 無需通知，行程將被取消。
(C) 會被額外收費。
(D) 將更改行程結束的時間。

最後一段說到：「If your group does not show up at the appointed time, the ending time of your trip will remain the same」，表示觀光結束時間不會改變，所以晚到的人的觀光時間會縮短，故正確答案為 (A)。

## 173–175 手冊資訊

| | |
|---|---|
| ### Visiting Hershey County<br>### Don't miss the chance to experience a fantastic world! | ### 赫希郡一遊<br>### 別錯過體驗夢幻世界的好機會！ |
| **Chocolate World Tour** | 巧克力世界之旅 |
| Open daily, 10 A.M.–5 P.M. / $5 admission | 每天上午10點到下午5點開放，入場費5美元 |
| The Chocolate World Tour brings you the historical scenes of Hershey County by bike-coaster with a lot of stages and figures. | 巧克力世界之旅帶您乘單車穿越多個歷程和雕像，一覽赫希郡的歷史景點。 |
| **Charlie's Chocolate Factory** | 查理的巧克力工廠 |
| Open to the public at no charge, Business Days, noon – 3 P.M. | 營業時間為平日中午到下午3點，免費對全民開放 |
| Constructed by the founder, Mr. John Hershey. Visitors can get a chance to see the chocolate-making procedures and receive some free chocolate items. Guided tours are available for $1 per person. | 由創辦人約翰·赫希先生所建立。遊客有機會一窺巧克力的製造過程，並免費獲得巧克力產品。導覽行程向每個人酌收1美元。 |
| **Hershey Amusement Park** | 赫希遊樂園 |
| Open daily, 9 A.M.–10 P.M. / $10 admission, $40 unlimited pass for the rides. | 每天上午9點到晚上10點開放，入場費10美元，無限暢遊所有設施只要40美元。 |
| This amazing theme park is suitable for the whole family. A lot of fantastic rides are available, including roller coasters. Special discounts for the park are given in specific seasons. | 超棒的主題公園適合闔家光臨。包括雲霄飛車等多項極棒的遊樂設施。特定季節入園享有特別優惠價。 |
| **County Chocolate Museum** | 郡巧克力博物館 |
| Open Tuesday to Sunday, 9 A.M.– 4 P.M. / Free of charge, but donations are welcome. | 週二到週日，上午9點到下午4點開放，免入場費，但歡迎贊助。 |
| A variety of impressive chocolates are exhibited in chronological order. Also, the Hershey family's history is played on a big LCD monitor on the ceiling. This museum is located adjacent to the North Gate of the amusement park. | 各種巧克力讓人難以忘懷，依年分順序陳列展覽。天花板的大液晶螢幕回顧赫希家族史。博物館地點鄰近遊樂園北大門。 |

**詞彙** figure 雕像　in chronological order 依時間（年代）順序

**173**

**What is the purpose of the information?**

(A) To describe a list of events

(B) To help visitors to tour certain spots

(C) To give directions to local attractions

(D) To announce some special monuments

這則資訊的目的為何？

(A) 描述一份活動清單

(B) 協助遊客參觀某些景點

(C) 提供前往當地景點的路線指引

(D) 公告一些特別的紀念館

從標題的「Visiting Hershey County」可知，此為介紹「赫希郡」一地的手冊，且後文提供許多當地景點名勝的資訊，故這份手冊最可能是在協助遊客觀光此地，故正確答案為 (B)。

**174**

**What is indicated about Hershey Amusement Park?**

(A) Its admission fee is not the same year-round.

(B) It varies from the opening time periodically.

(C) It uses a mini-trailer for watching the historical movie.

(D) It is only popular with teenagers and children.

文中提到赫希遊樂園什麼事？

(A) 整年的入場費用並不完全一樣。

(B) 營業的時間會定期更動。

(C) 播放歷史電影的簡短預告。

(D) 只受到青少年和兒童歡迎。

根據「Special discounts for the park are given in specific seasons」，特定季節入場將享有特別的優惠，故本題正確答案為 (A)。

**175**

**According to the information, what do the chocolate factory and the museum have in common?**

(A) Both charge no admission fee.

(B) Both require guided tours.

(C) Both show historical events.

(D) Both are located near the shore.

根據資訊，巧克力工廠和博物館有何共同之處？

(A) 都不用入場費。

(B) 都需要導覽。

(C) 都展示歷史事件。

(D) 都坐落在海岸旁邊。

巧克力工廠為「Open to the public at no charge」，博物館則是「free of charge」，表示這兩個景點都是免費的，故本題正確答案為 (A)。

(B) 文中只提到巧克力工廠提供導覽，並須收費 1 美元；(C) 只有巧克力世界之旅有提到歷史景點參觀；(D) 文中未提及此事。

## CAAA's Twentieth-Annual Athletic Equipment Fair, June 1–10
### Progressive Convention Center, Cleveland, Ohio

The CAAA (Cleveland Area Athletic Association) invites companies to join this fair, which was attended by over 200 businesses last year. This event is related to effective approaches and methods for using the right exercise equipment.

The CAAA is pleased to offer corresponding benefits based on the degree of corporate sponsorship.
(For inquiries, contact Ms. Gloria Sanders at 932-451-3894. To register, e-mail supports@caaa.org.)

•**Workshop Sponsor** — $1,200

A representative of your company will have a chance to promote your company by speaking as a keynote speaker in one of the workshop sessions.

•**Stage Sponsor** — $2,000

At each stage displaying equipment, your company's name will be displayed in front of the demonstration booth.

•**Bag Sponsor** — $3,000

Your company's logo and name will be on fabric tote bags that are distributed to all visitors.

•**General Program Sponsor** — $6,000

Three executive members of your company will be introduced in a banquet, named "CAAA Night," on the first day of the fair.

---

**From:** gloria@caaa.org
**To:** hsyoon@knetwork.com
**Date:** May 20
**Subject:** Thank you

---

Dear Ms. Yoon,

I would like to show my appreciation for your registration of the Remote Interval Exercise Program as a supporter of the Cleveland Area Athletic Association (CAAA) Fair.

---

## CAAA 二十週年體育器材展
### 6月1日到10日
### 俄亥俄州克里夫蘭市革新會議中心

CAAA（克里夫蘭地區體育協會）邀請各公司參展，去年有超過200家企業與會。這場活動讓您更快找到合適的運動器材，並教您正確使用。

根據企業贊助的額度，CAAA很榮幸給予相應的回饋（如需詢問請洽格洛麗亞‧桑德斯女士，電話是932-451-3894。如需登記，請寄信到supports@caaa.org）

研討會贊助—1,200美元

您的公司代表將在其中一個研討會中擔任主講人，有機會為您的公司宣傳。

舞台贊助—2,000美元

在每個展示設備的平台上，貴公司的大名會出現在展示攤位前方。

提袋贊助—3,000美元

發送給參展訪客的布製手提袋，全都會印上貴公司商標和名稱。

活動整體規畫贊助—6,000美元

展覽首日的「CAAA之夜」晚宴上，將介紹貴公司三位的經理人給大家。

---

寄件人：gloria@caaa.org
收件人：hsyoon@knetwork.com
日期：5月20日
主旨：感謝

---

親愛的尹女士：

感謝您登記贊助遠距間歇訓練計畫，以支持克里夫蘭地區體育協會（CAAA）展。您的贊助不但讓我們

Your sponsorship not only enables us to make this event possible, but also stimulates interest in exercise.

Your donation of $2,000 has been credited to our account. In addition, we are attaching your company's name to the demonstration booth at no extra cost. It is a token of our appreciation for the long-standing support of CAAA and its programs. To finalize the promotional materials, please e-mail me your official CI (corporate identity) or BI (business identity) images.

Gloria Sanders
CAAA Fair Coordinator

策展順利，也能讓大家對運動更感興趣。

您捐贈的2,000美元已經成功入帳。此外，我們也會特別將貴公司名稱秀在展示攤位上，不收取額外費用。以此向您長久以來對CAAA和我們計畫的支持，致上我們的感謝之意。為確認宣傳用的素材，請您回傳貴公司企業或商業識別的圖片。

CAAA展統籌
格洛麗亞·桑德斯

**詞彙** athletic 體育的　keynote speaker 主講人　tote bag 手提包；托特包　token 象徵
long-standing 長久的　finalize 最後定下　coordinator 統籌者

**176**  --------------------------------------------------------

**What is the purpose of the flyer?**

(A) To announce the success of these successive events
(B) To encourage participants to try out equipment
(C) To promote the benefits of joining an event
(D) To report financial issues to their sponsorship board

這篇傳單的目的為何？

(A) 宣布一系列的活動有多成功
(B) 鼓勵參加者試用器材
(C) 推廣加入活動的好處
(D) 向贊助委員會回報財政狀況

傳單第一句即寫道：「The CAAA (Cleveland Area Athletic Association) invites companies to join this fair」，表示邀請公司行號參加博覽會，接著給予聯絡方式，並列舉各種回饋贊助的方式，故正確答案為 (C)。

**177** --------------------------------------------------------

**According to the flyer, when should a call be placed to CAAA's office?**

(A) When additional information is needed
(B) When a donation cannot be processed
(C) When participation is required
(D) When a change is made at their level

根據傳單，什麼時候需要打電話到 CAAA 的辦公室？

(A) 需要更多資訊時
(B) 沒辦法處理捐款作業時
(C) 需要參加活動時
(D) 當他們層級有所變動時

從第二段的「For inquiries, contact Ms. Gloria Sanders at 932-451-3894.」可知，欲詢問企業贊助額度的人，可以電話聯絡諮詢，故本題最合適的答案為 (A)。

**178** ----------------------------------------------------------------

**What will happen on June 1?**

(A) An athletic game will be started.

(B) A formal gathering will be held.

(C) New board members will be appointed.

(D) Display stages will be set up at the fair.

6 月 1 日會發生什麼事？

(A) 一場運動賽事即將開始。

(B) 將舉辦一場正式的集會。

(C) 將指派新董事會成員。

(D) 將設置好展覽展示台。

從傳單上可以看見 6 月 1 日為器材展的開幕日，根據最後一點：「Three executive members of your company will be introduced in a banquet, named "CAAA Night," on the first day of the fair.」，贊助 6,000 美元的企業會在展覽首日的晚宴會上受到介紹，故 6 月 1 日晚上應會舉行宴會，正確答案為 (B)。

**179** ----------------------------------------------------------------

**What is suggested about CAAA's event?**

(A) It is intended to promote interest in exercise.

(B) It attracts more than 200 companies annually.

(C) It is partially funded by the Cleveland City Council.

(D) It is held at a different location every year.

文中提到 CAAA 展什麼事？

(A) 它的目的是為了推廣運動。

(B) 它每年都吸引超過 200 間公司參展。

(C) 由克里夫蘭市議會部分贊助。

(D) 每年都在不同地點舉辦。

根據傳單第一段的第二句：「This event is related to effective approaches and methods for using the right exercise equipment.」，此展覽與找尋合適運動器材與正確使用有關，故本題答案為 (A)。

(B) 傳單上只提到去年有 200 多家公司參加，並不知道是否每年皆如此，(C) 與 (D) 則皆未在文中提及。

**180** ----------------------------------------------------------------

**In the e-mail, what is Ms. Yoon asked to do?**

(A) Check the amount of supporting budget for taking part in the event

(B) Send an e-mail including the company's logo designs to the fair.

(C) Organize an event booth to promote their new items at the fair

(D) Call the customer service center to ask more information about the fair

電子郵件中，尹女士被要求做什麼？

(A) 確認企業為了參加這活動所贊助的預算金額

(B) 回信附上參展用的公司商標設計

(C) 安排一個展區在展場上宣傳新產品

(D) 聯絡客服中心詢問更多有關展覽的資訊

從郵件最後一句中的「please e-mail me your official CI (corporate identity) or BI (business identity) images」，可知尹女士應在回信中附上企業或商業識別的圖片，故正確答案為 (B)。

## 181–185 電子郵件

**To:**
berry@linguisticconference.org
**From:**
customerservice@holidaylodge.us
**Date:** 25 July
**Subject:** Re: Reservation TC1270

---

Dear Dr. Berry,

Thank you for choosing Holiday Lodge Hotel. As requested before, you have made a reservation of 12 rooms for your group. Since you will attend the National Applied Linguistics Forum here this August, you are receiving a special rate of $90 a room per night.

We have you checking in on 3 August, and checking out on 10 August. The room reservations are confirmed under your name. Please be aware of your reservation code, TC1270, which you must use if you need to contact us about these arrangements for any reason.

We are confident that you will enjoy our amazing amenities such as an outdoor pool, a spa, a gym, and a variety of dining options. For a casual dining experience, you may want to try the Romeo's Café terrace, located next to our lobby. If you are interested in dining at Donnatello Restaurant, which was given a 5-star rating from *Trip Advisory Guide*, we strongly recommend that you make a reservation in advance.

Please let us know if you need more information.

Thank you again for choosing Holiday Lodge Hotel.

Sincerely,
The Holiday Lodge Hotel Staff

---

收件人：
berry@linguisticconference.org
寄件人：
customerservice@holidaylodge.us
日期：7月25日
主旨：關於：TC1270預約

---

親愛的貝里博士：

感謝您選擇度假小屋飯店。如您稍早的要求，為您的團體預約了12間房。由於您將到這裡參加八月分的全國應用語言學論壇，您將享有每個房間一晚90元的優惠價。

我們需要您在8月3日辦理入住，並在8月10日退房。房間預約都登記在您名下。請記得您的訂房號碼為TC1270，當您對這些安排有任何需要聯絡的事，都需要使用這組號碼。

我們有信心您會很喜歡這裡很棒的設施，像是戶外游泳池、水療、健身房和多樣化的用餐選擇。如果想要悠哉一點的用餐環境，您可以嘗試位於大廳旁邊的羅密歐露天咖啡廳。如果您有興趣在《旅遊推薦指南》中，評等為五星的多那太羅餐廳用餐，我們強烈建議您事先預約。

如果您需要了解更多資訊，請告訴我們。

再次感謝您選擇度假小屋飯店。

度假小屋飯店員工 敬上

| **To:** | **收件人：** |
|---|---|
| customerservice@holidaylodge.us | customerservice@holidaylodge.us |
| **From:** | **寄件人：** |
| berry@linguisticconference.org | berry@linguisticconference.org |
| **Date:** 27 July | **日期：**7月27日 |
| **Subject:** Re: Reservation TC1270 | **主旨：**關於：TC1270預約 |

To Whom It May Concern,

My reservation number is TC1270, and I am writing to correct some errors I noticed in the previous e-mail.

Firstly, the number of reserved rooms is 10, not 12. Also, I will not be arriving until August 4, even though almost all members will get there one day before the conference.

I clearly stated these points on my original reservation request form. Please correct these and contact me in order to confirm that this has been resolved. Thank you in advance for your immediate response to this matter.

Sincerely,
Dr. Bonds Berry

致相關人士：

我的訂房號碼為TC1270，我致信的目的是想更正我在上一封電子郵件中所發現的一些錯誤。

首先，我預訂的房間是10間，而非12間。而且，我也要等到8月4日才會抵達，即便大多數人都會提前在會議前一天到。

我在原來的訂房需求表單裡，已很明確地提出上述這些事項。請予以修正，並和我聯繫確認這個問題已經解決。先謝過您對這件事的即時回應。

龐茲・貝里博士 敬上

**詞彙** applied linguistics 應用語言學　amenity 設施

**181**

**What is the main purpose of the first e-mail?**

(A) To confirm the details of a reservation
(B) To notify a customer of a change in hotel price
(C) To explain a variety of amenities
(D) To announce a hotel's temporary construction

第一封電子郵件的目的為何？

(A) 確認訂房細節
(B) 提醒房客客房價格有更動
(C) 解釋多樣設施
(D) 宣布飯店要暫時整修

第一封郵件第二句提到：「As requested before, you have made a reservation of 12 rooms for your group」，並在下文說到入住與退房日期、訂房號碼、飯店設施等，故可知這封郵件是飯店為了確認訂房細節而傳送的，正確答案為 (A)。

**182**

**What is suggested about the Donnatello Restaurant?**

(A) It was recently opened.
(B) It has been remodeled.
(C) It is usually busy.
(D) It is next to Holiday Lodge Hotel.

文中提到多那太羅餐廳什麼事？

(A) 最近才開張。
(B) 剛整修好。
(C) 通常客人很多很忙碌。
(D) 位於度假小屋飯店的旁邊。

第一封郵件最後說到：「Donnatello Restaurant . . . was given a 5-star rating from *Trip Advisory Guide*」，並說到「we strongly recommend that you make a reservation in advance.」，可知餐廳剛得到旅遊指南的五顆星評價，欲用餐最好先訂位，故可知道餐廳常有眾多客人，本題正確答案為 (C)。

**183**

**What information in the hotel reservation is wrong?**

(A) That Dr. Berry will check in on August 3
(B) That Dr. Berry has organized the forum
(C) That Dr. Berry has paid for all rooms
(D) That Dr. Berry will depart before the conference ends

哪個訂房資訊有錯誤？

(A) 貝里博士會在 8 月 3 日入住
(B) 貝里博士主辦論壇
(C) 貝里博士已為所有訂房付款
(D) 貝里博士會在會議結束之前提前離開

從第一封郵件中的「We have you checking in on 3 August」，及第二封郵件裡的「I will not be arriving until August 4」，可知飯店預約者貝里博士因為 8 月 4 日才會抵達，故無法在 8 月 3 日入住，所以入住日期有誤，正確答案為 (A)。

**184**

**What is stated about the hotel reservation?**

(A) The reservation code is misprinted.
(B) The number of rooms is not correct.
(C) The attendants for the forum are not enough.
(D) The room rates are different.

文中提到關於這次飯店訂房什麼事？

(A) 訂房號碼印錯了。
(D) 訂房數量不正確。
(C) 出席論壇的人數不夠。
(D) 客房價格有別。

第二封郵件第二段指出：「the number of reserved rooms is 10, not 12」，表示飯店誤將房數多給了兩間，故正確答案為 (B)。

**185**

**In the second e-mail, the word "matter" in paragraph 3, line 3, is closest in meaning to**

(A) situation
(B) substance
(C) material
(D) publication

第二封電子郵件中，第三段、第三行的「matter」最接近下列哪個意思？

(A) 情況
(B) 物質
(C) 材質
(D) 刊物

第二封郵件主要在要求飯店修正錯誤，並事先對飯店即刻處理表示感謝，因此此處的「matter」應為「問題」、「情況」的意思，本題答案為 (A)。

# Athens Gazette

## Local Companies Need More Staff
by Sophia Lauren

Athens (April 10)—It is difficult for us to seek suitable candidates for a position. To make their hiring process easier, some companies make a request to staffing agencies. By finding part-time employees for the peak season or handling the whole application procedure through these agencies, companies save money and time in many ways.

Jane Foster, the general manager of Hellocrew Recruiting, which is one of the oldest staffing agencies in Georgia, said that a number of companies can get an advantage while hiring temporary staff from the agency. "They have a chance to resolve certain hiring matters. Another benefit is that they can train a potential member before they offer him/her full-time employment," Foster said.

To support local companies through this process, we have posted a list of staffing agencies. You can find it on the upper right-hand side of this page at www.athensgazette. com.

# Hellocrew Recruiting
## TEMPORARY EMPLOYEE REQUEST FORM

**Company Information**
- **Name**: Brad Triana
- **Company**: MSC Business Accounting
- **Field**: Accounting
- **Phone**: 412-237-9400
- **E-mail**: btriana@mscbiz.com

**Task Information**
- Need number of staff: minimum 8
- Opening Position: office workers
- Expected duration: 2–3 weeks

**Specifications:**
We have a lot of government-led projects on auditing city councils' accounts in many districts. Because of these projects, we have stored up too many documents and

---

# 《雅典公報》

當地企業需要更多員工
索菲亞·羅倫撰文

雅典（4月10日）—對我們來說，要找到適合的應徵者並不容易。有些公司為了簡化聘僱流程，會轉往人力仲介找人。公司透過這些仲介尋找旺季的兼職員工，或處理整個應徵流程，多方面省下金錢和時間。

喬治亞歷史悠久的一家人力仲介公司，「哈囉幫人力」的總經理珍·佛斯特說，很多公司經由仲介聘僱臨時工，並從中獲得優勢。「他們有機會解決某些聘僱問題。另外一個好處是，他們可以先訓練有潛力的員工，再給予他或她全職職位。」佛斯特說。

為了支持當地企業使用這個流程，我們公告了人力仲介公司的名單。您可以在www.athensgazette.com網頁的右上角找到資訊。

# 哈囉幫人力
## 臨時雇員需求表

公司資訊
- **姓名**：布萊德·崔安納
- **公司**：MSC商業會計
- **領域**：會計
- **電話**：412-237-9400
- **電子郵件信箱**：
  btriana@mscbiz.com

職務資訊
- 員工需求數：最少8人
- 職缺：職員
- 預計聘僱期間：2到3週

特別說明：
我們接了很多政府計畫，審計市議會多區的帳務。因為這些計畫，我們堆積了太多的文件和檔案需要整

files that we need to arrange. These documents and files should be categorized and scanned more quickly in order to meet a deadline. We are seeking meticulous applicants who are able to follow instructions well.

**How did you find out about us?**
I saw your agency in yesterday's online column in the Athens Gazette.

**Thank you for your registration!**
One of our staffing agents will contact you within 24 hours through e-mail.

理。這些文件和檔案需要分門別類歸檔，並在期限前儘快完成掃描。我們徵求的應徵者需要非常細心，且要能聽從指示辦事。

您如何知道我們的？
我在《雅典公報》昨天的線上專欄看到貴公司。

感謝您的登記！
我們的人事專員將在24小時內透過電子郵件與您聯繫。

---

**From:** Brad Triana
<btriana@mscbiz.com>
**To:** Heather Lowry
<hlowry@hellocrew.net>
**Subject:** Thank You
**Date:** April 15

寄件人：布萊德·崔安納
<btriana@mscbiz.com>
收件人：海瑟·洛瑞
<hlowry@hellocrew.net>
主旨：感謝
日期：4月15日

---

Dear Ms. Lowry,

I would like to extend my sincere gratitude for your help. It was my first time working with a staffing agency, so, frankly, I did not have confidence in this process. Because of your agency, we are ready to complete our tasks with the temporary employees you matched with us. You responded to my request form within just three hours and made a list of employees available within just a day! The employees you recommended were really industrious, hardworking, and devoted to our assignments. For that reason, we made a decision to interview two of them for offering them full-time positions.

Best wishes,
Brad Triana

親愛的洛瑞女士：

我誠摯感謝您的協助。這是我第一次和人力仲介公司合作，所以坦白說，我對這個流程不是很有信心。因為貴公司所找到的合適臨時工，我們已經快完成工作了。您在短短三個小時內回覆我的需求，而且一天內就提出人員名單！您推薦的人員真的很勤奮認真，對於我們指派的任務也很投入。有鑑於此，我們決定要面試其中兩個人，提供他們全職員工的職缺。

祝好，
布萊德·崔安納

---

**詞彙** **staffing agency** 人力仲介　**duration** 期間　**government-led** 政府主導的　**audit** 審計
**city council** 市議會　**meticulous** 細心的　**industrious** 勤奮的

**186** ----------------------------------------

**In the article, what advantage is NOT indicated about part-time staff?**

(A) Getting specialized and professional support
(B) Saving more than the company's budget planned
(C) Making the recruiting process smoother
(D) Supporting companies in handling some issues

關於兼職員工，文中沒有提到哪一項好處？

(A) 得到專門或專業的協助
(B) 比公司原先規劃的省下更多預算。
(C) 讓聘僱程序更加流暢
(D) 協助公司處理某些問題

文章第一段的第三句提到：「companies save money and time in many ways」，可知僱用兼職員工能使公司省下金錢與時間，故 (B) 有被提及。再從同段第二句開頭的「To make their hiring process easier」，可知兼職員工的僱用流程相較簡單，故 (C) 的內容有被提及。

而從郵件中可以看出，兼職員工的確可完成公司的需求，故 (D) 也能從文中推知。綜合上述，文中未提及的只有 (A)，所以正確答案為 (A)。

**187** ----------------------------------------

**What is implied about Mr. Triana?**

(A) He read Ms. Lauren's article on the Web.
(B) His company is included in the list on the *Athens Gazette*'s page.
(C) His company has worked with Hellocrew Recruiting before.
(D) He did an interview with the *Athens Gazette*.

文中提到崔安納先生什麼事？

(A) 他在網站上讀了羅倫女士的文章。
(B) 他的公司也被列在《雅典公報》網頁的清單裡。
(C) 他的公司曾和哈囉幫人力合作過。
(D) 他接受《雅典公報》的採訪。

從臨時雇員需求表上的「I saw your agency in yesterday's online column in the *Athens Gazette*」，可以得知崔安納先生曾於報紙的線上專欄看到廣告文章，而對照第一篇文章的作者可知，崔安納先生看到的就是羅倫女士撰寫的文章，故正確答案為 (A)。

**188** ----------------------------------------

**In the form, the word "duration" in paragraph 2, line 2, is closest in meaning to**

(A) length
(B) strength
(C) growth
(D) path

在表格中，第二段、第二行的「duration」，最接近下列哪個意思？

(A) 時間長短
(B) 強度
(C) 成長
(D) 路線

從 duration 後方接的「2–3 weeks」，以及整篇需求表的內容，可推測此處的 duration 與工作的「期間長度」有關，故正確答案為 (A)。

**189** ----------------------------------------------------------------

**What is the main purpose of the e-mail?**

(A) To offer both staff members new permanent positions

(B) To confirm a request the sales team made

(C) To express thanks for an issue they dealt with

(D) To complain about some errors in the article

這封電子郵件的目的為何？

(A) 給予兩名成員新的正職

(B) 確認銷售團隊所提出的需求

(C) 對於他們所處理的事表示感謝

(D) 抱怨文章中的一些錯誤

根據郵件的第一句「I would like to extend my sincere gratitude to your help」可看出，由於人力仲介公司協助配對臨時員工，寄件人想要表達感謝而撰寫了郵件，故正確答案為 (C)。

**190** ----------------------------------------------------------------

**Who most likely is Ms. Lowry?**

(A) A part-timer in the MSC Business Accounting

(B) An official in a city council

(C) A staffing agent at Hellocrew Recruiting

(D) A news writer at the *Athens Gazette*

洛瑞女士最可能的身分是？

(A) MSC 商業會計的兼職員工

(B) 市議會的官員

(C) 哈囉幫人力的人事專員

(D)《雅典公報》的新聞撰稿人

洛瑞女士為郵件的收件人，而郵件內容講述對人力仲介公司的讚許，且說道「You responded to my request form within just three hours and made a list of employees available within just a day!」，表示洛瑞女士迅速回覆人力需求且提出人員名單，故可知道她應是人力仲介公司的職員，且從郵件收件者的信箱網址「llowry@hollocrew.net」也可以知道她隸屬於哈囉幫人力公司，故正確答案為 (C)。

### 191–195 文章和電子郵件

## New Local Landmark Construction

At a meeting on Thursday, Hattiesburg officials discussed a local improvement plan that would enable the town to attract more students and visitors. According to Gian Pagnucci, the chair of Hattiesburg College, construction of a multi-complex convention center should be fully considered within both the local council and college's budget. Hence, the city council decided to encourage local companies to join a public bid for this construction project. In addition, local residents are encouraged to submit an entry for a contest to name the center.

Some proposed projects include an outdoor sports park, depending on whether it would be located near the center on Oak Grove Street. According to Mr. Pagnucci, the council will ask all community members to share their ideas. Interested people may

## 當地新地標的建設

週四的會議上，哈蒂斯堡的官員討論了一項地方改善計畫，可以讓城鎮吸引更多的學生和遊客。根據哈蒂斯堡學院院長金安・帕格努奇的說法，建設一個多功能綜合會議中心，需要全面考慮當地議會和學院的預算。因此，市議會決定鼓勵當地企業公開競標這項建設計畫。此外，也鼓勵當地居民報名參加中心命名的比賽。

部分提案提議建設戶外運動公園，但是否選址在中心旁邊、位在橡樹林街上還有待決定。帕格努奇先生表示，議會將請所有當地社區成員分享意見。感興趣的民眾可以帶著自己的意見，於6月18日下週四下午四點，到議會週例會分享，或在6月22日前寄電子

bring their opinions to the next weekly meeting on Thursday, 18 June, at 4 P.M. or send an e-mail to the task force team before 22 June. After fully considering extensive opinions from citizens, the planning committee will put forth a final draft to the council for an official discussion. The expected date of the decision is no later than 30 June.

郵件給任務執行團隊。籌委會將通盤考量眾多的公民意見，並向議會提出最終版草案，進行正式的討論。預計最晚會在6月30日前做出決議。

---

**From:** selindiana@stormmail.com
**To:** citycouncil@hattiesburg.org
**Date:** 20 June
**Subject:** Additional Projects

寄件人：selindiana@stormmail.com
收件人：citycouncil@hattiesburg.org
日期：6月20日
主旨：附加計畫

---

Dear Council Official,

I was notified that you are accepting suggestions for the use of the town's budget to build new convention center. Due to another appointment in my schedule, I was not able to attend the weekly meeting for the project, but I would like to express my support for the plan to make our town more attractive. Although the cost of the construction is likely to be reasonable, project planners should fully take into account the effectiveness and proximity to the center, and the benefit of all our community members. This project will be a good source of civic pride and a brand-new landmark where we can enjoy a diversity of activities. Even though it is important for the town's image, its advantages should be evenly distributed among our citizens.

Selin Diana

親愛的議會官員：

我知道對於使用市鎮預算建設新的會議中心一事，您正在徵詢建議。由於我已有行程安排，不克參加這項計畫的週會，但我仍想表態支持這項可以讓地方更具吸引力的計畫。雖然建設的成本可能還算合理，專案規畫人員還是得全面考量會議中心的成效、地理方便性，還有它對於我們全體在地居民的助益。這項計畫將成為市民驕傲，中心也將會是我們可以享受各類活動的全新地標。即便它對市鎮形象舉足輕重，它的效益還是應該均衡地回饋給所有在地人。

塞林‧戴安娜

---

**From:** fangyu@solomonunitas.com
**To:** citycouncil@hattiesburg.org
**Date:** 21 June
**Subject:** City Projects

寄件人：fangyu@solomonunitas.com
收件人：citycouncil@hattiesburg.org
日期：6月21日
主旨：市政計畫

---

To Whom It May Concern,

I was happy to hear that the new development was decided for our town. Because the town's public facilities are not suitable for a variety of activities for

致相關人士：

我很開心我們鎮上有了新的發展方向。因為鎮上的公共設施不足以提供各式各樣的活動，滿足各年齡層的需

all citizens of all ages, this multi-complex space can give the public many opportunities to enjoy a wide range of events such as NCAA basketball games, local job fairs, and so on. I have just one issue to consider, and it concerns older people.

This project should not just focus on teenagers and young adults. According to the city population distribution data, the elderly form 30 percent of the citizenship in Hattiesburg. Therefore, we should never overlook considering their needs. It would be a remarkable improvement to the town if all of us can enjoy this facility—both young and old—without any inconvenience. Please make sure these benefits are equally shared among all people.

求，這個全新的綜合空間可以讓大家有更多機會享受更廣泛的活動，像是國家體協籃球聯賽、當地就業博覽會等等。但我只有一個和老年人相關的考量。

這項計畫不應該只著重在青少年或年輕人身上。根據市鎮的人口分布數據，高齡人口佔哈蒂斯堡公民的三成。因此，我們絕對不能忽視他們的需求。如果我們全體，不分老少都能夠便利地享受這個設施，這會是一項了不起的進步。請確保所有人都可以平等共享好處。

**詞彙** **chair** 主席　**multi-complex** 多功能綜合大樓　**entry** 參賽作品　**task force team** 任務執行團隊　**put forth** 提出　**take into account** 考量　**civic pride** 市民驕傲　**image** 形象

**191**

**Why does the town of Hattiesburg need a new project?**

(A) The city council canceled a previous project.
(B) The town has raised tax on property.
(C) The area is planning to attract more people.
(D) Citizens have debated a development issue.

為什麼哈蒂斯堡需要新的計畫？

(A) 市議會取消了前一項計畫。
(B) 鎮上最近提高了地產稅。
(C) 該地區計劃能吸引更多人。
(D) 鎮民已爭論了一項發展議題。

根據第一篇報導文章中的第一句話：「Hattiesburg officials discussed a local improvement plan that would enable the town to attract more students and visitors.」，可以得知建設計畫是為了吸引學生與遊客，故正確答案為 (C)。

**192**

**In the article, the phrase "put forth" in paragraph 2, line 6, is closest in meaning to**

(A) publish
(B) promote
(C) propose
(D) plant

在文章中，第二段、第六行的「put forth」，最接近下列哪個意思？

(A) 出版
(B) 推廣
(C) 提案
(D) 栽種

從「the planning committee will put forth a final draft to the council for an official discussion」可以看見「籌委會」、「最終版草案」、「議會」與「正式的討論」，故可推知，「put forth」此處應為「提出，提議」之意，表示提交草案給議會，故最相近的詞彙為選項中的 propose，正確答案為 (C)。

## 193

**When did Ms. Diana have an appointment?**

(A) June 18
(B) June 20
(C) June 21
(D) June 30

戴安娜女士何時有約？

(A) 6 月 18 日
(B) 6 月 20 日
(C) 6 月 21 日
(D) 6 月 30 日

先從郵件中的「I was not able to attend the weekly meeting for the project」得知，戴安娜女士在建設計畫的週會時間另有安排，故對照回報導文章，其中說到：「Interested people may bring their opinions to the next weekly meeting on Thursday, 18 June, at 4 P.M.」，表示週會是在 6 月 18 日星期四舉辦，故正確答案為 (A)。

## 194

**What is the second e-mail mainly about?**

(A) Celebrating civilian projects
(B) Questioning the directions to the new facility
(C) Complaining about incorrect information
(D) Raising a potential issue

第二封電子郵件主旨為何？

(A) 慶祝市鎮計畫
(B) 質疑新設施的方向
(C) 抱怨錯誤資訊
(D) 提出潛在問題

第二封郵件在第一段的最後一句即寫到：「I have just one issue to consider, and it concerns older people.」，表示有與老年人相關的顧慮，並在第二段詳細說明，故可知第二封郵件是為了點出其他潛在問題而寄出，正確答案為 (D)。。

## 195

**What will happen by June 30?**

(A) A final planning outline will be made with public opinions and officials' research.
(B) The city will have a groundbreaking ceremony for the new multi-complex.
(C) The council will announce a competitive bid for the facility development.
(D) Some citizens will instigate demonstrations against the construction issue.

6 月 30 日前將會發生什麼事？

(A) 根據公民意見和官員研究，完成最終版企畫大綱。
(B) 鎮上將為新綜合場館舉行開工典禮。
(C) 市議會將為了開發新設施宣布競標。
(D) 有些鎮民將發動抗議，反對建設計畫。

第一篇的報導文章在最後提到：「The expected date of the decision is no later than 30 June.」，表示會在 6 月 30 日前做出決議，且前句也提到「fully considering extensive opinions」以及「official discussion」，表示決議將建立在民眾意見與官方考量的基礎上，因此正確答案為 (A)。

**From:** John Dyson
**To:** Ben Tannacito
**Subject:** Trucking Company
**Date:** March 2

Hello Mr. Tannacito,

I am so glad that you have signed up for deliveries of our furniture — initially a couch for four, a desk in white, two chairs in black, a queen-sized bed — made here at our LINKer Furnishings Factory. I can assure you that you and your customers will be pleased with the products we provide.

Your store is in an area that is new to us, and we are looking forward to delivering our items into a new store. Please let me know if you are interested in this moving service. Our licensed drivers in Stonybrook do not go out to Albany, so a different company should be hired. U-Haul moving company Is the best choice that fits your conditions. We would like to work with a company of your choice to keep the service for you as safe as possible.

Sincerely,
John Dyson

寄件人：約翰‧戴森
收件人：班‧塔南西多
主旨：貨運公司
日期：3月2日

哈囉，塔南西多先生：

我很高興您登記了我們的家具運送服務，您訂了由我們聯客家具工廠所生產的四人座沙發、白色辦公桌、兩張黑色椅子和一張大號的床。我可以保證，我們提供的產品將讓您和您的客戶感到滿意。

您店面所在的地區，對我們來說是個新地點，我們很期待可以把商品送到新的店家。請讓我知道您是否對這項運送服務感興趣。我們在石溪的合格駕駛員不會派送到阿伯尼，所以會聘請其他公司協助。考量您的情況，優禮搬運是最合適您的選擇。我們很願意和您所選擇的公司合作，盡力提供給您安全的服務。

約翰‧戴森 敬上

## ALTOONA HOME DECO SYSTEM

NEW THIS WEEK!
March 20
**Items from LINKer Furnishings Factory**

Dear Customers,

We would like to call your attention to the latest additions to our product lines. You've asked for durable and inexpensive home furniture, and now we're carrying it. We can bring these items directly to you from LINKer Furnishings Factory, located just two hours from here in Buffalo.

– Family-Size Couches
– White Desks with Durable Wood
– Well-Being Black Chairs
– Various Bed Designs and Sizes
– Mobile Closets
– Antibacterial Area Rugs

## 阿爾圖納居家裝潢系統

本週最新！
3月20日
**來自聯客家具工廠的產品**

親愛的客戶：

我們籲請您注意我們產品線上的最新產品。您諮詢過耐用且價格實惠的家具，現在我們有提供了。我們可直接從聯客家具工廠出貨，該廠位於水牛城，到這裡只要兩個小時車程。

—家用尺寸沙發
—耐用木製白色書桌
—安康黑色椅子
—各種設計和尺寸的床
—可移動式櫥櫃
—抗菌地毯

| | |
|---|---|
| Next season, we will develop user-friendly office furniture in our Amherst branch. If you have any questions about the items, please feel free to contact linkercustomer@lffactory.com. | 下一季，在我們阿姆赫斯特分公司，將開發貼近使用者需求的辦公室家具。如果您對這些商品有任何疑問，請儘管聯繫 linkercustomer@lffactory.com。 |

## LINKer Furnishings Order Form　　聯客家具訂貨表

**Customer:** ALTOONA HOME DECO SYSTEM
**Order Date:** March 25
**Delivery Date:** April 10

**Delivery Details:**
Repeat the initial order with the following changes.
- No couch for four. (Couch for five needed)
- Instead of white items, please send me black items.
- Add one more chair

P.S. You asked me to let you know if there were any issues with the U-Haul Trucking delivery. The arrival was on time, the driver was friendly, and the items were in good condition.

客戶：阿爾圖納居家裝潢系統
訂單日期：3月25日
配送日期：4月10日

配送內容：
維持原訂單但修改內容如下：
—沒有四人座沙發（需要五人座）
—請配送黑色書桌，而非白色的。
—加一張椅子

備註：您向我詢問優運貨運有沒有狀況。他們準時到貨、駕駛友善，運送抵達時商品的狀況也良好。

詞彙 **queen-sized bed** 大尺寸的床（但小於 **king-sized bed**）　**durable** 耐用的　**carry** 有提供
**well-being** 安康的　**antibacterial** 抗菌的　**follow up on sth** 對某事採取進一步行動

**Why did Mr. Dyson send the e-mail?**

(A) To advertise new products
(B) To request a delivery estimate
(C) To announce a policy change
(D) To follow up on an order

為什麼戴森先生要寄這封電子郵件？

(A) 為新產品打廣告
(B) 詢問運費的估價
(C) 公告政策異動
(D) 追蹤訂單

根據郵件第一句的「I am so glad that you have signed up for deliveries of our furniture」，以及戴森先生條列出的家具品項，可知收件人向戴森先生的公司要求了家具運送服務，而這封郵件的目的是為確認產品訂購與配送資訊，故正確答案為 (D)。

**Where is Altoona Home Deco System probably located?**

(A) In Stonybrook
(B) In Albany
(C) In Buffalo
(D) In Amherst

阿爾圖納居家裝潢系統可能位於哪個地方？

(A) 石溪
(B) 阿伯尼
(C) 水牛城
(D) 阿姆赫斯特

本題首先要知道塔南西多先生為阿爾圖納居家裝潢系統的員工。在第一封郵件中，戴森先生說：「at our LINKer Furnishings Factory」，表示戴森先生應為聯客家具工廠的員工，再從通知上的「We can bring these items directly to you from LINKer Furnishings Factory」知道，阿爾圖納居家裝潢系統的商品是向聯客家具工廠訂購的，故第一封郵件的收件人塔南西多先生應為阿爾圖納居家裝潢系統的員工，也可對照兩篇內容條列出的品項應證此事。

接著回到第一封郵件，其中說到：「Your store is in an area that is new to us」，表示公司並不熟悉收件人的所在地，且後文提到「Our licensed drivers . . . do not go out to Albany」，公司的司機無法送達阿伯尼地區，意即收件人阿爾圖納居家裝潢系統就位於阿伯尼，故本題正確答案為 (B)。

 **198**

In the notice, what is implied about LINKer Furnishings Factory's products?

(A) They are delivered within just two hours of ordering.

(B) They are likely to best suit small houses.

(C) They are reasonably priced.

(D) They are out of stock because of their popularity.

關於聯客家具工廠的產品，這篇告示中暗示什麼？

(A) 訂貨後兩小時就會出貨。

(B) 最適合小坪數房子。

(C) 價格實惠。

(D) 因為太受歡迎而缺貨。

告示內第二句說到：「You've asked for durable and inexpensive home furniture, and now we're carrying it.」，表示他們引進的家具既堅固又不貴，而他們的家具又是聯客家具工廠製造的，故可推知聯客家具工廠的產品耐用且價格不高，故本題正確答案為 (C)。

 **199**

What will Altoona Home Deco System probably receive on April 10?

(A) Antibacterial Area Rugs

(B) King-Size Beds

(C) Four Black Chairs

(D) Black Big Desks

在 4 月 10 日，阿爾圖納居家裝潢系統可能會收到什麼？

(A) 抗菌地毯

(B) 加大尺寸的床

(C) 四張黑椅子

(D) 黑色大書桌

先參照第一封郵件中的「a couch for four, a desk in white, two chairs in black, a queen-sized bed」，再從訂貨表上的列點得知，訂單有些更動的內容，故最後要送達的產品應為五人座沙發、黑色書桌、三張黑色椅子以及大床，正確答案為 (D)。

**200**

**What does Mr. Tannacito indicate in the order form?**

(A) He had a good experience with the trucking service.
(B) The U-Haul service has a lot of clients.
(C) He was disappointed with the items he got.
(D) Some wear and tear could be found in the products.

在訂貨表格中，塔南西多先生指出什麼事？

(A) 貨運服務使用經驗不錯。
(B) 優運貨運的客戶很多。
(C) 他對收到的商品感到失望。
(D) 產品上有部分刮傷和毀損。

從訂貨表的備註可知：「The arrival was on time, the driver was friendly, and the items were in good condition」，表示配送準時、駕駛友善且商品完整，故本題正確答案為 (A)。

# ACTUAL TEST
# 7

## PART 5

**101**

Felix Armstrong, the owner of the Indonesian restaurant, chose to order flatware and other ------- directly from the producer.

(A) supply
(B) supplies
(C) suppliers
(D) supplied

題型 位置──名詞

翻譯 印尼餐廳的老闆菲力克斯·阿姆斯壯選擇直接和製造商訂購餐具和其他用品。

詞彙 flatware 扁平類的餐具

空格出現在限定詞 other 之後，因 other 後面應出現可數複數名詞或不可數名詞，所以 (A) 與 (D) 可先刪去。

(B) 與 (C) 的區別在於事物和人物，而前面的 flatware 與空格之間使用對等連接詞「and」進行連接，所以空格字義應與 flatware 相關，故選意思為「用品」的事物名詞 supplies 最為適合，正確答案為 (B)。

**102**

Every Monday, we ------- tours of the production facilities to ensure they are in order.

(A) arrive
(B) visit
(C) conduct
(D) inspect

題型 詞彙──動詞

翻譯 我們每週一都會進行生產設備巡視，確保它們運作正常。

詞彙 in order 運作正常

句中提到「生產設備」、「巡視」、「確保」與「運作正常」，故可推測出此處缺少的動詞，其字義應為「進行」，表示進行生產設備巡視，以確保運作正常，故正確答案為 (C)。

(A) arrive 為不及物動詞，故後面不可緊接著受詞 tours；(B) visit 後面應接表示場所的受詞；(D) inspect 的字義為「檢查」，與字義為「巡視」的受詞 tours 在意義上並不相符，故無法成為答案。

**103**

Ms. Grant sees to it that she advises the new workers in order to carry out ------- duties efficiently.

(A) they
(B) their
(C) them
(D) theirs

題型 位置──所有格代名詞

翻譯 格蘭特女士一定會給予新進員工建議，讓他們的工作執行得有效率。

詞彙 see to it 留意到；保證做到
carry out 執行

由於空格在名詞 duties（義務；任務）之前，故空格要能夠修飾名詞，唯一可選的只有身為所有格的 their，故正確答案為 (B)。

**104**

---

**Due to the increase in the availability of mobile technology, landlines have become ------- in many domestic homes.**

(A) obsolete
(B) extracted
(C) insolent
(D) contemporary

| 題型 | 詞彙──形容詞 |
|---|---|
| 翻譯 | 行動科技的使用愈來愈普及，室內電話在很多家庭已是淘汰的。 |
| 詞彙 | landline 市內電話<br>domestic 家內的；國內的 |

本題應選出符合句意的形容詞。本句提到「行動科技」、「普及」與「室內電話」，故可以推測此處應填入字義為「沒有用處的、淘汰的」的形容詞，故選項中最適合的為 obsolete，正確答案為 (A)。

**105**

---

**The Dart Entertainer Academy holds open auditions every month for those ------- in participating in the annual singing contest.**

(A) interest
(B) interested
(C) to interest
(D) interesting

| 題型 | 文法──分詞 |
|---|---|
| 翻譯 | 達特演藝學院每個月舉行公開試鏡，給有興趣參加年度歌唱大賽的人。 |

空格前後形成「for those . . . in participating in」的結構，those 一般以「those (who are)＋形容詞或分詞」的型態出現，表示「做……的人」，注意本題 those 後面省略了 who are，所以空格內應直接代入形容詞或分詞。

選項中，(B) 為過去分詞，(D) 為現在分詞。interest 為表示情感的及物動詞，在修飾人物時應使用過去分詞，表示「感到……的」，修飾事物時則使用現在分詞，表示「令人……的」，故空格內應代入過去分詞 interested，正確答案為 (B)。

**106**

---

**Mr. Spencer has received an appreciation plaque at a retirement ceremony for ------- dedication to the company where he has worked for over 25 years.**

(A) he
(B) his
(C) him
(D) himself

| 題型 | 位置──所有格代名詞 |
|---|---|
| 翻譯 | 斯賓塞先生最近在退休典禮上獲頒銘牌，感謝他在公司超過 25 年的貢獻。 |
| 詞彙 | plaque 銘牌；匾額 |

空格的位置在名詞 dedication 前面，故要選能修飾名詞的，選項中只有所有格代名詞 his 適合，故正確答案為 (B)。

## 107

Cox Industries' latest career announcement ------- notes that the managerial position is only accepting current line supervisors.

(A) specify
(B) specific
(C) specifying
(D) specifically

題型 位置——副詞

翻譯 考克斯工業最近的職缺公告特別地指出，管理職位只會考慮錄取目前在職的生產線主管。

觀察空格夾在主詞與動詞之間，應為修飾動詞的副詞，因此只有 specifically 適合填入，故正確答案為 (D)。

The latest novel from Brian Bennett has had positive ------- from the critics.

(A) matters
(B) repairs
(C) reviews
(D) collections

題型 詞彙——名詞

翻譯 布萊恩·班納特新出的小說獲得評論家的好評。

本句提到「小說」、「正面的」（positive）以及「評論家」，故可推測空格處的名詞字義應為「評論」，表示小說得到來自評論家的正面評論，故正確答案為 (C)。

Ms. Cunningham was supposed to purchase the tickets to the concert, but she thought that they were too -------.

(A) expense
(B) expensive
(C) expensively
(D) expensiveness

題型 位置——形容詞

翻譯 坎寧漢女士早該去買演奏會的票，但她覺得太貴了。

空格位於 be 動詞後，可接續名詞或形容詞，但此處的 they 指的是名詞 the tickets，故此處填入 (A) 與 (D) 兩個名詞皆不正確，故最適合的答案為 expensive，正確答案為 (B)。

## 110

The government has urged everyone to renew their annual tax return online ------- to avoid incurring a financial penalty.

(A) early
(B) hardly
(C) enough
(D) usefully

**題型** 詞彙──副詞
**翻譯** 政府敦促大家及早上網更新年度退稅資料，以免被罰錢。
**詞彙** urge 敦促
tax return 退稅
incur 遭受

本題提到政府督促大家上網更新資料，故此處的副詞應具有「早」的意思，表示及早更新資料，故正確答案為 (A)。

## 111

At Mason Hospital, all medical records are strictly ------- and can only be released upon permission of the patient.

(A) confiding
(B) confidence
(C) confidential
(D) confidentiality

**題型** 位置──形容詞
**翻譯** 梅森醫院所有的醫療紀錄都是嚴格保密的，唯有取得病患同意才能調閱。
**詞彙** permission 同意

本題空格位於副詞之後，應代入可被其修飾的形容詞，故 confidential 最為適合。注意 confidential 字義為「機密的」，而 confident 為「自信的」，兩者並不相同。本題正確答案為 (C)。

## 112

The results from recent client questionnaires ------- in the file attached to this e-mail.

(A) summarizes
(B) summarized
(C) are summarizing
(D) are summarized

**題型** 文法──被動
**翻譯** 近期顧客問卷的結果，摘要於電子郵件的附檔中。
**詞彙** summarize 摘要
questionnaire 問卷
attach 附加

判斷動詞型態，須考慮動詞是否及物，以及單複數與時態是否一致。summarize 為及物動詞，但後方沒有受詞，故可知道此處動詞為被動，所以正確答案為 (D)。

**113**

Under the ------- of Dr. Owen, the Engineering Department of Patel Precision Industries performs a number of material examinations every year.

(A) prediction
(B) indication
(C) completion
(D) supervision

題型 詞彙──名詞

翻譯 帕托精工工程部每年都會在歐文博士的監督下檢驗多項材料。

詞彙 precision 精準
perform examinations 進行檢驗

本句提到公司會進行材料檢驗，故空格處應填入帶有「監督、管理、指導」意思的名詞，表示在公司的監督下進行檢驗。本題最適合填入 supervision，故正確答案為 (D)。

**114**

The Cornell Ski Resort employed 12 additional safety guards ------- at its Yellowwoods Valley branch during the hectic winter season.

(A) assists
(B) assisted
(C) to assist
(D) have assisted

題型 文法──不定詞

翻譯 康乃爾滑雪休閒中心黃林谷分店加聘了 12 名保全人員，協助冬天旺季的生意。

詞彙 safety guard 保全人員
hectic 忙碌的

選項為動詞 assist 的各種型態。句子中已經出現動詞 employed，空格中不可再代入一般動詞，所以 (A)、(B) 與 (D) 皆不正確，(C) 不定詞帶有「要去做某事」的意思，故此處填入 to assist 最為合適，正確答案為 (C)。

**115**

In its latest newspaper advertisement, Prime Bank ------- the general complaint by the public that its interest rates are too high.

(A) tended
(B) refuted
(C) imposed
(D) recuperated

題型 詞彙──動詞

翻譯 首席銀行在其最新一期的報紙廣告上，反駁民眾批評它的利率太高。

詞彙 interest rate 利率

(A) tend 照顧；(B) refute 反駁；(C) impose 強加；(D) recuperate 恢復。

本題要選出動詞，需確認空格與主詞、受詞間的意義與關係。本句提到民眾抱怨銀行利率太高，但由銀行當作主詞，故此處最可能填入帶有「反駁」意思的動詞，表示銀行反駁民眾抱怨的事情，故正確答案為 (B)。

**116**

The Health Bureau has assured the public that it will expand the number of medical activities ------- in the following year.

(A) distantly
(B) recently
(C) currently
(D) significantly

| 題型 | 詞彙——副詞 |
| --- | --- |
| 翻譯 | 健康局向民眾承諾，會在明年大幅增加醫療活動。 |
| 詞彙 | Health Bureau 健康局 |

副詞修飾動詞，故要找出字義上適合修飾 expand 的選項。本句提到承諾增加醫療活動，所以空格處應該填入帶有「大幅地、顯著地」的意思的副詞，以表示大幅增加數量，故正確答案為 (D)。

注意 recently（最近）與 currently（現在）在意義上不可與未來式一起使用。

**117**

When checking a safety device, please also ensure that the doors and windows are ------- before leaving the office.

(A) security
(B) securely
(C) securing
(D) secured

| 題型 | 文法——被動 |
| --- | --- |
| 翻譯 | 檢查保全設施時，也請確保離開辦公室前，所有門窗都關緊了。 |
| 詞彙 | safety device 保全設施 |
| | secure 拴緊；扣緊 |

secure 在此作為及物動詞，當主詞為 doors and windows，後方又沒有其他受詞時，動詞要改為被動式。此處已有 be 動詞，故空格處應填入過去分詞，正確答案為 (D)。

**118**

Workers who make use of company vehicles must ------- a legal and up-to-date driver's license.

(A) expel
(B) assign
(C) specify
(D) possess

| 題型 | 詞彙——動詞 |
| --- | --- |
| 翻譯 | 員工駕駛公司車輛時，須持有最新版的合法駕照。 |
| 詞彙 | make use of sth 使用某物 |
| | up-to-date 最新版的 |

(A) expel 驅逐；(B) assign 分配、指派；(C) specify 明確指出；(D) possess 擁有。

本句提到「使用」、「公司車輛」以及「駕照」，故可推測空格處應填入帶有「擁有、持有」意思的動詞，表示要使用公司車輛必須持有駕照，故正確答案為 (D)。

## 119

**According to a newsletter published today, a significant ------- of employees welcome the chance to feature their newly developed dietary supplement at the upcoming expo.**

(A) major
(B) majored
(C) majoring
(D) majority

| 題型 | 位置──名詞 |
|------|-----------|
| 翻譯 | 根據今天發布的電子報，絕大多數的員工都歡迎在近期展覽會上，主打新開發的營養補充品的機會。 |
| 詞彙 | newsletter （按時送出的）電子報<br>feature 主打<br>dietary supplement 營養補充品<br>expo 展覽會 |

空格前有形容詞 significant，故應為可被其修飾的名詞，正確答案為 (D)。

★記住下列用法：
**major**〔形容詞〕主要的；〔名詞〕主修
**major in (a subject)**〔動詞〕（主修某科目）
**a majority of**（大多數的）

## 120

**The fire drill will start at 2:00 P.M. in the Minnesota facility, and its manufacturing process cannot recommence ------- it has been finished.**

(A) while
(B) until
(C) that
(D) upon

| 題型 | 詞彙──連接詞 |
|------|-----------|
| 翻譯 | 明尼蘇達工廠的消防演習將在下午兩點開始，產線直到演習結束前都不能重新運作。 |
| 詞彙 | drill 演習<br>recommence 重新開始 |

觀察空格後句為具有主詞與動詞的完整句子，可將 (D) 介系詞先行剔除。本句提到「演習」、「生產」、「重新開始」，故此處應填入具有「直到」意思的連接詞，表示直到演習結束前都無法開始生產，正確答案為 (B)。

## 121

**To prevent any further delays in the delivery process, the production team had to work ------- to fix the broken machines.**

(A) swift
(B) swiftly
(C) swiftness
(D) swiftest

| 題型 | 位置──副詞 |
|------|-----------|
| 翻譯 | 為避免出貨延遲，生產團隊必須迅速地修理故障的機械。 |

空格在不及物動詞 work 之後，故應填入修飾動詞的副詞 swiftly，以表示迅速工作，因此正確答案為 (B)。

## 122

Kaur Designs ------- staff satisfaction a top priority since its inception 10 years ago.

(A) has considered
(B) will consider
(C) considering
(D) is considered

題型 文法——動詞

翻譯 考爾設計自 10 年前創立以來，就視員工滿意度為第一優先。

詞彙 a top priority 第一優先
inception 創立

consider 在此有「將 A 視為 B」的意思，用法為「consider A (to be) B」，但現在使用時通常都會省略 to be，直接寫作「consider A B」。

此句重點為「since」，表示「自……以來」，故搭配動詞要使用現在完成式，正確答案為 (A)。

## 123

The Walker's Chicken has a number of chain stores ------- Australia and is planning to extend its business abroad.

(A) behind
(B) among
(C) across
(D) despite

題型 詞彙——介系詞

翻譯 沃克炸雞有很多間連鎖店遍及全澳洲，並正計劃到其他國家展店。

詞彙 chain store 連鎖店
extend its business 拓展業務範圍

(A) behind （位置上）在後面；(B) among 在（數個個體）之間；(C) across 橫越；(D) despite 儘管。

根據句意，此處應使用帶有「遍及、橫跨」意義的介系詞，表示連鎖店已遍及澳洲全境，故公司計劃將到國外展店，正確答案為 (C)。

## 124

It is a ------- procedure to delete all confidential files from your computers at the end of the day.

(A) routine
(B) fastened
(C) difficult
(D) mistaken

題型 詞彙——形容詞

翻譯 每天下班前刪除電腦裡的機密檔案是例行的程序。

詞彙 at the end of the day 一天工作結束時

本題需選出可修飾名詞 procedure 的形容詞，而僅憑形容詞與名詞的字義，便可得知除了 (B) 之外，其餘選項皆合理，故需要理解整句的脈絡。本句應是表示工作完畢後清除機密檔案乃「例行的」程序，故正確答案為 (A)。

**125**

The Adams Hotel installed energy-saving LED lighting ------- all of its rooms last month.

(A) of
(B) on
(C) in
(D) before

題型 詞彙——介系詞

翻譯 亞當斯飯店上個月在所有房間裡安裝了省電的 LED 照明。

詞彙 energy-saving 省電的

介系詞題型可能考字義本身，或是考介系詞與動詞的固定搭配，本題屬於前者。本句提到飯店在房間裝設 LED 照明設備，故應使用 in，表示在房間「裡面」，正確答案為 (C)。

**126**

The employees ------- intend to undergo an interview for transfer have to apply today.

(A) where
(B) who
(C) whose
(D) when

題型 文法——關係代名詞

翻譯 有意參加調任面試的員工，必須在今天提出申請。

詞彙 undergo 進行；經歷
transfer 轉職

空格後沒有出現主詞，而是立即接續動詞與受詞，因此此處應代入主格關係代名詞，正確答案為 (B)。

**127**

The ------- has announced that cameras will be allowed in the courtroom for the first time.

(A) patron
(B) reputation
(C) spokesperson
(D) outcome

題型 詞彙——名詞

翻譯 發言人宣布，將首次允許在法庭上使用相機。

詞彙 courtroom 法庭

(A) patron 客戶；(B) reputation 名譽；(C) spokesperson 發言人；(D) outcome 結果。

空格為句子主詞的位置，且因為動詞 announce 為由人物進行的動作，故可先刪除 (B) 與 (D)。本句提到允許在法庭上使用相機，故應是由「發言人」宣布消息比較適合，本題正確答案 (C)。

**128**

---

Train 404 to Minox County departed two hours
------- than expected due to heavy snow in
Foxtown.

(A) late

(B) later

(C) latest

(D) lately

| 題型 | 文法——形容詞比較級 |
|---|---|
| 翻譯 | 因為佛克斯鎮的大雪，開往米諾克斯郡的 404 號列車晚了兩小時發車。 |
| 詞彙 | due to N 因為某事 |

由於空格後出現關鍵的 than，故可知道此處的形容詞要使用比較級，表示比預期晚，本題正確答案為 (B)。

**129**

---

------- the battery runs out quicker than expected
after being fully charged, contact our authorized
service center.

(A) If

(B) So

(C) Even

(D) Such

| 題型 | 詞彙——連接詞 |
|---|---|
| 翻譯 | 假如電池充飽後耗電比預期得快，請聯繫我們授權的服務中心。 |
| 詞彙 | battery runs out 電池沒電<br>charge 充電 |

本題前句表示電話的電池比預期中更快消耗，後句則請對方與服務中心聯絡，故根據句意，此處應填入 If，表示「如果」前句發生，則後句發生；正確答案為 (A)。

**130**

---

Any inquiries ------- travel expense claims should
be sent to the accounts department.

(A) through

(B) according to

(C) related to

(D) upon

| 題型 | 詞彙——片語 |
|---|---|
| 翻譯 | 和差旅費核銷有關的疑問都應轉往會計部門。 |
| 詞彙 | claim 報銷單 |

空格處應填入能夠連接「疑問」以及「差旅費核銷」的詞，故填入 related to，表示「有關」核銷的疑問，在句意上較為適當，正確答案為 (C)。

## PART 6

**131–134 新聞發布**

**To:** John Turner
<Johnturner@fastmail.com>
**From:** Charles Stone
<Cstone@walshlaws.com>
**Subject:** Letter of interest
**Date:** June 12

收件人：約翰・特納
<Johnturner@fastmail.com>
寄件人：查爾斯・史東
<Cstone@walshlaws.com>
主旨：求職信
日期：6月12日

---

Dear Mr. Turner,

Upon reading your letter of inquiry, we **131** in scheduling you for an interview for a career position with our company. **132**. As a result, we would like to consider you for an internship that will run from July 1 to September 30.

The program is intended to develop one's legal research expertise by means of training and hands-on practice, and if one becomes successful, he or she may choose from the **133** positions that we offer after the completion of the program. We advise you to think about this prospect, and if you wish **134** the internship, please get back to us by e-mail at a time that suits you.

Sincerely,
Charles Stone, Walsh Business Associates

親愛的特納先生：

讀過您的來信，我們有意安排您面試本公司的一項職務。您在信中提到您想應徵的職務是法務專員。因此，我們考慮提供您一份從7月1日到9月30日的實習。

這項計畫的目的在於透過訓練和實務操作，培養實習生鑽研法律知識的專業。如果受訓有成，實習生可以在計畫結束後，選擇我們提供的正職。我們建議您考慮這個機會，如果您有意把握這次實習，請在您方便時回信給我們。

沃爾什商會
查爾斯・史東 敬上

**詞彙** schedule 為……安排　run 持續（一段時間）　means 方法　hands-on 實務的
prospect 機會；可能性　get back to sb 回覆某人

**131** --------------------------------------------------------------------------------

(A) interest
(B) interested
(C) are interested
(D) are interesting

(A) 興趣
(B) 感興趣的
(C) 是感興趣的
(D) 是很有趣的

**題型 位置——動詞**

先觀察本句缺少動詞，故空格處為動詞。空格前有人物主詞 we，而 interest 用在形容人的感受時，要使用過去分詞 interested，表示「感到有興趣的、有意願的」，且分詞前要加上 be 動詞，故本題答案為 (C)。

## 132 (NEW)

(A) Your letter suggests that you are looking for a position as a legal associate.
(B) Please submit your application to our legal team by tomorrow.
(C) I think you should reconsider your decision.
(D) We ask for your permission to file your application for future consideration.

(A) 您在信中提到您想應徵的職務是法務專員。
(B) 請您在明天前向我們的法務團隊提交申請表。
(C) 我想您應該重新考慮一下您的決定。
(D) 我們徵求您的同意，能否讓我們將您的應徵申請留待未來再作考慮。

**題型 填入句子**

前句表示讀過收件人的信件，有意為他安排面試，後句則説到實習時間，所以空格應的句子應具有「應徵」、「收件人的資格」等內容，(A) 不只描述到收件人想應徵的職位，還點出前句信件一事，故本題正確答案為 (A)。

## 133 (NEW)

(A) persistent
(B) permanent
(C) habitual
(D) durable

(A) 持久的
(B) 長期的
(C) 習慣性的
(D) 耐久的

**題型 詞彙──形容詞**

選項中最適合修飾名詞 positions（職位）的形容詞應為 permanent，本題正確答案為 (B)。

permanent position 字面上為「長期的、常設的職位」，也就是「固定的工作」的意思，也常用來表示「正職」。

## 134

(A) pursuit
(B) pursuing
(C) to pursue
(D) pursued

(A) 追求
(B) 正在追求
(C) 去追求
(D) 追求了

**題型 位置──不定詞**

先觀察空格前有動詞 wish，後有名詞受詞 the internship，而選項全為動詞 pursue 的變化型。動詞 wish 若需接續動詞，應使用 to 隔開，故本題正確答案為 (C)。

| | |
|---|---|
| **From:** David Watts<br>**To:** Marshall Design Studio Staff<br>**Date:** March 1<br>**Subject:** Mary Ryan's Farewell Party | 寄件人：大衛·華茲<br>收件人：馬歇爾設計工作室員工<br>日期：3月1日<br>主旨：瑪麗·萊恩的餞別宴 |

You may be aware that Mary Ryan is leaving the Marshall Design Studio after having been our top designer for many years. A celebration in honor of **135** substantial commitment to our company is to be held next Friday, March 10, at 6 P.M. in the boardroom.

In my last e-mail, I requested some ideas for a **136** gift for the function. **137**. I'm sure that it would make the best gift for her.

In order for us to buy the gift in time for the party, I ask that all donations **138** by Monday, March 6. Please give donations to the associate design director, Claire Lewis, who is located in the main design studio.

Many thanks,
David Watts
Director of Human Resources

你們應該知道，我們資深的頂尖設計師瑪麗·萊恩即將離開工作多年的馬歇爾設計工作室。慶祝活動預計在下週五3月10日傍晚六點在董事會會議室舉行，以茲紀念她對我們公司的巨大奉獻。

我在上一封電子郵件中曾徵詢餞別禮的意見。大家的共識是想送瑪麗一個黃金可攜式時鐘。我確信這會是最適合她的禮物。

為了讓我們可以趕在派對前買到禮物，我要求在週一，也就是3月6日以前集資完畢。請把錢交給工作室總部的副設計總監克萊兒·路易斯。

非常感謝，
人資主任
大衛·華茲

**詞彙** **substantial** 巨大的　**boardroom** 董事會會議室　**function** 典禮；儀式

**135** - - - - - - - - - - - - - - - - - - - - - - - - - - - - - - - - - - - - - - - - - - - - -

(A) our
(B) her
(C) your
(D) whose

(A) 我們的
(B) 她的
(C) 你的
(D) 誰的

**題型** **詞彙**——所有格代名詞

空格前句提到設計師瑪莉·萊恩女士將離開公司，故此句應要填入女性的所有格代名詞 her，表示「她的」貢獻，正確答案為 (B)。

**136** - - - - - - - - - - - - - - - - - - - - - - - - - - - - - - - - - - - - - - - - - - - - -

(A) parting
(B) similar
(C) hopeful
(D) gratified

(A) 臨別的
(B) 相似的
(C) 抱有希望的
(D) 感到高興的

**題型** **詞彙**——形容詞

前文提到要為將離去的同事舉辦餞別會，故此處應使用與全文相應的形容詞 parting，表示要送她「離別的」禮物，正確答案為 (A)。

**137** NEW

| | |
|---|---|
| (A) We have not decided what we should do with the gift yet. | (A) 我們還沒決定要怎麼處理禮物。 |
| (B) I will start to search for her replacement. | (B) 我會開始找接替她的人。 |
| (C) Everyone is invited, and refreshments will be served. | (C) 每個人都受邀參加，現場會提供茶點。 |
| (D) The general consensus is that you want to give Mary a gold carriage clock. | (D) 大家的共識是想送瑪麗一個黃金可攜式時鐘。 |

題型 填入句子

後句提到「it would make the best gift for her」，其中的「it」指的應該就是禮物，但此處僅以代名詞出現，表示空格處應首次提到禮物。(D) 明確提到要送黃金可攜式時鐘，故正確答案為 (D)。

**138**

| | |
|---|---|
| (A) make | (A) 做 |
| (B) makes | (B) 做 |
| (C) be made | (C) 被做 |
| (D) will have made | (D) 將做完 |

題型 文法──動詞

make 為及物動詞，但空格後面沒有出現受詞，故此處應已改為被動，(A)、(B) 與 (D) 皆不適合代入，正確答案為 (C)。

在表示要求、命令、主張與提議的動詞後面，當以 that 子句作為受詞時，that 子句的動詞通常會以省略 should，以動詞原形出現，所以本題可以理解為「(should) be made」。

## 139–142 文章

| | |
|---|---|
| Canberra (February 22) – Regional airports are planning to **139** the amount of luggage on board the week after next. | 坎培拉（2月22日）—地區機場計劃要從下下週起限制登機的行李數量。 |
| Beginning on March 4, the luggage control will be put in force at every airport from Melbourne to Sydney. "Banning more than two suitcases will help us to better monitor the amount of luggage used in order to avoid the congestion that occurs **140** the baggage carousels," said Director of Services Dorothy Bailey. | 從3月4日起，從墨爾本到雪梨的所有機場將強制實施行李數量控管。「禁止攜帶兩件以上的行李箱，有助我們管控行李的數量，以避免行李轉盤發生阻塞。」服務處處長桃樂絲·貝里說。 |
| Passengers should pack fewer than two suitcases. **141**. Alternatively, they can leave unwanted items in the secure lockers, **142** to hold up to 5kg of luggage. | 旅客不得攜帶超過兩件行李。否則，每件行李須支付額外費用。或者，他們可以選擇把不需要的物品留在安全儲物櫃，可以容納多達五公斤的行李。 |

詞彙 **monitor** 控管　**ban** 禁止　**baggage carousel** 行李轉盤　**alternatively** 或者，要不然

**139** ------------------------------------------------

(A) propose                 (A) 提議

(B) relate                  (B) 使……有聯繫

(C) enhance             (C) 強化

(D) restrict              (D) 限制

**題型** **詞彙——動詞**

本題要閱讀完後文才能知道答案。從第二段的「Banning more than two suitcases」，可知機場限制行李最多只能兩件，故此處空格應要填入字義為「限制」的動詞，與後文一起表示「限制數量」，正確答案為 (D)。

**140** ------------------------------------------------

(A) after                  (A) 在……之後

(B) among              (B) 在……之間

(C) around             (C) 附近

(D) through            (D) 穿過

**題型** **詞彙——介系詞**

本題空格處的介系詞要能夠串連「阻塞」、「發生」、「行李轉盤」三個詞。而選項中只有 around 能表示行李轉盤「附近」發生的阻塞，故正確答案為 (C)。

**141** NEW ------------------------------------------------

(A) All extra boxes will be delivered for free.    (A) 所有多餘的箱子將免費運送。

(B) Otherwise, they may have to pay extra per bag.   (B) 否則，每件行李須支付額外費用。

(C) In fact, they have relaxed the regulations.    (C) 事實上，規則已經鬆綁。

(D) And the passengers are asked to leave their suitcases in the lockers.    (D) 而且旅客得把行李箱留在儲物櫃裡。

**題型** **填入句子**

前句提到不得攜帶超過兩件行李，後句卻使用了副詞 alternatively 提到超過兩件行李時的處理方法，故可知道空格處的句子應同樣與處理方法有關。(B) 提到支付額外費用，同為處理方法的一種，故正確答案為 (B)。

(A) 表示可以免費寄送超過限額的箱子，與「行李數量限制」的整體脈絡相互矛盾，故不適合。
(D) 此句內容與後句相同，但後句開頭有關鍵詞 alternatively 表示「或者」，所以兩者應要有所不同，故此句也不適合填入文中。

**142** ------------------------------------------------

(A) equipment           (A) 設備

(B) equipped            (B) 備有……的

(C) equip               (C) 裝備

(D) equips              (D) 裝備

**題型** **文法——關係代名詞**

本句已擁有主詞 they 與動詞 can leave，但沒有連接詞，所以無法再代入第二個動詞，(C) 與 (D) 不正確。

equip 意為「裝備」，「A be equipped to V」則意為「A 被備有某功能」，因為儲物櫃是人設計的，所以此處使用被動，表示擁有容納行李的功能。

而本句原本應為「the secure lockers, (which are) equipped to hold up to 5kg of luggage」，但由於「主格關係代名詞＋be 動詞」可以一起省略，所以此處省去了 which are，只剩下分詞型態的 equipped，正確答案為 (B)。

## 143–146 信件

| | |
|---|---|
| Dear Mr. Evans, | 親愛的伊凡斯先生： |
| I appreciate your interest in **143** our marketing department. | 感謝您有意加入我們行銷部門。 |
| **144**. To apply for a position as a service marketing team member with us, you need to send us your updated résumé, together with a proposal **145** your own marketing approach. | 我們會很高興收到您的應徵申請表。欲成為我們服務行銷團隊的一員，您需要寄給我們您最新的履歷，以及一份描述您自身行銷方式的提案。 |
| We will be contacting you in two weeks **146** accepting your application to set up an interview from the materials you sent us about your background and career. You are likely to be an ideal candidate for the position we talked about before. | 收到您的應徵申請後，我們將根據您所寄的背景資料和職場經歷，在兩週內聯繫您安排面試。就我們先前談過的職位，您似乎是非常合適的應徵者。 |
| Best regards, | 祝好， |
| Anderson Brooks<br>Marketing Director, Norton Electronics | 諾頓電子行銷主任<br>安德森·布魯克斯 |

**詞彙** updated 最新的

**143**

(A) joining
(B) promoting
(C) evaluating
(D) organizing

(A) 加入
(B) 推廣
(C) 估價
(D) 組織

**題型 詞彙**——動名詞

信件第二段要求提供履歷，第三段針對應徵流程解說，因此可推測收信人應是對公司的職缺有興趣的人。

本句空格前感謝對方有意願，空格後則提到行銷部門，故可推測出中間的空格應填入具有「加入」字義的詞，表示有意加入行銷部門，本題正確答案為 (A)。

## 144

NEW - - - - - - - - - - - - - - - - - - - - - - - - - - - - - - - - - - - - -

(A) However, I'm afraid we have already filled the position.

(B) We enjoyed meeting you at your job interview.

(C) We would be pleased to receive your application form.

(D) I'm attaching my résumé as requested.

(A) 然而，恐怕該職位已經有人補上。

(B) 我們很高興與您面試。

(C) 我們會很高興收到您的應徵申請表。

(D) 如您所要求，我將隨信附上履歷。

題型 **填入句子**

空格前句感謝對方對職缺有興趣，後句則要求對方提交履歷表及行銷提案，且下一段還提到
「your application」，故空格處的句子應與「履歷」、「申請」有關，最適當的答案為 (C)。

(B) 雖然文中也有提及面試一事，但是此為下一段的內容，且此選項的時態為過去式，代表面試
已經完成，也與全文不符。

**145** - - - - - - - - - - - - - - - - - - - - - - - - - - - - - - - - - - - - - - - - - - - - - - - - - - - -

(A) describe

(B) describing

(C) described

(D) will describe

(A) 描述

(B) 描述

(C) 被描述

(D) 將描述

題型 **文法**——關係代名詞

選項皆為 describe 的不同型態。根據句意，空格到 approach 的內容是在補充說明前面的
proposal，表示是能「描述行銷方式的」提案，故此句應使用關係代名詞連接，成為「a
proposal that describes your own marketing approach」。

關係代名詞其中一個句型是可以省略 that，並將主動動詞改為「V-ing」，被動動詞改為
「V-ed」，如同此處將 that describes 改成 describing，所以正確答案為 (B)。

**146** - - - - - - - - - - - - - - - - - - - - - - - - - - - - - - - - - - - - - - - - - - - - - - - - - - - -

(A) around

(B) until

(C) by

(D) after

(A) 附近

(B) 直到

(C) 藉由

(D) 在……之後

題型 **詞彙**——介系詞

空格前表示會在兩週內聯絡，空格後則提到接受對方的申請表，故此處的介系詞應要帶有
「在……之後」，表示在收到申請表後聯絡，故正確答案為 (D)。

# PART 7

**147–148 優惠券**

| Limited Offer | 限時優惠 |
|---|---|
| Enjoy Climber Route with your friend for the price of one! | 用單人價和朋友共享登山之樂！ |
| Present this coupon at the ticket booth and you will receive one more ticket for free when purchasing a full-price adult ticket. | 在售票處購買成人票時，出示此優惠券將免費獲得一張票。 |
| Enjoy the scenery and the refreshments – complimentary food and drink are available at our mountain-top café. | 享受風景和茶點—附贈的餐飲在山頂咖啡廳可供取用。 |
| – Cannot be used in conjunction with other coupons<br>– Expires on 31 December<br>– Children must be accompanied by their parents | — 不可以和其他優惠券併用<br>— 12月31日到期<br>— 小孩需父母陪同 |

**詞彙** route 路線　booth 小亭子　ticket booth 售票處　refreshment 茶點
A in conjunction with B 同時發生 A 與 B

## 147

**What is the coupon for?**

(A) A sightseeing venue
(B) A cafeteria
(C) A boating site
(D) A sports tournament

**這是什麼的優惠券？**

(A) 觀光場所
(B) 自助餐廳
(C) 乘船處
(D) 運動賽事

本題詢問優惠券用途。從下半部分可看出，只要出示此券，就能「Enjoy the scenery and the refreshments」，故可知此券最可能是在觀光景點使用，正確答案為 (A)。

## 148

**What restriction is placed on the coupon?**

(A) It can be used by adults only.
(B) It can be used on weekends.
(C) It cannot be used before 31 December.
(D) It cannot be used with another coupon.

**這張優惠券有何限制？**

(A) 只有成人可以使用。
(B) 只能在週末使用。
(C) 不得在 12 月 31 日前使用。
(D) 不得和另一張優惠券一起使用。

折價券下半部提及三點注意事項，其中包括「Cannot be used in conjunction with other coupons」，表示無法與其他優惠券一起使用，故正確答案為 (D)。

## Relocation and Care

When moving animals to a new place, particular care has to be taken to ensure their safe arrival and enhance their ability to fit into their new environment. Always remember they can be very unpredictable. Place them in the designated container, as carrying them without one may allow them to escape. Follow our specific directions on the brochure when relocating animals, as there are a variety of containers for different animals. These leaflets are free and can be found at the cashier.

## 搬移和照顧事項

搬移動物到新的場所時,需要特別照顧以確保牠們能安全抵達,並加強牠們適應新環境的能力。請牢記牠們是非常難以捉摸的,要將牠們置入特定箱籠,否則可能會導致逃脫。為牠們搬家時,請遵守手冊上特定的指示,因為不同的動物適用的箱籠都不同。這些手冊可以在結帳櫃檯免費索取。

**詞彙** relocation 搬移　fit into 適應　designated 特定的　at no cost 免費

**149**

**Who is the information most likely intended for?**　這些資訊最可能是想提供給誰?

(A) Storekeepers　(A) 店長
(B) Animal owners　(B) 飼主
(C) Container manufacturers　(C) 箱籠製造商
(D) Safety inspectors　(D) 安檢人員

開頭的「When moving animals to a new place, particular care has to be taken」,提到將動物移到新場所時應給予特別的關心,從此處看來,這篇文章的撰寫對象最可能為有飼養動物的人,因此最適合的答案為 (B)。

**150**

**What is available at no cost?**　什麼東西可以免費取得?

(A) Carriers　(A) 運輸工具
(B) Written instructions　(B) 紙本說明
(C) Containers　(C) 箱籠
(D) Canned food　(D) 罐頭食品

文章最後提到:「These leaflets are free and can be found at the cashier.」,由此可知,結帳處放置了可免費索取的手冊,選項中與 leaflet 意思最相近的為 written instructions,故正確答案為 (B)。

**151–152 收據**

Hawkins Uniforms
DELIVERY RECEIPT
**Thank you for your order.**

**Order Number:** 452198732
**Date Placed:** June 21
**Date Shipped:** June 25

**Customer Name:** Duncan Restaurant
**Customer Number:** 24

Item 1: Custom-made shirts, logo on the left sleeve
Color: Blue / Size: Large / Quantity: 13

Item 2: Chefs Hats
Color: White / Size: N/A / Quantity: 4

Item 3: Head Scarves
Color: Red / Size: N/A / Quantity: 27

Visit us online at http://www.hawkinsuniforms.com.

霍金斯制服
送貨收據
感謝您訂貨。

訂單號碼：452198732
訂貨日期：6月21日
出貨日期：6月25日

顧客姓名：鄧肯餐廳
顧客號碼：24

物品一：客製襯衫，商標於左袖
顏色：藍　尺寸：大　數量：13

物品二：廚師帽
顏色：白　尺寸：單一尺寸　數量：4

物品三：頭巾
顏色：紅　尺寸：單一尺寸　數量：27

造訪我們的官網：
http://www.hawkinsuniforms.com

**詞彙** custom-made 客製的　head scarf 頭巾

**151**

**How many shirts were ordered?**

(A) 24
(B) 13
(C) 4
(D) 27

襯衫訂了多少件？

(A) 24
(B) 13
(C) 4
(D) 27

本題詢問襯衫的訂購數量，答案就在 item 1 那欄，Quantity 後的數字 13，正確答案為 (B)。

**152**

**What is stated on the receipt?**

(A) The order was made online.
(B) Duncan Restaurant is a regular customer.
(C) Thirteen waiters are working at Duncan Restaurant.
(D) The logo of a company appears on the clothes.

收據上寫了什麼？

(A) 這是張網路訂單。
(B) 鄧肯餐廳是常客。
(C) 有 13 名服務生在鄧肯餐廳工作。
(D) 公司商標秀在衣服上。

(A) 收據上只寫到可以造訪網站，沒有說訂單是使用網路完成；(B) 內文未提及此事；(C) 雖然客製襯衫的數量為 13 件，但無法確定此即代表服務生的數量；(D) 從 Item 1 後方描述的「logo on the left sleeve」可知商標會出現於左袖，故此選項描述正確，本題答案為 (D)。

| | | | |
|---|---|---|---|
| **Jeremy Ashton** | 10:46 A.M. | 傑瑞米・艾西頓〔上午10:46〕: | |
| Guys, we've got a problem with the dyes again. | | 大家，我們又遇到染料問題了。 | |

**Nancy Parish** 10:46 A.M.
Not again! What's the problem this time?

南茜・帕里許〔上午10:46〕:
不會吧！這次是什麼問題？

**Jeremy Ashton** 10:47 A.M.
The 80 purple towels came out in the wrong color. These are more like pink.

傑瑞米・艾西頓〔上午10:47〕:
80條紫色毛巾的顏色錯了，反而像粉紅色。

**Nancy Parish** 10:48 A.M.
That's terrible. We have to deliver all the towels by tomorrow.

南茜・帕里許〔上午10:48〕:
糟糕。我們明天前得寄出所有毛巾。

**Dustin Hyde** 10:48 A.M.
I don't think I have enough time to do it over. Is the rest of the order ready to go out?

達斯汀・海德〔上午10:48〕:
我想我沒時間重新來過。剩下的訂單全都準備好出貨了嗎？

**Jeremy Ashton** 10:49 A.M.
Yes. All the other colors are ready to go.

傑瑞米・艾西頓〔上午10:49〕:
是的。其他所有顏色都好了。

**Nancy Parish** 10:51 A.M.
Why don't we send them first so that Lisa's team can start preparing for the upcoming event? In the meantime, you can dye the remaining 80 towels again.

南茜・帕里許〔上午10:51〕:
何不先把製好的毛巾寄出，這樣麗莎的團隊就可以開始準備即將到來的活動？與此同時，你可以重染剩下的80條。

**Dustin Hyde** 10:51 A.M.
That'd save us some time. But we'll have to check the dye before we rework them.

達斯汀・海德〔上午10:51〕:
這可以爭取一些時間。但這次重新開始前，我們得先檢查染劑。

**Nancy Parish** 10:52 A.M.
Sure thing. I'll call Lisa and ask for the color samples.

南茜・帕里許〔上午10:52〕:
當然。我會打給麗莎，並和她要樣色。

**詞彙** dye〔名詞〕染料；〔動詞〕染色　do sth over 重做某事　save (sb) some time 為（某人）省下時間

**153** --------------------------------------------------------------------------------

**What problem is being discussed?**

(A) Some labels were printed incorrectly.
(B) Some dyeing results were unexpected.
(C) An inspector is unavailable.
(D) Some machines are running too slowly.

他們正在討論什麼問題？

(A) 有些標籤印錯了。
(B) 有些染色結果出乎預料。
(C) 一名檢查員沒空。
(D) 有些機器運作得太慢。

從 10 點 47 分時艾西頓先生説的「The 80 purple towels came out in the wrong color. These are more like pink.」可知，原本應為紫色的毛巾因為染色錯誤，變成了粉紅色，故答案為最符合此情形的 (B)。

## 154 (NEW)

**At 10:48 A.M., what does Mr. Hyde imply when he writes, "I don't think I have enough time to do it over"?**

(A) The schedule is tight.
(B) They cannot help sending the pink towels.
(C) He doesn't have enough towels to dye again.
(D) The upcoming event should be postponed.

在上午 10:48 時，海德先生寫道：「我想我沒時間重新來過」，他的意思是？
(A) 時程很趕。
(B) 他們寄出粉色毛巾。
(C) 他沒有足夠的毛巾重新染色。
(D) 接下來的活動得延期。

前文提到有 80 條毛巾染錯顏色，而 10 點 48 分時帕里許女士卻說：「We have to deliver all the towels by tomorrow.」，表示明天前要寄出毛巾，故此時海德先生所謂的「I don't think I have enough time to do it over.」最可能表示沒有時間重做毛巾，也就是時間緊迫的意思，正確答案為 (A)。

## 155–157 廣告

### Reid & Ross Inc. Job Openings

Applications are for the night shift (6:00 P.M. to 5:00 A.M.), unless otherwise stated.

**Facilities Manager**
Must hold relevant qualifications, in-depth understanding of inventory process, and knowledge of health and safety policies. Also desirable are basic skills in computing and budgeting. Previous experience in mechanical factory work is preferred but not essential.

**Forklift Truck Technician**
Must be educated to high school level or higher, with two years' experience working in a busy warehouse operating heavy machinery. Must be trained in forklift truck driving. Some day shifts required.

**Computer Assistant**
Must have a BA degree, with experience of operating SAGE software in an industrial environment. Some day shifts required.

**Inventory Assistants and Stock Clerks**
Must be conscientious and hard-working. Stock clerks may be required to work the day shift.

Please send résumés to : The Recruitment Manager

Reid & Ross Inc.
472 Southern Lake Drive
Austin, TX 78753

No recruitment agency calls or e-mails.

### 里德＆羅斯公司職缺

若無特別說明，職缺均為晚班（傍晚6點到早上5點）

**工廠經理**
須持有相關資格，深入了解倉儲運作流程，且熟知健康與安全規定。期望能有計算和制定預算的基本技能。機械工廠工作經驗尤佳，但非必要。

**堆高機駕駛技術人員**
須有高中以上學歷，並有兩年在繁忙的倉庫裡操作重機具的工作經驗。必須曾受訓操作堆高機。有若干早班需求。

**資訊助理**
須有大學學歷，曾在工業環境操作SAGE軟體。有若干早班需求。

**倉儲助理和倉管人員**
須認真勤奮。倉管人員要能配合早班工作。

請將履歷寄給：招募經理

里德＆羅斯公司
78753 德州奧斯汀市南湖路472號

謝絕人力仲介來電或電郵。

night shift 晚班　in-depth 深入的　inventory 倉儲存貨　day shift 日班
BA degree 大學學歷（BA = Bachelor of Arts 文學士）　conscientious 認真的
recruitment agency 人力仲介

**155**

**What is a requirement for the facilities manager position?** | 工廠經理的應徵條件是什麼？
--- | ---
(A) A degree in finance | (A) 金融學位
(B) Knowledge of health and safety policies | (B) 健康與安全規定的知識
(C) Previous experience in conducting inspections | (C) 進行檢查的工作經驗
(D) A valid driver's license | (D) 有效駕照

requirement 表示必要條件，所以從文中找出有寫到 must 的內容應該就能得到答案。故可從第一句知道，工廠經理必須擁有「a relevant qualification」、「in-depth understanding of inventory processes」和「knowledge of health and safety policies」，也就是要持有相關資格、理解庫存處理，以及具備健康安全的相關知識，故正確答案為 (B)。

**156**

**What position does NOT involve day shifts?** | 哪項職務沒有早班需求？
--- | ---
(A) Forklift truck technician | (A) 堆高機駕駛技術人員
(B) Stock clerks | (B) 倉管人員
(C) Inventory assistants | (C) 倉儲助理
(D) Computer assistant | (D) 資訊助理

文章開頭部分提到「Applications are for the night shift (6:00 P.M. to 5:00 A.M.), unless otherwise stated.」，表示如果沒有另外註明，皆為晚班職缺。

選項 (A)、(B) 與 (D) 四個職缺中，分別提到了「Some day shifts required」、「Stock clerks may be required to work the day shift」以及「Some day shifts required」，故只有 (C) 沒有特別提及早班需求，本題正確答案為 (C)。

**157**

**How will candidates apply for the positions?** | 應徵者要如何應徵？
--- | ---
(A) By online | (A) 線上申請
(B) By mail | (B) 寄信
(C) In person | (C) 面對面
(D) By telephone | (D) 透過電話

文章尾聲提到地址，並說「Please send résumés」，表示請對方將履歷寄送到該處，且最後一句表明「No . . . e-mails」，可知公司並不接受電子郵件，因此正確答案為 (B)。

**158–160 電子郵件**

**To:** All Staff
**From:** Elizabeth Webster
<Ewebster@gilbertfashion.com>
**Subject:** Re: Spring Collection
**Date:** December 9

On behalf of the management at Gilbert Fashion, I would like to invite you to a special showing of our new Spring portfolio to be held on December 18 from 4 P.M. to 9 P.M. at Silver Hall. —[1]—. We expect every employee to attend and enjoy a buffet meal on the balcony. —[2]—. There will also be entertainment in the form of Ella Kay and her band.

—[3]—. Please note that although this is a free event to preview our new collection, we need to provide numbers for the caterers, so if you can attend, please give your name to Kate Parry or Henry Rhodes by the end of the week. If you have any tunes that you wish the band to play, we welcome any suggestions. —[4]—.

I look forward to seeing everyone on December 18.

Elizabeth Webster
Human Resources Manager

---

收件人：全體員工
寄件人：伊莉莎白・韋伯斯特
<Ewebster@gilbertfashion.com>
主旨：關於：春裝系列
日期：12月9日

謹代表吉爾伯特時尚的管理階層，邀請您參加我們最新春裝系列的特別秀，將在12月18日下午4點到晚上9點於銀廳舉行。我們期待每位員工都可以前來，並在陽台上一起享用自助餐。現場也會有艾拉・凱和她樂團的表演。

請留意，雖然這是一場可以提前觀賞我們最新系列服飾的免費活動，我們還是要提供人數給外燴業者。所以如果您可以出席，請在這週以前向凱特・派瑞或是亨利・羅德斯報名。如果您有什麼歌曲想請樂團演出，我們也歡迎任何建議。只要把選曲用電子郵件寄給我就可以了，或者想知道更多資訊也可以來信詢問。

很期待在12月18日見到大家。

人資經理
伊莉莎白・韋伯斯特

---

**詞彙** one behalf of 作為……的代表　portfolio 作品集　caterer 外燴業者　tune 曲子

**158**

**What is the purpose of the e-mail?**

(A) To invite employees to an event
(B) To ask for volunteers to assist with a party
(C) To encourage employees to hold their show
(D) To order food for a celebration

這封電子郵件的主旨為何？

(A) 邀請員工參加活動
(B) 詢問有沒有人志願幫忙籌辦派對
(C) 鼓勵員工舉辦自己的秀
(D) 訂慶祝要用的餐點

先觀察郵件收件人為「All Staff」，且在開頭部分，寄件人寫道：「I would like to invite you to a special showing of our new Spring portfolio」，表示想代表經營團隊邀請全體員工參加春季新裝特別秀，由此可知，此郵件的目的是為了邀請員工參加活動，所以正確答案為 (A)。

**What is NOT indicated about the event?**

(A) It is organized by the company.
(B) It will preview a fashion collection.
(C) It will feature live music.
(D) It is held every season.

關於這場活動，文中沒有提到什麼？

(A) 由公司主辦。
(B) 可以搶先看到一個時裝系列。
(C) 現場音樂演出是一大特色。
(D) 每一季都會辦。

從開頭第二句的「I would like to invite you to a special showing of our new Spring portfolio」可看出春裝發表秀為公司舉辦，故 (A) 與 (B) 有被提及。另外，在同段最後一句也說到「There will also be entertainment in the form of Ella Kay and her band」，表示會請樂團到場表演，故也可推知 (C) 的內容。綜合上述，文中未提及的只有 (D)，故本題答案為 (D)。

 **NEW**

**In which of the positions marked [1], [2], [3], and [4] does the following sentence best belong?**

**"Simply e-mail me with the song choice or for any further information on the event."**

(A) [1]
(B) [2]
(C) [3]
(D) [4]

下列句子最適合出現在 [1]、[2]、[3]、[4] 的哪個位置中？

「只要把選曲用電子郵件寄給我就可以了，或者想知道更多資訊也可以來信詢問。」

(A) [1]
(B) [2]
(C) [3]
(D) [4]

題目引述的句子提到「song choice」，故此句應該出現在與音樂、歌曲有關的段落。第二段尾聲提到：「If you have any tunes that you wish the band to play, we welcome any suggestions.」，表示若有推薦樂團演奏的曲目，歡迎提出建議。句子放於此處繼續說道可寄送含選曲的郵件，符合段落脈絡，故句子最適合放在 [4] 的位置，正確答案為 (D)。

**161–163 信件**

| Emerald Town of Northern Territory | 北領地的翡翠鎮 |
| --- | --- |
| 55 Turner Street<br>Engawala, Australia 0872 | 0872 澳洲恩嘎瓦拉市特納街55號 |
| February 11<br>Mr. Ford Lucas<br>426 Girraween Road<br>Palmerston City, Australia 0830 | 2月11日<br>福特·路卡斯先生<br>0830澳洲帕默斯頓市<br>芝拉溫路426號 |
| Dear Mr. Lucas, | 親愛的路卡斯先生： |
| We have received your application at Emerald Town regarding the position that was advertised last week in the *Darwin Times* for a mining assistant. We are sorry to inform you that this position has already been filled. Nevertheless, | 關於我們上週在《達爾文時報》徵求採礦助理的廣告，我們已收到您寄來翡翠鎮的求職信。很抱歉通知您該職缺已經關閉。不過， |

we are planning to begin mining in another location in April, and we believe that you would be suitable for this position. With your permission, we would like to keep your details on file. The location is not far from our main production facilities in Darwin, but it will require some travel to Pine Creek, Mataranka, and other areas. Please keep checking our website for any future vacancies that arise with our organization. We wish you luck with your job search.

Kind regards,
Jaxon Bates, Personnel Supervisor

我們計劃要在四月開採新礦坑，相信您會是適合的人選。如果您允許，我想把您的詳細資料留檔。新地點距離我們達爾文的主要礦區不遠，但由此前往松溪、馬塔蘭卡或其他地區會花些時間。未來請持續關注我們官網所開出的新職缺。我們祝您求職順利。

祝好，
人事主管
傑克森‧貝茲

**詞彙** vacancy 職缺　job search 求職　arise 出現

---

**161**

**What is the main purpose of the letter?**

(A) To let an applicant know that he failed to meet the qualifications for the position
(B) To ask an applicant for further details of his career
(C) To arrange an interview with an applicant
(D) To inform an applicant that the position he applied for is no longer available

這封信的主旨為何？

(A) 讓一名應徵者知道他不適合這個職缺
(B) 詢問應徵者更詳細的工作經歷
(C) 安排應徵者面試
(D) 告知應徵者該職缺已經關閉

從信件署名看來，此信由人事主管貝茲先生寄出，且根據內容，收件人路卡斯先生為求職者。信件在第二句的提到：「We are sorry to inform you that this position has already been filled.」，表示路卡斯先生應徵的職缺已經徵滿，後文也是承接此事展開，故本題正確答案為 (D)。

---

**162**

**Where are the main facilities of Emerald Town of Northern Territory located?**

(A) In Darwin
(B) In Pine Creek
(C) In Mataranka
(D) In Palmerston City

北領地的翡翠鎮主礦區位於哪裡？

(A) 達爾文
(B) 松溪
(C) 馬塔蘭卡
(D) 帕默斯頓市

信件中間的部分提及：「our main production facilities in Darwin」，故可知道主要礦區位於達爾文地區，正確答案為 (A)。

另外，(B) 和 (C) 為礦區附近的地區，(D) 則為收信人路卡斯先生居住的地區。

What does Mr. Bates suggest that Mr. Lucas do?

(A) Check the website for additional job openings
(B) Send in more information about his qualifications
(C) Contact the main facilities for employment changes
(D) Read the job advertisements in the newspaper

貝茲先生建議路卡斯先生做什麼？

(A) 查看官網後續開出的新職缺
(B) 寄出更多關於他資格的資訊
(C) 聯絡主礦區要求換僱員
(D) 在報紙上看求職廣告

在信件結尾部分，貝茲先生提到：「Please keep checking our website for any future vacancies that arise with our organization.」，表示請路卡斯先生關注官網開出的新職缺，故正確答案為 (A)。

### 164–167 訊息串

| | |
|---|---|
| **Morgan Leek** 02:32 P.M.<br>Hello, James. I saw several flowerpots in your shop yesterday. Where did you get them? | 摩根·里克〔下午02:32〕：<br>哈囉，詹姆斯。我昨天在你店裡看到一些花盆。它們從哪來的？ |
| **James Pipe** 02:33 P.M.<br>Hello, Morgan. You mean the ones on the table by the window? | 詹姆斯·派普〔下午02:33〕：<br>哈囉，摩根。你是指窗邊桌上那些嗎？ |
| **Morgan Leek** 02:33 P.M.<br>Yes. They had a lovely, sweet scent and also looked nice. So, I want to put some of those in my apartment. | 摩根·里克〔下午02:33〕：<br>是的。它們味道很甜美，看起來也不賴。所以我也想要在公寓裡擺設一些。 |
| **James Pipe** 02:35 P.M.<br>From the garden center on St. George Street, next to Thomas' Bakery. | 詹姆斯·派普〔下午02:35〕：<br>是從花卉中心買來的，在湯馬斯烘焙旁邊的聖喬治街。 |
| **Morgan Leek** 02:36 P.M.<br>Oh, I know where the flower shop is. By the way, what are they called? | 摩根·里克〔下午02:36〕：<br>喔，我知道那家花店。順便問一下，它們叫什麼？ |
| **James Pipe** 02:37 P.M.<br>It slipped my mind. Anyway, they have a lot of wildflowers and herbs. Just take a closer look and check the scent. | 詹姆斯·派普〔下午02:37〕：<br>我一時想不起來。總之店內有很多野花和藥草。就靠近看看也能試聞香味。 |
| **Morgan Leek** 02:37 P.M.<br>But, I don't know much about wildflowers and herbs. Are they easy to maintain? | 摩根·里克〔下午02:37〕：<br>但我不是很懂花草。照顧起來容易嗎？ |
| **James Pipe** 02:38 P.M.<br>Yes, absolutely. They grow well indoors, and they don't need much water. | 詹姆斯·派普〔下午02:38〕：<br>對，很容易。放室內也長得很好，也不需要太多水。 |
| **Morgan Leek** 02:39 P.M.<br>That's great! I'm not able to be at home every day. | 摩根·里克〔下午02:39〕：<br>太好了！我也沒辦法每天在家。 |

詞彙 **flowerpot** 花盆 　 **sth slipped one's mind** 某人忘了某事 　 **herb** 藥草

**164**------------------------------------------------------

**What is mainly being discussed?**

(A) Ms. Leek's new apartment
(B) Some plants for the Ms. Leek
(C) A bakery on St. George Street
(D) Sowing some herb seeds

他們主要在討論什麼？

(A) 里克女士的新公寓
(B) 里克女士想要的植物
(C) 聖喬治街的烘焙坊
(D) 播種一些香料種子

開頭對話中，里克女士便問派普先生他店裡的花盆從何而來，里克女士還在 2 點 33 分時說道：「I want to put some of those in my apartment」，故可知對話主題主要圍繞在花卉植物，本題正確答案為 (B)。

**165**------------------------------------------------------

**What does Mr. Pipe suggest that Ms. Leek do?**

(A) Stop by the bakery
(B) Meet him at the garden center
(C) Water the flowers every day
(D) Smell the plants

派普先生建議里克女士做什麼？

(A) 順道去烘焙坊
(B) 在花卉中心和他見面
(C) 每天澆花
(D) 聞聞看植物

2 點 36 分時，里克女士詢問派普先生種的花的名字，派普先生接著表示他忘記了，並說：「Just take a closer look and check the scent.」，代表他建議里克女士聞聞花香以確認品種，故正確答案為 (D)。

**166** **NEW** ------------------------------------------

**At 2:37 P.M., why does Mr. Pipe write, "It slipped my mind"?**

(A) He doesn't know how much the plants would cost.
(B) He forgot the names of the flowers.
(C) He thinks Ms. Leek cannot take care of the plants.
(D) He doesn't mind how much water they need.

下午 2:37 時，為什麼派普先生寫道：「我一時想不起來」？

(A) 他不知道植物多貴。
(B) 他忘記花朵的名稱。
(C) 他認為里克女士不會照顧植物。
(D) 他不在意它們需要多少水。

即使沒聽過這個用法，也能從前後文推測答案。里克女士詢問花名，但在派普先生的回答中並沒有明確說出名字，反而是直接要里克女士用氣味辨認，故可推測出此處的「it slipped my mind」應該是有「遺忘」的意思，正確答案為 (B)。

另外，slip 作為動詞時本身是滑走、溜走的意思，故可以想成某事從記憶中溜走不見，有忘記的意思。

**★記住下列用法：**
**sth slip one's mind/memory**（某人忘記某事）

**Why would Ms. Leek find the plants suitable for her?** 為什麼里克女士覺得這些植物適合她？

(A) They are inexpensive.

(B) She is going to grow them outdoors.

(C) The flower shop is located near her apartment.

(D) She doesn't need to water them every day.

(A) 它們不貴。

(B) 她要將植物種在戶外。

(C) 花店位於她的公寓附近。

(D) 她不用每天澆花。

派普先生在 2 點 38 分時說，他種的植物「don't need much water」，隨後里克女士回覆：「That's great! I'm not able to be at home every day.」，故可推知，由於里克女士不常在家，無法常常澆水，因此不用太多水的植物很適合她，故本題答案為 (D)。

(A) 與 (C) 皆未在文中提及，(B) 由於對話中只有提到「They grow well indoors」，但是無法看出里克女士想將植物放置的位置，故不適合作為答案。

## 168–171 文章

### BORDEAUX, FR.

May 2 — Alan Debois, President of the Agricultural Union, is to be awarded the Géant Prize on May 10. —[1]—. This is an annual award to a deserving and active member of the Bordeaux business community, whose achievements have enhanced the region.

As a lifelong farmer, Mr. Debois has a keen interest in the local environment and put forward a proposal to the regional government for the installation of flood barriers to prevent crops and livestock from being affected by annual flooding in Bordeaux. Five years ago, his proposal for flood barriers began to be implemented and the Debois Barriers, as they are known, are now a well-known attraction for tourists. The first set was installed three years ago with a grant from the Environmental Agency. —[2]—. Since then, the barriers have prevented crops from being ruined, saved many cattle from drowning, and raised awareness of the dangers of tidal power. Completed last year in Bordeaux, the barrier installation scheme is now being considered by many coastal regions in France.

—[3]—. This program offers funding for apprenticeships to young adults who want to learn how to become farmers and work on the land. So far, over a hundred people have completed the program and have found employment on farms within the region.

—[4]—. The awards ceremony will take place in the Bordeaux Town Hall from 7 P.M. to 9 P.M. All residents of the town are welcome to attend, and details will be posted on the website, www.bordeaux.fr/awards.

### 波爾多，法國

5月2日—農業聯盟主席亞倫·德布瓦，將在5月10日獲頒巨擘獎。這項年度獎項頒給積極促進波爾多產業界、且其貢獻有益於地區發展者。

德布瓦先生一生務農，對在地環境抱有熱忱，推動地方政府設置防洪設施，讓波爾多作物和家畜免於受到每年的洪災波及。他提出的防洪計畫始於五年前，也就是現在名聞遐邇的觀光景點德布瓦堤防。第一道堤防在三年前由環境部門出資建設。從那時起，堤防保護了作物免於摧毀，牲畜倖免於難，也提高了當地對潮汐的危難意識。這座堤防去年落成於波爾多後，法國許多沿岸地區也考慮跟進這項堤防建設計畫。

不僅如此，德布瓦先生還創立德布瓦學院。這項計畫資助訓練有志成為農夫、在地深耕的年輕人。目前已有超過一百人完成課程，並受僱於當地農場。

頒獎典禮將在波爾多市政廳，晚上7點到9點舉行。歡迎鎮民蒞臨參加，詳情請見官網：www.bordeaux.fr/awards。

**詞彙** crop 作物　livestock 家畜　implement 執行　cattle 牲畜　tidal 潮汐的 apprenticeship 學徒制度

**168** ----------------------------------------

**What is the purpose of the article?**

(A) To explain why a particular person won a community award

(B) To describe the role of the farming community

(C) To invite the townspeople to a seminar on flood plains

(D) To welcome a new member of the Bordeaux business community

這篇文章目的為何？

(A) 說明特定人物獲社區獎的原因

(B) 描述農業社群的作用

(C) 邀請鎮民參加洪氾區的研討會

(D) 歡迎波爾多產業界的新進成員

文章第一段提到一名叫做「Alan Debois」的人獲頒獎項，並提到：「This is an annual award to a deserving and active member . . . whose achievements have enhanced the region.」，表示獎項是頒給對地方積極貢獻的人，接著在後文描述了他的作為，由此可知，這篇報導文章是在說明德布瓦先生獲獎的原因，正確答案為 (A)。

**169** ----------------------------------------

**What is NOT mentioned as a benefit of Dubois Barriers?**

(A) Saving the lives of certain livestock

(B) Drawing travelers in Bordeaux

(C) Organizing a recycling program

(D) Raising awareness of tidal power

德布瓦堤防帶來的好處，文中沒有提到的是？

(A) 拯救某些家畜

(B) 吸引觀光客來波爾多

(C) 籌劃一項回收計畫

(D) 提醒民眾小心潮汐

本題要從文章中找出有提及「Dubois Barriers」的部分。在第二段第一句即提到「the installation of flood barriers」，並在第二句說：「Dubois Barriers . . . are now a well-known attraction for tourists」，可知堤防吸引了觀光客，故 (B) 有出現在文中。

第三段倒數第二句也說：「the barriers have . . . saved many cattle from drowning, and raised awareness of the dangers of the tidal power」，表示堤防拯救牲畜不受水災影響，且提高人們對潮汐危難的關心，提及了 (A) 與 (D) 的內容。

綜合上述，只有 (C) 的內容未出現在文中，故本題正確答案為 (C)。

**170** ----------------------------------------

**When was the Dubois Barrier project completed?**

(A) Five years ago

(B) Three years ago

(C) The previous year

(D) On May 10

德布瓦堤防的計畫什麼時候完成？

(A) 五年前

(B) 三年前

(C) 去年

(D) 5 月 10 日

第二段最後一句提到「Completed last year in Bordeaux」，故可知堤防在去年終於落成，本題正確答案為 (C)。

(A) 從第二段第二句的「Five years ago, his proposal for flood barriers began to be implemented」可知，此為堤防計畫開始進行的時間點；(B) 此為環境部門出資建設第一道堤防的時間點；(D) 為頒獎典禮舉辦的日期。

In which of the positions marked [1], [2], [3], and [4] does the following sentence best belong?

"In addition, Mr. Debois has also set up the Debois Academy."

(A) [1]
(B) [2]
(C) [3]
(D) [4]

下列句子最適合出現在 [1]、[2]、[3]、[4] 的哪個位置中？

「不僅如此，德布瓦先生還創立德布瓦學院。」

(A) [1]
(B) [2]
(C) [3]
(D) [4]

先觀察文章的段落組成：第一段介紹德布瓦先生得獎一事，第二段簡述他推動的防洪堤防計畫，第三段說到他幫助訓練有意在地深耕的年輕人，第四段則是典禮相關的資訊。因此，注意題目引述的句子提到「Debois Academy」，並且使用關鍵的「In addition」，代表前文有提及相關的某事，故此處才會說「不僅如此」。

已知第二段是堤防建設，第三段則與農業教育有關，故此句最適合放在兩段落交界處，也就是 [3] 的位置，以達到承先啟後的作用，本題正確答案為 (C)。

## 172–175 廣告

### PTZ Component Testing

PTZ Component Testing provides a full testing service for all those involved in the radiology industry, as well as hospitals. We offer extensive testing on all equipment using up-to-date machinery. We consider each application individually, tailoring the testing procedure to each specific client. In addition to being a brand-new testing facility, we also provide a mobile service to test the equipment in your workplace.

**Our services:**
- Analyzing and testing outcomes of new equipment for hospitals and healthcare facilities
- Examining reports following testing procedures
- Advising and implementing alterations to any equipment offsite or in the facility, if necessary

**Facilities and Personnel**
Our main facility is located in Shanghai, China, with supplementary offices in West Java Province and Szechuan. We have links with government-run testing firms globally, which enables us to provide an international service not available anywhere else in the country. Every member of our staff is trained to internationally accepted standards, with an average of 15 years' experience in the testing of radiology equipment.

### PTZ 零件測試

「PTZ零件測試」為放射醫學的業者和醫院提供全方位的測試服務。我們使用最新的儀器測試所有設備，為每一位客戶著想，量身打造適合您的測試流程。不但擁有嶄新的測試機構，我們也提供到府服務，到您的工作場所測試設備。

**我們的服務：**
- 醫院或醫療設施新設備運作的分析測試
- 測試流程後的檢驗報告
- 如有必要，給予顧客建議，以及提供院內或院外設備的安裝替換服務

**設施和人員**
我們的總部位於中國上海，在西爪哇省和四川也設有辦公室。我們和全球各地的政府測試機構有交流，讓我們得以提供當地所缺乏的國際服務。我們全體員工均受符合國際標準的訓練，在放射學的設備測試診斷有平均15年的工作經驗。

| Report | 報告 |
|---|---|
| Our software provides results in internationally formatted data reports. | 我們軟體提供的資料報告均符合國際規格。 |
| Results are printed in hard copy and provided digitally as well. | 測試結果均會印出紙本也能提供電子檔。 |
| All information can be accessed on the website using a client-protected coded password. | 所有的資訊都可以在官網上以加密的客戶密碼取得。 |
| For more information, contact Vivian Lawson at vivian@ptzcomponents.com. | 欲知更多資訊請透過電子郵件聯繫薇薇安・羅森，vivian@ptzcomponents.com。 |

**詞彙** component 零件　radiology 放射醫學　tailor〔動詞〕量身打造　personnel 人員

---

**172**

The word "tailoring" in paragraph 1, line 3, is closest in meaning to

(A) sewing
(B) adapting
(C) presenting
(D) evaluating

第一段、第三行的「**tailoring**」，最接近下列哪個意思？

(A) 裁縫
(B) 調適
(C) 呈現
(D) 評估

前半句說到「We consider each application individually」，表示為個別用戶考量，後半句也說到「each specific client」，表示每一位特定的客戶，故可推知此處的動詞 tailor 應具有「特別製作、量身打造」的意思，故最近於選項中的 adapt，因為 adapt 也有「調整以適應不同狀況」的意思，本題最適合的答案為 (B)。

---

**173**

What service does PTZ Component Testing NOT advertise?

(A) Examining radiology equipment
(B) Providing a mobile service
(C) Inspecting healthcare cleanliness
(D) Analyzing results of some machinery

PTZ 零件測試沒有宣傳哪一項服務內容？

(A) 檢驗放射醫學的設備
(B) 到府服務
(C) 檢查醫療衛生
(D) 分析儀器的結果

廣告開頭便說：「provides a full testing service for all those involved in the radiology industry」，故有提及到 (A)；之後在服務列點中的第一項說到：「Analyzing and testing outcomes of new equipment」，表示會分析結果，故有提及 (D)；最後在第一段末也可看到「provide a mobile service to test the equipment in your workplace」，表示提供到府安裝服務，故 (B) 也有提及。

綜合上述，文中並未提及的只有 (C)，故正確答案為 (C)。

**According to the advertisement, what makes PTZ Component Testing unique?**

(A) It works with similar companies throughout the world.

(B) It is the oldest company in the industry.

(C) Its scientists graduated from internationally renowned universities.

(D) It has a presence in every major city.

根據廣告，什麼讓 PTZ 零件測試獨一無二？

(A) 和遍布全球的類似公司有合作。

(B) 是業界最老牌的公司。

(C) 公司裡的科學家都是國際知名大學畢業。

(D) 出現於各大城市。

在「Facilities and Personnel」的標題下說到：「We have links with government-run testing firms globally」，並寫道這項特點「not available anywhere else in the country」，表示此為絕無僅有的服務，故本題正確答案為 (A)。

另外，選項中也只有 (A) 的內容曾在文中出現，故也可因此選出正確答案。

**What is indicated about the reports generated by PTZ Component Testing?**

(A) They are witnessed by independent experts.

(B) They are available online to the public.

(C) They are presented to customers in two formats.

(D) They can be kept on file for an extra fee.

文中提到關於 PTZ 零件測試所產出的報告什麼事？

(A) 由第三方專家驗證。

(B) 在網路上對外公開給大眾。

(C) 提供給客戶兩種報告格式。

(D) 額外付費可以存放檔案。

在廣告的最後部分提到：「Results are printed in hard copy and provided digitally as well.」，表示分析結果可透過紙本印刷或數位方式提供，所以共有兩種格式，本題正確答案為 (C)。

**176–180 電子郵件**

---

**From:** Nolan Parker <Nparker@toyfactory.com>
**To:** Khloe Swann <Kswann@toybox.com>
**Date:** January 25
**Subject:** Sales update
**Attachment:** Report-01.xls

---

Dear Ms. Swann,

I am replying to your inquiry about this month's sales updates. As you can see, I have attached a list of the stock that we sold in December together with a profit and loss spreadsheet. You can see that most of the items sold extremely well. In particular, we sold a record number of the ceramic dolls from Minakawa Inc. The branded stuffed animals from Harpers also continue to

寄件人：諾蘭・帕克 <Nparker@toyfactory.com>
收件人：科勒・史旺 <Kswann@toybox.com>
日期：1月25日
主旨：銷售更新
附件：報告－01.xls

---

親愛的史旺女士：

我來信答覆您詢問有關這個月的銷售資訊更新。您可以看到附件中有一份十二月存貨的銷售清單，還有一份損益試算表。您可以看到大多數的商品都賣得非常好。尤其是源川企業的陶瓷娃娃，銷售量破紀錄。哈潑牌的填充動物玩偶也仍為暢銷商品，還有

be bestsellers, as well as the consoles and electronic games from ELF Ltd. What I find surprising is the lack of sales of the children's wooden building sets. I think the quality was extremely inferior to those of other competitors and we had many complaints that they broke easily. This is shown in the sales figures as refunds.

However, I have sourced a different supplier, so hopefully sales figures for the next few months will reflect this. I am looking forward to meeting you at the annual sales convention next Monday. If you need any further information before then, please let me know.

Sincerely,
Nolan Parker
Sales Manager

ELF股份有限公司的家用遊戲機和電玩也是。令我感到驚訝的是，兒童積木組合的銷售下滑。我想是因為和其他競爭商品相比，我們的商品品質落後非常多，我們也接獲很多抱怨，說它們很容易壞掉。這在銷售數字的退款部分可以見得。

不過，我已經找上另一家供應商，希望幾個月之後的銷售數據可以反應出效果。我很期待在下週一的年度銷售會議上和您見面。如果在這之前您需要更多資訊的話，請告訴我。

銷售經理
諾蘭・帕克 敬上

---

**From:** Khloe Swann <Kswann@toybox.com>
**To:** Nolan Parker <Nparker@toyfactory.com>
**Date:** January 26
**Subject:** Re: Sales update

Dear Mr. Parker,

Thank you for your prompt reply. As you are aware, we have signed a large contract to supply children's toys for the retail stores in Boston and Springfield, both very high-profile areas. From our research, we know that the locals in these areas demand very high-quality merchandise, and they have an even higher than average number of schools and children's clubs. Therefore, I think we should order more stock from Minakawa Inc. Can you supply me with a product list from this company and a contact name and number? I understand the meeting has been rescheduled to Tuesday. Can you confirm this as well?

Khloe Swann
Marketing Manager

寄件人：科勒・史旺 <Kswann@toybox.com>
收件人：諾蘭・帕克 <Nparker@toyfactory.com>
日期：1月26日
主旨：關於：銷售更新

親愛的帕克先生：

感謝您迅速答覆。如您所知，我們已和波士頓和春田的零售業者，簽了一筆供應兒童玩具的大訂單，這兩地都是備受關注的地區。根據我們的研究，我們得知該地區的人對商品品質的要求很高，而且當地有高於平均數量的學校和兒童俱樂部。因此，我想我們應該向源川企業訂購更多商品。可以請您提供一份這間公司的產品清單，還有聯絡人的姓名和電話給我嗎？就我所知，會議已經改期到週二舉行了。您可以同時確認這事嗎？

行銷經理
科勒・史旺

---

**詞彙** ceramic doll 陶瓷娃娃　stuffed animal 填充動物玩偶　console 遊戲機　sale figures 銷售數字　source 得到　high-profile 備受關注的

331

## 176

**Why did Mr. Parker send the first e-mail?**

(A) To provide Ms. Swann with information

(B) To request a list of available playthings

(C) To supply a new date for a meeting

(D) To respond to a proposed change

為什麼帕克先生要寄出第一封電子郵件？

(A) 提供史旺女士資訊

(B) 要求一份庫存玩具的清單

(C) 提供會議的新日期

(D) 回覆一項提議的變更

第一封郵件的開頭部份提到：「I am replying to your inquiry about this month's sales updates.」，表示這封郵件的目的是為了回覆對方針對銷售量的諮詢，且在後句附註已將 12 月存貨的銷售清單放於附件中，由此可知，這封郵件主要是在提供資訊，正確答案為 (A)。

## 177

**According to the first e-mail, what items will be provided by a new supplier?**

(A) Electronic games

(B) Stuffed animals

(C) Building sets

(D) Ceramic dolls

根據第一封電子郵件，哪項商品將由新的供應商供應？

(A) 電玩

(B) 填充動物玩偶

(C) 積木組合

(D) 陶瓷娃娃

第一封郵件的中間部分，寄件者表示發現「the lack of sales of the children's wooden building sets」，並認為兒童積木組合是因品質落後才銷售量下滑。在第二段他繼續提到：「However, I have sourced a different supplier」，由此可知，兒童積木組合將更換供應商，故正確答案為 (C)。

## 178

**In the second e-mail, the word "locals" in line 3, is closest in meaning to**

(A) residents

(B) regions

(C) items

(D) sales

第二封電子郵件中，第三行的「locals」，最接近下列哪個意思？

(A) 居民

(B) 地區

(C) 商品

(D) 銷售量

此句使用「the locals in these areas demand very high-quality merchandise」，而就句意判斷，demand（要求）這個動作只可能由人物產生，故只要找出選項中與人物相關的名詞即可，正確答案為 (A)。

local 作為形容詞時意思為「當地的」，而作名詞時字義為「當地居民」。另外，雖然本題不在此例，但英文中有一種用法，是以「the ＋形容詞」代表特定群體，如 the poor（窮人）、the rich（富人）、the foolish（庸人）與 the wise（智者）等。

## 179

**What is suggested about the ceramic dolls?**

(A) They are expected to sell well in the Boston area.

(B) They are not available during the summer season.

(C) They were purchased from Harpers.

(D) Their price has decreased from last month.

文中提到陶瓷娃娃什麼事？

(A) 預期將在波士頓地區賣得很好。

(B) 在夏季缺貨。

(C) 是從哈潑買來的。

(D) 售價比上個月低。

第一封郵件提到源川企業的陶瓷娃娃銷售破紀錄，第二封郵件則說公司與波士頓及春田兩地的零售商簽訂契約，並提到：「we know that the locals in these areas demand very high-quality merchandise」，其中的 the locals 就是指這兩地的居民，且後續還表示：「Therefore, I think we should order more stock from Minakawa Inc.」，從上述可知道，由於居民對品質的要求，以及源川企業娃娃大賣的經驗，公司應會向源川企業訂購更多商品賣往此兩地，故本題最適當的答案為 (A)。

 **180** ----------------------------------------------------------------

**About what do Mr. Parker and Ms. Swann have different information?**

(A) The date of a meeting
(B) The contact information for ELF Ltd.
(C) The sales figures for December
(D) The refund details of a client

帕克先生和史旺女士擁有的資訊，哪一項不一樣？

(A) 會議日期
(B) 和 ELF 股份有限公司的聯繫資訊
(C) 12 月的銷售數據
(D) 一位顧客的退款細節

帕克先生在第一封郵件的結尾提到：「I am looking forward to meeting you at the annual sales convention next Monday.」，表示希望在下週一的會議上見到史旺女士，但對方確認回信中說道：「I understand the meeting has been rescheduled to Tuesday. Can you confirm this as well?」，表示她認為會議已改到週二，並請對方確認，由此可知，兩人對會議時間認知有出入，故正確答案為 (A)。

**181–185 信件和保固文件**

August 15
Customer Service Department
Wells Home Appliances Inc.
22 Saunders Road
San Francisco, CA 94016

8月15日
客服部門
韋爾斯家用設備股份有限公司
94016 加州舊金山市桑德斯路22號

To Whom It May Concern,

When my coffee maker (serial code CFM 436) failed to work recently, I took it to the WHA service center in the Morris Shopping Mall, which is listed as one of your repair outlets. I was very annoyed when the shop declined to provide a free repair to my appliance although I have a valid warranty of more than six months. I had to pay for the repairs personally as there are no other local shops listed on your warranty. Here is a list of the charges from the repair center:

此致有關人士：

我的咖啡機（產品序號CFM436）最近壞了，我把它帶到莫里斯購物中心的韋爾斯服務中心，也是就貴公司列出的其中一個維修門市。我非常生氣，雖然我還有超過六個月的有效保固期，店家卻拒絕免費維修我的咖啡機。因為附近沒有保固證書列出的其他維修點，我只能自己花錢修理。這是維修中心跟我索取的費用明細：

| Parts : | | 零件： | |
|---|---|---|---|
| Filter ........................ | $12 | 濾網.................... | 12元 |
| Power unit ................ | $17 | 電源.................... | 17元 |
| Labor: $10 per hour...... | $20 | 勞務費（每小時）............. | 20元 |
| Dispenser nozzle.......... | $21 | 噴嘴管.................... | 21元 |
| Total........................ | $70 | 總計.................... | 70元 |

Please find attached the invoice and my guarantee I received when I bought the coffee maker. If you need any further information, please contact me.

Regards,
Ian Travers
23 Cherrystone Drive
San Jose, CA 95120

隨信附上我購買咖啡機的發票和保證書。如果還需要更多資訊，請和我聯絡。

祝好，
伊恩・崔佛斯
95120 加州聖荷西市櫻桃石街23號

## Guarantee

Welcome to your new Wells Coffee Maker. We have been supplying quality kitchen appliances throughout the world for over 30 years, and we pride ourselves on our quality and customer service.

All appliances are manufactured to the highest standards of craftsmanship. We offer a two-year warranty that covers the repair and replacement of your appliance in the event of a malfunction of parts. This warranty covers repairing labor and the replaceable parts only; please be aware that we take no responsibility for the damage to the dispenser nozzle or damage incurred by mishandling.

Attached is a list of authorized repair centers. Should you experience any problems with your new appliance, please take it to one of these WHA service centers for repair together with the original receipt and warranty. These centers have all been approved by Wells for the quality of their service and repairs.

## 保證書

歡迎使用您的新款韋爾斯咖啡機。我們在全球供應高品質的廚房電器已逾30年，我們以產品品質和顧客服務自豪。

所有的產品都是遵循最高標準的工藝製造。我們提供兩年保固，包括維修和替換故障的零件。這份保固僅涵括維修的勞務費用和可供替換的零件；請您留意，噴嘴管的毀損或操作不當造成的損壞，我們一概不負責。

附件清單是我們所授權的維修中心。如果您的新產品有問題，請攜帶原收據與保證書，前往其中任何一家韋爾斯公司的服務中心維修。這些中心的維修和服務品質都經由韋爾斯公司認可。

**詞彙** **repair outlet** 維修門市　**valid warranty** 有效保固書　**charge** 費用　**invoice** 發票　**pride oneself on sth** 某人以……為傲　**craftsmanship** 工藝技術　**malfunction** 故障　**incur** 造成　**mishandling** 不當操作　**authorized** 被授權的

**181**

**Why did Mr. Travers write the letter?**

(A) To request reimbursement of his expenses
(B) To request a copy of his guarantee
(C) To ask for a replacement for his broken machine
(D) To complain about a mistake on his receipt

為什麼崔佛斯先生要寫這封信？

(A) 要求補償他的花費
(B) 要求取得一份保固書副本
(C) 要求替換他故障的商品
(D) 抱怨他收據上的一項錯誤

在信件中，崔佛斯先生提到，自己因為咖啡機故障而前往保固卡上的服務中心，並說道：「I was very annoyed when the shop declined to provide a free repair to my appliance although I have a valid warranty of more than six months.」，表示明明保固未到期，服務中心卻拒絕免費維修，使得他須自費處理，崔佛斯先生也在信上附上費用收據，故可推知，這封信件應是為了要求費用償還而寫，最適合的答案為 (A)。

## 182

**In the letter, the word "declined" in paragraph 1, line 3, is closest in meaning to**

(A) descended
(B) rejected
(C) weakened
(D) modified

在信中第一段、第三行的「declined」，最接近下列哪個意思？

(A) 下降了
(B) 拒絕了
(C) 弱化了
(D) 修改了

動詞 decline 除了「減少、縮減」的意思外，也可以表示「（鄭重地）拒絕」。該句提到：「I was very annoyed when the shop declined to repair my appliance」，其中說到他很生氣，故可推測應是店家拒絕了他的要求，所以字義最相近的為 (B)。

## 183

**What does Mr. Travers mention about the WHA service center?**

(A) It offered the service at a reduced rate.
(B) It completed the task quickly.
(C) It carried out unnecessary work.
(D) It is an approved service center.

關於韋爾斯公司的服務中心，崔佛斯先生提到什麼？

(A) 它降價提供服務。
(B) 它很迅速完成工作。
(C) 它做了非必要的工作。
(D) 它是經認可的服務中心。

信件開頭提到：「I took it to the WHA service center . . . which is listed as one of your repair outlets.」，表示自己帶著故障的咖啡機前往官方認證的 WHA 服務中心。另外從保證書最後一段的「Should you experience any problems with your new appliance, please take it to one of these WHA service centers for repair. . . . These centers have all been approved by Wells」也可知道服務中心是官方認證的維修站，故本題正確答案為 (D)。

## 184

**What did Wells Home Appliances include with the product warranty?**

(A) A customer registration form
(B) A catalog of Wells products
(C) A register of clients
(D) A list of service centers

韋爾斯家電的產品保固包含什麼？

(A) 顧客註冊表格
(B) 韋爾斯的產品型錄
(C) 客戶名冊
(D) 服務中心的名單

保證書第一段介紹公司，第二段說明提供兩年保固與注意事項，第三段則說到授權維修中心，其中用了「Attached is a list of authorized repair centers.」，attached 就是「附上的」，故可知道保證書上有服務中心的名單，正確答案為 (D)。

| What expense amount reported by Mr. Travers will the warranty NOT cover? | 崔佛斯先生所反應的哪項支出，沒有含在保固內？ |
|---|---|
| (A) $12 | (A) 12 元 |
| (B) $17 | (B) 17 元 |
| (C) $20 | (C) 20 元 |
| (D) $21 | (D) 21 元 |

先看保證書的第二段，保固服務僅包含「repairing labor and the replaceable parts」，且「we take no responsibility for the damage to the dispenser nozzle」，表示只有維修的勞務費與替換零件費可免除，噴嘴的毀損不在保固範圍。再對照信件中崔佛斯先生提供的明細，其中卻寫到了「Dispenser nozzle」，故可知道不在保固的就是噴嘴費用 21 元，正確答案為 (D)。

**186–190 表格和電子郵件**

| City of Jacksonville | 傑克遜維爾市 |
|---|---|
| Council Office: Street Performer Permit Application | 議會辦公室：街頭藝人許可申請 |
| The following applicant seeks a license to perform on the streets of Jacksonville as an "artist" and submits the following information as required: | 下表中的申請人請求傑克遜維爾街頭「藝人」的演出執照，並提交下述必要資訊： |
| **Artist's Name:** Jace Payne<br>**Legal Address of Applicant:** 2194 Richardson Road, Jacksonville | 藝術家姓名：傑斯‧佩恩<br>申請人的法定地址：傑克遜維爾市，理查森路2194號 |
| **Location of performance:** Ed Austin Park | 表演地點：艾德‧奧斯丁公園 |
| Completed application forms must be accompanied by: | 完成的申請表格須附下列資料： |
| • Copy of birth certificate issued by Government Births Bureau<br>• A recording of the applicant playing the relevant instrument or singing<br>• License fee of $30 for each member, item of equipment, and stage<br>• A list of all equipment to be used at the venue<br>• If the music requires an amplifier, please send details of the decibel levels to our noise pollution officer, Mr. Gavin Freeman, to ensure it meets the permitted levels. | • 民政局所核發的出生證明副本<br>• 申請人演奏相關樂器或歌唱的錄影錄音檔<br>• 每一名成員、設備和舞台的執照費30美元<br>• 場地所需的設備清單<br>• 如需使用擴音器，請將分貝等級的細節寄給負責噪音汙染管制的官員，蓋文‧弗里曼先生，以確保符合規定。 |
| The applicant states that the above statement is true and he/she has read and agrees to comply with the provision of Section 44 of the code of the city of Jacksonville as it applies to artists. | 申請人聲明上述內容皆為真，並已閱讀及同意遵守傑克遜維爾市政法第44款，適用於藝人的規定。 |
| **Signature of applicant** *Jace Payne* | 申請者簽名：傑斯‧佩恩 |
| **Date** *July 24* | 日期：7月24日 |

**To:** Gavin Freeman
<Gfreeman@admin.jacksonville.org>
**From:** Jace Payne
<Jacepayne@bigmail.com>
**Date:** July 27
**Subject:** Re: Noise permission

Dear Mr. Freeman,

I wish to obtain permission for a street performance to be held at Ed Austin Park from August 1 to 3. I understand that I will need permission to use amplifiers, which are currently capable of emitting 100 decibels maximum. I am planning to use three amplifiers at the event. If you wish to check the noise levels, I'm performing at three venues in the downtown area on weekdays: Marrs Bar, Venure Restaurant, and Streetlife Café. I'll provide free entrance tickets if you want to come along and check that the decibel levels are acceptable.

Regards,
Jace Payne

---

**To:** Jace Payne
<Jacepayne@bigmail.com>
**From:** Gavin Freeman
<Gfreeman@admin.jacksonville.org>
**Date:** July 29
**Subject:** Re: Noise Permission

Dear Mr. Payne,

To assess the noise level, I need to operate the measuring equipment on-site. Among the places you've mentioned, Streetlife would work for me. You wrote you are performing on weekdays. When can I come over to see you?

And regarding your application, the person in charge says she hasn't received the recording of your playing yet. If you don't mind, I can record your performance when I visit there to check the amplifiers. Since we don't have much time before August 1, please call me at 500-5157 at your earliest convenience.

Gavin Freeman
Noise Pollution Officer

---

收件人：蓋文・弗里曼
<Gfreeman@admin.jacksonville.org>
寄件人：傑斯・佩恩
<Jacepayne@bigmail.com>
日期：7月27日
主旨：關於：音量許可

親愛的弗里曼先生：

我想要取得8月1日到3日在艾德・奧斯丁公園舉行街頭表演的許可。我了解我需要得到使用擴音器的許可，它目前的音量最高達100分貝。我打算在演出時使用三座擴音器。如果您想要確認噪音等級，我週間在市區的三個地點有演出：馬爾斯酒吧、維紐爾餐廳和街頭生活咖啡店。如果您要前來確認分貝數是否合乎標準，我可以提供您免費入場券。

祝好，
傑斯・佩恩

---

收件人：傑斯・佩恩
<Jacepayne@bigmail.com>
寄件人：蓋文・弗里曼
<Gfreeman@admin.jacksonville.org>
日期：7月29日
主旨：關於：音量許可

親愛的佩恩先生：

我需要在現場操作測量設備來評估噪音等級。從您先前所提及的地點中，街頭生活對我來說較為可行。您說您週間會演出。那您方便我何時過去呢？

另外關於您的申請，負責人說她沒有收到您演出的影音檔。如果您不介意，我到現場檢測擴音器時可以一併錄影。由於我們在8月1日前沒有太多時間，請您方便的話，儘早透過電話500-5157聯絡我。

噪音汙染部官員
蓋文・弗里曼

詞彙 **street performer** 街頭藝人　**birth certificate** 出生證明　**amplifier** 擴音器　**decibel** 分貝　**provision** 條款

**186** --------------------------------------------------------------------

**What is Mr. Payne applying for?**

(A) A permit to sell drinks

(B) A sound check

(C) A safety certificate from the council

(D) A license to perform

佩恩先生要申請什麼？

(A) 販賣飲料的許可

(B) 音效檢測

(C) 議會的安全證書

(D) 表演執照

從表格上的藝術家姓名，以及最後申請者簽名後方的「Jace Payne」皆可知道，佩恩先生是想申請街頭藝人許可，故正確答案為 (D)。

**187** --------------------------------------------------------------------

**Where will Mr. Freeman most likely see Mr. Payne play?**

(A) At a park

(B) At a bar

(C) At a café

(D) At a restaurant

弗里曼先生最有可能在哪裡看到佩恩先生的演出？

(A) 在一處公園

(B) 在一間酒吧

(C) 在一間咖啡廳

(D) 在一間餐廳

從佩恩先生在第一封郵件上寫的「I'm performing at three venues in the downtown area on weekdays: Marrs Bar, Venure Restaurant, and Streetlife Café.」可知道，他將在一個叫「Streetlife」的咖啡店表演，而在弗里曼先生的回信上提到「Streetlife would work for me」，表示他應該會去觀賞咖啡店的演出，故正確答案為 (C)。

**188** --------------------------------------------------------------------

**What required references does Mr. Freeman say Mr. Payne has missed?**

(A) A birth certificate

(B) A video clip

(C) A list of equipment

(D) Some money

弗里曼先生提到，佩恩先生漏了哪一項資料？

(A) 出生證明

(B) 一段錄影畫面

(C) 設備清單

(D) 一些錢

弗里曼先生在郵件中提到：「regarding your application, the person in charge says she hasn't received the recording of your playing yet.」，表示尚未收到佩恩先生演出的錄影，故正確答案為 (B)。

**189** --------------------------------------------------------------------

**What is the purpose of the first e-mail?**

(A) To submit an application

(B) To offer directions

(C) To ask for permission to use equipment

(D) To advertise some venues

第一封電子郵件的目的為何？

(A) 遞交一份申請

(B) 提供路徑指引

(C) 取得使用設備的許可

(D) 推廣某些場地

可先看第一篇的申請表裡的第五項，說到若使用擴音器需將詳細內容寄給負責人員弗里曼先生。
再回到佩恩先生的郵件，他開頭便說道：「I understand that I will need permission to use
amplifiers」，表示他想要使用擴音器，所以他才會邀請弗里曼先生來看演出，以確認分貝水
準，故正確答案為 (C)。

**190** ----------------------------------------------------------------------

**What will Mr. Payne most likely use at the event next month?**

(A) Electric guitars
(B) Microphone stands
(C) Editing equipment
(D) Loudspeakers

下個月的活動裡，佩恩先生可能會使用什麼東西？

(A) 電吉他
(B) 麥克風架
(C) 剪輯設備
(D) 喇叭

佩恩先生的郵件是在 7 月 27 日寄出的，裡頭提到會在 8 月 1 日至 3 日的表演中使用擴音器。
選項中與擴音器最相關的是 loudspeaker，故本題最適合的答案為 (D)。

## 191–195 文章和電子郵件

| International Business Newsletter | 國際商貿訊 |
|---|---|
| **MJ Foodville Appoints New Head of Research Team** | **MJ美食村指派新任研發團隊主管** |
| MJ Foodville (MJF) which has its headquarters in Singapore, has appointed Colton Choi as the new head of its research team. "I am very excited about the new opportunities to open up for me here in Singapore, even though I am sad at having to leave my homeland in Korea," said Mr. Choi in a statement released in the MJF newsletter. | 總部設在新加坡的MJ美食村（MJF）最近指派了卡爾登‧崔擔任研發團隊的新主管。「我感到很興奮，我在新加坡這裡有了全新的機會，雖然要離開家鄉南韓有些難過。」崔先生在MJF通訊的聲明裡表示。 |
| He went on to say that he had been interested in the work done at MJF for many years and is delighted to join the team. His first task once he assumes the position, according to the newsletter, will be to strongly highlight the importance of healthy eating in the Philippines and Indonesia. | 他接著說，他多年來對於MJF所做的工作很感興趣，很高興能加入這個團隊。根據本訊，他就任後首要任務，將更重視菲律賓和印尼健康飲食的重要性。 |
| Mr. Choi graduated with a master's degree in food and nutrition from the University of London. His previous employment was with Bristol Food Company, where he worked as a research assistant to the company's development director, Julian Baker. He will begin his new role in October at MJF. | 崔先生在倫敦大學取得食品與營養學的碩士學位。他之前在布里斯托食品公司就職，擔任研發部主任朱里安‧貝克的研究助理。他將在10月開始MJF的新職。 |

**To:** Colton Choi
<coltonchoi@gomail.com>
**From:** Ariana Rose
<arianarose@bfc.com>
**Date:** September 9
**Subject:** Congratulations

Dear Mr. Choi,

Well done on your new appointment once again. This is an excellent opportunity for you, and I have no doubt that you will make a valuable contribution to the MJ Foodville. When you resigned, I was asked by Mr. Baker to fill in for your position as research assistant. I intend to accept the offer even though I have not given him an answer yet. I have wanted to join the research team since I began working here last year. I extend my heartfelt gratitude to you for putting me forward for the job.

I would very much like to keep in touch and would appreciate your sending me your new address and phone number in Singapore.

Kind regards,

Ariana Rose
Bristol Food Company

---

**To:** Ariana Rose
<arianarose@bfc.com>
**From:** Colton Choi
<coltonchoi@gomail.com>
**Date:** September 11
**Subject:** Re: Congratulations

Dear Ms. Rose,

I'm very pleased to know that you're accepting the offer. Although we had no chance to work on the same team, I heard a lot about you from your manager, Mr. Cox. I'm sure that your experience in the material division would be a great help to the research team. When I nominated you to the position, Mr. Baker readily agreed to give you the opportunity. So, you should return your thanks to Mr. Baker.

---

收件人：卡爾登‧崔
<coltonchoi@gomail.com>
寄件人：雅瑞安娜‧羅斯
<arianarose@bfc.com>
日期：9月9日
主旨：恭喜

親愛的崔先生：

您又再次獲得很棒的工作，這對您來說是個絕佳的機會，我確信您會在MJ美食村有傑出貢獻。當您請辭後，貝克先生請我接替您研究助理的位子。雖然我還沒給他答覆，但我想要接受這份工作。從去年開始在這裡工作，我就想加入研究團隊了。我衷心感謝您推薦我這份工作。

我希望我們能保持聯絡，如果您願意讓我知道您在新加坡的新地址和電話號碼，我也會很感謝。

祝好，

布里斯托食品公司
雅瑞安娜‧羅斯

---

收件人：雅瑞安娜‧羅斯
<arianarose@bfc.com>
寄件人：卡爾登‧崔
<coltonchoi@gomail.com>
日期：9月11日
主旨：關於：恭喜

親愛的羅斯女士：

我很高興得知您要接受這份工作。雖然我們之前沒有機會在同一個團隊裡共事，但我從您的主管考克斯先生聽到很多關於您的事。我相信您在材料部門的經驗，對研究團隊會有很大的幫助。我向貝克先生推薦您接任時，他很快便同意要給您這個機會。所以，您應該向貝克先生轉達您的感謝。

I haven't moved to Singapore yet. I found a house to settle in but still don't have a phone number. And my e-mail is to be changed; you can contact me at coltonchoi2793@mjfgroup.com if you need my advice on your new duties that start next month.

Sincerely,
Colton Choi

我還沒搬到新加坡。我已找到安頓的房子，但還沒有電話。我也會更換電子信箱；假如下個月開始新職務，您需要我的建議的話，您可以透過coltonchoi2793@mjfgroup.com聯絡我。

卡爾登‧崔 敬上

**詞彙** highlight the importance of sth 強調某事的重要性　extend one's gratitude 表達某人的感謝
heartfelt 衷心的

---

**191**

**Why was the article written?**

(A) To announce the appointment of a staff member
(B) To publicize the findings of a questionnaire
(C) To release information about a new product
(D) To inform staff of an upcoming research project

為什麼要寫這篇文章？

(A) 公告一名新員工就職
(B) 公布問卷結果
(C) 釋出新產品資訊
(D) 通知員工接下來的一項研究計畫

文章撰寫的目的或埋由，通常會在前半部出現。第一篇文章的開頭提到：「MJ Foodville (MJF), which has its headquarters in Singapore, has appointed Colton Choi as the new head of its research team.」，表示崔先生將成為 MJ 美食村的新主管，並在第三段詳細介紹崔先生的經歷，故可推知這篇文章的目的是告知人事資訊，正確答案為 (A)。

---

**192**

**Where are the headquarters of MJ Foodville located?**

(A) Korea
(B) Singapore
(C) Malaysia
(D) Philippines

MJ 美食村的總部位於哪裡？

(A) 南韓
(B) 新加坡
(C) 馬來西亞
(D) 菲律賓

從報導文章第一句中的「MJ Foodville (MJF), which has its headquarters in Singapore」即可知道 MJ 美食村總部位於新加坡，正確答案為 (B)。

---

**193**

**What does Ms. Rose ask Mr. Choi to do?**

(A) Write a letter of recommendation
(B) Join a research team
(C) Provide contact information
(D) Speak at a meeting

羅斯女士要求崔先生做什麼？

(A) 寫推薦信
(B) 加入研究團隊
(C) 提供聯絡資訊
(D) 在會議中發言

在羅斯女士撰寫的郵件中，她說：「I would very much like to keep in touch and would appreciate your sending me your new address and phone number in Singapore.」，表示想和崔先生保持聯絡，並請對方告知住新加坡的地址、電話等聯絡資訊，因此本題正確答案為 (C)。

## 194

**What is mentioned about Mr. Choi?**

(A) He is currently working for MJ Foodville.
(B) He will replace Mr. Cox for the research assistant position.
(C) He recommended Ms. Rose for his previous position.
(D) He decided to stay in his home country.

文中提到崔先生什麼事？

(A) 他目前在 MJ 美食村就職。
(B) 他會接替考克斯先生擔任研究助理。
(C) 他推薦羅斯女士接任他之前的職位。
(D) 他決定待在家鄉。

羅斯女士在郵件中說，貝克先生請她接替崔先生成為研究助理，並說：「I extend my heartfelt gratitude to you for putting me forward for the job.」，表示感謝崔先生推薦她接任職位。且在崔先生的回信上也寫到「When I nominated you to the position」，間接透露出他推薦了羅斯女士接任職位一事，故正確答案為 (C)。

## 195

**What is implied about Ms. Rose?**

(A) She is a client of MJ Foodville.
(B) She currently lives in Singapore.
(C) She majored in food and nutrition.
(D) She is currently working for Mr. Cox.

文中提到羅斯女士什麼事？

(A) 她是 MJ 美食村的客戶。
(B) 她現在住在新加坡。
(C) 她主修食品和營養學。
(D) 她目前為考克斯先生工作。

第一封郵件中，羅斯女士說自己被邀請加入研究團隊，但是「I have not given him an answer yet.」，表示她尚未正式回覆，而根據崔先生在回信中說的「I heard a lot about you from your manager, Mr. Cox.」，可知羅斯女士目前的主管為考克斯先生，正確答案為 (D)。

**196–200 資訊、表格和信件**

## Hatton Business Update

Trust us for up-to-the-minute news and events

Information to subscribers:

Requests for subscription renewal are sent automatically one week prior to your current subscription's expiration date, subject to the conditions below. If your subscription finishes prior to a renewal request but you wish to continue to renew your subscription within two months of the actual expiry date, you can purchase any missed issues of the business magazine for 25% off the cover price.

Clients who ask for a renewal or extension prior to April 30 will be offered a 10% reduction on a two-year subscription or a 5% reduction on a 12-month subscription. All online offers cease with the expiration of any subscription, including the search-and-find database, which enables

## 《哈頓商業最新訊息》

信賴我們帶給您分秒必爭的新聞和事件

向訂戶報告：

續期訂閱的需求，除了會在您現有訂閱過期日的前一週自動通知，也視下述情況而定。如果您的訂閱在您申請續訂前就已經結束，但在過期的兩個月內您還想要繼續訂閱的話，可以用比定價便宜25%的折扣，購買您錯過的任何一期商業雜誌。

訂戶如果在4月30日前要求續訂或展延，訂閱兩年期將折扣10%，12個月期將折扣5%。訂閱過期後的所有線上服務，包括可以讓您瀏覽之

you to browse through the past catalogs of previously published Hatton Business Update issues. Visit www.hattononline.com for more information.

前每一期《哈頓商業最新訊息》的目錄搜尋資料庫，都將跟著停止。請造訪www.hattononline.com取得更多資訊。

---

## Hatton Business Update

------------------------------------

Account Number: 34073
Current Login: March 6
Previous Login: February 27

------------------------------------

### Hatton Business Update Online Subscription

- **Name:** Austin Crocker
- **Subscription status:** Current subscription expires on March 6.
- **Requested renewal period:** 24 months
- **Payment method:** Bank transfer

Thank you for renewing your *Hatton Business Update* subscription.

---

**Written by:** Austin Crocker
**Date:** March 6
**Subject:** Subscription Renewal

---

Dear sir,

I've checked the information about the discount on your website today. I've been very satisfied with your service, so I decided to renew my subscription right away, even though I still have one month left before the expiration date. However, I was surprised to read the message, which states my expiration date is today, March 6. It must be April 6, according to your webpage. Other information on the message seems to be right.

I also checked if I applied for a new subscription instead of renewing it. But it says, "Thank you for renewing your *Hatton Business Update* subscription." Please take care of this issue as soon as possible.

## 《哈頓商業最新訊息》

------------------------------------

帳戶號碼：34073
最近登入：3月6日
上次登入：2月27日

------------------------------------

### 《哈頓商業最新訊息》線上訂閱

- 姓名：奧斯丁·克羅克
- 訂戶狀態：目前訂閱將在3月6日到期
- 請求更新訂閱期間：24個月
- 付款方式：銀行轉帳

感謝您續訂《哈頓商業最新訊息》。

---

來自：奧斯丁·克羅克
日期：3月6日
主旨：續期訂閱

---

您好：

我今天查看您官網上的優惠訊息。我很滿意您的服務，所以即便距離到期還有一個月，我馬上決定再次訂閱。不過，我收到訊息時很驚訝，上面說我的到期日是今天，也就是3月6日。根據您的網頁，應該是4月6日才對。其他訊息裡的資訊看起來都是對的。

我也確認過是不是我按成「新訂戶」，而不是「續期訂閱」。但它寫到「感謝您續訂《哈頓商業最新訊息》。」請儘快處理這個問題。

---

**詞彙** expiration date 過期日　　**subject to** 取決於　　**cover price** 定價　　**cease** 終止

**196**

**What is the purpose of the information?**

(A) To announce further discounts on subscriptions

(B) To explain subscription renewal policies

(C) To notify subscribers of changes to online subscriptions

(D) To request that subscribers complete a survey

這則資訊的目的為何？

(A) 公告訂閱的額外優惠

(B) 解釋續期訂閱的規定

(C) 通知訂戶線上訂閱的異動

(D) 要求訂戶完成問卷

資訊在開頭便說到「Requests for subscription renewal」，接著也通篇講述與續訂相關的規定，故可知道這是為了解釋規定而發送的公告，正確答案為 (B)。

**197**

**In the information, the word "conditions" in paragraph 1, line 2, is closest in meaning to**

(A) ends

(B) proposals

(C) terms

(D) names

在資訊中，第一段、第二行的「conditions」，最接近下列哪個意思？

(A) 結束

(B) 提案

(C) 條件

(D) 名字

前文提到「Requests for subscription renewal are sent automatically one week prior to your current subscription's expiration date」，表示續訂有一種是會在到期前一週發送通知，後文則說明到期後才續訂的狀況，故兩句中間的「subject to the conditions below」，其中的 conditions 應要具有情境、條件的意思，以表示續訂也取決於下列的「狀況」，因此選項中最相近的為 terms，正確答案為 (C)。

**198**

**What is indicated about *Hatton Business Update*?**

(A) Its reporters have won several publishing awards.

(B) Its website provides some information to subscribers.

(C) It published its last issue two months ago.

(D) It recently increased its subscription fees.

文中提到《哈頓商業最新訊息》什麼事？

(A) 它的記者得過很多出版獎。

(B) 官網提供訂戶部分資訊。

(C) 兩個月前出了最後一期。

(D) 它最近漲了訂閱費。

第三段提到：「All online offers cease with the expiration of any subscription, including the search-and-find database, which enables you to browse through the past catalogs of previously published Hatton Business Update issues.」表示訂閱期間屆滿時，包含檢索過去刊號等原先可在網站上進行的線上服務將會中斷。由此可知，這篇文章以網站訂閱者為對象，提供相關資訊，因此正確答案為 (B)。

**199** ----------------------------------------

**What problem does Mr. Crocker report?**

(A) He cannot log on to the website.

(B) He hasn't received any notice about the event.

(C) He got a message with the wrong information.

(D) He wants to get a full refund.

克羅克先生反應了什麼問題？

(A) 他沒辦法登入官網。

(B) 他沒有接到任何該活動的通知。

(C) 他接獲的訊息裡有錯誤資訊。

(D) 他想要全額退款。

在克羅克先生撰寫的信件裡，他說到：「I was surprised to read the message, which states my expiration date is today, March 6. It must be April 6, according to your webpage.」，表示系統將他的訂閱到期日誤寫為 3 月 6 日，但應該是 4 月 6 日才對，故正確答案為 (C)。

**200** ----------------------------------------

**How much of a discount will Mr. Croker receive?**

(A) 5%

(B) 10%

(C) 20%

(D) 25%

克羅克先生會得到多少折扣？

(A) 5%

(B) 10%

(C) 20%

(D) 25%

根據第二篇表格中的「Requested renewal period: 24 months」，可知克羅克先生續訂了 24 個月，也就是兩年。回到公告資訊，上頭寫著：「Clients who ask for a renewal or extension prior to April 30 will be offered a 10% reduction on a two-year subscription」中，表示續訂兩年即可獲得折扣 10%，故本題正確答案為 (B)。

# ACTUAL TEST
# 8

## PART 5

**101**

The nutritional instruction program in Addis Ababa was so ------- that some countries are intending to introduce similar initiatives in their cities.

(A) success
(B) successive
(C) successful
(D) successfully

| 題型 | 位置──形容詞 |
| --- | --- |
| 翻譯 | 阿迪斯·阿巴巴的營養指導課程非常成功,有些國家也考慮在其都市內引進類似的計畫。 |
| 詞彙 | introduce 引進　initiative 計畫 |

本句主詞為「The nutritional instruction program in Addis Ababa」、動詞為 was,故此處應接續形容詞。選項中,(B) 雖然也是形容詞,但是因為字義為「連續的、接二連三的」,故此字只用在名詞前面,後方不適合加 that,故字義最符合題目的為 successful, 正確答案為 (C)。

**102**

Affiliates of Prime.com will now receive unlimited ------- to the organization's exclusive online data pool.

(A) accesses
(B) access
(C) accessing
(D) accessory

| 題型 | 位置──名詞 |
| --- | --- |
| 翻譯 | Prime.com 的隸屬機構可以無限制地取得該組織專屬的線上資料庫。 |
| 詞彙 | data pool 資料庫 |

空格位在形容詞 unlimited 後方,所以應代入受形容詞修飾的名詞。選項中,名詞為 (B) access,故正確答案為 (B)。

★請記住下列 access 相關用法:
have/gain access to N(接近;使用)

**103**

The brochure highlights the sequence of ------- is happening over the two-day event.

(A) that
(B) what
(C) who
(D) when

| 題型 | 文法──關係代名詞 |
| --- | --- |
| 翻譯 | 這本小冊子特別強調這兩天的系列活動。 |
| 詞彙 | sequence 系列活動 |

由於空格前是介系詞,並沒有先行詞,所以要使用不定關係代名詞 what,正確答案為 (B)。

## 104

Two years ago, Mr. Walker ------- college to join his current company.

(A) leave
(B) left
(C) will leave
(D) was left

題型 **文法**——動詞

翻譯 沃克先生兩年前離開大學，加入現在的公司。

從選項可判斷本題要選出 leave 正確的時態。本句的主詞為人物，動詞 leave 同為人物進行的動作，故應為主動式，再根據開頭表示過去時間的 Two years ago，可知動詞應為主動過去式，正確答案為 (B)。

## 105

------- maintenance work on the Kaur Drive, workers at the Mahir Library have to enter via the north entrance to get to work.

(A) Now that
(B) Moreover
(C) Wherever
(D) Because of

題型 **位置**——介系詞

翻譯 因為考爾路的維修工程，梅西爾圖書館的員工必須從北入口進來上班。

先從本題句意判斷，此處填入的詞應具有「因為」的涵義，故答案就在 (A) 與 (D) 中。 (A) 中的 that 為從屬連接詞，後方要接完整的句子，而 (D) 的 of 則為介系詞，後方接名詞即可。觀察空格後的「maintenance . . . Kaur Drive」，其中並沒有主詞與動詞，故可知道此處並不是填入連接詞，故正確答案為 (D)。

## 106

Those who have ------- about their missing baggage have to visit the claim office located next to the luggage carousel.

(A) features
(B) connections
(C) properties
(D) inquiries

題型 **詞彙**——名詞

翻譯 詢問行李遺失的人，必須到行李轉盤旁邊的行李提領處洽詢。

以下將選項以單數呈現：(A) feature 特點；(B) connection 關聯；(C) property 財產；(D) inquiry 詢問。

本句提到「行李遺失」、「到行李提領處」，故此處應是要填入和「詢問」相關的詞，表示要詢問行李遺失的人須前往提領處，故正確答案為 (D)。

## 107

Those who feel dizzy in the heat of the day will realize that the best way to make ------- feel better is to drink some water.

(A) they
(B) them
(C) their
(D) themselves

題型 位置——反身代名詞

翻譯 在大太陽底下熱昏頭的人,會發現讓自己感到舒服的最佳方式就是喝點水。

句子的主詞為 Those who feel dizzy,而本句是在說明讓這些人恢復的最佳方法,由於主詞與受詞的意義一致,所以空格應代入的是反身代名詞。因此,正確答案為 (D)。

---

108

The pay increase this year for all employees is the ------- as that incentive last year.

(A) same
(B) repeat
(C) equal
(D) one

題型 詞彙——形容詞

翻譯 今年度全體員工的加薪,和去年的激勵方式是一樣的。

詞彙 pay increase 加薪
incentive 激勵人心的事物

本句提到「今年」、「加薪」以及「去年」,故空格處應填入表示「程度」的形容詞,(C) equal 雖然在字義上也符合本題,但是搭配的介系詞應為「to」,故本題最適合填入 same,正確答案為 (A)。

★請記住下列表示「相同」的用法:
be the same as
be equal to

---

109

Farmers in Shamrock are overwhelmed by the enormous demand for ------- organic potato products.

(A) they
(B) themselves
(C) them
(D) their

題型 位置——所有格代名詞

翻譯 有機馬鈴薯產品的大量需求,使酢漿草農場的農民感到無法負荷。

詞彙 be overwhelmed 感到無法負荷

空格後為形容詞片語 organic potato products,所以此處適合填入所有格代名詞 their,表示「他們的」農產品,故正確答案為 (D)。

**110**

The majority of shoppers at Camden supermarket will readily pay extra for food that is produced -------.

(A) local
(B) locality
(C) locals
(D) locally

題型 位置——副詞

翻譯 康登超市的大部分顧客都願意為在地生產的食物多付一點錢。

由於空格前的動詞為被動式 is produced，所以空格應該代入修飾動詞的副詞，表示「在地」生產，故正確答案為 (D)。

**111**

Although public admission to the Anaheim Society's award ceremony is allowed, the after-party is by ------- only.

(A) collection
(B) invitation
(C) operation
(D) function

題型 詞彙——名詞

翻譯 雖然全民都獲准參加安那翰協會的頒獎典禮，但續攤宴會只限受邀請者參加。

詞彙 admission 參加
after-party 續攤宴會

從屬子句的連接詞為 although（雖然），表示兩個子句需為互相相反的意思。從屬子句表示頒獎典禮開放給大眾參加，而主要子句則提到「續攤宴會」、「憑藉」、「只」，故可推測空格處的字義應為「邀請函」，表示續攤宴會不隨意開放，而是需要邀請函，故正確答案為 (B)。

**112**

Company employees have been advised that the new product range's market is highly ------- and will face fierce rivalry from other companies.

(A) competitive
(B) competitors
(C) competition
(D) competitively

題型 位置——形容詞

翻譯 公司員工被提醒，新產品的市場是高度競爭的，且將面臨來自其他公司的強烈較勁。

詞彙 highly competitive 高度競爭的

空格位於 be 動詞後面，並受副詞 highly 修飾，故應該代入形容詞，因此正確答案為 (A)。

**113**

The customer conference was ------- delayed as the projector had an operational malfunction in the course of the seminar.

(A) enough
(B) many
(C) quite
(D) ever

題型 詞彙——副詞

翻譯 投影機在研討會上運作失常，造成客戶大會延遲頗久。

詞彙 malfunction 故障

本句提到「客戶大會」與「延遲」，從空格位置判斷，空格處填入的副詞應要修飾延遲的程度，故填入 quite 表示「相當地」延遲最為適合，正常答案為 (C)。

**114**

The ------- annual manufacturing costs of the company were estimated to be $12 million as a result of structural renovations.

(A) totaling
(B) totaled
(C) totals
(D) total

| 題型 | 位置——形容詞 |
| 翻譯 | 因為公司大樓結構整修，其年度生產總成本預估會是一千兩百萬美元。 |
| 詞彙 | structural renovation 結構上的整修 |

從空格位置來看，此處應填入能修飾名詞 manufacturing costs 的形容詞。選項中，(A) 與 (B) 為分詞，(D) 為形容詞，但此處使用普通的形容詞即可，且在商業用語中也很常使用「total cost」表示總成本，故本題答案為 (D)。

**115**

Visitors ------- to show their passport or photo identification whenever they have to check-in at a hotel.

(A) requests
(B) are requested
(C) to request
(D) requesting

| 題型 | 文法——被動 |
| 翻譯 | 訪客在飯店辦理入住時，會被要求出示護照或是有照片的身分證件。 |
| 詞彙 | identification 身分證件 |

觀察全句可知缺少動詞，故空格處應填入的是動詞，剩下 (A) 與 (B) 可選；又因為主詞 Visitors 為複數名詞，而單數動詞 (A) 違反單複數一致，所以正確答案為 (B)。

(A) 就算改成複數型態 request 也不能成為答案，因為 request 後面的不定詞應為受詞補語，只有使用被動式 are requested 時，才能直接接續不定詞。

**116**

The board of directors is considering ------- the headquarters to Vancouver.

(A) to relocate
(B) relocation
(C) relocating
(D) has relocated

| 題型 | 位置——動名詞 |
| 翻譯 | 董事會正考慮將總部搬遷到溫哥華。 |

本題的關鍵在於空格前的動詞 consider，這個動詞後接的動作固定是以動名詞的狀態出現，所以正確答案為 (C)。

其他一樣要以「動詞＋動名詞」出現的動詞還有 avoid、deny、enjoy、finish、mind、practice、resist 等。

## 117

**The Sales Manager, Cody Flynn, insisted that marketing the merchandise ------- online is not a profitable way of attracting young customers.**

(A) closely
(B) otherwise
(C) solely
(D) almost

**題型** 詞彙——副詞

**翻譯** 業務經理寇帝‧佛林堅稱，僅在網路上行銷這項商品不能有效吸引年輕消費者。

從位置判斷，空格處要能修飾空格後的副詞 online，選項中符合的只有 solely，表示「僅只」在網路上行銷商品，故正確答案為 (C)。

## 118

**Kemp Apparel's second quarter growth rate was higher than originally -------.**

(A) anticipates
(B) anticipated
(C) anticipating
(D) anticipation

**題型** 文法——準關係代名詞

**翻譯** 肯普服飾第二季的成長率比預期來得高。

**詞彙** growth rate 成長率

在比較級的子句中，有時 than 可作為關係代名詞，代替主格代名詞或受格代名詞。本句中的成長率是「被預期」對象，所以應搭配被動動詞，故寫成「growth rate was higher than it was originally anticipated」並不正確，而是該寫成「higher than was originally anticipated」，其中的 be 動詞又可再省略，成為「higher than originally anticipated」，故本題正確答案為 (B)。

★ than 後省略主詞與 be 動詞的用法常常出現，類似的還有 than necessary、than needed

## 119

**Applicants who passed the initial selection tests for the supervisor position ------- by the company recruiter next week.**

(A) will contact
(B) would contact
(C) will be contacted
(D) have been contacted

**題型** 文法——動詞

**翻譯** 應徵主管職位並已通過初試的人，下週將由公司人事招募處聯繫。

**詞彙** initial 初期的

從句子最後出現 next week 看來，空格應代入未來時態的 (A) 或 (C)。又因為句中主詞 Applicants 為要「被聯繫」的人物，故要使用被動式，正確答案為 (C)。

**120**

Bainbridge Public Library visitors may check out a total of 5 publications ------- 3 multimedia items per week.

(A) than
(B) just as
(C) so
(D) and

題型 位置──對等連接詞

翻譯 民眾每週可以在班布里治公共圖書館借出總共五本書和三片多媒體光碟。

詞彙 multimedia 多媒體

空格前後皆為名詞，且具有對等的字義，故此處填入的為對等連接詞 and，表示書「和」光碟，正確答案為 (D)。

**121**

During their stay, guests have the option of participating in various outdoor activities ------- cycling, fishing, and swimming.

(A) similarly
(B) such as
(C) as far as
(D) likewise

題型 詞彙──介系詞

翻譯 留宿期間，房客可以選擇參加多項戶外活動，像是騎單車、釣魚和游泳。

(A) similarly 相似地；(B) such as 像是；(C) as far as 只要；(D) likewise 同樣地。從句意看來，此處要填入具有「例如、列舉」意義的詞語，故正確答案為 (B)。

**122**

Travelers are asked to collect all of their ------- belongings before exiting the train.

(A) personal
(B) accurate
(C) unlimited
(D) believable

題型 詞彙──形容詞

翻譯 旅客下火車前，必須帶走所有的個人物品。

詞彙 personal belonging 個人物品

本句提到「旅客」、「帶走」、「物品」、「下火車」，故可推測此處修飾物品的形容詞應具有「個人的」的意思，表示旅客下車前要帶走個人物品，正確答案為 (A)。

**123**

Changes in LK Telecom's billing policy are ------- determined by how much demand there is.

(A) large
(B) largest
(C) larger
(D) largely

題型 位置──副詞

翻譯 LK 通訊公司開立帳單規定的變動，主要根據其需求來決定。

空格位於被動中的 be 動詞和過去分詞 determined 之間，所以應代入可修飾動詞的副詞 largely，以表示「主要地」，故正確答案為 (D)。

**124**

The estimate covers all the labor and materials for building a parking ------- on Boulder Road that can accommodate 1,000 vehicles.

(A) structure
(B) structures
(C) structural
(D) structurally

**題型** 位置──名詞

**翻譯** 關於建設波德路上可容納1,000 台車的停車場，其估價包含所需的人事和材料支出。

**詞彙** estimate〔名詞〕估價
accommodate 容納

從句意看來，此處應是要表示建設「停車場」。空格前有 parking，故此處適合填入名詞 structure，組成複合名詞，正確答案為 (A)。

★複合名詞為兩個或兩個以上的名詞組成，其中有一種形式為「V-ing ＋名詞」，這時的 V-ing 通常用在說明後方名詞的功能，例如 drinking water、turning point、parking lot 等。

**125**

Mr. Reynolds should certainly be praised for ------- a welcome reception for the new employees at Orange Software.

(A) correcting
(B) applying
(C) organizing
(D) connecting

**題型** 詞彙──動詞

**翻譯** 雷諾斯先生為橘子軟體的新進員工籌辦了歡迎會，應該獲得稱讚。

此處考的是動詞詞彙，但也要留意因為空格前有介系詞 for，故動詞要變成 V-ing 的形式。從空格後方的 a welcome reception 可知，此處的動詞應具有「舉辦、籌辦」的意思，故最適合填入 organizing，正確答案為 (C)。

**126**

The retailers on Simpson Street are prohibited from displaying items outside ------- prior consent.

(A) around
(B) without
(C) owing to
(D) as opposed to

**題型** 詞彙──介系詞

**翻譯** 沒有事先取得同意的話，辛普森街上的零售商店禁止在外展示商品。

**詞彙** prior 在先的
consent 同意

本句提到「禁止」、「展示產品」、「事前同意」，故可推測空格處應填入具有「沒有、缺乏」意思的介系詞，表示沒有事前同意就無法展示產品，正確答案為 (B)。

------- impresses the board of directors the most is that the White Timber Company has established its presence in the hardwood furniture market.

(A) Nothing
(B) Neither
(C) What
(D) Which

題型 **文法──關係代名詞**

翻譯 讓董事會印象最深刻的是，白木公司在硬木家具市場建立了它的一席之地。

詞彙 establish one's presence 建立一席之地

不定關係代名詞 what 可以代替 the thing that 或 anything that，領導的子句會同時缺少主詞與關係代名詞。先觀察整個句子，動詞其實是後方的 is，而主詞為空格處到 most 的部分。

如果空格代入 what，此句主詞可看成「The thing that impresses the board of directors the most」，代表「那件令董事會印象深刻的事」，然後接了 is 以及 that 子句，解釋「那件事」就是 that 子句中提到的白木公司的事情。綜合上述，空格最適合填入 what，因此正確答案為 (C)。

## 128

While a majority of customers think that the new model is easy to use, those ------- familiar with the original operating system have to look through the user's manual before using the item.

(A) little
(B) none
(C) less
(D) fewer

題型 **文法──比較級**

翻譯 即使大部分顧客都覺得新產品操作簡易，還是有不太熟悉之前操作系統的人，必須在使用前詳讀使用說明書。

先抓出空格前的 those，此處其實是省略用法，可還原成「those who」，意為「……的人們」，「those who are familiar with . . .」則解釋為「對……熟悉的人們」，而空格位於 familiar 前，應填入可形容熟悉程度的副詞。

由於句子中出現連接詞 While，所以前後句應有相反之意；前句提到大部分人覺得使用容易，可推測後句是要轉而說明較不熟悉操作的人的情形，所以此處要使用副詞比較級 less，表示「比較不」熟悉的人們，正確答案為 (C)。

(D) fewer 形容數量較少，後方要接可數名詞，像是 fewer people、fewer complaints 等。

## 129

Because of her outstanding performance, Ms. Russell has been ------- to a manager position at Higgins Inc.

(A) promoted
(B) registered
(C) pleased
(D) increased

題型 **詞彙──動詞**

翻譯 因為表現出色，羅素女士最近被晉升為希金斯公司的經理。

從句中的「表現出色」、「經理」及被動 has been 可推測，此處缺少的動詞應具有「升職」的意思，表示因出色表現而被升職為經理，故正確答案為 (A)。

**★記住下列用法：**

**promote A to B**（使 A 晉升為 B）

**130**------------------------------------------------

**Vending machines containing beverages and snacks are strategically situated ------- the company premises.**

(A) between
(B) down
(C) throughout
(D) except

| 題型 | 詞彙──介系詞 |
|---|---|
| 翻譯 | 飲料和點心的販賣機，策略性地設置在公司內各處。 |
| 詞彙 | premises 公司所在處；生產廠區 |

觀察空格後面出現地點名詞 the company premises，且從句意看來，此處應填入具有「貫穿、在各處」的意思的介系詞，表示在公司各處設置販賣機，故最適合填入的介系詞為 throughout，正確答案為 (C)。

## PART 6

**131-134 廣告**

## New Exhibition at Sierra Art Museum

In recent years, Sierra Art Museum has been popular in holding exhibitions on Junk art, innovative art **131** the great artistic talent shown by famous local artist Diego Harding and his colleagues.

According to Mr. Harding, his activity would every now and then be termed as "Junk art." **132** "Junk art", as his work is called, is once-abandoned items **133** are utilized to come up with a new creation.

The exhibition will be open to anyone interested from April 1 to June 30. **134**, on the evening of Wednesday, March 23, there will be a reception that will include the staff members of the art center only. A website is also set up in case someone needs more clarification. The website is at museum.sierraart.org.

## 席亞拉美術館新展覽

席亞拉美術館近年來藉著舉辦廢物藝術展大受歡迎。它是創新的藝術,特色標榜知名在地藝術家迪亞哥‧哈丁和他團隊所展現的藝術才能。

根據哈丁先生的說法,他的創作活動有時被稱為「廢物藝術」。他想到要利用人們每天丟掉的東西。「廢物藝術」誠如其名,指的是一度廢棄的物品用來從事新的創作。

展覽從4月1日到6月30日開放,歡迎任何感興趣的人蒞臨。此外,3月23日週三晚間將舉行接待會,僅限藝術中心的員工參加。欲知詳情者請參見官網,網址是museum.sierraart.org。

**詞彙** junk 廢物;垃圾　every now and then 有時;偶爾　be termed as 被稱作　abandon 拋棄
utilize 使用　come up with 想出;提出　clarification 說明

**131** --------------------------------------------------------------------------------

(A) feature
(B) featured
(C) featuring
(D) features

(A) 特色
(B) 有……特色
(C) 以……為特色
(D) 以……為特色

**題型 位置——分詞**

觀察空格前後,空格後的內容是在補充說明前面的 innovative art,故此處原本是用關係代名詞連接,為「innovative art that features the great artistic talent」,但由於將關係代名詞省略,並把主動動詞改為現在分詞 featuring,所以空格處要填入的是 featuring,正確答案為 (C)。

**132** (NEW) --------------------------------------------------------------------------

(A) But the materials for those sculptures are not junk in fact.
(B) This was once believed to be possible, but Mr. Harding thought otherwise.
(C) Mr. Harding is now collecting a lot of junk to turn his idea into a reality.
(D) He came up with the idea of utilizing the things that people throw away every day.

(A) 但這些雕塑的材料事實上並非垃圾。
(B) 它一度被認為是可行的,但哈丁先生不這麼想。
(C) 哈丁先生現在蒐集大量廢棄物,來實現他的創意。
(D) 他想到要利用人們每天丟掉的東西。

題型 **填入句子**

空格前句提到，哈丁先生的藝術常被稱為「junk art」，後句則說明他的作品是利用曾被丟棄的物品作為材料，因此空格中應填入命名背景，或是有關該創作活動的內容，所以 (D) 最為合適，本題正確答案為 (D)。

(C) 乍看之下無誤，但句中提到「now」，表示哈丁先生還在蒐集廢物要實現想法，但文中提到他已經創作出作品，並舉行過多次展示會，故與內容不符。

**133** -------------------------------------------------------------

(A) what            (A) 凡是……的事物
(B) that            (B) 那東西
(C) how           (C) 用……的方式
(D) each          (D) 每一

題型 **文法**──關係代名詞

從句意判斷，空格後的主詞應為空格前的 once-abandoned items，故此處要填入可作為主格關係代名詞的 that，正確答案為 (B)。

(A) what 可看成 the things that，為包含先行詞的不定關係代名詞，所以前面不可出現作為先行詞的名詞。

**134** -------------------------------------------------------------

(A) In addition      (A) 此外
(B) Instead         (B) 反而
(C) Thus          (C) 因此
(D) As a result     (D) 結果

題型 **詞彙**──連接副詞

從選項可以看出，本題要考的是連接空格前後句的連接副詞。空格前句說到展覽舉辦的時間，後句則提到接待會，故空格處應填入帶有「順帶一提、另外」等字義的副詞以提供附加資訊，故最適合填入 In addition，正確答案為 (A)。

## 135–138 信件

Dear Stellar Store customer,

We appreciate you very much for your interest in joining the Stellar Store Rewards loyalty program. Participating in this program **135** you to enjoy a lot of wonderful rewards. The benefits of being a member of this program are that you will have early **136** about discount deals, access to special exclusive occasions, and the opportunity to be awarded a gift certificate worth $50 for every $400 spent on product purchases.

親愛的星星商店顧客：

我們非常感謝您加入星星商店的忠誠獎勵計畫。參加本計畫將讓您享受很多優質獎賞。成為計畫會員的好處是可以提早取得優惠資訊、參加獨家活動，每次購買商品消費滿400元也有機會贈與50元禮券。

**137**. An individual is only required to submit the enclosed application form to the nearby store, where a membership card can be issued for you. Updates on your account detailing the points you have accumulated and discount coupons you have earned will be provided **138** six weeks after you start using your membership card.

Membership is free and can be canceled at any time. Welcome and start earning your rewards today!

Sincerely,
Amy Henderson
Customer Loyalty Program Director

Enclosure

加入計畫一點都不難。只需填寫好隨函附上的申請表，並交至鄰近的星星店面，當場就能發會員卡給您。開始啟用會員卡後，就會在六週內提供您帳戶更新的資訊，它會詳列您累積的點數和賺到的優惠券。

免費登記會員，且隨時都能取消。歡迎從今天起開始賺取獎勵！

顧客忠誠計畫主任
艾美・韓德森 敬上

隨函附上

**詞彙** **loyalty** 忠誠　**exclusive** 獨家的；專屬的　**gift certificate** 禮券　**accumulate** 累積

---

**135** --------------------------------------------------------

(A) has allowed
(B) is allowing
(C) allowed
(D) will allow

(A) 已允許
(B) 正在允許
(C) 允許了
(D) 將允許

**題型 文法**——動詞

從信件開頭的「We appreciate you very much for . . . joining . . . loyalty program」，可知道收信者剛加入了店家的獎勵計畫。空格前後提到「參加計畫」與「享有優惠」，可推測中間的動詞應是未來式，表示「之後」可以獲得優惠，因此正確答案為 (D)。

另外也可以從下句中的「you will have」知道，因為兩句敘述的方式與內容相似，故此句也同樣使用未來式。

**136** --------------------------------------------------------

(A) performance
(B) evaluation
(C) information
(D) referral

(A) 表現
(B) 評估
(C) 資訊
(D) 轉介

**題型 詞彙**——名詞

空格前提到可享受優惠，後句則列舉幾個優惠內容，故此處填入 information 以表示搶先獲得優惠「資訊」最為適當，正確答案為 (C)。

## 137 NEW

(A) Once you cancel, all your coupons will become invalid.

(B) There are no complications in signing up for this program.

(C) You are not on our customer list; however, we will service you as our most important member.

(D) You'll need to visit one of our affiliates to get an application form.

(A) 一旦取消，您所有的優待券就會失效。

(B) 加入計畫一點都不難。

(C) 您不在我們的顧客名單上；然而，我們仍視您為最重要的會員服務您。

(D) 您需要到我們其中一間分店拿申請表。

**題型 填入句子**

空格為第二段的開頭。第一段中提到優惠計畫，而空格後面提到，只要填寫申請表即可加入，因此此處若表示加入會員相當簡單，具吸引收信者加入的作用，所以選項中最適合的答案為 (B)。

(D) 提到要到分店拿取申請表，但空格後句的內容表示申請表已隨信件附上，故此選項與內文矛盾，不適合作為答案。

## 138

(A) within
(B) since
(C) until
(D) due to

(A) 在……期間內
(B) 自從
(C) 直到
(D) 因為

**題型 詞彙——介系詞**

根據文意，此處提到「六週」、「累積的點數」與「賺到的優惠券」，可推測此處的介系詞應有「某範圍內」的意思，表示在六週「內」會有點數與優惠券的更新，故本題填入 within 最適當，正確答案為 (A)。

## 139–142 文章

Bangkok (2 April) — Superior Athletics, a prominent Canadian clothing company, will soon **139** its fashion items in Thailand.

Richard Kent, the president of Superior Athletics, declared in an interview with *Thai Business News* that the company intends to ship its first batch of the newest sports apparel and fashion accessories to Bangkok, Thailand, in several weeks. Thai **140** can acquire the products in May, when the goods are put up for sale in the market.

Mr. Kent credited the business move of the company to a **141** demand for sports apparel in Thailand and its neighboring countries. **142**. According to Mr. Kent, the current trend in Southeast Asia is that more and more people have become interested in workout clothing, and this is precisely what Superior Athletics aims to provide.

曼谷（4月2日）—加拿大服裝主要品牌「優秀運動」的潮流商品，很快就要在泰國促銷。

「優秀運動」總裁李察‧肯特在《泰國商業新聞》的訪談中宣布，公司打算在幾週內，將第一批最新的運動服裝和時尚配件運到泰國曼谷。商品五月上市，屆時泰國消費者就能拿到貨。

肯特先生認為，這次的商業行動，是因為泰國和其鄰近國家在運動服飾方面成長的需求。特別是在菲律賓賣得非常好。肯特先生表示，依東南亞日前的趨勢，有愈來愈多人對健身服飾感興趣，而這也正是「優秀運動」的目標市場。

### 139

(A) recall
(B) market
(C) reduce
(D) design

(A) 回憶
(B) 促銷
(C) 減少
(D) 設計

**題型 詞彙——動詞**

根據第二段的第一句：「the company intends to ship its first batch of the newest sports apparel and fashion accessories to Bangkok」，可知公司要進一批新貨到泰國，故此處的動詞應具「銷售、販售」的意思，故最適合填入 market，正確答案為 (B)。

### 140

(A) consuming
(B) consumers
(C) consumable
(D) consumed

(A) 正在消費
(B) 消費者
(C) 消耗品
(D) 消耗過的

**題型 位置——名詞**

在助動詞 can 前為主詞的位置，此空格處應填入名詞，以表示泰國的「消費者」，故正確答案為 (B)。

### 141

(A) rising
(B) controlling
(C) long-standing
(D) questionable

(A) 成長的
(B) 決定性的
(C) 存在已久的
(D) 可疑的

**題型 詞彙——形容詞**

本題要選適合修飾名詞 demand 的形容詞。前面提到公司要在泰國販賣流行服飾，因此本句應表示泰國與鄰近國家有「成長的」需求，故正確答案為 (A)。

### 142 NEW

(A) No wonder the company is withdrawing its business from Southeast Asia.
(B) He is now worried that the Asian market might begin to shrink.
(C) As a result, its business may be more beneficial in European countries.
(D) In particular, its business in the Philippines was a huge success.

(A) 難怪那間公司正在撤出東南亞的事業。
(B) 他現在擔心亞洲市場會開始萎縮。
(C) 因此，在歐洲的生意或許更有利可圖。
(D) 特別是在菲律賓賣得非常好。

題型 **填入句子**

空格前句說到運動服飾在泰國與鄰近國家賣得好，後句則提到「the current trend in Southeast Asia」，更擴大範圍地說明東南亞的趨勢，因此此處若填入 (D)，就能表示不只泰國，在菲律賓也有人氣，故正確答案為 (D)。

## 143–146 備忘錄

**To:** Production workers and inspectors
**From:** Fred Wilson, Production Manager
**Date:** February 9
**Subject:** EZ2Drink Juicer

I am writing to promptly inform you that we **143** several reviews from our customers regarding the detachable squeezers on our new EZ2Drink Juicers.

**144**. While this may seem like an unimportant detail, I feel these complaints would negatively affect our reputation in the long run. As a reminder, production workers must make sure that the squeezer is **145** manufactured. Inspectors must also double-check these **146** prior to distribution.

Please call me at 764-8314 if you need further details about the EZ2Drink Juicer.

收件人：製造員和品管員
寄件人：弗雷德・威爾森，生產製造經理
日期：2月9日
主旨：簡單喝榨汁機

我想要立即通知大家，對於新款簡單喝榨汁機的可拆式榨汁器，我們已收到一些顧客的意見。

有些顧客擔心榨汁器不能完整貼合機身。雖然這細節好像不是很重要，但我覺得這些抱怨長遠來看對我們的商譽有害。提醒一下，製造員必須確保榨汁器製造無誤。品管員於配送前也必須再三檢查這些零件。

如果還需要知道簡單喝榨汁機的更多細節，請來電764-8314。

詞彙 **promptly** 立即　**detachable** 可拆式的　**squeezer** 榨汁器　**in the long run** 長遠看來
**be disconcerted** 擔心的

**143**

(A) will receive
(B) have received
(C) receive
(D) receiving

(A) 將收到
(B) 已收到
(C) 接收
(D) 正在接收

題型 **文法──動詞**

先觀察句子結構，空格處為 that 子句的動詞，所以可先將現在分詞型態的 (D) 刪去。本句說到，公司收到顧客對榨汁器的意見，此處若使用現在完成式，可強調動作從過去持續到現在，故為最適合的時態，正確答案為 (B)。

**144** NEW --------------------------------------------------------------

(A) There are no complaints reported by the customers yet.

(B) I'm pleased to know that the newest model is earning favorable reviews.

(C) Despite the poor sales figures, the company has to continue to increase the production.

(D) Some customers are disconcerted as the squeezer does not fit in the body completely.

(A) 尚未收到顧客抱怨。

(B) 我很高興知道最新款商品獲得好評。

(C) 儘管銷售額很差，公司還是得要增加產量。

(D) 有些顧客擔心榨汁器不能完整貼合機身。

題型 **填入句子**

空格後文提到：「While this may seem like an unimportant detail」、「these complaints」，其中使用代名詞「this」代指榨汁器的問題，表示空格處應有和問題相關的描述，且是來自顧客的抱怨，故此處最適合填入 (D)。

**145** --------------------------------------------------------------

(A) rapidly

(B) comfortably

(C) properly

(D) certainly

(A) 很快地

(B) 舒服地

(C) 正確地

(D) 無疑地

題型 **詞彙**——副詞

前文提到榨汁器無法貼合機身，所以此處應是要提醒製造員，確認榨汁器有被「正確地」製作，故填入副詞 properly 最為合適，正確答案為 (C)。

(D) certainly 多用來強調意見、推測、想法的「明確程度」，不適合修飾動詞 manufacture。

**146** --------------------------------------------------------------

(A) parts

(B) vehicles

(C) schedules

(D) payments

(A) 零件

(B) 車輛

(C) 行程

(D) 付款

題型 **詞彙**——名詞

從本句提到的「再三檢查」與「配送前」，可推測空格處應要填入與榨汁器相關的名詞，故最適合填入的為 parts，表示在配送前要再次檢查榨汁器的零件，正確答案為 (A)。

## PART 7

**147–148 通知**

Iron Jones Gym is now due for renovation. The gym is to be closed for two weeks in July for building repairs.

The dates below are important:

| | |
|---|---|
| June 20 – June 30 | Renewal of annual membership |
| July 1 – July 6 | Room refurbishment |
| July 7 – July 14 | External window replacement |
| July 15 | Gym reopening |

To check our full calendar for the year, go to www. ironjones.com. Membership can be renewed over the telephone. If you are renting sports equipment, the lending period can also be renewed if you'd like. If not, please return the items before June 20. You may reapply for the equipment on July 15. Even if you are renewing a rental agreement, all equipment has to be removed from your previous lockers by June 30, as they will be changed. Anything left in the lockers will be removed after this date. Contact us with any questions at 777-4644 extension 14.

鋼鐵瓊斯健身房預計要整修。健身房將在七月關閉兩週以便建築維修。

幾個重要日期如下：

| | |
|---|---|
| 6月20日—6月30日 | 年度會員資格更新 |
| 7月1日—7月6日 | 房間翻修 |
| 7月7日—7月14日 | 外窗更換 |
| 7月15日 | 健身房重新開張 |

如欲查看今年度的全部行事曆，可上www.ironjones.com。會員資格可透過電話更新。如果您正租用運動設備也能隨時更新租期。如果不需要，請在6月20日前歸還。等到7月15日即可重新申請。儘管您更新了租約，但因為將要更換置物櫃，您放在裡頭的所有器材需在6月30日前清空。任何留在置物櫃裡的東西在6月30日後將被丟棄。如有任何疑問請致電777-4644分機14聯絡我們。

**詞彙** be due for 預計要　refurbishment 翻修

**For whom in the Iron Jones Gym is the notice intended?**

(A) Management
(B) Members
(C) Fitness trainers
(D) Gym staff

鋼鐵瓊斯健身房的通知想要告知的對象是誰？

(A) 管理階層
(B) 會員
(C) 健身教練
(D) 健身房員工

通知在開頭便提到健身房將進行整修，並在段落中説了「Membership」、「if you are renting sports equipment」、「You may reapply for the equipment」、「your previous lockers」等字詞，故可推測這則通知最主要是寫給健身房會員的，正確答案為 (B)。

## 148

**How should membership be renewed?**

(A) In person
(B) By phone
(C) By e-mail
(D) Through the website

想更新會員資格應該怎麼做？

(A) 面對面辦理
(B) 打電話
(C) 寫電子郵件
(D) 上官網

從日期下方段落第二句的「Membership can be renewed over the telephone.」可知道，會員資格可透過電話延長，故正確答案為 (B)。

## 149–150 訊息串

| | |
|---|---|
| **Katie Hart** 　　　　3:29 P.M.<br>Jake, Delta Office Supplies called. They won't be able to deliver the projector on Wednesday. | 凱蒂·哈特〔下午3:29〕：<br>傑克，德塔辦公用品打電話來。他們不能在週三送投影機過來。 |
| **Jake Wood** 　　　　3:31 P.M.<br>It can't be. We need that projector for the training session. | 傑克·伍德〔下午3:31〕：<br>這不行啊。我們訓練課程會用到投影機。 |
| **Katie Hart** 　　　　3:32 P.M.<br>I'm aware of that. Perhaps I should find another shop where I can pick up a new projector in person. | 凱蒂·哈特〔下午3:32〕：<br>我知道。也許我應該再找一間我可以親取投影機的店。 |
| **Jake Wood** 　　　　3:33 P.M.<br>Terry says there's an office supply store that has recently opened on Main Street. I think I can give you a ride. What time should I pick you up? | 傑克·伍德〔下午3:33〕：<br>泰瑞說，主街上最近新開了一間辦公用品店。我想我能載你一程。什麼時候接你？ |
| **Katie Hart** 　　　　3:34 P.M.<br>Thank you so much! I'll meet you at five o'clock in front of the north entrance. | 凱蒂·哈特〔下午3:34〕：<br>非常感謝！我五點在北入口前面等你。 |
| **Jake Wood** 　　　　3:35 P.M.<br>Sure thing. Don't forget the company credit card. | 傑克·伍德〔下午3:35〕：<br>沒問題。別忘了帶公司信用卡。 |

**詞彙** give sb a ride 載某人一程　　sure thing 沒問題

## 149

**What problem are the speakers discussing?**

(A) The new projector is not working properly.
(B) They cannot attend the workshop on Wednesday.
(C) An order cannot be delivered in time.
(D) Mr. Wood needs a ride to Main Street.

談話的人討論到什麼問題？

(A) 新的投影機運作失常。
(B) 他們不能出席週三的研討會。
(C) 有筆訂購商品不能及時送到。
(D) 伍德先生到主街需要搭便車。

3 點 29 分時哈特女士說：「Delta Office Supplies called. They won't be able to deliver the projector on Wednesday.」，表示訂購的投影機無法準時送達，後文便針對此事討論解決辦法，故正確答案為 (C)。

**150** (NEW)

**At 3:31 P.M., what does Mr. Wood mean when he writes, "It can't be"?**

(A) He can't find another supplier.
(B) He can't fix the projector.
(C) He can't agree to Ms. Hart's opinion.
(D) He can't accept the failure.

下午**3:31** 時，伍德先生寫道：「這不行啊」，他的意思是？

(A) 他找不到其他供應商。
(B) 他修不好投影機。
(C) 他不同意哈特女士的意見。
(D) 他無法接受貨品未寄達。

3 點 29 分時，哈特女士先告知了投影機無法在週三前送達的消息，所以此時伍德先生回覆的「It can't be」最可能是表示他無法接受此事，且從後句的「We need that projector for the training session.」也可知道他需要使用投影機才能進行課程，故本題最合適的答案為 (D)。

## 151–152 公告

Dear Residents of Henderson,

From August, Sunset Station Dance Hall will become known as the Rainbow Paradise Nightclub. There is a major refurbishment taking place, which will include a new dining area as well as an extension to the dance floor to make it larger. The new owner, Larry Stone, will still maintain the same high quality of food and entertainment that you have been used to in the past. We look forward to seeing you again.

親愛的韓德森居民：

暮站舞廳從八月起將改名為彩虹天堂夜店。目前正在大翻修，將增建新的用餐區並擴大舞池。新店家賴瑞・史東將維持大家過往所熟悉的高水準餐點和娛樂活動。期望很快與您再相見。

詞彙 extension 擴大

 **151**

**According to the announcement, what is being changed about the establishment?**

(A) Its name
(B) Its location
(C) The menu
(D) The prices

根據公告，工程將帶來什麼改變？

(A) 店名
(B) 地點
(C) 菜單
(D) 價格

從開頭第一句的「From August, Sunset Station Dance Hall will become known as the Rainbow Paradise Nightclub.」即可知道，8 月起暮站舞廳將改名，故正確答案為 (A)。

 **152**

**What is suggested about Mr. Stone?**

(A) He plans to change the menu.
(B) He owns other properties in the area.
(C) He used to work in a nightclub.
(D) He plans to extend a dance area.

文中提到史東先生什麼事？

(A) 他計劃換菜單。
(B) 他在當地有其他房產。
(C) 他過去曾在夜店工作。
(D) 他計劃擴大舞池。

中間部分提到：「There is a major refurbishment taking place, which will include . . . an extension to the dance floor to make it larger」、「The new owner, Larry Stone」，因此可知道史東先生是舞廳老闆，且舞池將會在他的改建下變得更寬敞，正確答案為 (D)。

## 153–154 文章

<table>
<tr><td>

### London Economist
### Business News

September 12, London — Ethan Fletcher, Chief Executive Officer at Filton Heating Components, has announced that the company will be expanding within the country over the next six months. He plans to open stores in Glasgow, Leeds, and London. —[1]—.

Mr. Fletcher admitted that the planned expansion is behind schedule due to complications in the manufacturing plant. He said that the recession "had taken everyone by surprise." Following the installation of new advanced machinery in its production headquarters in Bristol, Mr. Fletcher is confident that the company's expansion will merit the investment. —[2]—.

Filton Heating Components was established by the current CEO's father, who began by recycling metal to make the boiler parts. —[3]—. And it has led to a massive rise in market share for the company over the years.

Next year, the company is hoping to expand into the air conditioning market, and the industry will be closely monitoring its performance. The move will be supplemented by an aggressive advertising and marketing campaign. —[4]—.

</td><td>

### 倫敦經濟家
### 商業新聞

9月12日，倫敦—「費爾頓加熱零件」執行長伊森·佛萊契宣布，公司未來六個月將在全國展店。新店計劃開在格拉斯哥、里茲和倫敦。

佛萊契先生坦承，擴張計畫因為工廠的複雜問題而落後。他說經濟衰退「嚇了大家一跳」。隨著其布里斯托的製造總部安裝了更先進的機具，佛萊契先生有信心，展店有利於投資。

「費爾頓加熱零件」由現任執行長的父親所創立，始於他開始回收製作鍋爐的金屬零件。這種回收行動使得市面上的製造零件變得便宜很多。所以公司的市場占有率也在幾年間大幅提升。

公司希望可以在明年把業務擴展到空調市場，業界也會密切注意其表現。這項商業行動將搭配積極的廣告行銷活動。

</td></tr>
</table>

**詞彙** **behind schedule** 進度落後　**recession** 經濟衰退　**take sb by surprise** 嚇某人一跳　**merit** 有利於　**market share** 市場占有率　**supplement** 增加

**153**

**What is suggested about Filton Heating Components?**

(A) It has lost significant market share over the years.
(B) Its founder passed the business to his son.
(C) It will expand into the commercial sector.
(D) It closed down its manufacturing plant.

文中提到費爾頓加熱零件什麼事？

(A) 市占率在幾年間大幅衰退。
(B) 創辦人把生意傳給他兒子。
(C) 業務將擴展到商業領域。
(D) 製造工廠關閉。

從「Filton Heating Components was established by the current CEO's father, who began by recycling metal to make the boiler parts.」可以知道，公司是由現任執行長的父親所創立，並以回收金屬製作鍋爐零件起家，所以最相符的描述為選項 (B)。

★建議記住下列與景氣衰退相關的字詞：

fluctuation（波動）
stagnation（停滯）
recession（衰退）
depression（大衰退，如 1929 年發生的 The Great Depression〔經濟大恐慌〕）

 **154** NEW ------------------------------------------------

**In which of the positions marked [1], [2], [3], and [4] does the following sentence best belong?**

下列句子最適合出現在[1]、[2]、[3]、[4]的哪個位置中？

**"This recycling initiative led to cheaper components exclusively for the industrial market."**

「這種回收行動使得市面上的製造零件變得便宜很多。」

(A) [1]
(B) [2]
(C) [3]
(D) [4]

(A) [1]
(B) [2]
(C) [3]
(D) [4]

此句的主詞為「This recycling initiative」，其中使用代名詞「This」，表示前文應有與回收相關的內容。文章中，recycle 出現在第三段：「the current CEO's father, who began by recycling metal to make the boiler parts.」，表示創業初期回收金屬製作零件，故將句子接在後方，可進一步解釋這項回收計畫讓公司得以生產價格低廉的零件，故句子最適合填入 [3]，正確答案為 (C)。

**155-157 手冊**

## Journey in Style through the Highlands with Express Trains

## 特快車遊高地的時尚旅程

Experience the sights and sounds of a coastal journey along the Highlands route on a three-hour train journey with Express Trains. The 200-kilometer coastal trail encompasses three counties, with beautiful scenery and lush vegetation. Our trip will take you through the high terrain with the option of a tour guide to explain the area. Lunch will be aboard the train passing through the industrial district of the Highlands. Then the journey ends with a visit to a hidden beach where you can see seals and dolphins at play off the coast.

沿著高地海岸三小時的特快車行程，體驗視覺聽覺的饗宴。兩百公里的海線軌道穿越三郡，沿途風景宜人，綠意盎然。本行程帶您穿越高地，自由選擇是否要導遊隨行。穿過高地工業區時是車上的午餐時間。旅途的終點造訪密境海灘，沿岸可以看到玩耍的海豹和海豚。

The train leaves the station at 11:30 A.M. from Manchester Station and returns at 2:30 P.M., Mondays to Fridays. Tickets are £40 for adults, £25 for students with valid ID cards, and £20 for children under the age of 12.

火車在週一到週五上午11:30從曼徹斯特站出發，下午2:30回來。成人票價40英鎊，學生票持有效證件為25英鎊，12歲以下兒童20英鎊。

**詞彙** **coastal trail** 海線軌道　**encompass** 包含　**lush** 綠意盎然的　**vegetation** 植被　**district** 街區
**at play** 在玩耍

**155**

---

**For whom is the brochure most likely intended?**　這手冊想要告知的對象是誰？

(A) Tour guides
(B) Historians
(C) Train drivers
(D) Tourists

(A) 導遊
(B) 歷史學家
(C) 火車駕駛
(D) 旅客

從文章標題的「Journey in Style through the Highlands with Express Trains」、開頭部分的
「Experience the sights and sounds of a coastal journey」以及最後提供的票價資訊與聯絡方
式，可知道這篇文章應是為旅客、觀光客所寫，故正確答案為 (D)。

**156**

---

**The word "hidden" in line 6, is closest in meaning to**　第六行的「**hidden**」最接近下列哪個意思？

(A) restricted
(B) obscure
(C) notorious
(D) crowded

(A) 禁止的
(B) 隱匿的
(C) 惡名昭彰的
(D) 擁擠的

該句提到：「a visit to a hidden beach where you can see seals and dolphins at play off the
coast」，推測能夠看見海豹與海豚玩耍的海灘，應該是相當隱密的，故正確答案為 (B)。

**157**

---

**How much is the fee for a ten-year-old?**　10 歲遊客的車費是多少錢？

(A) £12
(B) £20
(C) £25
(D) £40

(A) 12 英磅
(B) 20 英磅
(C) 25 英磅
(D) 40 英磅

文章第二段說明，12 歲以下兒童的車票是 20 英鎊，故本題正確答案為 (B)。

## 158–160 廣告

### Melrose Business College

If you are seeking an International Master's Degree in business, then contact the Melrose Business College for details of courses.

The college offers a two-year program, beginning in September, and has a range of courses in international relations and business studies. The courses are taught by reputable faculty members, all of whom have significant hands-on experience in international businesses and trade industries. Together with an innovative exchange program with major companies overseas, this has placed the college in the top three educational establishments in the International Business College rankings.

The application fee is $150 for domestic students and $250 for applicants from abroad. If you quote this advertisement, the price will be halved, as long as you submit the application by the end of June. The application deadline for the upcoming course is July 15. There are also a number of grants and scholarships available. For more information and an application form, visit our website at www.melrosebusiness.edu.

### 梅爾羅斯商學院

如果您正在尋找國際商學碩士學位，請聯繫梅爾羅斯商學院了解課程細節。

本學院提供兩年制的課程，課程包括各類國際關係和商學研究，將於九月開學。課程由享譽盛名的教授授課，他們在國際商貿產業有豐富的實務經驗。本院同時也有和海外大公司合作的創新交流計畫，讓本學院在國際商學院評鑑名列前三。

國內學生的申請費為150美元，國際學生則為250美元。如果您出示這則廣告並於6月底前申請入學，申請費將減免一半。新課程的申請截止日期為7月15日。也有多種獎助學金可供申請。如欲了解更多資訊並取得入學申請表，請上官網www.melrosebusiness.edu。

**詞彙** reputable 享譽盛名的　grant 補助金

**158**

---

**What is suggested about the International Master's Degree course?**

(A) It recently added new faculty members.
(B) It has three enrollment periods.
(C) It has a renowned reputation.
(D) It takes one year to complete.

文中提到國際碩士學位課程什麼事？

(A) 最近來了新進教職員。
(B) 有三個註冊時間。
(C) 享譽盛名。
(D) 一年可以修完。

從第二段最後一句的「the college in the top three educational establishments in the International Business College rankings」，可看出商學院國際排名前三，故最符合的選項為 (C)。

文章中並未提到有新的教授，只說到教授享有盛名，故 (A) 不能選；另外，文中只提到在 6 月底前申請入學能夠獲得優惠，且申請於 7 月 15 日截止，所以 (B) 也不能選；再從第二段開頭：「The college offers a two-year program」可知，課程為兩年制，故 (D) 也不正確。

## 159

**According to the advertisement, what is NOT available to students?**

(A) An opportunity to work abroad
(B) Access to lecturers with international expertise
(C) The possibility of getting financial assistance
(D) The ability to take courses over the Internet

根據廣告，學生不能得到什麼機會？

(A) 到海外工作
(B) 修到關於國際專業的課程
(C) 取得財務資助的機會
(D) 能夠線上上課

本題要注意題目問的是不能得到的東西。第一句的「The college . . . has a range of courses in international relations」即表示提供國際專業課程，故 (B) 不可選。第三句中的「an innovative exchange program with major companies overseas」則是代表學院與海外公司合作，有提供交流課程，故 (A) 也不可選。另外，第三段說到「There are also a number of grants and scholarships available.」，表示提供獎助學金，故 (C) 也不可選。

綜合上述，文中並未提及的只有網路課程，故本題正確答案為 (D)。

## 160

**What is indicated about the application fee?**

(A) It is different for national and international applicants.
(B) It will increase next year.
(C) It must be paid by June 30.
(D) It can be paid online or via credit card.

文中提到申請費什麼事？

(A) 本國人和國際人士申請費用有別。
(B) 明年會漲。
(C) 6 月 30 日前要付款。
(D) 可以線上或信用卡繳款。

根據最後一段：「The application fee is $150 for domestic students and $250 for applicants from abroad.」，可知本國籍學生的申請費用比外籍學生便宜 100 美元，故正確答案為 (A)。

**161–163 備忘錄**

## Memo
## Irvine Hotel

In an effort to try to reduce expenses, the management of the Irvine Hotel will no longer be supplying free toiletries. Guests must specifically ask for them to be supplied, and there is an additional charge. This is part of our cost-cutting initiative. Please make sure that you inform guests of this change when they check in. However, guests can purchase essential toiletries at a reasonable cost from our shop in the foyer. Guests can pre-order well-selected toiletries to await them when they arrive and the cost of these items will be added to the final bill. Please ensure that this message is clearly stated to any person who books over the telephone. We will post notices of this change in every hotel room and also in the lobby so that the message is clear.

## 備忘錄
## 爾灣飯店

為了減少開支，爾灣飯店管理部門將不再免費提供盥洗用品。房客必須特別要求並額外付費，始能提供盥洗用品。這是我們減少成本計畫的一部分。請您於房客登記入住時確實告知這項改變。不過，房客可以在大廳的商店裡，用合理價格買到必要的盥洗用品。房客也能預購嚴選盥洗商品並於抵達時取用，費用將結算在帳單上。請確實、清楚地告知每一位電話訂房的客人。我們也會在飯店全部的房間和大廳張貼異動通知，明確傳達此訊息。

**詞彙** toiletry 盥洗用品　cost-cutting 減少成本的　initiative 計畫　foyer 門廳

## 161

**For whom is the memo most likely intended?**

(A) Hotel guests
(B) Maintenance staff
(C) Housekeeping staff
(D) Hotel receptionists

這則備忘錄想要告知的對象是誰？

(A) 飯店房客
(B) 維修人員
(C) 打掃人員
(D) 飯店接待人員

本題為詢問公告對象的題型。從右上角的「Irvine Hotel」可以看出這是一則來自飯店的公告，且開頭提到，為了節省開支，飯店不再免費供應盥洗用品。解題關鍵在於接下來的「Please make sure that you inform guests of this change when they check in.」，表示要閱讀備忘錄的人，在客人登記入住時告知這項異動。最可能告知客人飯店資訊的為接待人員，故本題正確答案為 (D)。

## 162

**According to the memo, why has a new policy been adopted?**

(A) To save the cost of disposable items
(B) To improve training for employees
(C) To use less energy and water
(D) To reduce requests for extra maintenance

根據備忘錄，為什麼要採取新規定？

(A) 節省一次性耗材成本
(B) 改進員工訓練
(C) 節約用水用電
(D) 減少其他的維修需求

備忘錄在開頭便提到：「In an effort to try to reduce expenses」，表示新規定是為了減少開支，且後文也有說到「This is part of our cost-cutting initiative.」，故選項中最相符的為 (A)。

## 163

**What are hotel employees instructed to do?**

(A) Inform guests that toiletries are not complimentary
(B) Charge guests for any water and electricity used
(C) Provide guests with a variety of items at reception
(D) Notify guests of an increase in room rates

飯店員工被指示要做什麼？

(A) 告知房客不附贈盥洗用品
(B) 向房客收使用的水電費
(C) 在接待處提供房客多種商品
(D) 提醒房客房價調漲

全文的重點就在「不免費提供盥洗用品」一事，故在「Please make sure that you inform guests of this change」這段話中，「this change」指的就是「不附贈盥洗用品」，所以正確答案為 (A)。

373

April 30 — Designer Carla Whittle of the Whittle Design Agency has made a donation of half a million pounds to the Soweto Town Direct Disability project. This is a huge boost for the charity as funding for the project has been reduced since last year. "We are truly delighted with Ms. Whittle's contribution," commented David Campbell, the director of the Direct Disability program. —[1]—.

Direct Disability was established a decade ago by local businesspeople to help disabled people to use public facilities. Although it was originally supposed to receive a grant from the government, funding was cut earlier this year due to pressure by the Treasury to reduce public spending. —[2]—. The project now relies upon donations.

Last month, Direct Disability began a fundraising campaign targeting local businesses. "Together with requests for donations, we sent pictures of some facilities we have established," continued Mr. Campbell. —[3]—. One of the installations was fitting a wheelchair ramp to the local library, which is frequented by Ms. Whittle's family. "I had no idea that Ms. Whittle's family used the library until she rang and asked if she could assist in some way," Mr. Campbell said.

Supporters and businesses are delighted with the donation, with local councilor Tom Brady praising the work done by the charity to raise awareness and funding for other projects. Ms. Whittle released a press statement saying, "I have loved the library since I was a child, and although I have now moved abroad, I still have fond memories of it. —[4]—. It is not just about installing access ramps. It means that more local people are now able to access the facilities."

Amy Wellington, Local Contributor

4月30日—惠特爾設計工作室的設計師卡拉·惠特爾最近捐款50萬英鎊,給索維托鎮「直接身障補助計畫」。該慈善活動的捐款自去年起減少以來,這著實是一大挹注。「惠特爾女士慷慨捐獻,我們真的很高興。」「直接身障補助計畫」主持人大衛·坎培爾說。「這確實有助於我們在社區裡,為身障者增設更多身障設施。」

在地商人十年前創設了「直接身障補助計畫」,以協助身障人士使用公共設施。儘管一開始拿到政府補助,不過今年礙於財政部要減少公共支出的壓力,預算在今年初被砍。該項計畫而今仰賴捐款。

「直接身障補助計畫」上個月開始向當地商家展開募款活動。「除了提出捐款要求,我們也寄送我們建設的設施照片。」坎培爾先生繼續說,其中一項設施是通往當地圖書館的無障礙坡道,也是惠特爾女士的家人經常使用的一項設施。「我從不知道惠特爾女士的家人會使用圖書館,直到她打電話給我,詢問能否提供任何協助。」坎培爾先生說。

支持者和企業對於這項捐款均感欣慰,地方議員湯姆·布萊迪也稱讚說,慈善機構的作法連帶提高其他計畫的知名度和募得款項。惠特爾女士在新聞稿發表聲明:「我從小就很愛這座圖書館,即便現在我搬到國外,還是有很多美好的回憶。這不只是裝設無障礙坡道,這意味著如今有更多當地人可以使用設施。」

艾美·威靈頓
在地撰稿人

---

**詞彙** **disabled** 肢體障礙的　**the Treasury** 財政部　**fundraising campaign** 募款活動
**wheelchair/access ramp** 無障礙坡道　**raise awareness** 提高關注　**fond** 美好的

**164**

---

**When was the Direct Disability project started?**

(A) Two years ago
(B) Three years ago
(C) Five years ago
(D) Ten years ago

直接身障補助計畫從何時開始？

(A) 兩年前
(B) 三年前
(C) 五年前
(D) 十年前

第二段開頭提到：「Direct Disability was established a decade ago by local businesspeople」，表示計畫是由該地的企業家在十年前創立，故正確答案為 (D)。

**165**

---

**According to the article, why has the project lost funding?**

(A) Local businesses refused to help.
(B) Building material costs increased.
(C) The local population had declined.
(D) The government reduced its financial support.

根據文章，這項計畫為什麼失去資金？

(A) 當地商家拒絕協助。
(B) 建築材料的成本增加了。
(C) 當地人口減少。
(D) 政府減少資助。

第二段說了「it was originally supposed to receive a grant from the government」，表示計畫本應獲得政府補助，但是「funding was cut earlier this year . . . to reduce public spending」，故可知政府為了減少公共支出而砍去補助，正確答案為 (D)。

**166**

---

**Who is currently NOT a resident of Soweto Town?**

(A) Carla Whittle
(B) David Campbell
(C) Tom Brady
(D) Amy Wellington

誰現在不是索維托鎮的居民？

(A) 卡拉‧惠特爾
(B) 大衛‧坎培爾
(C) 湯姆‧布萊迪
(D) 艾美‧威靈頓

本報導以索維托鎮為背景，故有提及「local」（在地的）皆為此地的居民。

(A) 從「Designer Carla Whittle of the Whittle Design Agency」可知她為惠特爾設計工作室公司的設計師，且在最後一段她說到：「although I have now moved abroad」，可看出她已經移居海外，故現已不是索維托鎮的居民，本題正確答案為 (A)。

(B) 從「David Campbell, the director of the Direct Disability program」可知他是計畫主持人，而計畫是十年前由在地商人創設，故他是索維托鎮的居民；(C) 從「local councilor Tom Brady」可知他是地方議員；(D) 從署名的「Amy Wellington, Local Contributor」可知她為當地撰稿人。

**In which of the positions marked [1], [2], [3], and [4] does the following sentence best belong?**

**"It will certainly help us to install more facilities for disabled people in the community."**

(A) [1]
(B) [2]
(C) [3]
(D) [4]

下列句子最適合出現在[1]、[2]、[3]、[4] 的哪個位置中？

「這確實有助於我們在社區裡，為身障者增設更多身障設施。」

(A) [1]
(B) [2]
(C) [3]
(D) [4]

題目引述的句子中使用了代名詞「It」，可判斷在句子之前有提及過相似的內容，故此處不再贅述僅以代名詞表示。而根據句意，此處說的是「It . . . help us install more facilities」，故所謂的「It」是能夠幫助計畫的事情。

從段落大意來看，第一段描述計畫收到贊助款項，第二段解釋資金來源，第三段說明捐款經過，第四段則是當事人自述捐款原因，故句子放於第一段最為合適。且 [1] 的前句提到：「We are truly delighted with Ms. Whittle's contribution」，若句子填入此處，則可知道前句的「contribution」就是此句說的「It」，故本題正確答案為 (A)。

## 168–171 電子郵件

**To:** Chad Rogers <chadrogers@gomail.com>
**From:** Carrie Slater <carrieslater@widemail.com>
**Date:** September 5
**Subject:** Cost Summary
**Attachment:** estimate_ChadRogers.xls

收件人：查德·羅傑斯 <chadrogers@gomail.com>
寄件人：凱莉·史萊特 <carrieslater@widemail.com>
日期：9月5日
主旨：成本彙總表
附件：估價單_查德羅傑斯.xls

Dear Mr. Rogers,

I enjoyed meeting with you last week and hearing your ideas for the expansion of your automatic car wash business. As I mentioned, my financial team has been preparing a financial estimate, which is attached to this e-mail.

You said you plan to open business on the site opposite from the Baxter Building to allow a drive-through car wash service. The team has figured the cost of this into the estimate, including an estimate for the renovations and rental that will be required prior to any agreement. I would still recommend the vacant site next to the Prime Building behind Anton Elementary School as a more viable option. As it has already been renovated, this will reduce your costs.

親愛的羅傑斯先生：

很高興上週和您見面，並聽您分享您擴展自動洗車事業的想法。如我所言我的財務團隊已經準備好估價，請參考本電子郵件附件。

您說您計劃要在百特大樓對面設置自動洗車通道。團隊已把成本列入估價，其中包括簽訂任何合約前的整修和承租費用。我仍然建議安東小學後面、一流大樓旁的一塊空地是更佳選擇。因為它已經經過整修，可以降低您的成本。

| | |
|---|---|
| If you want us to carry out the work, we can begin immediately. Please do not hesitate to contact me with any queries. I look forward to hearing from you soon.<br><br>Sincerely,<br><br>Carrie Slater | 如果您想要我們執行計畫，我們可以馬上動工。有任何問題都請儘管聯繫我。我期待很快聽到您的看法。<br><br>凱莉·史萊特 敬上 |

**詞彙** drive-through 得來速；不用下車就能接受服務的地方　viable 可行的　carry out 執行
contractor 承包商　breakdown 細目

 **168**

| **Who most likely is Ms. Slater?** | 史萊特女士最可能的職業是？ |
|---|---|
| (A) A car wash company owner | (A) 洗車公司老闆 |
| (B) A building contractor | (B) 建築承包商 |
| (C) A financial consultant | (C) 財務顧問 |
| (D) A landscaping professional | (D) 環境美化專家 |

先觀察收件人與寄件人，可知這是史萊特女士寄給羅傑斯先生的電子郵件，且第一段便提到：
「I enjoyed . . . hearing your ideas for the expansion of your automatic car wash business」
以及「my financial team has been preparing a financial estimate」，表示史萊特女士知道羅傑斯先生想擴展洗車事業，且她的財務團隊已準備好估價，故只剩下 (B) 與 (C) 適合作為答案。

然而，從最後一段的「If you want us to carry out the work, we can begin immediately.」可以推斷，史萊特女士最可能是建設的承包商，正確答案為 (B)。

 **169**

| **According to the e-mail, what was discussed at last week's meeting?** | 根據電子郵件，上週的會議裡談了什麼？ |
|---|---|
| | (A) 新餐廳的設計 |
| (A) Designs for a new restaurant | (B) 車隊擴編 |
| (B) Expansion of a fleet of vehicles | (C) 搬遷店面計畫 |
| (C) Plans for a business relocation | (D) 可能的整修計畫 |
| (D) Potential renovation projects | |

由於羅萊特女士在開頭說到：「I enjoyed meeting with you last week and hearing your ideas for the expansion of your automatic car wash business.」，所以可推測上週兩人討論了洗車場的擴建計畫，故選項中最相符的應該是 (D)。

 **170**

| **What is mentioned as being included in the attachment?** | 關於附件內容，文中提到什麼？ |
|---|---|
| | (A) 詳細藍圖 |
| (A) Detailed blueprints | (B) 價格細目 |
| (B) A breakdown of prices | (C) 整修材料的收據 |
| (C) Receipts for renovation materials | (D) 工作進度表 |
| (D) Work schedules | |

第一段提到：「my financial team has been preparing a financial estimate, which is attached to this e-mail」，表示附件裡有估價單，而估價單的細項可從第二段的「The team has figured the cost of this into the estimate, including an estimate for the renovations and rental」，知道裡頭包含建設自動洗車通道的成本、整修與承租費用，故正確答案為 (B)。

**171**

---

The word "figured" in paragraph 2, line 2, is closest in meaning to

(A) exceeded
(B) discounted
(C) incorporated
(D) transformed

第二段、第二行的「figured」，最接近下列哪些意思？

(A) 已超過
(B) 已折扣
(C) 已併入
(D) 已轉變

動詞 figure 後面用金額作為受詞時，其字義為「計算……」，因此該句應是表示財務團隊已經將整修與承租費用「算入」估價單中。選項中最相近的字為 incorporated，故本題正確答案為 (C)。

## 172–175 網路討論區

| | |
|---|---|
| **Kayla Maxwell**　　10:01 A.M.<br>Hello, everyone. I would like to check on the progress of the product development. You are inviting some participants to test the new soap today. Is that correct? | 凱伊拉·馬克士威〔上午10:01〕：<br>哈囉，大家。我想確認產品研發的進度。你們正在邀請新肥皂的試用者，對嗎？ |
| **Jordan Moss**　　10:02 A.M.<br>But we haven't managed to get enough volunteers yet. Twelve people so far have come forward but we need eight more. | 喬丹·摩斯〔上午10:02〕：<br>不過我們找到的志願者還不夠。目前有12個人會來，但還需要8個人。 |
| **Erin Parker**　　10:02 A.M.<br>Then we have no option but to postpone the testing for a few days. | 艾琳·帕克〔上午10:02〕：<br>那我們只好將測試延後幾天。 |
| **Kayla Maxwell**　　10:03 A.M.<br>Can't we just do it with twelve subjects? | 凱伊拉·馬克士威〔上午10:03〕：<br>12人難道不能將就用嗎？ |
| **Erin Parker**　　10:03 A.M.<br>We'd better not. Currently we have only two subjects between the ages of 41 and 50. This can distort the results of the findings. | 艾琳·帕克〔上午10:03〕：<br>最好不要。我們現在只有兩組介於41歲和50歲間的族群。這會扭曲測試結果。 |
| **Kayla Maxwell**　　10:04 A.M.<br>There's nothing that we can do if it doesn't work. Can you ensure that the testing is carried out as soon as possible, with the results sent directly to me? I will need some sort of written report by the end of next week. | 凱伊拉·馬克士威〔上午10:04〕：<br>我們如果弄不起來就沒輒了。你可以確保測試儘快完成，並將測試結果直接寄給我嗎？我需要在下週末前拿到書面報告。 |

| | |
|---|---|
| **Jordan Moss** 10:05 A.M.<br>Yes, it was my general plan. I can assure you that you will receive a report by next Friday. | 喬丹・摩斯〔上午10:05〕：<br>是啊，我的大致計畫是這樣。我可以保證讓你在下週五前收到報告。 |

**詞彙** manage to 設法辦到　distort 扭曲（事實）　drive 計畫活動　product trail 產品測試

**172** ----------------------------------------

**What are the speakers mainly discussing?**　　對話者主要是在談什麼？

(A) A recruitment drive　　　　　　　　(A) 人才招募活動
(B) A marketing report　　　　　　　　(B) 行銷報告
(C) An advertising campaign　　　　　(C) 廣告活動
(D) A product trial　　　　　　　　　(D) 產品測試

開頭馬克士威女士便問道：「I would like to check on the progress of the product development.」，表示想知道產品開發的進度，隨後也問：「You are inviting some participants to test the new soap today. Is that correct?」，確認對方今日是否招募志願者試用新肥皂，後文也持續環繞在產品測試的主題上，故可知正確答案為 (D)。

**173** ----------------------------------------

**What does Ms. Parker tell Ms. Maxwell?**　　帕克女士對馬克士威女士說了什麼？

(A) The test has to be delayed.　　　　(A) 測試必須延期。
(B) She'll send a report by the end of the week.　(B) 她會在週五前寄出報告。
(C) They have to move up the test date.　(C) 他們得提前測試。
(D) She'll proceed with the test with 12 people.　(D) 她會進行 12 人的測試。

帕克女士在 10 點 2 分時說：「Then we have no option but to postpone the testing for a few days.」，代表她認為測試必須延期，且即使馬克士威女士想妥協只使用 12 名測試人員，她仍說：「We'd better not.」，表示最好不要這麼做，所以正確答案為 (A)。

**174** (NEW) ----------------------------------------

**At 10:04 A.M., why does Ms. Maxwell write, "There's nothing that we can do if it doesn't work"?**　上午10:04 時，為什麼馬克士威女士寫道：「我們如果弄不起來就沒轍了」？

(A) She doesn't want to volunteer for the test.　(A) 她不想自願參與測試。
(B) She understands why the test has to be postponed.　(B) 她了解測試要延期的原因。
(C) She can help them gather more participants.　(C) 她可以幫忙召集更多受測者。
(D) She will work on the research herself.　(D) 她將自行研究。

前文中馬克士威女士先問：「Can't we just do it with twelve subjects?」，表示想在只有 12 名試用者的情況下測試，但帕克女士解釋道：「Currently we have only two subjects between the ages of 41 and 50. This can distort the results of the findings.」，代表 40 歲到 50 歲的試用者過少，試用結果將會失真。

故此時馬克士威女士說的「There's nothing that we can do if it doesn't work.」最可能代表已經「無能為力」，必須將測試延期以招募更多試用者，故正確答案為 (B)。

**What does Mr. Moss say that he will do?**

(A) Convince Ms. Parker to reschedule the test
(B) Send the report to Ms. Maxwell by next Friday
(C) Check the release date of the new soap range
(D) Advertise for more people in a newspaper

摩斯先生說他會做什麼？

(A) 說服帕克女士重新安排測試時間
(B) 在下週五前寄報告給馬克士威女士
(C) 確認新肥皂系列的上市日期
(D) 在報紙上刊廣告找更多人

摩斯先生最後説的「I can assure you that you will receive a report by next Friday.」，代表他保證會在下週五前將報告寄給馬克士威女士，故正確答案為 (B)。

## 176–180 電子郵件

**To:** Philippe D'Anjou
<pdanjou@shellie.com>
**From:** Cassie Swift
<cswift@shellie.com>
**Date:** August 23
**Subject:** Shellie's products

Philippe,

I wish to draw your attention to negative feedback posted on a number of websites across Asia and Australia in particular about our Shellie range of windbreakers. You should pay particular attention to www.uniquesales.com and www.ratedornot.au. It seems that there are numerous complaints about the quality of the material used for the items. Shellie is going to be featured strongly in our new advertising campaign, so it is imperative that we find out more about the problem. Could you ask your department to look into this matter? At the same time, could your department undertake some further research into the Shellie range to find out if customers have any other concerns? Please make this a priority and report back to me with your findings by the end of next week.

Many thanks for your cooperation,

Cassie

收件人：菲利普・丹朱
<pdanjou@shellie.com>
寄件人：凱西・絲薇芙特
<cswift@shellie.com>
日期：8月23日
主旨：雪莉系列產品

菲利普：

我想請你注意一下，亞洲和澳洲的幾個網站上針對雪莉系列風衣的負評。需要特別留意的是www.uniquesales.com和www.ratedornot.au。看起來有很多針對商品材料品質的抱怨。雪莉是我們新的廣告活動打算力推的特色商品，所以有必要找出更多有關問題。你可以請你的部門了解這個狀況嗎？同時，可否請你的部門進一步研究，消費者對於雪莉系列有沒有其他疑慮？請把這視為首要任務，並在下週結束以前回報我的發現。

感謝你的配合。

凱西

**To:** Cassie Swift
<cswift@shellie.com>
**From:** Philippe D'Anjou
<pdanjou@shellie.com>
**Date:** August 30
**Subject:** Re: Shellie's products

Cassie,

We have investigated the issues that you mentioned in your e-mail dated August 23. We have discovered that there is indeed a global concern about the quality of the material used in the Shellie range. In particular, it seems to be restricted to the all-in-one item, Shellie XK1. Customers are complaining that the material is too thin and prone to ripping. I would ask your manufacturing department to find a solution to this problem.

Additionally, we have found some dissatisfaction with the Shellie YL bra sets. Customers are uncomfortable about the lack of color choice. The website lists any color other than white as out of stock. I will  e-mail you with more details by Friday.

The good news is that the level of satisfaction with both the sizing options and the price are very high. Once we sort out the issues raised by our customers, we will be just fine.

Philippe

---

收件人：凱西‧絲薇芙特
<cswift@shellie.com>
寄件人：菲利普‧丹朱
<pdanjou@shellie.com>
日期：8月30日
主旨：關於：雪莉的產品

凱西：

我們調查了妳在8月23日郵件中提到的問題。我們確實發現，雪莉系列的材質品質引起全球的疑慮，特別是雪莉XK1多合一那一款。顧客抱怨材質太薄而且容易裂。我會要求妳的生產部門找到解決方法。

此外，我們發現顧客對雪莉YL胸罩組也有不滿，就是該產品顏色選擇不多，除了白色，其他在官網上都顯示缺貨。我週五前會再發封電子郵件解釋詳情。

好消息是，關於尺寸選擇和價格的滿意度都很高。只要我們處理好顧客提出的意見，應該就沒問題了。

菲利普

---

**詞彙** draw one's attention to sth 請某人注意某事　windbreak 風衣　imperative 迫切重要的
look into 調查　undertake 從事　priority 首要任務　all-in-one 多合一　be prone to 容易
rip 撕裂

**176**
----

**Why does Ms. Swift write to Mr. D'Anjou?**

(A) To promote two new websites
(B) To complain about the quality of an item
(C) To propose a new advertising campaign
(D) To ask him to research a problem

為什麼絲薇芙特女士寫信給丹朱先生？

(A) 宣傳兩個新網頁
(B) 抱怨產品品質
(C) 提出新的廣告行動
(D) 請他研究問題

在第一封郵件中，絲薇芙特女士在第三句寫道：「It seems that there are numerous complaints about the quality of the material used for the items.」，代表她注意到有許多關於材質的負評，接著詢問丹朱先生：「Could you ask your department to look into this matter?」，請他的部門對這個問題進行調查，故可知這就是絲薇芙特女士寄送郵件的目的，正確答案為 (D)。

## 177

**In what field does Ms. Swift work?**

(A) Manufacturing
(B) Advertising
(C) Customer relations
(D) Product development

絲薇芙特女士在哪個領域工作？

(A) 製造
(B) 廣告
(C) 顧客關係
(D) 產品開發

丹朱先生在回信第一段最後提到：「I would ask your manufacturing department to find a solution to this problem.」，從其中的「your manufacturing department」便可看出絲薇芙特女士隸屬製造部門，故正確答案為 (A)。

**What is NOT stated about Shellie?**

(A) Its products are mainly reviewed on two websites.
(B) Its headquarters are in Asia.
(C) It produces women's clothing.
(D) It has a research-related department.

關於雪莉系列產品，文中沒有提及什麼？

(A) 主要在兩個網站上討論到它的產品。
(B) 總部在亞洲。
(C) 生產女性衣物。
(D) 有研究相關部門

從第一封郵件中開頭的「negative feedback posted on a number of websites」、「You should pay particular attention to www.uniquesales.com and www.ratedornot.au.」，便可知道主要有兩個網站在討論他們的產品，故 (A) 有被提及。再從第一封郵件提到的「windbreakers」與第二封第二段提到的「bra sets」，可知公司的確生產女性衣物，故 (C) 也有出現在文中。最後回到第一封郵件，其中提到「could your department undertake some further research into the Shellie range」，故可知道 (D)。

綜合上述，唯一無法在文中找到相關內容的為 (B)，故本題答案為 (B)。

## 179

**What does Mr. D'Anjou note about Shellie XK1?**

(A) The material is of an inferior quality.
(B) The color choices are not as many as customers want.
(C) The price is too high for the customers.
(D) The item is no longer in fashion.

丹朱先生提及雪莉XK1 什麼事？

(A) 材料品質低落。
(B) 可供選擇的顏色不如顧客期望。
(C) 價格對顧客來說太高。
(D) 商品不再時尚。

尋找本題的關鍵字「Shellie XK1」，可在第二封郵件第一段看到。其中丹朱先生說：「there is indeed a global concern about the quality of the material used in the Shellie range」、「In particular, it seems to be restricted to the all-in-one item, Shellie XK1.」，故可知道雪莉系列的確有材質問題，尤其雪莉 XK1 特別明顯，故正確答案為 (A)。

**180** NEW

In the second e-mail, the word "restricted" in paragraph 1, line 3, is closest in meaning to

(A) reduced
(B) exceptional
(C) limited
(D) confidential

在第二封電子郵件中，第一段、第三行的「restricted」，最接近下列哪個意思？

(A) 減少的
(B) 傑出的
(C) 限制的
(D) 機密的

前句提到的確發現雪莉系列有材質問題，並説：「In particular, it seems to be restricted to the all-in-one item, Shellie XK1」，其中的「In particular」表示「特別是」，故此處的 be restricted to 意思是「限制在」，就全句的脈絡看來，是表示「問題僅限於雪莉 XK1 上」，所以本題最適合的答案為 (C)。

---

### 181–185 文章和顧客意見

| | |
|---|---|
| **Excellence in Technology**<br>**Amanti Boost**<br><br>by Alice Cryer, New Delhi News | **科技上的卓越**<br>**安馬緹手機**<br><br>《新德里新聞》艾莉絲·克萊爾撰文 |

April 2 — Amanti is renowned for the quality of its mobile technology, and the New Boost mobile phone — due for launch on April 10 — is no exception. It has the capacity to store approximately 3,000 photos and 20 thirty-minute videos at the same time, and in addition, the external memory card provided with it is able to accommodate up to 5,000 tunes.

As an incentive, contract purchasers of the New Boost will receive a free set of state-of-the-art headphones. They were extensively tested by Amanti's research center, and the sound is far superior to the standard earphones supplied with its mobile phones. Moreover, Amanti is offering a new application that will enable users to download music and films faster and cheaper than before.

The New Boost is all new to us. It has a brighter screen as well as a much longer battery life. The New Boost is expected to supersede the company's previous flagship mobile phones and has a bright future ahead.

4月2日—安馬緹行動科技以品質聞名，即將在4月10日亮相的New Boost新手機也沒有例外。它擁有大容量可以同時存放近3,000張照片和20支半小時的影片，此外，附贈的外插式記憶卡也能儲存高達5,000首歌曲。

作為促銷，簽約購買New Boost將隨機附贈最先進的頭戴式耳機。經過安馬緹研究中心大量測試，音質遠遠超過原機標準配備的耳機。不只這樣，安馬緹也提供一個新的應用程式，讓用戶以比先前更快、更划算的價格下載音樂和電影。

New Boost是一場全新的體驗。螢幕更亮，電池更耐久。New Boost預計將取代先前的旗艦機種，展望光明的未來。

| Feedback | Products | Services | Purchase |
|---|---|---|---|

**User Feedback:** Amanti Boost Mobile Phone
**User:** Ranjit Khan, Mumbai
**Posted:** 7:12 P.M. May 23

User rating: ★★★★☆

I really like the New Boost, and I have no regrets about waiting in line to purchase it on the day it was launched. I particularly like the headphones that came free with the phone. I also highly recommend the new application that enables you to download music and films for only 100 rupees a month. At the moment, there aren't many options, though I understand from the company that they will resume adding more contents from May 30.

My only real complaint is the new screen. Although it is brighter and bigger than Amanti's previous models, watching movies is a problem as there is a significant glare.

| 回饋 | 產品 | 服務 | 購買 |
|---|---|---|---|

使用者回饋：安馬緹手機
使用者：朗吉特·汗，孟買
張貼時間：晚上7:12，5月23日

用戶評價：四顆星

我真的很喜歡New Boost，一點都不後悔在上市那天開始排隊搶購。我特別喜歡隨機附贈的頭戴式耳機。我也非常推薦新的應用程式，每個月只要花100盧比，就可以下載音樂和電影。現在上面有的選擇還不多，我從公司得知他們將會從5月30日起加入更多內容。

我唯一想抱怨的是新螢幕。雖然是比以前亮也比較大，但反光很嚴重，看電影時是個問題。

**詞彙** **sth be no exception** 某事不在例外中　**tune** 歌曲　**incentive** 激勵措施　**supersede** 取代　**flagship** 旗艦商品（表示最主打、最重要的商品）　**have a bright future** 前景看好　**have no regrets** 不後悔　**rupee** 盧比（印度、印尼、巴基斯坦等地的貨幣）　**resume** 重新開始；繼續　**glare** 反光

**181**

**What is the purpose of the article?**

(A) To announce a company's brand name has been changed
(B) To preview a new mobile device
(C) To explain how to download media onto a memory card
(D) To introduce testimonials from customers

這篇文章的目的為何？

(A) 宣布公司的品牌名稱異動
(B) 提前介紹新行動裝置
(C) 解釋如何下載影音到記憶卡
(D) 介紹來自顧客的使用推薦

第一篇報導文章在開頭便提到：「Amanti is renowned for the quality of its mobile technology, and the New Boost mobile phone — due for launch on April 10 — is no exception.」，表示以品質聞名的安馬緹行動科技公司即將推出 New Boost 手機，之後第一段說明手機的容量，第二段介紹促銷贈送的耳機與應用程式，第三段則說到螢幕與電池，故可知道本文的撰寫目的是介紹新產品，正確答案為 (B)。

**182**

---

**What is NOT mentioned about the New Boost?**

(A) Its larger screen
(B) Its accessories
(C) Its storage capacity
(D) Its carrying case

**關於 New Boost，文中沒有提到什麼？**

(A) 更大的螢幕
(B) 配件
(C) 容量
(D) 手機殼

從顧客意見最後一段的「the new screen」、「bigger than Amanti's previous models」可知道新手機的螢幕有變大，故可在文中找到 (A)。且報導文章也有提到「the external memory card」、「standard earphones」，外部記憶卡與耳機皆是手機的配件，故有提到 (B)。再從文章第一段說的「the capacity to store approximately 3,000 photos and 20 thirty-minute videos」可知道手機的容量，所以 (C) 也有被提到。

綜合上述，唯一在文章無法找到的就是手機殼相關的資訊，故本題正確答案 (D)。

**183**

---

**When did Mr. Khan most likely purchase his New Boost?**

(A) On April 2
(B) On April 10
(C) On May 23
(D) On May 30

**汗先生最可能在何時購買 New Boost？**

(A) 4 月 2 日
(B) 4 月 10 日
(C) 5 月 23 日
(D) 5 月 30 日

從汗先生在顧客意見表上寫的「I have no regrets about waiting in line to purchase it on the day it was launched.」可知，他是在手機上市當天購買的，而根據第一篇報導文章提及的「due for launch on April 10」，New Boost 是 4 月 10 日上市，故本題正確答案為 (B)。

**184**

---

**What is indicated about the mobile application?**

(A) It is a combined effort between two mobile phone companies.
(B) It is gradually adding more choices to its inventory.
(C) It has been in existence for several years.
(D) It is offered to New Boost purchasers for free.

**文中提到關於手機應用程式什麼事？**

(A) 是兩間手機公司的合作成果。
(B) 慢慢增加清單上的選項。
(C) 已經存在多年。
(D) 免費提供給 New Boost 的買家。

在顧客意見中，汗先生說了：「the new application . . . enables you to download music and films for only 100 rupees a month」、「At the moment, there aren't many options」、「they will resume adding more contents from May 30」，故可知應用程式上只要付 100 盧比便可以下載音樂與電影，雖然現在選擇不多，但公司將從 5 月 30 日起添加內容，所以本題正確答案即為 (B)。

## 185

**What is Mr. Khan's complaint about the screen?**

(A) It is too bright.
(B) It is easily damaged.
(C) It doesn't switch to horizontal mode.
(D) It turns off unexpectedly.

汗先生不滿螢幕的什麼？

(A) 太亮。
(B) 容易毀損。
(C) 不能切換成水平模式。
(D) 無預警自動關機。

汗先生在顧客意見的最後一段提到「My only real complaint is the new screen.」、「Although it is brighter」「watching movies is a problem as there is a significant glare」，表示新螢幕有反光的問題，故本題答案為 (A)。

## 186–190 文章、評論和電子郵件

### FASHION SHOW

Kanta Fashion Show was instrumental in revealing a number of innovations in today's fashion. Since last year, designers have been focusing heavily on natural materials.

"The latest designs from fashion houses are an indication of the new trend. If people had not want the designs, they would not have appeared in the show," commented Ms. Grainger, fashion show organizer.

For some companies, including Essie Sew and Laramar, the show gave them the chance to showcase their portfolio for the first time. Another new company, Pantala, revealed a brand-new concept in outerwear, which earned them the coveted Best in Show award, which has been previously won by Mackowns, who have been exhibiting for nearly five years.

Over 10,000 people attended the show at the Downton Hotel, which is located in the center of the town.

### 時裝秀

勘太時裝秀在當今時尚展現大量創新元素上，有舉足輕重的地位。從去年起，設計師非常重視天然材質。

「時裝店最新的設計款式，是潮流的一項指標。如果人們不想要這些設計，那它們就不會出現在這場時裝秀上。」時裝秀負責人格蘭傑女士說。

某些公司，像是艾西縫紉、拉瑞馬爾，藉著這場秀的機會，初次展露它們的作品集。另一家新公司「蜻蜓」展示了外套的全新概念，為它贏得夢寐以求的時裝秀最佳獎。這個獎項之前是由參展將近五年的麥可孔斯所拿下。

時尚秀在市中心的唐頓飯店舉行，有超過一萬人前來共襄盛舉。

### Fashion Review of Pantala

#### By Suzy Rees

Operating for only twelve months, Pantala produces very well-known designs such as the Oasis Collection. Unlike other start-up companies, the organization is unique in not following the traditional designs of the industry.

Personally, I like the Dress Collection, which is a combination of lace, silk, and hemp — not a common choice but one that certainly attracts attention.
The dresses come with a free pair of gloves and a handkerchief of the Grace Silver brand.

### 蜻蜓時尚回顧

#### 蘇茲·芮意絲撰文

雖然才營運12個月，「蜻蜓」生產了非常知名的設計，像是綠洲系列。和其他新創公司不同，這間公司獨到之處，在於不追隨產業的傳統設計。

我個人較喜歡洋裝系列，結合蕾絲、絲和麻—不是常見的選擇，但肯定引人注目。洋裝搭配免費的手套以及優雅銀的品牌手絹。

Their new collection, Autumn Dream, is the only one that uses leather: up to now, the company has only used soft materials. However, one look at their gorgeous jacket with a leather belt, straps, and silk lining will make you notice its quality.

他們的新系列，秋夢，是唯一用到皮革的系列：到目前為止，這間公司只使用軟性材質。但是只要看一眼他們極好的夾克搭配皮帶、束帶和襯絲，就能注意到它的好品質。

---

**To:** Suzy Rees <Suzyrees@fashiontoday.com>
**From:** Joanne Kay <Joannekay@pantala.com>
**Date:** May 7
**Subject:** Upcoming Event

收件人：蘇茲·芮意絲 <Suzyrees@fashiontoday.com>
寄件人：喬安·凱 <Joannekay@pantala.com>
日期：5月7日
主旨：下次活動

---

Dear Ms. Rees,

I'm writing to express deep gratitude for your favorable review on our Dress Collection, exhibited at the Kanta Fashion show last month. The show was the second event we've ever participated in, and I'm so glad to know that our collection has drawn much attention from fashion experts so soon.

In particular, I would like to thank you for your warm reviews about Autumn Dream as well as the Dress Collection. And I would like to invite you to our next event at Hummingbird Hotel, which is scheduled to be held on the 11th of next month. This will be the first fashion show hosted by Pantala, featuring the Autumn Dream collection accompanied by several more collections we are launching for the next season.

Thank you in advance for your time and participation.

Joanne Kay
Senior Designer
Pantala Fashion

親愛的芮意絲女士：

對於我們上個月在勘太時裝秀上的洋裝系列，您所寫的精采評論促使我寫這封信表達深切的感謝。那場秀是我們第二次參加這種活動，很高興得知我們的系列這麼快就受到時尚專家的關注。

我尤其想要感謝您給予秋夢系列以及洋裝系列如此熱情的評論。我想邀請您參加我們位於蜂鳥飯店的下一場秀，將安排在下個月11號舉辦。這將是由蜻蜓時尚所主辦的第一場時尚秀，以秋夢系列為主軸，同時呈現數個我們下一季要推出的新系列。

提前感謝您撥冗參加。

蜻蜓時尚
資深設計師
喬安·凱

---

**詞彙** instrumental 起作用的　showcase 展露　coveted 令人夢寐以求的　hemp 麻料（材質）　strap 束帶　silk lining 襯絲

**186**

What did Ms. Grainger imply about the fashion designs made of natural materials?

(A) They have been the only clothes on show.
(B) It is hard to design new trends.
(C) Their prices have been falling.
(D) Interest in them has been high.

關於時尚設計採用天然材質，格蘭傑女士說了什麼？

(A) 是時裝秀上的唯一服裝。
(B) 很難設計出新的趨勢。
(C) 價格正在下滑。
(D) 受到高度關切。

「Ms. Grainger」出現在第一篇的報導文章中。第一段最後先提到了「Since last year, designers have been focusing heavily on natural materials.」，故可知天然材質開始在設計師間受到重視並開始使用。

第二段結尾出現「Ms. Grainger, fashion show organizer.」，她說：「The latest designs from fashion houses are an indication of the new trend. If people had not want the designs, they would not have appeared in the show.」，代表她認為設計趨勢是先受到人們歡迎，才會出現在時裝秀上，所以在時裝秀上展示的衣物運用天然材質，是因為受到人們的關注，故選項中最適當的答案為 (D)。

**187**

**Which company participated in the Kanta Fashion Show last year?**

(A) Essie Sew
(B) Laramar
(C) Pantala
(D) Mackowns

哪家公司去年參加了勘太時裝秀？

(A) 艾西縫紉
(B) 拉瑞馬爾
(C) 蜻蜓
(D) 麥可孔斯

根據報導文章的第三段：「the coveted Best in Show award . . . has been previously won by Mackowns, who have been exhibiting for nearly five years」，可知道麥可孔斯公司已參加時裝秀近五年，所以去年也有參加，故本題正確答案為 (D)。

另外，Essie Sew 和 Laramar 在文中是「showcase their portfolio for the first time」，而提到 Pantala 更是直接說是「new company」，所以可知道這三家都是第一次參賽，(A)、(B) 與 (C) 皆不正確。

**188**

**What is indicated about the first fashion show hosted by Pantala?**

(A) It was organized by Ms. Grainger.
(B) The place of the event has not been decided yet.
(C) It will be held on June 11.
(D) It will be the second fashion event hosted by Pantala.

關於蜻蜓主辦的第一場時裝秀，文中提到？

(A) 由格蘭傑女士籌辦。
(B) 還沒決定舉辦的地點。
(C) 將會在 6 月 11 日舉行。
(D) 這是蜻蜓主辦的第二場時尚活動。

本題要從郵件尋找解題線索。凱女士在郵件第二段說道：「I would like to invite you to our next event at Hummingbird Hotel, which is scheduled to be held on the 11th of next month.」、「This will be the first fashion show hosted by Pantala」，故可知道，蜻蜓時尚首次主辦的時裝秀將在蜂鳥飯店舉行，又因為寄件日期為 5 月 7 日，所以句中的「next month」指的就是 6 月，故時裝秀是在 6 月 11 日舉辦，正確答案為 (C)。

**189** - - - - - - - - - - - - - - - - - - - - - - - - - - - - - - - - - - - - - -

**Which design collection received an award at the show?**

(A) Oasis Collection
(B) Spring Collection
(C) Autumn Dream
(D) Grace Silver

哪一個系列在時裝秀上得獎？

(A) 綠洲系列
(B) 春系列
(C) 秋夢系列
(D) 優雅銀

先注意報導文章第三段，其中說到蜻蜓時尚公司「revealed a brand-new concept in outerwear, which earned them the coveted Best in Show award」，重點在於「outerwear」，表示公司得獎的是外套相關的衣服。

再看到芮意絲女士撰寫的評論中，出現了「Their new collection, Autumn Dream」、「their gorgeous jacket」，代表秋夢系列有夾克，故可以知道得獎的最可能是秋夢系列，正確答案為 (C)。

**190** - - - - - - - - - - - - - - - - - - - - - - - - - - - - - - - - - - - - - -

**What does the reviewer suggest about Pantala?**

(A) It has been operating for over two years.
(B) It avoids using ideas from other companies.
(C) It has relocated to another location.
(D) It uses only natural materials.

評論家暗示蜻蜓時尚什麼事？

(A) 營運超過兩年。
(B) 並不使用其他公司的構想。
(C) 最近搬到新地點。
(D) 只使用天然材質。

評論的第一段說了：「the organization is unique in not following the traditional designs of the industry」，表示不遵循業界傳統是蜻蜓時尚公司的特點，所以正確答案為 (B)。

### 191–195 電子郵件和行程表

| | |
|---|---|
| **To:** Chloe Page<br><chloepage@edmonds.com><br>**From:** Kevin Goodwin<br><kevingoodwin@edmonds.com><br>**Date:** February 17<br>**Subject:** Candidate Interview<br>**Attachment:** Interview_Schedule.doc | 收件人：蔻羅依・佩婭<br><chloepage@edmonds.com><br>寄件人：凱文・古德溫<br><kevingoodwin@edmonds.com><br>日期：2月17日<br>主旨：應徵者面試<br>附件：面試行程.doc |

Chloe,

Can I ask a favor of you? Luke Bowden is coming over on Thursday as a prospective candidate for the directorship of the drama school. However, I have double-booked with foreign clients from China at the same time. I cannot reschedule this meeting. Can I swap interview times with you? The original schedule for Mr. Bowden is attached. I hope you can accommodate the changed times.

蔻羅依：

可以請妳幫忙嗎？路克・鮑登是一位很有潛力的應徵者，週四會來面試戲劇學校的主管職。但是我在同一時間要和兩位中國客戶見面。我不可能重新安排會議。我可以和妳交換面試時間嗎？鮑登先生原訂的面試時間安排如附件。我希望妳可以接受更改後的時段。

389

Mr. Bowden has an impressive résumé, particularly his work with the Oscar Theater, which has been recognized as the top drama teaching academy in the country and is a major rival. I hope he will be a great asset to us. We have also had an excellent reference from Ian Hicks for his outstanding contribution on the board of the Arts and Music Corporation. Mr. Hicks is also coming to join us for lunch.

Thank you,
Kevin Goodwin
Acting Head of Drama
Edmonds Entertainment

鮑登先生的履歷讓人印象深刻，特別是他和奧斯卡劇院的作品。奧斯卡劇院被視為是國內頂級的戲劇教學學院，也是我們的主要勁敵。我希望他可以成為我們的重要資產。對於鮑登先生擔任藝術與音樂企業董事的出色表現，我們也接獲伊恩·希克斯的極力推薦。希克斯先生也會和我們一起午餐。

感謝，
埃德蒙茲娛樂
戲劇學校代理主任
凱文·古德溫

## Edmonds Entertainment
## Candidate Interview Schedule

**Candidate Name:** Luke Bowden
**Potential Position:** Director of Drama School
**Interview Date:** February 20

| Meeting | Time | Location |
|---|---|---|
| Interview: Chloe Page | 11:00 A.M. – 12:00 P.M. | Building A, Room 205 |
| Lunch with Ian Hicks | 12:20 P.M. – 1:20 P.M. | Building B, Cafeteria |
| Interview: Kevin Goodwin | 1:30 P.M. – 2:30 P.M. | Building A, Room 303 |

**NOTE:** Upon arrival, please show your driver's license to the parking attendant next to the main entrance so that he can check on the necessary information and park your car in a designated area.

## 埃德蒙茲娛樂
## 應徵者面試行程

應徵者姓名：路克·鮑登
應徵職位：戲劇學院主任
面試日期：2月20日

| 會議 | 時間 | 地點 |
|---|---|---|
| 面試：寇羅依·佩姬 | 上午11:00到中午12:00 | A棟，205室 |
| 和伊恩·希克斯午餐 | 中午12:20到下午1:20 | B棟，自助餐廳 |
| 面試：凱文·古德溫 | 下午1:30到下午2:30 | A棟，303室 |

提醒：抵達時，請向大門旁的停車服務員出示您的駕照，他才能確認必要資訊，以便將您的車輛停在指定區域。

**To:** Kevin Goodwin <kevingoodwin@edmonds.com>
**From:** Chloe Page <chloepage@edmonds.com>
**Date:** February 17
**Subject:** Interview reschedule

Kevin,

Don't worry about the interview schedule. I'm available on Thursday afternoon. And I also informed Mr. Bowden about the change as soon as I received your e-mail. Upon arrival, he will meet you at Room 303. I have high expectations of him, too. He'd be a great person to work with.

收件人：凱文·古德溫 <kevingoodwin@edmonds.com>
寄件人：寇羅依·佩姬 <chloepage@edmonds.com>
日期：2月17日
主旨：重新安排面試時間

凱文：

不用擔心面試時間表。我週四下午有空。我在收到你來信的同時，也馬上通知了鮑登先生。他到了就會先在303室和你見面。我對他也抱有高度期待。他應該會是個很棒的同事。

We're going to have lunch together, with Mr. Hicks and Mr. Bowden, right? Then I think Greenwoods restaurant is better than the cafeteria, since this will be the first time for us to meet Mr. Hicks. The restaurant is right next to the company building, so you won't be late for your meeting at 1:30. I'll reserve a table for four.

Good luck with your meeting with the Chinese clients. I'll see you on Thursday.

Chloe Page
General Manager
Edmonds Entertainment

我們會和希克斯與鮑登先生一起共進午餐，對嗎？既然如此，我想綠林餐廳比公司自助餐廳更好，畢竟這是我們首度和希克斯先生見面。餐廳就在公司大樓旁邊而已，所以你下午1:30的會議不會遲到。

我會預訂四個人的位子。祝你和中國客戶的會議順利。週四見。

埃德蒙茲娛樂
總經理
蔻羅依‧佩姬

---

**詞彙** ask a favor (of sb) 請人幫忙　**directorship** 主管職　**double-book** 與多人有約　**swap** 交換
**accommodate** 通融；接納　**rival** 敵人　**asset** 資產　**reference** 推薦信
**have high expectation of sb** 對某人有高度期待

---

### 191

**What is implied about Mr. Bowden?**

(A) He has worked for a competitor of Edmonds Entertainment.

(B) He used to work for Edmonds Entertainment many years ago.

(C) He is being recruited for his acting skills.

(D) He has visited Edmonds Entertainment in the past.

文中提到鮑登先生什麼事？

(A) 他曾在埃德蒙茲娛樂的競爭者那裡工作。

(B) 他好幾年前曾在埃德蒙茲娛樂上班。

(C) 他因為演出技巧而被招募。

(D) 他過去曾參訪過埃德蒙茲娛樂。

第一封郵件中，古德溫先生在第二段說：「Mr. Bowden has an impressive résumé, particularly his work with the Oscar Theater」，並提到鮑登先生曾就職的奧斯卡劇院對公司來說是「a major rival」，也就是勁敵的意思。從古德溫先生的信件署名可知道，他工作的公司名為「Edmonds Entertainment」，所以本題正確答案為 (A)。

---

### 192

**When does Mr. Goodwin indicate he wants to interview Mr. Bowden?**

(A) At 11:00 A.M.
(B) At 12:20 P.M.
(C) At 1:30 P.M.
(D) At 2:30 P.M.

古德溫先生說他想在哪個時間面試鮑登先生？

(A) 上午 11:00
(B) 下午 12:20
(C) 下午 1:30
(D) 下午 2:30

古德溫先生在寫給佩姬女士的郵件中，先表示有一位面試者要到訪，又說：「I have double-booked with foreign clients from China at the same time.」、「Can I swap interview times with you?」告知對方為了和客戶開會，他不方便在那個時段面試，希望兩人的面試時間可以互換。對照面試行程表可知道，佩姬女士的面試時間原是上午 11 點至中午 12 點，故可知道古德溫先生是想在這個時段面試，正確答案為 (A)。

## 193

**What is Mr. Bowden expected to do?**

(A) Leave earlier than originally informed

(B) Book a restaurant

(C) Meet Mr. Hicks at the main entrance

(D) Bring a form of identification

**鮑登先生預期會做什麼事？**

(A) 比原先被告知的時間更早離開

(B) 預約餐廳

(C) 和希克斯先生在大門見面

(D) 攜帶某個證件

面試行程表上的「NOTE」説了：「Upon arrival, please show your driver's license to the parking attendant」，所以鮑登先生需要出示駕照，故他得攜帶這個證件前來，正確答案為 (D)。

(A) 鮑登先生依然需要面試到下午 2 點 30 分，只是變成先與古德溫先生面試，再和佩姬女士面試。(B) 根據佩姬女士的回信，她已經訂好餐廳了。(C) 從面試行程表看來，鮑登先生在大門口會遇見的只有停車服務員。

## 194

**Who will meet with Mr. Bowden in Room 303?**

(A) Ms. Page

(B) Mr. Hicks

(C) Mr. Goodwin

(D) Ms. Oscar

**誰會在303 室和鮑登先生見面？**

(A) 佩姬女士

(B) 希克斯先生

(C) 古德溫先生

(D) 奧斯卡女士

本題有陷阱，關鍵線索在佩姬女士的回信中。古德溫先生信上説過想更改時間，但沒有説面試地點也要跟著互換，但佩姬女士卻説：「Upon arrival, he will meet you at Room 303.」，由此可知，古德溫先生不只換到 11 點面試，連地點也會換成 303 室，故本題正確答案為 (C)。

**What will Ms. Page likely to be doing at 1 P.M. on February 20?**

(A) Taking a tour of the Edmonds premises

(B) Dining at a nearby restaurant

(C) Having a meeting at the company cafeteria

(D) Interviewing Mr. Bowden

**佩姬女士在2 月20 日下午1 點，可能在做什麼？**

(A) 在埃德蒙茲建築參訪

(B) 在附近的餐廳吃飯

(C) 在公司自助餐廳開會

(D) 面試鮑登先生

先看時程表，中午 12 點 20 分到 1 點 20 分是鮑溫先生與希克斯先生的午餐會面，但根據佩姬女士的郵件，她説了：「We're going to have lunch together, with Mr. Hicks and Mr. Bowden, right?」、「I think Greenwoods restaurant is better than the cafeteria」、「The restaurant is right next to the company building」，故可知道她也會共進午餐，且她將餐廳改為公司附近的綠林餐廳，故下午 1 點時她正在綠林餐廳用餐，本題正確答案為 (B)。

## Peacock Office Supplies

**Voted by the *Business Times* as the best supplier of office supplies!**

To celebrate our 5th anniversary in May, we are offering a special service to all our valued customers. On your request, we will imprint your company and personal information on your purchases, including file folders, envelopes, boxes, whiteboards, and all kinds of ballpoint pens. It is completely free!

Please put a checkmark by the items you want on the ordering form. Also, you'll need to fill in the design layout code, which can be checked on our website. And don't forget to update your customer information so that we can imprint them correctly.

Thank you for choosing Peacock Office Supplies!

## 孔雀辦公用品

**《商業時報》票選為最佳辦公用品供應商！**

為了慶祝五月的五週年慶，我們向全體尊貴的顧客提供一項特別服務。只要您提出需求，我們將在您購買的商品上刻印公司和個人資訊，包括文件夾、信封、盒子、白板或任一款原子筆。完全免費！

請在訂購單上您想要的商品欄位打勾註記。並且填上設計版型代碼，相關資訊可以在我們官網上查看。也別忘了更新您的顧客資訊，我們才可以正確刻印。

感謝您選擇孔雀辦公用品！

## Peacock Office Supplies

**Send order to:**
**Name:** Christopher Dixon
**E-mail:** chrisdixon@foxcox.com
**Company:** Fox&Cox Inc.

Please indicate which information you would like to have on your office products and how you want it laid out.

|  | File folders | Pens | Business Cards |
|---|---|---|---|
| Company name | ✓ | ✓ | ✓ |
| Company address |  |  | ✓ |
| Company logo | ✓ | ✓ | ✓ |
| Company website | ✓ |  | ✓ |
| Individual name | ✓ |  | ✓ |
| Individual phone number |  |  | ✓ |
| Individual e-mail address |  |  | ✓ |
| Design layout code | AD7 | GK3 | HL4 |
| Quantity | 20 | 500 | 100 |

## 孔雀辦公用品

**請將訂購商品寄到：**
**姓名：** 克里斯多福・迪克森
**E-mail:** chrisdixon@foxcox.com
**公司：** 佛克斯＆考克斯股份有限公司

請指明您想要印哪些資訊在您的辦公用品上，以及您期望的版型。

|  | 文件夾 | 筆 | 名片 |
|---|---|---|---|
| 公司名稱 | ✓ | ✓ | ✓ |
| 公司地址 |  |  | ✓ |
| 公司商標 | ✓ | ✓ | ✓ |
| 公司官網 | ✓ |  | ✓ |
| 個人姓名 | ✓ |  | ✓ |
| 個人電話 |  |  | ✓ |
| 個人電子信箱 |  |  | ✓ |
| 設計版型代碼 | AD7 | GK3 | HL4 |
| 數量 | 20 | 500 | 100 |

After one week of your order being placed, one of our design team members will contact you via e-mail. They will attach a digital copy of the images that you have chosen to go on your office equipment. Please approve these designs or inform us of any changes that you wish to make. We will not go ahead with the order unless we receive confirmation that all images are correct.

Remember to complete the form in its entirety and return it with all the information, including your individual and company details as well as your company logo.

下訂單一週後，我們設計團隊的成員將透過電子郵件信箱和您聯絡。針對您選擇要放在辦公用品上的圖樣，他們會附上一份數位設計圖檔。請您同意或者告知我們任何想要修改的地方。除非確認圖樣正確無誤，訂單才會進一步作業。

請記得完整填寫表格，寄回時提供所有資訊，包括您個人和公司的詳細資料和公司商標。

---

**To:** Bryan Gibbs
<bryangibbs@peakcocksupplies.com>
**From:** Christopher Dixon
<chrisdixon@foxcox.com>
**Date:** 6 May
**Subject:** Re: Order for Fox & Cox Inc.

收件人：布萊恩·吉布斯
<bryangibbs@peakcocksupplies.com>
寄件人：克里斯多福·迪克森
<chrisdixon@foxcox.com>
日期：5月6日
主旨：關於：佛克斯＆考克斯股份有限公司訂單

---

Dear Mr. Gibbs,

Having reviewed the information you provided last week, I have decided to change the design layout code of the pens. I would prefer to apply BG33 instead, and add our company website, www.foxcox.com. Once you have made the changes, can you send me the updated version? Everything else is perfect.

Additionally, I am making a presentation at a marketing conference in Berne next month and would like to take some products with the new design with me. Other agencies will be attending, and I want to make an impact. I know your company carries customized corporate items, such as T-shirts, for promotion. Please e-mail me your latest brochure with the prices for these items. In addition, is it possible to add my new choice to this order for one invoice payment, or is it necessary to raise a separate purchase order? Please advise me.

Many thanks.

Christopher Dixon
Marketing Manager
Fox & Cox Inc.

親愛的吉布斯先生，

我已經看過您上週提供的資訊，並決定換掉原子筆的設計版型代碼。我偏好用BG33取代原來的，並加入我們公司官網網址www.foxcox.com。您修改後可以寄一份更新檔給我嗎？其他部分都很完美。

還有，我下個月將在伯恩的一場行銷會議上做簡報，我想要帶一些設計好的產品過去。其他代理商都將出席，所以我想讓他們留下印象。我知道您的公司販售很多可用來宣傳的客製化商品，像是T恤。請您用電子郵件寄給我最新版、上面有標價的商品手冊。此外，有可能讓我加購的訂單也併入目前這個訂單，用同一張發票，還是有需要另外下單呢？請您給我建議。

非常感謝。

佛克斯＆考克斯股份有限公司
行銷經理
克里斯多福·迪克森

詞彙 imprint 刻印　ballpoint pen 原子筆　checkmark 勾勾符號　layout 版型
in its entirety 完整地　make an impact 使人印象深刻

## 196

**What is suggested about Peacock Office Supplies?**

(A) It will open a new branch in May.
(B) It will host a marketing conference next month.
(C) It doesn't have a team of designers.
(D) It was voted as the best supplier of office products.

文中提到孔雀辦公用品什麼事？

(A) 新分店將在五月開幕。
(B) 下個月將舉辦一場行銷會議。
(C) 它沒有設計團隊。
(D) 被票選為最佳辦公產品的供應商。

根據廣告標題「Voted by the *Business Times* as the best supplier of office supplies!」即可知，正確答案為 (D)。

(A) 文中只說到五月是公司的五週年慶，並沒有提到分店一事；(B) 將舉辦行銷會議的是來自佛克斯＆考克斯股份有限公司的迪克森先生；(C) 訂購單下方第一行寫了：「one of our design team members will contact you via e-mail」，表示公司有設計團隊。

## 197

**Who submitted the order to Peacock Office Supplies?**

(A) A manager at a marketing agency
(B) A logo designer of a design team
(C) An office equipment manufacturer
(D) An editor at the *Business Times*

誰向孔雀辦公用品訂貨？

(A) 一家行銷公司的經理
(B) 一個設計團隊的商標設計師
(C) 一家辦公用品製造商
(D) 一名《商業時報》的編輯

先記住訂購單上的姓名「Christopher Dixon」，再從郵件的署名知道，迪克森先生就是「Fox & Cox Inc.」的行銷經理，所以最適當的答案為 (A)。

## 198

**What are the customers asked to do to confirm their orders?**

(A) Reply to an e-mail
(B) Update their information
(C) Sign an order form
(D) Visit a website

顧客要做什麼來確認訂單？

(A) 回覆電子郵件
(B) 更新資訊
(C) 在訂購單上簽名
(D) 造訪官網

訂購單下方的指示寫了：「After one week of your order being placed, one of our design team members will contact you via e-mail.」、「Please approve these designs or inform us of any changes that you wish to make.」，表示公司會使用電子郵件與顧客聯絡，故顧客最有可能是用回覆郵件的方式來確認訂單，所以本題最適當的答案為 (A)。

**In the e-mail, what does Mr. Dixon request?**

(A) A copy of the invoice for a previous order

(B) A brochure from Peacock Office Supplies

(C) Shipment of his order to Berne

(D) Changes to the quantities of orders he placed

迪克森先生在電子郵件中要求什麼？

(A) 前一次訂單的發票副本

(B) 孔雀辦公用品的商品手冊

(C) 把訂購品運到伯恩

(D) 修改他的訂購數量

迪克森先生在郵件第二段寫著：「Please e-mail me your latest brochure with the prices for these items.」，表示希望收到最新的商品手冊，故正確答案為 (B)。

**What is suggested about Mr. Dixon?**

(A) He has organized an online meeting.

(B) He is designing a new company's logo.

(C) He produced an innovative advertisement.

(D) He hopes to bring promotional items to a conference.

文中提到迪克森先生什麼事？

(A) 他安排了線上會議。

(B) 他正在設計公司的新商標。

(C) 他做過很有創意的廣告。

(D) 他希望可以帶一些宣傳品去開會。

迪克森先生在郵件第二段表示下個月有一場行銷會議，且他想要「take some products with the new design with me」，所以選項中最適合的答案為 (D)。

# ACTUAL TEST
# 9

# PART 5

101

------- his one year abroad, Mr. Feltman visited London, Amsterdam, and Brussels.

(A) Behind
(B) During
(C) From
(D) Between

**題型** 詞彙——介系詞

**翻譯** 費爾特曼先生過去一年在海外的期間,造訪了倫敦、阿姆斯特丹和布魯塞爾。

本題提到「one year abroad」,表示在國外的一年間,故前方介系詞應具有「期間」的意思,所以最適合填入的是 During,正確答案為 (B)。

102

Luxembourg Electronics has ------- on a couple of selected brand-name appliances each week.

(A) discount
(B) discounts
(C) discounted
(D) discountable

**題型** 位置——名詞

**翻譯** 盧森堡電子每週都會挑選幾個品牌的電器提供折扣販賣。

**詞彙** brand-name 有品牌的

本題重點在於區分可數與不可數名詞。先觀察空格為動詞 has 的受詞,所以名詞答案應是 (A) 或 (B) 之一。discount 為表示「優惠」的可數名詞,如果前面沒有出現 a、an、the、所有格等限定詞,則應以複數型態出現,因此正確答案為 (B)。

另外從句意上來看,本句敘述的應該是多部機器的優惠,所以也應該使用複數型。

103

Tacoma Computer's in-store promotion ------- customers a selection of cut-price laptops.

(A) recommends
(B) offers
(C) suggests
(D) instructs

**題型** 詞彙——動詞

**翻譯** 塔科馬電腦的店內促銷提供顧客精選的折價筆電。

**詞彙** in-store 店內的
cut-price 折價的

本句提到「促銷」、「顧客」、「折價」,故可知道此處應填入具有「提供、給予」意思的動詞,以表示促銷提供顧客折價商品,且空格後面出現間接受詞 customers 與直接受詞 a selection 的句構,可知空格處為「授與動詞」,故正確答案為 (B)。

**104**

Mr. Devlin insisted that in order to meet the deadline, ------- must work extra hours together.

(A) no one
(B) someone
(C) everyone
(D) one another

題型 **詞彙——代名詞**

翻譯 戴夫林先生堅持，為了趕上截止日期，每個人都得加班。

詞彙 **meet the deadline** 趕上截止日期

本句提到「趕上截止日期」、「加班」，故此處的代名詞應具有「每個人」的意思，表示每個人都要加班，故正確答案為 (C)。

(B) 句中出現副詞 together，強調要一起加班，所以前方若填入 someone 會不符合句意，若沒有 together 則此選項可為正確答案；(D) one another 是用在群體中，兩人之間或多人彼此間有某動作的時候，用來指涉人物的代名詞，與此處不符合。

**105**

What is notable about the Taipei locality is that travelers will take pleasure in eating ------- yet inexpensive dishes and foodstuff.

(A) delicious
(B) hungry
(C) brief
(D) definite

題型 **詞彙——形容詞**

翻譯 台北成為著名景點，是因為遊客可以愉快享用美味又不貴的食物。

詞彙 **notable** 著名的
**locality** 特定地區
**foodstuff** 食物

注意空格後的對等連接詞 yet，作用是連結空格處的形容詞與 inexpensive，而這兩個形容詞則是在修飾名詞 dishes 和 foodstuff，故選項中最符合句意的是 delicious，表示食物好吃又不貴，所以正確答案為 (A)。

**106**

The Experimental Design Company produced a range of clothes using silk and leather in an ------- popular fashion statement.

(A) astonishingly
(B) astonished
(C) astonishment
(D) astonish

題型 **位置——副詞**

翻譯 實驗設計公司發表一項驚人流行時尚宣言，用絲和皮革生產了一系列服飾。

空格修飾後面的形容詞 popular，所以要選副詞 astonishingly，正確答案為 (A)。

**107**

The customer support team checked your purchase and will immediately inform you ------- the product has been placed for shipment.

(A) but
(B) once
(C) than
(D) so

| | |
|---|---|
| 題型 | 詞彙——連接詞 |
| 翻譯 | 客戶支援團隊已確認您的訂單,一旦出貨時馬上通知您。 |
| 詞彙 | place〔動詞〕放置 |

觀察空格前後皆句有主詞、動詞,所以空格中需填入可以連結兩個子句的連接詞。本句提到「確認訂單」、「通知」、「出貨」,故此處的連接詞應要有「一旦、只要」的意思,表示已確認訂單,只要出貨便會通知,所以正確答案為 (B)。

(A) 對等連接詞 but 或 (D) 連接副詞 so 也可以放在子句間,但是此處字義不符。

★與 once 相關的用法:

once〔副詞〕一次;曾經;〔連接詞〕一旦……就會……　　once in a lifetime(一生一次)
at once(立刻;同時)　　once in a while(偶爾)
for once(難得)　　once or twice(幾次)

**108**

Stock of fresh produce should ------- earlier than the market opening time tomorrow morning.

(A) arrival
(B) arriving
(C) arrive
(D) arrived

| | |
|---|---|
| 題型 | 位置——原形動詞 |
| 翻譯 | 生鮮農產品的存貨在明天早上抵達的時間,應該會比市場開市來得早。 |
| 詞彙 | produce〔名詞〕農產品 |

空格前有助動詞 should,所以要填入的是動詞原形 arrive,正確答案為 (C)。

**109**

If the fire alarms go off at any time, please contact Mr. Perry in the security office for -------.

(A) assisted
(B) assistant
(C) assistance
(D) assist

| | |
|---|---|
| 題型 | 位置——名詞 |
| 翻譯 | 如果火災警報器在任何時間作響,請聯繫保全辦公室的佩瑞先生協助。 |
| 詞彙 | fire alarm 火災警報器<br>at any time 任何時間 |

空格位於介系詞後面,扮演受詞的角色,所以應代入名詞。選項中屬於名詞的有 (B) 人物名詞 assistant(助理)及 (C) 事物名詞 assistance(協助),但句意上,本句應是表示聯絡保全以獲得協助,故正確答案為 (C)。

另外要注意,當人物名詞為單數時,前面必須出現 a、an、the、所有格等限定詞。

## 110

The committee finally chose the design provided by Interlotze Architecture for their new workplace in Moscow following ------- reviews of the six proposals submitted to them.

(A) cares
(B) careful
(C) cared
(D) carefully

題型 **位置**——形容詞

翻譯 經過仔細審查六件提案後，委員會最終選用了因特路建築事務所的設計，以打造他們在莫斯科的新辦公場所。

空格位於名詞 reviews 前，所以應填入修飾該名詞的形容詞 careful，另外，following 一般被當作介系詞使用，具有與 after 相似的意思與功能；本題正確答案為 (B)

## 111

In order for Ines Marketing to keep up with competitors, all its departments have to ------- perform to the highest manufacturing standards.

(A) finely
(B) continually
(C) lately
(D) straightly

題型 **詞彙**——副詞

翻譯 為了讓伊能斯行銷能夠趕上競爭對手，所有部門必需持續地以最高生產標準執行工作。

詞彙 keep up with sb 追趕上某人
perform to the highest standards
以最高標準執行

本句提到「執行工作」，故選項中最適合修飾此動作的副詞應是 continually，表示「持續地」執行，正確答案為 (B)。

## 112

Readers depend upon *Medical Updates Weekly* for ------- information on the latest medical news.

(A) rely
(B) reliable
(C) relying
(D) reliably

題型 **位置**——形容詞

翻譯 讀者仰賴《醫療週刊新訓》獲得最新醫療新聞的可靠資訊。

空格後面接續名詞 information，故應填入可修飾名詞的形容詞。選項中 (B) 形容詞與 (C) 現在分詞皆可能成為答案，但是 reliable 的字義為「可靠的」，而 relying 則是「依存的」，所以最符合句意的是 reliable，正確答案為 (B)。

**Although she passed the first examination, Ms. Chan failed to get the job as it ------- to someone with better work experience.**

(A) gave
(B) has given
(C) was given
(D) will have given

題型 **文法──動詞**

翻譯 雖然陳女士通過了初試,她還是未獲錄取,因為這份工作給了另一位工作經驗較多的人。

選項為 give 的各種型態,所以要根據句意確認主被動、時態與單複數一致等條件。從句意來看,此處在講工作「被給予」他人,所以動詞要用被動,故正確答案為 (C)。

也可以觀察前面的動詞 passed 與 failed,為了前後一致,本句的時態應該也使用過去式。此外,(D) 為未來完成式,用在表示某動作「發生在過去,現在未完成,但未來將會完成」,但此刻陳女士已經「failed to get the job」,所以可看出「工作給別人」這個動作現在已完成了。

**Only after ------- becomes qualified for the accounting certificate is Omar Jenkins subject to promotion.**

(A) he
(B) his
(C) him
(D) himself

題型 **文法──倒裝**

翻譯 只有等到歐馬爾‧傑金斯取得會計證照,他才能獲得升遷。

本題重點為看出句中倒裝。Only 放在句首,後接上 after,此即為 only 倒裝句型的其中一種。若沒有 only,句子應還原成:「Omar Jenkins is subject to promotion after he becomes qualified for the accounting certificate.」,此處為了加入 only,強調某事「只有」在某種條件下發生,所以變成倒裝句,但也不是全句都有倒裝,「after he becomes . . . certificate」這段時間副詞子句沒有倒裝,只有主句從「Omar Jenkins is subject to promotion」變成了「is Omar Jenkins subject to promotion」,這就是 only 倒裝句型的規則。

從還原的句型來看,空格處要填入的是一般的主格代名詞 he,故正確答案為 (A)。

★ **only 倒裝句型的規則:**

**使用時間:**
句首出現「only +時間子句/時間副詞/介系詞片語(if、when、after、before、then、in this way)」

**規則:**主句的主詞、動詞倒裝,若為一般動詞,則將動詞變成「助動詞+原形動詞」,主詞就放在兩者之間。注意並不是所有 only 開頭的句子都要倒裝。

**例句:**After Lily had worked with John, she remembered that she had met him a long time ago.
→ **Only** after Lily had worked with John **did she remember** that she had met him a long time ago.

## 115

**The five fabric conditioners surveyed in the latest ------- were found to have the same effect on clothing.**

(A) development
(B) study
(C) history
(D) subject

題型 **詞彙——名詞**

翻譯 最近的研究發現，五款衣物柔軟精的效果一樣。

詞彙 **fabric conditioner** 衣物柔軟精
**survey** 〔動詞〕調查

從過去分詞 surveyed 以及空格後的 were found 可以知道，本題的空格處應填入與「研究、調查結果」相關的名詞，表示最新的研究中，發現受調查的五款衣物柔軟精效果相同，所以正確答案為 (B)。

## 116

**The board of directors chose ------- a leading entrepreneur, Simon Rogers, for his outstanding contribution to the organization.**

(A) will honor
(B) to honor
(C) would honor
(D) to be honored

題型 **文法——動詞**

翻譯 考量大企業家西蒙·羅傑斯對組織的傑出貢獻，董事會決定向他致敬。

詞彙 **honor** 〔動詞〕致敬；公開表揚

觀察空格前方已出現動詞過去式 chose，所以空格中若想再代入動詞，應使用不定詞 (B) 或是 (D)，而其中 honor 是向某人致敬的意思，常後面接續人物名詞，只要使用主動即可，故正確答案為 (B)。

## 117

**If you have any questions ------- our items or carriage services, please do not hesitate to communicate with John's Floral World.**

(A) regard
(B) regards
(C) regarding
(D) regarded

題型 **位置——介系詞**

翻譯 如果您對於我們的產品或運輸服務有疑問，請儘管聯繫約翰植物世界。

詞彙 **carriage service** 運輸服務

空格位於名詞 questions 與名詞片語 our items 之間，所以空格需填入介系詞以連結兩者，故本題答案為 (C)。

★ **regard 的用法：**
**regard**〔動詞〕（視為）；〔名詞〕關心；尊重
**regarding**〔介系詞〕關於
**regard A as B**（將 A 看作 B）
**best regards**（常作為書信結尾的問候語，表示致上問候）

**118**

Because of the complaints filed by foreign clients, Gorden Stanley assured them that he intends to ------- the matter.

(A) go ahead
(B) show up
(C) look into
(D) act out

題型 詞彙——片語

翻譯 由於外國客戶提出抱怨，高登·史坦利保證他會調查這件事。

詞彙 file 提出（抱怨、訴訟、離婚）

(A) go ahead 引領；(B) show up 現身；(C) look into 調查；(D) act out 付諸行動；表演。

本句提到「抱怨」、「保證」、「事件」，故此處的動作應帶有「調查」的意思，以表示保證會調查引起抱怨的事件，故正確答案為 (C)。

**119**

The Santiago Photocopier Company has issued a press release, which is targeted at ------- clients to take their old machines in for repair.

(A) encouraging
(B) to encourage
(C) encourage
(D) encourages

題型 位置——動名詞

翻譯 聖地牙哥影印公司發布新聞稿，目的是要鼓勵顧客拿舊機器來維修。

詞彙 press release 新聞稿

選項皆為動詞 encourage 的變化，且觀察空格位在系詞 at 之後，故一般動詞應改為動名詞，所以正確答案為 (A)。

**120**

Workers require written ------- from their manager in order to borrow equipment.

(A) authorizes
(B) authorized
(C) authorization
(D) authorize

題型 位置——名詞

翻譯 員工想要借用設備，必須取得主管的書面授權。

先觀察空格前面已有動詞 require，之間又沒有連接詞，所以此處不可能再出現動詞，再看空格前方有形容詞 written，表示空格受其修飾，故最應當填入的是名詞，正確答案為 (C)。

**121** ---------------------------------------------------

The Talking Leaves Corporation ------- provides customers with the latest information about its organic syrup products.

(A) perfectly
(B) regularly
(C) equally
(D) considerably

| 題型 | 詞彙——副詞 |
|---|---|
| 翻譯 | 「說話葉企業」經常提供顧客最新的有機糖漿產品資訊。 |
| 詞彙 | syrup 糖漿 |

本句提到公司會提供顧客最新資訊，而從各選項的字義來看，最適合用來修飾 provide 的是 regularly，表示「經常、定期」提供的意思，故正確答案為 (B)。

(D) considerably 主要是修飾比較級，以及表示數量或程度的動詞，如 vary、lessen、improve、reduce、increase 等，所以此處不適用。

**122** ---------------------------------------------------

The following is a list of the conditions that were most commonly ------- by the employees within the company.

(A) stipulating
(B) stipulated
(C) have stipulated
(D) stipulation

| 題型 | 文法——被動 |
|---|---|
| 翻譯 | 下列是這間公司員工最常提起的狀況。 |
| 詞彙 | stipulate 明確說出 |

觀察前方依序出現了 be 動詞與 most，可知此句最可能是使用最高級，所以空格要填入 stipulated，而此處會變成「the conditions that were most commonly stipulated」，表示最常被提起的狀況，故本題正確答案為 (B)。

**123** ---------------------------------------------------

Mr. Vasquez will open the Pierce mobile phone's production branch ------- it is fully prepared.

(A) as well as
(B) thanks to
(C) due to
(D) as soon as

| 題型 | 詞彙——片語 |
|---|---|
| 翻譯 | 只要皮爾斯手機的製造分工廠完全準備好，瓦斯奎茲先生就會讓它開始運作。 |

(A) as well as 也；(B) thanks to 多虧；(C) due to 由於；(D) as soon as 一……就……。

空格前後的內容皆為擁有主詞、動詞的完整子句，所以空格前應會出現連接詞。(B) 與 (C) 裡頭的 to 是介系詞，後方只能填入名詞，故不可選。再從句意可知，此處應是要表示準備好了就會讓分工廠運作，所以最適合填入的是 as soon as，正確答案為 (D)。

**124**

Owing to the recent oil price surge, all production of excessive stocks ------- until further notice.

(A) are deferring
(B) have deferred
(C) have been deferring
(D) will be deferred

| 題型 | 文法──動詞 |
| --- | --- |
| 翻譯 | 由於近期油價上漲，所有過剩商品都先將暫緩生產，除非等到進一步通知。 |
| 詞彙 | surge 上漲<br>excessive 過多的<br>defer 推遲，延期 |

從本句的脈絡來看，此處應是表示因為近來油價驟升，生產活動將被延遲，而 production 為被延後的事物，動詞要使用被動式，所以答案為 (D)。

(C) have been deferring 是完成進行式，用在動作持續至今或動作最近不斷重複等等狀況，與此處不符。

**125**

When it comes to purchases, Townsend Industries assures its customers that they will receive their items ------- two business days.

(A) through
(B) within
(C) around
(D) behind

| 題型 | 詞彙──介系詞 |
| --- | --- |
| 翻譯 | 談到買賣，鎮送工業確保其客戶都能在兩個工作天內收到商品。 |
| 詞彙 | when it comes to 談到 |

本句提到「客戶」、「收到」、「兩個工作天」，而選項中 (B) within 常與「期間」連用，具有「在……內」的意思，所以空格處應要填入 within 最為適當，表示客戶會在兩個工作天內收到產品，故本題正確答案為 (B)。

**126**

Thanks to the ------- number of foreign customers, Lloyd Bank is fast becoming one of the most promising financial groups.

(A) growing
(B) unknown
(C) costly
(D) closed

| 題型 | 詞彙──形容詞 |
| --- | --- |
| 翻譯 | 靠著大量成長的外國客戶，羅伊德銀行很快成為前景最為看好的金融集團之一。 |

根據句意，本題要選出最適合修飾 number 的形容詞，且要有「成長的」或「許多的」之意，故選項中最適合的是 growing，本題正確答案為 (A)。

## 127

Perfect for presents, Allan's Premium Coffee Beans are packaged in a ------- colored case.

(A) bright
(B) brightly
(C) brightness
(D) brighten

題型 **位置**——副詞

翻譯 艾倫頂級咖啡豆以色彩鮮豔的禮盒包裝，是完美的贈禮。

過去分詞 colored 具有形容詞的功用，表示「上色的」，所以空格應填入可修飾形容詞的副詞，正確答案為 (B)。

(A) 本題若選形容詞 bright 變成 bright colored case，句意上是表示「明亮的、彩色的包裝盒」，但用明亮形容盒子並不適合，所以此處的「明亮」應該用 brightly 修飾，變成「色彩鮮豔」的意思，故 (A) 不是正確答案。

## 128

------- is especially convincing about the proposed rail link is its proximity to the airport.

(A) Which
(B) That
(C) Why
(D) What

題型 **文法**——不定關係代名詞

翻譯 這項鐵路網計畫特別有說服力的點在於它離機場很近。

詞彙 **rail link** 鐵路網

從選項組成可以看出，本題要考的是關係代名詞。先觀察空格後直接是 be 動詞，故空格應是主詞的角色，又看到句子後面再次出現 be 動詞，所以空格中的關係代名詞還需要包含先行詞，表示「The thing that is especially convincing . . . is its proximity」，選項中只有 what 能還原成 the thing that，是包含先行詞的關係代名詞，所以正確答案為 (D)。

## 129

Without ------- from the author, no part of the article can be used elsewhere.

(A) permission
(B) reluctance
(C) identification
(D) association

題型 **詞彙**——名詞

翻譯 沒有作者的允許，哪裡都不准使用這篇文章任何一部份。

根據題意來看，此處應該是要說，沒有作者的「允許」不得使用文章，所以最適合填入 permission，正確答案為 (A)。

**130** - - - - - - - - - - - - - - - - - - - - - - - - - - - - - - - - - - - - - - - - - - - - - - - - - - - -

The Flying Panda Travel Agency, specializing in honeymoon travel packages, is at its ------- between April and June.

(A) busy
(B) busier
(C) busily
(D) busiest

題型 文法──最高級

翻譯 飛行熊貓旅行社專門規劃蜜月旅行套裝行程，在四月到六月是最忙的時候。

最高級原本就會出現在定冠詞 the 或所有格之後，此處的 at its busiest 可說是慣用語，代表「最忙」，所以正確答案為 (D)。

★記住下列最高級用語：
at one's busiest （最忙）
at one's best/finest （最棒）

# PART 6

**131–134 通知**

The main objective of the Image Nature Stocks publication is to __131__ taking photos in the natural surroundings of the wilderness. __132__. Apparatus and methods used to capture these images are also discussed in this editorial. Hobbyists and freelance __133__ are the ones responsible for submission to this publication, which is issued once every two months.

Snapshots and articles on matters that happened from September are currently being considered. __134__, due to the pressure and the workload that we deal with every day, no feedback is given to individuals who send materials to us. For more information, please visit our website at www. imagenaturestocks.com.

自然圖庫刊物的主要目標是推廣荒野環境的攝影，以出色的戶外風景和野生動物為主。本刊評論也討論拍攝這些影像所需的器材和手法。由業餘愛好者或自由攝影專家負責供稿給這本雙月刊。

九月拍攝的照片和文章目前還在評估。然而，因為每天的工作壓力和負荷，我們將不會個別回饋意見給個人所提供的素材。欲知詳情請上官網www.imagenaturestocks.com。

**詞彙** objective 目標 wilderness 荒野 apparatus 器材 hobbyist 業餘愛好者
freelance 自由接案的 snapshot 照片 workload 工作量

**131** ----------------------------------------------------------------

(A) impress
(B) promote
(C) impose
(D) fund

(A) 給……留下深刻印象
(B) 推廣
(C) 把……強加於
(D) 資助

**題型 詞彙——動詞**

空格後方提到照片攝影，句子開頭又說這是某刊物的主要目標，所以最適合填入 promote，代表目標為推廣拍照，故正確答案為 **(B)**。

**132** NEW ----------------------------------------------------------------

(A) This can be a good piece of evidence supporting industrial evolution.
(B) Those images captured by the space telescope reveal the wonders of outer space.
(C) Remarkable outdoor scenery and wildlife are the main things concentrated on by this publication.
(D) We've been looking for feedback from various users who have rated these magazines on our website.

(A) 這可能是支持產業發展的好證據。
(B) 天文望遠鏡拍攝的照片揭露外太空的奧秘。
(C) 以出色的戶外風景和野生動物為主。
(D) 我們查看了眾多讀者在官網上對這些雜誌的評價。

**題型 填入句子**

空格前說刊物的主要目標是推廣荒野攝影，空格後句則提到「Apparatus and methods used to capture these images」，而選項中只有 (C) 寫的「Remarkable outdoor scenery and wildlife」，恰好可以對應到後句裡的「these images」，表示所謂的這些影像（these images），就是拍攝戶外風景與野生動物的照片，故本題最適當的答案為 **(C)**。

409

## 133

(A) professional
(B) profession
(C) professionally
(D) professionals

(A) 專業的
(B) 職業
(C) 內行地
(D) 專業人士

**題型** 位置──名詞

空格位於主詞的位置，需要代入名詞，且由於動詞為複數 are，所以應該填入複數名詞 professionals，正確答案為 (D)。

**134**

(A) However
(B) Likewise
(C) For example
(D) Therefore

(A) 然而
(B) 同樣地
(C) 舉例來說
(D) 因此

**題型** 詞彙──副詞

空格前句提到，刊物正在評估九月期間的照片與文章，空格後則說了，因為每天工作壓力與業務量，無法給予個別回覆。此處填入 However 最能表示語氣上的轉折，故正確答案為 (A)。

## 135–138 電子郵件

**To:** Bobby Wright <wbobby@bigmail.com>
**From:** International Association of Miners <admin@associationofminers.com>
**Date:** August 2
**Subject:** Membership information

收件人：巴比・萊特 <wbobby@bigmail.com>
寄件人：國際礦工協會 <admin@associationofminers.com>
日期：8月2日
主旨：會員資訊

---

Dear Mr. Wright,

The International Association of Miners would like to congratulate you on joining our organization, which **135** the well-being and security of the global mining community by means of conducting numerous programs and services that address the needs of miners worldwide.

Our **136** mission is to make mining construction better by promoting strict safety measures in the industry. **137**, we offer professionally developed materials for new and experienced miners on our website, which includes the latest information on the subject of mining rules and regulations.

親愛的萊特先生：

國際礦工協會恭喜您加入本協會，我們支持全球礦業同行的安全健康，並為全球礦工的需求進行多項計畫和服務。

我們主要的任務是推廣更嚴格的礦業安全措施，讓礦場建設臻於完善。此外，我們也在官網上，向新進或經驗老道的礦業從業人員提供職業發展的資料，其中包括最新版的採礦法規。

**138**. We hope to help you to become a better and safer mining expert.

Sincerely,
International Association of Miners

隨信附件說明了會員的權益。希望能幫助您成為更好、更安全的採礦專業人士。

國際礦工協會 敬上

詞彙 **address the needs** 處理需求

**135** ----------------------------------------------------------------

(A) supports
(B) supported
(C) having supported
(D) would be supporting

(A) 支持
(B) 支持了
(C) 已支持
(D) 會支持

題型 **文法**——動詞

本題需考慮動詞時態、主被動及單複數一致。先觀察空格前有關係代名詞 which，且空格後的內容為修飾先行詞 organization 的主格關係代名詞子句，再解讀句意，可知此處應是要表示協會支持礦業團體，故使用簡單現在式表示事實，本題正確答案為 (A)。

**136** ----------------------------------------------------------------

(A) frequent
(B) primary
(C) early
(D) previous

(A) 頻繁的
(B) 主要的
(C) 早的
(D) 先前的

題型 **詞彙**——形容詞

本題要選出最適合修飾空格後的 mission 的形容詞。本句要闡述協會的任務，故使用 primary 強調為「主要的」任務，是最適當的寫法，所以正確答案為 (B)。

**137** ----------------------------------------------------------------

(A) However
(B) By the way
(C) Furthermore
(D) As far as I know

(A) 然而
(B) 順道一提
(C) 此外
(D) 就我所知

題型 **詞彙**——副詞

空格前句提到協會幫助推廣礦業安全措施，後句則說到網站提供相關資料，故空格處要填入帶有「補充說明」意思的詞，所以最適當的答案為 (C)。

**138** NEW --------------------------------------------------

| | |
|---|---|
| (A) An application for admission is attached to this e-mail. | (A) 電子郵件附上入會申請書。 |
| (B) This is the first time that we are offering this exceptional opportunity to local miners in Ghana. | (B) 這是我們首次給予迦納當地礦工的特別機會。 |
| (C) We want you to join our organization in the future, to keep updated with the latest. | (C) 我們希望您未來會加入我們組織了解最新狀況。 |
| (D) Attached herewith is a document that outlines the advantages of membership. | (D) 隨信附件說明了會員的權益。 |

題型 **填入句子**

解讀內容後可知，萊特先生因為加入了國際礦工協會，才會收到這封郵件。選項中，(A) 與 (C) 是鼓勵尚未加入者加入協會時，可能出現的內容，不符合文章脈絡。再從信件第一段提到的「conducting numerous programs and services that address the needs of miners worldwide」可知，表示協會是為處理全球礦工的需求所設，但 (B) 卻說是給特定地區的服務，所以也與文意矛盾。

(D) 表示附件含有說明會員權益的資料，最適合作為信件的結尾，故正確答案為 (D)。

### 139–142 文章

| | |
|---|---|
| Vice president Randolph Ward has unveiled that his ambitious project, Grand Bloom, is expected to be completed in May in Columbia, Missouri. Presently in the finishing stages of construction, the project consists of a brand-named shopping center and leisure complex. **139** will be located on Olson Boulevard. | 副董事長藍道夫·華德所揭露的遠大計畫「遍地開花」，預計五月在密蘇里州哥倫比亞市落成。計畫現階段已接近完工，包括一棟自有品牌的購物中心和複合休閒中心，雙雙坐落在歐森大道上。 |
| Mr. Ward is organizing a competition to find the best name for the facilities, which will occupy approximately 1,000 square meters and which will have a great **140** of Dawn River. | 華德先生舉行了命名大賽，要為佔地1,000平方公尺、坐擁曙光河美景的建築找到最合適的名稱。 |
| When asked what tips he would give to participants, Mr. Ward commented, "Bear in mind that the premises are surrounded by the river. The successfully-chosen name **141** that." The results will be announced at the end of next month. **142** . | 被問到給予參賽者的相關建議，華德先生表示：「要記得這些場所外有河流環繞。命名要反映出這點才有勝算。」比賽結果將在下個月底公布。優勝者將獲得該中心一年份的會員資格。 |

詞彙 **unveil** 揭露　**bear in mind** 記得　**premise** 場所

**139** --------------------------------------------------

| | |
|---|---|
| (A) Both | (A) 兩者 |
| (B) Few | (B) 很少 |
| (C) Several | (C) 數個 |
| (D) Some | (D) 有些 |

412

**题型 文法──代名詞**

空格為句子的主詞位置，需根據前一句的內容選出適合的代名詞。前面的內容提到，「遍地開花」建設計畫包括購物中心與複合休閒中心，所以使用 Both 作為代名詞最為合適，故正確答案為 (A)。

**140** ----------------------------------------

(A) preference
(B) exterior
(C) appearance
(D) view

(A) 偏好
(B) 外部
(C) 外表
(D) 景色

**题型 詞彙──名詞**

先找出關係代名詞 which 的先行詞，應是出現在逗號前的 the facilities，所以可知道此處兩個 which 引導的子句都是在描述某建築的特徵，故空格填 view 以表示建築能夠坐擁河岸「景致」最為適當，本題正確答案為 (D)。

**141** ----------------------------------------

(A) reflects
(B) reflected
(C) is reflecting
(D) should reflect

(A) 反映出
(B) 反映過
(C) 正在反映
(D) 應該反映

**题型 文法──動詞**

此處是在給予命名的建議，故根據句意，應填入 should reflect 較為適當，因此正確答案 (D)。

**142** (NEW) ----------------------------------------

(A) Mr. Ward is now looking for a site to build this facility.
(B) The prize winner will receive a one-year membership to the complex.
(C) The drawing was held in the new shopping center, and the result was surprising.
(D) The names will be announced at the groundbreaking ceremony.

(A) 華德先生還在找地點蓋這棟建築。
(B) 優勝者將獲得該中心一年份的會員資格。
(C) 新購物中心舉行抽籤活動，結果讓人大感意外。
(D) 名稱將會在開工儀式上公布。

**题型 填入句子**

從第二段的「Mr. Ward is organizing a competition to find the best name for the facilities」中，可知將舉行某設施的命名大賽，再從空格前句：「The results will be announced at the end of next month.」，知道比賽結果會在下個月底公布。因此，空格應代入與比賽結果有關或之後將發生的事，故選項中，告知頒獎事宜的 (B) 最為適當，正確答案為 (B)。

(A) 提到正在選址，但文章第一段中的「expected to be completed in May in Columbia, Missouri」，已說過建設計畫會在密蘇里州哥倫比亞市落成，故此選項非正確答案；(C) 使用過去式，代表結果已經出爐，與文意不符；(D) groundbreaking ceremony 指的是動工前進行的儀式，但文章中提到工程已接近尾聲，所以此選項也與文意不符。

| | |
|---|---|
| **To:** Reginald Reed <reginaldreed@umail.com> **From:** Aneroid Rental Shop <manager@arentals.com> **Date:** Wednesday, August 13 **Subject:** Overdue DVD items | 收件人：雷吉納德·里德 <reginaldreed@umail.com> 寄件人：安納羅伊德影視出租店 <manager@arentals.com> 日期：8月13日，週三 主旨：逾期DVD |
| Our rental records show that the following items were supposed to be returned to the rental shop on August 5: Raining Dark Night and An Isolated Island. Please take **143** back here by the end of the week. | 我們的租借紀錄顯示下列商品：《暗夜風雨》和《孤立島》，應該要在8月5日歸還。請在這週結束前把它們歸還商店。 |
| **144**. However, the items mentioned in the following list are not **145** for the extension: new arrivals, overdue items, and those which have been booked by other rental customers. | 請記得您可以透過電話向店家續借DVD七天。然而，下列DVD並不適用續借規則：新DVD、逾期DVD和其他顧客已預訂的影片。 |
| **146** we have sent you this notification as a reminder, please note that it is the customer's responsibility to return or renew our items by the deadline. | 雖然我們會寄送提醒通知，但請留意準時歸還或續借商品是顧客的責任。 |
| Thank you. | 謝謝您。 |

**詞彙** overdue 逾期的

**143** ----------------------------------------

(A) it
(B) ours
(C) this
(D) them

(A) 它
(B) 我們的
(C) 這個
(D) 它們

**題型 文法──代名詞**

「take sth back」意思是「歸還某物」，而空格前句提到 Raining Dark Night 與 An Isolated Island，可知這兩樣就是要歸還的物品，故此處使用可代稱複數名詞的 them 最為合適，正確答案為 (D)。

**144** NEW ----------------------------------------

(A) You may not lease, sublicense, rent, or resell this DVD.
(B) If so, we can renew the due date as long as they are new arrivals.
(C) Remember that rented DVDs can be renewed up to seven days by calling the shop.
(D) It is our responsibility to return the overdue items.

(A) 您不應出租、轉授權、租借或轉售這片 DVD。
(B) 如果是這樣的話，只要是新進光碟，我們都可以續借。
(C) 請記得您可以透過電話向店家續借 DVD 七天。
(D) 歸還逾期品是我們的責任。

題型 填入句子

注意空格後使用的是具有轉折語氣的 However，且後句提到未包含在續借規則裡的物品，故可推測此處的句子應也和「續借」這個主題有關。選項中 (B) 與 (C) 都有提到相關內容，但 (B) 表示新的 DVD 可以續借，此句與後方文意不符，故本題最適合的答案為 (C)。

**145** ----------------------------------------------------------------

(A) eligible             (A) 適用的

(B) displayed        (B) 被展示的

(C) finished          (C) 完成的

(D) capable          (D) 有能力的

題型 詞彙——形容詞

從句中使用的 not 和 extension 可以推測，此處是要表示「不可續借」，選項中只有填入 eligible 能表達出「不適用續借規則」的意思，故正確答案為 (A)。

**146** ----------------------------------------------------------------

(A) Except           (A) 除了

(B) Although        (B) 雖然

(C) Likewise        (C) 同樣地

(D) In case         (D) 以防萬一

題型 詞彙——副詞連接詞

空格後面接續著子句，而逗號後面也連接了子句，故空格應代入的是連接詞。此題也可直接從選項的字義判斷，因為此句應是要表示「雖然」有寄發此通知，但顧客應該自己在期限內返還或續借物品，故最適合填入的是連接詞 Although，正確答案為 (B)。

## PART 7

**147-148 資訊**

### Healing Dream Training Gym Uniforms

Newly appointed personal trainers at the Healing Dream Training Gym will be issued with three uniforms that they must wear when training clients. Two are indoor uniforms, and the third is to be kept for outdoor training. These uniforms are free to employees for the mandatory probation period of two months. However, employees who leave within this time will be required to pay for the cost of them. This money will automatically be deducted from the final paycheck as per our terms and conditions of employment. Uniforms must be kept clean at all times; please note that personal trainers have free access to our on-site laundry, which is located in the basement of the building.

### 夢想療癒健身中心 制服

夢想療癒健身中心將核發三件制服給新進私人教練,為訓練客戶時必穿的服飾。兩件是室內制服,第三件則適合戶外訓練使用。在兩個月的法定試用期期間,這些制服是免費提供給員工的。然而員工如果在這段期間離職,必須支付制服費用。根據我們的僱用條款和規則,金額將從最終薪資單自動扣除。制服必須隨時保持乾淨;請記得私人教練可以自由使用我們地下室的洗衣間。

**詞彙 mandatory** 法定的  **probation** 試用期  **as per** 按照

**147**

**Where would the information most likely be found?**  這項資訊最可能在哪裡看到?

(A) In a travel brochure
(B) In an expense claim
(C) In an employee handbook
(D) In a clothing store

(A) 旅遊小冊子裡
(B) 索賠單上
(C) 員工手冊上
(D) 服飾店內

先觀察最上方出現的公司名稱為 Healing Dream Training Gym,再看到文章內容的多次提到 uniforms,可知道這篇資訊和健身中心的員工制服有關,且文內提到「mandatory probation」、「terms and conditions of employment」、「Uniforms must be kept clean at all times」等內容,故可知道此文最可能出現在給員工閱覽的手冊上,正確答案為 (C)。

**148**

**What is mentioned about the Healing Dream Training Gym?**  文中提到夢想療癒健身中心什麼事?

(A) It only offers indoor training.
(B) It has its own laundry.
(C) It manufactures the uniforms itself.
(D) It is closed for two months of the year.

(A) 只提供室內訓練。
(B) 有自己的洗衣間。
(C) 自己生產制服。
(D) 今年關閉了兩個月。

文章下半部提到，制服需時常保持乾淨，並說到：「personal trainers have free access to our on-site laundry, which is located in the basement of the building」，由此可知，健身中心內部的確設有洗衣店，因此本題正確答案為 (B)。

(A) 文章中提到：「the third is to be kept for outdoor training」，表示第三套制服為戶外訓練專用，所以 (A) 不正確；(C) 的內容文中並未提及；(D) 文中說到 two months 的部分是指試用期，所以 (D) 也不正確。

## 149–150 通知

| | |
|---|---|
| **7th Used Furniture Fair with Annual Secondhand Goods Auction** | **第七屆二手家具市集 暨年度二手商品拍賣** |
| Featuring hundreds of mahogany antique furniture pieces including chairs, desks, beds, and many more | 上百件特色桃花木古董傢俱，包括桌椅、床和更多選擇。 |
| Saturday, 22 November 32 Reuben Street, Brisbane | 週六，11月22日 布里斯本，魯賓街32號 |
| **Admission:** from 11:00 A.M. to 7:00 P.M. **Reception:** from 5:00 P.M. to 7:00 P.M. Auction begins at 7:30 P.M. | 入場：上午11點到晚上7點 接待會：下午5點到晚上7點 拍賣從晚上7:30開始 |
| **Tickets:** $5 before 17th November; $7 at the door | 票價：11月17日前預購5元； 現場購票7美元 |
| For advance tickets, visit our website www.uff.com or call us at (643) 367-3475. The ticket price includes the catalog of auction items. | 預購票請上官網查詢www.uff.com或者 電話聯絡我們(643)367-3475。 票價已包括拍賣會型錄。 |
| All proceeds of the event go to Greenslopes Community Hospital. | 活動收益將全數資助綠坡社區醫院。 |

**詞彙** **auction** 拍賣　**mahogany** 桃花木　**advance ticket** 預售票　**proceeds** （拍賣得來的）收益

**149** - - - - - - - - - - - - - - - - - - - - - - - - - - - - - - - - - - - - - - - - - - - - - - - - - - - - - - - - - - -

**What is the purpose of the notice?** | **這則通知的目的為何？**

(A) To promote the visit of a famous craftsman | (A) 宣傳一位工藝名匠的到訪
(B) To advertise the sale of unique furnishings | (B) 為獨特家具的拍賣打廣告
(C) To announce the opening of a furniture store | (C) 公布一家家具店的開幕時間
(D) To publicize a community hospital | (D) 宣傳一間社區醫院

從標題的「Used Furniture」、「Secondhand Goods」及內文的時間、地點、票價等資訊，可看出這是二手物品拍賣的廣告訊息，再從內文第一句：「Featuring hundreds of mahogany antique furniture pieces」可知，拍賣品皆為桃花木製成，故選項中最符合的為 (B)。

## 150

**What is suggested about the event?** 　文中提到這個活動什麼事？

(A) There is an additional fee to attend the reception. 　(A) 參加接待會要額外付費。

(B) Students receive a special discount. 　(B) 學生享有特別折扣。

(C) Antique furniture will be displayed beginning at 　(C) 古董家具將在晚上七點開始展示。
    7:00 P.M.

(D) Tickets cost less if purchased online. 　(D) 網路購票比較便宜。

文中指出拍賣會是在 11 月 22 日舉辦，而票價資訊上寫著：「Tickets: $5 before 17th November; $7 at the door」，故可知道，提前在 17 日前買好預售票，會比現場購票便宜 2 美元，且從後文可知，預售票能透過網路或電話購買，故本題正確答案為 (D)。

---

### 151–152 收據

| Michael's | | 麥可家 | |
|---|---|---|---|
| 665 West Broadway | | 加拿大溫哥華市西百老匯街665號 | |
| Vancouver, Canada | | | |

| February 12 | 4:31 P.M. | 2月12日 | 下午4:31 |
|---|---|---|---|
| **Gym Gear** | | 運動穿著 | |
| Sports Direct: jogging pants | 19.99 | 立馬運動：運動用慢跑褲 | 19.99 |
| **General Items** | | 一般商品 | |
| Brand Zest: boxing gloves and pads | 16.99 | 品牌興趣：拳擊手套和護墊 | 16.99 |
| Subtotal | 36.98 | 小計 | 36.98 |
| Tax-8% | 2.96 | 稅8% | 2.96 |
| **Total** | **39.94** | **總計** | **39.94** |
| Cash tendered | 50.00 | 收現 | 50.00 |
| Change | 10.06 | 找零 | 10.06 |

**Returns and Exchanges Policy**

Unworn items may be returned for a refund or exchanged for credit vouchers within 30 days of purchase. These items must be in like-new condition, and the original receipt of purchase must be included. Items purchased on sale cannot be refunded at any time. These items may, however, be exchanged for goods of the same value and must be accompanied by the original receipt.

**退換貨政策**

未穿過的商品可以在30天內退款，或換成有效的現金券。商品必須幾近全新狀態，並附上購買時的收據。特價商品均不得退款，但可以保留原收據兌換其他等值商品。

**詞彙** **voucher** 現金券　**like-new** 接近全新的

---

**151**

---

**What type of store most likely is Michael's?**

(A) A souvenir shop
(B) A sports store
(C) A music store
(D) A rental store

參可家最可能是什麼商店？

(A) 紀念品店
(B) 運動用品店
(C) 樂器行
(D) 出租店

因為收據上的品項有慢跑褲、拳擊手套和護墊，故這最可能是間販售運動用品的商店，正確答案為 **(B)**。

---

**152**

---

**What is true about the store's policy?**

(A) All exchanges require an original receipt.
(B) All returned items incur an 8 percent restocking fee.
(C) All purchases must be paid in cash.
(D) All sale items must be in original packaging.

關於店家政策，何者為真？

(A) 換貨都需要原收據。
(B) 所有退貨商品酌收 8% 的入庫處理費。
(C) 只接受現金交易。
(D) 所有特價商品都得在原包裝內。

本題詢問「store's policy」，故答題時要鎖定「Returns and Exchanges Policy」部分。此處提到未穿過的商品與特價商品，其中針對未穿過的商品，文內說當要退貨時，「the original receipt of purchase must be included.」；而針對特價商品，則表示無法退款，但是可以「be exchanged for goods of the same value and must be accompanied by the original receipt」，也就是特價商品若保留收據，可以兌換等值商品。

綜合上述，**(A)** 是唯一可從文中找到的內容，其餘三個選項皆未在文中提及，故小題正確答案為 **(A)**。

---

### 153–154 訊息串

| | | | |
|---|---|---|---|
| **Norah Turner** | 03:43 P.M. | 諾拉・特納〔下午3:43〕： | |
| Jayden, can I talk to you about the advertising revenue? I personally only managed to sell 20% of my monthly target. | | 傑登，我可以和你談一下廣告收益嗎？我個人只能達成這個月目標的 20%。 | |
| **Jayden Watts** | 03:44 P.M. | 傑登・瓦茲〔下午3:44〕： | |
| I haven't managed to achieve my allocation either. Since Hendel Publishing launched a similar magazine recently, many businesses have been moving to advertise in that. | | 我也沒能達到額度。自從韓德爾出版最近發行了類似雜誌，很多公司都跑去那裡登廣告了。 | |
| **Norah Turner** | 03:44 P.M. | 諾拉・特納〔下午3:44〕： | |
| What shall we do? Don't we need to reduce the advertising pages and save the cost? | | 我們該怎麼辦？我們需要減少廣告頁以節省成本嗎？ | |
| **Jayden Watts** | 03:44 P.M. | 傑登・瓦茲〔下午3:44〕： | |
| We're not supposed to do that. There's much to be lost if we reduce the pages | | 不行，減少頁數的損失太大。 | |

**Norah Turner**                                03:45 P.M.

Then, why don't we lower the advertisement rates as an incentive for our existing clients?

**Jayden Watts**                                03:46 P.M.

That would be worth trying. We are going to lose even more revenue next month if we don't do anything about it.

諾拉·特納〔下午3:45〕：
那何不降低廣告價格，來吸引我們的現有客戶呢？

傑登·瓦茲〔下午3:46〕：
值得試試。如果我們再不採取行動，下個月會損失更多收益。

 **詞彙** allocation 配額　existing 現有的

---

**153**

**What problem is being discussed?**

(A) A product's development has been delayed.
(B) Advertising revenue is falling.
(C) The magazine circulation has been reduced.
(D) Staff turnover has been increasing.

他們討論到什麼問題？

(A) 產品開發的進度落後。
(B) 廣告收益下滑。
(C) 雜誌發行量下滑。
(D) 員工一直增加。

特納女士在一開頭便已提到「the advertising revenue」，並說：「I personally only managed to sell 20% of my monthly target.」，表示自己未達本月目標，隨後瓦茲先生也說自從類似雜誌發行後，許多公司都去那邊刊登廣告，後續兩人便針對廣告收益下降的問題討論解決辦法，故本題正確答案為 (B)。

---

**154** NEW

**At 3:46 P.M., What does Mr. Watts mean when he writes, "That would be worth trying"?**

(A) The company shouldn't make any changes.
(B) He has to cut down the cost by reducing the pages.
(C) They can offer discounts to current advertisers.
(D) He wants Ms. Turner to try harder next month.

下午3:46 時，瓦茲先生寫道：「值得試試」，他的意思是？

(A) 公司不會嘗試任何改變。
(B) 他必須減少頁數來降低成本。
(C) 他們可以提供折扣給目前的廣告主。
(D) 他希望特納女士下個月更努力

特納女士最後說到：「why don't we lower the advertisement rates as an incentive for our existing clients」，提議降低現有客戶的廣告費用作為優惠，故此處瓦茲先生說的「That would be worth trying.」，應該是認為這項提議值得一試，本題正確答案為 (C)。

**155–157 資訊**

| | |
|---|---|
| ## Tapas La Mancha | ## 拉曼查小菜 |

| | |
|---|---|
| *Sanchez Pietro, Owner*<br>*Reviewed by Helene Labore* | 店長桑切斯‧彼耶羅<br>海倫‧拉波爾評論 |
| Overall rating: 3 out of 5 stars ★★★☆☆ | 整體評價：三顆星（滿分五顆星）<br>★★★☆☆ |
| **Atmosphere: 3 stars**<br>Sanchez Pietro refurbished the venue last month. —[1]—. It is spacious inside and has a distinct Spanish theme. However, the noise from the kitchen was loud, and there seemed to be a lack of privacy for couples who were dining. | 氣氛：三顆星<br>桑切斯‧彼耶羅上個月才整修場地。空間大，西班牙主題風格突出。不過廚房的聲音太吵，情侶用餐的隱私也不夠。 |
| **Service: 4 stars**<br>The service was very good with the serving staff extremely polite and efficient. —[2]—. The food arrived quickly and dishes were cleared as soon as we finished our meal. | 服務：四顆星<br>服務非常好。服務生有禮貌效率高，出餐很快，我們剛吃完很快就清空桌面。 |
| **Food: 2 stars**<br>The menu was not very varied and had not really changed from the last time I visited the restaurant, three years ago. —[3]—. I enjoyed the main meal, although the fish was slightly overcooked. The desserts were a big disappointment, as there was little choice and they were tasteless. | 食物：兩顆星<br>菜單選擇不是非常多，和我三年前來的時候相比沒什麼變化。分量太少，開胃菜味道不太好。我覺得主餐不錯，但魚煮得有點太老。甜點非常令人失望，不但選擇少還沒味道。 |
| **Value : 4 stars**<br>Although some of the items on the menu are overpriced, on the whole, the meals are relatively inexpensive. —[4]—. The wine list is also very pricey, but the main dishes are true bargains. | 價位：四顆星<br>菜單上有些菜色定價太高，不過餐點整體來說都相對便宜。酒水也很貴，不過主餐真的很划算。 |

**詞彙** spacious 寬敞的　distinct 突出的　on the whole 整體來說　bargain 划算的交易

**155** --------------------------------------------------------------

| | |
|---|---|
| **What is the purpose of the information?** | 這篇資訊的目的為何？ |
| (A) To announce the reopening of a restaurant | (A) 公告一家餐廳重新開張 |
| (B) To summarize the expansion plans of a restaurant | (B) 總結一間餐廳的擴建計畫 |
| (C) To promote special menus that will be introduced at a restaurant | (C) 推薦一家餐廳即將推出的特別菜單 |
| (D) To assess the quality of a restaurant | (D) 評估一家餐廳的品質 |

從段落標題可知，文內分成氣氛、服務、食物與價位，並以星等給予餐廳評價，故本題正確答案為 (D)。

**What is suggested about the restaurant?**

(A) Its menu items are overall value for money.

(B) It hosts live musical events.

(C) Its menu has significantly changed over these years.

(D) It is located within a city center.

文中提到這間餐廳什麼事？

(A) 整體菜色值得這個錢。

(B) 舉辦現場音樂活動。

(C) 菜單在過去幾年有明顯變化。

(D) 位於市中心。

最後 Value 的標題下提到：「on the whole, the meals are relatively inexpensive.」，表示整體來說餐點算是相對平價，並給予 4 顆星的高分數，故本題最相符的選項為 (A)。

(B) 與 (D) 皆是文中未提及的內容；(C) 在 Food 的標題下有提到「The menu . . . had not really changed from the last time I visited the restaurant, three years ago」，表示菜單已三年未更換，故此選項也與內文不符。

157 (NEW)

**In which of the positions marked [1], [2], [3], and [4] does the following sentence best belong?**

**"The portions were small, and the tapas starters were not very tasty."**

(A) [1]

(B) [2]

(C) [3]

(D) [4]

下列句子最適合出現在[1]、[2]、[3]、[4]的哪個位置中？

「分量太少，開胃菜味道不太好。」

(A) [1]

(B) [2]

(C) [3]

(D) [4]

題目引述的句子提到餐點的分量與開胃菜的味道，故應放在與食物相關的標題下，也就是 [3] 的位置，所以本題正確答案為 (C)。

## 158–160 信件

| | |
|---|---|
| Alltrue Digital Equipment<br>355 Tree Drive<br>Sacramento, CA 94203 | 全真電子設備<br>94203 加州沙加緬度市<br>大樹街355號 |
| 16 March | 3月16日 |
| Alexander Soskin<br>2541 Angel Place<br>Santa Barbara, CA 93109 | 亞歷山大·索斯金<br>93109 加州聖塔芭芭拉市天使地<br>2541號 |
| Dear Mr. Soskin, | 親愛的索斯金先生： |
| We have enclosed the radio that you returned to us for repair. Unfortunately, we are unable to complete the repairs as the fault to the appliance is not covered under our two-year general guarantee. | 隨包裹附上您送修的收音機。很遺憾，我們沒有辦法修理它，因為這項機械故障並不含在兩年保固的範圍內。 |

We have ascertained that the original sound box has been replaced by a component that is not compatible with our brand of audio equipment. Please see the enclosed report from our repair officer for clarification. Our guarantee is also enclosed, which clearly states that should any part be replaced or altered, the work must be carried out by our repair team using our own approved components. The guarantee does not cover unauthorized tampering with the appliance and, therefore, we are unable to repair this appliance under the terms and conditions of the guarantee. If, however, you still wish to have the item repaired, we can do so at a cost of $100.

Many thanks for your cooperation in this matter and for purchasing an item from Alltrue Digital Equipment.

Yours sincerely,
Kevin Constant
Customer Services Manager
Enclosures

我們確認原來的音箱已經換成和我們品牌收音機不相容的零件。請參閱附件中維修人員的說明報告。也附上保固書，其中載明如果需要更換或改裝內部零件，必須由我方維修團隊執行，並使用我方核准的零件。未經授權的拆裝將不提供保固，因此根據保固條款，我們無法修理這項產品。但如果您仍想維修，我們會酌收100美元維修費。

非常感謝您的合作，也謝謝您在全真電子購買產品。

客服經理
凱文・康斯坦特 敬上
附件

**詞彙** **ascertain** 確認 **compatible** 相容的 **tamper** 折裝

**158** ----------------------------------------

**What is the main purpose of the letter?**

(A) To explain why a request was not fulfilled
(B) To thank a customer for a recent purchase
(C) To request a call back from a repairperson
(D) To request information about digital equipment

這封信的目的為何？

(A) 解釋為什麼沒有辦法達成要求
(B) 感謝顧客近期的購買
(C) 請求維修人員回電
(D) 詢問某個電子產品的資訊

從信件第一句的「We have enclosed the radio that you returned to us for repair.」，可以看出索斯金先生將收音機送給全真電子設備維修，再從之後的「Unfortunately, we are unable to complete the repairs」可知，公司無法如他所願的修理機器，故把收音機寄回。

而信件第二段則是具體說明無法維修的原因，並提到「the original sound box has been replaced by a component that is not compatible with our brand of audio equipment.」，表示收音機因為使用非原廠的零件修理過，已不符合保固規定。綜合上述可知，這封信件的目的是要說明無法維修的原因，因此正確答案為 (A)。

**159** ----------------------------------------

**What is NOT included with the letter?**

(A) A guarantee
(B) A findings report
(C) A refund
(D) A radio

這封信中沒有包括什麼？

(A) 保固書
(B) 報告書
(C) 退款
(D) 收音機

信件開頭便說了「We have enclosed the radio that you returned to us for repair.」，代表收音機有隨包裹附上，再從第二段的「Please see the enclosed report from our repair officer for clarification.」與「Our guarantee is also enclosed」，可以看出說明報告及保固書也有隨信附上，故信中沒有包含的只有退款，本題正確答案為 (C)。

## 160

**What is Mr. Soskin advised to do?**

(A) Repair the item himself

(B) Pay for repairs

(C) Purchase an extended warranty

(D) Call an Alltrue Customer Service manager

索斯金先生被建議怎麼做？

(A) 自行維修商品

(B) 付費修理

(C) 付費展延保固期

(D) 打電話給全真電子的客服經理

第二段敘述無法維修的原因，最後一句說到：「If, however, you still wish to have the item repaired, we can do so at a cost of $100.」，表示若索斯金先生仍然希望物品能順利修復，需要負擔 100 美元的維修費用，故本題正確答案為 (B)。

## 161-163 訊息串

| | |
|---|---|
| **Allison Green** 09:43 A.M.<br>Good morning, Timothy. I heard you are meeting our Spanish guests when they come on Monday. | 艾莉森・格林〔上午9:43〕：<br>早安，提摩西。我聽說你下週一會接待我們來自西班牙的訪客。 |
| **Timothy Moore** 09:43 A.M.<br>Hello, Allison. That meeting's giving me a headache. | 提摩西・摩爾〔上午9:43〕：<br>哈囉，艾莉森。這讓我很頭痛。 |
| **Allison Green** 09:44 A.M.<br>What's the matter? You speak Spanish pretty well. | 艾莉森・格林〔上午9:44〕：<br>怎麼了？你西班牙文說得很好。 |
| **Timothy Moore** 09:45 A.M.<br>As a matter of fact, you know I have to prepare for the sales presentation on Tuesday. I just don't have enough time to take care of the Monday meeting. | 提摩西・摩爾〔上午9:45〕：<br>事實上，我得準備週二的銷售簡報。我沒有時間準備週一的接待。 |
| **Allison Green** 09:46 A.M.<br>That must be very hard. Is there anything I can do to help you? | 艾莉森・格林〔上午9:46〕：<br>這真的很難。有什麼我可以幫你的嗎？ |
| **Timothy Moore** 09:47 A.M.<br>Hmm . . . I need to find a caterer to provide lunches and some refreshments. Do you have any suggestions? | 提摩西・摩爾〔上午9:47〕：<br>嗯……我需要找到廠商提供午餐和茶點。妳有什麼建議嗎？ |
| **Allison Green** 09:48 A.M.<br>I would say Mortime Caterers. They are very reputable, and they provide an excellent lunchtime buffet. Shall I take care of the food service? | 艾莉森・格林〔上午9:48〕：<br>我推薦多食餐飲。他們評價蠻好的，午餐自助吧也很棒。需要我負責處理餐點嗎？ |

| | | | |
|---|---|---|---|
| **Timothy Moore** | 09:49 A.M. | 提摩西‧摩爾〔上午9:49〕： | |

That would be great. Thank you, Allison. I owe you one.

那就太好了。謝了，艾莉森。我欠妳一次。

| | | | |
|---|---|---|---|
| **Allison Green** | 09:50 A.M. | 艾莉森‧格林〔上午9:50〕： | |

Don't mention it. I can call them now and see if they are available.

不客氣。我馬上打電話問看看他們方不方便。

---

**詞彙** **sth give sb a headache** 讓人頭痛、傷腦筋　**owe** 欠款；對……有虧欠
**I owe you one** 我欠你一次　**don't mention it** 不客氣；不用謝

**161** ----------------------------------------

**What will Mr. Moore do on Tuesday?**

(A) Visit a restaurant
(B) Prepare for a business trip
(C) Give a presentation
(D) Conduct a job interview

摩爾先生週二要做什麼？

(A) 去餐廳看看
(B) 準備出差
(C) 做簡報
(D) 面試

9 點 45 分時，摩爾先生在話中提到「I have to prepare for the sales presentation on Tuesday」，表示週二有銷售簡報，故本題正確答案為 (C)。

**162** [NEW] ----------------------------------------

**At 09.44 A.M., what does Ms. Green mean when she writes, "You speak Spanish pretty well"?**

(A) She believes Mr. Moore is able to do his job perfectly.
(B) She has a suggestion for Mr. Moore.
(C) She thinks the guests will love Spanish food.
(D) She wants to help Mr. Moore prepare for the Tuesday meeting.

上午9:44 時，格林女士寫道：「你西班牙文說得很好」，她的意思是？

(A) 她相信摩爾先生可以完美勝任這個任務。
(B) 她想向摩爾先生提出建議。
(C) 她認為訪客會喜歡西班牙菜。
(D) 她想幫忙摩爾先生準備週二的簡報。

格林女士說這句話時，還不知道摩爾先生遇到什麼困難，她只知道他週一需要接待來自西班牙的訪客，故在此狀況下，格林女士說的：「You speak Spanish pretty well.」應是表示她認為摩爾先生能成功接待西班牙來的貴賓，故本題最適合的答案為 (A)。

**163** ----------------------------------------

**What does Ms. Green offer to do?**

(A) Provide a buffet
(B) Contact a service
(C) Recommend a restaurant
(D) Purchase a new phone

格林女士主動提供什麼幫助？

(A) 提供自助餐點
(B) 聯絡某項服務
(C) 推薦一家餐廳
(D) 買新電話

9 點 47 分時，摩爾先生向格林女士尋求供餐廠商的建議，格林女士則回答道：「Shall I take care of the food service?」，且之後還說了：「I can call them now and see if they are available.」，表示她能幫忙聯絡業者處理餐點，故正確答案為 (B)。

## Company Library Cards

The Law Society's library system enables members of the business community to use its facilities.

Employees of businesses within the local area will be eligible for a company library card. The cost is just $40 a year, although the fee is waived for charities and nonprofit organizations.

A company library card can be used by local businesses for research purposes, and employees should take responsibility for any books or papers they might borrow. The cardholder is responsible for any fines incurred for late or lost materials.

To apply for a company library card, you must fill out an application form at the library's reception desk. This must be accompanied by a photo identification, a letter confirming your position at your organization, and the fee to join. We will then provide you with a receipt.

If you have any queries, contact us at the main law office at 555-9284.

## 商務圖書證

法律協會的圖書館系統允許商會會員使用它的設施。

當地企業的員工可以申請商務圖書證。年費40美元,但若為慈善機構或非營利組織則免年費。

商務圖書證可以讓當地企業基於研究目的使用,企業員工有責任保管借出的書籍或文獻。如有逾期未還或資料遺失,持卡人將面臨罰款。

如欲申請商務圖書證,您必須在圖書館接待處填妥申請表格。申請需檢附有照片的身分證件、公司就職證明和會費。我們將會提供收據給您。

如果您有任何疑問,請聯絡法律協會主辦公室555-9284。

---

詞彙 eligible 有資格的　paper 文獻　incur 遭受;招致　query 疑問

**What is the purpose of the notice?**

(A) To explain a service
(B) To propose an idea
(C) To correct a mistake
(D) To announce an opening

這則告示的目的為何?

(A) 解釋一項服務
(B) 提出點子
(C) 修正錯誤
(D) 公告開張

從標題的「Company Library Cards」即可知道內容會與商務借書證相關,且之後文章的第一句:「The Law Society's library system enables members of the business community to use its facilities.」,解釋了圖書館的設施開放商會會員使用,之後第二段提到費用,第三段則是借書規定,第四段説明申請方式,故可知道全文旨在介紹商務圖書證這項服務,本題正確答案為 (A)。

**What is stated about annual fees?**

(A) Certain organizations are exempt.
(B) They can be paid by credit card.
(C) They are higher for out-of-town businesses.
(D) They are refunded after a year.

文中提到年費什麼事?

(A) 特定組織得免繳。
(B) 可以用信用卡付款。
(C) 外地的企業會比較貴。
(D) 一年後會退款。

費用相關的資訊要從第二段得到。本段提到：「The cost is just $40 a year, although the fee is waived for charities and nonprofit organizations.」，也就表示年費為 40 美元，但慈善機構與非營利組織不須付費，故本題正確答案為 (A)。

(B) 第四段提到必須在圖書館接待處付費，但沒有提及信用卡；(C) 從第二段無法得知外地企業的年費，故無法比較；(D) 文中未提及此事。

---

**166**

According to the notice, what must a borrower do if materials are lost?

(A) Waive their membership
(B) Report the loss to their supervisor
(C) Return their company library card
(D) Pay a fine to the library

根據告示，如果資料不見，借閱者必須做什麼？

(A) 取消會員資格
(B) 向主管回報損失
(C) 交還商務圖書證
(D) 向圖書館繳交罰款

第三段中提到：「The cardholder is responsible for any fines incurred for late or lost materials.」，表示如有逾期未還或資料遺失，衍生的罰金為卡片持有者的責任，由此可知，如果遺失了資料，借閱者需要繳納罰金，正確答案為 (D)。

---

**167**

What is NOT required at the time of application?

(A) Proof of identity
(B) Payment
(C) Confirmation of employment
(D) A signed contract

申請時不需要什麼東西？

(A) 身分證明
(B) 付款
(C) 確認員工身分
(D) 簽訂合約

第四段整段都在講解申請圖書證的規則，其中說到需要「fill out an application form」，且申請表上包含了「a photo identification」與「a letter confirming your position at your organization」，最後還要帶著「the fee to join」，故可以知道申請時需要有照片的身分證件、公司就職證明與會費，故選項中唯一不需要的是簽訂合約一事，所以本題答案為 (D)。

**168–171 文章**

| Manager's Behavior | 管理者行為 |
|---|---|
| In his new book, *Etiquette in the Workplace*, Manuel Rodriguez gives advice to managers on how to earn and gain respect from employees by behaving in the appropriate manner. —[1]—. Mr. Rodriguez explains that managers who hold a responsible position should conduct themselves in a manner that befits their status, not just in an office environment but in social situations, especially those organized by the company for which they work. | 曼紐爾‧羅德里格斯在他的新書《職場禮儀》內建議管理者舉止合宜，才能贏得員工的尊重。羅德里格斯先生解釋，擔任重責的管理者，其所作所為應該要與他們的地位相稱，不單單只限於辦公環境，也要考量社交情況，尤其是所屬公司安排的場合。 |

For example, a manager should be in attendance at a social event such as an awards ceremony where other senior employees are invited. This is part of a manager's role. However, a social event such as a sports tournament with more junior members of staff can be avoided. Nevertheless, managers should decline any such invitations with a polite refusal.

—[2]—. A manager should always appear neat and well-groomed. Punctuality is mandatory. When a manager is attending an event arranged by the company, he or she must acknowledge coworkers who are not seen often and ensure that he or she is familiar with their names as a matter of courtesy. Also, it is compulsory for a manager to praise the organizers of events and acknowledge the effort that has gone into making an event successful for all attendees.

Mr. Rodriguez has been writing online for many years and has been recognized as one of the leading authorities on workplace etiquette. —[3]—. He is a regular contributor to television and his book, *Etiquette in the Workplace*, has already sold over 200,000 copies since its publication six months ago, through Mitchell Hamden. —[4]—. It can be ordered online through www.mitchellhamden.com.

舉例來說，管理者應該出席社交場合，像是一場邀請了其他資深員工的頒獎典禮。這是管理者職責的一部分。不過，像是大多數由年輕員工參加的運動比賽，則可以避免。然而，管理者拒絕這種邀請時務必婉轉。

另外，外表美觀至關重要。管理者外表要整齊乾淨。準時是義務。管理者參加公司安排的活動，必須認得不常見的同仁，也要禮貌性知道他們的姓名。此外，管理者必須稱讚安排活動的人，讓他們知道他們的努力付出促使活動成功，參加者都很愉快。

羅德里格斯先生在網路上書寫多年，被視為談論職場禮儀的一位重要權威人士。他經常上電視分享，而且他由米契爾·哈姆登出版公司出版的新書《職場禮儀》，出版六個月以來已暢銷超過20萬本。可以在www.mitchellhamden.com線上訂購。

詞彙 etiquette 禮儀　behave 表現　conduct 舉止　befit 與……相稱　be in attendance 出席
sports tournament 運動比賽　refusal 拒絕　neat 整齊的　well-groomed 外觀整潔的
punctuality 守時　mandatory 義務的

 **168**

**What does the article primarily discuss?**

(A) A book about appropriate behavior for managers
(B) A guide to solving improper workplace issues
(C) A leaflet about organizing social events
(D) A brochure about maintaining employment levels

這篇文章主要是討論什麼？

(A) 一本關於管理者舉止合宜的書
(B) 一本解決不當職場問題的指引
(C) 安排社交活動的傳單
(D) 維持員工職業水準的小冊子

先觀察文章的標題為「Manager's Behavior」，且開頭隨即提到：「In his new book, *Etiquette in the Workplace*, Manuel Rodriguez gives advice to managers on how to earn and gain respect from employees by behaving in the appropriate manner.」，點出《職場禮儀》一書能教導管理者透過適當的舉止贏得員工的尊重，之後的內容也與書籍或主管態度建立有關，且最後還給與訂閱書籍的網址，故可知道這篇文章是在介紹一本管理者舉止相關的書，正確答案為 (A)。

**169** - - - - - - - - - - - - - - - - - - - - - - - - - - - - - - - - - - - - - - - - - - - - - -

**What is suggested about Mr. Rodriguez?**

(A) He has worked for the same company for years.
(B) He is a very successful writer.
(C) He will finish writing his book within six months.
(D) He organizes the company's social events.

文中提到羅德里格斯先生什麼事？

(A) 他在同一間公司工作多年。
(B) 他是個非常成功的作家。
(C) 他將在六個月內寫完書。
(D) 他安排公司的社交活動。

根據第四段的內容，羅德里格斯先生寫作多年，且「has been recognized as one of the leading authorities on workplace etiquette」，表示他被視為談論職場禮儀的權威人士，故選項中最適合他的描述應為 (B)。

(A) 文中未提及此事；(C) 根據第四段，《職場禮儀》是在六個月內賣出超過 20 萬本，且此處使用未來式與文意不符；(D) 社交活動只是書中其中一個主題，文中沒有提到他安排活動一事。

**170** - - - - - - - - - - - - - - - - - - - - - - - - - - - - - - - - - - - - - - - - - - - - - -

**What kind of business does Mitchell Hamden specialize in?**

(A) Event organizing
(B) Online design
(C) Employment benefits
(D) Book publishing

米契爾・哈姆登專職什麼事業？

(A) 活動企畫
(B) 線上設計
(C) 就業福利
(D) 書籍出版

第四段提到：「*Etiquette in the Workplace*, has already sold over 200,000 copies since its publication six months ago, through Mitchell Hamden」，表示《職場禮儀》是透過「Mitchell Hamden」出版的，故可推測這應該是一間出版社的名字，因此最適當的答案為 (D)。

**171** NEW - - - - - - - - - - - - - - - - - - - - - - - - - - - - - - - - - - - - - - - - - - -

**In which of the positions marked [1], [2], [3], and [4] does the following sentence best belong?**

**"In addition, a good appearance is essential."**

(A) [1]
(B) [2]
(C) [3]
(D) [4]

下列句子最適合出現在[1]、[2]、[3]、[4]的哪個位置中？

「另外，外表美觀至關重要。」

(A) [1]
(B) [2]
(C) [3]
(D) [4]

文中只有第三段出現針對外貌的討論，其中說到「A manager should always appear neat and well-groomed.」，表示管理者應要有整潔的外表，故題目引述的句子最適合放在 [2] 的位置。

另外也可從句子開頭的「In addition」著手；由於第二段討論的是出席社交場合的舉止禮儀，第三段則轉為討論外表、準時與和同仁相處的態度，故兩段之間適合插入「In addition」表示社交場合之外的日常對應，為管理者自我管理的話題的接續。綜合上述，本題最適當的答案為 (B)。

# Gordon Industries

**To:** All staff
**From:** Grace Elliott
**Date:** June 11
**Subject:** Re: Holiday Schedule

Well done for helping Gordon Industries successfully complete its largest contract in the company's nine-year history. As a reward for your hard work, we are organizing a Family Week in the month of July. For one week during the summer vacation, we are holding numerous events to which you and your family are invited free of charge. We hope that the next few years will bring as much success to Gordon Industries, and we are showing our appreciation with the week of events. See below for a day-by-day schedule.

| DATE | EVENT | LOCATION | TIME |
|---|---|---|---|
| Monday, July 25 | Water play | Magic Springs Water Park | 11 A.M. to 6 P.M. |
| Tuesday, July 26 | Family picnic | Hot Springs Park Campsite | All Day |
| Wednesday, July 27 | Outdoor activities | Hot Springs Park (See department notice boards for a breakdown of locations) | All day |
| Thursday, July 28 | Field Day (Basketball, Softball, Soccer) | Park Recreation Center | 1 P.M. to 5 P.M. |
| Friday, July 29 | Dance party and children's entertainment | Hot Springs Park Campsite | 3 P.M. to 6 P.M. |

My personal secretary, Amanda Cole, has already booked the children's entertainment and caterers for the event. Before it reaches the fixed number, please call her at extension 256 as soon as possible. There will also be a barbeque party after the sports competition. To sign up for the tournaments, please give your name to Jared Murphy in management support. There will be prizes for the winning teams.

# 高登工業

收件人：全體員工
寄件人：葛瑞斯·埃利奧特
日期：6月11日
主旨：關於：假期行程

各位做得好！協助高登公司成功簽下公司九年來，史上最大筆的合約。為感謝您的辛勞，我們將在七月舉辦家庭週。於暑假舉辦為期一週的各式活動，免費邀請您的家人蒞臨參加。希望未來幾年也能為高登工業帶來更多成功，以一週的活動表達我們的感謝。逐日行程如下。

| 日期 | 活動 | 地點 | 時間 |
|---|---|---|---|
| 7月25日（一） | 水上遊戲 | 魔術噴泉水上樂園 | 上午11點到下午6點 |
| 7月26日（二） | 家族野餐 | 溫泉公園露營區 | 全天 |
| 7月27日（三） | 戶外活動 | 溫泉公園（詳細地點請見部門布告欄） | 全天 |
| 7月28日（四） | 運動場日（籃球、壘球、足球） | 公園休閒中心 | 下午1點到5點 |
| 7月29日（五） | 舞會和兒童娛樂 | 溫泉公園露營區 | 下午3點到6點 |

我的私人祕書亞曼達·科爾已經預約好兒童娛樂活動和活動餐點。指定人數額滿前，請儘快撥分機256和她聯絡。運動比賽之後會舉辦烤肉大會。如欲參賽請向負責運動項目的傑瑞德·墨菲報名。獲勝隊伍將有獎賞。

I hope you are all looking forward to the Family Week, as it will be a chance for you to relax and enjoy the company of your family and colleagues. I hope to see everyone there.

Grace Elliott
President
Gordon Industries

我希望您們也都引頸期盼家庭週，這將是在家人和同事的陪伴下，好好放鬆享受的機會。我希望可以在那裡見到各位。

高登工業
總裁
葛瑞斯·埃利奧特

**詞彙** **day-by-day** 逐日的

---

**172**

**Why was the memo written?**

(A) To inform employees of management changes
(B) To introduce a week of family-oriented events
(C) To announce the signing of a major contract
(D) To recruit teams for a sporting event

為什麼會寫這則備忘錄？

(A) 通知員工管理方式有異動
(B) 介紹以家庭為主的一週活動
(C) 公告簽下一筆大合約
(D) 為體育活動招募隊伍

根據開頭第二句：「As a reward for your hard work, we are organizing a Family Week in the month of July.」，以及文章中的日程表，可知公司為了犒賞同仁，將在七月舉辦「家庭週」的活動，且此篇公告的目的就是介紹這個活動，因此正確答案為 (B)。

---

**173**

**How are staff members asked to contact Ms. Cole?**

(A) By making a phone call
(B) By registering online
(C) By visiting her office
(D) By sending an e-mail

員工要用什麼方式聯絡科爾女士？

(A) 打電話
(B) 線上登記
(C) 到辦公室找她
(D) 寄電子郵件

在日程表下方可看見：「please call her at extension 256 as soon as possible」，故根據文章，要用電話聯絡科爾女士，本題正確答案為 (A)。

---

**174**

**When is the barbeque party?**

(A) On Monday
(B) On Tuesday
(C) On Wednesday
(D) On Thursday

烤肉大會在什麼時候？

(A) 週一
(B) 週二
(C) 週三
(D) 週四

烤肉大會的行程無法直接在日程表中找到，而是要根據日程表下方的段落，其中的「There will also be a barbeque party after the sports competition.」說到，運動比賽後就會舉辦烤肉大會，而對照日程表，運動比賽是在星期四舉辦，故本題正確答案為 (D)。

**What is suggested about Ms. Elliot?**

(A) She is the founder of Gordon Industries.

(B) She won't be able to join the Family Week.

(C) She has a nine-year-old son.

(D) She wants to reward her employees with a special event.

文中提到埃利奧特女士什麼事？

(A) 她是高登工業創辦人。

(B) 她沒辦法參加家庭週活動。

(C) 她有個九歲兒子。

(D) 她想要藉特別活動獎勵員工。

從最後署名在「Grace Elliott」名字後的「President」可知，埃利奧特女士是公司總裁，且根據開頭的「Well done for helping Gordon Industries successfully complete its largest contract」、「As a reward for your hard work」，可知因為公司簽下一筆大生意，總裁決定舉辦活動犒賞員工，故本題正確答案為 (D)。

(A) 只能知道她是目前的總裁，但是無法確認是否為公司創辦人；(B) 從文章最後的「I hope to see everyone there」，可以得知她也會出席這個活動；(C) 文中並未提及此事。

### 176–180 文章

## Supreme Economy News
## Top Gambling Companies See Expansion in Workforce

January 7 — Many of the major gambling companies in the Blenheim district have seen a rapid increase in their workforces over the past six months. These are the findings of a report released yesterday from the Conglomeration of Online Casinos. In total, each of the district's top five companies employed 15% more employees compared to the period between July and December last year.

The leading company is Offshore Developments, currently the market leader in the gambling industry. More than 150 staff members were employed at casinos in Blenheim in the latter half of last year. Most of these employees were headhunted from Blake Soft, a small software company specializing in financial program development, which Offshore Developments acquired last June. Two other companies in the industry, Lucky Thistle and Crown Rooms (both specializing in online poker), also joined forces.

## 《最高經濟新聞》
## 多家頂尖博奕公司擴編人事

1月7日—線上賭場集團昨天發布的報告中發現，布倫亨區多家主要博奕公司在過去六個月，員工數大幅成長。與去年7月到12月同期相比，該區的前五大公司多聘了15%的員工。

博奕產業的市場龍頭「離岸發展公司」，是這波聘僱潮的領先者。布倫亨區的賭場去年下半年間，僱用了超過150名員工。大多數員工挖角自布雷克軟體公司。該公司在去年六月為離岸發展收購，是一家專門研發財務軟體的小型公司。業界另兩家公司「幸運薊」和「皇冠廳」（均專營線上撲克）也決定聯手。

The Conglomeration of Online Casinos only takes revenue from gambling establishments in Blenheim into account when publishing its rankings. Each of the top five companies accrued over $1.2 million in annual revenues. Lucky Thistle generated profits of approximately $1.2 million, with Offshore Developments reporting a $1.3 million net profit.

Marcel Prost

線上賭場集團發布的排名,只考慮布倫亨區賭場事業的營收。前五大公司年營收都超過120萬美元。幸運薊總營收大約120萬美元,離岸發展的淨收入為130萬美元。

馬歇爾·保魯斯

## Offshore Developments to Invest in Latest Technology

March 30 — David Carruthers, Chairman of Offshore Developments, is reportedly investing in new software: Marking Up, an online corporate financial program that was tested earlier this year.

This is the first time that Offshore Developments has entered the corporate market. In the past, the company has dealt solely with the individual consumer gambling market. Mark Owen, the business strategy director of Offshore Developments, says, "So that we can develop the technology that will enable corporations to enter the gambling market, we had to hire a number of experts in financial software."

The company has been listed as one of the leading five firms by the Conglomeration of Online Casinos for a number of years, with an average annual profit margin of $1.3 million. This year, the turnover has increased since January with profits of $0.7 million already generated and an additional $4.5 million expected by December.

G. Harker

## 離岸發展將投資最新科技

3月30日—據報導,「離岸發展」主席大衛·卡魯瑟斯正在投資新軟體:「增值」,是一款今年初才測試過的企業財務線上軟體。

「離岸發展」過去只針對博奕市場的個人消費者,這是它首度進軍企業市場。「離岸發展」事業策略經理馬克·歐文說:「我們得僱用幾位財務軟體的專家,如此一來,我們才能發展科技,鼓勵企業投入博奕市場。」

該公司多年來名列線上賭場集團評比的五大領先企業,年平均淨利潤為130萬美元。今年的營業額從一月開始成長,獲益高達70萬,預估在12月前會再增加450萬美元。

G·哈克

---

**詞彙** **gamble** 賭博　**conglomeration** 集團　**market leader** 市場龍頭　**headhunt** 挖角
**acquire** 併購　**profit margin** 淨利　**turnover** 營業額

---

**What is the first article about?**

(A) New gambling products released in the marketplace

(B) Marketing methods for gambling firms

(C) Employment growth in large gambling companies

(D) Employee satisfaction in the gambling industry

第一篇文章主旨為何?

(A) 市場上出現新的博奕商品

(B) 博奕公司的行銷方式

(C) 大型博奕公司的員工數成長

(D) 博奕產業的員工滿意度

根據第一篇報導文章的標題可以知道，有幾家頂尖的博弈公司擴編人事，且文章內的第一句也提到：「Many of the major gambling companies in the Blenheim district have seen a rapid increase in their workforces over the past six months.」，表示布倫亨地區的主要博弈公司在過去六個月間增加了許多員工，故正確答案為 (C)。

**177** -------------------------------------------------------------------

**In the first article, the word "period" in paragraph 1, line 5, is closest in meaning to**

(A) growth
(B) interval
(C) conclusion
(D) exercise

在第一篇文章中，第一段、第五行的「period」最接近下列哪個意思？

(A) 成長
(B) 間隔
(C) 結論
(D) 運動

此處使用的是「the period between July and December last year」，表示在 7 月到 12 月之間的「period」，故可推測此字在這應是表示「期間」，選項中字義最相似的只有 interval，故正確答案為 (B)。

**178** -------------------------------------------------------------------

**What is indicated about Offshore Developments?**

(A) It is an Internet-based company.
(B) It sells casino supplies.
(C) It has several international offices.
(D) It took over a software company.

文中提到「離岸發展」什麼事？

(A) 是間以網路為基礎的公司。
(B) 販賣賭場用品。
(C) 有一些國際辦事處。
(D) 它接管一間軟體公司。

第一篇報導文章的第二段提到「離岸發展」公司增聘許多員工，而且說到：「Most of these employees were headhunted from Blake Soft . . . which Offshore Developments acquired last June」，表示多數員工都是從去年公司收購的布雷克軟體公司挖角而來，故本題正確答案為 (D)。

**179** -------------------------------------------------------------------

**What is suggested about Marking Up?**

(A) It is the first product designed by Mr. Carruthers.
(B) Almost two million dollars in sales has already been achieved.
(C) It has been designed for the corporate market.
(D) Customers have criticized it for not being user-friendly.

文中提到關於「增值」什麼事？

(A) 是卡魯瑟斯先生設計的第一個產品。
(B) 銷售額幾乎已達兩百萬美元。
(C) 設計給企業市場使用。
(D) 顧客批評不好用。

根據第二篇報導文章第一段的「Marking Up, an online corporate financial program」，可知由離岸發展公司投資的「增值」是線上企業財務軟體，且第二段也提到：「This is the first time that Offshore Developments has entered the corporate market.」，表示這是公司第一次進入企業市場，代表這個軟體是給企業市場使用的，故正確答案為 (C)。

## 180

How much revenue does Offshore Developments anticipate from January to December?

(A) $1.3 million
(B) $4.5 million
(C) $5.2 million
(D) $6.5 million

離岸發展一月到十二月的營收預估為多少？

(A) 130 萬美元
(B) 450 萬美元
(C) 520 萬美元
(D) 650 萬美元

從第二篇文章的最後一句，可以看到「This year, the turnover has increased since January with profits of $0.7 million already generated and an additional $4.5 million expected by December.」，表示 1 月以來獲益已達 70 萬美元，在 12 月前會再增加 450 萬美元，故本題只要將兩者相加即可知道，全年預估營收為 520 萬美元，正確答案為 (C)。

## 181–185 電子郵件和資訊

**To:** Dieter Van Hugen
<dvh@pph.com>
**From:** Avril Labasse
<avrilla@pph.com>
**Date:** May 12
**Subject:** Exhibition
**Attachment:** Minefall Conference Center download

收件人：迪特·凡·休根
<dvh@pph.com>
寄件人：艾薇兒·拉巴斯
<avrilla@pph.com>
日期：5月12日
主旨：展覽
附件：礦瀑布會議中心下載

Dear Dieter,

Many thanks for your offer to help with PPH Limited's preparations for the forthcoming Technical Exhibition. This year's show will be from June 21 to 24 and, as in the previous year, the venue will be the Minefall Conference Center. For past exhibitions, I have rented the Benton Room, which allowed us to present our new products and stage a number of seminars. Over the four days, we attracted nearly 1000 people, on average 250 a day. We expect the exhibition to be even bigger this year.

In order to prepare for this eventuality, I would ask you to rent a bigger space. Although the room accommodated all attendees comfortably, the presentation facilities were inadequate. We had to rely upon the center's staff to supply and set up the presentation equipment. Although the feedback was excellent for the most part, a number of attendees complained about the quality of the visual material. This must be rectified this year.

親愛的迪特：

非常感謝您協助PPH有限公司準備即將到來的技術展。本年度的活動日期為6月21日到24日，地點和去年一樣，都辦在礦瀑布會議中心。過去幾次參展我都租用本頓廳來展示新產品和舉辦研論會。我們四天內就吸引了近千人，平均一天250人。我期待今年的展覽會比去年更盛大。

為提前做好準備，我想請您租一個更大的空間。雖然本頓廳可以容納所有與會者，但還要放展示設備的話，空間就不太足夠了。我們只能靠中心提供的器材，請中心員工協助架設。儘管大多數評價都很好，還是有些與會者對影像素材的畫質不滿意。今年一定要改正這個問題。

Previously, we held a reception for invited guests in the Manila Suite at the end of the week. This time, we prefer to take them somewhere more upmarket. I suggest either Brown's Restaurant or the Quayside Brasserie to avoid self-catering. Please note, I will make the necessary arrangements and forward the details to you.

Please check the enclosed brochure for the most suitable room for our requirements. As the deadline is only two weeks away, you will need to reserve a suitable room with a deposit as quickly as possible.

Please contact me with any questions or problems that may arise.

Avril Labasse

之前我們會在一週行程的尾聲，在馬尼拉套房接待受邀賓客。這次，我們想要帶他們到更高檔的地方。我建議布朗餐廳或是碼頭小館，也不用我們準備餐點。我會把必要的事安排好，再寄給您細節，還請您多加留意。

請看過隨信附上的小冊，選出最適合我們需求的房間。再兩週就要開展了，你需要僅快訂房並支付訂金。

如果還有疑問或遭遇到任何困難，請跟我聯絡。

艾薇兒·拉巴斯

# Minefall
## CONFERENCE CENTER

### ROOM RENTAL

**Manila Suite:** This is our biggest room, with daylight ingress to three sides. It is able to accommodate up to 400 guests for any celebration or business event. Catering is supplied by the in-house Minefall Catering Department. Costs begin at $300 for morning or afternoon hire, $500 for the full-day hire. Catering costs are additional.

**The Fortune Room and Day Room:** These are perfect for small private meetings or seminars, with a capacity of 50 people. Equipped for business, these rooms include telephone, computer with Internet access, overhead projector, and dark-colored curtains. Fees for the Fortune Room begin at $200 for a half day and $300 for a full day. The Day Room is slightly larger and has audio facilities. Prices for the Day Room are $220 for a half day and for a $320 full day.

**Sentinel Suite:** Ideal for large-scale presentations, events, and seminars. This room is equipped with a floor-to-ceiling projection screen, stage, lighting, and an all-around sound system. This luxurious suite holds up to 350 guests comfortably. Prices begin at $500 per half day and $700 per day. There is an added fee for catering services.

# 礦瀑布
## 會議中心

### 房間租用

**馬尼拉套房：**我們所提供最大的房間，三面採光，最多可以容納400名賓客，適合舉辦任何慶祝酒會或商貿活動。餐飲由礦瀑布的外燴部門提供。早上或下午的租金為美金300元起，全天租用則為500元。餐飲需另外付費。

**富貴房和日照房：**適合小型私人會議或研討會，可容納50人。房間內有電話、可上網的電腦、高架投影機和深色布幕等商務設備。富貴房的租金為半天美金200元、全天300元。日照房空間稍微大一些，備有音響設備。租金為半天美金220元、全天320元。

**衛哨套房：**舉辦大型演講、活動和研討會的理想場地。房間配備有落地投影螢幕、舞台、燈光和環繞立體音響系統。舒適豪華的房間可以容納高達350名賓客。租金從半天美金500元、全天700元起。餐飲須另外付費。

> **Polar Patio:** Adjacent to the Sentinel Suite, this outdoor venue is available for receptions and refreshments. The cost is $310 for three hours but comes free with the hire of the Sentinel Suite. There is an added fee for catering services.

> 天極露台：鄰近衛哨套房，適合舉辦歡迎會，或擺設會議餐點的戶外場地。租金為每3小時310美元，如果租用衛哨套房則可以免費使用天極露台。餐飲需另外計費。

**詞彙** forthcoming 即將到來的　venue 活動地點　rectify 改正　upmarket 高檔的　ingress 進入

---

### 181

**What most likely was Ms. Labasse's role in last year's exhibition?**

(A) She organized PPH Limited's event.
(B) She chose a catering service.
(C) She set up some equipment.
(D) She gave a presentation.

拉巴斯女士在去年的展覽中，最可能扮演的角色是？

(A) 由她安排 PPH 有限公司的活動。
(B) 由她決定餐點。
(C) 由她架設裝備。
(D) 由她發表簡報。

根據拉巴斯女士寄給休根先生的郵件，她在開頭便感謝休根先生協助準備展覽，段落中間還說到：「For past exhibitions, I have rented the Benton Room, which allowed us to present our new products and stage a number of seminars.」，表示之前的展覽中，都是由拉巴斯女士負責租用場地，故可推知她去年最可能也有幫忙承辦公司的展覽活動，因此本題最適合的答案為 (A)。

---

### 182

**How is this year's exhibition expected to be different from last year's?**

(A) It will be opened by a celebrity.
(B) It will attract even more visitors.
(C) It will be held at an alternative venue.
(D) It will include additional exhibitors.

今年的展預期會和去年的有何不同？

(A) 將由名人開場。
(B) 將吸引更多賓客。
(C) 將在備用場館舉辦。
(D) 會有額外的展出者加入。

根據郵件第一段，去年活動的參加人數將近千人，而拉巴斯女士預計「the exhibition to be even bigger this year」，表示今年應會有更多人到訪，故本題正確答案為 (B)。

(A) 與 (D) 未能在文中找到相關內容；(C) 根據拉巴斯女士，展覽會和去年一樣辦在礦瀑布會議中心。

---

### 183

**What problem probably occurred at last year's show?**

(A) Some people could not see the presentation screen clearly.
(B) The event location was changed before the exhibition.
(C) The reserved room was too noisy.
(D) A presenter didn't make it in time.

去年的展覽可能遇到了什麼問題？

(A) 有些人看不清楚投影螢幕。
(B) 展覽前更改地點。
(C) 訂到的房間太吵。
(D) 報告人沒有及時到達。

根據郵件第二段，去年租借的會議室雖然空間夠大，但是「the presentation facilities were inadequate」、「a number of attendees complained about the quality of the visual material」，也就是有發表設施不足及影像畫質不夠的問題，因此選項中與內文最相符的答案為 (A)。

**184**

**Who provided the food services at PPH Limited's reception last year?**

(A) Minefall Catering
(B) Polar Patio
(C) Quayside Brasseries
(D) Brown's Restaurant

PPH 有限公司去年的歡迎會上，餐點由誰提供？

(A) 礦瀑布外燴部門
(B) 天極露台
(C) 碼頭小館
(D) 布朗餐廳

根據郵件第三段：「Previously, we held a reception for invited guests in the Manila Suite」，可知去年的歡迎會是在馬尼拉套房舉辦，再對照租用房間的資訊，其中馬尼拉套房的內容提到：「Catering is supplied by the in-house Minefall Catering Department.」，表示餐點是由會議中心內的外燴部門提供，因此本題的正確答案為 (A)。

**185**

**Which space will PPH Limited be likely to reserve this year?**

(A) Day Room
(B) Manila Suite
(C) Fortune Room
(D) Sentinel Suite

PPH 有限公司今年可能會預約哪個房間？

(A) 日照房
(B) 馬尼拉套房
(C) 富貴房
(D) 衛哨套房

郵件的第一段中說到，預估今年的展覽會訪客會比去年多，而去年是平均一天 250 人，故今年的場地需要容納 250 人以上。另外，第二段提到因為發表設施的不足，造成部分與會者不滿，故今年的場地應要具有更好的影音設備。第三段則提到去年在馬尼拉套房舉辦，但是今年「we prefer to take them somewhere more upmarket」，也就是想選在更高級的場所舉辦。

接著參照房間資訊，只有衛哨套房既有完善影音設備，又能容納 350 人，且還能免費使用天極露台，故今年最可能預約的房間應是衛哨套房，正確答案為 (D)。

**186–190 職缺、電子郵件和信件**

# The London branch of Melton Manufacturing is seeking an experienced manager to join the production team!

Melton Manufacturing has been a leading manufacturer and distributor of top-quality automotive parts in the U.K. for half a century. We provide automobile companies both here and abroad with hundreds of car and truck parts.

The production manager will have the responsibility of training and monitoring a production team of 50 full-time staff members as well as many temporary and seasonal workers. The manager is also in charge of the factory environment, ensuring the health and safety of all employees. We are looking for someone with at least four years of relevant experience who has spent one year in the same industry. The successful candidate is expected to work out of hours to oversee deliveries and shipments.

Candidates must be familiar with the production and distribution of materials as well as have a working knowledge of handling requirements. Computer expertise on SPA 43 is also required. Interested parties should send their applications along with a cover letter and references to Tony Beach, Melton Manufacturing, 13 Ryville Crescent, London WR11 4BD.

---

**To:** Tony Beach <tonybeach@melton.com>
**From:** Adam Stern <adamstern@gomail.com>
**Date:** September 8
**Subject:** A letter of reference
**Attachment:** Adam_Stern_Reference.doc

---

Dear Mr. Beach,

I was surprised by your e-mail. I thought I had enclosed the reference with my résumé; it seems I missed it. I append Mr. Bushell's letter herewith. I'm glad to hear that my résumé is impressive. As to the SPA 43 you inquired about, I qualified for it 5 years ago. I had undertaken an evening course after work for it, and now I am in charge of employee computer training.

---

# 梅爾頓製造商的倫敦分部正在徵求有經驗的經理加入製造團隊！

梅爾頓製造商半世紀以來，一直是英國高品質汽車零件製造和批發的領導者。我們供應數百個汽車和貨車零件，給本地和海外的汽車公司。

生產製造經理有責任訓練和監督，由50名全職員工、臨時工和季節工所組成的製造團隊。經理也要管理工廠環境，確保全體員工的健康和安全。我們正在找的人要有至少四年的相關經驗，且其中一年同樣要在製造業。我們也期待獲選的應徵者，可以加班監督出貨和運送。

應徵者需熟悉材料的製造和批發，也要有處理規定相關的知識，並具備電腦技能SPA 43。有意的應徵者請將申請書附上求職信與推薦信，寄給湯尼‧比奇，地址是WR11 4BD倫敦市萊韋爾新月街13號梅爾頓製造商。

---

收件人：湯尼‧比奇 <tonybeach@melton.com>
寄件人：亞當‧斯騰 <adamstern@gomail.com>
日期：9月8日
主旨：推薦信
附件：亞當_斯騰_推薦.doc

---

親愛的比奇先生：

收到您的來信讓我很驚訝。我以為我有把推薦信附在履歷上；看來我是忘了。我隨信附上布希爾先生的信。我很高興聽到我的履歷讓人印象深刻。關於您詢問的SPA 43，我五年前已經取得資格，我之前在下班後的晚間課程研習該軟體，現在也負責員工的電腦訓練。

Please let me know when I should visit you for an interview. As London is far away from here, I'll need to find a place to stay one night. Again, thank you for considering me for this position.

Sincerely,

Adam Stern

---

August 27
Mr. Beach
Melton Manufacturing
13 Ryville Crescent
London WR11 4BD

Dear Mr. Beach,

This is a reference for Adam Stern, who is applying for the job of production manager within your organization. I have worked with Mr. Stern for five of his seven years at Packaging Express, where he began as a temporary worker before I took him on full time. Mr. Stern is an extremely competent employee and is currently employed as production supervisor here. He has been particularly instrumental in the implementation and commissioning of new production line equipment that has sped up the production process and reduced wastage.

Mr. Stern is fully qualified for the position advertised and, in addition, has extensive work experience. He has just completed an HNQ in management at Kings Cross College as well as numerous in-house courses.

I have every faith in Mr. Stern's capability for this job, as he has the ability to adapt to any work demands. Please contact me for any further information.

Sincerely,

Trey Bushell
Production Director

---

請讓我知道和您面試的時間。倫敦離我有段距離，我必須找到地方留宿。再次感謝您考慮錄用我。

亞當‧斯騰 敬上

---

8月27日
比奇先生
WR11 4BD 倫敦市萊韋爾新月街13號梅爾頓製造商

親愛的比奇先生：

這是一封推薦信，向您推薦亞當‧斯騰，他正在申請貴公司的生產製造經理一職。斯騰先生在打包快遞曾有七年工作經驗，他從臨時工開始做起，直到我讓他轉正職，我們共事了五年。斯騰先生是一名非常稱職的員工，目前在這裡擔任生產製造監督。他曾引進新的生產線設備器材，並讓它順利運作，加快了生產流程也減少浪費。

斯騰先生十分適任貴公司所招聘的職缺，此外，他也有豐富的工作經驗。他最近在王十字學院完成管理學HNQ課程，也進修過多項在職訓練課程。

我對斯騰先生有信心，他可以勝任這個職位，因為他能妥善應對任何工作需求。欲知更多資訊，歡迎您聯絡。

生產製造主任
特雷‧布希爾 敬上

---

**詞彙** oversee 監督　cover letter 求職信　append 附上　herewith 隨信　competent 稱職的　instrumental 起作用的　implementation 啟用　commissioning 安排操作　wastage 浪費　adapt to 應對；適應

**186**

**What is suggested about Melton Manufacturing?**

(A) It distributes safety equipment.
(B) It offers computer training.
(C) It recently expanded into the U.K.
(D) It specializes in automotive parts.

文中提到梅爾頓製造商什麼事？

(A) 批發安全設備。
(B) 提供電腦訓練課程。
(C) 最近擴展業務到英國。
(D) 專門製造汽車零件。

在第一篇的職缺資訊的第一段便寫到：「Melton Manufacturing has been a leading manufacturer and distributor of top-quality automotive parts」，故可知梅爾頓製造商應是生產汽車零件的業者，因此正確答案為 (D)。

**187**

**According to the job posting, what must the production manager be willing to do?**

(A) Handle heavy machinery
(B) Hire team members
(C) Work overtime
(D) Sign a one-year contract

根據職缺公告，生產製造經理要願意做什麼？

(A) 操作重機械
(B) 招募團隊成員
(C) 超時工作
(D) 簽一年的合約

職缺資訊的第二段最後提到：「The successful candidate is expected to work out of hours to oversee deliveries and shipments.」，表示為了監督出貨與運送，獲選的應徵者需要加班，所以正確答案為 (C)。

**188**

**Why does Mr. Bushell write the letter?**

(A) To explain a delay in a shipment
(B) To welcome a new team member
(C) To apply for a new job
(D) To recommend an employee

為什麼布希爾先生要寫那封信？

(A) 解釋為什麼延後出貨
(B) 歡迎新成員加入團隊。
(C) 應徵新工作。
(D) 推薦一名員工。

布希爾先生在郵件的第一句便寫：「This is a reference for Adam Stern」，說明這是一封斯騰先生的推薦信，並在文中著述斯騰先生工作上的優點與良好表現，故本題正確答案為 (D)。

**189**

**What is indicated about Mr. Stern?**

(A) He has experience in overseas sales.
(B) He teaches a course at Kings Cross College.
(C) He is skilled in the use of a computer software program.
(D) He is looking for a part-time position at Melton Manufacturing.

文中提到斯騰先生什麼事？

(A) 他有海外銷售的經驗。
(B) 他在王十字學院教書。
(C) 他擅長使用某個電腦程式。
(D) 他想找梅爾頓製造商的兼職工作。

先找到職缺資訊最後提到的「Computer expertise on SPA 43」，再對斯騰先生撰寫的郵件，其中第一行說到：「As to the SPA 43 you inquired about, I qualified for it 5 years ago.」，表示他擁有這項電腦技能，且之後還說到自己目前擔任員工電腦訓練教育的負責人，故可知最符合斯騰先生的描述應是 (C)。

(A) 文中未提及此事；(B) 推薦信上只說他在王十字學院完成管理學的課程，並沒有說他有負責教學；(D) 他應徵的生產製造經理應是全職員工，且文中斯騰先生也並未確切提到兼職工作一事。

**190** --------------------------------------------------------------

**What does Mr. Stern ask Mr. Beach to do?**

(A) Visit him at his earliest convenience
(B) Write him a letter of reference
(C) Inform him of a date
(D) Send him an application form

**斯騰先生要求比奇先生做什麼？**

(A) 在他方便時儘快前來拜訪
(B) 為他寫封推薦信
(C) 通知他日期
(D) 寄給他申請表

從斯騰先生的郵件結尾，可以看見他寫了：「Please let me know when I should visit you for an interview.」，表示需要比奇先生告知他方便面試的時間，故本題的答案為 (C)。

**191–195 電子郵件和表格**

---

**To:** <service@kramindustries.org>
**From:** Gerard Graff <gg@deutschei21.org>
**Date:** January 5
**Subject:** Customer complaint

---

Dear Sir/Madam,

I wish to report a problem with a new wardrobe (catalog number #92). I followed the assembly instructions strictly. However, the wardrobe tilts to one side as the wrong panel was supplied, which is one inch too short. I would like you to replace the panel so that I can reassemble this piece of furniture.

I apologize for the delay in contacting you. I purchased the wardrobe on November 2 but, due to a hospital placement abroad of over two months, I was unable to attempt to assemble the item. I have the packaging in which the item was supplied and can send the receipt issued by your store if necessary.

Sincerely,
Gerard Graff

---

**收件人：** <service@kramindustries.org>
**寄件人：** 傑拉德·格拉夫 <gg@deutschei21.org>
**日期：** 1月5日
**主旨：** 客戶投訴

---

親愛的先生／女士：

我想要反應新衣櫃（型號#92）的問題。我嚴格遵循安裝說明，但是衣櫃還是歪一邊，因為有一塊隔板送錯了，它短了一吋。我希望您可以替換這塊隔板，好讓我可以重新把這個家具裝好。

很抱歉我太晚聯絡。我在11月2日買了衣櫃，但因為被醫院外派海外超過兩個月，期間我沒能組裝它。如果有需要的話，我保有商品運送時的包裝，也可以寄回店家收據。

傑拉德·格拉夫 敬上

**To:** Gerard Graff <gg@deutschei21.org>
**From:** Joseph Pieters <peiters@kramindustries.org>
**Date:** January 6
**Subject:** RE: Customer Complaint

Dear Mr. Graff,

Thank you for the e-mail regarding your purchase. We apologize for the difficulties you have had with assembling this item and will send you a replacement part free of charge. We operate a store policy stating that if the item purchased is less than two months old, it can be returned with the original receipt and in its original packaging. For items bought over two months ago, our policy is that they can only be returned if discovered to be damaged at the time of purchase. This necessitates a Faulty Return Form to be completed. This can be found on our website complaints page: www.kramindustries.org/returns. After the form is filled out and submitted, a Merchandise Return Code will be e-mailed to you. For full details on the policies, please see the website.

I hope this is useful information. We would request that you complete a feedback form attached about your experience with the customer service department. Once completed, you will receive a voucher for 15% off your next purchase with our store.

Joseph Pieters
Manager

---

## Customer Feedback

**Name:** Gerard Graff
**Overall rating:** ★★★★☆ (Good)
**Comments:** I reported a problem with a wardrobe by e-mail, and I received a reply on the following day. I followed the faulty return procedure as informed and got a replacement for the defective part. Thanks to your help, I was able to finish assembling it correctly. However, the illustration on the manual was not very accurate, and I experienced inconvenience in recognizing the problem with the panel. I think that should be corrected as soon as possible. Except for that, I was generally pleased with your service.

---

收件人：傑拉德·格拉夫 <gg@deutschei21.org>
寄件人：約瑟夫·彼特斯 <peiters@kramindustries.org>
日期：1月6日
主旨：關於：客戶投訴

親愛的格拉夫先生：

感謝您的來信說明您購買的商品。針對您安裝商品時遇到困難，我們向您致歉，並且將免費寄給您替換的零件。根據我們所實施的店面營業規定，商品在購買兩個月內，可以持收據和原包裝退貨。如購買已超過兩個月，根據公司規定，要能證明商品是在購買時已有毀損方能退貨。且有必要填寫缺失回報單。該表單可以在我們官網的客戶投訴頁面找到：www.kramindustries.org/returns。填完表單並送出之後，會寄給您一份商品退換碼。如需了解規定全文，還請上官網查看。

我希望這對您有幫助。我們想請您填寫一份隨信附上的客戶回饋單，以了解您對客服部門的經驗感受。填完後，您將收到一張15%的折扣券，可供下次在我們的店裡購買時使用。

經理
約瑟夫·彼特斯

---

## 客戶回饋

姓名：傑拉德·格拉夫
整體評價：四顆星（好）
意見：我用電子郵件回報了衣櫃的問題，隔天就收到答覆。我按照信中告知的缺失回報流程，並在之後收到了替換零件。感謝您的協助，我才可以順利安裝。不過，手冊上的說明圖示不是非常精確，讓我在找出隔板問題時感到不便。我希望可以儘快改正。除了這點，整體服務讓我很滿意。

詞彙 **wardrobe** 衣櫃　**assembly** 組裝　**tilt** 歪斜　**necessitate** 使⋯⋯有必要

**191**

---

**What problem with the product does Mr. Graff report?**

(A) A part is defective.
(B) An instruction manual is missing.
(C) The size is wrong for his bedroom.
(D) It is the wrong color.

格拉夫先生回報了產品的什麼問題？

(A) 一個零件有缺陷。
(B) 說明手冊不見了。
(C) 對他的寢室而言尺寸有誤
(D) 顏色錯了。

在第一封郵件中，格拉夫先生開頭便寫：「I wish to report a problem with a new wardrobe (catalog number #92).」、「the wardrobe tilts to one side as the wrong panel was supplied」，表示想要回報隔板的問題，故本題正確答案為 (A)。

**192**

---

**What most likely is Mr. Graff's job?**

(A) Teaching woodwork
(B) Working within a hospital
(C) Preparing meals
(D) Constructing furniture

格拉夫先生最有可能的工作是？

(A) 教木工
(B) 在醫院工作
(C) 準備餐點
(D) 製作家具

本題的線索只有一個，就在第一封郵件的第二段，其中格拉夫先生解釋自己延遲回報問題的原因，並寫了「due to a hospital placement abroad」，表示自己當時受醫院外派異國，故可推測格拉夫先生最可能在醫院工作，所以本題最合適的答案為 (B)。

**193**

---

**What benefits would Mr. Graff receive from the furniture shop?**

(A) A discount coupon
(B) An honorarium
(C) A new piece of furniture
(D) Free delivery

格拉夫先生從家具店得到什麼好處？

(A) 折價券
(B) 謝禮
(C) 一件新家具
(D) 免運費

第二封郵件最後說，若是幫忙填寫回饋單，就可以得到「a voucher for 15% off」，也就是折扣券。而根據第三篇文章的標題：「客戶回饋」，可知格拉夫先生的確填寫了回饋單，故他可以從家具店得到折價券，本題正確答案為 (A)。

**194**
----------------------------------------------------------------

In the feedback form, the word "recognizing" in line 5, is closest in meaning to

(A) watching
(B) finding
(C) informing
(D) reporting

在回饋表中，第五行的「recognizing」，最接近下列哪個意思？

(A) 看
(B) 發現
(C) 知會
(D) 報告

從前文可知，格拉夫先生發現衣櫃隔板尺寸有誤，故希望可以得到替換的新隔板，而此句提到「inconvenience」、「the problem with the panel」，可推測他應該是想說在「找出」隔板問題時感受不便，故此處的「recognizing」應該是「發現、辨識出」的意思，故最適合的答案為 (B)。

**195**
----------------------------------------------------------------

According to Mr. Graff, what should be revised?

(A) The assembly instructions
(B) The return code
(C) The website address
(D) The packaging

根據格拉夫先生的說法，什麼需要改正？

(A) 組裝說明
(B) 商品退換碼
(C) 官網網址
(D) 包裝

在客戶回饋單上，格拉夫先生提到：「However, the illustration on the manual was not very accurate」、「I think that should be corrected as soon as possible.」，表示他認為安裝說明上的圖示不夠精確，需要儘快趕正，故正確答案為 (A)。

**196–200 廣告和電子郵件**

| | |
|---|---|
| **Jason Falls** | **傑森瀑布** |
| in the center of Urban Melbourne<br>business, residential, and commercial space to rent | 位於墨爾本市中心<br>公司、住宅以及商業區空間出租 |
| A contemporary, up-to-date structure surrounded by existing shops and businesses. Close to the train station. Adjacent to the War Memorial with urban park and sports stadium close by. | 走在時代尖端的建築結構，周遭有多間商店和公司行號。<br>靠近車站。<br>緊鄰戰爭紀念碑，一旁還有都會公園和體育場 |
| **Residential (Floors 2–7):** Two and three-roomed apartments comprising two bathrooms, one en-suite, kitchen-dining room, and living room. For an extra charge, parking is available in the underground car park. Shared rooftop garden as well as on-site laundry facilities. | **住宅（2到7樓）：**兩房或三房公寓，均有兩間衛浴、一間附衛浴套房、廚房餐廳和客廳。可以使用地下室停車場，需另外繳交停車費。屋頂花園和曬衣場共用。 |
| **Offices (Floor 8–14):** Large and small offices available. Modular layout with open-plan space that can be compartmentalized. Choice of furnishings. | **辦公室（8到14樓）：**大小辦公室都有。方塊格局的開放空間可供隔間。辦公家具可供選擇。 |

**Commercial (Street level):** Four shop fronts. Retail only, each 500 square meters in floor space. No dining establishments.

**Details on pricing and availability:**
Please direct residential inquiries to Garry Mason, (08) 3014-7610 or residential@jasonfalls.com.au.

Please direct commercial inquiries to Finola Castiel, (08) 3014-7620 or commercial@jasonfalls.com.au.

---

**To:** Finola Castiel
<commercial@jasonfalls.com.au>
**From:** Thomas Christian
<tchristian@christianbrooks.com>
**Title:** Jason Falls
**Date:** 10:01, September 2

---

Dear Ms. Castiel,

My business has recently expanded, and we will be employing new recruits to help with the future workload. We are currently located close to Jason Falls, but there is not enough space for new employees. I would be interested in finding out if the available office space at Jason Falls is sufficient to house 17 staff members, in Administration and Sales. I will need to see the offices for myself sometime next week.

Many thanks.

Thomas Christian

---

**To:** Elias Innes
<e_innes@terralink.org>
**From:** Finola Castiel
<commercial@jasonfalls.com.au>
**Subject:** Urgent renovation work
**Date:** 11:30, September 2

---

Dear Mr. Innes,

My colleague Garry Mason referred you to me. I require a quote to remove three internal walls from an office, which are all two meters tall, with one being 20 centimeters thick. The other two are only

商業區（地面樓）：四間店面。只供租賃使用，每間樓地板面積500平方公尺。謝絕餐廳。

租金細節和出租狀況：如有住宅承租需求請詢洽蓋瑞·梅森(08)3014-7610或電郵residential@jasonfalls.com.au。

如有商辦需求請詢問費諾拉·斯蒂爾(08)3014-7620或電郵commercial@jasonfalls.com.au。

---

收件人：費諾拉·卡斯蒂爾
<commercial@jasonfalls.com.au>
寄件人：湯馬斯·克里斯丁
<tchristian@christianbrooks.com>
主旨：傑森瀑布
日期：9月2日10:01

---

親愛的卡斯蒂爾女士：

我最近將事業擴大營業，我們會聘請新員工分擔未來的工作。我們目前位於「傑森瀑布」附近，但已經沒有空間容納新員工。我想知道在「傑森瀑布」裡有沒有辦公室空間，可以容納行政部和業務部的17名同仁。我需要親自看看辦公室，會在下週找個時間過去。

非常感謝，

湯馬斯·克里斯丁

---

收件人：埃利亞斯·因尼斯
<e_innes@terralink.org>
寄件人：費諾拉·卡斯蒂爾
<commercial@jasonfalls.com.au>
主旨：緊急整修作業
日期：9月2日11:30

---

親愛的因尼斯先生：

我的同事蓋瑞·梅森轉介您給我。我打算要拆除辦公室裡的三面牆，想要跟您詢價。牆壁均為兩公尺高，其中一面20公分厚。另外兩面牆則只有15公分厚。

15 centimeters wide. These walls were not there originally, but set up by the last tenant's request.

The office is on the twelfth floor of the building, and there's an elevator available. I will need a team of workers who can undertake the work as soon as possible. I have a client who is interested in this office; I think those walls must be removed to accommodate all his staff. I want this renovation work to be done by Sunday.

I hope to hear from you soon.

Regards,
Finola Castiel

這幾面牆不是一開始就有的，而是依照上一個承租戶的要求加裝的。

辦公室位於12樓，大樓內有電梯。我需要一個可以儘快動工的團隊。有客戶想要這間辦公室，我得拆了這些牆才能容納他所有的員工。我希望整修作業可以在週日前完成。

希望很快能收到您的回信。

祝好，
費諾拉‧卡斯蒂爾

**詞彙** comprise 包括　en-suite 套房　modular 格狀的　open-plan 開放式的
compartmentalize 分隔　street level 地面樓　refer A to B 轉介 A 給 B　quote 報價

---

**196** ------------------------------------------------

**What is indicated about the Jason Falls building?**

(A) It is near a train station.
(B) It is far from the War Memorial.
(C) It is on the outskirts of the city.
(D) It is under construction.

文中提到傑森瀑布大樓什麼事？

(A) 位於車站附近。
(B) 距離戰爭紀念碑很遠。
(C) 在城郊。
(D) 正在興建中。

從內容看來，第一篇廣告文章就是「傑森瀑布」的出租廣告。文中提到「Close to the train station.」，表示建築靠近火車站，故本題答案為 (A)。

(B) 根據「Adjacent to the War Memorial」，建築靠近戰爭紀念碑；(C) 根據「in the center of Urban Melbourne」，建築位於城市中心；(D) 大樓已經完工，並非正在施工的建築。第二封郵件中雖然提及拆牆工程，但是不代表整棟樓都還在興建。

---

**197** ------------------------------------------------

**According to the advertisement, what is available to residential tenants for an additional cost?**

(A) Cleaning facilities
(B) Underground parking
(C) An extra bedroom
(D) Use of a rooftop garden

根據廣告，住宅區的租戶額外付費的話，可以使用什麼？

(A) 打掃用具
(B) 地下停車場
(C) 額外的寢室
(D) 屋頂花園

廣告文章上寫了：「For an extra charge, parking is available in the underground car park.」，表示支付額外費用即可使用地下停車場，故本題正確答案為 (B)。

**What type of tenant is not allowed to occupy the building?**

(A) A law firm
(B) A sales office
(C) A retail store
(D) A restaurant

這棟大樓不允許哪種承租戶使用？

(A) 法律事務所
(B) 業務辦公室
(C) 零售商店
(D) 餐廳

在廣告文章的 Commercial 標題下，有寫出「No dining establishments.」，表示不接受餐廳承租，故正確答案為 (D)。

**What is suggested about Mr. Christian's company?**

(A) It is relocating out of Melbourne.
(B) It recently lost some staff.
(C) It has become increasingly successful.
(D) It is changing its main business plans.

關於克里斯丁先生的公司，文中提到什麼？

(A) 正要搬出墨爾本。
(B) 最近失去一些員工。
(C) 漸漸發達起來。
(D) 正在改變主要的商業計畫。

根據克里斯丁先生寫的郵件，他在開頭部分提到「My business has recently expanded」，並說因此需要增聘員工，故最符合克里斯丁先生公司的答案是 (C)。

**Why does Ms. Castiel want to renovate the office so urgently?**

(A) She does not work on Sundays.
(B) A tenant will come to see the property soon.
(C) The walls can be hazardous for the new tenant.
(D) A tenant requests to set up some partitions.

為什麼卡斯蒂爾女士這麼急著想要整修辦公室？

(A) 她週日不上班。
(B) 承租戶很快要來看租賃空間。
(C) 對新的承租戶而言，這些是危牆。
(D) 承租戶要求做些隔間。

從克里斯丁先生撰寫的郵件中可知，他對於傑森瀑布有興趣，有意租下裡頭的空間，並且「will need to see the offices for myself sometime next week」，也就是他會在寄信的隔週親自去看場地。

對照卡斯蒂爾女士的郵件，她要求儘速拆除牆壁，並說：「I have a client who is interested in this office」，所以這裡的 client 指的就是克里斯丁先生，也就可推知，因為克里斯丁先生即將前往看房，卡斯蒂爾女士才會急著整修，故本題正確答案為 (B)。

# ACTUAL TEST
# 10

# PART 5

**101**

Dinner will be served by Walsh House ------- Hokuto Grill.

(A) but
(B) nor
(C) and
(D) yet

題型 **文法──對等連接詞**

翻譯 晚餐將由威爾斯屋和北斗碳烤提供。

本題需要能對等連結兩個名詞的連接詞，由於此處在解釋晚餐廳供的餐廳，且兩個地方皆可以用餐，故應代入 and，正確答案為 (C)。

**102**

Diadora's new running shoe, the Runner Blade, is ------- named for its shape and agility.

(A) suitably
(B) suitable
(C) suitability
(D) suitableness

題型 **位置──副詞**

翻譯 迪亞朵拉的新款慢跑鞋，照它的外型與機動性命名成「刀鋒跑者」很恰當。

詞彙 agility 機動性

be 動詞與過去分詞之間，唯一可代入的為副詞，且此處是想表示鞋款被「恰當地」命名，故正確答案為 (A)。

**103**

------- in Davison Restaurant, including the expansion of its parking lot, have attracted more customers.

(A) Improved
(B) Improvement
(C) Improvements
(D) Improving

題型 **位置──名詞**

翻譯 戴維森餐廳的進步，包括擴建停車場，吸引了更多客人。

本句是想表示餐廳的改善措施吸引許多客人，故空格處是主詞的位置，且因為後方動詞是 have attracted，故要使用複數名詞作為主詞，選項中最適合填入的是 (C)。

## 104

**The Nooseburg Society Association will be in charge of tours of historical sites every day ------- Saturday.**

(A) other
(B) except
(C) than
(D) some

題型 **詞彙──介系詞**

翻譯 努斯堡組織協會負責每日歷史景點的導覽，除了週六以外。

本句的空格在 every day 與 Saturday 之間，可推測應是想表示週六以外的日子，因此，選項中只能選 except，正確答案為 (B)。

★請熟記下列表示「除了」的用法：
except〔不可放句首〕（除了……之外，其他都）
except for N〔可放句首〕（除了……之外，其他都）
besides〔常放句首〕（除了……之外，還有）
apart from〔可放句首〕（除了……之外，還有）

## 105

**San Marino Steel is now ------- a wide range of steel products for building facilities outside the city.**

(A) manufacturer
(B) being manufactured
(C) manufactured
(D) manufacturing

題型 **文法──動詞**

翻譯 桑馬利諾鋼鐵目前正生產各種鋼鐵製品來興建市外的建築設施。

空格後面出現受詞 a wide range of steel products，且前面有 be 動詞，所以此句的時態應該是現在進行式，表示公司「正在」生產鋼鐵製品，故正確答案為 (D)。

## 106

**Ms. Dennings ------- gives a hand to those in charge of the press conferences.**

(A) often
(B) early
(C) less
(D) far

題型 **詞彙──頻率副詞**

翻譯 丹寧斯女士經常協助負責舉辦記者會的人。

注意頻率副詞通常位於一般動詞前，或是 be 動詞及助動詞後面。本題應是要表示丹寧斯女士「經常」協助人，故正確答案為 (A)。

## 107

You may answer questions ------- the space provided on the enclosed survey form.

(A) up
(B) out
(C) in
(D) of

題型 詞彙——介系詞

翻譯 您可以在附上的問卷表裡回答問題。

詞彙 enclosed 隨信附上的

本題應是想表示將答案填入問卷表「內」，所以要使用 in 最為正確，本題答案為 (C)。

## 108

New training methods that could improve productivity -------.

(A) to develop
(B) developing
(C) are being developed
(D) to be developed

題型 文法——動詞

翻譯 目前正在開發新的訓練方法來提升生產力。

本題先觀察由關係代名詞 that 引導的子句，只是補充說明前方先行詞 new training methods 是個能夠提升生產力的方法，而暫時不看這個 that 子句，就會知道空格處是這個句子的動詞，且本句是要說訓練方法「正被開發」，故正確答案為被動進行式的 (C)。

## 109

To receive a full refund, please ------- your items in original condition.

(A) returns
(B) returned
(C) return
(D) returning

題型 文法——動詞

翻譯 退貨時請保持商品原貌，以取得全額退款。

空格前出現 please，可知這是表達命令的祈使句句型，故隨後接續的動詞應為原形，因此正確答案為 (C)。

## 110

Both Saitrich and Petrov electronics companies are financially stronger than many of ------- rival companies.

(A) theirs
(B) they
(C) their
(D) them

題型 位置——所有格代名詞

翻譯 塞伊德李奇和彼得洛夫兩家電子公司的財力，都比他們的許多競爭對手來得強。

根據句意，此處要說的是 Saitrich 和 Petrov 這「兩家公司的」競爭對手，故空格處要填入所有格代名詞 their，正確答案為 (C)。

**111**

Mr. Vettel broke the record ------- the fastest lap time in the German Grand Prix.

(A) at
(B) within
(C) above
(D) for

| 題型 | 詞彙——介系詞 |
| --- | --- |
| 翻譯 | 威特爾先生在德國國際賽車大賽打破單圈的最快紀錄。 |
| 詞彙 | break the record 打破紀錄<br>lap 單圈 |

描述打破的紀錄時要搭配的介系詞是 for，故正確答案為 (D)。

另外 in 也常常使用，故可直接背下「break the record in/for sth」。

**112**

The energy committee has determined that building a roof in a brighter and more reflective blue color will ------- reduce heat, especially in cities.

(A) significantly
(B) extremely
(C) utterly
(D) countlessly

| 題型 | 詞彙——副詞 |
| --- | --- |
| 翻譯 | 能源委員會已經證實，用較明亮且有反光效果的藍色蓋屋頂能大幅降低室溫，城市裡效果尤佳。 |

空格出現在動詞 reduce 前面，所以應該要能夠修飾減少程度，故最適合用 significantly 表示「大幅地」降低，本題正確答案為 (A)。

(B) 與 (C) 因為字義太極端，所以通常在這種題型中不太可能成為答案。從句意看來，此部分是説藍色屋頂可以降低室溫，但要「極度地、徹底地」降低溫度應是不可能的。

★下列為常用來修飾程度的副詞：

significantly、considerably、substantially 帶有「顯著地、相當地」的意思，故可放在表示增減的動詞，如 increase、decrease、reduce、raise 等的前面進行修飾。

**113**

Ashanti Travel Agency provides the ------- flights available from Tokyo to Beijing and Seoul.

(A) cheapness
(B) cheapen
(C) cheaply
(D) cheapest

| 題型 | 位置——最高級 |
| --- | --- |
| 翻譯 | 亞香提旅行社提供最便宜的東京到北京和東京到首爾機票。 |

注意空格前出現定冠詞 the，表示後方出現的形容詞應是最高級的狀態，且根據句意，表示「最便宜的」航班也符合邏輯，故正確答案為 (D)。

## 114

The board of directors ------- approved the plan to make inroads into the overseas market, which was aimed at young adults in Asian countries.

(A) conditions
(B) conditioned
(C) conditional
(D) conditionally

題型 位置──副詞

翻譯 董事會有條件地採納了以亞洲國家青年為目標的進軍海外市場計畫。

詞彙 make inroads into sth 採取行動

空格出現在動詞 approved 前，故應是能修飾動詞的副詞，且表示「有條件地」採納計畫，也符合文意與邏輯，故正確答案為 (D)。

## 115

Publics Dynamics has three facilities with a combined floor space ------- 51,500 square meters.

(A) processing
(B) totaling
(C) finishing
(D) enduring

題型 詞彙──動詞

翻譯 公眾動態有三座工廠，總樓地板面積達51,500 平方公尺。

本句提到「地板」、「51,500 平方公尺」，故空格處填入的現在分詞應要具有「加總」的意思，而選項中只有 total 作為動詞使用時，意思是「合計為……」，因此本題正確答案為 (B)。

## 116

When requesting full refunds, customers have to show ------- records including the purchase date.

(A) accurate
(B) delayed
(C) accepting
(D) distant

題型 詞彙──形容詞

翻譯 要求全額退費時，顧客必須出示正確的消費紀錄，包括消費日期在內。

句意上提到「全額退費」、「出示」、「消費紀錄」，故空格處的形容詞應該要具有「正確的」之意，表示全額退費時要出示正確的消費紀錄，故正確答案為 (A)。

## 117

Walgreen Alliance deals with a high ------- of claims every day, so it needs capable employees.

(A) set
(B) size
(C) extent
(D) volume

題型 詞彙──名詞

翻譯 沃綠聯盟每天處理大量索賠，所以它需要能力很強的員工。

詞彙 alliance 聯盟
claim 索賠

表達「大量」時，可使用 high volume 這個説法，另外，要描述量或尺寸時，則可用 a volume of 表示。本題應該要説處理「大量」索賠，故空格適合填入 volume，本題正確答案為 (D)。

**118** - - - - - - - - - - - - - - - - - - - - - - - - - - - - - - - - - - - - - - - - - -

**Recent research findings for Tisler Cookware's new prototype were ------- encouraging.**

(A) well
(B) near
(C) freely
(D) very

| 題型 | 詞彙——副詞 |
| --- | --- |
| 翻譯 | 針對提斯勒烹調用具的新產品樣品，近期的研究發現非常鼓舞人心。 |

本題應是要表示研究發現「非常地」鼓舞人心，故正確答案為 (D)。

此外，well、near 和 very 也可用作為形容詞，但 freely 不行。

**119** - - - - - - - - - - - - - - - - - - - - - - - - - - - - - - - - - - - - - - - - - -

**------- several suggestions have been made to improve Manchester City's transportation system, none of them is within budget.**

(A) Why
(B) Whether
(C) Although
(D) Unless

| 題型 | 詞彙——連接詞 |
| --- | --- |
| 翻譯 | 雖然為了改善曼徹斯特市的運輸系統已接獲很多建議，但沒半項符合預算。 |

逗號前句提到接獲許多建議，後句卻說沒有一項符合預算，故此處的連接詞應要具有「雖然」的意思，以表達前後句的轉折關係，所以正確答案為 (C)。

**120** - - - - - - - - - - - - - - - - - - - - - - - - - - - - - - - - - - - - - - - - - -

**Please check ------- of your order #1282712, which will be shipped by Wednesday.**

(A) receipt
(B) receive
(C) received
(D) receiving

| 題型 | 詞彙　　名詞 |
| --- | --- |
| 翻譯 | 請確認您1282712 號訂單的收據，商品將在週三前送到。 |

空格位於及物動詞 check 後的受詞位置，選項中只有 (A) 名詞與 (D) 動名詞最合適，而根據句意，此處應是要確認訂單的「收據」，故正確答案為 (A)。

**121**

Mr. Shinohara, a plant manager, recently ------- a tour of the facilities for brewing beer for the company's important clients.

(A) conduct
(B) conducted
(C) to conduct
(D) will conduct

題型 **文法──動詞**

翻譯 工廠經理篠原先生為了公司的重要客戶，最近帶了釀啤酒工廠的導覽。

詞彙 brew beer 釀啤酒

觀察本句並沒有受詞，故空格為動詞的位置。(C) 為不定詞，不是一般動詞。另外，因為句子中出現 recently，故動詞不可能為未來時態，所以 (D) 也不適合。

最後根據單數主詞可知道，動詞不能使用複數的 conduct，但選項中最適合的答案為 (B)。

**122**

The owner of Hamilton Art Gallery recruits volunteers who enjoy helping ------- with their need for tour guides.

(A) ones
(B) others
(C) any
(D) that

題型 **詞彙──代名詞**

翻譯 哈米爾頓藝廊的老闆聘用了一群喜歡幫助他人的志工，滿足他們對導覽員的需求。

空格處的代名詞要能夠扮演 helping 的受詞角色，且此句應該是要表示喜歡幫助「他人」的志工，故此處最適合填入的是 others，正確答案為 (B)。

**123**

The board of directors interviewed five top candidates before making the ------- decision about whom to choose as a vice president.

(A) final
(B) finals
(C) finally
(D) finalize

題型 **位置──形容詞**

翻譯 在最終決定誰是副總裁之前，董事會面試了五名頂尖應徵者。

空格位於名詞前，應為能修飾名詞的形容詞，故選項中最適合的為 final，且 final decision 這個說法也很常見，建議可直接背起來；本題正確答案為 (A)。

**124**

All fountain pens ------- at Sunday's auction will be open to buyers starting on Saturday at 9:00 A.M.

(A) to be sold
(B) has been sold
(C) is selling
(D) was to sell

題型 **文法──動詞**

翻譯 週日拍賣會上所有將出售的鋼筆，都會在週六上午9點開放給所有買家鑑賞。

詞彙 fountain pen 鋼筆

一個句子若沒有連接詞，則只能出現一個動詞，本句主詞為 All fountain pens，而動詞為助動詞 will，所以就算空格要代入的是動詞的變化型態，故本題正確答案為 (A)。

## 125

**Official ------- is required for all of the airplanes arriving at the airport.**

(A) documentation
(B) administration
(C) freight
(D) agency

題型 **詞彙**——名詞

翻譯 抵達機場的所有班機都需要出示官方文件。

(A) documentation 資料；(B) administration 管理、經營；(C) freight 貨物；(D) agency 代理機構、仲介、媒介。

本句提到「官方的」、「需要出示」，故空格處的名詞應是能夠被要求出示的官方「證件、文件」等，所以本題最適合填入的是 documentation，正確答案為 (A)。

## 126

**As the number of travelers visiting China rises, ------- the demand for tour guides to lead them.**

(A) as long as
(B) whereas
(C) so does
(D) as to

題型 **文法**—— so 倒裝

翻譯 造訪中國的旅客增加，帶隊導遊的需求也隨之增加。

本句應是要表達，當遊客增加，對觀光導遊的需求也跟著增加。後句中，the demand 出現在空格之後，且該子句並未有到動詞，推測空格處應填入動詞，這個子句是個倒裝句，因此要選 so does，正確答案為 (C)。

so、neither、nor 等有時會需要部分倒裝，此處原本是要說 the demand for tour guide rises，因為前句已提過 rises，故此處變成 so does the demand for tour guides，其中助動詞 does 是根據原本子句主詞 the demand 而定，若此處是複數主詞，則改為使用 do。

## 127

**ThermoSafe, a large packaging company, specializes in ------- packaging services for insulated shipping boxes and containers.**

(A) absolute
(B) savory
(C) protective
(D) expired

題型 **詞彙**——形容詞

翻譯 安熱是一間大型包裝公司，專門為隔熱箱子或容器提供保護性包裝服務。

詞彙 insulated 隔熱的

(A) absolute 絕對的；(B) savory 美味的；芬芳的；(C) protective 具保護性的；(D) expired 到期的。

選項中最適合與空格後的 packaging service 連用的為 protective，表示具保護性的包裝服務，故正確答案為 (C)。

**128**

Neil Berret's new S/S collection features pants in a ------- variety of colors.

(A) wide
(B) width
(C) widen
(D) widely

題型 位置──形容詞
翻譯 尼爾·柏瑞特新的春夏褲款系列，以多樣顏色可供選擇為主打特色。

觀察空格位於不定冠詞 a 以及名詞 variety 之間，故應該填入形容詞，修飾多樣的程度，所以最適合的是 wide，正確答案為 (A)。

**129**

Unfortunately, research indicated that the increase in oil prices will ------- economic recovery.

(A) interfere with
(B) correspond to
(C) fall behind
(D) rely on

題型 詞彙──片語
翻譯 不幸的是，研究指出油價上漲會干擾經濟復甦。

(A) interfere with 妨礙；(B) correspond to 與……一致；(C) fall behind 落後；(D) rely on 依賴。

本句前面已提到 Unfortunately，可推測應該是負面的資訊，所以此處應是要表示油價上升會「干擾、妨礙」經濟復甦，最適合填入的是 interfere with，正確答案為 (A)。

**130**

All department stores should ------- with regulations regarding sales at special events.

(A) comply
(B) adhere
(C) authorize
(D) follow

題型 詞彙──動詞
翻譯 所有百貨公司都得遵守特賣活動的相關規定。

本題必須填入可和介系詞 with 連用的動詞，並表示「遵守」的意思，所以正確答案為 (A)。

(B) adhere 應該和 to 連用；(C) 與 (D) 皆為及物動詞，後面不用接續介系詞，應直接連接受詞。

★記住以下表示「遵守」的用語：
comply with / adhere to / stick to / follow

## PART 6

**131–134 電子郵件**

**To:** Maria Gomez
<mgomez@samail.com>
**From:** Taylor Fisher
<tfisher@lapubliclibrary.com>
**Date:** May 5
**Subject:** Your inquiry

Dear Ms. Gomez,

Thank you for your inquiry about your **131** library book, The Blossom Girl. Although the book is now one week overdue, I renewed it through May 12 so that the library will not keep charging you a late fee.

I did ask my colleagues to check if they could find it on the shelves, just in case someone could have found or **132** the book. **133**.

If you cannot return the book by May 12, we will **134** a new one. In that case, you should bear the expenses.

Sincerely,
Taylor Fisher
Los Angeles Public Library

---

收件人：瑪麗亞‧戈梅茲
<mgomez@samail.com>
寄件人：泰勒‧費雪
<tfisher@lapubliclibrary.com>
日期：5月5日
主旨：您的詢問

親愛的戈梅茲女士：

感謝您詢問您所遺失的借閱書本《花開女孩》。這本書現在雖然逾期一週了，但我已更新借閱到5月12日，所以圖書館不會再繼續收取逾期罰款。

我已請同事確認這本書是否有在書架上，以防有人可能找到它並協助歸還。但很遺憾，我們並沒有找到。

如果您無法在5月12日前還書，我們將會訂購一本新書。那就必須由您負擔這筆支出。

洛杉磯公共圖書館
泰勒‧費雪 敬上

---

**詞彙** charge a late fee 收逾期罰款　in that case 那樣的情況發生的話

**131** ------------------------------------------------

(A) miss
(B) to miss
(C) missing
(D) missed

(A) 錯過
(B) 去想念
(C) 遺失的
(D) 錯過的

**題型 位置——現在分詞**

空格位於所有格與名詞之間，應為形容詞。從後文看來，此處應是要表示「遺失的」書本，故要填入具有「遺失的、弄丟的」之意的 missing，因此正確答案為 (C)。

**132** ------------------------------------------------

(A) return
(B) returned
(C) be returned
(D) will return

(A) 歸還
(B) 已歸還
(C) 被歸還
(D) 將歸還

觀察空格前方的有連接詞 or 及動詞 could have found，可知道受 or 連接的應該要是同樣時態的動詞，故此處原本應是 someone could have found or could have returned，只是 could have 重複可省略，所以可以變成 could have found or returned，正確答案為 (B)。

**133** [NEW] ----------------------------------------------------------------

| | |
|---|---|
| (A) All library patrons are issued a membership card. | (A) 會員卡會發放給所有來圖書館的訪客。 |
| (B) You can find the location on our website. | (B) 您可以在我們官網上找到圖書館地點。 |
| (C) Unfortunately, we failed to find it. | (C) 但很遺憾，我們並沒有找到。 |
| (D) However, we are closed on Sunday. | (D) 但是我們在週日閉館。 |

題型 **填入句子**

第二段提到圖書館一方也在幫忙尋找書籍，第三段則告知對方，若無法在指定日期前找到，後續會發生的處理流程。因此兩段之間，應該先告知對方沒有在圖書館找到書本，所以如果對方自己也找不到，最後將面臨罰款，故正確答案為 (C)。

**134** ----------------------------------------------------------------

| | |
|---|---|
| (A) order | (A) 訂購 |
| (B) recognize | (B) 認出 |
| (C) acknowledge | (C) 承認 |
| (D) identify | (D) 認出 |

題型 **詞彙**──動詞

本句前半段設想 5 月 12 日前無法找到書本，故後面應告知對方在此情況下的後果。從文意來看，本句提到「we」、「a new one」，最可能是圖書館將「訂購」一本新書，故應填入 order，正確答案為 (A)。

### 135-138 文章

San Francisco (March 29) — For two weeks only, Starbean will launch a limited edition of retro packaging for their products, which dates back to thirty years ago, when the brand **135** became popular. This promotion will not apply to Starbean's existing coffee lineup. The company will be introducing new drinks, including Iced Cinnamon Almond Milk Macchiato, Coconut Milk Mocha Latte, and Caramel Cocoa Frappuccino, **136** the size compared to the existing options.

Starbean president Kim Perry says the packaging shows the history of the brand. **137**. "We feel this promotion will attract both long-time and new customers," she said. Starbean's retro packaging products will be available in April. And its new **138** will hit stores in May.

舊金山（3月29日）──再等兩週，星豆公司將推出限量復刻版產品，可追溯到30年前品牌首度流行的時候。這次活動將不會包括星豆公司現有的咖啡系列。公司將會推出新飲品，像是冰肉桂杏仁牛奶瑪奇朵、椰奶摩卡拿鐵和焦糖可可特調冰沙，容量將是現在的兩倍。

星豆公司董事長金・派瑞說，包裝展示了品牌歷史。這正是星豆暢銷的原因。「我們覺得這次的推廣活動，會受到舊雨新知的青睞。」她說。星豆復刻商品將在四月上市。至於新飲品則會在五月開賣。

**詞彙** retro 復刻的　date back to 追溯到　apply to 推及；適用於　existing 現有的　lineup 系列　Frappuccino 特調冰沙；星冰樂　long-time 長時間的　hit stores 開賣

**135** ----------------------------------------------------------------------

(A) once

(B) all

(C) first

(D) thus

(A) 一度

(B) 全部

(C) 首度

(D) 因此

**題型 詞彙——副詞**

前文提到公司將推出復刻版產品，並提到「30 年前」、「品牌」、「流行」，故可推測此處的副詞應帶有「首度、初次」的意思，代表此產品的發行是在 30 前品牌首度變得受歡迎時，所以空格處最適合填入 first，正確答案為 (C)。

**136** ----------------------------------------------------------------------

(A) double

(B) doubles

(C) will double

(D) doubling

(A) 使加倍

(B) 使加倍

(C) 將使加倍

(D) 使加倍

**題型 文法——分詞片語**

double 除了當形容詞表示「雙倍的」，也可作動詞表示「使……翻倍」，此處就是作為動詞。

由於空格前沒有出現連接詞，前方又已出現 will be introducing，所以此處不可再填入動詞的一般型態。除了 (D) 之外，其他三個選項皆為一般動詞，故不可能是答案。

另外，分析句子結構可知，「including . . . Frappuccino」這個子句是作為補充，解釋 new drinks 包含的種類，若先省略不看，全句的主詞在 The company，動詞 will be introducing，而空格後的「double the size . . .」其實是在說明 new drinks 的容量增大，所以兩句之間應該有關係代名詞 that，故此句原本是：「The company will be introducing new drinks that double the size compared to the existing options」，此處只是把 that 省略，主動動詞 double 改為 doubling，而全句變成：「The company . . . new drinks, doubling the size . . .」，故空格處要填入的是 doubling，正確答案為 (D)。

**137** (NEW) ----------------------------------------------------------------------

(A) Market analysts predict that it will show disappointing quarterly earnings.

(B) The price of coffee is expected to steadily increase this year.

(C) That is why Starbean has become so popular.

(D) It also appeals to customers who don't have time to enjoy coffee.

(A) 市場分析師預期，這季的利潤將讓人失望。

(B) 今年咖啡的價格預期將持續成長。

(C) 這正是星豆暢銷的原因。

(D) 這也吸引到沒時間享用咖啡的顧客。

**題型 填入句子**

前文提到，復古包裝能夠展現品牌的歷史，故空格處應接續包裝的話題最適當，(C) 說明包裝是品牌受歡迎的原因，也是選項中唯一與包裝相關的內容，故此處最適合填入的答案為 (C)。

(A) services
(B) functions
(C) equipment
(D) beverages

(A) 服務
(B) 功能
(C) 裝備
(D) 飲品

題型 詞彙——名詞

從上段可知公司不只推出復刻版包裝，也會推出新飲品，故此句應是在説明新飲品的上市時間，因此空格應填入 beverages，正確答案為 (D)。

## 139–142 備忘錄

**To:** All staff
**From:** Accounting Department
**Date:** February 4
**Subject:** Revised Procedures

收件人：全體員工
寄件人：會計部門
日期：2月4日
主旨：程序更正

Please be aware that the reimbursement program for travel expenses has been changed. **139**, the Travel Expense Form was submitted within one month after the trip. Now, employees must submit the form within at least two weeks after traveling. All expenses **140** by the company, providing that they are properly used and have been approved beforehand. Once the request for travel expenses has been processed, **141** of incurred expenses that have been approved by the company will be sent to the employee. **142**. If you need further information, please visit our website at www.tesoro.com/reimbursementprogram.

請注意最近差旅費的核銷方案有異動。這之前，差旅支出表要在行程結束後一個月內提交。而今，員工最遲必須在行程後兩週內提交。只要合理使用且事先取得許可，所有開銷都將由公司負擔。一旦差旅費申請通過，公司將會寄送核准開銷的通知給員工。差旅費會經由正當程序核發。如果您需要更多資訊，請上官網www.tesoro.com/reimbursementprogram。

(A) Consequently
(B) Exceedingly
(C) Previously
(D) Eventually

(A) 所以
(B) 非常地
(C) 之前
(D) 最終

題型 詞彙——副詞

前句提到方案有所變更，此句動詞時態為過去式，而下句開頭使用 Now，且説明「現在」改變後的流程，因此空格處的副詞應具有「之前」的意思，以與後句呈現今昔對比，故正確答案為 (C)。

**140** ------------------------------------------------

(A) pays
(B) paid
(C) have been paying
(D) will be paid

(A) 付款
(B) 已付款
(C) 一直在付款
(D) 將被付款

題型 **文法**──動詞

本句的主詞 All expenses 應是「被支付」的東西，所以動詞要使用被動。選項中只有 (D) 是被動，故本題正確答案為 (D)。

**141** ------------------------------------------------

(A) notifies
(B) notified
(C) notifying
(D) notification

(A) 通知
(B) 已通知
(C) 正在通知
(D) 通知

題型 **位置**──名詞

觀察句子結構可看出，空格處應該是此句的主詞，而動詞則是後方的 will be sent，其中夾著的 that 子句，是用來補充說明前方的空格處至 expenses。既然空格處為主詞，則應該填入名詞，正確答案為 (D)。

(C) notifying 為動名詞，是及物動詞 notify 加上 ing 的形式，但是 notify 後面需要接續受詞，而此句後方並沒有受詞。

**142** (NEW) --- ------------------------------------

(A) Please e-mail this form to the accounting department.
(B) The company has been encouraging all staff to travel abroad.
(C) The travel expenses will be reimbursed by the proper procedures.
(D) Business trips are restricted due to the financial problems the company has faced.

(A) 請將表格以電子郵件寄到會計部門。
(B) 公司一直鼓勵員工出國旅遊。
(C) 差旅費會經由正常程序核發。
(D) 由於公司目前面臨財務問題，商務出差有所限制。

題型 **填入句子**

此處在解釋差旅費申請通過後的程序。前句說到公司會寄送核銷通知，故接續脈絡，此處應是說明之後旅費發款一事，故最適當的答案為 (C)。

## About the Award

Organizations with top performance throughout the U.S. give a boost to the country's economy. Over the years, we've witnessed that **143** success is mostly attributable to having an engaged workforce. Enthusiastic employees tend to have a positive impact on their coworkers. **144**. The Staples Best Workplace Award was **145** fifteen years ago to honor successful companies whose employees are dedicated to their work. **146**, hundreds of organizations throughout the U.S. have already received the award. If you would like to know about a complete list of award winners, go to the Recipient page.

## 獎項說明

績效表現頂尖的公司給美國經濟注入了一針強心劑。過去幾年來,我們見證很多成功的公司,其成功大多歸功於員工對工作的投入。有熱忱的員工可為同事帶來正面影響。這可從更高的工作產出上見得。史泰博最佳職場獎於15年前創立,為的是獎勵成功企業,他們的員工全心為工作貢獻。從那時起,數百家遍布全美的公司已獲獎項肯定。如果您想知道更完整的得獎名單,可以到「獲獎者」頁面查看。

**詞彙** **give a boost** 為……注入強心劑;帶動發展　**attributable** 可歸功的　**engaged** 投入的

(A) his
(B) when
(C) where
(D) their

(A) 他的
(B) 何時
(C) 哪裡
(D) 它們的

**題型** 位置──所有格

此句空格後為名詞,故此處應是填入能修飾名詞的所有格代名詞。前句説到績效良好的公司提振美國的經濟,故此句應該是要表示「那些公司的」成功是員工的功勞,所以代名詞要用複數型的 their,正確答案為 (D)。

**144** **NEW**

(A) Sometimes this can cause customer complaints.
(B) The award ceremony will be held in June.
(C) Only large companies are entitled to receive the prize.
(D) This can be seen in higher productivity.

(A) 有時候這會引起顧客的抱怨。
(B) 頒獎典禮將在六月舉行。
(C) 只有大企業會獲頒這個獎項。
(D) 這可從更高的工作產出上見得。

**題型** 填入句子

前句提到熱忱的員工可為公司帶來正面效果,所以後句應與此相關。(D) 提到「正面效果」體現在高工作產出上,此為最適當的接續,故本題正確答案為 (D)。

**145** - - - - - - - - - - - - - - - - - - - - - - - - - - - - - - - - - - - - - - - - -

(A) established           (A) 被建立

(B) appealed            (B) 被訴諸

(C) asked               (C) 被詢問

(D) inspired            (D) 被啟發

題型 **詞彙**——動詞

此句提到「獎項」、「15 年前」，故空格處的動詞應該具有「設立、創立」的意思，以表示獎項是在 15 年前創立的，故正確答案為 (A)。

**146** - - - - - - - - - - - - - - - - - - - - - - - - - - - - - - - - - - - - - - - - -

(A) Now that           (A) 既然

(B) On the other hand    (B) 另一方面

(C) Since then          (C) 從那時起

(D) Nevertheless        (D) 然而

題型 **詞彙**——片語

前句使用過去式動詞，講到獎項於 15 年前創立，此句則使用了現在完成式，説明有許多機構獲獎。現在完成式可用在某事從過去發生，並一直延續至今的情況，因此選項中最適合填入的應是 Since then，以表達「從那時起」便有許多機構獲獎，正確答案為 (C)。

(A) Now that 文意不符，且詞性為連接詞，無法獨立存在。

## PART 7

### 147–148 廣告

| Nucor Center | 紐克中心 |
|---|---|
| • More than 40 exciting outdoor sports | • 超過40種刺激的戶外運動 |
| • More than 50 amazing games with reasonable prices | • 50種以上物超所值的驚奇遊戲 |
| • Special music festival all year round | • 全年度的特別音樂節 |
| • The country's largest indoor food court | • 國內最大的室內美食街 |
| • A play area designed only for children under five | • 專為五歲以下兒童設計的遊樂區 |
| Nucor Center is open throughout the year, Monday through Sunday. Tickets can be purchased online or at the main gate. Group discounts apply for groups of 12 or more. | 紐克中心週一到週日全年無休。可由網路或在大門處購票。12人以上團體享折扣。 |

**What is being advertised?**

(A) A music concert
(B) A competition
(C) An amusement park
(D) A design festival

這篇是要廣告什麼？

(A) 音樂會
(B) 競賽
(C) 遊樂園
(D) 設計嘉年華

廣告內容寫到此場所有戶外活動、遊戲、音樂節，還有為兒童設計的遊樂區，故最可能包含上述所有項目的應該是遊樂園，正確答案為 (C)。

**Who is eligible for a discount?**

(A) People buying tickets as a group
(B) People visiting more than five times a month
(C) People purchasing tickets online
(D) People under five years of age

誰適用折扣？

(A) 團體購票的民眾
(B) 單月來訪超過五次的民眾
(C) 網路購票的民眾
(D) 五歲以下的民眾

在廣告最後寫著「Group discounts apply for groups of 12 or more.」，可知只有 12 人以上的團體享有購票優惠，故本題正確答案為 (A)。

**149–150 資訊**

| Omnicom S9 Mobile | 全通 S9 手機 |
|---|---|
| Thank you for purchasing the Omnicom S9 mobile phone. Your new phone includes state-of-the-art features to make your life more enjoyable. This user manual offers you easy-to-follow instructions for your new mobile phone. If you want to avoid any possibility of damaging your Omnicom S9, please check the list of precautions on page 25 concerning accessories, including battery chargers, phone cases, batteries, and earphones. | 感謝您購買全通S9手機。您的全新手機具備最先進的功能，讓您的生活更好玩。這本使用說明書提供簡單好上手的手機使用說明。如果您想避免全通S9受損，請翻閱第25頁與配件有關的注意事項，內容包括充電器、手機殼、電池和耳機。 |

**詞彙** **easy-to-follow** 簡單好上手的　**precaution** 注意事項；預防措施　**accessory** 配件（常為複數型）

**149**

**What is the purpose of the information?** 這則資訊的目的為何？

(A) To promote the mobile phone's warranty program (A) 推銷手機的保固方案
(B) To offer a discount on electronic devices (B) 提供電子產品的折扣
(C) To advise customers to take a look at the manual (C) 建議顧客翻閱使用書
(D) To encourage consumers to buy a new phone (D) 鼓勵顧客買新手機

第二句說到「This user manual」，表示這則資訊應該來自手機使用說明書，且後面還提到「If you want to avoid any possibility of damaging your Omnicom S9, please check the list of precautions on page 25」，提醒消費者詳閱說明書以避免手機受損，故這則資訊的目的應是建議顧客詳閱手機使用說明，正確答案為 (C)。

**150**

**What is suggested about mobile phone accessories?** 文中提到手機配件什麼事？

(A) Omnicom S9 includes all of them at no extra cost. (A) 全通 S9 通通附贈。
(B) Using them incorrectly might damage the phone. (B) 不當使用可能會損害手機。
(C) They come with a one-year warranty. (C) 有一年的保固。
(D) Authorized dealers can replace the damaged ones with new ones. (D) 經授權的經銷商可將毀損的商品換成全新的。

第四句中說到：「If you want to avoid any possibility of damaging your Omnicom S9, please check the list of precautions on page 25 concerning accessories」，表示為了避免手機受損，需要查閱與配件相關的說明，故可推測手機配件若未好好使用，可能損害手機，本題正確答案為 (B)。

本題在解題時，有可能不小心以常識判斷而造成失誤。(A) 提到手機會附贈所有配件，作答時可能因為平常購買手機時的確會附上配件，而誤將此選項選為答案，然而文章內容並未提到附件是會隨產品附贈還是需要另外購買，故此選項不能選。

Scarlett Portman
51–59 Chester Ave.
Garden City, NY 11530

January 5

Angela West
667 3rd Ave. Welaka, FL 32193

Dear Ms. West,

I am writing to thank you for your professional reference. I believe that your recommendation letter supporting my application was of great help in securing the position of news interpreter at SBTY.

The experience I have gotten during graduate school, particularly through translating Korean and Japanese into English, made me well suited for this job. Aside from the interpretation, I am now enjoying the challenge of translating medical news program as well.

Again, I really appreciate your help.

Yours sincerely,
Scarlett Portman

---

史嘉莉·波特曼
11530 紐約花園市雀斯特大道
51–59號

1月5日

安琪拉·威斯特
32193 佛州韋拉卡第三大道667
號

親愛的威斯特女士：

感謝您的專業推薦。我相信您的推薦信對我應徵上SBTY新聞口譯一職，有很大的幫助。

我在研究所的所學，特別是將韓文和日文翻譯成英文的經驗，讓我勝任這份工作。除了口譯，我也很享受翻譯醫療新聞節目的挑戰。

再次非常感謝您的幫忙。

史嘉莉·波特曼 敬上

---

**詞彙** reference 推薦信　　graduate school 研究所

---

 **151** ----------------------------------------

**Why did Ms. Portman write the letter?**

(A) To approve some information
(B) To express gratitude
(C) To ask for a translation
(D) To offer a position

為什麼波特曼女士要寫這封信？

(A) 表示同意一些資訊
(B) 表達感謝
(C) 請求翻譯
(D) 提供職位

信件開頭第一句便說了：「I am writing to thank you for your professional reference.」，感謝對方幫忙撰寫推薦信，故正確答案為 (B)。

---

**152** ----------------------------------------

**Where does Ms. Portman most likely work?**

(A) At a broadcasting network
(B) At a pharmaceutical company
(C) At a language school
(D) At a hospital

波特曼女士最可能在哪裡工作？

(A) 電視網
(B) 製藥公司
(C) 語言學校
(D) 醫院

第一段最後使用了「news interpreter」，第二段則是提到「translating medical news program」，表示除了口譯之外，也負責翻譯醫療新聞節目，故波特曼女士最可能是在播報新聞相關的電視台等處工作，選項中最適合的答案為 (A)。

## 153–155 電子郵件

**From:** Brad Bourne
<b.bourne@jbconsulting.com>
**To:** Natasha Miller
<n.miller@jbconsulting.com>
**Date:** 14 July
**Subject:** Paris meeting

Hello Natasha,

I'm in Tokyo to supervise the overall inspection process and make sure it is properly carried out, but it's taken longer than I expected. So, I'm going to extend my stay here in Japan for a further two weeks, meaning that I need you to reschedule my appointment on Thursday in Paris.

If you do so, I could prepare for the client meeting with Mr. James next month. And could you send me a copy of the contracts that I drew up? They're probably either in my file cabinet or on my desk. I will not be reachable by phone today. If you need me, please e-mail or message me.

Thank you for your help.

Brad Bourne,
President, Bourne Consulting

---

寄件人：布萊德・伯恩
<b.bourne@jbconsulting.com>
收件人：娜塔莎・米勒
<n.miller@jbconsulting.com>
日期：7月14日
主旨：巴黎會議

哈囉娜塔莎：

我現在在東京監督整個檢驗流程，並確保一切運作正常，不過花的時間比我預期得還要久。所以我想要在日本再多待兩週，這表示我需要你重新安排我週四在巴黎的會議。

如果可以的話，我可以準備下個月和詹姆斯先生的客戶會議。可以請你給我一份我擬好的合約副本嗎？要是它們不在我的檔案櫃裡，就是在我桌上。我今天沒辦法講電話。如果需要跟我聯絡，請寄電子郵件或傳訊。

感謝你幫忙。

布萊德・伯恩
伯恩諮詢總裁

**詞彙** draw up 草擬　**file cabinet** 檔案櫃　**reachable** 能聯絡上的

**153** ----------------------------------------------------------------

**What is the purpose of the e-mail?**

(A) To approve a request for an inspection
(B) To summarize a report
(C) To complain about the inspection results
(D) To request assistance in changing a schedule

這封電子郵件的目的為何？

(A) 核准檢驗的要求
(B) 總結一份報告
(C) 抱怨視察結果
(D) 請求協助更改行程

伯恩先生在郵件的第一段中間提到，自己必須在日本多待兩週，並說：「I need you to reschedule my appointment on Thursday in Paris」，表示希望收信的米勒女士幫忙重新安排行程，故本題正確答案為 (D)。

**154**

**Why is Mr. Bourne most likely in Japan?**

(A) To open a new facility
(B) To sign a contact
(C) To oversee a project
(D) To interview a candidate

伯恩先生待在日本可能是因為什麼？

(A) 開設新廠
(B) 簽合約
(C) 監督一項計畫
(D) 面試應徵者

第一段第一句提到：「I'm in Tokyo to supervise the overall inspection process and make sure it is properly carried out」，表示伯恩先生是為了監督檢驗流程才留在日本，故本題答案為 (C)。

**155**

**What is suggested about Mr. James?**

(A) He is a factory manager.
(B) He is Ms. Miller's administrative assistant.
(C) He is Mr. Bourne's business client.
(D) He helped Mr. Bourne with the inspection process.

文中提到詹姆斯先生什麼事？

(A) 他是工廠廠長。
(B) 他是米勒女士的行政助理。
(C) 他是伯恩先生的企業客戶。
(D) 他在檢驗過程中幫助伯恩先生。

郵件第二段開頭提到「the client meeting with Mr. James」，由此可知，詹姆斯先生應是伯恩先生的客戶，故正確答案為 (C)。

### 156–158 信件

| Aramark Electronics | 愛瑪客電子 |
|---|---|
| www.aramarkelectronics.com | www.aramarkelectronics.com |
| Michael Dawson | 麥克·道森 |
| 1C Vestry Road London, E17 9NH England | E17 9NH 英格蘭倫敦教會路1C |

Dear Mr. Dawson,

親愛的道森先生：

Thank you for contacting Aramark Electronics for your air-conditioner repair (No. 2912012). To provide the best quality service to our customers, we ask you to take a few minutes to complete the survey. Please send us your completed survey sheet by using the enclosed self-addressed stamped envelope. Thank you for your cooperation.

感謝您聯繫愛瑪客電子來維修您的空調（單號2912012）。請您花幾分鐘完成問卷，讓我們能夠提供顧客最好的服務。請使用隨信附上的回郵信封寄回您填答完畢的問卷表。感謝您的配合。

| | Strongly Agree | Agree | Disagree | Strongly Disagree |
|---|---|---|---|---|
| Aramark Electronics replied to your request quickly. | ✗ | | | |

| | 非常同意 | 同意 | 不同意 | 非常不同意 |
|---|---|---|---|---|
| 愛瑪客電子迅速答覆您的需求。 | ✗ | | | |

| A service technician precisely explained what the problem is. | | × | | |
|---|---|---|---|---|
| Your Aramark Electronics product was immediately repaired and returned. | | | | × |

| 維修技師正確說明問題所在。 | | × | | |
|---|---|---|---|---|
| 您的愛瑪客電子產品很快修好歸還。 | | | | × |

**Customer Name:** Michael Dawson
**Repair Request Number:** 2912012
**Comments:**
It was better to use Q&A's on your website than to chat with a technician. That's because I could get a quick answer about troubleshooting. The answer written by the technician had detailed information about what to do to solve the problems. My air conditioner, however, was not fixed properly and arrived five days later than the estimated shipping date.

顧客姓名：麥克‧道森
修理單號：2912012
其他意見：
在官網上看問題集都比和維修技師溝通來得好。我會這樣說，是因為我從疑難排解就可以迅速知道故障的原因。關於怎麼解決問題，技師寫得很詳細。不過，他沒有修好我的空調，且歸還時間還比預計時間晚了五天。

詞彙 self-addressed 回郵的　technician 維修技師　troubleshooting 疑難排解

---

**156** ----------------------------------------

**Why was the letter written to Mr. Dawson?**

(A) To complain about what he went through
(B) To announce the recall of defective models
(C) To notify him of policy changes
(D) To get information about customer service

為什麼會寫這封信給道森先生？

(A) 抱怨他經歷過的一切
(B) 公告回收有瑕疵的產品
(C) 提醒他政策變動
(D) 了解有關顧客服務的資訊

本題解題時應仔細閱讀題目。本題詢問的是「寫信給道森先生的原因」，而非「道森先生寫信的原因」，沒看清楚的話可能就會將答案選成了 (A)。信件在第二句提到：「To provide the best quality service to our customers, we ask you to take a few minutes to complete the survey.」，可看出這封信的目的是想請道森先生填寫問卷，以供日後服務參考，因此正確答案為 (D)。

---

**157** ----------------------------------------

**What does Aramark Electronics offer?**

(A) Online assistance
(B) Free shipping
(C) A warranty extension
(D) A troubleshooting manual

愛瑪客電子提供什麼？

(A) 線上協助
(B) 免運費
(C) 保固展延
(D) 故障檢修手冊

「Comments」標題下的第一行提到：「It was better to use Q&A's on your website than to chat with a technician.」、「I could get a quick answer about troubleshooting」，代表愛瑪客電子有提供線上 Q&A，可與顧客直接溝通並解決問題，由此可知公司最可能提供的是線上協助服務，正確答案為 (A)。

**158**

---

**What does Mr. Dawson mention?**

(A) The technician perfectly fixed the air conditioner.

(B) The repair took longer than expected.

(C) The air conditioner was defective at the time of purchase.

(D) The manual was difficult to understand.

**道森先生提到什麼？**

(A) 技師將空調維修得很完美。

(B) 維修時間比預期還久。

(C) 空調買的時候就有瑕疵。

(D) 說明書很難理解。

在信件最後可看到，道森先生寫了：「My air conditioner . . . arrived five days later than the estimated shipping date」，表示冷氣的維修時間比預估的還要久，因此正確答案為 (B)。

根據「My air conditioner . . . was not fixed properly」可知冷氣並沒有被修好，故 (A) 不正確，另外文中並未提及 (C) 與 (D) 的內容。

### 159–160 訊息串

| | |
|---|---|
| **Ashton Williams** 10:50 A.M.<br>The clients have just arrived! Where are you? Is it OK to start the meeting without you? | 艾希頓‧威廉斯〔上午10:50〕：<br>客戶剛剛到了！你在哪？你沒到的話我們可以先開會嗎？ |
| **Collins Reynolds** 10:51 A.M.<br>Yes, please. I'll be there in 15 minutes. | 柯林斯‧雷諾斯〔上午10:51〕：<br>可以啊。我15分鐘內到。 |
| **Ashton Williams** 10:52 A.M.<br>OK. I'll give an overview of trends in the industry and begin talking about the features of our new products. | 艾希頓‧威廉斯〔上午10:52〕：<br>好。我會先談整體產業趨勢，再講我們新產品的特色。 |
| **Collins Reynolds** 10:52 A.M.<br>I'm pretty sure you'll do an excellent job. | 柯林斯‧雷諾斯〔上午10:52〕：<br>我相信你會做得很好。 |
| **Ashton Williams** 10:53 A.M.<br>Thanks, but you had better give the presentation for the estimated costs. It's your area of expertise. | 艾希頓‧威廉斯〔上午10:53〕：<br>謝了，但你最好負責報告估價，那是你的專業。 |
| **Collins Reynolds** 10:54 A.M.<br>All right, see you soon. | 柯林斯‧雷諾斯〔上午10:54〕：<br>沒問題，等等見。 |

**詞彙** one's area of expertise 某人的專業領域

**159** NEW

At 10:51 A.M., what does Mr. Reynolds most likely mean when he writes, "Yes, please"?

(A) He needs more information about the product.

(B) He wants Mr. Williams to stay on schedule.

(C) He wants them to take a fifteen-minute break now.

(D) He recommends that the presentation be delayed.

上午**10:51**，雷諾斯先生寫道：「可以啊」，他最可能的意思是？

(A) 他需要更多產品資訊。

(B) 他想要威廉斯先生照進度走。

(C) 他想要他們現在先休息 15 分鐘。

(D) 他建議延後簡報。

在 10 點 50 分時威廉斯先生先問了：「Is it OK to start the meeting without you?」，詢問雷諾斯先生能否在他未到場的情況下先開始會議，故此時雷諾斯先生回覆的「Yes, please.」是代表肯定，讓威廉斯先生可按流程先與客戶開會，因此正確答案為 (B)。

**160**

According to Mr. Williams, what is Mr. Reynolds most knowledgeable about?

(A) Manufacturing

(B) Product specification

(C) Marketing strategy

(D) Budgeting

根據威廉斯先生的說法，雷諾斯先生最熟悉什麼？

(A) 製造生產

(B) 產品規格

(C) 行銷策略

(D) 預算評估

威廉斯先生在最後說道：「you had better give the presentation for the estimated costs」、「It's your area of expertise.」，表示希望由雷諾斯先生報告估價相關的內容，因為那是他的專業領域，故選項中最適當的答案是 (D)。

**161–163 文章**

## Business Inside

Lincoln Bookstore recently has acquired the retail space right next to the store's original location at 877 High Road Leytonstone in London. The popular spot will finally launch an expansion project by using the new space. "Since opening our doors five years ago, we have been on the fast track," says Seth Johnson, cofounder and president of Lincoln Bookstore. "We were told that successful stories for offline bookstores are a thing of the past. —[1]—."

Johnson went on to say that the renovated Lincoln Bookstore will be approximately double the size. "The much-anticipated reopening ceremony will be held on November 8," says Johnson. "—[2]—. We're thrilled with the revamped bookstore. —[3]—. It means we could have many books and host various events like book signings. —[4]—."

## 商情內幕

林肯書店最近收購了原先是零售業者的店面，地點緊鄰它倫敦雷頓斯通高路877號原店址。這個熱門地點總算要運用新空間進行擴展計畫。「自五年前開業以來，我們發展得很快。」林肯書店共同創辦人暨總裁塞斯·強生說。「常常有人跟我們說成功的實體書店是過去式了。我們證明了事實剛好相反。」

強生繼續說道，林肯書店整修完成後約莫是原店面的兩倍大。「眾所期待的重新開幕儀式將在11月8號舉行。」強生說，「書店改頭換面讓我們很興奮。這表示我們可以收納更多書，舉行各式各樣的活動，像是簽書會。」

詞彙 **on the fast track** 進度快　**cofounder** 共同創辦人　**offline bookstore** 實體書店　**a thing of the past** 過時的事物　**much-anticipated** 眾所期待的　**be thrilled with** 感到興奮　**revamped** 改進的；改頭換面的　**host** 主辦

## 161

**What is the purpose of the article?**

(A) To introduce a local business owner

(B) To announce changes to a bookstore

(C) To advertise a new book

(D) To promote a book signing event

這篇文章的目的為何？

(A) 介紹當地一家商店老闆

(B) 宣布書店改裝

(C) 推銷一本新書

(D) 推廣一場簽書會

文章開頭便提到：「Lincoln Bookstore recently has acquired the retail space right next to the store's original location」、「an expansion project by using the new space」，表示林肯書店收購新店面，並要進行擴展計畫，同時在第二段的第一行也能看到「the renovated Lincoln Bookstore」，表示書店經過整修，故本文章的目的應是公告一家書店的整修改裝，故最適當的答案為 (B)。

## 162

**Who is Mr. Johnson?**

(A) A bookseller

(B) A popular writer

(C) An online book supplier

(D) A real estate agent

誰是強生先生？

(A) 書商

(B) 知名作家

(C) 網路書籍供應商

(D) 房仲業者

第一段中間的部分提到：「Seth Johnson, cofounder and president of Lincoln Bookstore」，表示強生先生是書店的共同創辦人與總裁，若答題時不確定 cofounder 與 president 的意思，也可以觀察他的話語；他在提及書店時總是使用「we」，表示他應該是書店方的經營相關人員，本題正確答案為 (A)。

## 163 NEW

**In which of the positions marked [1], [2], [3] and [4] does the following sentence best belong?**

**"We have proved that the opposite is true."**

(A) [1]

(B) [2]

(C) [3]

(D) [4]

下列句子最適合出現在[1]、[2]、[3]、[4]的哪個位置中？

「我們證明了事實剛好相反。」

(A) [1]

(B) [2]

(C) [3]

(D) [4]

從句意來看，在這句之前應該提出某個大眾相信的論點，所以此刻才會接上「我們證明了事實剛好相反」。第一段最後強生先生說：「We were told that successful stories for offline bookstores are a thing of the past.」，表示有人告訴他們現今已難經營實體書店，但前文才提過林肯書店擴展店面、發展快速，所以此處若接續題目引述的句子，代表雖然眾人看衰，但林肯書店證明了自己經營實體書店的能力，因此此句放於 [1] 位置最為適當，正確答案為 (A)。

**164–167 資訊**

## Manchester Music Festival

Are you interested in participating in one of the famous music festivals as a committed volunteer while enjoying great music? Then, why don't you volunteer at the 25th annual Manchester Music Festival! This year's festival starts from on 1 and runs until August 5 at the Heaton Park in Manchester, and more than 15 professional groups and 25 talented amateur groups — including local favorites Roland Byrd, Jazzmatazz, Acadia Beat — will show off their great performances during the event.

**Volunteers are needed to**

• Help with creating, distributing all posters and flyers, and handing out press releases, which starts July 1.

• Greet and interpret for the musicians from July 28 to August 8. All out-of-town musicians will stay at the designated hotel.

• Operate the ticket office and the information desk as well as guide guests to the parking lots during the festival.

To show our appreciation for volunteers' dedication, the rewards are bountiful! Volunteers will receive an official limited-edition Manchester Music Festival T-shirt, VIP invitation to the official after party, a season festival pass, and more.

If you are interested in volunteering, please contact Hilary Roberts at hroberts@manchestermusicfestival.co.uk by June 15.

## 曼徹斯特音樂節

您有興趣擔任志工參與知名音樂節，共享音樂盛宴嗎？那您何不自願來第25屆曼徹斯特音樂節！今年音樂節將從8月1日到5日，在曼徹斯特的希頓公園舉行，超過15個專業團體和25個才華洋溢的業餘團體—包括當地人最喜愛的羅蘭・柏德、爵士馬塔茲、阿卡迪亞節拍—都將共襄盛舉，在活動中展現高超表演。

志工需要做的事：

•協助所有海報和傳單的創作和發放，並從7月1日開始處理新聞稿。

•7月28日到8月8日期間接待音樂家並擔任口譯。來自其他城市的音樂家均住在指定旅館。

•音樂節期間，管理售票亭和服務台，並引導遊客到停車場。

為了感謝志工的付出，我們提供豐富獎勵！志工將收到曼徹斯特音樂節官方限量版的T恤、官方慶功宴的貴賓邀請函、一整季的音樂通行證等。

如果您有興趣擔任志工，請於6月15日前聯絡希拉蕊・羅伯茲hroberts@manchestermusicfestival.co.uk。

**詞彙** committed 願意奉獻的　amateur 業餘的　interpret 口譯　bountiful 豐富的

---

**164**

**What is indicated about the festival?**

(A) It will begin on August 1.
(B) It features various music genres.
(C) It is run by the local government.
(D) It may be postponed due to rain.

文中提到音樂節什麼事？

(A) 從 8 月 1 日開始。
(B) 特色是有多種音樂類型。
(C) 由當地政府舉辦。
(D) 可能因為下雨延期。

從第一段的「This year's festival starts from on 1 and runs until August 5」可看出音樂節從 8 月 1 日到 5 日展開，故本題正確答案為 (A)。

(B) 文中雖然提到有許多表演團體參加，但是並未提及音樂類型，故無法確定此事，(C) 與 (D) 同樣無法在文中找到相關內容。

## 165

**What is suggested about some of the performers?**　文中提到某些表演者什麼事？

(A) They will be donating used musical instruments.　(A) 他們將捐出二手樂器。

(B) They will be offering autographed CDs.　(B) 他們將提供簽名唱片。

(C) They will be staying at homes in Manchester.　(C) 他們會住在曼徹斯特的民宅裡。

(D) They will be receiving some interpretation services.　(D) 他們會接受一些口譯協助。

從志工工作內容的第二項可以看到「Greet and interpret for the musicians」，表示志工需要為表演者口譯，也就是表演者會接受口譯服務的意思，故正確答案為 (D)。

(A) 與 (B) 皆為文中未提及的內容，另外可從列點第二項的「All out-of-town musicians will stay at the designated hotel.」知道，外地的表演者會住在指定旅館，故 (C) 不正確。

## 166

**What task will NOT be done by volunteers?**　哪項任務不會由志工來做？

(A) Selling tickets for the festival　(A) 販售音樂節的票

(B) Transporting musicians to their hotels　(B) 將音樂家送到飯店

(C) Informing visitors of parking locations　(C) 告知旅客停車位置

(D) Distributing some documents　(D) 發送一些文件

從志工工作內容第一點的「distributing all posters and flyers」可知志工需要發送文件，再從第三點的「operate the ticket office」、「guide guests to the parking lots」知道，志工也需要管理售票亭與引導旅客往停車場，故以上可依序確認 (A)、(C) 與 (D) 皆為志工的業務，因此選項中只有 (B) 不是志工的工作，本題正確答案為 (B)。

## 167

**What will volunteers receive for free?**　志工可以免費收到什麼？

(A) An article of clothing　(A) 一件衣服

(B) A voucher for the designated hotel　(B) 特定飯店的住宿券

(C) A ticket for an awards banquet　(C) 頒獎晚宴的票

(D) Food and beverages on festival days　(D) 音樂節期間的餐飲

倒數第二段說到志工可以獲得「an official limited-edition Manchester Music Festival T-shirt」，也就是官方限量 T 恤，故正確答案為 (A)。

## The Renovation of Marine Park

By Jack Davenport

San Diego (April 15) — San Diego's city council has adopted a resolution to renovate Marine Park with unanimous approval. The issue of the renovation project was initially raised three years ago and has been under discussion. After Mayor Natalie Witherspoon took office, the plan was finally approved. She said in an interview, "I told the city that this would be my first act after coming into office, and I plan to fulfill my pledge." —[1]—.

After the park was opened, its two-kilometer trail along the lake became one of the places of interest in San Diego. However, it was not long before residents came to know that the park is not an ideal place for their children. —[2]—.

"We walk the trail on a daily basis, but our kids want to kick a ball around," said city resident Ivanka Aniston. The park is indeed lacking spaces for children to run freely. "We sometimes thought of having lunch at the park, but there are no tables and benches." —[3]—.

As a part of the project, Marine Park will have more green space for outdoor activities. A space will be designed for children to play in safety as well. —[4]—. This was for the convenience of residents who prefer to walk or exercise later in the evening. The renovations will be finished by the end of this year at the latest.

## 海洋公園整修

傑克・戴文波特撰文

聖地牙哥（4月15日）—聖地牙哥市議會全數通過海洋公園的整修決議。整修計畫的議案最早在三年前提出，經過長時間討論，直到娜塔莉・薇斯朋接任市長，計畫才終於通過。她受訪時表示：「我向市民說過這是我當選後的首要任務，我也打算兌現承諾。」

公園開張後，沿著湖邊兩公里長的步道成為聖地牙哥的一大景點。不過，當地居民不久就才發現，公園對他們的小孩來說，並不是個理想的地方。

「我們每天都會使用步道，但我們的小孩只想到處踢球。」當地居民伊凡卡・安尼斯頓表示。公園內確實缺乏讓小孩自由奔跑的空間，「我們有時候想在公園吃午餐，但卻沒有桌子和長椅。」

計畫一部分就是要讓海洋公園有更多綠地，供戶外活動使用。並規劃讓小朋友可以安全遊玩的空間。市議會也通過提案，將沿著步道兩側裝設路燈，方便喜歡在傍晚散步或運動的居民。整修最晚會在今年底完成。

---

**詞彙** adopt 接受；通過　resolution 決議　unanimous 一致通過的　take office 上任
come into office 上任　pledge 承諾　on a daily basis 每天　at the latest 最晚

**168** ----------------------------------------------------------------

**What is indicated about the park's renovation?**

(A) It will end next summer.
(B) Mayor Witherspoon first proposed it.
(C) It will take three years to finish.
(D) All members of the council agreed to it.

文中提到公園整修什麼事？

(A) 明年夏天會結束。
(B) 由市長薇斯朋率先提出。
(C) 需要三年才會完工。
(D) 取得議會全體同意。

文章開頭便提到：「San Diego's city council has adopted a resolution to renovate Marine Park with unanimous approval.」，表示議會全數通過公園整修案，故本題正確答案為 (D)。

(A) 文章最後提到：「The renovations will be finished by the end of this year at the latest.」，故可知最晚整修最晚會在今年年底結束；(B) 文中未提及整修計畫的提議者，只說到在市長薇斯朋任期內通過；(C) 文中未提到耗時多久才完工。

 **169**

**The word "plan" in paragraph 1, line 5, is closest in meaning to**

(A) intend
(B) keep
(C) agree
(D) concentrate

第一段、第五行的「**plan**」，最接近下列哪個意思？

(A) 有意
(B) 保持
(C) 同意
(D) 專注於

本句說到「I plan to fulfill my pledge」，其中「plan to V」具有「計劃做……」的意思，故選項中最相近的應該是 intend，另外，intend 也是以「intend to V」表示「企圖做……」；本題正確答案為 (A)。

**170**

**How have residents been using the park?**

(A) To eat something
(B) To sell their handmade products
(C) To go for walks
(D) To ride a bicycle

居民如何使用公園？

(A) 吃東西
(B) 販賣他們的手工商品
(C) 去散步
(D) 騎單車

第三段引述居民的話，其中有居民提到「walk the trail」，表示他們會在公園裡散步，故正確答案為 (C)。

(A) 根據居民所言，雖然他們想要在公園裡吃東西，但是「there are no tables and benches」，也就是公園內沒有桌椅，故人們無法於此進食，另外 (B) 與 (D) 的內容皆未出現在文章中。

**171** (NEW)

**In which of the positions marked [1], [2], [3], and [4] does the following sentence best belong?**

**"And the city council has also approved the installation of lampposts along the trail."**

(A) [1]
(B) [2]
(C) [3]
(D) [4]

下列句子最適合出現在[1]、[2]、[3]、[4]的哪個位置中？

「市議會也通過提案，將沿著步道兩側裝設路燈。」

(A) [1]
(B) [2]
(C) [3]
(D) [4]

題目引述的句子提到「裝設路燈」，由此推測此句應放於說明公園設施的段落。第四段說到整修計畫會讓公園有更多綠地可從事戶外運動，且 [4] 前句說到：「A space will be designed for children to play in safety as well.」，表示公園會有兒童遊樂空間，由此便可看出此段就是講述設施細節的段落。

另外 [4] 的後句也說了：「This was for the convenience of residents who prefer to walk or exercise later in the evening.」，其中使用代名詞「This」，表示 [4] 處的句子應已提過這個方便傍晚運動的設施，故可知道句子應該填入 [4]，表示路燈能方便居民晚上運動，因此本題正確答案為 (D)。

## 172–175 網路討論區

| | |
|---|---|
| **Cindy Hilton** 9:45 A.M.<br>I have to arrange transportation from the airport for our annual conference next week. So, I want you to provide me with flight information. As we are holding the conference for the first time, I sincerely hope there aren't any problems during the event. | 辛蒂‧希爾頓〔上午9:45〕：<br>我需要為下週的年度會議，安排從機場到會場的交通事宜，所以我希望你們提供你們的班機資訊。由於這是我們第一次舉行會議，我真心希望過程中不要出錯。 |
| **Mary Kate** 9:46 A.M.<br>I've been waiting for this for a long time. Unfortunately, I forgot to reserve a flight. Will the company reimburse me for the travel expenses if I drive my own car? That's because the flights from San Francisco are full. | 瑪麗‧凱特〔上午9:46〕：<br>我期待這會議很久了。但很遺憾我忘了訂機票。如果我自己開車過去，公司會補貼車馬費嗎？因為從舊金山出發的班機都客滿了。 |
| **Ben Ford** 9:47 A.M.<br>I'll be on Clover Airlines, flight 803 from Dallas to New York at 7:35 A.M. | 班‧福特〔上午9:47〕：<br>我搭乘四葉草航空803班機，從達拉斯飛紐約，上午7:35抵達當地。 |
| **Cindy Hilton** 9:48 A.M.<br>Oh, that's too bad, Mary. I'll check on that. | 辛蒂‧希爾頓〔上午9:48〕：<br>喔，真糟糕，瑪麗。這件事我會再確認。 |
| **Ariana Crawford** 9:49 A.M.<br>All flights from Houston were full as well. So, I have no choice but to take a bus to Philadelphia and then fly to New York, arriving at 7:50 A.M. I managed to get the last ticket. | 亞歷安娜‧克勞福〔上午9:49〕：<br>從休士頓飛往紐約的班機也都滿了。所以我別無選擇，只能搭客運到費城再轉搭飛機，到紐約的時間是7:50。我來得及搶到最後一張票。 |
| **Cindy Hilton** 9:55 A.M.<br>I've just been told by the finance department that costs of travel by car will not be reimbursed according to the company policy. Why don't you take a train instead? I would appreciate it if you book it immediately and let me know the time of your arrival. | 辛蒂‧希爾頓〔上午9:55〕：<br>我剛才從財務部得知，根據公司政策，自行開車前往不給與補貼。妳要不要改搭火車？如果妳現在馬上訂票，讓我知道妳抵達的時間，我會很感謝。 |
| **Mary Kate** 9:56 A.M.<br>Sure. | 瑪麗‧凱特〔上午9:56〕：<br>當然。 |

479

| Cindy Hilton | 9:57 A.M. | 辛蒂‧希爾頓〔上午9:57〕： |
|---|---|---|
| Thank you for the information, Mr. Ford and Ms. Crawford. See you then. | | 福特先生和克勞福女士，感謝你們的資訊。到時見。 |

 **172** (NEW) ---------------------------------------------------------

**At 9:46 A.M., what does Ms. Kate most likely mean when she writes, "I've been waiting for this for a long time"?**

(A) She is waiting for the details about flight information.

(B) She did not realize flights are fully booked.

(C) She is glad the speakers will finally meet next week.

(D) She has prepared a presentation for the conference.

上午9:46 時，凱特女士寫道：「我期待這會議很久了」，她最可能的意思是？

(A) 她等著知道詳細的班機資訊。

(B) 她沒發現班機訂位滿了。

(C) 她很高興下週講者們終於要見面了。

(D) 她準備會議演講已久。

解讀對話後可知，希爾頓女士先說了：「I have to arrange transportation from the airport for our annual conference next week. So, I want you to provide me with flight information.」，表示她要為了下週的年度會議安排機場到會場的接駁，並需要與她對話的人提供航班資訊給她，因此可以知道，希爾頓女士是舉辦會議的一方，而凱特女士、福特先生與克勞福女士應該是參加會議的一方。

本題可以使用刪去法；根據內文希爾頓女士才是需要知道班機資訊的人，故 (A) 不會是正確答案；從凱特女士之後的言論可知，她知道機位已滿，甚至已經擬好替代方案，所以 (B) 也不正確；最後基於上述判斷，凱特女士不是準備會議的一方，她只需要參加會議，所以 (D) 也不能選。因此可知，本題正確答案為 (C)。

另外，由於凱特女士、福特先生與克勞福先生都是參加會議的人，且主辦方特地確認他們的交通狀況，故可推測他們最可能是受邀與會的講者，且「I've been waiting for this for a long time.」，透露出期待會議已久，應帶著興奮語氣，故 (C) 是最適合成為答案的選項。

 **173** ---------------------------------------------------------

**At 9:48 A.M., what is Ms. Hilton going to check on?**

(A) A flight ticket from San Francisco

(B) The company's reimbursement policy

(C) Ms. Ford's flight information

(D) The start time of the conference

上午9:48 時，希爾頓女士要確認什麼事？

(A) 從舊金山起飛的機票

(B) 公司的車馬費補助政策

(C) 福特先生的班機資訊

(D) 會議開始的時間

本題解題時很可能以為是在回應前一個人，然而前句中，福特先生只是單純在告知自己的班機時間，所以希爾頓女士真正要確認的，應該是凱特女士在 9 點 46 分時問的：「Will the company reimburse me for the travel expenses if I drive my own car?」，代表她要為凱特女士向公司確認是否補助自駕的費用，故正確答案為 (B)。

## 174

**How will Ms. Kate most likely travel to the annual conference?**

(A) By car
(B) By air
(C) By train
(D) By bus

凱特女士最可能用什麼方式參加年度會議？

(A) 開車
(B) 搭飛機
(C) 搭火車
(D) 搭客運

9 點 55 分時，希爾頓女士告知凱特女士公司無法補助自駕費用，並說：「Why don't you take a train instead?」，建議她搭乘火車前來，故從凱特女士隨後回答的「Sure.」可知，她將搭火車與會，正確答案為 (C)。

## 175

**What is true about the speakers?**

(A) They are all flying out of the same city.
(B) They will take the same flight.
(C) They met at the conference last year.
(D) They are all attending a conference in New York.

關於演講者，下列何者為真？

(A) 他們都從同一個城市起飛。
(B) 他們會搭乘同一班飛機。
(C) 他們去年一起開過會。
(D) 他們都要參加在紐約舉行的會議。

先從希爾頓女士開頭說的「As we are holding the conference for the first time」知道，這是第一次舉行會議，所以無法知道三名演講者去年是否一起開過會，故 (C) 不適合作為答案。

接下來從凱特女士說的「the flights from San Francisco」可知她是要從舊金山出發，而從福特先生說的「flight 803 from Dallas」可知他會從達拉斯出發，最後再從克勞福女士話中的「All flights from Houston」看出她會從休士頓出發。三人並非從同一城市起飛，故不可能搭乘同班機，所以 (A) 與 (B) 皆不正確。

另外福特先生與克勞福女士的話中皆提到「to New York」，表示他們會在紐約開會，又因為凱特女士也是與會者，所以可推測她也會到紐約集合，故正確答案為 (D)。

### 176–180 文章和電子郵件

| Weekly Business Insight: Trustworthy Brothers | 一週商業洞察：誠信兄弟 |
|---|---|
| Five years ago, Jay and Gavin Damon set up a company called Trustworthy Brothers, which is truly unique and a game-changing firm in the real estate industry in Barcelona. To renovate older properties, the small firm has much experience working with existing landlords in the city. The brothers have concentrated on an increase in value and rental income potential by effectively evaluating properties and determining what improvements are needed. From building exterior to interior design, Trustworthy Brothers hires skilled | 五年前，傑·戴蒙和蓋文·戴蒙創立了「誠信兄弟」，它是很獨特的公司，顛覆了巴塞隆納的不動產業。為了整修老舊建築，這間小公司有和城裡房東合作的豐富經驗。這對兄弟有效評估建築物的價值，並決定需要改善的部份，專注於提高房地產價值和租金潛力。從外部裝潢到室內設計，誠信兄弟聘僱老練專業的工人來完成工程。至今他們所有的工程只集中在巴塞隆納中部。 |

and professional laborers to get the project done. Until now, all of their work has been done only in central Barcelona.

One of the local landlords, Jay Manuel, who recently signed a contract with Trustworthy Brothers to renovate his old buildings, said, "Thanks to working with Trustworthy Brothers, I have experienced an increase in tenant demand and rental profits. Furthermore, the renovation has led to cost savings for power and water. Tenants of my building enjoy their leisure time on the new rooftop terrace. I'll definitely recommend Trustworthy Brothers to others."

If you want to contact Trustworthy Brothers, visit their website, trustworthybrothers.com.

---

**From:** Michael Keane
<mkeane@amail.com>
**To:** Jay Damon
<jdamon@trustworthybrothers.com>
**Date:** March 24
**Subject:** New Proposition

---

Dear Mr. Damon,

I am writing to request a renovation for a building I recently purchased, which is located in a seaside town near Barcelona. I am pretty sure that you would be interested in the renovation project. The building is not currently in good condition because it has been abandoned for several years. So I was able to purchase it at a very low price. The building is, however, very close to a subway station, which I believe is an advantage. I would like to make a request to you to transform my building into a new attractive residence for rent. Please let me know if you are available to talk about it.

Thank you,

Michael Keane

---

傑‧曼努埃爾是當地一名房東，最近才和誠信兄弟簽約整修他的舊建築。他表示：「多虧了和誠信兄弟合作，我才感受到租屋需求的成長和租金收益的增加。不只如此，整修也節省了水電開銷。我的住戶很享受，閒來沒事就待在頂樓天台。我絕對會向其他人推薦誠信兄弟。」

如果您想要聯絡誠信兄弟，可以上他們的官網trustworthybrothers.com。

---

寄件人：麥克‧基恩
<mkeane@amail.com>
收件人：傑‧戴蒙
<jdamon@trustworthybrothers.com>
日期：3月24日
主旨：新提案

---

親愛的戴蒙先生：

我想請求您協助整修我最近新買的房子，它鄰近巴塞隆納的海岸城市。我確信您會對這項整修計畫感興趣。這棟建築荒廢數年，目前屋況並不好。所以我才能低價買下。房子倒是離地鐵站很近，我相信這是個優勢。我想請您改造我的房子，讓它能夠吸引房客入住。如果您有空談談這件事，請告訴我。

感謝，

麥克‧基恩

---

詞彙 **game-changing** 顛覆大局的；破天荒的

**176**

**What does the article NOT indicate about the Trustworthy Brothers?**

(A) They have worked in the real estate industry for 10 years.
(B) They improve profits for their clients.
(C) They have worked with landlords in Barcelona.
(D) They employ workers to carry out their plans.

關於誠信兄弟，文中沒有提到什麼？

(A) 他們在不動產業界已工作十年。
(B) 他們讓顧客的收益增加。
(C) 他們一直和巴塞隆納的房東合作。
(D) 他們找工人來完成計畫。

從報導文章第一段的「The brothers have concentrated on an increase in value and rental income potential」，與第二段顧客說的「I have experienced an increase in tenant demand and rental profits」，可以知道經過誠信兄弟的改造，顧客的租金收益的確有所增加，故 (B) 可在文中找到。

再從第一段最後的「all of their work has been done only in central Barcelona」知道，他們目前只在巴塞隆納整修建築，也就是只有和此地的房東有合作關係，故 (C) 也有提及。最後從前句的「Trustworthy Brothers hires skilled and professional laborers」可知他們會僱用專業工人，所以 (D) 也在文中。

綜合上述，文中未提及的只有 (A) 的內容，故本題正確答案為 (A)。

**177**

**What is suggested about Mr. Manuel's buildings?**

(A) They attract more tenants than before.
(B) They are new buildings.
(C) The rooftop terrace is not open to the tenants.
(D) Mr. Manuel has to pay more for their electricity bills now.

文中提到曼努埃爾先生的房子什麼事？

(A) 它們較以前吸引更多房客。
(B) 它們是新建築。
(C) 頂樓天台沒有開放給房客使用。
(D) 曼努埃爾先生現在必須替房子負擔更多電費。

從文章第二段可以看出，曼努埃爾先生的房屋曾讓誠信兄弟整修，且他也說了：「Thanks to working with Trustworthy Brothers, I have experienced an increase in tenant demand」，表示整修後租屋需求增加了，故本題的答案為 (A)。

**178**

**What does the article indicate potential clients should do?**

(A) Ask for an estimate
(B) Visit a website
(C) Negotiate the price
(D) Send a request

關於潛在客戶，文章建議他們怎麼做？

(A) 請求估價
(B) 上網查看
(C) 議價
(D) 提出請求

報導的最後部分寫著：「If you want to contact Trustworthy Brothers, visit their website」，並留下一串網址，故文章建議有意聯絡誠信兄弟的人造訪他們的網站，本題正確答案為 (B)。

## Why was Mr. Keane able to purchase the building at a low price?

為什麼基恩先生能夠用低價買到房子？

(A) It is in a remote area.

(A) 地處偏遠。

(B) It does not have access to a water supply.

(B) 沒有供水。

(C) It was on sale as a special promotion.

(C) 特價拍賣。

(D) It could not be rented out in its present state.

(D) 因為它的現況沒有辦法提供出租。

基恩先生在郵件的第三句先寫了「The building is not currently in good condition」，表示現在屋況不佳，並解釋「(The building) has been abandoned for several years」、「So I was able to purchase it at a very low price.」，表示因為建築荒廢已久，他才得以低價入手，並在後文提出希望改造房屋的請求。

綜合上述，可以推測房屋當時廢棄多時，應該並非可出租的狀態，所以才會低價售出；本題正確答案為 (D)。

## How is Mr. Keane's proposal different from typical works for Trustworthy Brothers?

基恩先生的整修計畫，和誠信兄弟之前做過的案子有何不同？

(A) The work would be done outside Barcelona.

(A) 這項工程將在巴塞隆納外作業。

(B) Mr. Keane would like to hire a renowned designer.

(B) 基恩先生想僱用知名設計師。

(C) The fee for the renovation would be paid after the project is finished.

(C) 整修費用要等到完工以後才會付款。

(D) The project should be finished within a strict time limit.

(D) 計畫必須在緊迫的時間內完成。

報導文章第一段的最後一句提到：「Until now, all of their work has been done only in central Barcelona.」，意即誠信兄弟至今所有工程都只在巴塞隆納中部進行，而基恩先生卻在郵件開頭寫到：「I am writing to request a renovation for a building ... which is located in a seaside town near Barcelona」，表示他想請誠信兄弟整修房子，且房子位於巴塞隆納附近的臨海城鎮，也就是並不在巴塞隆納，而這就是這件案子與誠信兄弟以往的案子不同之處，故本題答案為 (A)。

**181–185 型錄備註與型錄內頁**

### Penske Books
### Winter Catalog

Dear Customers,

Please enjoy looking over our latest catalog. If you look at the Cookbooks, Food, and Wine section on page 5, you will find some bestsellers that let you know recipes from famous restaurants. Our Travel and Tourism section on page 7 guides you to enjoy your winter vacation wherever you go. For all the latest in the Science Fiction section on page 9, imaginative writers will lead you into

### 潘世奇書店
### 冬季型錄

親愛的顧客：

請盡情瀏覽我們最新的型錄。如果您看第5頁的食譜、飲食美酒類別，您會找到知名餐廳食譜的暢銷書籍。我們第7頁的旅行和旅遊類別，帶領您享受各地的冬季假期。第9頁有所有最新的科幻小說，充滿想像力的作者引導您進入科幻世界。

the world of fantasy. Highly experienced writers will tell you about the latest trends in the Business and Management section on page 11. You can also see the best-loved books including *Risk Management for Small Businesses*, winner of the Jamison Award (page 13).

Please note that this catalog has only a small number of samples. If you want to see a full list of our titles, go to our website, www.penskebooks.com. For those who live in Pennsylvania, please visit our store for a wealth of additional books that you cannot find on our website.

在第11頁的商管類別，經驗豐富的作者將告訴您最新趨勢。您也可以看到備受喜愛的書籍，包括賈米森獎得主的《小企業的風險管理》（第13頁）。

請您留意這本型錄裡的樣書不多。如果您想要看到完整的書目標題，請造訪我們官網www.penskebooks.com。歡迎賓州居民到我們實體書店來看看，有連官網上也找不到的豐富書籍。

---

### Business Perspective
by Yuri Tielemans and Jane Carter

An impressive introduction to business strategy, full of specific cases and entertaining pictures and illustrations to explain key points. The easy-to-follow instructions will give you a better understanding of the business world.

Condition: Very good. $39.95

### 《商業展望》
作者尤里・蒂耶萊曼斯和珍・卡特

帶您認識商業策略，引人入勝，充滿具體案例和有趣的圖片插畫，來解釋其中關鍵重點。便於理解的說明，讓您更了解商業界。

書況：非常好。39.95美元。

### Finance Management Analysis
by Thiago Malcom

This book features combining new financial theory with practical examples. Malcom uses real-world scenarios to analyze theoretical principles of finance management. Highly recommended for both businesspeople and students.

Condition: Like new. $25.95.

### 《金融管理分析》
作者蒂亞戈，馬康

本書特色結合實際案例和新的財務理論。馬康用真實世界的場景，分析金融管理的理論原則。強烈推薦給商務人士和學生。

書況：近全新。25.95美元。

### Risk Management for Small Businesses
by Alicia Dunst

Essential books for small business owners who take care of high-risk situations effectively. The book contains several interviews with owners running a successful business.

Condition: Fair with some wear to corners and edges. $32.95

### 《小企業的風險管理》
作者艾莉西亞・鄧斯特

小企業主必讀的書，有效處理高風險的情況。本書內有多個商業成功人士的訪談。

書況：一般，書角和書緣有折損。32.95美元。

| Encyclopedia of Business Marketing<br>by Anthony Martial<br><br>With more than 5,000 definitions of business marketing terms, this book is a must-have item for those who are starting their own business for the first time.<br><br><u>Condition: Good with signs of cover wear. $49.95</u> | 《商業行銷百科》<br>作者安東尼‧馬夏爾<br><br>本書有超過5,000個商業行銷術語的定義，對於首度投身創業的人，是必定收藏之作。<br><br>書況：好，書封有些破舊。49.95美元。 |

詞彙 **perspective** 觀點　**practical** 實際的　**scenario** 場景　**wear** 〔名詞〕折損
**encyclopedia** 百科全書　**must-have** 一定要有的

## 181

**Based on the note, what book would Penske Books most likely have in stock?**

(A) A biography of a famous musician
(B) A history of Africa
(C) An introduction of the new computer models
(D) An information on top vacation spots in East Asia

根據備註，哪本書在潘世奇書店最可能有庫存？

(A) 知名音樂家的自傳
(B) 非洲史
(C) 新電腦模型的概論
(D) 東亞度假勝地的資訊

根據型錄備註提供的資訊，只能知道書店提供包括飲食、旅行、科幻小說及商管四種主題的書籍，而選項中只有 (D) 符合旅行書籍的類別，故本題正確答案為 (D)。

## 182

**In the note, the word "wealth" in paragraph 2, line 3, is closest in meaning to**

(A) value
(B) quality
(C) sense
(D) abundance

在備註中，第二段、第三行的「wealth」，意思最接近下列何者？

(A) 價值
(B) 品質
(C) 感覺
(D) 大量

此句提到「please visit our store for a wealth of additional books that you cannot find on our website」，表示如果無法在網路上找到書籍，可以直接造訪店面，並以「a wealth of」形容書籍。故從前後文可推知，此處的「a wealth of」應該是「數量豐富」的意思，以表示店面有大量的書籍，因此本題正確答案為 (D)。

## 183

**What is suggested about the catalog?**

(A) It advertises used books.
(B) It has a complete listing.
(C) It includes mainly academic books.
(D) It is released twice a year.

文中提到這本型錄什麼事？

(A) 推廣二手書。
(B) 有完整的清單。
(C) 主要都是學術書籍。
(D) 每年出版兩次。

從型錄內頁的書況描述，可知道這本型錄應是刊登二手書籍，故正確答案為 (A)。

184

**Who received an award?**

(A) Mr. Tielemans
(B) Mr. Malcom
(C) Ms. Dunst
(D) Mr. Martial

誰得了獎？

(A) 蒂耶萊曼斯先生
(B) 馬康先生
(C) 鄧斯特女士
(D) 馬夏爾先生

備註文章的第一段最後說到：「*Risk Management for Small Businesses*, winner of the Jamison Award」，代表《小企業的風險管理》這本書是獎項得主，而根據型錄內頁，這本書的作者是「Alicia Dunst」，故本題正確答案為 (C)。

185

**What feature is NOT mentioned among the descriptions of the books on the catalog page?**

(A) Drawings to clarify key points
(B) Interviews with those involved
(C) Examples from real world
(D) Checklists for starting a small company

關於書本的描述，型錄頁面上沒有提到哪個特色？

(A) 用圖畫闡明重點
(B) 有關人士的訪談
(C) 真實世界的案例
(D) 創業的勾選清單

本題要從型錄內頁找出答案。第一本書的介紹提到「full of . . . entertaining pictures and illustrations to explain key points」，表示書內以有趣插圖解釋重點，故 (A) 為有被提及的內容；第三本書的介紹則有「The book contains several interviews with owners running a successful business」，表示書內有與多位成功商業人士的訪談，且從書名可看出，書的主題與企業經營有關，故此為相關人士的訪談，(B) 有被提及。最後可從第二本書的介紹看到「practical examples」、「uses real-world scenarios to analyze theoretical principles」，表示作者加入實際案例，以真實世界的場景分析理論，故 (C) 也是有被提及的內容。

綜觀上述，唯一無法在文中找到的是 (D)，故本題正確答案為 (D)。

### 186–190 電子郵件、行程表和資訊

**From:** James Rodriguez
<jrodriguez@ita.com>
**To:** Brian Mendy
<bmendy@altriagroup.com>
**Date:** December 1
**Subject:** Invitation for speaker

寄件人：詹姆斯‧羅德里格斯
<jrodriguez@ita.com>
收件人：布萊恩‧門迪
<bmendy@altriagroup.com>
日期：12月1日
主旨：致講者的邀請函

Dear Mr. Mendy,

I am writing to invite you to be a keynote speaker at the 5th annual Information Technology Association Conference, which is scheduled for May 1-3 in Charlotte, North Carolina. Thousands of business leaders and industry experts will participate in the event, which will

親愛的門迪先生：

我想要邀請您出席5月1日到3日，於北卡羅萊納州的夏洛特舉行的第五屆資訊科技協會會議，並擔任會議的主講人。數千名商業領導人和產業專家都將出席，這是建立人脈的

be an ideal venue for networking. This conference will be held at the Hyatt Charlotte Hotel, and business leaders will share their insights into the latest trends in the IT industry.

We would appreciate it if you would agree to make a speech on the flexible pricing options you introduced to boost profits for the Internet security program created by the Altria Group. Please let me know your availability.

James Rodriguez
President
Information Technology Association

理想場合。會議將在凱悅夏洛特飯店舉行,商業領導人將分享,他們對資訊科技產業最新趨勢的深入見解。

如果您同意蒞臨演講,談談您為了提高奧馳亞集團網路安全程式的利潤,所引進的彈性定價選擇,我們將不勝感激。請告訴我您能否撥空前來。

資訊科技協會
總裁
詹姆斯・羅德里格斯

---

## Information Technology Association Conference Program

(May 1 – Schedules)

| | |
|---|---|
| 8:30 A.M. | Visual Communication – A more effective and better way of communicating as well as saving money and effort <br><br> Speaker: Elizabeth Cohan, Cofounder of Micron Technology |
| 9:30 A.M. | Revolutionary Change – The vice president of Supervalu speaks on how her team brought the company back from near bankruptcy and made the company turn a profit through innovative product design <br><br> Speaker: Anna Kirby, Vice President of Supervalu |
| 10:30 A.M. | Creating a Product – The secret behind the Altria Group's unique strategy to increase the sales revenues of its computer programs <br><br> Speaker: Brian Mendy, CEO of Altria Group |
| 11:30 A.M. | Leadership in an IT company – How to react quickly and efficiently to rapidly changing circumstances <br><br> Speaker: Laurel Allen, Professor of Charlotte Business School |
| 12:30 P.M. | Lunch |

## 資訊科技協會 會議行程

(5月1日行程)

| | |
|---|---|
| 上午8:30 | 視覺化傳播—更好且更有效率的傳播方式,省錢又省力 <br><br> 講者:伊莉莎白・科漢,密可龍科技共同創辦人 |
| 上午9:30 | 革命性變革—超價公司副總裁分享她的團隊如何帶領公司,藉由產品的創新設計從破產邊緣轉虧為盈。 <br><br> 講者:安娜・卡比,超價公司副董 |
| 上午10:30 | 創造產品—揭密奧馳亞集團提高旗下電腦軟體銷售量的獨家策略 <br><br> 講者:布萊恩・門迪,奧馳亞集團執行長 |
| 上午11:30 | 資訊產業公司的領導力—如何即時、有效地因應迅速變動的局勢 <br><br> 講者:羅瑞爾・艾倫,夏洛特商學院教授 |
| 下午12:30 | 午餐 |

## Information Technology Association Conference

### Registration fees

Information Technology Association members — $1,000
Nonmembers – $1,500

Registration fees include hotel vouchers for use — during the event as well as meals and refreshments. Registration online in advance is required to attend the conference. Presentation videos will be available on our website to all participants the following month.

## 資訊科技協會會議

### 報名價

資訊科技協會會員—1,000美元
非會員—1,500美元

報名費包括旅館的消費券—可用於活動期間餐食和點心。欲出席會議須提前上網登記。講座影片將在下個月放上官網，供所有與會者觀看。

 **詞彙** IT 資訊科技，為 Information Technology 的縮寫

---

### 186

**What is mentioned about the Information Technology Association Conference?**

(A) It takes place annually.
(B) An on-site training will be scheduled.
(C) It is a one-day event.
(D) The latest products will be on display.

關於資訊科技協會會議，文中提到什麼？

(A) 每年都會舉辦。
(B) 會安排現場的訓練課程。
(C) 是為期一天的活動。
(D) 會展示最新的產品。

從郵件第一句的「5th annual Information Technology Association Conference」可知，會議每年都會舉辦一次，且今年是第五年舉辦，故本題正確答案為 (A)。

(C) 會議是從 5 月 1 日到 3 日舉行，為期三天；(B) 與 (D) 的內容皆未在文章中提及。

---

### 187

**When will product pricing most likely be discussed?**

(A) At 8:30 A.M.
(B) At 9:30 A.M.
(C) At 10:30 A.M.
(D) At 11:30 A.M.

什麼時候最有可能討論到產品定價？

(A) 上午 8:30
(B) 上午 9:30
(C) 上午 10:30
(D) 上午 11:30

郵件最後一段寫著：「We would appreciate it if you would agree to make a speech on the flexible pricing options you introduced」，由於收件者為門迪先生，因此可知門迪先生的演講內容應會和定價相關，而對照行程表，門迪先生是在上午 10 點 30 分演講，故本題正確答案為 (C)。

## 188

**What is indicated about Supervalu?**

(A) It will merge with a rival company.

(B) It has overcome difficulties.

(C) It has changed the company logo.

(D) It moved its headquarters last year.

文中提到超價公司什麼事?

(A) 將和對手整併。

(B) 它克服困難。

(C) 最近換了公司商標。

(D) 總部在去年搬遷。

本題要看從行程表裡找答案。行程表上,9 點 30 分開始的演講主題為「Revolutionary Change」,內容則提到:「The vice president of Supervalu speaks on how her team brought the company back from near bankruptcy」表示超價公司的副總裁將分享團隊如何從破產邊緣東山再起,意即超價公司克服了瀕臨破產的困境、扭轉了情勢,故選項中最符合描述的為 (B)。

## 189

**What is a benefit available only to Information Technology Association members?**

(A) A private dinner for networking

(B) Free transportation

(C) Upgraded hotel accommodations

(D) Reduced registration fees

哪項優惠只提供給資訊科技協會的會員?

(A) 人脈拓展的私人晚餐

(B) 免費交通

(C) 飯店住宿升等

(D) 報名費用減少

從第三篇提供的資訊可以發現,協會會員的報名價比非會員便宜 500 美元,故本題正確答案為 (D)。

**What will Mr. Mendy receive access to in June?**

(A) Recordings

(B) Articles

(C) Receipts

(D) Photographs

門迪先生在六月可以得到什麼的使用權?

(A) 錄影

(B) 文章

(C) 收據

(D) 照片

最後一篇內容提到講座影片會在「下個月」放上官網,而從前兩篇可知道,會議是在五月,所以六月時就能看見演說的影片,因此本題正確答案為 (A)。

# Discount Coupon

## END-OF-SEASON SALE for One Day Only!
Wednesday, 2 April

- 20% off one regularly priced item
- 30% off one clearance item

Thousands of items in stock, including coats, shirts, pants, shoes, accessories, and more. We will extend our business hours for this event: 9:00 A.M. – 9:00 P.M.

This coupon is not able to be combined with other promotions. We limit one coupon per customer. Please note that the coupon is not valid on pants. Once the item is purchased, no refunds or exchanges are allowed. Coupon is valid on 2 April only.

**Monstanto**
1040 Grand Concourse
Bronx, NY 10456
Telephone: (718) 681-6000

---

**To:** Monstanto Employees
**From:** William Singer, Manager
**Date:** April 1
**Subject:** Re: Upcoming sale

---

Today's edition of the *New York Daily* failed to mention that accessories are excluded from the regularly priced items. So, if a customer makes a purchase of the item, please explain the issue and make an apology. And then, please inform the customer of the fact that we'll nevertheless offer 10% discount as a courtesy.

Also, as the promotion has been advertised through all media, more customers are expected to visit our store than usual, especially from 5 P.M. to the closing time. So, we will need more sales associates on duty during that time. Please let me know if you are available for an extra shift.

Thank you.

# 折價券

季末出清，只有一天！
4月2日週三

- 一般價格商品打八折
- 出清商品打七折

數千種庫存商品，包括外套、襯衫、長褲、鞋子和配件等。活動期間我們將延長營業時間，從上午9點到晚上9點。

本折價券不能和其他優惠活動合併使用。每名顧客限用一券。請留意長褲並不適用本折價券。商品一經購買，就不能退款和換貨。僅限4月2日當天使用有效。

孟斯坦都
10456 紐約布朗克斯中央大廳1040號
電話：(718)681-6000

---

收件人：孟斯坦都員工
寄件人：經理威廉·辛格
日期：4月1日
主旨：關於：即將到來的特賣

---

今天出版的《紐約日報》沒有提到一般價格商品不包括配件。所以如果顧客購買配件，請向顧客解釋清楚並道歉。也請通知顧客為表誠意，我們特別提供九折優惠。

另外，因為廣告已透過媒體宣傳，預期會有比平常更多的顧客到店選購，尤其是下午5點以後到關店這段期間。所以到時候，我們將需要更多銷售人員值班。如果您願意加班，請告訴我。

感謝。

**From:** Service Department
<service@monstanto.com>
**To:** Jill Elkins
<jelkins@mmail.com>
**Date:** 2 April, 4:26 P.M.
**Subject:** Your receipt

Dear Ms. Elkins,

Here is the purchase receipt you recently requested from Monstanto.

| Quantity | Item | Price |
|---|---|---|
| 1 | Soft Jacket<br>30% promotion discount<br>Item price | $400.00<br>-$120.00<br>$280.00 |
| 1 | Ring and necklace set<br>10% promotion discount<br>Item price | $160.00<br>-$16.00<br>$144.00 |
| 1 | Long denim pants | $28.00 |

Total $452.00
Total Saved $136.00

Thank you for shopping at Monstanto.

寄件人：服務部門
<service@monstanto.com>
收件人：吉兒‧埃爾金斯
<jelkins@mmail.com>
日期：4月2日 下午4:26
主旨：您的收據

親愛的埃爾金斯女士：

這是您向孟斯坦都索取的購物收據。

| 數量 | 商品 | 價格 |
|---|---|---|
| 1 | 軟夾克<br>七折特賣折扣<br>商品價格 | 400.00美元<br>-120.00美元<br>280.00美元 |
| 1 | 戒指和項鍊組<br>九折特賣折扣<br>商品價格 | 160.00美元<br>-16.00美元<br>144.00美元 |
| 1 | 丹寧長褲 | 28.00 美元 |

總計452.00美元
總折扣136.00美元

感謝您在孟斯坦都購物。

---

**詞彙** regularly priced item 一般價格商品　clearance item 出清商品　concourse 中央大廳
sales associate 銷售人員　shift 值班

**191** ----------------------------------------------------------------

**According to the coupon, what will happen on April 2?**

(A) New product line will be unveiled.

(B) The store will remain open longer than usual.

(C) Additional coupons will be handed out in front of the store.

(D) Customers will be able to see a fashion show.

根據折價券，4月2日會發生什麼事？

(A) 揭幕新的生產線。

(B) 開店時間較長。

(C) 店家門口會發放多的折價券。

(D) 顧客可以看到一場時尚秀。

從折價券上可看到特賣會是 4 月 2 日舉行，且第一段上寫著：「We will extend our business hours for this event」，表示當天將延長營業時間，故正確答案為 (B)。

## 192

**In the first e-mail, what are sales associates requested to do?**

(A) Arrive early to work

(B) Volunteer to work extra hours

(C) Hand out flyers

(D) Take an inventory

在電子郵件中，銷售人員被要求做什麼？

(A) 提早到班

(B) 自願加班

(C) 發放傳單

(D) 盤點存貨

郵件的第二段提到，預計將有許多顧客光顧，所以「we will need more sales associates on duty during that time」，也就是需要更多銷售人員，且最後一句也寫：「Please let me know if you are available for an extra shift.」，即請有意加班的員工與自己聯絡，由此可知，本題正確答案應為 (B)。

## 193

**In the first e-mail, the word "advertised" in paragraph 2, line 1, is closest in meaning to**

(A) updated

(B) released

(C) attracted

(D) promoted

在第一封電子郵件中，第二段、第一行的「advertised」，最接近下列哪個意思？

(A) 被更新

(B) 被放送

(C) 被吸引

(D) 被推廣

本句提到「promotions」、「through all media」，可以推測句中的「has been advertised」應該是只活動在各媒體上「被宣傳」的意思，而原形動詞 advertise 就是廣告、宣傳之意，故與之最相近的是 promote，本題正確答案為 (D)。

## 194

**What is suggested about Ms. Elkins?**

(A) She purchased a clearance item.

(B) She recently moved to Bronx.

(C) She paid for her purchase with a credit card.

(D) She frequently visits Monstanto.

文中提到埃爾金斯女士什麼事？

(A) 她買了一項出清商品。

(B) 她最近搬到布朗克斯。

(C) 她用信用卡付費購物。

(D) 她經常去孟斯坦都。

折價券上提到，原價商品可享有八折優惠，而出清商品可獲得七折優惠。對照收據，其中有一項商品享有七折優惠，故可知埃爾金斯女士有購買一件出清商品，正確答案為 (A)。

## 195

**What did Ms. Elkins probably NOT receive when she purchased the ring and necklace set?**

(A) A discount

(B) A gift certificate

(C) An apology

(D) An explanation

埃爾金斯女士買戒指和項鍊組時，可能不會收到什麼？

(A) 一項折扣

(B) 一張禮券

(C) 一個道歉

(D) 一個解釋

本題要從郵件中獲得線索，並使用刪去法找出答案。郵件開頭提到，報紙上忘了說明，配件並不在一般價格商品的範圍中，因此如果顧客購買了配件，要先「explain the issue」、「make an apology」並「inform the customer of the fact that we'll nevertheless offer 10% discount」，也就是要和顧客解釋此事、向他們道歉，並且仍舊給予顧客九折優惠。

本題問的是不會收到的東西，所以購買了配件的埃爾金斯女士不會得到的東西只有 (B)，故本題正確答案為 (B)。

**196–200 公告、電子郵件和表格**

| | |
|---|---|
| **Student Liaison Officer**<br>**Chicago University**<br><br>The university is looking for student liaison officers (SLOs) to work in the Student Support Department. The SLOs will meet two times every month to support international students who make up the Student Committee, taking care of services that can assist with various issues including personal problems, academic issues, accommodation, and career advice. The SLOs will also organize monthly meetings in different places on campus to promote a sense of community.<br><br>If you are interested, please send us an e-mail at ssd@chiuni.edu.com. | **學生事務聯絡員**<br>**芝加哥大學**<br><br>校方正在徵求能在教務處工作的學生事務聯絡員。他們每個月要和學生委員會中的國際學生會面兩次，協助他們的各種疑難雜症，包括個人、學業、住宿和生涯規畫等問題。學生事務聯絡員每個月也要在校園各處舉行聚會，來凝聚向心力。<br><br>如果您有興趣，請寄電子郵件到 ssd@chiuni.edu.com。 |
| **From:** Bankole Johnson<br>**To:** Robert Rivest<br>**Date:** February 15<br>**Subject:** Welcome | 寄件人：班科勒‧強森<br>收件人：羅伯特‧里弗斯特<br>日期：2月15日<br>主旨：歡迎 |
| Dear Mr. Rivest,<br><br>Thank you for accepting our offer for the position of SLO (Student Liaison Officer). There is some paperwork you should complete before your first day of work. Within a week, you will receive a welcome box containing our university's official documents that you need to fill out by the end of this month. This will also let you know the details about your orientation.<br><br>Furthermore, we do need an official transcript from your last university. So please send me an official one by the end of this month as well.<br><br>Sincerely,<br>Bankole Johnson<br>Director of Student Support Department, Chicago University | 親愛的里弗斯特先生：<br><br>感謝您接下學生事務聯絡員的職務。在您開始工作前，您需要完成一些文書作業。您將在一週內收到校方歡迎您的公文匣，請在這個月底前填完裡面的正式文件。這也幫助您瞭解更多關於迎新的資訊。<br><br>此外，我們還需要您在上一間大學的正式成績單。也麻煩您在這個月底前寄給我正本。<br><br>芝加哥大學 教務處主任<br>班科勒‧強森 敬上 |

<table>
<tr><td>

## San Diego University
## Transcript Request Form

Transcripts will NOT be released if:
    Money is not yet paid to the university.
    There is a hold on your student record.

**Last Name:** <u>Rivest</u>      **First Name:** <u>Robert</u>
**Degree Obtained:** ☐Undergraduate
                     ☑Graduate (Communication)
**Street Address:** <u>5801 S Ellis Ave</u>
**Post Code:** <u>60637</u>    **City:** <u>Chicago</u>    **State:** <u>Illinois</u>

When do you want your transcript proceeded?
☑Immediately      ☐Hold for Final Grades

**Signature:** *Robert Rivest*

</td><td>

## 聖地牙哥大學
## 成績單申請表

如果學生沒有向學校繳費，或是學生紀錄有所疑慮，成績單將不予發放。

姓：里弗斯特      名：羅伯特
學歷：☐ 大學部
         ☑研究所（傳播）
住址：南艾力斯街5801號
郵遞區號：60637
城市：芝加哥    州：伊利諾

您希望何時發放成績單？
☑即刻     ☐待最後成績公布

簽名：羅伯特・里弗斯特

</td></tr>
</table>

**詞彙** liaison 聯絡　**a sense of community** 團隊向心力　**orientation** 迎新活動　**transcript** 成績單

---

 **196** ------------------------------------------------------------------

**What is the purpose of the notice?**

(A) To recruit international students for a university
(B) To announce the employment of a new professor
(C) To solicit applications for an open position
(D) To publicize the creation of a new organization

這篇公告的目的為何？

(A) 幫助大學招募國際學生
(B) 公告招聘新教授
(C) 徵求職缺的應徵者
(D) 宣傳新團體的創作

公告開頭便提到：「The university is looking for student liaison officers (SLOs)」，表示學校正在招募學生事務聯絡員，並在後文描述業務內容與聯絡方式，因此可知這篇公告的目的是徵求此職缺的應徵者，正確答案為 (C)。

---

 **197** ------------------------------------------------------------------

**How frequently does the Student Committee meet with the student liaison officer?**

(A) Once a week
(B) Once a month
(C) Twice a week
(D) Twice a month

學生委員會和學生事務聯絡員開會的頻率是？

(A) 一週一次
(B) 一個月一次
(C) 一週兩次
(D) 一個月兩次

從公告的第二句：「The SLOs will meet two times every month to support international students who make up the Student Committee」，即可知道學生委員會由國際學生組成，而學生事務聯絡員每個月要和他們見面兩次，故正確答案為 (D)。

**What will Mr. Rivest do at Chicago University?**

(A) Help relocate the student center
(B) Help all students select appropriate courses
(C) Lead the department of student support
(D) Provide support to international students on campus

里弗斯特先生將在芝加哥大學做什麼？

(A) 協助學生中心搬遷
(B) 協助所有學生選擇合適的課程
(C) 領導教務處
(D) 提供協助給校內國際學生

從郵件開頭提到的「Thank you for accepting our offer for the position of SLO (Student Liaison Officer).」，可看出里弗斯特先生被錄取成為了芝加哥大學的學生事務聯絡員，故回頭對照公告可知，他的業務內容包含與國際學生會面、提供協助以及在校舉行聚會，故正確答案為 (D)。

**What will Mr. Rivest receive within a week?**

(A) A package of documents
(B) A receipt of a payment
(C) A copy of his school transcript
(D) A letter of acceptance

里弗斯特先生會在一週內收到什麼？

(A) 裝有文件的包裹
(B) 付款收據
(C) 成績單副本
(D) 錄取通知書

郵件第一段最後提到：「Within a week, you will receive a welcome box containing our university's official documents」，表示在郵件寄出的一週內，里弗斯特先生會收到校方的正式文件，故本題正確答案為 (A)。

**What is suggested about San Diego University?**

(A) It does not have a medical program.
(B) It does not have a graduate course.
(C) It recruits a large number of international students.
(D) It is the last university Mr. Rivest attended.

文中提到聖地牙哥大學什麼事？

(A) 沒有醫學課程。
(B) 沒有研究所課程。
(C) 錄取很多國際學生。
(D) 是里弗斯特先生最後就讀的大學。

根據成績單申請表上的「San Diego University」，以及上頭寫著的申請人姓名，可以知道里弗斯特先生曾就讀於聖地牙哥大學。另外也能從給里弗斯特先生的郵件看到「we do need an official transcript from your last university」，表示需要他的大學成績單，故本題正確答案為 (D)。

(A) 文中並未提及此事；(B) 里弗斯特先生就是從聖地牙哥大學的傳播研究所畢業的，故此校有研究所課程；(C) 錄取國際學生的是芝加哥大學。

# TOEIC 成績換算對照表

| LISTENING 答對題數 | LISTENING 分數 | READING 答對題數 | READING 分數 |
|---|---|---|---|
| 96-100 | 480~495 | 96-100 | 460~495 |
| 91-95 | 435~490 | 91-95 | 410~475 |
| 86-90 | 395~450 | 86-90 | 380~430 |
| 81-85 | 355~415 | 81-85 | 355~400 |
| 76-80 | 325~375 | 76-80 | 325~375 |
| 71-75 | 295~340 | 71-75 | 295~345 |
| 66-70 | 265~315 | 66-70 | 265~315 |
| 61-65 | 240~285 | 61-65 | 235~285 |
| 56-60 | 215~260 | 56-60 | 205~255 |
| 51-55 | 190~235 | 51-55 | 175~225 |
| 46-50 | 160~210 | 46-50 | 150~195 |
| 41-45 | 135~180 | 41-45 | 120~170 |
| 36-40 | 110~155 | 36-40 | 100~140 |
| 31-35 | 85~130 | 31-35 | 75~120 |
| 26-30 | 70~105 | 26-30 | 55~100 |
| 21-25 | 50~90 | 21-25 | 40~80 |
| 16-20 | 35~70 | 16-20 | 30~65 |
| 11-15 | 20~55 | 11-15 | 20~50 |
| 6-10 | 15~40 | 6-10 | 15~35 |
| 1-5 | 5~20 | 1-5 | 5~20 |
| 0 | 5 | 0 | 5 |

註：上述表格僅供參考，實際計分以官方分數為準 。